Hats off to Brandenburg

To Rose, my Friend

Happy Birthday.

Happy Reading

With Love

2012

First published in 2012 by TheNeverPress

Cover design by Leighton Johns.
www.leightonjohns.co.uk

ISBN 9780956742230

www.theneverpress.com

www.theroxyplayhouse.com

ACKNOWLEDGMENTS

With grateful and loving thanks to my family for their encouragement and support. To my friends, in particular Wayne Crawford, Brett Antill, Ryan Wootten, Leighton Johns, Chris Rolfe, Mr John B. Peacock and Donatella Marena.

Special thanks to the following patrons of *'Hats off to Brandenburg'*

Colleen Thomas, Deborah Thomas, Donatella Marena, Victoria Jane Blakemore, Kevin Hattam, David John Watton and Linda Owen – with you around, everything is possible.

Thank you

For The Bishop and all who drink in her

Hats off to Brandenburg

Part One

A Fate Worse Than Debt

Chapter One

Mary Middleton's Garret, St Giles Rookery, London, 1815

The creature of the night recoiled in horror as the curtains were thrown open and the bright springtime rays flooded the room.

"Up! Up, up dear Archie!" chirped Mary Middleton in her usual early morning optimism that grated with his contrasting demeanour.

Archie groaned and clamped his eyes shut. Opening the curtains was a barbaric act. He tried to go back to sleep. It was too late; the hubbub from the city had already paraded its way into the room and brought with it that cursed stench of the rookery. The evil broth of pestilence, rotten intentions and sulfuric bile mixed in with cabbage permeated the air and contaminated his soul. He wanted to slam the window shut, draw the curtains, drag that woman back into his arms and forget all about her transgression. '*Some people never consider other peoples hangovers*', he thought as he looked over to her standing in the corner of the room, half naked and glorious.

Mary knew that Archie was angry with her, and she knew just how to get out of the doghouse. She winked and blew him a kiss.

"Call me Giselle," she whispered in a beguiling accent that had no fixed abode. Job done; a silky bit of feminine distraction tailor-made for the gentleman lying on her bed, soaking in self-pity and truculence.

"I know you want to call me Giselle. I don't mind Archie. I don't mind a jot."

She walked over to the bed and knelt beside it, looking up at his rakish face; slightly sunken, slightly shadowed and slightly pungent. He was lying with his arms arranged corpse like upon his chest. Mary gently took his hand.

"You look like you're laying in state, my dear," she whispered, as she gently mopped his brow with his own hanky. He turned and looked at her; kohl-ringed eyes, sharp cheeks, and gentle nose. He had a wealth of seduction in every feature. A perfect tear rolled down his cheek.

"Sit up," she commanded.

He turned his head from her and winced as if the very notion rattled his soul to destruction.

"No! I am dying," he whispered, "The Devil will have a new bedfellow tonight, and, oh! How I am dying."

Mary's smile dropped as her eyes scanned his face for any indication of deception. He looked incredibly ill all of a sudden. Archie peeked out of the corner of his eye to make sure she was looking at him and curled a smile. Mary slapped his chest.

"A terrible ruse!" she cried. "Some actor you are, Archibald Enfield."

Archie rolled onto his side, grabbed her, and hoisted her up onto him.

"Gin me, woman!" he declared, "before I waste away and wander lost and lonely through a desert of sobriety."

Mary rolled her eyes.

"Never, you cheeky fraudster. You've had quite enough, you soak, you. Plus it's late in the morning and its curtains up in a few hours." She climbed off him.

"Curtains up? Rhubarb! We have not even had a dress rehearsal, so it cannot be. Besides, it is curtains up on his birthday and today is not his birthday. I won't be fooled." Archie Enfield stretched out on the bed, happy that his day would demand little work.

"It *is* his birthday," said Mary as she began to collect up the clothes that littered the floor of the tiny garret.

Archie's eyes widened. "What?"

"'Tis the fifth, my dear."

"Lies, lies, pretty eyes! If anything it's at least the second, at a push the third. If it's the fourth I will eat my cravat, and if it's the fifth then I, Mary Middleton, am in trouble."

She turned to him and sighed. "Then you, Archibald Enfield, are in trouble".

"Buggeration! Really?"

Mary half frowned and raised her eyebrows in that 'sorry to be the bearer' kind of way.

"*Really*?" he stressed in defiance.

Mary nodded and threw the rest of his threadbare articles to him.

"You'd better get dressed and shift yourself to the playhouse, play with the Irregulars and cheer up dear old Ananas. The poor man has been in the gutter for too long. Oh, and, to think from where he came, too! It pains the heart…"

"And the lug-holes", interrupted Archie, "at least you don't have to listen to the idiot bang on about it all day."

"Oh, you love him, and do not say otherwise. Now, you rakish fool, get up and scarper before him outdoors becomes him indoors."

Archie leapt to his feet with surprising agility and swung his coat round on with a theatrical flourish. Mary, with her pleasant brown eyes and matching hair looked at him with an affectionate gaze. Archie had an immaturity to him that appealed to her greatly; a demeanor that cared not for all the ills of the time. Grime didn't muddy Archie Enfield and she deeply believed that he had the wonderful and unique ability to walk between the raindrops. Archie with his bloodshot eyes and explosive hair looked at her with an equally affectionate gaze. She had an inner strength to her that ran deeper than she would ever let on and a confidence that was a marvel to behold. Nothing broke down Mary Middleton and Archie knew that if he could somehow harness her laugh and bottle it, he could give it to London and bring some light into the lives of the put upon.

He stepped forward, took her by the hands and together they begun to waltz around the room which was barely big enough to blink in. With a soft and gentle whisper, he said; "Mary, you are the apple of my eye, truly."

Mary love-smiled at him and laughed that golden laugh.

"Archie, dearest Archie, in this room I am the apple of your eye. I am your apple tree it is true. But outside this room, ah, them barmaids, and gutter girls, them mollies and butter-beans, thems what make up your orchard." She kissed him. They stopped dancing and Archie bowed a ridiculous bow which filled her with joy.

"Alas, I must depart, lest that frog-backed husband of yours returns and makes a grave boy of me."

"The window as always?" she said, gesturing towards it as if directing a guest toward a room.

Archie smiled hopped over the bed like a jackrabbit, landing next to the window. He swung one leg over the ledge and stopped, half in and half out of the room. He looked back at her. She was glorious in her underclothes, her shoulders exposed, hair tussled and still with a flushed chest.

"Until the next time," he said, "stay just as you are." And with that ridiculous signoff, Archie Enfield exited the room. Mary

Middleton swooned and slumped down on her bed giddy at the hours she had spent with her lover. Archie didn't see the effect of his exit, but he imagined to be exactly how it was. Some people have that effect on others.

Having never looked before he leapt in his entire life, one would think the amount of injuries he had sustained in performing that exit would have taught him otherwise. Benjamin Ananas, his beloved friend had advised him on several occasions to think about climbing rather than leaping out of windows. "Or perhaps use a door," he would say. "Or maybe even court the girls who dwell on the ground floor." Sound advice indeed, however Archie didn't want to dangle out of windows, or stroll out of front doors. He wanted to leap and land hard on the ground.

"Like a leopard, Benji," he would say, "a deadly leopard."
Benjamin would roll his eyes, apply another bandage to the strained limb and pour an extra large drink for his hopeless friend.

As was his desire, Archie landed hard and landed well. He missed the gutter by a few inches, which didn't really save him for any distasteful feculence, as the streets of the rookery were pretty much a river of foulness. The calamitous hustle of the place was insane. Every corner seemed to harbour some sort of villainy. There was always some chancer or coiner, some burglar or mugger, some murderer or rapist lurking in the shadows. Of course, on some days when he had perhaps cheated a few beers out of someone, or he had struck on the idea for a new devised piece of theatre Archie would actually feel somewhat enamored with The Seven Dials. Sometimes in those halcyon hours, the nightmare would wash away and on every corner of that lively area he would see salt-of-the-earth characters and pretty women of wit and reverence, unified in their hardships, simply mucking in and getting on with it. How Archie loved the

Mighty Londoner on those days. Today however, the Seven Dials was an eel-infested reservoir of pus.

He looked around, taking a few minutes to gather his bearings; his hangover was still dancing around inside his body. *'The Seven Dials; what a shithole,'* he thought before spitting on the floor. Archie pulled his lapels up around his neck, looked to the floor and stepped out into the street. He had to get to Borough and to The Roxy Playhouse, rehearse, perform, bring the house down and give Benjamin Ananas the birthday he deserved. The thought of The Roxy filled him with warmth and batted back the sensory onslaught of The Seven Dials. Indeed, although Archie enjoyed his nights seeking out new and wonderful men and women to conquer, come the morning all he ever wanted was to get home to that theatre; that dilapidated, shitty, wonderful theatre, filled with those broken-down drunks, that collection of misfits and oddities, those glorious performers. The Roxy Playhouse Irregulars were his friends and lovers.

As he weaved through the great unclean, his thoughts drifted from the playhouse and back to Mary Middleton and how she had tasted. He had not lied when he said she was the apple of his eye. She was indeed one of his favourites and the only one who understood the concept of 'Giselle', that unobtainable ideal that was his life's pursuit. Mary was not 'Giselle' and she knew it, but she was more than happy to play along for a few hours when she could. After all, both of them knew that she would not be able to stand Archie much longer after their sessions anyway. He was fine enough for her in small doses. They both knew it and felt blessed to have that mutual understanding. Mary was one hell of a woman.

Archie was about to smile when four large men, factory built to intimidate stepped out of a doorway and surrounded him. Archie recognized them instantly: Each, Peach, Pear and Plum; the villainous heavies under the employ of one Richard Sheridan. They stood, surrounding Archie, each one hitting their clubs into their hands and chewing tobacco in unison.

"'Ello there, Master Enfield, my my, you are an easy one to find, ain't yer?" snarled Each, the 'brightest' of the four.

"Gentleman, good day to you and what a fine day it is, no time to talk I'm afraid, I have an 11:30 with the Regent, can't keep." Archie attempted to slink through the gang when Peach halted him with his club and shook his head.

"Oh no, Mr Enfield, don't be rushin' off just yet, not when you have more pressin' engagements," said Peach as he jabbed the point of his club into Archie's chest.

"Of course, my lovelies, I would love to stop and chat, I would, but... holy smokes, is that Wellington? What's he doing touching that woman?" Archie pointed to some vague character in the distance. Pear and Plum turned to look. Archie attempted to make a dash for it. He got about a yard before Each tripped him up. Archie fell hard, squelching into the mud and grime. The impact knocked the wind clean out of him. Pear and Plum turned back and, angry at falling for his ruse, administered a kick apiece to the poor man's ribs. Archie was lifted two feet into the air with the force. He spun over and landed down hard on his back. His vision blurring slightly, bells chiming in his ears.

"Can I conclude," he wheezed "that my cunning ruse did not payoff? Gentlemen, you are cleverer than I thought." He tried to get to his feet. "I do you a disservice."

Each smiled at the fool. "Help the spanner up," he said almost kindly. Peach and Pear helped Archie to his feet and dusted him off. Plum stood watch.

"Now, Mr Sheridan is not in the habit of granting clemency to them who bring him bad news. So don't send us back to him empty 'anded," said Each, enjoying his moment.

"That whole 'don't shoot the messenger' fing don't mean diddly-piss to old Sheridan…now, you don't want him to get the grouch with us, do you?"

Archie pondered the question. Peach grew impatient very quickly and wacked him in the stomach with his club. The little air Archie had managed to re-coup was expelled once more.

"Don't send us back to Mr Sheridan with bad news, Archie or we might have to come back. And not just for you," said Each. He turned to address Pear. "What's the name of that little one who hangs about with them lot? That little bit of Spanish crumpet."

"Claudia," said Pear, grinning like drain cover.

"Oh yes, Claudia," smiled Each. "Lovely, innocent Claudia." He stepped forward to Archie and clamped his filthy claws around the actors face. "Now we don't hit women, do we lads?" The lads shook their heads.

"No," he continued, his voice almost a whisper. "We do things much worse… don't we lads?"

"Yeah, much worse," they cackled together.

"You owe what you owe, and if you ain't paid up, we'll get hold of that Spanish whore and by the time we've all finished with her, there won't be an imagination in the land that can imagine her as a woman." Each's face was close to Archie's.

The thug's foul breath made Archie's stomach turn. Each began to chuckle and released his grip on the actor's face. Archie instantly head-butted Each and cracked his nose in the most satisfying way. Each staggered backwards, blinded by the blood and tears. Peach, Pear and Plum stepped into attack Archie when a rapier shot out of dark alleyway and halted their advance. The blade turned and rested against Archie's throat. The attackers halted, smiled and stepped back.

"Tut tut, tish and pish," floated an effeminate voice from the alleyway. Archie grimaced in recognition.

"Kemble, I should have known, you vile louse," he snarled.

"Silly, silly man," said Kemble, from the shadows, "you have cost yourself a little extra by hitting my man there. What will tell I Mr Sheridan?"

Archie, with his neck craned back to avoid the edge of the blade was breathing hard. Anger rose inside of him. He clenched his jaw and briefly contemplated taking them all on at once but he would not win. He knew that much.

"You tell that areswipe 'No-Not' Sheridan that he'll get his money when he gets his money."

Kemble stepped out of the shadows. He was a thin, fey man, covered in thick make-up and dressed in the clothes of a dandy. The makeup was chipped and faded, but still clung heavy to the nest of boils on his left cheek. He strafed Archie, turning so that the blade against his throat changed from edge to point. They stood face to face.

"Call him 'No-Not' Sheridan again Archie, I dare you," he hissed, twisting his rapier and burrowing the point into Archie's throat. The four heavies gathered behind Kemble. A tiny trickle of blood ran down Archie's throat. He clenched his jaw and buried the pain.

"I have the money," he said quietly. "Tomorrow, St Catharine's docks."

Kemble smiled and released the point. The heavies stepped backwards as Kemble bowed ornately, sticking his leg out and flourishing his hanky.

"There, that was not so ghastly, was it?" he said, standing back up and pocketing his hanky. "Good day to you Archie, off you trot now dear boy," and with that, Kemble flounced off into the uncaring hustle of the Seven Dials. Peach, Pear and Plum followed. Each was about to join them when he stopped, turned back and squared up to Archie.

"You were lucky that…"

Archie head-butted him again and Each staggered back cursing and stamping his feet. Archie was about to escape when Each recovered his senses and swung out at the actor. The thug connected sharply with the actor's jaw. Archie's eyes rolled back and he fell down onto the filthy street. As he drifted into unconsciousness Archie hoped that when he came to, he wouldn't be quite so hungover.

Chapter Two

The Roxy Playhouse Irregulars

Herschel Barnabus stood in the centre of the dark stage, rolled a cigarette and looked up into the eaves of the theatre. The old playwright inhaled the sweet orange flavoured tobacco and shook his head.

"Jesus," he said, "Those rafters are banjoed and no mistake."

The ballerina next to him looked also. "Danilov will be fine," she said in her warm, thick Umbrian accent. Herschel shook his head again. The ballerina silently moved into a handstand position and rested her foot underneath Herschel's chin. He nuzzled her sole and kissed the ball of her foot three times. "I hope you're right, Desiree, I hope you're right," he said.

Danilov, the taut lean man in question, was standing across the stage from Herschel and Desiree, tying a thin wire around himself which disappeared up into the gloomy rafters. Once it was tight, he gave it a little tug and looked upwards towards the beam it was tied to. There, above them all, high up on the rafters and glinting like a star, cartwheeled Danilov's younger sister; a lithe and graceful beauty named Anya Kamilcova.

"But Danilov *and* Anya up there?" said Herschel, with genuine concern. Desiree smiled, transferred her weight to one arm, effortlessly lifted the other and reassuringly patted him on the small of his back.

"Oh, she weighs less than a breath," she said softly. Herschel kissed her foot again and closed his eyes for nerves as Danilov began his ascent.

"If he gets up there," he warned, eyes still shut, "the chances are they'll be coming down with the whole place fast behind."

Desiree stood upright and kissed his cheek, soaking in his tobacco infused aroma.

"Either way, we'll bring the house down," she said before cartwheeling away. Herschel muttered under his breath and rolled another cigarette. Behind Herschel, half hidden in the wings stood a meek young boy of sixteen years holding an over-sized butterfly net. His name was Gertie and he was looking up at Anya with worried eyes. His mouth whispered, "Please don't fall, please don't fall, please don't fall," but what his heart really said was, *'fall so I can catch you, fall so I can catch you, fall so I can catch you.'*

Desiree cartwheeled across the stage, passing a moustachioed man who was trying on two identical hats in quick alternate succession and farther into the backstage area passing through the fug of perfume and make-up debris falling from the gargantuan opera singer named Lupe Darling. Nobody paid any attention to the duel-sword wielding Dalmatian fighting the eight-armed monster in the middle of the stage.

———•·•———

The Roxy Playhouse stood on Borough High Street wedged in between two ramshackle tenements that bore no resemblance to the vision held by their architect. This was due to numerous and seemingly random additions of wooden box-rooms and garrets plonked on the outside at nauseating angles. The theatre itself was largely ignored by the local populous and totally ignored by the artistic universe, save for those that lived within its crumbling walls and creaking beams. Local legend had it that The Roxy had once housed an actual performance. A real one, with curtains going up, people talking really loudly, and if that wasn't enough, actual applause from members of the paying public. Of course it was apocryphal, and in 1815 the building was simply there and it never demanded any attention. Like a mole on one's body that is in an inoffensive place; on the inside upper arm, or the shin perhaps. It just was. Far more heartbreaking than a theatre demolished or a theatre burnt down is a theatre forgotten. Locked in an oubliette of the public's conscience was a fate worse than death. However, the tragedy of The Roxy Playhouse was no more tragic than the state Borough was in, which in turn was no better off than the state of London. Reform was around the corner, but the spirit of hope and perseverance held little currency. The city was rife with vice and crime with nothing but decrepit old watchmen patrolling the unlit warrens of inequity. Life was a dangerous gauntlet for the Londoner. There were no country retreats with windy lakeside walks filled with hushed impropriety and stolen glances over the edge of laced fans. There were no balls or banquets or parlour games to play, just the drudgery of a hard and hopeless life. London was a brutal city.

However, even in the darkest parts of London there sometimes shone a little glint of life and one such glint made her way through the melee of hard living. Claudia, a sixteen year old Spanish girl pulled her little handcart laden with drink towards The Roxy, the jingle-jangle of the bottles she was ferrying creating a chaotic symphony that was almost lost in the din of the streets. She walked with the slightest spring in her step, a whisper of joviality, and a quiet, yet noticeable 'up-yours' to adversity. Her large, brown-eyes seemed not to see the dirt and toil all around her. She had a far-away manner; she was elsewhere, but in the most wonderful and reassuring way possible. If one were to look at her and notice that satisfied and distant gaze, you would assume she was recalling a sweet dream, or reminiscing over a time spent in the sunshine, in an orchard or an orange grove. It was so intoxicating to be orbiting such a calm innocence, that one felt as if one were right there with her, in whatever blissful land she was in. Some people are calm seas, it is true.

Anya Kamilcova was still high up in the rafters when Claudia entered the theatre. Below Anya, Danilov was swinging pendulously to and fro, suspended twelve feet above the ground by the wire caught around his ankle, which had prevented a fatal fall. Below him, Herschel and Gertie were running back and forth trying to grab Danilov's arm and pull him down safely to the ground. All the while, Gertie kept one eye on Anya.

The Spanish girl pulled her cart down the aisle towards the stage, the jingle-jangle of the bottles in her cart, where once was a chaotic symphony, was now a harmonious melody that caught the attention of everyone. Upon seeing the Claudia, Anya smiled broadly and leapt from the rafter. Gertie abandoned Herschel in his task of getting Danilov down and grabbed his butterfly net. Anya, in freefall, grabbed Danilov's wire and swung around it like a top, wrapping her legs around and scuttling down head first like a spider. She reached Danilov, untangled him and sent her brother crashing down twelve feet onto Herschel. Anya then let go and fell softly into Gertie's butterfly net. Claudia, with her goods, arrived and began to unload the baskets of bottles onto the stage. When she had finished, she held up her arms and Danilov climbed off of Herschel (who wriggled around like an upturned beetle), walked over to her, grabbed her wrists and whipped her up onto the stage in the blink of an eye. He bowed deeply and honestly to her, and she curtsied back, before turning to Anya and doing the same, and then to Gertie too. She turned to Herschel who was still beached.

"Hello dear Claudia! Just a second please," said the old man while gesturing to Gertie and Danilov who helped him up. He stood proudly before the Spanish girl.

"My dear sweet Little Mouse. You have returned in the nick of time and with the gifts of Dionysus himself. Oh! May the sun rise only to show your beauty to the world, forever more." And at that he bowed deeply and slowly. As he did so his back cracked five times. Luckily his bow was so deep, that nobody could see the pained expression on his face. He remained at the nadir of his bow for a few seconds. Everyone else looked quizzically at each other until Gertie cleared his throat.

"I'm fine...just...showing...my respect...," Herschel winced. Gertie and Danilov took some bottles and, linking their arms under Herschel's, helped the old man off stage.

Anya smiled and stroked Claudia's hair before taking a bottle and darting back up the wire to recline upon the beam and relax in her private universe that were the eaves of The Roxy. Below her, Claudia picked up some baskets and walked off towards the strange moustachioed man in the corner of the stage who was still exchanging the two hats on his head in a steady succession. Claudia looked up at him held out a bottle. He stopped, spun on his heels and looked at her. His bow was unlike the others as he stuck one foot out, and bent low on his calf, keeping his back straight.

"Antoine Le Magnifique thanks you, mon petite souris," he said in a French accent so overblown that it sounded like a vaguely offensive impersonation. He kissed Claudia's forehead, took the bottle, ripped the cork out with his teeth and spat it out across the stage at a great velocity. He smiled at Claudia who smiled back with bright eyes. He took one of his hats and put it on her head. He lilted his head, unsure if the hat suited her or not. Antoine rubbed his moustache and then took his own hat from his head and swapped the two over. He tilted his head the other way. Unsure still, he swapped the hats back around, then again and again and again. Claudia began to giggle, which made the Frenchman work faster, and faster, his hands becoming a blur. Claudia was giddy with excitement as the Frenchman dazzled her with his fast hands and she tried to keep up with which hat was on her head and which was on his. Suddenly, Antoine stopped. He looked at her with a confused expression. He furrowed his brow and felt his head, feigning surprise that the hats had gone. Claudia touched her head. Nothing. She smiled. He pondered. She laughed. He shrugged comically and turned away from her. She walked away beaming and not realising that the hats were now perched atop two bottles in one of her little baskets.

Lupe Darling was still putting on her face when Claudia reached her. The little girl tugged at Lupe's bustle and the huge woman turned to her, shrieking with mad joy upon seeing Claudia. Lupe had never had children, and never wanted them, until the day she met the little Spanish girl and as such had always held her close to her heart in the way mothers do. She kissed the girl a hundred times before she swiped a bottle from the basket. Claudia gasped as she noticed Antoine's hats on the bottles and turned back to him. From across the stage, he winked mischievously and blew her a kiss. He was trying on two new ridiculous hats in quick alternate succession.

"Darling Claudia," said Lupe, "you must take some to Benji, he is in his quarters. Keep him busy until we are ready. Now hurry, scurry Little Mouse!"

Claudia nodded and walked off into the warm, dark backstage area. It was a cramped and cluttered honeycomb of makeshift 'rooms' and vestibules for private and professional use, sectioned off by dirty sheets and blankets, damaged canvases, stacks of boxes, crates and backdrops of past productions. It had a charming homeliness to it that beggared love from everyone who lived there. Claudia had painted ivy over the 'doorway' of her dressing room. Not wanting to be selfish, she had also painted flowers and trees on those of everybody else using her preternatural talent to recall in exacting detail any scene, image or memory she cared to chose. Lupe had lilies, as they reminded her of the time she sang at the national opera in Prague and was pelted with them. Danilov had a forest and Herschel had sprigs of rosemary to remind him of his dearly departed wife and the smell of the sprigs she used to wear in her hair.

Claudia walked further along. She offered a bottle to Desiree who was reclining in a hammock, totally naked and rubbing some rose water into her legs as was her thrice daily routine. Claudia left the backstage area and came to a rickety old staircase. She ascended and stopped on the first level to peer into one of the few 'proper' rooms on a landing. It was a dark, candle lit chamber filled with busts, masks, costumes, weapons and all manner of props and tools designed to create whatever world the Players desired. The sign on the door read, 'Tobias Strong: Props Department'. Claudia knocked politely and waited by the door.

There was a shuffling inside the room and an extremely tall, thin man with a steep widow's peak and a gaunt face appeared from behind a large stuffed bear. He was hunched over and inspecting a small metal object though a madcap pair of glasses what had at least 35 different lenses, each one attached to its own arm, in turn attached to the frame. The lens he was looking through made his sharp grey eyes appear as big as the moon. Tobias Strong stood in the centre of the room amongst his costumes and props, slightly startled by Claudia's sudden appearance. He lifted his glasses from his head and bowed politely, and she followed suit before leaving a bottle on the floor by the doorway. She was about to leave, when he held up his finger to halt her. She halted. He turned to his cluttered work station, fumbled around and turned back to her smiling.

"Close your eyes, Claudia," he whispered in a soft and timid voice.

She smiled, closed her eyes and held out her hands.
Tobias approached her, bent and kissed her forehead, which left a slight oil-mark. The metallurgical smell of alchemy hung close to him and was as welcome and recognizable to the Spanish Girl as the smell of Desiree's rosewater skin, Archie's gin-breath or Antoine's moustache wax.

Tobias placed a small metal object in her hands and closed them shut. She opened her eyes and looked down at the prize the propmaker had given her; a perfect pearl, held in the most delicate silver bedding imaginable; a tiny circular mesh of silver thread, interwoven and spun to create a perfect 'birds nest' for the pearl to sit in. Claudia never failed to be amazed by the prop-makers magical ability to fold base metal and make it appear as gold or silver. She placed the pearl earring in her right ear before hugging Tobias's waist.

"Off you go to Benji, dear Claudia," he said, stroking her hair. "It's his birthday!"

Claudia released her hold of his waist and stepped out of the room and looked up the staircase. At the very top of the theatre stood an imposing, heavy dark-stained door with fake gothic trimmings and the words 'Benjamin Ananas: Crown Prince of the Wishful Drinkers.

Poet, Playwright, Artist…no circulars' scrawled across it. A polished violin hung next to the door. She ascended the staircase, picked up the violin, knocked on the door and waited. There was a rustling, a tumble, a crash of glass, a profanity. And then silence.

"Come," rumbled a deep, powerful voice from behind the door. Violin under her arm, Claudia picked up two bottles and opened the door to Benjamin Ananas private chambers.

"Happy birthday," she whispered as she stepped into the room and closed the door behind her.

Chapter Three

The Drunken Bear

Desiree stood, wrapped in a threadbare shawl and quietly watched Herschel pray by his bed. She could lip-read and her heart was full with sorrow as she watched him pray, not to God but to Annabel, his dearly departed wife. She had died in childbirth twenty five years before and left him a shattered man for the first six years after her death and a rebuilt man in the latter nineteen spent inside the comfort of The Roxy. Desiree dearly loved that ancient, fat and aching man and at a quarter to seven, every day, come happy hour or hellish hangover, she would watch him pray.

On this day, Herschel added a slight addendum to his usual prayer of love and hope. On this day, he asked Annabel to bless their production from on high, and to let her radiance and beauty illuminate each performance and touch the hearts of each of his beloved friends as she touched his heart every second of every day…oh, and to keep an eye on that rafter.

He got to his feet, crossed himself, and blew a kiss heavenwards. Desiree smiled and took him by the hand, the shawl falling slightly off her shoulder and exposing a perfect collarbone. She leant forward and they kissed deeply and longingly. The kiss was what they lived for. Herschel's love for his Annabel was sacred to both of them, but their love for each other was another heaven altogether.

"Is Archie back?" enquired Herschel, his blue eyes slightly bloodshot and tired, but still carrying a hint of his not-forgotten youthful devilry. Desiree shook her head. Herschel tutted. He took her by the hand and they walked over to the empty stage.

They stood there in the middle of the boards and looked out over the empty auditorium. Desiree thought back to her youth, and the roar of her father as he watched the clowns and buffoons perform in the open piazza in Perugia, and herself captivated by the strength and grace of the ballerinas. Herschel brought forth the rapturous applause of the twenty three people who had seen the legendary opening night of his adaptation of 'The Medea'. The memories were glorious and searing and no amount of cheap gin and lousy pipedreams since had dulled them.

Antoine's thunderous clap from the wings snapped Desiree and Herschel out of their daydream.

"Almost time and no Archie!" he bellowed, "Almost time! Where are Anya, and Lupe? I need making up." Antoine dashed backstage, displaying his usual pre-performance nerves.

Herschel and Desiree were about to follow when the doors to The Roxy were flung open and Archie Enfield flopped through the opening and staggered about the aisles until he reached the stage. Herschel and Desire stood dumbstruck as the libertine lover, bruised jaw, muddied and bloodied attempted to hoist himself up on the stage three times before losing his grip and falling backwards. The ballerina and the playwright dashed to him to help him to his feet.

"What in Athena's undercrackers happened to you?" said Herschel, as Desiree attempted to wipe the matted hair from Archie's brow, all the while kissing his cheek with worry, in the way Italian women do.

"It's nothing, honestly, Herschel, I'm fine."

"You've come a right cropper," replied the playwright, shaking his head.

"It's fine."

"Were you out hunting Giselles again?" asked Desiree.

"God loves those that try, right?" smiled Archie, his indomitable eyes, bloodshot and bright. He stepped back from his two friends, fixed his hair, took a deep bow, and stood upright in a flash, magically transforming his demeanor back to normalcy.

"Show time," he declared and hopped onto the stage like a jackrabbit. Archie stood on the stage and looked at the backdrop; a marvelously painted panorama, the left side depicting the inside of a study, resplendent with a suit of armour, coat of arms bearing the name 'Ananas', a floor to ceiling library and globe bar. The right side of the backdrop displayed an idyllic English countryside. Archie nodded his approval and walked behind the curtain.

Backstage was bustling with activity. Danilov was stretching off while Lupe Darling was applying lipstick and rouge onto his face, a task which she seemed to be more than capable of doing, despite Danilov's movements. Indeed, the two worked together in a rather pleasing symmetry. It would have been poetic and soothing, if Lupe Darling wasn't 'warming' up her pipes by racing up and down the scales at a volume that would a make dead dog howl. Archie slapped a portion of her posterior and took the bottle out of Danilov's hand as he passed them by.

Rounding the back of the stage, he passed Anya who was walking over a trial wire, erected three feet off the ground. Archie limbo danced under the wire and flashed a smile at Anya, who winked back as she performed a jimmy flip. He carried on around the backstage area all smiles, until he received a butterfly net in the stomach. He flipped forward and fell into the net. Gertie apologised profusely for the accident, tipped him out and carried on thrusting and jabbing, practicing every pose imaginable in which to catch Anya should she fall.

Archie clicked his heels and strolled through the path of the Dalmatian who was still fighting the eight-armed monster, blades flashing, parrying and riposting and with each thrust millimetres from nicking Archie. Onward he walked until he reached the end of the backstage area. He turned around and looked back at the commotion he had strolled through. His friends were in their own little world, and Archie's heart was filled with joy to know these oddities and lovelies were alive in *his* world. He felt his jaw, which was killing him, and ventured further into the bowels of the theatre.

The darkness and gloom shrouded the echo of Lupe's scales. The only sound other than Archie's boots was the worry in the back of his mind that had returned to invade his solitude. Sheridan and his goons truly would be the death of him, and Archie Enfield really hoped that he wouldn't die. Why had he said to meet him the next morning? He knew he couldn't outrun the debt forever. He took a second for himself and rested upon a beam. The avenues of redemption seemed closed and, in the darkness, he knew that it was almost over for him. His bottle was empty. But, it was his friend's day. It was Benjamin Ananas's birthday and Archie would rather die a death worse than the one that was upon him than let down the drunken bear of a man. He rallied once more and clambered through the gloom until he got to the edge of the stairwell. And then it hit him full in the heart, and his jaw hurt no more. Claudia's violin was alive.

Archie smiled and sat upon the bottom stair and listened. It did not take long before Tobias Strong left his workshop on the landing and wandered down to join Archie. They shook hands and sat together, sharing a bottle and listening. The luminous melody of

Claudia's violin floated down to the pair of friends and hung in the air, sweeping and diving around them. It carried all the hope and spirit of the young, and was, when it was heard, the glue that bound their hearts. However, the perfection of the melody was not simply in its single line, but in its accompaniment. Underneath that melody, sobbed a deep and melancholic lament from Benjamin Ananas' heart which filtered through his cello. The waltzing instruments united to question and answer each other, to contradict and collude, and to sing and sigh. Ananas' years of unwanted wisdom and enforced life and Claudia's spirited naivety were everything.

Strong closed his eyes, the faintest smile crossing his face, his fingers rippling through an imaginary stream. Archie sipped his drink and dangled his feet over a pier as Sheridan and his cronies were cast into the fog of his memory, each one of the bastards paid off and never to return, the slender hand of a Giselle on his shoulder. Times were easy and London was mighty when Claudia and Benjamin spoke to each other with their instruments. Finally, the conversation ended with Ananas and Claudia sustaining a single, sad note beyond reason until the sound fell asleep and Tobias and Archie fell awake. They looked at each other and smiled. Strong stood up and returned to his work.

Claudia opened Ananas' door and saw Archie standing there, dirty, bedraggled and ravishing. At only sixteen, Claudia was green to the vagaries of love and lust. To her, it was a near indecipherable charter of the unknown. But something about Archibald's manner lit a beacon inside her. He represented that glimmer of temptation to jump headlong into the ravine of desires. As ever she held her secret confusions deep inside her and the outside world remained oblivious to her inner conflicts. Claudia had not even told Lupe Darling, that huge oracle in matters of the heart about it all. It was her mystery alone.

Claudia smiled and descended to meet Archie who rose instantly, dusted himself off and sorted out his hair. He fixed her with a thankful smile for the music and bowed earnestly. Claudia curtsied before leaping from the fourth step onto Archie, who grabbed her and spun her round, forcing her to burst out laughing. He gave her a huge kiss on her forehead and she walked away into the gloom of the backstage loaded with an even greater galaxy of questions thanks to his lips. Archie watched her leave before turning to the walk up to his pal's room.

The room was dark and dank and the air hung oppressively low. The few candles guttering on the wonky fireplace afforded little evidence to prove that the room was really there and that it wasn't some awful void. There were no windows. Well, that's not entirely true, there may well have been windows somewhere, but the walls were covered with tacked up boards and papers, every inch covered with childish scrawls and drunken messages, ideas, thoughts, brainwaves. It was a living notebook. The candles flickered and threw up random words on the walls and hinted at objects in the room. There were stacks of books, papers and props everywhere. There was a desk, a cello, a bed, and a figure lying upon it.

Archie knew his way around the room and made his way to the busted chair in the corner. The cushioning was shot away so when he slumped down in it, he almost disappeared completely. He looked over at the outline on the bed. It was breathing. Good sign. The candles picked out a pair of glinting eyes, focused way passed the ceiling and far away into space and memory.

Archie looked down at all the bottles that lay strewn about his feet. He found one that was still, miraculously, corked. He picked it up and opened it. The sound of the uncorking made the outline on the bed move a little more. The smell of the drink drifted over to its nostrils and there was a slightly more aggressive movement from the shape.

"What time is it?" said the outline in a voice that sounded like it had been filtered through a tombola of gravel.

"Birthday time," said Archie in his usual chipper tone.

The outline replied with a wet and fluey cough. It sat up. The candles took that as a sign to illuminate the character a little more. Hairy and mad, wrapped in a moth-eaten bearskin rug sat Benjamin Ananas. He sported a large, proud hooked nose, rather high forehead, full lips, greasy hair and an unruly and matted beard. He was a mess before one even considered his personal hygiene.

"Showtime my friend," said Archie smiling kindly.

Benjamin Ananas nodded and reached for his cane. He stood to his full six foot three inches.

"How do you feel?" *'Pointless question'* thought Archie, *'pointless'*.

Ananas looked down at him. Archie nodded, stood up and hugged the drunken bear.

"Happy birthday my friend."

Benjamin coughed once more and took the bottle from Archie and drank heavily from it. Archie looked him over and, seeing a spark of life returning to the bear, decided he was ready to leave his chamber and face the world. He crooked his arm and Benjamin grabbed hold of it.

"Ready, Old Love?"

Ananas wheezed.

"Close enough. Show time," and Archie kicked open the door and led Benjamin out of the room and towards the auditorium.

The backstage area was spookily bereft of activity as Archie led his friend through, down the side of the stage, through the orchestra pit and into the stalls. Benjamin found his way to a suitable seat and collapsed into it. He looked around and smiled as he noted that all around him lay fresh bottles of drink. '*A kind and considered gesture*', he thought as he cracked one open and sat back to watch his friends perform for him. After the first sip he let out a sigh and the words "life is good" fell from his mouth. And then the curtains went up.

Hats off to Brandenburg

Chapter Four

The Fortunes and Misfortunes of Our Friend Benjamin Ananas'

An original play by Herschel Barnabas (Extracts)

Extract – Act One, Scene One

The study of Benjamin Ananas as a young man. A simple modest study piled with canvases and papers. There is a desk in the middle of the room. Slumped over is Benjamin Ananas - young, beautiful, working.

Enter the narrator.

Narrator

See here, gentle audience, bright of eye
and warm of heart, see here our hero.
Note how he is stooped over his desk,
note how his quill flurries. Note, if you
see with your mind and not your eyes,
how the dreams and wonders fall all
around him.

Dreams and visions made real enter the stage and dance around him. Colourful birds, dancing maidens, flying machines and mythical creatures. All in silent dance.

> Narrator (cont'd)
> Mark and remember our hero's definite posture: that of the artist! Low to the paper, low to the canvas. Note how much he toils, with the dreams all around who tease and weave! Note all you lovers, note all you audience for here is how we all are. The artist in love, but in love with nary a note of hope.

(Clearly vexed, Ananas stands up and begins pacing around the study.)

> Narrator (cont'd)
> But note now, how this artist is pacing, note now with your eyes, not your mind, how the artist's brow is troubled and furrowed, for what could possibly trouble him so? Could it be the instrument? A blunt chisel? A dulled quill? Weak canvas? Hark now with those audience ears as we find out.

(Narrator steps aside)

Ananas

Ah! The vex of my mind, the break of my
heart! For lack, lack, lack and quadruple
the lack of my art! How can the true artist
be, if one cannot set the bondage artist
free? Behold the clock and the hour it
near will chime, I think I'll die in despair
in this solitude of mine.

The dreams made real fade. Benjamin is left alone in his study.

Ananas (cont'd)

For what if we break apart the word that
is 'heart'? We find only the word 'he'
and the word 'art'. But it is this he, this
man of me that cannot live in this world
without his art nor heart. But a way out
of this gloom, this prison of mine I
cannot see! I just cannot seem to make
real, all my ideas, dreams and the love I
feel. I am a useless artist.

Benjamin slumps down against his desk and throws his quill across
the stage

———•◦•———

The Benjamin Ananas in the audience was sideswiped by the
'Benjamin Ananas' on stage in front of him. Srdjan, the actor in the
lead role and who had previously been sword-fighting the eight
armed monster, had somehow reached into the soup of memory and

pulled out something miraculous. The stoop over the desk, the frantic scribbling over the parchments, even the breathing was impeccable. For a fleeting moment, the audience member was enraptured with the feeling that Mnemosyne herself had flown down from Olympus and held up a mirror to him. But not a mirror that showed the drunken birthday bear in his contemporary form, but a mirror that showed the fierce and passionate man of his youth. He instantly began to weep, quietly and gracefully. One eye cried for the astonishing portrayal from Srdjan and how he well he must have known his character, despite never meeting him in the time of life from which he was performing, and the other eye cried for all those awful moments when one remembers how beautiful and apocalyptic their verve used to be and how, over vicious time, they had offered themselves up to a dulled and blunt life.

In an instant, Benjamin was youthful and angry once more and it was not the twisted and bile-filled anger of his adult years, but the passionate anger of his youth that used to marshal armies of conviction ready to do battle with the world around him.

The simple stage setting triggered the romanticism of memory inside Benjamin and he conjured up his little study, hidden away in an almost forgotten wing of his parent's mansion house in Hampshire. He had spent over twenty-five years burying his past and now, on his birthday, he was confronting it. He relented and fell deeply into memory.

Though in his youth, he had never had to worry about money, or hardship, he had never been in anyway content with anything around him, especially his 'art'. Watching Srdjan portray his struggling artist on stage caused hundreds of ideas, theories and forgotten dreams to spring up in his mind. Benjamin swooned at just how versatile and fast his creativity used to be. But, more acutely, he grimaced at just how mediocre his art was in retrospect. At the time, he believed he moved at a speed too fast for his contemporaries to understand. Sometimes, at night, he couldn't keep up with himself. Every thought generated galaxies of questions, which, in turn, created solar systems within them of answers, problems, and contradictions. But in truth, even though he couldn't see it then, the compassionless march of time had convinced Benjamin Ananas that he had had no real talent at all, save for his gift for duping himself into believing that he held fire in his hands. The frustration that he couldn't marry idea to artistic execution was projected onto the world he saw. Everything around him, from the vulgar opulence of his parent's lifestyle to the bitter taste his peers' idiotic vanities left in his mouth.

Of course, the forty-five year old Benjamin Ananas now looked back and cringed at just how naive and misguided he'd been in thinking that his art was divine. While his young friends danced and drank, he would sit amongst them and objectively take part certain that at some point, the banality of the games they played would add some sort of ingredient for some great masterpiece waiting inside to be called forth. He was a foolish, foolish boy, he concluded.

As the play of his youth unfolded on stage, Benjamin couldn't help but concede that though he had been foolish, at least he wasn't wretched. Not like his friends were. While he had fallen from the grace of his art and his God, they had remained as they were, in amongst the comfort of their decanters, swelled by the satisfaction of their bellies. At least he tried to understand his existence, however unsuccessfully, he concluded, while those around him lived out their vulgar lives.

Ananas sighed at the romantic thought that he should've died young and vital, instead of old and haggard. Still, he concluded, if his destiny was the gutter, at least he could die amongst the filth, on his back, bottle in hand, surrounded by his true friends and looking up at the stars.

He laughed his booming laugh at the tragic comedy on stage, and was tickled pink at the revelation of how his true friends saw him. Clearly, presenting a play detailing his miserable past could've tipped him over the edge, especially on his birthday, and (double-specially) when one considered his booze filled mental state. Instead, he was enthralled and knew that his friends knew he would be. To an outsider, it would have seemed a deadly risk and may have garnered a simple two word review that read 'too soon' but to The Roxy Playhouse Irregulars, sticking their heads in the bear's mouth and forcing him to confront his past was nothing short of artistic derring-do.

"Bravo!" he shouted as Srdjan sank to his knees weeping, after delivering a heartfelt soliloquy that captured the essence of Benjamin's youth and anguish. He was awestruck at the precision of the writing and the delivery and found himself clapping wildly. And that was before the entrance of Archie and Desiree dressed to the nines in finery. Playing Lord and Lady Ananas respectfully (after a lightning fast costume change on Archie's part to get him out of his narrator's garb), the two threw themselves around the set, blowing a fresh gust into the play and changing the pace considerably. Benjamin smiled broadly at Desiree's interpretation of his mother and was very impressed with her considered walk and rigid poise. His mother had always held herself as if her spine were made of iron. Moving from one pose to another always seemed awkward. Benjamin had always assumed that she had been schooled, if not born to believe that she was a statue, and that any sort of movement was unnatural and unthinkable.

Of course, he had loved his mother as all boys do, but as he grew up and began to become aware of himself, his world, her world, and the rest of the world, he had quickly realised that, much to his lament, all three were completely different planets in completely different universes. His natural love for his mother was boxed away and looked after, but his respect for her gender was not learned through her at all.

The alarming transformation Desiree had achieved, simply in the way she had impersonated the rigidity of his mother, rattled Benjamin. Had he expressly told her about his mother? It was possible. At the backend of a ten day drinking spree, Benjamin could have told her anything. There was no denying the uncanny resemblance in her silhouette, even down to the calculated lilt of the head. Desiree was dead and Lady Ananas was alive. The very thought made Benjamin drink harder. His mother had died long ago, burnt to a crisp in that terrible house fire and whatever afterlife she now posed in, she was certainly better off there.

———•—

Extract - Act One, Scene Eight: (Cont'd)

Benjamin returns from the cellar, sits at his desk and attempts to draw. He soon grows frustrated with his efforts and tears up the parchment.

Ananas

Damn you heart, and damn you art! What
can I do, what can I offer so that unto me

talent you will proffer? Is there no deal, no accord that we can reach? Help me Lord!

(The stage dims and a ghostly green light appears.)

Ghostly Voice

I am here, I always have been.

Ananas

Hark, what can that voice be? For both my father and mother are far from me. And my lordly kin are at sport and play, for I have been locked in solitude all of this day.

Ghostly Voice

Summon me up, bring me near and I will cure your doubling fears.

Ananas

(Laughing at the obvious practical joke.)

A pitiful ruse but a playful try, to instill some fear into this heart of mine. Fair enough, I'll play along and summon them out. I call their bluff. Come out Messrs Whit, Belling and Clough.

Silence.

Ghostly Voice
Those boys you summon, those boys you accuse have no part in this for 'tis no ruse.

Ananas smiles and raises his hands and bellows dramatically.

Ananas
So then devil or angel, or who e're you be. Show yourself now and come parley with me!

Ananas freezes with his arms outstretched.

Enter The Narrator.

Narrator
So the die was cast and the demon was summoned, that Being whom, in tradition past, carried quiver and arrows which into hearts cast. But those who know and I'm sure as you do, that Demon carries also thumb-locking screws. Not all kindness love and joy, for he is also a black-hearted boy. He arrives. See him now. Behold! Cupid!

———•◦•———

Already two bottles into the play, Benjamin's heart was totally in step with his surroundings. The set, the writing, the performances, all of it was a wonderful circus. His posture had shifted from slouched to upright and alert. His eyes had widened and had shattered the crust of sleep that had previously all but entombed them. Now they were young and active, darting around the stage, picking apart every iota of detail. His heart was beating fast and his hands were shaking. He was clutching his second bottle so tightly that the booze inside was almost boiling. He was alive. And then, Danilov appeared and Benjamin gasped.

With a preternatural grace Danilov, playing Cupid, swooped in from the rafters and dipped and dove around the space two feet above Young Ananas' head. His costume was a simple construction of feathered wings, no doubt mined from Lupe Darling's extensive boa collection. His eyes were closed, but Lupe had painted over his eyelids two huge, wondrous angelic eyes; the eyes of a babe, the eyes of love. But she had also painted his mouth and made it carry a pained and disturbing smile - something altogether sadistic.

As he flew around the stage, accompanied by a heavenly aria courtesy of the hidden Lupe Darling, Ananas couldn't help but feel a burning sensation of love and repressed desire for the acrobat. Danilov, in his Cupid's attire, was naked save for his wings and quiver. In the candlelight his body was breathtaking. He was taut, muscular and powerful and despite the unsettling make-up, his grace and poise conjured up a volcanic expression of lust within Benjamin.

Extract - Act One, Scene Eight: (Cont'd)

Narrator
See that cupid armed to the teeth and
grinning like a beast, ready to strike a deal, a

barbarous accord. Who will help dear
Ananas, are you hiding in the cupboard dear
Lord?

Exit Narrator. Our scene unfreezes.

Cupid

Ah dear mortal and troubled young soul
before you see not demon nor troll. But the
beauteous babe and lover of loves, winged
bliss sent from above. You are troubled
young man, the plight of Benjamin I cannot
ignore! I see you are vexed and broken of
mind, fallen upon such doubtful times. For
you see that your art has not a true note, a
stingless harp, and neckless lute.

Ananas

Yes and yes, and a third time yes.

Ananas goes to his desk and holds up his drawings and paintings in
dismay. Cupid looks over them.

Ananas (cont'd)

See the work, how flat it sits. I would say to
you to behold the colours, but so dull and
bland that the name 'colour' seems wrong.
Pray babe of babes, lover of loves, help me
here and help me now.

Cupid
Well the answer is simply and perfectly
clear, come step forward and stand around
here.

Cupid directs Ananas to stand in the centre of the stage. He pulls
back his bow and arrow and lets one fly straight into the troubled
artist's heart.

———•◦•———

Benjamin battled internally with the lust and the lava Danilov stirred
inside him as it made him fall into his memory and dare, beyond all
his battle plans, to allow his mind's voice to utter the name of his
destroyer and, as soon as his mind's voice had dared to whisper that
heathen name, his mind's eye also betrayed him and blew forth her
image. Time had done nothing to diminish or heighten her beauty and
Benjamin Ananas remembered her exactly how she was: *'the one'*.
Then, like the collapse of a cathedral only played back in reverse, the
world around that vision rebuilt itself and after a quarter of a century
of repression, he was now looking upon the face of his one true love:
Abigail Hardwoode.

Chapter Five

Abigail Hardwoode
(With further extracts)

It wasn't until that apocalyptic month of May in his twentieth year that Benjamin Ananas was struck in the heart by Cupid's arrow. Only a few parties into the calendar and his weak constitution could not take much more. He had drunk wantonly during the beginning of the month partly because he was expected to, partly because he had to get through the events but mainly because he was trying desperately to unlock the secrets of his failing talents. He had read somewhere, or possibly heard something (he couldn't remember which) that all the great artists, thinkers, lovers and dreamers of the age had somehow honed their gifts through their prodigious intake of drink, drugs, food and fornication. He was young and could never have known the ridiculousness of his theory, or that the artist's path is not known even to the artist and that they all simply bumbled from one idea to the next much like everyone else.

Even so, the pace of the beginning of the month had caught up with him and before the Whit ball had begun, he had a terrible feeling in his bowels that any excess would be exceedingly unwise. As he had travelled in the coach with his ridiculous father and rigid mother, every bump and jolt of the carriage had sent frantic warning signs through his digestive system in every direction. He had gripped the carriage handle so tightly that by the time they had arrived his fingers had all but cramped up and he had to use his other hand to unclamp them.

After the third week of endless balls, parties, dinners and dances, they all seemed to blur into one. Conversations went beyond being merely repeated and into the realms of the archetype. At the time, Benjamin couldn't differentiate one party, one supper, one lord or lady from the countless others, let alone recollect any of them years later. But, because of what happened at that party, on that day, somehow it had galvanized in his mind and the seemingly inconsequential or indeed regular occurrences had stuck along with it, orbiting that one event, held in by the gravity of its importance, forever revolving around the hours he spent in the maze with *her*. He had felt awfully ill, that much he remembered. The scented sherry and the juniper and ginger twisted liquor hadn't settled his stomach. Some monstrous woman with a heavily made up face like a bulldog dipped in flour had been barking at him, her pine yellow teeth smeared with caviar looming into him as she spat and slurped on about her wealth and reverence. He remembered the portraits on the wall which looked exactly like every other portrait in every other home. Each stern and aloof, casting judgment on the fanciful debutantes gorging beneath them. He only remembered those particular portraits because he remembered that gorgon woman, and he only remembered her, because he remembered the drink, and he only remembered the ineffectual drinks because he remembered his volcanic stomach, and he only remembered that because he remembered running out of that party and seeking solace in the huge topiary maze in the grounds of Eveltham House and he only remembered that maze, because he remembered the central star in that memorial solar system. That star whose name was Abigail Hardwoode.

———•·•———

Extract - Act One Scene 27 – The Maze in the Grounds

Ananas wanders lost through the maze. Cupid's arrow still juts from his heart. Topiary animals stare at him. As he wanders, the hedges and animals move behind him: an ever-changing labyrinth. Though he is lost, he is lost more so in thought.

Ananas

> This arrow in me, what use? What good?
> I still see and feel as a normal man
> should. I notice the leaves and feel the
> sun on my face. I know every privet and
> every leaf in this, a most secluded place.

———•·•———

In the empty auditorium, Benjamin Ananas gleefully smiled as the actors on stage, covered in branches and bracken moved about the stage in sharp, sudden, feline movements, shifting and morphing with each other to create new topiary animals, both real and mythical. Archie, with branches and leaves sticking out from every conceivable pocket, sleeve and seam, climbed onto Gertie's back and held up his arms and lo, before Benjamin towered a mighty Phoenix. The Benjamin on stage was oblivious to the eerie and slightly melancholic dance sequence going on around him. This filled the real Benjamin with a warm glow. The Phoenix fell apart, moved snake-like on the floor, and joined with Claudia, Lupe and Antoine to create freeze frames of a goose taking flight. Then Anya descended from the roof, foliaged like the others, and hung there at the zenith of the goose's flight path, arms outstretched, head craning to the heavens. The image of a goose in the different moments of take-off sparked a curio inside Benjamin and he was struck by the sublime idea to make a series of relief wood carvings of that very image to decorate his chamber wall. *'What'* he thought *'symbolises hope, nature and freedom better that a bird taking flight?'* He smiled at the novel idea and smugly flicked the lid off of another bottle.

Extract - Act One, Scene Twelve - The Maze in the Grounds: (Cont'd)

Benjamin is sitting on the ground, around him the topiary animals have now merged to form a giant, open clam, much like the ones mermaids lounge about on. Our Hero is peacefully sleeping, the arrow still sticking out of his chest.

Enter Abigail Hardwoode, stage left – young, lithe and possibly beautiful. We cannot see for her face is covered by the mask of a porcelain doll. She is walking around looking in wonder at the sun, the clouds, and the hedges.

Then an eye in the clamshell opens and turns to Abigail. Just then, Cupid descends. He blows a kiss onto the Clamshell – gold and silver elements of stardust fall around it.

Slowly the shell breaks apart and moves towards Abigail. It reforms around her, creating new paths and forcing her towards the sleeping Ananas. She rounds a corner and spots him. The 'hedges' drift back.

She walks cautiously up to him, bends down and touches his cheek softly. His eyes open. Cupid readies his arrow. Ananas stands up, entranced at the vision before him. He seems to be haloed with a bright, warm light. He bows slowly and deeply. Cupid releases his arrow, straight into the heart of the masked Abigail.

———•••———

As he sipped his drink, Benjamin couldn't for the life of him recollect the discourse that had taken place on that evening in the maze all those years ago. The back and forth, while probably searing and complete at the time had been well and truly lost in the mire of memory. Instead it was the inconsequential details of the environment that still hung onto the inside of his head. He smiled in wonder at how he had vowed that when she said whatever it was that she said, he would remember it for all eternity. Instead he just remembered that a few feet behind her head, and to the left, there was an ugly little branch sticking out of the topiary peacock. He remembered that the clasp of her necklace had slid to the side and rested now in plain sight on her collarbone. He remembered looking down at his feet when she said something, and noticing a slight scuff to the inside left. As for the words that were spoken? He remembered nothing of them.

In the imagination of The Roxy playwright Herschel Barnabus, however, the courtship of Benjamin Ananas and Abigail Hardwoode on that bright, searing May afternoon was conducted in a rapid back and forth, each one instantly sparring and playfully handling their instantaneous rapport as if it were dough and they were both making a wondrous cake, the recipe of which was shared only by the two burgeoning lovers.

Across the stage Srdjan and Desiree (Ananas guessed it to be her behind the mask) poked and prodded each other verbally, sparring and dancing around in the most curious and dizzying display of verbal gymnastics he had rarely had the pleasure to witness. Herschel was really flying. On stage love was being born and Benjamin sank deeper into his chair and a dark melancholia suddenly blew through his soul, and as it passed its echo reverberated his heartstrings and they lamented *'if only it was like that, if only it was like that and it stayed like that, if only it was like that and it stayed like that and it was like that still and so for evermore'* He drank deeply, dropped the empty bottle on the floor and regressed to their second meeting, some weeks later at Rose Manor Hall.

Extract - Act Two, Scene Seventeen - The Rose Manor Dance

The great hall is resplendent with decorations. Great chandeliers with gold garlands wreathed around them like a great spiderweb. Everybody is dancing. Men are bowing, bosoms are heaving.

Enter Ananas, stage right, dressed well, perfect posture. The dance carries on, around him.

Enter Abigail Hardwoode, stage left dressed equally well and still wearing her porcelain doll mask.

The two meet in the middle of the stage - their Cupid's arrows still protruding. They dance around the stage, eyes locked on each other.

———•·•———

Benjamin laughed at the sight of him dancing around the stage as it was almost a flight of fancy too far. Of all talents he had as child, dancing could not be counted among them. His expression of concentration, his rigid posture and overly calculated moves rendered him an undesirable dancing partner. Indeed, his general shadowy nature and peripheral lurking rendered him more than undesirable as a partner for any sort of activity. As a child he played alone, as a teenager he wandered and wondered alone. As a young man, well, that was different. Though he naturally orbited around the fringes of the social clusters, he did genuinely want to participate in the jokes, gossiping and gorging.

He inwardly railed against the social practices of his friends, but in truth it was a contradiction within him, the contradiction that told him that he did, sometimes, need interaction. He needed to talk and dance and eat and kiss. *'If only to know how the other side live,'* he would suggest. So dance he tried, and fail he did, but again and again he would take to the floor, offer an arm or a hand and try desperately to at least appear to know what he was doing and to at least look like he was enjoying it. The result was an off-putting mix of expressions.

However, the ball at Rose Manor was different. In preparation he had taken twice as long bathing, twice as long dressing and a laughable amount of time fixing his collar before leaving that afternoon, in case Abigail Hardwoode might be there.

Extract - Act Two Scene Eighteen - A Balcony at Rose Manor

Benjamin and Abigail are alone on the balcony. All the stars are out, watching the lovers. Benjamin takes Abigail's hands. The moon grows brighter, the stars hold their breath.

Ananas

I speak from my heart if I may be so bold
to do as his bidding, as Cupid has told. I
have thought of nothing, not eaten nor
slept. It seems on an ocean away I've
been swept. So far from my home to a
raft I have clung, to drift through storms
to your island I've come. To the paradise
named Abigail with meadow and
mountain, to live off her land and drink
from her fountain that springs eternal
with grace and light, with each breath a
new star born in the night.

The two lovers kiss and all the stars sigh.

———•◦•———

Benjamin Ananas had never kissed Abigail Hardwoode on a balcony that much was for sure. The romanticism of their second encounter was much more fraught with nerves, much more awkward and with not quite as large a celestial audience as was presented on stage. However, Benjamin had shared many evenings with Archie listening to tales of his conquests, from wooing parlour girls and barmaids to his greatest achievement to date; the bedding of some sisters from an obscure family called Bennet in some backwater town called Meryton in a single evening.

Archie always peppered his stories with fanciful details mainly designed to heighten the romanticism or endanger the situation. He never lied about the grimy details of the events, but he certainly embellished the details of the occasion. Candles always dimmed 'conspiratorially' to avoid arousing suspicion while he was ravishing a chambermaid in the room next door to her master. Dresses seemed to undo themselves at his convenience. Swords drawn by rage-filled husbands were eight feet long. Bosoms were colliding planets and peacocks would squawk louder to mask the noise of congress emanating from gazebos as he stole brides' virtues on their wedding days.

And so Benjamin Ananas was sure his roguish friend had coaxed Herschel's interpretation of the first kiss from something adequate and into something far more ethereal. In reality, despite the awkwardness of that first kiss, Abigail and Benjamin had both dove headfirst into love's abyss. Letters, missives, meetings both secret and public, hands held, collarbones kissed, vows exchanged, gifts, poems, walks, dinners every manner of thing that lovers do when they are in love they did. And it was the real thing because, truly, they believed that nobody had done what they had done nor experienced what they had. Everything was original, fresh and theirs. They were the spinning around on love's great carousel.

The returning taste of Abigial's lips in Benjamin Ananas' memory lulled him into a light sleep and he travelled back in time to be with her but instead of the dream he had hoped for, he was greeted with the nightmare of her betrayal.

In his dreamscape, he was walking down the corridor leading to his little study. It was unusually cold for June and he could see his breath. He felt a pang of dread and his feet grew heavy as if sinking into the floor. He did not want to approach that door and yet he was compelled to. He looked around and winced in fear as the wood paneled walls appeared to be glistening. Water? Oil? Blood? What liquid ran down those walls? He dared not reach out to touch them and instead carried along. His vision began to distort. The door seemed to come forward while the walls pulled away in a contradictory motion. He felt a great nausea rise inside him and the coldness penetrated him deeply. On his brow the sweat was like ice. He reached the door and tried to open it, but it would not move. The feeling of dread did not fall away and, not fully aware that he was dreaming; Benjamin could not muster the fortitude to wake himself up. Against all logic, his feet moved forward and he walked through the door, the internal splinters scratching at his face as he passed through.

He was now standing in his study. The distortion in his vision corrected itself and the room appeared to be real. It was the normalcy that turned the dream into a nightmare because he knew instantly that no unreality could be as horrifying as the truth of what was about to happen. He stepped forward to his desk and saw the plain white envelope resting atop of his sketch pad. It bore his initials in the handwriting he had come to love. His heart broke as he picked up the envelope and pulled the note out. He closed his eyes tightly, but even then, the words upon the page appeared in his mind's eye. The note simply said:

'It was nothing. A lie. Forget it. A.H.'

Benjamin dropped the letter on the floor as, from outside the room came a piecing scream.

———•◦•———

Benjamin Ananas jolted out of his nightmare to the sound of Lupe Darling screeching so fiercely that the bottles by his feet rattled. On stage he saw his counterpart on his knees holding the letter and weeping. Abigail stood in front of him. The screech was mortifying. The Ananas on stage and the Ananas in the audience could not bear the noise and they both covered their ears. Abigail removed her mask and there was an almighty explosion of red flame all around the stage, as if the Inferno had been brought forth.

Before his eyes, Abigail sprouted six arms, each wire-controlled off stage and each brandishing swords. The screech continued. Anya, dressed in a black bodystocking to hide her appearance, almost invisibly descended from the rafter and attached a harness to the back of the Abigail Beast. The screech continued and suddenly, the whole damned monster floated up into the air, each arm waving ferociously.

Then, in a moment of classical heroism, the broken Ananas stood up and squared off to the Harpy. He drew his sabre and there began an epic duel that covered the entire stage. Srdjan's fencing skill was matched only by Gertie and Herschel's unified synergy in their wire work. They were frantically pulling wires to control the six arms of the harpy like a pair of demented bell ringers. The sword fight was incredible. The Ananas in the audience sank into his chair, struck with fear and awe at the magisterial duel conjured up before him. He opened another bottle and drank heavily from it. His internal nightmare thankfully replaced by this new theatrical one.

Chapter Six

Nathanial Whit and the fall of The House of
Ananas
(With further extracts)

The thoughts that speared his mind continuously over the three months since Abigail abandoned him were his only real comfort, despite their dark and torturous nature. Running a knife from the corner of his ear down and across his throat and to hell with life was chiefly upon his mind. And so, after Abigail deserted him leaving only that single line written on the paper without any hint of emotion, he took to his tortured lovelorn persona as if it were a coat of his own making, destined to be worn by him, and rightfully handed down from the legions of dead lovers who wallowed in the mires of misery eternal.

Upon seeing her forlorn son, Benjamin's mother softened her iron spine, bent towards him and held him tightly as often as she could. However, he was so introverted and enthralled to the will of his broken heart that he felt her cheeks to be cold and her embrace to be shallow. And as for his father, and all his life lessons he spouted while shooting or smoking were the worst kind of populist tripe to Benjamin's ears. Who was this man, this fop whose wigs troubled the top of the door frames, whose hankies dangled coquettishly from his signet ring? Who was this talentless glutton to sermonize about love to an artist of unknown borders?

Despite his moping and his angst, his friends rallied around, as friends do, but their maturity in matters of the heart extended no further than the pursuit of golden geese with ocean-deep dowries. Even his fortress hidden in the forgotten wing of his house yielded no comfort. It seemed that the revelation of the letter and the gust of wind she took with her as she swept out of his life had whipped up all his dreams, ideals and talents and sucked them straight out of his chamber. He could no longer paint, or dream, or sculpt or write. Of course, he couldn't before she had come into his life, but at least he could differentiate the colours on his palette. Now it seemed that his vision was monochrome, his art a void, his well dried up and his passion now a barren wasteland populated with emaciated and decaying dreams. Never had Benjamin Ananas felt as alone as he did in those months between Abigail Hardwoode leaving, the inferno in his house and the deaths of his parents.

———•·•———

Extract - Act Three, Scene Eight (Cont'd)

Benjamin and The Harpy are still fighting across the stage. The scenery has changed and they are now dueling on the roof of Ananas Mansion. Back and forth they thrust and parry. Below them the flames of the inferno lick higher and higher.

———•·•———

The flames in question were represented by the cast members writhing and twirling beneath the dueling fates, their faces in anguish, they limbs strained and manic. Lupe had created vibrant and flowing costumes that seemed to take on a life of their own. The fire was intense and Benjamin remembered the heat on his face, the shock of the discovery and the silent aftermath. Mostly, he remembered the sword. He slunk deeper into the chair and rested his cheek in his hand, forgetting the anguish of his broken heart and remembering the shame of his fall from grace.

Nobody knew how the fire that destroyed his mansion and killed his parents had started. It was late August and preparations for the Ananas Dance had begun in earnest as they did every year. Benjamin, of course, was in no mood to celebrate anything, so during the hustle and bustle of gazebo and marquee construction and the to and fro of caterers and house staff he had ensconced himself in his bedroom armed to the teeth with booze. Up until meeting Abigail his constitution had always been weak however, the shift in his persona since her abandonment had seemed to alter his capacity to handle his drink. His thirst was voracious.

He did not hear the guests arrive or the party start. He did not hear the music and fireworks nor hear the guests leave. He had barricaded himself in his room and drunk until he passed out on the floor. It was the heat that eventually awoke him. The smoke was already choking him and he could barely see. He remembered the portraits in his bedroom bubbling and twisting as the heat transformed the faces into demons. He scrambled to the barricaded door and pulled it apart with adrenalized strength. He staggered through the halls of the mansion calling out for his parents until he came to their bedroom door. The heat was unbearable but he managed to barge it down. From within the room belched flame and he shielded his eyes and looked inside. The four poster bed was on fire and there were two flaming bodies upon it, lying next to each other as if they were asleep. He remembered his scream and how it twisted in his throat and gave him a graveled tone for evermore. He remembered looking at his burning parents and feeling a pull on his shoulders. He remembered being dragged out of the house by some surviving staff.

He sat on the edge of a gazebo, wrapped in a blanket and watched as the house burned through the night until, come dawn, it was a charred and forlorn wreckage. He left the gazebo to walk amongst the ruins. As the sun's rays flicked over the smoking graveyard, Benjamin caught sight of something twinkling at him, something jeweled and bewitching, a tiny sparkle, glistening then vanishing. At first he thought his waterlogged eyes were catching the morning rays. He wiped them clear and the sparkle came back. It was just yonder, about twenty feet away almost fully concealed under a charred cabinet. He crawled over to the glinting star and pulled it from its smoking scabbard. He was holding his father's sword: The Sword of Ananas. It was remarkably unscathed. The burnished steel blade sang in the morning air, the gilded basket shaped like a pineapple had lost none of its brilliance. Despite the wasteland Ananas was in, as soon as he held that sword, a zephyr of hope passed through him. It was tangible, but unfortunately in the months after the great fire, that zephyr of hope was not nearly as tangible as the spiraling typhoon of debt, drink and despair that swept through him.

Extract - Act Three, Scene Fourteen – Regent Street

Benjamin Ananas stands in the middle of Regent Street. His clothes are tatty and he is dirty and bedraggled. Rich clothed and black hearted people hurry passed him.

Enter Nathanial Whit, Benjamin's 'best friend' and a few other stragglers. They begin to circle our forlorn hero.

> Nathanial Whit
> What's this, whose this? What dreg of
> the sewer? What's this, whose this? What
> filthy ill-doer?

Nathanial Whit lifts his cane to Ananas's chin and raises his head so they are eye to eye.

> Nathanial Whit
> Why Lord above and Devil below, 'tis
> that awkward rich boy we used to know.
> Remember the one who drank like a fish
> and danced like an ox? What happened to
> him? Oh yes! I forgot. His parents now
> live in a charcoaled box!

The gang all laugh.

> Former Friend #1
> Yes, I remember, I laughed at his plight!

> Former Friend #2
> Not as much as to his paintings, those
> piles of shite!

Former Friend #3

Didn't he also love some trolloping fish?
Some   buck-toothed   lizard,   some
hunchbacked bitch?

Nathanial Whit

All you say is true and more, he loved a
girl like his mother, a whore. She ran away
without looking back, and off she ran into
Nathanial's sack. For I did bed her and
more to boot. Oh, the things I did to her
womanly flute!

The gang laugh.

Nathanial Whit (cont'd)

And so Benjamin you pitiful boy, what
brings you round here? What is your
ploy?

Benjamin Ananas, holding back his rage and despair stands tall.

Benjamin Ananas

Sirs, you do spit upon my parent's grave.
I would strike you all down, you
miserable knaves. But alas I have
nothing, no strength to fight, for Satan is
reveling in my pitiful plight. No barbs or
spears can hurt me more, than the ones I
have endured in times before.

Nathanial Whit

So what is it, why are you here? Is it for money for yet more gin and beer? Ah it is! I should've known, in the depths of booze is where you call home. Well, I know you a man of word and truth that much is clear with no need to deduce. You will never accept a gift or act of charity, to your character t'would be an act of vulgarity.

Benjamin Ananas

It is true I have come seeking a deal, to sell you an item to garner a meal. It is the last thing I do possess and its beauty I show for you to attest.

Benjamin holds out his father's sword.

Benjamin Ananas was overcome with shame at being reminded of his lowest ebb. Selling the sword of his father just to keep himself alive for a few more days was his darkest moment. All the subsequent years of drinking had done little to silence the wails of disappointment from the spirit of his ancestors at that moment of indignity.

On stage, Antoine Le Magnifique playing Nathanial Whit was circling Benjamin and every time he completed a revolution, another piece of Benjamin's costume had been removed. Antoine's sleight of hand was so fast and so silky that it seemed as if the costume was disappearing. Underneath Benjamin's costume was then slowly revealed the clothes of a pauper. Antoine was a master at the peak of his profession and the Ananas in the audience was astonished at the magic show in front of him. He trained his eyes on Antoine's hands, trying to detect their movements, trying to unravel just how exactly he made objects vanish and then reappear somewhere else.

The memory of his darkest moment now thankfully stowed away and replaced with the childlike wonder of a boy trying to outfox a magician. Then the coup de grâce came. As Benjamin held out his father's sword, Antoine clapped his hands thunderously and against all the laws of the earth, the sword appeared in Antoine's belt - real magic in plain sight.

In the audience, Benjamin audibly gasped and then, with barely enough time for the dust to settle on the audacious trick, Antoine flicked a solitary coin at Ananas's feet and as the actor bent down to pick it up, Antoine strode passed him laughing maniacally and dished out the obligatory kick up the rump to the poor, broken Benjamin.

Antoine's portrayal of Nathanial Whit was not entirely accurate, but was more of a pantomime interpretation of him. Benjamin Ananas had never really spoken of his former best friend and how he had behaved. The Roxy Players only knew a few simple facts about it. They knew he refused to help Benjamin after the death of his parents, and that he practically stole his sword from him. They knew he ostracized him from their social circles and that, possibly, he was in the military. Benjamin's tendency to roar with anger at any mention of his name, or pressing for details about their relationship had convinced the Players that he was some sort of devil or nemesis. They were completely right. Benjamin's shame and guilt for what he had done was only matched by the anger he felt towards Whit and so, to keep himself alive and for the sake of being pleasant company around his friends, he had taken to burying Whit's name deep under years of drink and drug fuelled repression.

However, on his birthday, he was surprised at how easy it was to see Antoine bravely dare to represent Nathanial onstage. The overt archetype they had created had gone a long way to sidestep any possible involuntary explosions of rage on Ananas' part. He was almost happy to share this arch villain with his friends and he opened another bottle and drank to the thought that, perhaps, he should have trusted his friends with sharing the name 'Nathanial Whit' long ago. He drank to them all and watched as the play climaxed.

———•—

Extract - Act Three, Scene Nineteen – St Giles Rookery

Benjamin is crawling through the streets, people rush by. He is drinking as he crawls on his hands and knees.

Enter Cupid from above. Ananas stand and draws a dagger and begins lunging at him. Cupid dodges and weaves in the air around him. Nobody sees Cupid but Benjamin.

Ananas

Back, Demon, back you go to the pits of
hell to spear poor souls with your
miserable darts of pain. You vile wretch,
I would tear you apart, but I fear your
flesh to be as corrosive as the lies you
spit. No angel, pure Devilry stands before
me. Back you beast! Take my eyes Lord
God so I never have to look upon such a

fetid extrusion as that which hornets
around me now.

Ananas gets tired and sinks to the floor crying. Cupid hovers near
him, his eyes sympathetic, his mouth still twisted.

Cupid

My beautiful and tortured soul, I gave
you sight beyond sight, that vision to see
the divine in another soul. That vision to
love and that providence to do so, and do
so you did and you cry now at what
happened to you? Recount to me now,
and highlight the injustices that you
falsely attribute to Cupid and all his
angel-arrows.

Ananas

It is true, my art and instruments were
dull and blunt until I had newer eyes,
given by you Cupid. Eyes to see the
maiden that so enraptured me. And lo I
fell in too deep and she has left me alone,
barren and broken for she has taken
everything – and 'twas Cupid and the
barbed poisonous arrow that shot through
my heart, covered my eyes, and painted
over them with an image of love and
fairness, so as to mask the truth before
me: the truth that she was not beautiful

and serene, but in fact an eight-armed monster, wreathed in flame and menace. She killed me, and slew my parents, and innocent they were too! Took everything from me, she did, drove me into this gutter. What a bitch! And what a bastard you are, cute-winged and podgy-cheeked one; a babe of devils, not of angels. So indeed it is your fault and none of mine.

Cupid

And the art; what of the gift given to you? Not by Cupid, that babe of babes, but by God himself? That most precious of gifts, what have you done with that?

Ananas

Alas! No! I have forgotten my art! I saw only my love for the Harpy Bitch and I neglected my talents.

Cupid

You wanted to make art pure and true and love was the way to do so, if only you had married that gift of art with that gift of Cupid's arrow. But blind you were and neglect you did. Instead you forgot your part of the deal and packed away your easel and stared only at the maiden who enraptured you so.

Ananas

So, had I loved a love, and arted an art,
none of this blackness? We would never
have fallen apart?

Cupid smiles and walks over to Ananas, puts his hands on his heart. Ananas screams in pain. Slowly, Cupid pulls his hands away and seemingly extracts the arrow from Ananas.

Exit Cupid

Ananas (con't)

What devilry I have succumbed to! My
art is dead for now, and my love has
taken it. The monster she is, might never
have been had I not forgotten my original
plight. Maybe it is true that I fell for the
beauty and unmasked the villainy within.
Queen of witches because she took on
innocent Abigail's form! A woman more
cunning than most, but a woman
nonetheless. And I cannot blame Cupid,
though stinking and rotten he is. He is at
least true and honest. I can blame only
The Harpy who has stolen my heart – yes
the beating muscle, but much more, she
has stolen the components: the 'he', and
'art'. I am undone for my foolishness to
love the Harpy. I am alone.

The stage goes black.

Benjamin Ananas held the bottle to his mouth but did not drink. The abrupt end to the play had confused him greatly. Was that it? Where they going to leave the poor hero on his back, in the gutter and alone? He looked around the pitch dark auditorium and saw and heard nothing. He slowly tipped the bottle and let a little liquid run into his mouth. Then, as if that was the cue, a beam of light fell onto the stage and illuminated the forlorn actor. The Benjamin onstage looked up at the light, reaching for it as if it were a path to heaven. He slowly got onto his feet.

In the audience, the silence, coupled with the striking image of watching a version of himself caught in the heavenly beam caused Benjamin to gasp and clutch his bottle to his chest. What now was in store for his character?

The beam of light moved across the stage and Benjamin followed it as it weaved around, leading through a dark labyrinth until it came to halt, centre stage. The actor stood with his back to the auditorium, bathed in the light. Suddenly, the beam shot up and illuminated the stage backdrop, revealing a mockup of the front of The Roxy Playhouse itself. Benjamin, in the audience, chuckled to himself at the seamless and silent stage-change performed by Gertie and Herschel. The actor on stage walked towards the doors of The Roxy and pushed them open. As he did so, the actual doors to the real Roxy opened at the far end of the auditorium and the whole theatre was filled with light.

As the Benjamin on stage stepped into the fake doors, the cast of the play poured into the real doors and rushed down the centre aisle, singing, dancing and cartwheeling all the way.

Benjamin stood up from his chair and looked around to see all his friends rush over to him and hoist him up onto their shoulders. They cheered and clapped as they carried him onto the stage and threw confetti over him. From the rafters came Anya and Danilov on their wires. Lupe began to lead them all in a rousing chorus of *'For He's a Jolly Good Fellow'*.

After singing it twelve times in a row, they began to administer the birthday bumps to the drunken bear. They hoisted him high in the air, much to the joy of Claudia and Herschel who loudly counted each throw and catch. With each journey into the air and back into the arms of his friends, Benjamin realised what a wonderful birthday present they had given him. They had made him confront the past and made him realise that without it, he would not be there now, flying through the air and half cut on cheap booze in a decrepit theatre surrounded by a rag tag bunch of misfits. He was in heaven.

The forty fifth birthday bump was administered with much more vigour than anyone had anticipated and Benjamin flew clear out of their reach and landed some twelve feet away amongst the chairs, knocking himself unconscious instantly.

Chapter Seven

Behold! The Bishop!

Whenen one wishes to wake Benjamin Ananas from a catatonic state, the 'Seven Slaps to the Chops' is the recommended Roxy treatment and so The Roxy Players gathered to perform the dangerous revival technique. The slaps were administered in the usual way, via the wooden hand-shaped paddle attached to an eight-foot pole and controlled from a safe distance. Gertie and Herschel operated the waking mechanism while the rest of The Irregulars looked on from the relative safety of the wings. Wise is the gent who wakes a drunken bear from afar. Said bear stirred after the third whack, by the fifth he growled and on the seventh, as ever, he roared himself awake. Of course, his fearsome arousal was short lived and his anger subsided as soon as he saw Herschel and Gertie fearfully holding the end of the pole. He smiled, they smiled; everyone smiled. Benjamin opened his arms and puffed up his chest.

"An after-party!" he boomed. Gleeful smiles all round. "To The Bishop," declared the Birthday Bear and everybody huzzaed.

———◆•◆———

Standing inconspicuously between The Woolpack and The Lamb & Crown on Bermondsey street, The Bishop was the chosen haunt of The Irregulars ever since the day they stumbled through its optimistically exposed glass-fronted doors on that blustery October night three years prior.

Upon entrance they had been greeted with that wonderful aroma that only truly great pubs can offer; the timeless mix of spilt drinks soaking into fetid carpet, the dense fog of tobacco, out of tune piano playing, even worse singing and, of course, the requisite hive of desperate and lonely drinkers. The place was crammed with the beauties - tired workers here, happy drunks there, chattering mollies abound, sharp-eyed rakers in the shadows and, naturally, women of affordable virtue showing ankle at the slightest whiff of a gin. Archie and Benjamin had fallen in love with that den of divinity the moment they stepped across the urine-drenched welcome mat and had stayed until the morning by which time they had become intimately associated with every barmaid and patron therein. Regulars in only a few hours.

Since that October, not much had changed. The ceiling was a little more yellow but now with congealed rivers of tobacco-coloured slime amassing along the coving. The stool propping up Mr Soper had moved itself about four inches closer to the edge of the bar. The grandfather clock now tock-ticked and the piano had detuned itself even further. These tiny infractions in the otherwise timeless bar were only noticeable if one had been away for too long and, like the prodigal son, found his way home again. For The Irregulars, however, it was a sacrosanct bubble in which nothing changed but the seasons outside.

Benjamin led the troupe into The Bishop and they were greeted by large cheers and hugs from the other patrons – each performer humbly bowing to their friends (well, as humble as a bow to an adulating crowd can be). Archie took his cue and leapt effortlessly onto the long bar that ran the entire length of the establishment, stepping over drinks, ongoing transactions and of course Mr Soper, the perma-smashed butcher who spent so much time slumped over it that his breath and sweat had worn away the varnish and left an odd, pungent stain in his image. Archie waved and strode soaking up the adoration, the tails of his coat swishing gloriously.

"My Lords! My wonderful fellows! My colleagues and partners in Knavery! My beautiful Kings of Wishful Drinking! See before you a man whose very existence colours our lives. An artist of singular vision, a lion-heart who's had his fair share of knocks and bashes."
The Players all stood in a crescent behind Benjamin Ananas who looked genuinely humbled at his friend's speech.

"But has also had his fair share of victories; deserved victories. Monumental achievements – and it is through him that we can all see something a little more wondrous, perhaps a better job, or kinder life, a healthier heart or a brighter wife. Or maybe we see our own failings, our own inadequacies? The things we should, or could be..."
Archie took a moment for the remark to sink in. And sink in it did. Every man jack amongst them was suddenly granted the remembrance of a gift, or an oath or love-pact that they had once promised but never fulfilled.

"Remember now the dreams that we all bartered and sold in order to become what we became. My loves, it is in looking at our friend Benjamin Ananas, that reservoir of decency and quality, it is in looking at that man standing right there, that we can understand our failures because we see his successes. That we can unite, overcome and grow stronger...be better to each other and to ourselves. And so, today on this on this glorious day, I bid you raise your glasses with me."

Archie jumped down off the bar, grabbed a bottle from an adoring barmaid, casually walked up to his pal and poured him a drink.

"And join me," he concluded quietly and earnestly, "in simply saying: happy birthday, old friend."

The entire pub followed the toast with a cheer. Benjamin and Archie hugged, and the crescent of actors closed in around them. The patrons turned back to their conversations, the interruption from the troupe not fazing them in the slightest. Archie led the Players to the 'saloon section' of the bar which was basically just a large collection of broken settees and chaise longue couches haphazardly arranged to signify some sort of area for the elite. The Players made themselves at home with Herschel slumping down into an almost bottomless wingback chair, Desiree perching delicately on the arm, her legs intertwining with his like ivy and roses. Anya, always one to feel slightly off-kilter when walking on ground level, wedged herself in between the piano and the table lamp. Benjamin and Srdjan (now in his own attire and looking nothing like his stage character) sat down around a large oblong coffee table that, possibly, once had a baize finish. As soon as they had pulled up their chairs to the table, Tobias threw down a deck of cards and Danilov gleefully clapped his hands in expectation.

"A game!" announced the acrobat.

Suddenly everybody looked like they were lost and penniless. Herschel inspected his broken timepiece, Benjamin began to whistle and look about and Srdjan copied him.

"A game! The pack is down!" enthused Danilov, winking at Tobias.

"Indeed," agreed Tobias, "is it not Brigand's Law that once the deck is on the table, wagers will be wagered?"

"That's true! I read that, wagers on the table or a pox on your noses," came a sweet little voice from behind Herschel's chair.

Everybody looked over to see Claudia's face pop up from behind it, smiling her siren smile. Desiree reached behind the chair and put her arm around the Spanish girl and began to sweetly stroke her hair.

The men reluctantly remembered where they had put their wallets and onto the table top fell coins, buttons and a few IOUs. Tobias and Danilov shook hands, flipped out their coat tails like concert pianists and sat down together.

"Should we not wait for the fish?" urged Benjamin, gesturing towards the bar where Archie, Antoine and Gertie were gathered.

"Balls to the fish," said Tobias in a manner that seemed to flow from him only in public houses. "The fish come when they see the bait."

The men jokingly huffed at his inference and they all dug deeper in their pockets to throw more into the pot. Desiree, Anya and Claudia all shook their heads in unison at the foolish men so easily duped by the two card-sharps.

"Claudia, will you deal?" asked Tobias. Claudia coyly hummed and ah'd for a few moments, much to the delight of the men before she joined the table, picked up the cards and performed the sort of card shuffling tricks that are marginally more dazzling than they are time-wasting.

"Gentlemen," she said as she shuffled and re-shuffled, "I don't care who owes what, who knows what and you all know what goes. Savvy?"

"Yes ma'am" they cried in unison.

At the bar, Archie, Antoine and Gertie were smashing shots in a fast moving drinking game called 'Cad Calloway's Cadaver'. Quite why it was called that was anybody's guess. Quite why it even needed a name was even more of a mystery. It wasn't even a game as such but more a couple of rules with no real endgame. A round consisted of everybody drinking a shot at the same time with the first to smash his empty glass back on the bar being declared the round winner. The two rules are thus: Rule one: You can use any tactic you like to stop the other fellow beating you. Rule two: Drinks are drunk and not spilt. The 'winner' is not really determined by any attainment of a magical score as, in most cases, scores are forgotten by the tenth or twelfth round. The leader might pass out or might end up being the last man standing and therefore no doubt have to pay for the entire game which is most definitely not the rite of champions. It was a foolish game to say the least, but never once has the manifesto of drinkers troubled the court of King Sensible.

'Cad Calloway's Cadaver' dropped down to two Players around about the eighth round after Archie, who could have been the leader, respectfully bowed out after something caught his attention. His retirement was a serious gesture, as Antoine and Gertie had just suffered the 'Archie Enfield Backhand-Forehand' signature move which was simply a lightning fast slap in the face of each opposing player the moment the shot glass comes to their mouth, the surprise of the impact usually jolting the contents of the glass down the faces of the victims and into their eyes. A caddish manoeuvre no doubt, but then the game was designed for cads. So, the move was administered, the Players were half blinded and Archie was about to order the next round to capitalise on his ill-gotten advantages when his eyes met upon a sight that always warmed the heart and loins of that libertine drinker: The Bishop had a new barmaid.

While Antoine and Gertie were pinching the bridge of their noses, squinting and stamping their feet, Archie threw in his beer mat and retired from the game. He turned to the new barmaid and slunk like a velvet snake down the bar towards her.

"Brute! Cheat! I hate that English flower!" spluttered Antoine as his sight returned. "Are you ok dear boy?" he said as he put his arm around Gertie. Gertie nodded affirmatively and both of them laughed.

"I think I need a beer," continued Antoine, "an English beer so that when I piss it out, I can pretend it is Archibald Enfield."

"I heard that, Frog-breath," called back Archie from a distance beyond reasonable aural range. He somehow just knew that the manner of his retirement would have irked his friend.

Antoine held up his two fingers in the 'V' sign then, with his other hand, made the universal mime for 'pair of scissors' and with it, cut down the victory fingers. He blew a raspberry and turned to the bar. He was about to order some beers when Gertie grabbed his arm.

"The game isn't over, Antoine! I dare you to continue sir!" he challenged with a wink in his eye and a fierce tone. Antoine roared with laughter.

"Gertie, dear Gertie! How I love you in this phase of the evening. What a man! My lady," he said over his shoulder to a barmaid, "more shots! More shots! I have been met with a worthy challenge." The shots were dutifully delivered and the game continued.

Behind him, Archie could hear Gertie and Antoine's raucous drinking game continue, and behind them, he could make out the smash-and-grab fracas that accompanied every Roxy card game. He could picture each expression on each player, each tell and each bluff. He knew every nuance of his friends because he loved them. But he didn't play the cards because his attentions were focused always on a more immediate goal. The man was of a singular purpose, and that was to seduce. Eating, drinking, and breathing were just necessary cogs to operate his machine. As for art and performance, they were simply pleasing flourishes, like the gilding on carriage doors, the buttons on trousers, or the knots on a bodice. Everything outside his carnal desires was merely decoration.

However, Archibald Enfield was by no means from the academy of seduce and destroy. He was a lover yes, but a bastard? Not a bit. Every woman or man he lay with was within the sanctity of love; albeit for differing periods of time. He loved life, he loved men and he loved women and he never meant to hurt anyone and he certainly never, ever embarked on adventures with lovers without their consent.

He waited patiently at the bar, letting other drinkers go ahead of him in the queue, buying a few drinks on their behalf and generally being a jolly good regular. However, his secret weapon had already been deployed; the secret weapon being simply his presence. He was the sinkhole in the basin of any room he was ever in and while the new barmaid rushed around serving all the drinkers along the bar, gradually over ten or twenty minutes her 'field of service' shrunk and shrunk until she found herself solely operating four feet of bar of which Archie stood in the middle. Finally, when there was nobody left to serve, she asked for his order. Archie, who had been skilfully keeping himself busy with objects in his pockets and trivial conversations around him, looked up at her with those kohl-ringed eyes and sharp cheekbones and softly ordered his drink.

Nothing more; a simple, polite "may I please have a small carafe of red wine?" and her battlements were breached. She looked at him and she was undone. After just a glance into that dreamer's eyes and she was locked within his orbit. However, Mr Enfield was not short changed by any means, for you see that the barmaid named Valerie

Folk was very, very beautiful indeed. How was he to know what a tangle of trouble she would tie him in?

Chapter Eight

Fado!

Antoine was well and truly Agincourted, as was the way The Roxy Players oft described him in a good-hearted way. That was to say, he had been utterly smashed by the power of the British pub.

"What's the tally" he slurred as he gripped the bar as tightly as he gripped his consciousness.

"It's thirteen...something," guessed Gertie, "we must...keep going."

"My lovely," called the Frenchman to a nearby barmaid who scuttled over dutifully. He attempted to point to the empty glasses and beckon a refill when he stumbled backwards and fell over. As he did so, he sent a few nearby empties crashing to the floor, the resulting smash garnering the requisite cheer from the other drinkers. Gertie helped him up and, in doing so, declared himself to be the winner.

"Rhubarb, Dandelion and Burdock!" protested Antoine, "You cannot declare victory because of a stumble! Did Achilles declare the rock that tripped Hector to be the champion? No! He fought on until he was...what was I saying?"

"You were saying that you wanted to continue."

"Continue? Are you mad? The game is over...I won. What were we playing?"

"Cadavers."

"Whose idea was that? I need to sit down."

"Archie's. You are sitting down."

"Am I? Good. That saves time, now to business."

Gertie turned to the barmaid and ordered two large supping-drinks. He handed one to the Frenchman, who took it, placed his arm around his friend's shoulder and pulled him close in that sort of conspiratorial way drinkers do when they are about to offer up some pearls of wisdom.

"Listen," began Antoine, "You listen here young man. You are a good one and a noble one."

"Thank you."

"One of the best, one of my favourites...wait, what am I drinking?"

"Beer."

"Good...for a moment I thought I was holding an off-coloured crème de menthe really close. Perspective gone."

Gertie shook his head in resignation. This conversation was not intent on going anywhere, and yet he was bound to it. There was no escape.

"Perspective, boy, that's what you need," said Antoine as he slapped his hand on the bar.

"Do I?"

"You do! We all need it."

"And why would I need that?"

"The stars are small to us...but we know them to be giants, right?" said Antoine gesturing to an imaginary celestial blanket overhead.

"I suppose." Conceded Gertie.

"They are tiny and unreachable because of our perspective…but it needn't be so! We can reach them."

"You're drunk." Sighed Gertie.

"Yes. What of it? Keep up, Gertie, I've set sail now! My galleon is at sea and you're either a deck hand in this or you're driftwood."

"Apologies, sorry, go on - perspective?"

"Yes…so, why do we look up to the stars? Why do we look up? Why do you look up?"

"I don't know, Antoine, why do I look up?"

"You look up because inside, you believe you can reach out to your star," and with that, Antoine nodded in the direction of Anya, who was still wedged between the piano and the table-lamp, meditating in perfect solitude.

"What am I looking at?" feigned Gertie, fighting hard to suppress a volcano in his belly that told him that Antoine had discovered his secret. If the drunken Frenchman could do it, maybe others could? Maybe Anya could? He began to sweat as panic ruled his senses.

"Don't play dumb with me, boy. It doesn't suit you" slurred Antoine.

"I don't know what you mean, Antoine, I really don't," replied Gertie, retreating into his normal shy demeanour.

"You know exactly what I mean and you know that I know and you're wondering if she knows what you know and maybe even if she knows what you know and that I also know what you know and by the same token what she knows. Everybody knows."

Gertie surrendered. He tucked himself in closer to Antoine.

"Antoine, I love her!"

"I know," whispered the Frenchman. "It is written on your face. It is in your walk. It is in the way you hold your glass. You are in love; how wonderful!"

"What do I do?"

"Do? You go over there now, ignore the others, and tell her. 'Woman,' you say, 'woman, in Gascony, we make love all day and at night, well…we fuck!'"

"Jesus, Antoine, that's no help at all."

"You're right, you're right. We are not in Gascony at all, more's the pity!"

"Then what do I do?"

"Oh I don't know." He ordered another round. "Go recite her some poetry or something. Whatever it is you English do….I don't know…but whatever it is you people actually do, you cannot call it romance."

"Thanks Antoine, you've been a real help."

"I have! You don't even know it. Listen, if you're not man enough to go get the women you love; then prepare to lose her to a bolder man! Prepare, young Gertie." At that, Antoine snatched his drink from the bar and stood up.

"It is in this part of the evening, I really hate drinking with you. My family are balloonists, and you are the lead weight that brings us down. Ha!" And with that odd sign-off, Antoine swayed over to join the rest of the group.

Gertie, a little hurt, a little confused, and a little sad turned back to the bar.

"I should've asked Archie," he said under his breath.

The erstwhile Mr Enfield was, when Gertie needed him most, engaged in full blown conversation with Valerie. The barmaid carried on serving of course, she had a job to do after all, but the rapid fire question and answer session initiated by Archie continued unabated. It had started in the usual way: once he had got her attention with his piercing stare and ordered his drink, he then asked her to 'tell him something'. Valerie responded with the requisite answer of 'something' and was about to go about her business when for some inexplicable reason she found herself poking her tongue out at him and winking. Had she really done that? Was she dreaming? She couldn't be sure. All she knew was that the scruffy man with the kohl-ringed eyes was really something. Archie's volley of enquiries that followed his odd conversation starter flew over the heads of some drinkers and across the faces of others as they waited to be served and she bustled about behind the bar. The questions were standard: What is your name? What is your favourite vice? What is your darkest secret? What is your place of safety?

Archie gathered up Valerie's rapid answers hungrily. The picture she was painting of herself and of her outlook checked all his boxes. This woman was alive in the best way possible. She was inquisitive, eager, quirky and funny. Her theories and understandings formed from a wild-eyed enthusiasm for the minutiae of life. Archie was captivated. If you were to have tapped him on the shoulder during that back-and-forth, he would have shushed you away and said "not now, my beauty, can't you see I am falling in love?" And he was too. He would have told her there and then, and to hell with the bluff drinkers around him. When you're in love, you are in love and everything else is monochrome. The only other thought in his mind was that, should Gertie ever realise his love for Anya, then he should come see him because Archibald Enfield knew about love and all its galaxies.

He prepared to deliver his declaration of love eternal (eternal meaning usually the hours of moonlight) when the glass doors to the pub were almost blown off their hinges. Everybody looked to see the giant cake trundling in.

They looked harder. It wasn't a cake. It was Lupe Darling wearing a huge, yellow, white and pink dress and sporting a white bee-hive wig that clipped the top of the door frame. She had spent the entire evening taking off her face from the performance, and constructing the one the patrons were deciphering now. She stood in the entrance to stunned silence. She opened her mouth. Everybody grabbed their glasses in preparation.

The noise that detonated from her voicebox also detonated any poor bottles that had been left unattended. The glass plates in the doors held fast, but it was a torture for them. The ones that didn't make it were the cheap empty bottles and glasses littering the bar. She couldn't help it, it was her gift and it was the curse of all cheap glassware. The woman just loved to sing.

After her entry-note had fallen away and the ringing had stopped in everyone's ears, she flicked open a giant fan made of peacock feathers and sashayed through the bar. The older clientele as well as a few cheekier, more sexually adventurous regulars, made a grab for her. Some were successful and were able to go home that night, hot in the knowledge that they had a grope of that spitfire woman. The wondrous quality of Lupe Darling was her longevity. She had been around the world seven times, loved on seven continents and on the seven seas and in all her years, through all her ups and downs, she had simply grown and grown and grown. She was knocking on the door of sixty-five (forty-three on Playhouse press releases) but had the zest of an eighteen year old. It was common knowledge that, on her sixteith birthday, she had decided to teach Archie a thing or two. And she did. For a week. After that marathon, Archie had famously walked out of her boudoir looking like a thirteen year old after his first wet dream. When Lupe left the boudoir two minutes after him she was simply filing her nails and humming to herself.

Lupe winked as she passed Archie and he winked back, secretly harbouring the desire to one day show her the new tricks he'd learned. Everybody moved their chairs and tables out of her way such was the expanse of her dress and bustle. She waved to them royally, carefully selecting a few adoring older men to wink at along the way.

The singer arrived at the table in the saloon to find all The Roxy Players smiling at her. Benjamin stood up and asked for her hand, she gave it and he kissed it. The taste of her almond skin-crème sent the birthday bear into a wonderful swirl of memory. Almonds; how he used to love eating almonds. When he was an artist, he would have a little bowl of them in his study. Lupe knew this. That's why she applied it that day instead of her usual butterscotch crème.

"Almonds," he said distantly, "my favourite," and he bowed deeply and honestly. Lupe curtsied back.

"Lupe!" cried Tobias, "will you sing us a song?"

"Tobias, you have been drinking I can tell, for it is the only time I hear that voice. And what a timbre it carries. I would buy you all the wine in the world if meant you could keep on talking."

She looked at a chair and then looked at Claudia. Claudia smiled, ran round to her and helped her sit in it which was no small operation given the size of her dress. At one point, Desiree had to help lift the heavy hem over Danilov who swore to keep his eyes closed as he passed under the dress. Of course he lied and saw everything. Once she was seated, she folded away her peacock fan and handed it to Desiree. Claudia jumped up and sat on her lap, the folds of the dress like a duvet around her.

"In 1785," began the singer, "I found myself penniless in Egypt." Everybody closed in for the anecdote.

"I was in a touring theatre group called...I forget the name...but the troupe leader, one Jedidiah McHarrington, was the most devious of sorts. We had begun life as a troupe in Munich, under the school of Von Brandenburg, you may have heard of it [nobody had heard of it], well we had played every playhouse in Germany. We had performed the passion plays at Oderamagau, we had stuffed Lessing and Schiller and bested Goethe to great applause. We were everywhere. I was happy. Being a mere stagehand and trainee soprano, I was happy to just be around such lovelies and to perform on such stages. But this man McHarrington, he had the devil of debts fierce upon him – he drank and he smoked and he gambled and got into trouble upon trouble. And so, I will always remember the day, on the eighth of October, moments before we were about to perform for one Josef II of Austria. Just as we were about to go on stage, McHarrington comes belting into the wings, arms flailing and with this pale look about him. He began throwing clothes, props and costumes into trunks and running around like a mad man. Now, I was about to go on stage, this was my big moment, the first time I had performed a solo, and to Josef himself! And suddenly, there I was witnessing this madman trying to pack up the entire show. I asked him what the hell he was playing at. He said 'my dear, we are undone! We must flee to the land where they don't speak German. Or French. Or Spanish' I asked him why and where and he said that, in Coptic Egyptian, there is no word for 'debt' which is true, by the way, and in a country where there is no word for debt, nobody can ever find him. I said to him 'Jedidiah, I have no need to follow you to Cairo! A man can run from debt all his life, but the only debt one owes is to the Lord, to repay him with the payment of his gift. I must sing!' He looked at me like was I talking in tongues. Then he told me that every loan he had made was in my name. That I was accountable! Me! Lupe Darling! Well, needless to say, when the curtain went up, old Joseph was greeted with an empty stage. The rogue McHarrington and I were already on the night boat to Cairo, as the saying goes."

Everybody was enthralled to her rambling anecdote.

"So, there we found ourselves. In Cairo, with nothing but a few cases of random props and unusable costumes! It was then that I realised that, perhaps, running from the debt collectors might not have been so prudent. I mean, Egypt is lovely, but once you've seen the pyramids what else is there to do? Drink gin, spit on camels and make love! [The group laughed] I'm joking of course, Egypt held many wonders for us, and we truly found ourselves in a creative heaven. McHarrington wrote all day, we rehearsed all night. After three months we were the best known double act in all of the land. We even performed for The King. He was hung like mouse by the way."

The group were dizzy with her story, every avenue offering up a new possible route. She had really done it all and even the incidents like sleeping with the King of Egypt were brushed off with an astounding nonchalance.

"We performed for everyone but one memory stands out the most. I remember one day, in the intense summer heat, McHarrington was asleep on a dune, and I was swimming naked in an oasis, a little beggar-child came running toward us. No older than seven. He came over the dune and stood at the water's edge looking at me while I swam around. It took a while to notice him, but when I did I didn't even think to cover myself – that's what it is like in the desert. Anyway, he stood there, and I asked him what he wanted, and he said that he had heard about us, and that he had followed stories of our performance from town to town, trying to catch up with us. Well he had finally. I said that, for such devotion, I would do whatever he commanded, for I was rich and he was a poor beggar child – for my shame, I guessed that he was going to ask for money but he looked at me and smiled. He simply said, 'please Miss Lupe, will you sing me a song?'

She paused for a few moments. This was not done for dramatic effect, but through a burning need to recollect every grain of sand on that dune. She needed to bask in that memory for a few moments. Her sudden pang of nostalgia was writ large on her face, and everybody looked at everybody else, trying to gauge whether she was about to laugh or cry.

"What happened to McHarrington?" asked Herschel, eager to bring Lupe back from the brink of memory.

"He was bitten by an asp that very night," she said quietly, directing her words more towards her memory than to her audience.

"He died in my arms." Lupe shed two tears, one for McHarrington and one for the boy on the dune. She sighed and regained her composure.

"So! A song for you all! Benjamin, if you permit me, I would like tonight to sing Fado."

"I can do nothing but acquiesce to such a woman as you," said the birthday boy.

"It is a song I wrote especially for you actually and it was inspired by Herschel's great play. I call it simply *'Hats off to Benjamin'.*"

Lupe solemnly stood up and prepared herself to sing her Fado song, that style of music from Portugal which harnesses all the sorrow and mourning in the world and channels it through the singer's heart and out through their voice.

Chapter Nine

Valerie Folk

A s soon as Lupe Darling started to sing her Fado song, Archie and Valerie ceased their flirting and joined the other patrons in watching and listening to the singing cake. Lupe had learned the secrets of Fado singing during her impoverished teenage years spent in Lisbon. Though she slept rough and barely ate, those years were among her favourites. She was enslaved to poverty as were most, but she also held in her a sense of freedom and a belief that, however hungry she was, however much her feet ached, it was only temporary. It was the fervour of youth and enthusiasm for her future kept her keen and alive and come sunset, whether she intended to or not, Lupe would always find herself sitting on a patch of grass in the shadow of the Castle of Sao Jorge's east entrance, overlooking the port, listening to Amalia Rodriguez sing.

Amalia was a sixty-six year old waif who, from dawn to late afternoon, would stand on the grass and wait for her lover, a long-lost sailor to return home. As she sat and held vigil, she would empty her heart through song and as it normally is with lovers whose partners have sailed away, her heart sang melancholic words of longing and sadness and, when her last song was sung, Amalia would turn her attentions to the bright eyed wanderer and instruct her in the technical and emotional marriages one must match when performing true songs of sadness. And so Lupe learnt the secret art of Fado from

Amalia, and forever kept it inside her, releasing its potent sound only when the situation called for it.

Though Lupe secretly detested the popularity that the Fado style had accrued over time, she still loved the purity of its intentions and so, it was with pride and seriousness that she penned her Fado song for Benjamin loading it with bittersweet reflection, and hopeful sadness for a glorious future regained. Benjamin gave the song the respect it deserved. He let the emotion overcome him and, as she sang on, he let his tears flow. He wasn't the only one to do so. Everybody in The Bishop who listened to Lupe sing sailed through their memories to locate lost lovers and spend some time with them. It was while they listened to her sing that Valerie reached across the bar and gently stroked Archie's hand. He did not turn to her and acknowledge the gesture but smiled and kept on watching Lupe. But, both he and the barmaid knew that her touch was a signal of unification.

Lupe's song finished and, without saying a word to each other, Archie and Valerie walked out of The Bishop to seek a quite place where they could love each other.

They did not have to walk far. A dark and deserted alleyway by the side of The Bishop suited their requirements perfectly. Valerie backed into the shadows, her eyes bright beacons in the gloom. Archie locked onto them and stepped into the darkness too. All they had to sail by was their sense of touch, and the tiny gasps of pleasure and agreement at the other's actions. He knew that he was kissing her neck correctly because of her breathing, and by the way her hands ran through his hair. Words, like vision, were needless in the dark. They had touch, and that was all they needed. Their kisses became increasingly passionate, each one rivalling the other with their intensity, the scales rising, and the hands gripping harder, the chests breathing heavier. Step by step they ascended in their pleasure. It was not long before articles began to come undone, the seductive innocence in which they had started this game now being replaced with a lustful fury that was heaven for Archie and all but unknown to Valerie. She was a ship captained by a novice and caught in a swell and she tried to trammel her thoughts and behave with a modicum of decency, but every electric touch of skin on skin caused her to act more and more like a woman possessed. She was about to take to the podium and conduct the symphony when, suddenly, Archie ceased everything. The kissing stopped. The caressing halted. Her dress hung round her hips perilously, lacking that one fatal shake to send it down to her ankles. She reached out into the darkness. He was not there. She stepped into the light and stood there semi-naked in the alleyway shocked at the sight before her.

Archie stood, trousers round ankles, frozen solid. He was flanked by Each, Peach, Pear and Plum one of whom held a large cut-throat razor to Archie's neck.

"Cover yourself up, Val, for heaven's sake, you'll give 'em all ideas" said Each with a disdainful tone. Valerie quickly pulled up her dress and sheepishly looked to the floor, fearful that she might catch the look of disappointment and betrayal in Archie's eyes.

"Well, well, well, Mr Enfield, you 'ave been up to all sorts ain't yer?" said Peach, who was sitting on a barrel, slightly off to the side, and rolling a liquorice cigarette. He finished, and hopped over to Valerie and offered it to her. She took it, and he lit it for her with a cool strike of a match.

"She is a real work of art, isn't she?" He said as he ran his fingers over her cheek, his fetid breath coating her face. She baulked slightly, but hid it well.

"You did it great, my dear," and he kissed her. She turned her face so that he could kiss her cheek instead of her lips, and as she did she inadvertently caught Archie's eyes. He raised a single eyebrow. The guilt that had been churning in her gut turned to stone.

"Now, run along little lady, there is a dog these men need to see about."

"What are you going to do to him?" she trembled.

"Best you go, love," said Archie, "take care of yourself, keep that chin up." He winked at her, and his reassurance assuaged her concern greatly. She looked to the floor and walked back down the alleyway. Valerie had taken only twenty steps when the beating commenced and the dull thud of fist on rib and face and the wheeze of expelled air floated towards her and she began to cry. She didn't want to hurt anyone and only did what she was told, but this was the first time that her acquiescence to Sheridan's commands had brought into sharp relief her actions. She hated herself for being so easily recruited into the honey-trapping business by Sheridan. He had spotted her acting potential a few months previous and, instead of embracing it and nurturing her, he twisted her abilities to his vile ends and she had not the courage to escape him.

The thumps and thuds continued. Valerie rounded the corner and, instead of returning to The Bishop, she ran off into the London night, bawling her eyes out. In the alleyway, Archie Enfield was punched to the ground. Once he was face down in the mud the kicks arrived. At first they were directed to the ribs and, when his whole insides were burning and his mind in a state of flux, Pear brought his boot up sharply to his jaw. It was lights out for Archie Enfield.

The Roxy Playhouse Irregulars piled out of The Bishop arm in arm and full of love and joy. They stumbled into the night, passing the mouth of an alleyway without anyone casting a glance down it. Had they done so, they would have seen a body being dragged away by four large men. Had they investigated, they would have seen that the body was that of their beloved Archie Enfield. Instead, they trundled off towards the Playhouse.

———•·•———

When all her tears were spent, Valerie's resolve returned. What was done was done; her betrayal had gotten someone killed. That would always be with her. She could have denied the duty charged to her by Sheridan. She could have said, "No, I don't want to lead the lamb to the slaughter." She could have said many things, but instead she said nothing and simply went along with it.

Of course, she could never have guessed who exactly she was honey-trapping or that they were going to kill him. She had just assumed that her target would have been some miserable wretch who deserved a going over. However, Archie presented an altogether different beast. He was a nice chap and she really did fall in love with him in those moments but she, effectively, murdered him. What was she to do? Now that her tears were spent, she concluded that there were only two duties left to perform. Firstly, she would confess to his friends, and then take them to where they could reclaim his body and after that, she would throw herself from London Bridge. In the morning she would go to them.

Eleven in the morning is not an amicable hour by anybody's standards, but in the wake of an after-party it is a wasteland populated by lost and baffled souls who wander helplessly back to the land of sobriety with no memory of where they have been, and no charter of where they are going.

Valerie Folk stood outside the Playhouse at that exact time. The fog was almost impenetrable, yet Borough was alive. Carts carrying vegetable graveyards trundled passed, carriages rumbled to and fro and everywhere rang the calamitous orchestra of a thousand lives moving in every direction.

She looked up at the Playhouse and could just make out the crudely painted lettering. Above it was nothing but fog. She had never been to The Roxy before, and had only come now out of duty to Archie and for fear of the repercussions for all concerned. She glanced each way down Borough High Street and, as figures drifted from oblivion and passed by back into it, she felt a little melancholic to be seemingly the only soul in London not on the move. She stepped forward and slowly pushed open the door.

The pea-souper outside was matched only by the fog of opium and tobacco smoke from within the theatre. Inside was a chasm. Even the cold morning light thought twice about penetrating more than two feet into the gloom of The Roxy .

The smell from within was not just those of tobacco and opium. As Valerie stood in the doorway, all kinds of aromas had their chance to entertain her pretty nose. Firstly, and most unmistakably, marched the fanfare of gin, closely followed by the dirge of vomit. Then, oddly, waltzed the sweet smell of rosewater followed by saffron and vanilla (though Valerie only learned the name for the smell of vanilla years later when she found herself inexplicably naked save for the pods in her hair in the bed of Emperor Agustin De Iturbide of

Mexico). Once the carousel of odours had spun itself to sleep and her nose declared the coast to be clear, she prepared to step inside.

She was one footstep into the abyss when, devilishly, a final scent twisted out of the gloom, causing her to blush and look around nervously, before it wafted proudly into the street. It was the wanton, glorious bouquet of sated carnal desires. The voice of probity stung her instantly. *'There be libertines inside! Demons too no doubt,'* it whispered in her mind. *'Sins of the flesh, foul degradation fit only for the avaricious black-hearted rapscallions,'* it continued. Her mother had warned her about those types. The fact that she knew exactly what the aroma was, and could have drawn you a portfolio of sketches detailing every position in which to mix up the perfume contradicted her sudden sense of propriety. She steadied her heart and stilled her anticipations of what might happen should she step into the darkness. For the sake of appearances, she crossed herself, pulled her shawl around her neck and stepped inside The Roxy with the confidence of a priest about to perform an exorcism.

Valerie walked slowly up the centre aisle towards the stage, passing beyond the shafts of light from the outside world and through a few metres of darkness until the warm glow of the guttering candles along the stage took her hand and lured her closer. The theatre was as still as a painting and the only sound was that of soft, safe, breathing.

She gasped reflexively and touched her chest as the bodies came into view. Half in the darkness, half in the faltering light, blanket by tinted smoke, lay The Roxy Playhouse Irregulars, entwined, comatose and in varying states of undress. What went on during the after-after party was anyone's guess, though an educated person, and Valerie was indeed educated in the ways of the wicked, would surmise that it was less time consuming to deduce what hadn't occurred.

The composition of the heap was startling in its candidness, but also somewhat liberating and warming in its serenity. These sleeping artists, freed of the strictures of cloth and boot, propriety and morality had fallen into each other in a way that spoke deeply to her heart. She felt excited and enchanted to be allowed into this most sacred of tableaux. Above all, she was calmed by the sense of kinship she had with these figures, with their stillness and their silence. Valerie had not seen anything remotely resembling that companionship amongst Sheridan's troupe. She instantly yearned to climb in amongst them, leave behind Sheridan's Olympus Theatre and become a Roxy Playhouse Irregular forevermore.

She crept around to the side of the stage and tiptoed up the steps, taking great care not to disturb any candles or touch any deceitful floorboards. She moved around into the wings and was about to walk onto the stage, unsure whether to wake them or tie her caution to her clothes, throw the bundle to the wind and lie down amongst them, when her boot struck a chair leg. The crack and scrape was deafening and Valerie held her breath in an attempt to coerce the air in the theatre to withhold the echo. She looked down at the chair and saw a body sitting on it - a fully clothed body. She crouched down and moved in close to the figure squinting to make out its face. The light afforded by the stage candles revealed a young face untarnished and fair, but not beautiful or ugly: simply fair. However, it was clear to her that the illicit nature of her scrutiny, close beyond comfort should she be discovered, enhanced his features considerably. She felt like a sculptor examining every pore and mark on her creation. The slope of his nose, the angle of his chin and the ginger stubble were all immaculate in their vague illumination.

Valerie leant in closer to his face, her breathing so gentle that it barely flicked his eyelashes. She wanted to kiss him, so softly and gently that it would not have stirred a babe. It was going to be her private, secret kiss, and not one she would ever tell this strange, sleeping boy even if they met again in a time of diminished reverie.

She leant in closer still, her eyes beginning to close in preparation when a nearby candle flickered slightly and pulled back the still curtain of darkness around the boy's eyes. They were open. Valerie gasped and sat back, covering her mouth lest the next gasp become a scream. The body on the chair did not move. After a few seconds, she leant back in. The eyes were indeed open and, looking closely now at his chest, she could see that he was breathing. Looking back at his eyes, she saw that the hazel irises were not looking at her, but up high into the eaves of the theatre. Then, slowly as if a statue awakening, the body raised a hand up to its head, extended its index finger to its lips, and then, pointed to the rafter. Valerie looked up and in the darkness, she could just make out the warm tones of flesh, the slender feminine lines of a woman lying naked on her back high up on a rafter, one leg hanging freely in the air.

She looked back at the body and it was only then, that she noticed this watchful boy had a very large butterfly net held tightly by his opposite side.

"I'm sorry," she whispered and backed into the gloom. As she did so she disturbed a candelabrum which creaked and tipped, smashing into a large dress mirror. The resulting noise rattled the foundations of the theatre. Gertie tightened his grip on his net, expecting Anya to jolt awake and possibly fall to her doom.

The pile of bodies stirred. There were groans. From deep within the mass, an arm wormed free and stretched out from between two legs. It had the appearance of somebody climbing out of a cave or a womb. The top layer of bodies slowly rolled off the mound and soon, everybody lay strewn about the floor. In the centre of them all, lay Benjamin Ananas. Valerie stood in the dark wings, her hands over her mouth and watched as the naked bear stood up, yawned and ruffled his hair. She stepped into the light, her heart still beating fast at the display of nudity in front of her.

Benjamin looked at her, his early morning arousal proud and unbothered about the guest. Valerie battled hard to overcome her feelings, and her voice wobbled slightly.

"I've come about Archie." She said, her voice trembling.

Herschel, lying on his back, craned his head to see who was talking. He looked at Valerie and his head slumped back down.

"If it's about the pox," he said, "rub two cloves of garlic on your thighs and think a little harder in the future about whom you spread 'em for."

Valerie looked to the floor. "He is in trouble," she said.

"He is always in trouble," yawned Desiree, her early morning demeanour a little less alluring than her afternoon one.

"He's...he's...dead."

The Irregulars craned their necks to look at her. Valerie was wringing her hands tightly.

"I didn't know it was going to be like that. I didn't know. I didn't know," she said seemingly to herself.

"Sssh," said Benjamin, as he stepped over the bodies towards her. "I'm sure he is fine, he has died many times before. He is a wily one, is our Archie." He hugged her slightly awkwardly given his morning state. "Now tell me, my dear, where did you leave the little rascal?"

"Well....I left him outside The Bishop."

"Well there you go, if he isn't there now, it's probably because he got up and wandered off to find breakfast. A man has to eat."

"No you don't understand, I left him there…the others…they took him."

The Players recognised the seriousness of her tone and they sat up in unison. Benjamin broke off the hug.

"Who took him, and where?"

Valerie tried not to cry, but she couldn't help it.

"Sheridan's lads…they took him away, to the Olympus!"

The words shattered the hearts of the Players. Dread now hung heavy all around. Desiree cupped her mouth and shook her head in denial.

Benjamin, with a ferocious look on his face, grabbed her shoulders and stared deep into her eyes.

"Are you telling me that Archie Enfield is in Drury Lane?"

She nodded. Claudia began to whimper. Lupe held her close.

"Srdjan," said Benjamin, still looking at Valerie, "get me some clothes, a drink and a sword. Now."

Srdjan hurried off backstage.

"What are you going to do?" whimpered Valerie.

"I'm going to reclaim our dead," snarled Benjamin, "and you are coming with me."

Chapter Ten

Dead Man Hanging

V alerie sat on the steps outside the Playhouse waiting for Benjamin to emerge. Though she was enthralled by the beauty and warmth within the theatre, she knew she was not welcome and so while Benjamin got dressed, she had slunk out. She would have given up everything for the chance for forgiveness and a welcoming hand to extend from the theatre, take her by the arm and guide her back inside. But she knew it was an impossible dream. She had to return to that flea pit on Drury Lane.

After a ten minute wait, the door flung open, and Benjamin strode out into the street and flagged down a carriage. He was wearing his huge bearskin coat, tricorne hat and carrying a sleek black cane. He didn't pay any attention to her until the carriage pulled up and he stepped inside. Benjamin let the door swing open and Valerie knew that he meant for her to climb aboard.

"Come along," he growled. Valerie got inside the carriage and closed the door. As soon as it trundled into motion, she broke down in tears.

"Please Mr Benjamin, I didn't know, honest I didn't. I just did what I was told. I thought they were going to slap him about, I thought he was a rotter that needed it. But he's a sweetheart, a kind man, I could see it in his eyes soon as I saw him, and I didn't want to go through with it. I didn't want them to hurt him, truly I didn't. Oh, I feel so worthless!"

Benjamin couldn't look at her, but he knew she was earnest in her bawling confession. He was many things, but he wasn't heartless. He moved along his seat and offered the space next to him. She sniffed and moved over. When he put his arm round her and she buried her head into that tobacco and beer infused coat, she really let go. Benjamin held her tightly and looked out the window as the carriage trundled over London Bridge. He wanted to see the river. He wanted to see water, sky and a horizon. What he saw instead was life. Wooden shacks and garrets crammed on either side of the bridge. People everywhere, living in the great Purgatory of London neither north nor south of the river, but amassed on that ramshackle and decrepit bridge. Why they didn't migrate to either side of the bridge was a mystery to most but Benjamin believed that it was, perhaps, the lesser of two evils. Perhaps one day the bridge would collapse and they'd all get washed away. In that instance he would have given anything for it to have occurred. Anything instead of going to Drury Lane. Progress was slow and an endless stream of people came to the carriage window to beg, or thrust wares in his face, hoping for a barter or sale. He closed his eyes to it all.

'Drury Lane - what a cesspit.' Thought Benjamin as the chaos of the envoirment fell away slightly. To him Drury Lane was a strip of wretched theatres, populated by tribes of actors and artists, each one as deadly on their own as they were in their packs. Ananas scoffed in disgust at the thought of it all. They had no love for performance, or art; they had no love for love itself. They were opportunist bastards the lot of them. The cutthroat nature of the behind-the-curtains double dealings of managers and promoters was gleefully overlooked by the ghastly westend proles who flocked to

the grimy pits to lap up the 'artistic' extrusions spewed upon them. Neither theatre nor punter therein knew what *real* drama was. If they did, they might step out of their comfort zone once in a while, look over the fence and see the glory of The Roxy; fat chance of that.

Their destination was the worst of them all: The Olympus Theatre; which ironically given its name, stood in the shadow of the Theatre Royal. That didn't bother its owner and his cronies, for their modus operandi was borrowing and lending. 'No Not' Sheridan had no real love for art or performance. The plays they had bothered to put on years before were lacklustre and incoherent and Sheridan had fallen from his calling as a dramatist many years before on that black day when he discovered that his love for putting people in his pocket far outstripped his love for putting people in his theatre.

Since that day the theatre's programme all but ceased as Sheridan refocused his accomplices' talents towards the odious business of loan-sharking and blackmailing. His system didn't bother the other managers around Drury Lane because none of them had any honour anyway. In fact, it was common knowledge that everyone there was on 'No Not' Sheridan's books. They borrowed money from him for productions, and they paid back in profits. They hired him to spy and also to sabotage. Great works lasted only a night in some theatres because a rival had paid Sheridan to strong-arm an actor or director. It was a fluid system but to Benjamin and the Players the fluid was sewage.

'No Not" Sheridan, you bastard,' thought Ananas as he drifted into a light sleep, lulled by the rocking of the carriage. Valerie's wails had turned to quiet whimpers and she too was falling asleep. He had no time to really prepare for what was ahead, as the carriage jolted to a halt. They had arrived.

He sat there for a few minutes and composed his thoughts. A wonderful smell of almonds drifted under his nose. He jolted from his solitude to see a frosted cupcake hovering beneath his nose. He reached into his pocket and dug out a few coins. The toothless young boy was grateful and scampered off. Benjamin nudged Valerie gently and she sat up.

"We're here," he said, and opened the door. He got out of the carriage first and held up his hand to help her down the step. Valerie was accustomed to the sights and sounds of Aldwych but Benjamin's constitution was in revolt. He felt sick to his stomach with the thought of what was about to occur, he felt disgust in his mind for the state and attitude of the area and he felt cold sweat on his brow from the hangover.

"Are you alright, sir?" she asked genuinely concerned. The colour had gone from him completely and he had to steady himself on the doorframe. The moment passed and he rallied.

"Yes, my dear, carriage travel is not for me," and he held out the cupcake to her. "You must be starving," he said, "take it. The sight of a pretty girl eating cake is one of man's only guilt free pleasures." Valerie took the cake and began eating it hungrily. Her tears all but forgotten as she enjoyed the simple token of kindness. Benjamin smiled and offered her his arm. She took it.

"Now, while we are here," he said, trying his best to put on a chipper face, "we might as well enjoy ourselves. Tell me about the wonders of Aldwych."

Valerie looked a little taken back at his change of attitude.

"Don't worry," he said as he kissed her head, "I'm sure our scamp of a friend is quite safe. This has happened many times before and he always bounces back."

Valerie was warmed by Benjamin's nature and felt the glow of reassurance in his tone. He was a good actor.

———•◦•———

The Olympus had not changed in the three years since he had lightened its doorstep. It had no warmth to it. It looked more like a bank, which is effectively what it was. Valerie's chatter had died down when they had fallen under the theatre's shadow. For the first time she suddenly felt as if she was approaching a funeral parlour. They stood silent in front of the great doors.

They were about to enter when, behind them, they heard the sound of a steel blade being drawn. Benjamin froze and assessed his options. He could surrender immediately, and be taken into the theatre, or draw in return and fight in the street. Thankfully, he didn't have to make a decision. The swordsman stepped up and stood beside him. It was Srdjan.

"Can't let you have all the fun, now can I?" smiled the actor. They bowed to each other and then shook hands. Valerie's heart fluttered at the gallantry, unheard of to her. Srdjan offered right of way to Benjamin who took it and led them into the Olympus.

The interior was full of oppression. The paint had peeled off the walls and most of the threadbare chairs were piled to the sides. The aisles were littered with papers and refuse. Shafts of light breaking through the murky windows were like Dionysus's fingers pointing out in disgust all the areas of disrepair. It was heartbreaking to Srdjan and Benjamin to see so much potential and so much negligence. To Valerie, it was home.

They walked down the centre of the aisle, swords by their sides. It seemed prudent not to rush in, but to gauge the situation first. As they approached the stage, a teasing horror appeared; a long smear of blood. Someone had been dragged down the centre of the aisle. Every few steps there was a little pile or a splatter up a chair leg, no doubt from a boot or stick. Valerie felt sick and scared. Srdjan and Benjamin's swords rose up, in anger and in expectance.

They followed the blood trail to the stage proper. There it stopped. They looked all around them, their sword tips leading their eyes. Valerie was backing back down the aisle, her hands up to her face in terror.

Suddenly, there came a whistling from the wings. Srdjan and Benjamin spun around and trained their blades on either side of the stage. Another whistle emerged to join the other. Together they formed the two part melody of 'Love Song for the Undertaker', a tune so joyful that it played merry hell with its lyrical content. Two more whistles joined in from the wings and, out of the gloom with a surprising sense of drama stepped Each, Peach, Pear and Plum.

Benjamin and Srdjan took stance, ready to engage. The four heavies, each armed with hardened sticks, jumped off the stage, forcing Srdjan and Benjamin to retreat down the aisle. The whistling continued. Sticks were patted into hands. Swords were pointed straight and true at eye level, darting from target to target.

"'Ello Benji" sneered Each, leading the four heavies down the aisle. "Can't imagine why you've come all the way down 'ere, can you Mr Peach?"

"Nah, I can't," agreed Peach.

"Can't imagine," reiterated Pear.

"Well, you fellows have always wanted for a little imagination," retorted Benjamin.

"Indeed," followed Srdjan, "we all remember your Faust!"

Both actors glinted, as the four heavies took offence.

"Bollocks to this, hit him, would you Plum?" commanded Each, not realising Plum was at the back of the gang and a little beyond striking reach. Plum lunged forward nonetheless and swung downwards wildly, losing his balance and clattering into some chairs and onto the floor, grabbing his shin and wincing in pain. The actors and the heavies all turned and looked down at him. Even Valerie took her hands from her mouth, taken by the buffoonery that momentarily killed off the danger in the air. Clubs and swords were lowered slightly.

"Plum, you dopey git, what the hell are you doing?" enquired Each in a resigned tone. Plum didn't answer, instead choosing to roll around on the floor whimpering and clutching his shin.

"For a big fella, your boy is a bit of a Nancy," commented Ananas.

"You're telling me," agreed Each. "You try taking the bacon from his plate in the morning. You ain't seen a tantrum like it."

"Get up you silly fat sod," said Pear kicking his whining friend, which only proved to make him scamper away in a sulk. Everybody shook their head.

"For Christ's sake!" a booming voice came from the back of the theatre. The heavies and the actors were pulled back out of their little moment.

"I can't trust you morons to boil an egg, let alone duff up a couple of pisshead actors." The heavies suddenly resumed their threatening poses. The clubs began to hit their palms in musical unison. Benjamin and Srdjan turned around to see 'No Not' Sheridan standing in a beam of light, leaning on his cane and inspecting his nails. He looked up at them.

"Oh, I'm sorry. It's you Benjamin. I should have said 'one pissed up actor and one pissed up tosspot."

The heavies sniggered.

"Shut it, you lot," snapped Sheridan. The heavies shut it.

"Where is he 'No Not', you bastard" said Benjamin.

"Damn you, sir!" came a well projected voice from yet another gloomy spot from the stage. "I shall have your eyes and your lungs for this days insult!"

"Kemble, I presume?" said Benjamin to the floating voice. "Cover up that pug face of yours and step into the light, there's a good runt."

Kemble pranced out to join 'No Not' and with is hanky and foot extended, he threw out a ridiculously ornate bow.

"Your insults cannot harm me, sir! It is the dishonour you give good Sir Richard that stiffens my rancour!"

Good Sir Richard Sheridan bowed in thanks to Kemble, who bowed back, to which Sheridan bowed again. Benjamin and Srdjan hung their heads. This was going to take all night.

"Alright, enough of the pleasantries" called Benjamin. "where is he? Give him back, we'll be out of your wigs and you can go back to stealing toffee apples off kids and sniffing whippets' arses."

'No Not' signalled to Each and Peach, who suddenly grabbed the actors from behind, pinning them close by using their clubs across their chests. Srdjan and Benjamin struggled. Then, from two flanking aisles thrust a pair of rapiers that came to rest an inch from Benjamin and Srdjan's throats. The blades disappeared into the shadows of the aisles, but Benjamin and Srdjan both knew who owned them.

"Good morning, ladies," said Benjamin to the points of the blades. Then, rising like serpents from a basket, came Ms Sarah Siddons and Ms Alexia Adberg esteemed and talented actresses, especially the former, but like Kemble and the heavies, fallen under the misguidance of Sheridan.

"Hello there, Ms Adberg," smiled Srdjan, "you're looking well. Are you still singing? Did you ever finish that opera we started?"

"No my dear, no I never."

Sheridan cleared his throat.

"I mean, quiet you fool, or I'll pin cushion your codlings," spat Ms Adberg before halfsmiling at Srdjan as the memory of a warmer time briefly sprung up.

"So, you came for your boy," began 'No Not' Sheridan, advancing down the aisle with Kemble on one side who took odd, lunging strides. 'No Not' stopped and looked back at Valerie and raised his eyebrows. She stepped forward to join him.

"You have met sweet Valerie? She shows great promise! A fine actress! Maybe one day fine enough to take Ms Siddons' place as my number one honeytrap" He had reached Ms Siddons as he said this and kissed her cheek. She smiled a bent smile and a slight shudder, imperceptible to most, but an earthquake to Benjamin's keen eyes, rippled through her.

"I don't want any more bloodshed, Mr Ananas," Sheridan sighed, "nobody does…well accept maybe Pear [Pear grinned]. You can just give me what is mine and I'll give you what is yours and you can chip off and leave us to…what was it, again?"

"Whippet sniffing"

"Ah yes….how colourful". Sheridan punched Benjamin in the stomach which was a caddish blow given that all actors are fragile in the gut. Benjamin almost vomited as his churning hangover exploded inside him. He coughed and spluttered, spitting and dry heaving. Sheridan signalled for Each to release the actor. He did so and Benjamin fell to one side, grabbing a chair-back for support.

"Come on Benji, dear boy, don't let him hang about all day!" said Sheridan, his yellow teeth peeking out from the corner of his mouth. Benjamin looked up at him, analysing the exact phrasing of his enemy's statement. Sheridan gestured to the rafters. Benjamin, Valerie and Srdjan looked up to see Archie's body bound in rope, swaying from a creaking beam.

Benjamin launched at Sheridan, tackling him to the floor and sending the chairs clattering. Kemble was pushed to the side, gasping feyly as he tumbled. Srdjan drove his head backwards into Peach's face and split his nose. The heavy staggered back, releasing Srdjan. The Dalmatian instantly kicked Ms Adberg's sword out of her hand sending it spinning into air. The other heavies dived for Srdjan and Ms Siddons' thrust at him with her rapier. Srdjan leapt up onto the back of a chair, missing the bundle of heavies and causing Ms Siddons' rapier to pierce Each's shoulder. Srdjan stood straddling two chairs, drew his own sword and caught the spinning rapier that he had kicked out of Ms Adberg's hand. He pointed the swords towards his enemies who climbed up onto the chairs to engage him.

While Ananas and Sheridan rolled around the floor trading blows to the midsection, Srdjan fought of Each, Peach, Pear, Plum, Kemble and a well-skilled Ms Siddons. They stepped across the chair-backs as they fought as if they were dancing across a pond on stepping stones. Valerie crawled along the floor, trying to get out of the danger. The swords swung and clashed above her hand, chairs fell down and boots swung low.

Benjamin managed to land a good punch to Sheridan's jaw and get to his knees. He was half-upright when a low swing from Pear's club swung wildly across his face. Ananas dived backwards to avoid it. Peach, unaware of how close he had come to cracking the actor, continued with the joint assault on Srdjan.

Benjamin grabbed his sword and climbed up to assist his friend; two versus six. Ms Adberg, weaponless, backed away against the stage and watched the melee, enthralled at the majesty of the fight, and for a fleeting moment remembering what it was to feel the thrill of performance and the throb in her loins for the Dalmatian.

Sheridan wasn't about to mess around for much longer and he crawled towards the stage, leaving his heavies and Ms Siddons to hold the actors at bay. They surrounded them, forcing Benjamin and Srdjan to fight back to back.

Sheridan scampered up onto the stage and ran over to a tatty upright harpsicord. He flung open the lid and reached inside.

Benjamin and Srdjan were about to start dealing out more lethal blows due to the encroaching circle and the look in their opponents eyes that hinted that things were about to get a lot more real when a large crack thundered through the theatre. Everybody froze and looked to the stage.

Sheridan stood with a smoking pistol by his side. He was holding another pistol in his other hand which he slowly raised until it was pointed at the dangling Archie.

"Drop your swords or I really will send the bastard down to meet his maker," growled Sheridan. Srdjan and Benjamin dropped their swords and stepped down to the floor.

"Alright, you win," panted Benjamin, the fracas taking a lot out his middle-aged energy reserves. "What do you want?"

"I want only what is mine, only what is mine, dear boy," smiled Sheridan.

"Which is?" replied the actor, though he had a feeling he knew what it was.

Sheridan's smiled dropped away.

"I want my theatre back, you son of a bitch"

Chapter Eleven

Live Man Walking

Barely a word had had been spoken all day. While they waited, The Irregulars occupied their time in shared solitude. Danilov and Tobias sat on the stage playing their own games of solitaire, on the other side of the stage stood Antoine who was practicing a sleight of hand movement in front of his mirror. As he didn't want to break the peace in the theatre, he mimed clapping his hands. Every time he 'clapped', his watch would dangle from a different pocket. Sometimes, even he marvelled at his speed.

'If only Papa could have seen,' he thought as he recalled an evening back in Gascony when he was twelve years old. Antoine had been standing in his father's workshop watching him turn the lathe while in the garden his brothers were taking it in turns to jump out of a large tree holding a pillowcase above their heads to ease their descent. Antoine stood in front of his father performing a routine of dazzling tricks and showing preternatural skill but his father paid no attention. He never did. Antoine's routine grew faster and faster until his speed overtook his skill and he dropped a hammer into a bucket of paint, causing it to tip and spill everywhere. His father had administered two hundred raps on his knuckles with his steel rule. Antoine couldn't grip anything for weeks after that and it took years for his full dexterity to return. To this day, even in the winter he felt his knuckles seize up. It didn't stop him. Not much did. He had a gift.

While Antoine continued his routine, Desiree swung in her hammock rubbing rosewater into her soft skin over and over again. She counted the days she had left of her life. Since a little girl, she had been sure that she would die on her thirty ninth birthday. She had less than four years remaining. She sighed at the prospect and, as she swung gently, she began to calculate the number of months, days, hours and minutes left of her life. To the side of her, on his bed, lay Herschel. He was smoking his pipe and dividing his mind between Desiree and his beloved Annabel. Across from him, in a tattered wingback chair sat Lupe Darling. She was half wrapped in a large silk gown, the warm candlelight stripping years from her. She was still as the grave, unblinking, barely breathing. In her eyes a distant stare. She could have been in any one of her million memories; diving for pearls, seducing princes, hunting tigers in Bengal or keeping watch for pirates in the crow's nest of a spice clipper.

The only real activity came from Anya who silently walked on her practice rope. Back and forth she paced in a graceful, yet clockwork rhythm. Every once in a while, she would perform a flip and then continue to walk on. Of course, Gertie looked on. Not just at Anya, but at everyone. The silent tableaux threatened to dispel his concern for Archie with the reassurance that, whatever has happened, or was going to happen, would be palatable because they all had each other.

The only one not amongst them was Claudia. She had taken herself away to Archie's quarters and was curled on his bed under his coat, crying quietly. While the rest of them had the quiet expectancy of those in the cells by the guillotine, Claudia found herself in turmoil. She thought of some terrible fate for Archie and, trying to overcome it, would dart her imagination down a different alley, only to dream up an even worse outcome. Though she was the comforting heart and spirit to all The Irregulars, it did not mean she spent her days in a giddy delirium. When alone, night or day, she would oftentimes find herself adrift in a sea of confusion. Her calmness only really projected outwards. Her eyes were panicked and wide. If she closed them, she would imagine the bad things, but the longer she kept them open, the more the room became a shrine to her dead beloved. His coat! The smell of it! His shoes, crumpled and with holes! One of the laces had a knot in it. Everything was a cruel reminder that she would never see him again. She loved him, unequivocally, and wanted to marry him, have children with him and then grow old and fat together. She closed her eyes and buried her face into his pillow.

There was no way of knowing precisely what time it was when they came back to the Playhouse. The grandfather clock had been stuck at ten-to-ten for many years and Tobias saw little point in repairing it. Time was meaningless. However, on that particular day, his feelings towards time were much more volatile. He wanted to know the time. He wanted to at least know if it had been long enough to start worrying, or if it was still on the right side of positivity. They all wanted to know. However, they were all in silent agreement that they did not want to hear the ominous tick...tock...tick...tock of the thing. They knew full well that the Fates would drop years in between the tick and the tock and within those years most exquisite tortures would be wrought upon their nerves.

It must have been around late afternoon when they came back because, when the doors were opened, an ochre-hued sunset spilled into their crypt.

Danilov, Tobias and Antoine turned to the doors, for they were on the stage and the others in the wings. They shielded their eyes from the startling light, desperately trying to count the bodies coming towards them. At first, it was just a black mass, but soon, the mass began to break apart. Srdjan and Benjamin were back as their near identical height and frames were unmistakable. Then there formed another figure, a mass that did not stand as tall and was propped up betwixt Srdjan or Benjamin. Antoine roared with laughter and clapped his hands delightfully. Tobias and Danilov flicked their deck of cards into the air like confetti and shook hands, laughing too.

The sudden noise and breaking light that managed to penetrate backstage resuscitated the rest of the Players who had all but drowned in their communal melancholia. They looked at each other, not quite sure if one or all were dreaming, and moved onto the stage. Srdjan, Benjamin and the remains of Archibald Enfield were walking down the centre aisle. Lupe shrieked a note of exultant joy. Desiree threw her arms around Herschel and Anya's hand brushed everso slightly against Gertie's.

Lupe's note shot through the theatre, round the backstage living quarters, through the darkness of the storage section where the sets where kept and up the stairs to Archie's quarters. The note kicked down the door like a hero and dived onto the bed and kissed Claudia's ears ravenously. She sat bolt upright, her eyes widening and her face lighting up. She smiled so broadly and gasped so gleefully that she almost fell off the bed. She steadied herself and ran out of the chamber.

The Irregulars had become accustomed to the light when the returning heroes reached the stage. Despite a few scratches and nicks here and there, Srdjan and Benjamin seemed relatively unharmed. Archie, on the other hand, looked like he'd been embraced by a rhino. Srdjan and Danilov lifted the poor bastard onto the stage and he lay there, breathing erratically and letting out a painful wheeze.

Desiree knelt by his head and stroked the matted hair from his face. He smiled at seeing his friends.

"My my, you have been in the wars, haven't you, lad," said Herschel. "Come on then, let's get you cleant up."

They were about to pick him up when Desiree caught glimpse of a figure skulking at the back of the theatre. Valerie Folk was sheepishly looking on.

"What is she doing here?" Desiree whispered angrily to Benjamin. The Irregulars all looked over at Valerie, their glares creating an even greater divide between her side and theirs. Archie reached up and patted Desiree's knee.

"Desiree..." he wheezed, acting up slightly.

"Yes, my love?" she said, caressing his face.

"Your hair looks good today." He tried to smile and wink. His lack of physical ability to do so actually magnified his charm and Desiree sighed. She kissed his head.

Benjamin was about to call to Valerie to step into the light and join them, when Claudia came bounding in from the wings. She was not expecting to see Archie half dead on the stage and the shock stopped her in her tracks. Everybody looked to her.

"My darling" said Lupe in a tone of maternal concern.

"Is he... is he...?"

They couldn't hear the rest of her sentence on account of her hands covering her mouth and her tears welling up. Tobias bent down and cupped the back of Archie's head and raised it up so he could see her. This time, the half-dead man managed a full smile, his eyes firing again. He raised his hand slowly and wiggled his fingers at her.

"I'm still here, my darling Mouse, would I go to heaven without my angel?" he blew her a kiss which healed all her concerns. She began to walk to him when she too noticed the culprit lurking at the back of the theatre. She turned to Valerie.

"Clemency," Archie wheezed, "grant her clemency, she means no harm."

Claudia cleared her throat and diverted her course. She hopped off of the stage and began to walk down the aisle towards the skulking honeytrap barmaid.

Benjamin reached out to her. "Claud..." He was halted by a quick, silencing finger from the Spanish girl.

Valerie stood in the shadows, pacing from side to side and wringing her hands. The rest of the Players sat, stood and propped around the battered Archie. As Claudia approached, Valerie began to prepare herself for the unexpected. The Spanish girl was volatile and athough Valerie didn't know her, it didn't take a genius to figure out that much about her.

Valerie stopped pacing and stood in the centre aisle. Without pausing to take a breath, Claudia walked up sternly and slapped her across the face. The crack echoed across the theatre and the Players all winced. Valerie clutched her cheek, tears streaming. She bit her lip and stood back up to face her assailant.

"That was for me," said Claudia leaning forward. Valerie clenched her jaw in preparation for another strike. Claudia kissed her on the lips. The pain vanished from her cheek and a flutter rippled though her. Claudia broke off the kiss and stepped backwards. "That was from my Archie." And she returned to the Players. Valerie cautiously followed behind her, taking the kiss as a signal of wary acceptance.

"Did they kiss and make up?" asked Archie. Herschel held his hand and nodded.

"Was it sexy?"

Herschel smiled and looked over at the rest of the group. "I think he'll be alright after all," he said, "come on then, on your feet soldier."

Tobias and Danilov helped Herschel pick Archie up and when Claudia and Valerie joined them on stage, they took the actor to rest in his chamber.

"I will stay with him, please let me," the barmaid said when they had laid Archie on his bed. Claudia covered him with his blanket and gently took his boots off, placing them next to his other, more ragged, pair. She ignored Valerie's request and took the bowl of water by the bedside, dabbed a cloth in it to clean up the actor's face and began to quietly sing the little Spanish lullaby about El Coco, the monster who eats children who don't go to sleep.

"Come now, Little Mouse," said Tobias, "I fear we have much to discuss. Let us leave the poor fellow." Claudia ignored the metallurgist and repeated her lullaby and her cleaning. Archie's face was slowly being uncovered from the layer of blood and grime. He was also drifting into sleep.

"Will you be here when I wake up?" he whispered in weary delirium.

"I will, my Archie, I will."

He smiled and held her hand that was cleaning his cheek. He kissed it.

"You go my dear, go talk with the bear. Valerie can look after me." He kissed her hand again. Claudia shot a look to Valerie.

"Very well," she said reluctantly and leant in close to his ear. She whispered something inaudible to the others, but which made Archie smile a wonderful smile and fall asleep almost instantly. Pleased with herself, she stood up. Valerie held out her hand for the cloth so that she could take over the cleaning duties. Claudia dropped it back into the bowl and put the bowl back on the table as if Valerie was an unseen spirit in the room. Tobias, in the doorway, lifted his arm, and Claudia looped hers around his waist and they left together.

Danilov remained in the doorway and looked at Valerie.

"Valerie" he said. She looked at him. He smiled to her, "I didn't know your name."

"Pleased to meet you...," she said, hoping her open-ended sentence would illicit his name in response.

"Valerie" he said back, confusingly. "That's a nice name" and he left her. She looked around the room to see if there was somebody else he could have been talking to. The man had confused her.

"Odd man" she whispered to herself. *'Handsome too'* her inner-voice added.

—————•◦•—————

The Players were sat in each other's arms on the stage floor. Benjamin was standing before them. Everybody looked shellshocked.

"So, that about covers everything, I think." He concluded gravely.

"I can't believe it" said Lupe to herself. Claudia, in her lap, turned inwards and buried her head into the singer's belly.

"What happens if we boycott the payment?" asked Tobias.

"That's not going to work," replied Herschel, "I've known Sheridan long enough to know that when you're in his pocket, you pay....or you *really* pay."

"But we're safe together. We look out for each other. We are family," said Antoine, "Damn that bastard's eyes. Damn him, we shall not pay!"

"We could fight," said Srdjan, rallied by Antoine's defiance.

"And we might win," agreed Herschel with less enthusiasm, "once or twice maybe. But eventually, he'll get at us. Probably on our own, the same way he got Archie. Only we won't get a warning. All we'll get is a Cypriote Kiss. That's how them types do it."

"What's a Cypriote kiss?" asked Desiree.

"It's a long, thin metal needle, like a hair pin only about eight inches long and its jabbed into the baseof the neck, where the spine meets the skull," said Herschel as he rolled a cigarette. "It's usually administered to drunks who are pissing against a wall. Walk behind one, schnickt – needle goes in neck, comes out of face, pisshead drops down dead. Done and done."

"Remind me not to sleep on my front if we ever argue again, my dear," said Desiree as she kissed his cheek.

"How did the old fool rack up such a debt?" asked Gertie. The rest of the group rolled their eyes at the seemingly obvious question.

"Sorry, I was just....sorry"

Gertie shut up, as was best for him.

"It's all our debt," said Benjamin, "for the productions he miraculously pulled out of the bag when you wanted to put on a play, Herschel. For the make-up and boas, Lupe. To square away the bookies, Danilov. For the base materials for you Tobias when you want to make swords. And me...well, that goes without saying. It's our debt."

They knew it. Of course they did. They were all culprits having to come to terms with how things had got so bad.

"God knows why he went to that bastard in the first place," said Srdjan.

"Well," answered Benjamin, "he didn't technically. Archie got what he needed piecemeal from all over the place. Trouble is, he'd made a lot of enemies though his finances and his...well, let's just say that there are more than a few of irate husbands out there looking for his blood, too."

There was a murmur of agreement amongst them all.

"The point is," continued Benjamin, "'No Not' Sheridan's been weaselling around, as he does, buying up the debts and threats until now it has accumulated to this amount." He thumped his cane on the wooden floorboards, signifying that the amount mean the theatre itself.

"I can't believe he's finally going to get the Playhouse back" said Herschel, referring to a time years before most of the Players had joined the troupe and The Roxywas indeed owned by Sheridan.

"So, we'll have to sign over tomorrow then" said Desiree, the finality in her voice that suggested that her bags were already packed and there was no hope left.

"Can't we raise the money? I mean, if we asked for a week...and somehow, I don't know...." said an exasperated Tobias.

"Borrow from Peter to pay Paul?" scoffed Antoine, "I think that is how we got into this mess to begin with!"

"Well, he did say we could sign the theatre over tomorrow, or pay within a month," replied Benjamin.

"Oh, so we have a month to pay?" chirped Lupe, "well, no problem, I can send a message to Count Zendolafine of Moldovania asking for charity. He owes me from the whole..." she cleared her throat, "...Greenland affair."

"There is a caveat," interrupted Benjamin. "We sign tomorrow, job done. Or we pay in one month with 100% interest. And if we don't...well let's just say the theatre will no doubt meet with the same fate as the Theatre Royal...probably with us inside."

"He can't burn it down!" gasped Desiree, "surely not even a villain like him!"

"Then we are undone," said Antoine and he walked off into the wings.

"Where are you going?" called out Danilov.

"To get us some drinks," he called back, "If I am to be back on the streets tomorrow, I shall be so wearing my beer jacket."

"Oh Benjamin," sobbed Claudia, "and it was your birthday yesterday too."

And so there it was. The Roxy Playhouse Irregular's entered into the twilight of their theatre residency with drink, each other and little else but the certainty of a destitute future.

Chapter Twelve

Dark Times, For a Change

The Players slept as they usually did after a night's drinking, exactly where they fell. The difference this time was that their attitude to the evening was more like that of a wake, rather than with their usual sense of revelry. They lay entangled in a heap and each one fully clothed. The evening had seen grand tales spun by Lupe, solos and duets from Claudia and Benjamin, some acrobatics from the Kamilcova twins and some keen knife throwing and juggling from Antoine.

After the variety show, the performers fell about drinking and laughing, basking in their shared nostalgia for the times they had shared under The Roxy's roof and, as nostalgic conversation invariably does, the tone changed into a more melancholic, bittersweet one. That is how they ended their night. Nobody wanted to passout but sooner or later everybody did.

———•◦•———

Earlier that evening, just after Claudia and the two men had left Valerie alone to tend to Archie she had locked the door and removed all her clothes. She draped them over his large, tatty chair and stood completely naked and felt, perhaps for the first time in her life, naturally naked. Most people, in their day to day lives are naked for the briefest amount of time possible and usually with the least amount of people around. However, every once in a while, someone, somewhere, finds themselves in a place of absolute safety and warmth and, if they do manage to go one step further and remove their clothes, they may find themselves naturally naked. If there is a mirror in the room, they will not inspect their body. They will not suck in their stomachs nor flex their muscles. To be naturally naked is to be in the womb. It is to be in a dream. It is to be calmly in love with the universe.

That is how Valerie felt then. Archie was asleep and completely unaware that two yards from him a beautiful woman was having an epiphany. She looked at his clothes, and his articles. She looked at the mountain range of guttered candles on the window ledge. She looked at his paperwork and smiled at the scribbles here and half-baked ideas there.

After she had explored the world, she carefully climbed into the bed and lay there, head propped by hand, looking at him. In those few minutes she made countless vows regarding him, regarding her and vows regarding the world around her. She rested her milky thigh over his legs, draped her arm around him, felt utter peace for a few seconds and fell asleep presently.

———•◦•———

Archie woke to find the naked Valerie next to him. She had rolled to the side in the night and was snoring sweetly. His head throbbed. He didn't remember putting her there. His head hurt even more when he thought about it. He lay back down and looked up at the black ceiling. The room felt cold to him. Every joint ached, but he could not really feel it. He had to tell himself that everything hurt, and remember what had happened to him, in order to fire his nerves into confirming it. The cold numbness in his soul was all encompassing.

Unlike most people who come to the end of their lives, Archie knew exactly how he had gotten there. He was the architect of not only his doom, but of his friends and their legacy too. He lay there thinking the same thought over and over, and over. Finally he whispered aloud; "Why didn't Sheridan listen to Kemble?"

While in their custody, and before Srdjan and Ananas had rescued him, Archie remembered lying on his back upon their stage near drowning in his own blood with a rapier blade swinging pendulously across his face. Sheridan was holding it and talking to Ms Siddons. He could not remember what she was saying, but he could remember Kemble looming over him, the awful boils like meteorites pressing down on him. The bastard actor kept saying "kill him Sheridan, kill him now master. Gut him, fry him, jab him, stab him! Kill him!"

"You should have done it," whispered Archie once more and turned over to look at Valerie. She was wondrous when asleep, like some women are but she may as well have been a vase in a cabinet for the good her beauty did him. He felt a million miles from everything. He got out of bed slowly and slipped his bare feet into his boots. He dispensed with breeches and a shirt and just wrapped his long coat around himself. He was freezing. He could not feel it, but he knew that he was supposed to be because he could see his breath.

He left the room as silently as he could. Valerie stirred slightly and let out a lethargic moan. A peaceful half-smile resting on her lips like a butterfly.

Archie walked through the dark recesses of the theatre as if he was asleep. Ducking here and stooping there mechanically and without looking. When he reached the stage, he saw the pile of bodies sleeping in their drunken slumber. He folded his arms and walked over and looked at them. He was still numb. He quietly whispered his goodbyes to each of them before turning away from his friends and drifting off towards Herschel's study where he knew to be found the only working pistol in The Roxy Playhouse.

———•—

Valerie was making a daisy-chain in a meadow when the skies suddenly became overcast and she knew that something was wrong; something in the waking world and so, she pulled herself out of her dream to find herself alone in Archie's bed. She looked around. He was not in his huge chair, he had not fallen off the bed and he wasn't buried further down under the blankets. She took a moment to run through the possibilities. The obvious one, that he had gone to relieve himself, seemed strangely false. Her intuition told her that something was wrong. She threw on a shawl and hurried, barefoot, out of the room.

Like a ghost, she flitted from alcove to alcove and hidey-hole to hidey-hole looking for him. She carefully lifted the covers off of all the beds and she picked apart the limbs in the pile of actors to see if he had burrowed in. He had not. She was about to give up, thinking she had missed him, and he had returned to his bed, when the scent of vanilla hit her nose. She followed its winding trail into the depths of the backstage area and after a few minutes of tracing she found herself at the door to a hidden room. It was slightly ajar and she could smell that smell and see the flickering orange candlelight within.

She peered in to see Archie, kneeling down by the writing bureau. He seemed to be in a waking catatonia. He raised the pistol to his head. Valerie gasped and burst into the room, running at Archie and grabbing the gun. She managed to get her thumb in between the hammer and the cock, just as he pulled the trigger. The hammer stuck her thumb, causing great pain, but saving the gun from discharging. She wrestled it from him. He looked up her with vacant, dead eyes.

"What are you doing? What is this? What are you doing?" She was near hysterical. He did not change his expression. She began to shake him by the shoulders. He felt like a ragdoll. She slapped him twice as hard as Claudia had done to her. His eyes fluttered slightly.

"That was from your friends for what you just did," she said through her tears. She kissed him deeply on the lips. His fire reignited and the moments snatched outside The Bishop sprung up inside him. Valerie broke off the kiss.

"And that was for me."

He looked at her, and like the pages of a book caught in a breeze, hundreds of emotions flicked passed. She held him tight and covered him with kisses, not caring if they angered his wounds. They did, and this time he could feel it but he did not mind.

"I'm naked," he said, pathetically. For the first time in his life, he found himself unnaturally naked.

"Yes you are," she whispered, while her kisses became incrementally softer and longer.

"I must put on some clothes. I must."

"Yes, you must…but not till morning. I must make sure you are fully recovered. It is my duty, my charge." Valerie straddled him and gently lowered him onto his back upon Herschel's desk.

"I can see that you are a fast healer," she said with a wink as she let her robe fall of her shoulders. Valerie took Archie's hands and placed them on her breasts before leaning back in for another, deep kiss that did not end until they had finished making love.

Archie had found some tobacco amongst Herschel's papers and rolled Valerie a cigarette. She lay on the desk, exhausted and covered in the warm glow of perspiration. Archie sat in Herschel's chair rolling himself a cigarette.

"I won't tell them, you know," she said to the air.

"About what we did?"

"No about... how I found you."

"Thank you, I would greatly appreciate that."

"What is the name of the Spanish girl?"

"Claudia...or Little Mouse, why?"

"She is pretty."

"Yes, yes she is," said Archie as he lit his roll-up off of a vanilla scented candle.

"You know, she has quite the crush on you." Valerie looked over to see if her remark had registered with Archie. He sat in the candlelight looking at her.

"Speaking of names," she continued, "why did Mr Ananas call Richard 'No Not'?"

Archie laughed to himself. Valerie looked back at him and took a long drag on the cigarette.

"What, what's so funny?" she asked.

"Well, a few years ago, your Mr Sheridan..."

"He's not my Mr Sheridan. Not no more."

Archie reached out and ran his hand over her leg. His gesture told her that he meant nothing by his remark. She relaxed back into her glow.

"Anyway, a few years ago he was invited to some Royal function in Haymarket, completely out of the blue. Well, for everyone else it was. This chap was a half-baked theatre practitioner, and not a very good one I might add. Did you know he once put on a musical version of 'Faust', two days before we did to trump our sales? The cad stole Herschel's script and cobbled together some bastard version and put it on. Shit reviews. We never opened that play. It was awful; bloody pirate."

Valerie was luxuriating in the bliss of Archie's voice, the solitude of the lovers and the romance of the theatre. She was living a wonderful fantasy.

"Anyway, this pillock gets this invite and he's all 'so? What's your problem? Of course I got an invite, why wouldn't I get an invite? I'm the greatest,' blah, blah, blah cocky sod. So, he spends half the budget of his kabuki themed production of 'Coriolanus' on the most ridiculous suit and he presents himself to Drury Lane. By the way, this was before him and us had the, ahem, falling out, anyway he presents himself to us."

Archie stood up, took Valerie's hands and pulled her up so that she was sitting on the desk and he stood in front of her, chest puffed out like a cross between a Greek statue and a man straddling two horses charging in opposing directions. Valerie stifled her laughter and began to roll another cigarette. Archie, now animated and much more revived was feeling like his old self again.

"He says to us, 'the King requires me' and he swanned off out of the theatre." Archie walked like a man with a broomstick wedged between his knees. Valerie laughed.

"We go about our business of the day, rehearsing, performing etc, etc. And then, later that night, 'No Not' comes home utterly crestfallen. Poor sod looks like an erection that lost his invite, back into the breeches he comes. We ask him, 'how was it?' And he simply says 'great'. Really sounded like it was pretty far from 'great' but we can't press him for any more details, you know. He seemed so deflated."

Valerie began looking around herself. Archie knew instantly what she was looking for.

"In the second drawer down, my dear," he said helpfully.

Valerie reached down and opened the drawer and found a bottle of incredible cheap red wine, which as everyone knows is the perfect after-love drink. As she grabbed the bottle and pulled it out, the papers lying on top of it fell onto the floor unnoticed.

She uncorked the bottle, drank from it and gave it to Archie who swigged greedily, letting the wine run down his face. Valerie traced the trickles of wine down his body and bit her lip in anticipation as the wine-river collected around his groin.

Archie continued with his story; "We kept daring each other. 'You ask him, no you ask'. After a while of nobody asking him about the event the matter sort of went away. It was only a few weeks later when I found myself with...in the company of..."

Valerie smiled, "You can say it, and I can quite imagine and fully understand."

"I was with a lady, a teeny thing from Somerset, a Chambermaid."

"I bet you can't even remember her name."

"Claire, Livingbrown," He replied instantly. Archie could recall the names of all his lovers because he loved them and you don't forget the names of those you love.

"I was with her and she was talking about all the famous people she had served under, giving me some juicy little secrets here and there; lovely gossip. And then she starts laughing. I ask her what is so funny and she tells me about this event at Haymarket which she worked at. She rattled of the names of all the posh nobs that were there and then she said 'Sir Richard Sheridan' and I said, 'oh really?' and she said, laughing, 'yeah, both of them' and I go, 'what do you mean both of them?' and she goes 'well, the Sir Richard Sheridan, the MP and the bloke what owns the Theatre Royal turns up and everything's fine, and then later in the evening, I spy a commotion going on outside. I go to the window and I see this bloke, right, dressed in this suit that looks like someone had loaded a cannon with paint and shot it at the village idiot.'

Valerie began laughing loudly.

"I say, oh really? She says, 'yeah and he's arguing with the announcer. Anyway, to avoid embarrassment, they let the fella in. The announcer stands in the hallway – the King's there, right, mad as bag of frogs by the way, but he's there, Nosey's there, everyone right and the announcer comes in, with this madman next to him walking like he's ten feet tall, or what have you, he stands there and goes. 'Ladies and Gentleman, Richard Sheridan. There is silence right, and people look around. The announcer, wanting to nip the confusion in the bud, says loudly, with The King in the room, he says 'No Not That Sheridan!"

Valerie claps her hands and laughs loudly.

"I told the lads and within minutes of learning the jokes come out. Sheridan is going about his business and might ask someone where his hat is? 'I Know Not, Sheridan' would come the reply. Or when he was in earshot, someone would say to another, 'pass the hammer...No Not that one.' It didn't take long for that to spread. Within hours, the poor bugger couldn't walk down the street without people tipping their hat and saying 'morning No Not.'

"Ah, the poor thing."

"Poor thing, have you forgot, Miss, that he almost killed me today?" Archie stepped towards the desk and Valerie stuck out her legs, trapping him and bringing him in.

"I haven't forgotten, but with regards to your medical condition, I think you need a second opinion." She lay back down on the desk and Archie climbed on top of her. She stretched and smiled.

"This place is heaven. If I were rich I would give you the money to pay him off. If I were even that Claire Livingbrown, around all them posh nobs, I would pick their pockets to save this place." Archie was about to lean in and kiss her, when the papers on the floor caught his eye. He pulled back and stepped to the side, picking one up and looking at it.

"What did you say?" he said in a tone that said his mind was not on her.

"I said that you need a second opinion."

"No, about Claire."

"Oh, I said that I would get amongst the nobs and swipes some jewels for you. Not like they would miss them."

He turned and looked at her. His eyes were like the Northern Lights. She sat up.

"What is it Archie? What's wrong?" she cried.

"Genius. You are a genius!"

"What do you mean?"

"I mean, you have saved us, saved everything." He handed her the picture. She looked at it.

"I don't understand."

"You will. Now quick come with me, we must wake the others." With that he pulled her out of the room. She was still looking at the paper, trying to decode its meaning and decipher just the hell was what was going on and why it was so important as to force Archie from his medical examination.

Archie roused the Players like a child on Christmas morn, his giddy excitement abrasive against their grogginess. They scratched their heads, pinched the bridges of their noses, stretched and yawned. Archie was hobbling as fast as he could, banging a small gong and yelling their names in turn. Valerie busied herself pulling chairs into a semi-circle as instructed by the mad actor. When that task was done, she went about looking for unopened bottles because, as she was told, after they heard what Archie had to say, they would be in need a stiff drink. Everything concluded in synchronisation. The last player woke up as the last chair was placed and, as the last Iregular finally sat down, the final bottle was located. Despite the enthusiasm from Archie and Valerie, the tired Players remained unimpressed.

Danilov wanted to say, "What the hell is going on?" but instead mustered a throaty, wet, cough and a growl. It had pretty much the intended effect. The Irregulars sat and stared at Archie, who was commanding centre stage, standing proudly and smiling broadly. Valerie stood to the side of the stage.

"Tomorrow morning, I will go to Sheridan and tell him we'll take the month. We'll take two if we need. Because we are good for it!" he said proudly.

The group looked at each other in confusion. Archie had a devilish look in his eyes.

"I have had an idea. An idea that I was destined to have!" he boasted.

"Oh, Archie, I'm too tired for that," protested Lupe, "beside's I have a headache"

"Not that. Although that is another idea and a good one too, no, this is it. It's the answer to all our problems. All of them."

Herschel hung his head and sighed.

"Go on, then," he said, too tired to not indulge the man, "let's hear it."

"We're going to steal it."

Everybody looked at him as if he had gone mad.

"Not from common folk. But from those who won't miss it. Think what a silver candelabrum is worth, and think how many of them litter a mansion. Think of the pearls sewn into dresses as if they were buttons. We'll Robin Hood our way through the Social Scene swiping little bits and pieces here and there and, before you know it, we've paid of Sheridan and maybe got some left over. He looked around the theatre. We could give her a lick of paint. Put on a few shows...do what we've always dreamt of; open The Roxy as a free theatre!"

He had their attention. He walked into the centre of the semi circle and bent low to them.

"Maybe give some God damn joy back to the people who get spat on every day by those who sit in their castles growing fat off cakes and arrogance. Maybe even be able to swipe some nice booze too!"

"In theory, a solid plan," said Herschel, "but sooner or later someone is going to miss their signet ring, or their candelabra."

Archie was prepared for that one, the glint in his eye brighter still.

"Not if we do our homework, my man. Say we already know what Lord Numpty's signet ring looks like; say old Tobias here has knocked up a pretty replica; then suppose Antoine shakes said Numpty's hand. Say Antoine uses his magic to replace the ring!"

Antoine smiled and nodded,

"The little man has something," and he slapped Danilov's knee. "He really has something."

"But, the best bit of all," continued Archie, "imagine the performance! The whole of London is our stage. Our lives will be the performance. Our missions the play! Imagine it, my loves. Believe it can happen" he stood up and let the idea sink in.

"But," Gertie, timidly offered. "How will we get in? Don't think they let any old goat into these parties; got to be hoity toity."

Archie smiled in agreement, "true, true – a good point there."

"What we need is someone to get us into the parties, someone posh. What we need is a Lord," said Desiree.

"We already have one," said Archie, looking at Benjamin. He handed the piece of paper to him. Benjamin looked at it and something stirred inside. He furrowed his brow. Archie began rubbing his hands - his friend was getting the picture. The other Players looked on as Benjamin tried to decipher the mystery. A smile broke across the bear's face. A little murmur escaped his lips. He began to laugh. He looked up at Archie and winked.

"Good show old boy, good show," he said quietly.

Tobias, who was sitting next to Benjamin snatched the paper and gave it a look. It was a watercolour painting of Benjamin Ananas - middle-aged, tall and broad. But he did not look a bear. He looked like a dashing Prince. He was dressed in fine clothes, a sabre at his side and medals pinned to his chest.

Across the title of the paper were the words:

'Concept Art for 'The Misfortunes and Fortunes' No.14:
Benjamin Ananas and the Lord he could have been.'

It was a stunning portrait of a life that was supposed to be. Tobias got it. He passed it back along the line. They each looked at it then they looked up at the bear. In their minds that bedraggled, put upon grimy actor vanished, and the handsome, bold and beautiful gentlemen in fine clothes stood before them. One by one, as they beheld the image, they stood up and nodded.

To the side of the stage, Valerie was overcome with admiration and love for this group of friends. *'What immortals,'* she thought, *'what classic lovers!'*

"Archie, you are a smart one!" beamed Claudia. Archie shook his head.

"Not my idea, really," and he gestured to Valerie to join him. She timidly walked into the centre of the stage.

"Ms Folk here, she is the muse."

Valerie blushed as each Player bowed deeply towards her.

"Tomorrow, we begin," said Benjamin in a firm voice that carried an unmistakable wave of anticipation and excitement. He took a bottle, opened it and passed it round the group. They all began drinking again.

"Oh, but before we do," he said, turning to Archie and Valerie, "can you two put some clothes on?"

Archie and Valerie, in their excitement, had totally forgotten that they had pitched the idea to the group stark naked.

Part Two

Character Building

Chapter Thirteen

Pre-Production

Before Valerie had woken and without once looking over to her, Archie Enfield had washed, shaved and dressed. On any normal day he would spend a good half an hour watching whoever he was lucky enough to wake up next to. Those moments were among his most sacrosanct. On this day, however, there was business to attend to. When The Roxy Playhouse Irregulars commit to putting on a play, there is no time for luxuriating in private pleasures. He could be sure that while he had quietly forgone his usual routine everybody else had made similar sacrifices in the name of duty. It was certain that Danilov would have worked twice as fast in his early morning fitness regime, Desiree would have postponed her rose-water massage until later and Lupe would have selected the nearest boa regardless of whether it matched her dress. He was tying his cravat when Valerie woke, yawned and stretched.

"Good morning, dear Archie," she said with a wide, sun-kissed smile. Archie smiled back and winked at her.

"What time is it?"

"It's early, go back to sleep if you want."

"No, no...I get up," she said groggily as the sleep clung to her and buffeted her mind somewhat. She scratched her head and looked around for her clothes. Archie handed her a robe.

"Take your time," he said before leaving his quarters. Valerie, a little perturbed at his sharp morning manner, huffed as she put the robe on. She lay back down to collect her thoughts and fell back to sleep instantly.

She was awoken a short while later by both the gentle knock on the door and the smell of coffee wafting under the frame.

"Come in" she said, as she covered herself quickly. The door opened and Claudia walked in holding a cup of coffee and a little sticky bun.

"Good morning, Claudia."

The Spanish girl placed the breakfast on the dresser and turned to leave, making a point of turning away from Valerie, rather than toward. They'd both been trained in the stage arts and so both knew the true meaning of the seemingly innocent turn. To turn ones back on one's audience is to show utter disdain. Claudia left and Valerie poked her tongue out at the door. She wrapped herself up, ignored the bun but took the coffee and left the room.

Valerie was immediately disorientated by the noise and commotion that seemed to fill the theatre. How was it so silent in Archie's room? Was she dreaming? As she walked through the back section of the Playhouse she saw Srdjan and Antoine carrying huge wooden flats from the storeroom onto the stage. She looked at the flat they were carrying and smiled at the section of backdrop painted upon it; a vista of Egypt, complete with pyramids and an oasis on the horizon. The two men did not see her as they struggled in their labour, the sweat pouring off of their brows. Valerie hugged the coffee with both hands and blew over the rim as she looked at the multitude of uprights and flats stacked in the storage room, each one offering a tantalizing glimpse of some exotic locale and firing her imagination as to where the Players had ventured to on stage. There was a giant underwater scene with painted mermaids and clams, a tropical island, a gothic chamber, a dense jungle and every other conceivable location. She was drifting into her imagination when she was almost clobbered by a moving beam. She ducked reflexively as Srdjan hoisted it onto his shoulder.

"So sorry, my dear, didn't see you there." He marched off, straight passed Antoine who was coming back for more. Valerie smiled at him, and he tipped his imaginary hat and stood beside her.

"Good morning to you, how are you today?" he said, hands on hips and looking over the various uprights.

"These are wonderful," she said completely ignoring the question. "Did you do these?"

"Heavens no, I'm the magician,"

Valerie smiled and gleefully clapped her hands.

"A magician, oh please show me a trick."

"Madame, I only perform for an audience! Out there, not here in the dark, no, no, no!" He winked at her and walked off. Srdjan returned and looked twice at Valerie.

"You alright Miss?"

"Yes, why?"

Srdjan nodded his head towards her torso. She looked down and gasped. Her robe was on back to front and inside out.

"He's fast with his hands that Frenchman, watch out for him!" he said stifling a laugh. He covered his eyes while she sorted out the robe and only peeked through his fingers three times.

"These paintings, you can look now, these paintings, who did them?"

"These are the work of little Claudia."

"I see"

"Quite the artist, isn't she?"

"Yes, wonderful" said Valerie into her coffee. Srdjan leant in and whispered in her ear.

"Don't worry about her, she is feisty like all girls, but she is warm too, like all women. She'll come around to you."

Valerie smiled at Srdjan who smiled back and returned to moving the flats out of storage. Valerie walked through the store room and was about to move into the living quarters when she was rugby tackled by a flying dress. She dropped her coffee and tumbled to the floor, swamped in the huge garment. Another one piled on top of her, and another, and another. They were flying out of a doorway that, she presumed, was the doorway to the costume department. From within, she could hear the happy sing-song of Lupe Darling who was, obviously, having a bit of a spring clean. Valerie scrambled out from under the clothes-mountain and stood up. She dodged a few wigs and hats as they flew towards her and peered inside. The room seemed endless. Desiree was standing in the middle looking up at the ceiling, flanked by row upon row of costumes. She was about to say good morning when a dress fell from the ceiling towards the Umbrian dancer who caught it and flung it straight towards the door. Valerie leant out of the way as the dress flew past and looked back up to the ceiling. There, way up high, teetering on a wheeled ladder, trilled Lupe Darling. She was scooting back and forth like a mad librarian, searching through the ranks of costumes, and throwing down possible options to Desiree. Valerie decided not to interrupt the work and moved along to Herschel's study area. She was keen to say good morning to the writer and compliment him on his wonderful little study and although she had no plans of telling him of the positions she had assumed on his desk the night before, she was secretly eager to have another look inside the room and refresh her fantasy. The door was closed. She knocked once and put her hand on the knob.

"If that door opens, I'm burning the place down and shooting myself!" bellowed Herschel from within. Valerie released the handle and backed away, knocking into Gertie who tumbled forward and dropped the large tray of crystal glassware he was carrying. It shattered instantly. Valerie was beside herself with the instant whip of shame and embarrassment.

"Oh! Oh no! I'm so, so sorry! I really am!" she garbled has she tried to gather up the million little pieces. Gertie bent down to help her.

"It's alright Miss, it's alright, look," he said softly as he picked up a large piece of glass and stuffed it in his mouth. Valerie was taken aback by the crazy fool. He smiled.

"It's sugar glass! Try some," and he offered her the stem of a wine glass to nibble on. She took it and cautiously bit into it. It was lovely. Sugary sweet with just the hint of rose petal.

Gertie smiled and said; "Desiree makes them to Tobias's moulds…and she always puts in rose water to make them taste like Turkish Delight. When nobody's looking, we sometimes sneak off round the back and share a decanter. Don't tell nobody!"

They smiled at each other and he put a large stopper in her pocket. He tapped his nose.

"Mums' the word, eh!" and he scurried up the stairs to Tobias's workshop.

Valerie nibbled on the decanter-stopper and walked onto the empty stage, which seemed like the safest place for her. She did not notice that high in the rafters, Danilov and Anya were swinging around dismantling harnesses and braces.

Valerie was still standing on the stage, looking out at the seats when Archie and Benjamin strode out of the side-stage and up the aisle towards the exit. They were dressed and armed. She was going to call out, but decided not to as they appeared to be deep in conversation. They flung open the door and walked into the street. Valerie was startled to discover, judging by the tone and hue of the light entering from the doors, that it was dawn or just after. It seemed to her that The Roxy Playhouse Irregulars did not operate by any sensible or regular method of time keeping.

She nibbled on her stopper and contemplated the previous forty-eight hours, completely oblivious to the heavy brace dangling an inch above her head, held by Danilov who had dropped it, dived head first after the tumbling brace and caught it just in the nick of time. He swung silently, still attached to his wire, his arms straining under the weight of the brace. Above him, Anya stood on the rafter with her hands over mouth. Valerie finished her sweet and wandered back to the store area to try and put herself to good use. As soon as she was at a safe distance, Danilov released the brace and watched as it collapsed down onto the stage with a great metallic thud. He looked up at his sister; they both breathed a sigh of relief and laughed nervously.

———•·•———

Benjamin and Archie's carriage made slow progress over London Bridge. Benjamin had his eyes closed to the sights and smells as usual. He had already started working on his character. He had always found that, when creating a character, the best approach was to start from a detail: the right hat or the perfect ring and then from that seed, the flower would bloom. This time, however, he was about to face his biggest creative challenge; building a character based upon himself and what he could have been. He was beginning to conjure up memories of his past, recalling postures, gestures and witticisms. The tiniest details previously disregarded by him were now intrinsic to the construction. The past twenty five years had seen him relentlessly pile on neurosis and venom in a quest to bury the past so deep that it could never resurface but now he knew that he would have to dredge that reservoir and let the bodies float to the surface for inspection. He remembered the way his father drummed his fingers on his cane when he leant against it, how he arched his eyebrow when weighing up judgement on a comment. He remembered the way his friend Sebastian used to roll the wine glass in both hands while he told stories and the way the bastard Nathanial Whit used to curl his lip and suck through his teeth whenever something flew in the face of his opinion. Everybody looked up to Nathanial. He was dashing, sharp, strong and severe in his knowledge of the world as only young men are. Among that band of 'friends', Nathanial Whit led the way. Benjamin recalled his pose, regal and constructed; the obtuse angle of his jaw, the arch of his back; that was the detailing that Benjamin needed. He was loathe to admit it, but he was grateful for his 'friend' for providing such a wealth of detail. His creation was going to be a masterpiece.

While Benjamin built his character in quiet solitude, Archie was busy dishing out coins to every orphan who came begging as he saw himself in their muddy, desperate faces. Not only did he see his own face reflected back at him but also the faces of his four brothers and three sisters who never made it past the age of fifteen. Three brothers had died in the orphanage before they were ten, two by pneumonia and one beaten so badly he could only be identified by the fact that he had a birthmark in the shape of Orion's Belt on the small of his back. The fourth and eldest brother who, along with Archie the youngest, had survived the orphanage, had taken up 'employment' as a mudlark; the dangerous trade of scurrying around the various basins of The Thames at low tide and catching bags and crates tossed overboard by crooked sailors. He was crushed by an anchor, dropped by accident, killing him instantly. Of his three sisters, one died of influenza, one of dysentery and the eldest of the Enfield siblings had met her end on her fifteenth birthday at the hands of a vicious fiend who decided not to pay after she'd serviced him. When her body was discovered, they found an imprint of a crucifix in the palm of her hand. They concluded that she must have been holding it so tight in her last moments that it made an impression. It had been stolen shortly after she died.

As Archie gave the guttersnipes coins and jokes, they tried to run alongside the carriage shouting out to him their dreams and escapades, of which he listened to all and threw words of encouragement and advice. They all knew his name. Benjamin smiled whilst listening to his friend banter with the street kids. He felt that Archie was, himself, a street kid, but who just happened to be a little bit taller and imbued with a greater capacity for landing himself in trouble than they were. They finally made it over London Bridge and Archie nudged his friend awake.

"Time to get into character, Old Love," he said, unaware of what Benjamin had been doing for the entire journey. Benjamin tapped the roof of the carriage with his cane, bringing it to a jarring halt and they disembarked.

"Let me do the talking," said Benjamin as they strode away.

"Sure thing, Old Love," chirped his friend, momentarily distracted by a passing beauty who winked at him.

The afternoon was growing old and Valerie had not yet broken for lunch. After her dazzling introduction to how the Players operated in the beginning stages of a production, she had thrown herself whole heartedly into work. Desiree had given her some old overalls which she jumped into without a moment's hesitation. She had helped Desiree and Lupe ransack the costume department and they had amassed three impressive piles. After that, she had helped Tobias gut and organise his workshop. They firstly moved everything out, took inventory and then looked at it for an hour. Tobias picked up every single object and inspected it carefully through his multi-lensed goggles.

When she asked him what he was doing, he simply said, "Inventory. I need to inventory every marking and scrape. My fingers need to relearn."

Valerie didn't understand quite what he meant, but was still happy to watch the curious man go about his inspection. After the painstaking hour, he stood up and looked at her. His brow furrowed and his eyes flitted from side to side in a strange expression of distant confusion.

"Right," he said, finally, "back they go," and they put everything back exactly how it was. The exercise baffled Valerie, but she did not complain as she was too enthralled in the wonderful circus of gadgets and props which had been created by the reclusive Mr Strong. After that little adventure, she found herself working with Gertie, Anya and Danilov as they marked out all the wires and braces they had. From the rafters, Anya would throw down a wire and Danilov would test its length and durability and call out a strange code to Gertie who scribbled it down, as Danilov was illiterate. Once the wire had been inventoried, Anya unclipped it and sent it down to the ground, whereupon Valerie dutifully gathered it and wound it round her arm and stowed it away. Once all the wires where down, Gertie grabbed his butterfly net and took position. Danilov took Valerie's hand and led her to the side of the stage.

"Watch this," he whispered.

Valerie held her breath and Danilov held her hand a little tighter as Anya swan-dived off of the rafter. Gertie's breathing was relaxed and he mouthed a silent prayer, never once taking his eyes of the falling girl. She fell with her eyes closed, until such time as she was ready to open them. She did and smiled at Gertie. That was his signal. He thrust his butterfly upwards and caught her perfectly. As she impacted, he swung the net downward, absorbing the inertia and scooped her around and up so that she could step out safely. The whole manoeuvre was akin to dropping an egg from a building and catching it on the brow of a hill, thereby letting it roll to safety. Anya dismounted and calmly bowed to the wings, and to the audience. She winked and gently slapped Gertie's cheek before picking up the braces on the floor and walking off. Gertie exhaled, relieved to have survived another catch. Danilov and Valerie stood for a few seconds, still holding hands.

When lunch finally came around, Valerie found herself dispatching coffees, teas and biscuits to the workers. She was a little surprised at the lack of alcohol supplied. However what surprised her more, was that while performing this task, she was doing so beside Claudia. She could feel the cold tension between them and went about preparing the food and drinks. Then, suddenly and without any provocation, Claudia lifted up Valerie's shirt and blew a large raspberry on her stomach. Valerie screamed and dropped the plate of biscuits she was holding. She looked at Claudia who went about her business as if nothing had happened. Valerie didn't want to stand for it, and so flicked water at Claudia while she wasn't looking. Claudia flicked water back. And so it went on for the rest of the afternoon. Of all the wonders and activities she had partaken in that day that little exchange between the two girls had meant the most to her. Indeed, when she was in her twilight years, sixty years hence in that hovel in St Petersburg, starving but happy, Valerie suddenly recalled that moment and labelled it *'the first time I felt accepted.'*

<hr />

"How do you see it playing out, dear boy?" said Benjamin as the carriage rolled back over London Bridge, the sun starting to set over the river and casting a manipulative glow over everything that coerced the town's romantics into thinking that everything was right with the world.

"It's a three-tier cake," said Archie, looking over his little pocket book, "backstage, stage crew, and performers, possibly with an intermediary. A floor manager to co-ordinate,"

Benjamin nodded in agreement.

"Stage crew, well, Danilov and Anya on exit strategy," continued Archie, "Tobias and Gertie loading and transport. And backstage, Lupe, Herschel and Srdjan."

"Srdjan, really?" said Benjamin, surprised at the thought of leaving the accomplished actor behind in The Roxy.

"Well, it's a trade off. We need his steel and skill, but then we can't leave the theatre totally unguarded. Not just from 'No Not' Dickhead. Anyone else gets a sniff of what were up too, we'll have Tom, Dick and Harry's dad Larry having a crack at our digs."

"True."

"He'll have train you up, get you up to speed in buckling swashes in case...I don't know, you feel the need to measure swords with some prick"

Benjamin chuckled.

"And Herschel," continued Archie, "because, well, he's a bit too senior for these games. Plus he's a grumpy sod and when it's time to take the stage, I don't want him raining on my performance with his clouds of grouch."

"Good point. And performers?"

"Antoine, obviously, he'll be waiting tables, serving drinks and nicking cutlery, necklaces, rings and all that. I was also thinking Claudia as runner, shuttling the booty to wherever Danilov and Anya are. Plus point here, I once held conference with a chambermaid, had great access to areas. Moved unseen, saw it all. Claudia is the only choice."

"I think that works. But Claudia is first out, no questions."

"Of course, so that leaves you, the hero of the piece, working the room, escalating up the ladder getting the invites, scoping for future targets and generally keeping all eyes on you. Oh, and Desiree as your wife. I figure she can keep a few eyes on her as well, and hold court if she needs to."

"So that leaves you," said Benjamin.

"Indeed. I think I can be on point, as it were. Keep an eye on you."

"On me?"

"Making sure you are on message and not on the piss."

Benjamin thought about taking offence, but realised that reconciling the statement with the truth to be a better option.

"Good thinking. And it's going to be up to you to see it all: eyes and ears. If anything is looking a bit ropey, I want you to pull the plug and get them out of there; Claudia, Desiree and Anya first."

"Understood."

"So, that's everything about the performance," said Benjamin as the carriage rolled up outside The Roxy. Archie flipped up his pad and pocketed it.

"Yep," he said, "we just need to organise the entire show, shape you into some sort of convincing Lord, avoid 'No Not' and his dickheads, not get pinched by them Bow Street Runner arsewipes, not get rumbled by anyone else nosing about and get invites to all the best parties in town... in four weeks."

Benjamin alighted and spun his hat on to his head.

"God, I love the theatre," he said with genuine zeal and walked into the place.

"Amen to that, Old Love," Archie concurred as he followed him inside The Roxy.

Chapter Fourteen

Two Theatres

A rchie and Benjamin entered the theatre expecting to find things pretty much as they had left them. They almost stopped to check that they had the right address. The theatre was immaculate. The aisles had been swept and cleant, the stage polished and the curtains beaten and the Players were all sitting on the stage, sharing drinks after a hard day's work. Archie was filled with joy to see Valerie laughing and joking amongst them, filthy and bedraggled from the toil and never more beautiful. Srdjan, upon seeing the returning fellows, stood up and threw two bottles at them which they caught appreciatively.

"How did it go, badly no doubt," grumbled Herschel, upon seeing the approaching actors. Desiree tutted and gave him a playful shove.

"Quite the opposite actually Negative Nancy," said Archie as he supped his drink.

"The place is ready," chirped Gertie, "Lupe and Desiree sorted the costume department, the braces are all accounted for, the store-room is cleant, Tobias inspected his workshop, I cleared the grime, Valerie helped too…I think everything is ready."

Benjamin looked around the theatre. The Players watched expectantly as he milked his inspection, running his finger along the stage and the seats of chairs. He smiled.

"You have done fine work, fine work indeed," he boomed, finally. The group patted each other on the back. Benjamin hopped up onto the stage.

"So," he began, while uncorking his drink, "'No Not' has agreed to the extension, though his rat Kemble was none too happy about it. We'll deal with that later. Now, in order for this to work, we figure it will take more preparation than we are perhaps used too. Where shall I start?" He looked at Archie for help.

"Costume?" said Archie.

"Why not, so, costume. Those of you in the backstage area, that's you Danilov, and you Anya, you will need to be as shadows. Lupe, can you sort them out? They will no doubt be pulling off some incredible acrobatic feats so I would imagine durability is essential. Durable shadows, can you manage that?"

"No problem," shrilled Lupe.

"Perfect, now Antoine, I'm sure you can imagine your role in all this."

The Frenchman nodded proudly.

"So again, Lupe, we're going to need a customisable waiter's outfit. He's going to be stuffing his sleeves and pockets with knives rings and whatnot. They need to be concealed and he can't look like he's a walking suit of armour with a crap shirt draped over it."

"That is going to be tricky," she huffed, "I mean the cut of the shirt, tapered at the sleeve, tight at the waist. If you want it authentic then I'm afraid you're going to have to make some concessions."

"Afraid we can't do that, Darling" countered Archie "he has to blend in, but without compromise to his not inconsiderable skills." Archie winked at Antoine who tipped his hat in return.

"It is impossible! Not with the materials we have never mind the timeframe! No, no, no, it can't, can't be done, it shan't be done, not even if you begged me!" huffed the diva, turning her nose up at them all. The rest of troupe shook their heads in non-surprise at her usual no-can-do attitude to dressmaking compromise.

"I might be able to help," piped up Tobias, from the back of the group. "I designed Danilov's brace, I could see if I could fashion some sort of corset.

"No Frenchman wears a corset!" snapped Antoine. Everybody turned and raised their eyebrows at him in a unified 'beg to differ' objection. He took their point.

"Well, this Frenchman does not wear a corset!"

"Armour then, some sort of armour," appeased Tobias,

"Parfait, armour it is much more appropriate."

Tobias mouthed 'corset' to Archie who winked in understanding.

"Alright then," said Archie. "Antoine, get measured by Lupe and Tobias, that's a little project for you three. Now, Claudia, some sort of chambermaid outfit for you. You will be scurrying around like the mischievous little devil that you are, picking locks, stealing and concealing loot and so on. Think you can do that?"

Claudia saluted affirmatively to her beloved Archie. "Good mouse," he said.

"And for myself," said Benjamin, taking the baton from his friend, "and my wife, that's you Desiree. Sorry Herschel." Herschel gave a 'pah' and a flick of the wrist to which he received another shove from the Umbrian dancer. "We're going to need some passable costumes. Lupe, this is your time to shine. Go nuts. I need to blend in and stand out, if that makes sense. Desiree needs to look like an angel." Desiree cleared her throat. "*More* like an angel than she already does. Eyes need to be on us, while Antoine and Claudia do their business. We cannot be too inconspicuous, but we also can't look like the Fifth of November. Can you do that?"

"My dear boy," said Lupe, "when my needle is put to bed, you will look like you have just stepped out of the couturière of The Gods, and Desiree...oh my word! What dresses you shall have." Lupe was about to break into song when Benjamin curtailed the possibility.

"So that's costumes sorted. Weapons, Tobias, I'm going to need some steel, I will talk to you later about what I have in mind, savvy?"

Tobias nodded.

"Backstory," said Archie, "this is the big one. This bedraggled sack of piss here is going to have to break into the halls of the mighty, stand before them, rob 'em blind and have 'em say thank you afterwards. The confidence he is going to have to exude is only going to become real because of details. Who is he is, where he comes from, how he wipes his arse and why - that sort of gubbins. Herschel, this is you, this is your challenge. Can you write a play that encompasses every moment of one's life?"

"Of course he can! I just know it," gushed Valerie, desperate to get involved. Archie beamed at her.

"Well, if young Ms Folk believes it so much, maybe you can rise to the occasion, what say you old man? Can you make Lupe's fine clothes and Tobias's steel sit perfectly on this walking cabbage right here?" Herschel looked at Benjamin who puffed out his chest and tried to present himself as best as possible.

"As long," he eventually began in a gruff tone, "as I am left alone to write. It's going to take a lot of work. But yes, I believe I can write a script that might suit our needs."

"Good man. You can breathe out now Benjamin." The group giggled a little as Benjamin deflated himself. "Now then," continued Archie "on to one of the most important aspects of all of this. Gertie I'm looking at you here sunshine. This task I entrust to you, and only you."

"I can do it!" he eagerly rushed, half looking to see if Anya comprehended the magnitude of his forthcoming role.

"I'm sure you can, that's why I asked you."

"Great…what do I have to do?"

"You'll be getting us the hell out of there. You can drive a carriage can't you?"

"Err…no."

"Perfect, good man, Tobias will be there too, Toby, you will load the gear and get everyone on board. Good?"

"Sure," said the metallurgist.

Gertie looked confused and felt like he had been holding a different conversation to the one Archie thought he was having.

"How will we get a carriage?" he asked, hoping to reignite the debate and gain some clarity.

"We'll cross that bridge when we come to it," retorted Archie half heartedly.

Gertie folded his arms and went over the previous conversation word by word in his head, trying to figure out if anybody had understood him.

"Just a quick question," said Tobias, sweet enough to put his hand up in the air.

"Yes, please Tobias, go on."

"Say we do all this stuff. The costumes, the backstory, the pilfering, the escaping, I get all that. But, how do we get into the parties in the first place? How do we, or you Benjamin, get into the Ton? I could forge a voucher, but I don't think that will be enough. How do we get a foot in the door?"

The group all murmured in agreement at Tobias's sound question. Benjamin looked at Archie, for he too was slightly confused about that one.

"Don't you worry my old muckers; I have the answer to that one. It's all under control." He winked at them, and they took that to mean that Archie was magically sleeping with some mythical woman who stood at the gates to the palaces of the rich and mighty and would slip them in thanks to his services rendered.

Archie, at that point, only had a vague idea of how they were going to actually get invited to any sort of social event. He figured he would brush over the detail until either the solution came to him, or they ran out of time and had to improvise. He walked over to stand next to Benjamin.

"And I think that's it, right?" said Archie as he and Benjamin looked around. Then they saw Srdjan who looked worried.

"Shit, Srdjan," said Archie. "Ah, mate, I'm so sorry, it's not the most glamorous role this time I'm afraid. Not so glamorous at all, but so, so necessary. It is thankless, but for that even more heroic." Archie tried to dress up the bad news as best he could. Srdjan and the Players saw through it. Srdjan wasn't going anywhere.

"I am to stay behind, aren't I?" he said, "train up Benjamin in the arts of steel then sit here while you go off to perform."

Benjamin and Archie looked sheepishly to the floor, as did the Players. Srdjan looked over his friends, thought for a moment and then spoke.

"It will be an honour," he said with a bold, noble voice. "We cannot fight abroad only to come home and find our lands conquered. I will stand on this stage and keep watch. You can be sure that this castle will be safe from anyone. I give you my word."

His simple declaration of solidarity and sacrifice for the plan choked everybody and they held the upmost admiration for the Dalmatian. Archie and Benjamin both bowed to him. And so, the scene was set, the play was cast and The Roxy Playhouse Irregulars cracked open some bottles, wasting no time in celebrating such a momentous occasion.

———•◦•———

Sheridan sat by the out of tune harpsichord and played a monotonous lament to the best of his near-forgotten abilities. He was once a master, but that time had since passed and he now played like a man who never could. The Olympus was empty save for himself. He was Zeus in a deserted palace. He hadn't bothered to light any candles, instead draping himself in an old red curtain for warmth. Each and Peach and been sent on an errand, Pear was out spying and Plum was fetching gin. He had released Kemble into the night with the express instruction to chaperone and keep eyes on Ms Siddons and Adberg who were operating a two-handed honey trap and who, of late, he had suspected of deviancy against him.

The constant suspicion of all around him wracked his brain and so he oft times found himself in need of solitude. It was in those quiet moments when he wasn't inspecting every slanted gaze, every shift in expression or nervous twitch writ large on those around him that he was able to strip it all away and see with clear vision, the secrets and advantages around him. It was like closing the window to the town outside in order to create a better work environment to plan its infrastructure. He wanted facts and figures, not suspicions and guesswork. Being a theatre-soul, he was ultra perceptive in absorbing the minutia of people's facial betrayals and decoding them for his benefit. This was his process in building a stage character, or at least it used to be. Now the tool was used to scan for exploitable weaknesses. But it came at a price; the constant noise and chaos of a magnified world. It always threatened to overthrow his senses and so, in order to quell the speculative variants and quantify the definite articles he needed peace. All debts pending and processed were quietly ordered in his mind as he played on.

He was nearing the completion of his work when the theatre doors were kicked open. He fumbled the last few keys of the lament and looked over, the pages of his ledger slamming shut in his mind. Plum trundled towards him with wooden crate of gin bottles.

"Ere we are guv," bellowed the fool showing no respect to the tranquillity he was bulldozing through. "Get your tit-sucker round these!"

Sheridan winced in disgust at the ex stagehand's vulgarity. He stood up from the harpsichord and made his way towards the idiot.

"Plum," he sighed, "you used to have such a cherubic tongue. I fear the years of street work have twisted it something rotten."

Plum breathed in heavily through his nose, pulling its contents to the back of his throat before hacking it out across the floor of the theatre. He handed Sheridan a bottle and he opened it instantly. As if opening the bottle had been some sort of dinnerbell, Each, Peach and Pear all suddenly sprung in through the front door, half drunk and singing. Peach was dragging a grandfather clock by its base, the window to the face cracked and the innards making a sound that a clock's innards, really, really shouldn't make.

"Boss!" jeered Each, "we did it, that molly Miss…what's her name?"

"I don't know…Middlearse?" offered Peach.

"Arse, arse. Ms Arse-arse?" slurred Pear.

Sheridan was unimpressed. "Middleton, Mary Middleton?"Each touched his nose with a finger and pointed at Sheridan with his other hand. "That's the coos," he said, "she paid up and…gave us this clock to boot! Imagine that!"

"Why on earth would she do that?"

The three drunken thugs got to the stage. Peach righted the Grandfather clock and leant against it.

"Well," began Each, "Pear wanted to have a go on her and, well, she didn't seem too keen, so Peach gave her a few things to think about and then we made a deal. Shame really, if she had been a little more pleasant she wouldn't look like panda so much now. She might 'ave even enjoyed a bit of a rodgering too." They sniggered to themselves.

"Jesus Christ!" shouted Sheridan, "explain to me what the hell I am supposed to do with a grandfather clock?"

The three inebriates looked at each other. An idea dawned, painfully slowly, over Pear's face.

"Give it your grandmother?" he said.

All four of the idiots began laughing. Peach leant a little too much on the grandfather clock and they both toppled to the ground, the clock smashing into pieces. Sheridan drew his sword and before the drunks had time to notice, he had slashed them each across the cheek and resheathed his blade.

"We don't hit nor rape women, and the next time I find out you have tried to get 'em out of your breeches you know what will happen," he roared. The four men had sobered up instantly. They were clutching their cheeks. The wounds were only slight and trickled a tiny amount of blood.

"Yes boss."

"And that is?"

"We all get the Cypriote Kiss when were 'aving a slash," said Each.

"Correct," said their master. Sheridan looked over the goons who looked like a bunch of school boys in the Headmasters room.

Kemble, Ms Siddons and Ms Adberg walked into the theatre. Sheridan was relieved to have 'civilised' company.

"Finish the gin, it's yours," he said to the heavies over his shoulder as he walked away from them. They each grabbed a corner of the crate and scampered off into the cold, dark recesses of the theatre to continue their binge.

Ms Siddons and Ms Adberg emptied their pockets as soon as Sheridan reached them. They lifted their arms so he could pat them down. He was still angry at the behaviour of his heavies and so felt into Ms Siddons hair a little too thoroughly and felt a sudden large sting of pain fork through his palm. She smiled and pulled out her hair-pin which looked less like a pin then it did a boar-spit. She pulled out three more and her hair cascaded down.

Sheridan looked over at Ms Adberg who did the same. She had a dozen eight inch needles in her hair. Sheridan inspected their takings and found a good amount of coins.

"Good work, my dears," he said quietly before turning to Kemble and flicking him a coin.

"Now then, friends, what do you think of all this Ananas business?"

"Me and her think it stinks," said Ms Siddons, "don't we, Ms Adberg? They owes what they owes."

"I see, well put, Ms Siddons. What about you, Kemble?"

The snarky fop danced the coin over his fingers. "Well, my Lord and Master, not wishing to speak out of turn but I beg you, may I speak frankly?"

"Of course, please do."

Kemble stopped dancing the coin. "I think we should have killed the lot of them cunts and taken the Playhouse and to hell with the rest."

"Delicately put, and on a normal day, I would be inclined to agree. But we are not animals, we are business men and we adhere to Brigand's Law and that is why we give them the extension. It is civil business all the way down the line…until it is time to not be civil and we are not there just yet."

Kemble sucked through his teeth.

"But that doesn't mean we can't keep an eye on them," said Sheridan, "hang around the theatre, my friends. Remain unseen. Just observe. Report back any findings."

"What about what goes on inside?" enquired Ms Siddons, "thems a tight knit group. Not like we can stroll in."

"Don't worry," Sheridan countered, "Valerie knows what to do. You just keep a watch over everything else."

The women smiled and walked off into the gloomy bowels of the theatre. Once they were out of earshot, Sheridan leant into Kemble.

"How were they?"

"They didn't put a foot wrong. I watched 'em well enough. No trickery there. Well, at least they didn't pull nothin' while they knew I was around," he hissed.

"Good, good. Keep an eye on the Playhouse and an eye on them two n'all. Would you do that for me?"

Kemble smiled his grotesque smile and bowed. Sheridan turned to leave, but stopped and looked back.

"Oh and Kemble, if they do give you any trouble or you suspect they are about to up sticks and hightail it into Hampshire…"

"Yes, my Lord?"

"Kill the lot of the cunts," he said, before leaving Kemble and walking back to his harpsichord.

Kemble bowed even more deeply than before and walked back out into the dark warren of Drury Lane.

Chapter Fifteen

Sleeping Dogs

Kemble spent the early portion of the night amongst the shifty denizens of The Two Brewers which was a wretched hole inbetween two other wretched holes on Monmouth Street. There was no pub loyalty in Covent Garden and the drinker was a migratory beast, swirling and barrelling from gin-house to gin-house. Indeed, in Covent Garden, the ration of booze-pit to residency was four to one so it was not surprising that the notion of loyalty was as alien as the sense of community.

After his dismissal from the Olympus, Kemble had skulked through Covent Garden, trying to avoid catching sight of the numerous posters advertising new and dynamic productions. Each pretty design pasted on the slats and billboards leered at him, and each one was a reminder of a life that should have been his. One single innocent mistake and he had fallen from grace. He felt great kinship with the Devil and held much sympathy for his plight. Why was he cast out? He, Kemble, the once beautiful and promising actor who held audiences enthralled, was thrown from the good graces of the public for one, simple fucking mistake. How he hated it all.

He rounded Earlham Street and was about to make a dash through The Seven Dials when he was barged by a drunk sailor, singing that Irish Shanty about the mariner who loved the mermaid. Kemble was knocked off his feet and landed face first in the gutter, the river of feculence trickling into his mouth and stinging his eyes. He got to his feet, coughed up the foulness and brushed himself off. His make-up had smeared down his face and he now resembled a half-melted wax figurine. He hid his face with his sleeve, fearful that someone might recognise his face and laugh at him. Nobody cared. He turned to face the wall, his rage volcanic in his twisted guts. He closed his eyes and desperately tried to recall a moment of happiness. He scanned back through the picture-book of memory and came up wanting; the years of simmering hatred and injustice had utterly stripped any memory of happiness or contentment. Even his privileged childhood now seemed like an overcast dirge to doomed youth. He opened his eyes. He was standing outside The Donmar Theatre, staring at a poster of some dashing stage actor holding a skull high in the air and looking overtly pensive. 'The Dane', Kemble bit his lip so hard that it began to bleed. He cursed God for thrusting that reminder in his face. The Dane was his destiny, it was his role, not this feckless rent boy who ponced about in front of him. Kemble felt like a man at the mercy of an omnipresent torturer. He hocked up some reddish brown sludge from his belly and spat it onto the poster, smearing the sludge over the actor's face with his sleeve. He turned to face the indifferent Dials. He needed a drink and the closest doorway was under the sign of The Two Brewers.

And so, he sat in the corner of the Two Brewers, smashing gin after gin with each one eroding some of the taste of the gutter from his mouth and simultaneously fuelling his rage. Nobody bothered him. No hawkers came to him, no soaks came to slur at him, and not one whore gave him a suggestive look. He was ignored, and it felt worse than being beaten. Nobody gave a shit about his fall from grace, about his future taken from him and his potential snuffed out. He was a shadow and so he drank, and he drank, and he drank until he had exhausted every possible scenario in which he could kill everyone in the room. He settled his bill with the coin Sheridan had given him and skulked out back into the night.

Kemble wandered through the rookeries, stopping for drinks every so often and, the further away from theatreland he ventured, the more his anger subsided and the more he succumbed to the near fatal condition of 'drinkers melancholia'. He was halfway across London Bridge when he realised that nobody loved him. Not even Sheridan. How could he? His master's heart beat to a monetary drum and Kemble no longer held any value. There used to be a time when Sheridan would look sweetly upon the failed actor and Kemble would catch that divine flash of love behind his eyes, but those days of glory had long since fallen away and that love crushed under the weight of time and misfortune. London Bridge is not a welcoming place at the best of times even less so when one finds oneself on that bridge of purgatory and unloved. Kemble shielded his face once more for fear that the public would see him crying. He hurried off the bridge and into Borough.

South of the river did not play a different tune to the North's; Kemble still felt despised and unloved. However, being further from Drury Lane galvanised something inside and he felt a strong conviction that if God hated him, then he'd hate him back. Added to that, the geographical proximity of the bastard Archie Enfield and his oh-so-lovely band of friends and lovers flicked a dark switch inside the actor. He rounded Borough High Street and saw a staggering drunkard approach. Kemble stepped into the shadows until the drunk was within range and as he stumbled passed the doorway, Kemble swung out, clocking the poor chap in the jaw, instantly sending him to Zanzibar. The drunkard flung his bottle into the air as he fell down and Kemble caught it. As he drank from the rancid gin, he rifled through the unconscious man's pockets, found some change and a pendant, pocketed them, kicked the unconscious man in the ribs and stalked off towards the Playhouse where, upon arrival, he crouched behind a pile of crates on the opposite side of the street and watched, eventually falling asleep under a dark blanket of bitter injustice.

———•◦•———

Benjamin Ananas had washed and dressed well before his normal waking hour. His enthusiasm for the mission ahead helped his eyelids to open and his ageing body to fire into action. He looked at himself in his mirror, his eyes looking deeply into the well of nostalgia. He had already begun to cultivate the soil in his memory and uproot elements to use in his creation but he had done so thus far with a weary trepidation. He knew that within that compost heap there lay buried deeply a skeleton he did not want to unearth. It was inevitable, however. Sooner or later, he would have to move apart the memories and revivify Abigail Hardwoode. Holding her name and face in his mind was hard enough, but to dare to unlock the emotions that she carried and the pain he had suppressed was tantamount to suicide. He closed his eyes and pushed her back into the mire and focused on the lesser of two evils; that of the mannerisms of Nathanial Whit who was rapidly becoming the main source of creative inspiration and also exorcism.

He had been standing in the mirror for twenty minutes, razor in hand and about to shave when Archie flung open his door and looked at him.

"Don't shave today, stay as you are. It's important," and he closed the door. Benjamin remained staring into the mirror. The door flung open again and Archie peered around the doorframe.

"And hurry-up, we haven't got all day". He closed it again and Benjamin slowly put the razor back into the dish. He washed his face again, revitalising himself, and threw on some clothes.

It was a particularly bright and warm morning and, as always, the city was alive with people. It was a Saturday and so, as was the way in Borough, the market was opening up. Every conceivable piece of fruit, vegetable, nut and root was housed on the covered grounds of Southwark Cathedral. Pushcarts and carriages came and went at a dizzying rate. Old Man Peacock, the guardsman of the stables, had flung open the green gates at the toll of five in the morning and the carriagemen had piled in to see to the horses and lead them out for work.

Kemble rose groggily after being slapped awake by the warm sun. His make-up was dry and flaking, his clothes filthy. He tried to recall how he came to be in the pile of refuse in The Borough but couldn't for the life of him remember. Something to do with The Playhouse, it must have been else he wouldn't be there. He sat up and rubbed his eyes. Through the hustle and bustle of the street in front he could make out the doors to the theatre. He decided to wait, at least for an hour or so. He had to wait only five minutes when he saw Archie and Benjamin stride out and onto the street. Archie was talking excitedly while Benjamin ate an apple. As they crossed the street, Kemble ducked down a little lower into the pile to evade being seen. He couldn't hear what they were talking about over the din of the street and was about to follow them, when he saw Tobias and Claudia leave the theatre and head off into the market. He was weighing up who to follow when Benjamin strode passed and threw his apple core into Kemble's rubbish pile. It hit him square in the face. His anger flared up instantly and he all but forgot about Tobias and Claudia and began to stalk after Benjamin and Archie.

———•◦•———

Claudia and Tobias had spent a good hour wandering around the multitude of stalls in Borough Market until they eventually came to the Dulwich Flower Company's little pitch. There, Tobias had reigned in the wayward Claudia who, as was her way, had spent the hour rushing around looking at everything and soaking in the sights and sounds all around. When they reached the Flower Market's stall, Tobias had gently taken her arm and turned her towards the trestle table, resplendent with every conceivable plant and flower. Claudia stopped her wild eyed dashing about and focused her attention solely on the stall. The sounds of the market fell away as the colour of the blooms took over her senses.

"How lovely," she whispered as she lifted a daffodil to her nose. Tobias was deep in thought, staring at the petals of flowers as if they were ancient scrolls to be deciphered. Claudia held the flower out to Tobias, the bell brushing against his cheek. He tilted his head to look at it and flicked a lens down on his glasses to inspect further.

"It's flawed. The yellow is wilting. Poor soil no doubt." He flicked the lens back up, and flicked down another set. He turned back to the other flowers. Claudia looked at the flower and stuck out her bottom lip.

"I think it's wonderful all the same. Anyway, what are we doing here is it some...."

She didn't have time to finish before Tobias turned to her and paraded seven different flowers in front of her face. He expression fell from her and her eyes widened. He held one up to her eyes and revolved it slowly in his fingers. Claudia looked on, almost hypnotised.

"Got it?" he said. She nodded.

"Good. Another" He held up another flower and repeated the motion.

"Got it?" She nodded again, her large and perfect brown eyes wide and unblinking like a doll's.

"Good. Another"

Valerie stood outside the door to Herschel's study. She was holding a little tray with some coffee and a small plate of biscuits. She was terrified to disturb him. Desiree walked past in a corset, with Lupe frantically walking after her, trying to make adjustments.

"Will you stop walking about?" protested Lupe.

"I need to speak to Herschel," countered Desiree, "it won't take long" and at that she walked into the study without paying any attention to Valerie who was still standing, holding the tray. Lupe sidled up to her and waited outside the study. She took a biscuit.

"Found a job yet, darling?" she said to Valerie. Valerie shook her head.

"Well, teagirl is a good enough place to start," said Lupe, spilling crumbs into her cleavage, "The world needs runners. When I was in the St Petersburg State Opera, I started out as a runner. Two years I spent making tea and drinking vodka."

"You were in St Petersburg? What a dream! I would be happy there!"

"Don't be too sure, it's bloody freezing…" she was cut off when Desiree flung to door open and walked out still adjusting her corset and looking flushed. She marched off back to the dressing room.

"Come on, let's get this sorted out," she called back. Lupe leant into Valerie and whispered "come have a chat with me tonight, I will tell you all about St Petersburg," and she rushed off back to her department, singing wildly as she went.

The door to Herschel's office was ajar. Valerie cleared her throat, timidly.

"Enter," said Herschel, sternly. She did so.

———————•·•———————

"How long has it been?" asked Archie.

"Twenty odd years give or take," replied Benjamin in a distant tone.

"What's changed?"

"Nothing, nothing at all. How depressing."

"Wrong. You've changed. How wonderful."

Archie and Benjamin where standing in Piccadilly, looking down the gauntlet of Regent Street. Ahead of them was a sight most uncommon to their eyes: cleanliness. The street was relatively clear and lined with gloss black wrought iron railings, the buildings shimmering an elegant cream in the sunshine. The carriages were well kept and their rider's hats tall and new. People didn't move as they did in the rookeries. They weren't rushing everywhere, evading or chasing, stealing or dealing. There was hardly any screams or shouts, no commotions or troubles at all. Archie and Benjamin felt as if they were on the edge of a pond looking into see the calm fish swimming along. It was a tranquil, alien world.

"Look at the twats," snarled Benjamin. "What do they know about love, or art, or life? They spend their days walking about just to be seen." He spat on the floor. A passing lady scoffed and lifted her hanky to her mouth. The gentleman accompanying her held her arm tightly and hurried her along.

"Look at the twats, indeed, dear boy," said Archie, "and look at us."

He turned Benjamin towards a window so that he could see his reflection. The very fact that he could see himself in a clean window was a novelty in itself. His hair was long and lank, collecting and ratty heap around his shoulders and over his threadbare collar. His brow was grimy and furrowed, despite his morning wash. Even the flashes of grey in his beard seemed to be dirty. Archie was no different, save for being the more youthful and virulent of the two.

"We are scum. Dirty, rotten arse blotches," said Archie. Benjamin turned each in the window to inspect himself from all angles. They turned back to the crowds of Regent Street.

"Jesus," uttered Benjamin, "we stand out like…"

"Two cat shits on an omelette?" offered Archie.

"Like two cat shits on an omelette" sighed Benjamin.

"But that's precisely the point. You haven't been here in so long you've forgotten what you were supposed to be like."

"I'm not like these people. Look at him," said Benjamin, pointing to a man with a ridiculous cane and hat combination.

"Well maybe not him," conceded Archie, "but the rest. That was your heritage. You used to able to walk down here and people would tip their hat. If you do it now, they're more likely to tip their breakfast over you. It's not just clothes Old Love; it's not just details you've picked out from your past. It's much deeper than that. It's your soul; who you are. Forget the riches and all that crap. I'm talking about the weight you didn't carry, the pain that wasn't inside. You lived among these fools, and dressed like them too…but you still stood out. That's your natural level. Clothes be damned! Get rid of your pain, get rid of that woman inside you and rise again my friend."

Archie's words cut Benjamin to the quick and he snarled his lips.

"All I want to do is pay *your* debt, get *you* out of the shit, save *our* necks and get *my* theatre back. What's in the past is dead," he spat. Benjamin instantly regretted his statement. He looked over at Archie, who had his cane across the back of his own neck, arms draped over it and looking to the floor like he was on a crucifix. Benjamin put his arm around him.

"I didn't mean it, dear boy," said Benjamin. "All of this trouble is ours. And if any of it was your fault, then I would thank you for it."

Archie looked up at him with a questioning filter over his pained expression. Benjamin smiled.

"I would thank you for breathing life into us," he said to Archie, "did you see how Srdjan fought against Sheridan's thugs? Did you see the light in Antoine's eyes? You've given us the idea to affect change. We are all heading into a dark abyss. But we're doing it together, and for each other."

Archie smiled. Benjamin bowed to him and said "come on dear Archibald, forgive this drunken fool."

Archie cuffed Benjamin around the head.

"Get up you streak of piss, before people think we're from Shoreditch."

Benjamin stood up.

"Now then," he said, resting his arm on his Archie's shoulder, "what is the next step?"

Archie smiled and winked. He pointed with his cane towards Regent Street.

"We're going to walk it," he chirped, "and you're going to realise how much work you have to do. You can't polish a turd Mr Ananas, but you can roll it in glitter."

Archie strolled off into Regent Street, instantly attracting so many looks and scoffs that he may as well have been naked. Benjamin watched him walk off into the melee of the ultra-clean.

"I really hate that man," he said, with a weary smile, before tucking his cane under his arm and walking into the lion's den of Regent Street for the first time in many years.

Neither of them noticed the rat like movements of Kemble, following them. He reached the mouth of the street and looked down. Fortunately, his quarry was quite conspicuous as they made their way into the ranks of the gentry.

Kemble was about to skulk down Regent Street when two women walked by him. One baulked at the sight of the disgusting, sewer-soaked clown and the other displayed the classic double-take of recognition he was used to. He looked at them with the corner of a yellowing eye and hissed. The women hurried on.

'Regent Street,' he thought, *'by rights you should be mine.'*

He tied a filthy handkerchief around his face to obscure any further bouts of recognition and made his way after the two actors.

Chapter Sixteen

Srdjan VS Antoine

The Roxy Irregulars instantly stopped working at the sound of the unprecedented occurrence. They all checked their minds and pinched themselves. They were not dreaming. They had heard it. Herschel was laughing. It had never happened before during one of his frantic writing sessions, and even if it had, they would have drunk to celebrate it and therefore awoken to have forgotten it.

Desiree, resplendent in a blue ball gown halted the fitting and looked at Lupe. They strained their ears. The laugh came again.

Anya froze mid cartwheel on a rafter and Danilov halted halfway down a press-up. Antoine's throwing knives flew errantly across the stage and embedded into a beam. Gertie stood motionless, his butterfly net extended fully and his legs stretched wide. The laugh came a third time, echoing around the theatre.

Inside his study, Valerie was sat upon the carpet while Herschel, in his chair, was stuffing his pipe. She was looking up at him like a child to grandfather at story time.

"And then the priest said, 'woman, God did not invent the organ for that! And if he had, the lid would have been padded!" he roared again and Valerie laughed and clapped.

"Anyway," he continued, "we got married a few weeks after that. Of course, we had to find a new parish to tie the knot in - one where the organist didn't leave his instrument unattended. She was a wonderful woman!" his laughter died down and he happily caught his breath and wiped a tear from his eye.

"What happened to her?"

"She died in childbirth"

The soul was sucked from Valerie. Herschel looked at her then looked up to see Desiree leaning against the doorframe smiling a smile of purest love.

"She is always there though, in here," he said tapping his heart, "and in here [tapping the floor] and here [picking up papers]. But you know, when you get to my age, and you have loved and lost you can only really do one more thing."

"What is that?" whispered Valerie.

Desiree entered the room and walked over to Herschel.

"Do it all over again" she said and they kissed.

The rest of the Players could somehow see, in their minds eye, what had just occurred and they smiled warmly to themselves and went about their duties.

Ms Siddons sat on a barrel outside The Roxy, her legs swinging and her heels clacking against the wood in a frustrated childlike rhythm. She was over the street opposite the theatre, spying on it and bored out of her little mind. She wanted to go to the market, smell the smells and walk amongst the people. She didn't even want to steal anything, she just wanted some interaction.

There had been little activity from the theatre. It was high noon and completely the wrong temperature to be out and about and bored. She began whistling the Cornish tune about the forester and wood-imps and looked up and down street, counting five pubs to the left of The Roxy, and seven to the right. She contemplated darting into one, having a few scoops and keeping an eye out from there. If she faced the window, then she would see if anyone walked passed, she reasoned. Of course, she knew that Murphy's Law was against her and she concluded that if she drank in a pub to the right of The Roxy, any sudden noteworthy activity would happen on its left, and vice-versa. She huffed and kicked her heels harder, resigned to her current position.

Fortunately Ms Siddons did not have to wait alone for much longer. Just after noon Ms Adberg came tottering along to join her. She held her hand behind her back suspiciously and whistling an annoyingly jovial tune.

"I'm bored," huffed Ms Siddons in a remarkable impression of a moody six year old.

"I thought you would be," said Ms Adberg and from behind her back produced a toffee apple for each. Ms Siddons clapped, this time like a happy six year old.

"I'm not bored!" she said and shifted to the side so as to share some of her barrel with her friend.

"So, nothing?" said Ms Adberg.

Ms Siddons shook her head.

"I was gonna go for a drink," she said, spraying debris from her mouth over the pavement.

"Which pub?"

Ms Siddons pointed to the Bunch of Grapes to the left of The Roxy.

"Well, one couldn't hurt," said Ms Adberg conspiratorially. The women hopped off their barrel and hurried across the road and into the pub.

———•◦•———

Tobias and Claudia lit two candles and placed them amongst the others. They had missed morning mass, to which Tobias was prepared to make up for with an hour of penitent prayer. He took Claudia's hand and they sat, as people do in churches, at the point furthest away from everyone else. Tobias knelt down and rested his head on the pew in front and began to whisper.

Claudia sat like a good girl and waited. She used the time not for prayer but to recall the flowers shown to her by Tobias. She had a rare and almost divine gift for memory. She could walk into a room, and months later recall every detail and she could look at painting and memorise every brush stroke. Unfortunately, to prove that only God is infallible, she found it near impossible to replicate what she saw in her mind, which is the curse of so many artists. She did not have the dexterity to marry vision with execution. She had to relay what she saw and rely on a craftsman's interpretation of it. She sat and pulled up every flower and spent a few moments looking in wonder at nature's art. Why Tobias had made her look at flowers was beyond her. She thought he might take her to jewellers or silversmiths to have a look at style and design. Instead, he chose to take her to see flowers. She didn't mind though, Borough Market was a feast for the senses.

Tobias prayed. Unlike Herschel, who scripted his prayers as he scripted his plays, Tobias used his divine connection to talk about anything and everything that was troubling him and for a solitary craftsman who spent his life crouched over a workbench fretting over the minutiae of his work, it was a lot. The big picture, as it were, was a canvas too large to comprehend for the ordered man. He was not blessed with Archie's skill for seeing an end-goal and careening towards it. He was not blessed with Antoine's skill for plate spinning and keeping everything going at once and so in the early stages of a production, he prayed that his friends had the fortitude to take care of the larger world around him and guide him through, and for him to have the skill and focus to construct the tiny details that would underpin everything. He would often quietly sit in an after-party and listen to the Players recounting how great each other had been and he would happily sit safe in the knowledge that God had helped him carve the perfect broach or buckle. It was in tiny details that may never be seen by the audience, but were indispensible to the whole effect, that Tobias lived. He prayed for the focus he needed to do the job right.

———•—•———

Running the gauntlet of Regent Street is hard enough at the best of times, but when you are a pilgrim in that unholy land, one certainly knows which way the wind blows. Archie and Benjamin were used to being buffeted and shunted by the general populous in the rookeries who were too busy to look where they were going. This did not happen in Regent Street. They were given a wide berth. Nobody went near them and everyone stared.

Benjamin and Archie had began their walk through Regent Street with a 'heads down' attitude which, after twenty-five yards had slowed right down from power walk to trudge. By fifty yards they were walking very, very slowly indeed.

"I feel like we are the newly dead, walking through the afterlife," whispered Benjamin.

"Not 'alf," Archie concurred, "getting their loot is going to be a doddle. It's getting near to the bastards, that's the rub". Archie took a sudden drastic lunge towards a group of passing gentry. The group took a sudden, drastic lunge backwards. The space between libertine and socialite maintained.

"And this ain't even the ones we have to crack!" said Archie.

"What do you mean?"

"These polished balloons are small chips. We have higher sights."

Benjamin halted and stepped in close to his fellow interloper.

"Where are we going?"

"All the way to the top my boy, all the way to the tippy top. Come on, let's press on and leave these ghouls behind."

They walked on with a slightly renewed sense of conviction. Behind them, like a hyena stalking an injured lion, Kemble crept along.

———•••———

"You are going to look good enough to eat," promised Lupe as she measured Srdjan's shoulders.

"Well, it's not for me, is it?" he replied, calmly but with an obvious underlying current of sadness. Lupe held his face with both hands and kissed him full on the lips, her almond-breath almost knocking him out.

"Don't worry my dear, I will make two of everything and you can wear yours out and about. You will be beating the girls off with…." She grabbed his crotch and smiled with impressed delight.

"With that beast, I imagine," she winked at him and went back to work. He stood, eyebrows raised and feeling slightly uncomfortable.

"Why did we not think of this before?" he queried.

"Well, we probably did but you know how a drunken man's scheming works. You have the most inspired ideas over wine then come the morning, you can't remember half of them. Think sober, do drunk. That's what I say anyway."

"Do you really think it can work?" he asked.

"I don't know. Most likely he'll be discovered in a pinch, taken out of whatever ball he is in and promptly shot," she replied in a matter-of-fact way that was oddly calming.

"And then what?"

Lupe stood up and jotted down the measurements in a little pad, closed it and stuffed it into her voluminous hair. She looked Srdjan over, smiled and shook her head.

"You are the spitting image of him when you want to be," she said, "why do you really think I'm making spares? So that when he is hanging from Traitors Gate, we can wheel you out in his place!" She winked and kissed him again. He felt better, though he did not know why. Since she had discovered him, under some covered cargo on that schooner in Portsmouth and brought him home, he had always found comfort in her ways even if he did not find comfort in her overactive hands.

Antoine had grown tired of practice. He had stuffed so many knives and forks up one sleeve and pulled them out of the other that he could have done it blindfold and under water. He looked around the theatre. Danilov and Gertie were tying a wire from a rafter to a chair in the far, far corner of a theatre for an unknown reason. Desiree was nowhere to be seen and Tobias was still away with the Spanish girl. There was nothing for it, he concluded. He walked to the edge of the stage and threw a blanket off of an umbrella stand. The dust flew up and he coughed. When it had settled, he reached to the stand and, instead of pulling out some brollies he pulled out two practice swords.

"You have fought your last fight, my friend," he said and marched backstage to find Srdjan.

The Dalmatian was pulling up his breeches when Antoine kicked open the door. He was slightly taken aback to see him in a state of undress and Lupe in the corner smiling devilishly. He leapt on the opportunity to improvise.

"So, cad!" he said angrily, "you have been laying siege to milady's battlements! I will not stand for it!"

Srdjan smiled and stood tall.

"Aye, sir!" he said, puffing his chest out, "I have! I have plundered her ports! Sacked her twin cities and ravaged her forested village!"

Lupe, in classic damsel in distress fashion, ran back and forth with the back of her hand on her forehead. She twirled before 'passing out' dramatically on the floor.

"And you have given her the syphilis too, I smell it from here!" roared the Frenchman, and he threw a practice sword and Srdjan who leapt in the air, caught the blade and landed in front of Antoine.

"You will not defeat me!" bellowed Srdjan, "I fight for something greater than love! Greater than the King! I fight for the death of all of France!"

The blades clashed and the play-duel commenced.

"Landlord, two more pints of cider and two large gins," ordered Ms Siddons as her accomplice sat on the knee of a sailor who was jigging her up and down a little too vigorously for comfort. But, like a trained ballerina on point, Ms Adberg showed no pain. She did, however, relieve him of a few coins and documents of residence. Ms Siddons returned.

"What do you think they are doing then?" Ms Siddons asked.

"They are probably thinking up ways to pay, or ways to run. Shame really, it was a nice place" replied Ms Adberg, ignoring the drunken sailor's busy hands.

"What do you mean, was?" asked Ms Siddons, sipping her pint.

"Well, I would imagine if they don't pay after the extension, it's a round of Cypriote Kisses and Sheridan will probably burn down the theatre."

"Why would he burn it?"

"Ain't worth nothing, plus he's a vengeful so-and-so and he hates that Ananas, more than death can quell. Something to do with cards," slurred Ms Adberg

"Aah scuttlers!" said the sailor. Siddons and Ms Adberg looked at him.

"They be in your pockets, yes?" he said with a sudden air of sobriety. "They be paying soon, by the Brigands Deal, yes? They be unable to pay, yes?"

"Yes Blackbeard, what of it?" said Siddons, already bored of the drunken sailor.

"Then they be scuttling the ship already! Come to seek your treasure tomorrow, you'll find driftwood. They be scuttlers!"

Ms Siddons and Ms Adberg looked incredulously at each other. They didn't believe sailors actually spoke like pirates. Then the thought hit them. They probably were scuttling the ship. Ms Adberg threw the coins she had pinched from the sailor across the bar and they both grabbed their drinks and rushed out.

Srdjan and Antoine's epic play duel had escalated into a full blown production. Anya had climbed down from the rafters and run to the side of the stage and gathered up the stack of old newspapers and ripped them into shreds. Danilov and Gertie had rushed up and fetched one of the giant tarpaulins from backstage and unravelled it. They shouted for the others to join, which they did. Herschel,

Desiree, Valerie, Lupe, Gertie and Danilov each grabbed and edge of the unfolded tarpaulin. Srdjan and Antoine understood what was about to happen. They walked into the centre of the giant mat.

Ms Siddons and Ms Adberg, aided by the Dutch courage from the booze, entered the theatre and froze in surprise. On stage, two men seemed to be fighting on water. They bobbed and ducked and sometimes flew into the air. The 'sea' was the large tarpaulin held taut by a group of stage-hands. They all worked together, running into the centre to give it some slack, forcing the men down to ground level, then they would run backwards, pulling the tarpaulin tight, thrusting the two men into the air. All the while, Antoine and Srdjan fought a vicious sword fight. To the side of the 'sea' they saw a stick-thin girl throw papers shreds at the fighters. The whole effect truly looked like to men fighting on water, or on a boat in a maelstrom. The two intruders dropped their bottles in unison, the resulting smash causing the Players to lose focus and stop their antics.

Antoine and Srdjan fell ten feet down and crashed onto the hard stage. Everybody froze and looked at the two intruders. Valerie, at the back, crept into the shadows. Srdjan scrambled from under Antoine and got to his feet to see why the game had stopped. He saw Ms Adberg. Ms Adberg saw him. They coyly waved to each other. Siddons looked at Ms Adberg, the Players looked at Srdjan. Ms Adberg and Srdjan looked at each other.

———————

Benjamin and Archie had fought through Regent St and had emerged at Oxford Circus covered in sweat and dazzled by the surreal experience they had just been through. They turned to look back at their passageway.

Oxford Circus was not so different, but at least it was more open. There was air, not rich clean air, but air nonetheless. They relaxed slightly. Benjamin came to his senses. He felt like a soldier home from a war, safe but also with the knowledge that something had been lost. In his case, it was not something lost, but something regained. That compost heap in his mind had, after that slog through, lost some of its consistency. In his mind he tried to compact it together to conceal his memories. But some bones had broken free. He knew then that the memory of Abigail Hardwoode was clawing its way back into his mind. He needed his sanity most for the coming adventure but this, he knew, would be their undoing. He had a prophetic soul.

Benjamin was snapped out of his foreboding sense of dread by Archie's slapping him on the back. The irrepressible rapscallion was keen for more.

"Right, that was easy enough," he said, "let's go and see the coup d'état" and with that he swanned off into the afternoon sun. Benjamin righted himself and dashed after him.

"Where are we going?" he said once he had caught up.

"For a pint first, you'll need one for what I have to say." Archie darted into the Crown and Sceptre on Langham Street and went straight to the bar.

Inside, the high ceilings and large windows light flooded the interior with a warm hue. They received their beers promptly and retired to the quiet corner at the back.

"Where are we going?" asked Benjamin, taking a third of his pint down in one go.

"We're going to The Gateway."

Benjamin halted, mid sup. He put his drink down. Archie nodded and took his drink.

"It's impossible. We have more chance of stealing the crown then getting in there."

"Poppycock," scoffed Archie.

"You need recommendations. You need approvals. You need a dammed voucher!"

"We'll get it, I have worked it out, it's fine," said Archie convincingly, "we'll get in. And once we're in, then we're away. I figured it out in bed last night. I was lying in bed thinking, *'how we gonna get into the parties? How we gonna get into the Social Scene?'* I was watching my hourglass and then it hit me. I imagined everything we were doing as grains within that hourglass. And we are doing what them grains do - falling from one bowl into another. If we want to transition from our bowl, into the next bowl, we have to go through the Gateway. Everybody who gets into the Social Scene gets in through there. Just like the sand in the hourglass. It's the only way to get our foot in the door, Old Love."

Benjamin understood Archie, despite his contrived analogy. Archie was right. Benjamin took a smaller sip of beer.

"The Almack Assembly Rooms," he said fearfully.

"Almack's Assembly Rooms" agreed Archie with no fear in his voice, "we'll get you through the door and into that club. We'll get you into the dining room, past that, into the card room. Herschel's script will get you so far into that club you'll be able to overwrite the name on the lease with your own. Now, how's that for a slice of tit-shaped cake?"

Archie clinked glasses with Benjamin, who remained unconvinced.

Across from the scheming men, unseen in a dark corner sat Kemble. He didn't know exactly what they where up to but he knew it was deviant. He drank harder when he heard the name of that club and he cursed God again as he had always known that somehow somewhere he would be brought back Almack's Assembly Rooms. God was a cruel joker and Kemble was the punchline. They were going back to the club. But why, what were they planning? Kemble sat hidden and agitated, his left leg jigging as he drank, eavesdropping on the actors.

Chapter Seventeen

Of Tall Ships and Dances

The unexpected sight that greeted Ms Siddons and Ms Adberg as they barged into the theatre was shocking and awe-inspiring. They were putting on a play! Of what, they did not know. But, for sure, The Roxy Playhouse Irregulars were not scuttling their ship but instead guiding her under full sails. No words had been spoken between player and intruder, instead all information needed was gleamed just from the sight of the bouncing swordfight. Ms Siddons and Ms Adberg had stood for a full minute, taking in the sight, before turning and rushing from the theatre, their minds a whir of thoughts. The Players did not rush after them. They knew that they had been caught out but that, hopefully, they had been caught out doing something that was not detrimental to their secret plans. Had Ms Siddons and Ms Adberg walked in while Benjamin was discussing the heist, they would have been done for. Luckily it was not so.

For Srdjan, seeing Ms Adberg and having her see him at the height of his capabilities fired a passion inside him. He allowed himself a moment to revel in the possibility that, perhaps, she missed him and that she wished she had not left and that she was still there with him, making art alongside her soulmate. The Dalmatian was not so far from the truth.

As she walked home, Ms Adberg allowed herself to lean into memory. It was a dangerous thing to do, but after seeing Srdjan twice in two days she had no choice but too. He looked good - strong, noble and still with the same wonderful stare. She, on the other had fallen foul under the hands of time. She felt old. Used up. Dry. Ms Siddons, however, did not stop talking from the moment they left The Roxyto the moment they entered The Olympus, her stream of consciousness falling from her mouth like a river down a mountain. While they were both unanimous in their shellshock they were polar opposites in their response to it. Witnessing the Players performing felt as if a veil had been lifted or a fever had passed for them both. They had forgotten just how liberating theatre could be. They were reborn.

Ms Siddons took this rejuvenation of spirit and let it overwhelm her. She spoke of her past for the first time, she recalled dreams and loves. She even smiled and it was a wonderful blossoming smile. She had been dead for too long. They walked instead of taking a carriage and Ms Siddons skipped along, making merry with any and everyone. Ms Adberg on the other hand, married her recovered sense of creativity to her awoken sense of painful lust. He was really something and she was a dry fish. It took the entire journey home to crawl out of the mire of self-loathing into the sunshine meadow of conviction. As she walked up the steps of the Olympus she made a solemn, unfaltering vow. She halted Ms Siddons with a stern grip on the shoulder, turned her around and looked in the eye.

"I have to get him back" she said and walked into the theatre, leaving Ms Siddons on the steps.

The Almack's Assembly rooms were housed in an inconspicuous white bricked building on Kings Street in St James. It did not need any fancy decoration or sign above its entrance. Everyone who needed to know what lay behind the plain black doors knew already. Archie and Benjamin stood across from it.

"What day is it?" asked Benjamin.

"Saturday."

"We should come back on Wednesday and scope it out properly. Wednesday is when the dancecard menagerie pile up, the ridiculous bastards."

"Speaking of dancing..."

"No." Snapped Benjamin

"You have to, Old Love."

"I can't dance."

"Don't be ridiculous," scoffed Archie, "everybody can dance. It's just walking about in a fancy way, is all. Grow up."

"Make me." Huffed Benjamin.

"Desiree will help you. If you can't dance, you can't stay in there. If you can't stay in there you can't do anything. It's social suicide to have the Almack Voucher taken from you. Lose that and you lose it all. Just ask twat-breath Kemble."

"Does the future of our lives really hinder on me dancing?"

"Yep. God help us all," sighed Archie.

"How do you expect to get through the door?"

"Well we, and by that I mean you, have to charm the seven Baronesses."

"Stygian witches," spat Ananas.

The Stygian Witches of the Almack assembly rooms were a group of seven women who presided over the club. Each one was well-to-do, vainglorious and vulgar. A single note of doubt from any one of them and a person could find themselves not only banished from the club, but banished from every social circle in London, and that meant every social circle in the world. These seven Queen Bees ruled with iron fists and held no currency for transgression. However, and to the advantage of Benjamin and the Players' needs, the seven witches did not care too much for nobility or lineage. They cared about prestige and they were astute enough to realise that prestige did not necessarily come with peerage. In fact, more often than not the two were mutually exclusive. And so, in order to gain entry into the Almack and, therefore, be allowed into the precious inner circle, all one needed was to tick their boxes.

"When they're all together we probably don't stand a chance," said Archie, "but if we get them on their own, sow some pretty seeds in their cabbage patches, we might get a foot in."

"That could work. How do we go about that?" asked Benjamin.

"I have a man on the inside. Well, I don't have him, but I know of him."

"The Irishman?"

"That's the chap. If we can get hold of him and bribe him to have a word, the little tyke might give us a leg up."

"Where is he nowadays?" said Benjamin with a smile on his face, "I haven't seen that lunatic in years!"

"Last I heard he was hanging around Camden, ducking about and causing all sorts of fracas."

"Hawley Arms?"

"One would assume. I shall go this evening," said Archie

"Take Herschel," advised Benjamin, "they used to run a poetry gazette a few years ago."

"Good tip...right, I'm thirsty. Shall we go home and check on the children?"

"Lead on, Archie, lead on." The two men walked into the afternoon sun.

Kemble stepped out of the doorway he was spying from. Though he had been out of earshot of their conversation, Kemble nevertheless knew that something was definitely amiss. He watched Archie and Benjamin walk away for a few seconds before turning back to the Almack's doors. He curled his lip at the sight of the Assembly rooms. He looked around. The street was deserted. He quickly darted over to the plain black doors, unbuttoned his breeches and urinated over the door, laughing maniacally to himself. When he had finished, he packed himself away, spat on the door for good measure and skipped off merrily, happy with himself for the little act of deserved retribution.

———•—

The sun had begun to set when Valerie Folk found the secret spot in the roof of the playhouse. After seeing Ms Siddons and Ms Adberg she had been reminded of her secret mission. The previous forty-eight hours had been a whirl and she had totally forgotten why she had been sent after Archie and Benjamin in the first place: She had fallen too deeply undercover.

Valerie had spent the afternoon deliberately avoiding the Players and shunning any activity that might come her way. The shying from the Players had seen her move from stage to wing, from wing to backstage, from there to storeroom, then to quarters, and then when even there had became compromised, she crept up the hidden staircase into the eaves of the theatre. There she had found a hatch which opened up into a cramped attic. There was barely any room to stand, but there was a large hole in the roof which enabled to her to peer out and look at London. She stuck her head out and gasped the air. The theatre was too intoxicating and she needed a release. The sight of the city's skyline at sunset overpowered her and she began to cry. How could she undermine the Players? How could she do right by Sheridan? How could she escape it all? She thought about Archie and how she found him with the pistol. Suddenly she felt a great affinity to his state of mind in his mad moment. She could leap. She could dash herself on the cobblestones at the back of the theatre and be undiscovered for days. It would be best for everyone. But of course she did not jump, instead held on to the pressure of betrayal. She was so lost in her sadness that she did not hear the hatch open behind her.

"Valerie," said a soft voice. In a daze she turned to see Danilov halfway through the attic hatch.

"What are you doing here?" he asked.

She could not answer and instead broke down in sobs. Danilov rushed to her and she fell into his arms.

"Why are you crying? What can I do?"

She felt his taut, strong arms brace her. She sobbed harder.

———•————

Kemble arrived back at the theatre confident that his findings would land him in good graces with Sheridan. He was wrong. Instead he found Sheridan sitting at his harpsichord being harangued by Ms Siddons and Ms Adberg who were filling his ears with piffle and lies about The Roxy Players putting on a production. Ms Siddons was telling him about a 'great production' and a 'wonderful performance' that was a 'licence to print money'. Not only did Kemble find the two honey-trappers spewing rubbish about what they had seen, but he also saw Sheridan's eyes wide with enthusiasm. Kemble listened for a moment before barging his way inbetween the two women.

"My lord, I must speak," he protested, "what these harridans tell you it is utter pig shit! They are producing nothing, Sire! Tis rhubarb!"

"They are!" countered Ms Siddons. "Me and Ms Adberg did see with our own fair eyes! We saw a stage fight, a sea, a maelstrom and wonders, wonders, wonders! They are doing something, I tell you!"

"I know what they are doing!" spat Kemble, "I was following them all day! They went to the Almack rooms!" Kemble's statement piqued Sheridan's attention.

"The Almack? Why?"

"I don't know" replied Kemble, bowing ornately as he spoke, "but for something backhanded and black hearted, my liege."

"Research, no doubt," countered Ms Siddons, "that Benjamin is methodical in his research, ain't he Mr Sheridan?"

"He is…he is," agreed Sheridan, clearly drinking the juniper gin of Ms Siddons' words.

Kemble was gobsmacked.

"You fools!" he shouted, hopping from one foot to the other in frustration, "don't be duped into thinking that they are putting on a simple play. There is more, more, more!"

"I think he's been out in the sun too long, that one," said Ms Siddons, draping her arm over Sheridan's shoulder, her soft honey-voice trapping him expertly.

"Oh begads!" huffed Kemble in resignation, "like these pus-coos know what the hell is going on! They spend their days getting sailors to blow their hate-paste up their fluteys!"

Sheridan stood up and slammed the lid down on his harpsichord, startling everybody.

"We do not talk about women like that!" he shouted.

Kemble fell forward, grovelling towards Sheridan, kissing the ground as he moved.

"Forgive me, my lord, it's just that I believe that they are masterful deceivers and that they have hoodwinked these two ladies. I mean no offense with my tongue. Sometimes it moves out of turn. Forgive me all!"

Sheridan felt his stomach turn upon seeing the wretched actor grovelling on the floor. He turned to Ms Adberg who had, until that point, remained more or less silent.

"Ms Adberg, what do you make of all this?" he asked. Siddons and Kemble looked over to her. Ms Adberg thought for a few moments and shrugged.

"I think maybe, if they are putting on a play, that maybe they might need some help?"

Nobody expected that. It felt as if the clocks had stopped. After a few awkward moments Ms Adberg excused herself.

Sheridan took that as leave to excuse himself also. Ms Siddons and Kemble remained. She curled and smile at him. The bile in Kemble's gut churned.

"You're a dumb cunt and it's going to cost you dear one day" he sneered and turned to walk away. Ms Siddons pulled one of her eight-inch hairpins out of her hair and inspected it.

"Be careful who you turn your back on," she said in a thinly veiled threat. Kemble looked back to see her running the needle's point down her face and across her throat.

"Sleep well, dear Kemble, sleep well."

Kemble swallowed in true fear. The coward knew that Ms Siddons, above all things, was a cold, vicious bitch.

"If you look over to the west, you can see the masts. Can you see?" asked Danilov pointing to the tall ships collected in the Thames Upper Pool.

"I cannot see," said Valerie, her tears drying, but her voice still wavering slightly. Danilov lifted himself out of the window and leant to the side, craning his neck to the masts. It was clear that Valerie was too small to see. He pulled himself back into the attic.

"Right, come here," he said and grabbed her round the waist.

"What are you doing?"

Danilov, displaying incredible strength, lifted Valerie up and held her out of the hole until she was dangling in mid-air. She began to kick wildly.

"Relax, relax, I have you," he said soothingly. She did.

Valerie looked down to the cobblestones. She was totally free of the theatre, hanging in the air, her life in the hands of the acrobat. She felt alive and weightless. Every dark thought fell away from her, like coins out her pockets.

"Alright, I'm going to turn you...are you ready?" he said.

"Alright...I am ready,"

If she had known what he meant by 'turn' Valerie would not have agreed. Danilov heaved Valerie up and let go and she flew into the air and spun over. For a moment she hung suspended in the air, looking up at the blue sky. Then she began to fall. Danilov caught her, his strong hands halting her descent with confidence. Valerie laughed nervously.

"Do not turn me again!"

Danilov smiled and twisted her slightly.

"Can you see now?" he asked. Valerie, held out in the open, could now see the masts of the tall ships.

"I can see them! I can see the ships!"

Danilov smiled.

"Can you see the tallest mast? It has the yellow flag of the Caribbean River Company flying? Can you see?"

"Yes! Yes I can see!"

"That is the 'Fermina Daza! She is the fastest clipper in the world. I have sailed on that boat. We stowed away on it, Anya and I, years ago, and it brought us here."

He lifted Valerie back into the roof and set her down.

"It was the most arduous journey, heavy seas and hard weather. Many people died. Sailors and stowaways alike but we made it. We arrived safely and we found The Roxy. Found everyone." He climbed back through the hatch, leaving Valerie alone in the attic.

"Whatever pains you," he said, before closing the door, "It will desert you in time... but The Roxy never will." He closed the door. Valerie broke down in tears once more, only this time, her tears were from relief. She really was home.

———•—•———

Sheridan sat in his private study with his feet on his battered desk and his ledger on his lap. He studied all the entries. Who owed what, whose debts he needed to call in, who he needed to place in his pocket, which secret belonged to who, predicted leverage percentages and all other manner of devious information his network of rats had gathered for him.

A small circular window lit the tatty office, the beam catching the dust as it shone down and finished its journey across the room. In the morning it illuminated the spittoon in the corner, at dusk it shone upon the three legged chaise longue. The enthused ramblings of Ms Siddons and the beleaguered nature of Kemble rattled him greatly. He needed solitude. He needed peace and so he studied. However, there was no joy in his work, no arch feeling of malice or avarice as his eyes scanned all the numbers and codes and the lives they denoted, it was simply business. The growing feeling of discontentment with his lot was now almost unbearable.

As had seemed to happen of late he grew bored of staring at the facts and figures. He closed the ledger and sat in quiet contemplation for a few moments. He looked around at the portraits on the wall, each one meaningless to him. They were not of relatives, or family heirlooms, but the product of years of debt collecting. People who had been short of that last coin or two had flung the pictures at him as payment and he had taken them readily. They might be worth something, monetarily speaking, one day. He felt the cold, gloomy, feeling of a bank manager sat in his office surrounded by bullion that held little currency to him. He was bored of secrets, bored of money, bored of life.

He stood up and walked over to a particularly stern portrait that, when the door was opened, was hidden. It was a competent portrait of a fop with long brown hair, angry eyes and rouged cheeks. He was holding a dachshund on his lap. When it was painted, it no doubt captured the glory and legacy of a once great name known for his decency and verve. Now it sat half unseen in some skanky den at the back of a misused theatre, cast off by its inheritors to save themselves a few coins and a beating. *'So much for legacy,'* Sheridan thought.

Sheridan lifted the portrait off its mounting and dropped it unceremoniously onto the cushionless chair below it. He returned back to his desk and sat back down, swinging his legs up and reclining once more. He looked back at the wall and smiled for the first time that day. Behind the portrait of the long dead fop hung a crumpled and faded poster, pasted up years before. It depicted a London street scene, with people bussing about as usual, but below the street level, rising up from the bottom of the page a giant insect-like monster. Emblazoned across the poster ran the title *'Sheridan & the Olympians Present...Creature From Beneath The Strand!'* Various plaudits and accolades were scattered around the central image. *'Best Monster play on Drury Lane this week – London Limelight'*, *'Good acting – Shoreditch Herald'* ran the largest. He reached into a side drawer and pulled out a small bottle of gin. He raised his glass to the poster and drank, falling into the well of memory in the cool, caressing evening sun.

As he drifted back to those glorious days when he actually gave a damn about anything, a honeyed voiced sloshed in his mind. *'I think maybe, if they are putting on a play, that maybe they need some help?'* it cooed. Ms Adberg's voice was a lulling tonic. It whirled and whirled and while it did, the debt collecting practitioner thought only that she was right, she was right, she was right.

Chapter Eighteen

Curtains

Tobias looked at the sketches and rubbed his stubble. He flicked down a lens and studied them closely. He flicked the lenses up then flicked down another set. Benjamin sat at his desk looking at some flat sheets of pressed metal. Upon the sheets, he could see the faint outlines of flowers. The detailing on the petals was exquisite. Eventually Tobias stood from his stoop and pushed his goggles from his head.

"I think I can do this," he said.

Benjamin smiled and shook his hand. Just then, Srdjan knocked on the door and entered.

"Benjamin, it's time," he said solemnly. He was about to leave, when he noticed the sketch on the workbench.

"May I?" he said.

"By all means," said Benjamin and handed the papers to him. Srdjan looked at them. They were designs for a sword. The scribing along the blade showed a twine of ivy, wrapping over the blade and collecting at the forte. The basket itself was a remarkable gilded spider. Its two front legs and mandibles made up the strong cross-guard, its belly made up the basket proper and its remaining legs wrapped around and met at the hilt. It was a beautiful design. Srdjan's eyes lit up when he saw it.

"It's exquisite" he said in a whisper as he handed it back to Tobias.

"If I can make such a thing!" said Tobias, "I have a suitable blade but the basket will be the greatest challenge I have met."

"I believe in you, old friend," said Benjamin. "You have never failed me. Just remember what we spoke about."

Tobias nodded, took off his apron and all three men left the workshop. They walked down the stair case and splintered off. Tobias and Benjamin walked off towards the stage and Srdjan went in the opposite direction towards the costume department.

Claudia was trying on her chambermaid outfit when Srdjan knocked on the dressing room door. He entered to see her standing on a chair, with Lupe fussing around the hem, attaching pins and hitches at a dizzying speed.

"It's time," he said and left.

Lupe and Claudia looked sadly at each other. Lupe helped the Spanish girl down from the chair and held her hand as they left the dressing room and headed for the stage.

When they stepped out of the wings, they saw the other Players standing in a solemn line. Claudia moved in closer to Lupe's dress almost disappearing into the folds as they joined the others.

Above the line of Players, Anya and Danilov were swinging around the huge curtain beam. Benjamin appeared from stage left, pushing a trolley with some wine and glasses upon it. He dutifully poured a large glass for each of his friends and they stood in silence, their heads bowed. Archie stepped forward and took the final glass from Benjamin and raised it in the air.

"My Lords and dreamers, my loves, my friends," he began in his Roxy Speechmaker voice, "it is with great sadness that I now call time for a great, noble and dutiful friend of ours. She has seen us through trials and tribulations, successes and failures. When we wanted solitude, she provided, when we wanted to see the world, she opened our eyes. But now, it is time she left us, to begin her new life in a new guise and with new sights to see. My Lords and Ladies, please join me now in a toast to our friend: to the curtain!"

"To the curtain" repeated everyone. They drank their wine and held each other's hands. Archie looked up and nodded to Danilov and Anya. Danilov swung low and grabbed a pull-rope. He gave it two tugs and the curtain unravelled from her holdings. The huge velvet drape tumbled silently to the floor. The Players had a few moments of introspective silence for their fallen friend.

After a few minutes, life returned to The Roxy. Lupe, Claudia and Valerie gathered up the curtains and quietly carried them off to the costume department ready for her to take the scissors to them.

Danilov descended from the rafter carrying a ream of wire slung over his shoulder. He was wearing a new, tight-fitting black body-stocking on which Benjamin complimented him.

"Durable shadows, indeed," said Benjamin before being led away by Desiree for his dance lesson. Gertie took the wire off of Danilov and looked back up the rafter. Anya was tying off the end. She nodded to the young man and he and Danilov led the wire off the stage and into the aisles, pulling it along, past all the rows and to the very front of the theatre. They pulled it as taut as possible before tying it off against the base of a pillar. The wire now stretched from the floor and diagonally up across the whole length of the building before disappearing into the eaves. Gertie gave it a tug to test its tightness. It held well. Neither Gertie, nor Anya, high up on the beam, heard the crack and groan coming from its stanchion.

Archie leant against the doorway to Herschel's study and looked at the maudlin writer scribbling away.

"You can hang around that doorway all night, Archibald, but I'm not going," he said without looking up from his notation.

"Come on, old bean! It will be fun! You, me, the beasts of Camden, drinks, fights, floozies!"

"My dear boy, I can think of nothing worse than drinking in Camden, with or without you!"

"Shame that...shame. Mr Moore would have liked to see you I'm sure," said Archie and, knowing that he'd played his best card, left the doorframe and walked off. Herschel looked up, taking in Mr Enfield's last statement.

Archie was about to leave the stage when Herschel marched straight passed him, throwing on his coat and picking up his walking stick.

"Come on," he called back, over his shoulder, "let's go see that fool and see if we can't get my watch back. Hurry up Archibald, I haven't got all night."

Archie doubled his pace to catch up with Herschel. He turned back to wave goodbye to the Players who were looking on in mild surprise to see the playwright storming out of the theatre. An act he very rarely performed.

———•••———

Antoine and Tobias left the stage and went to the metallurgist's workshop to tinker with the magician's harness. Desire and Benjamin remained behind.

"Alright then, this evening we're going to practice a quadrille," said Desiree as she supped some more wine. Benjamin looked at her with a blank expression.

"It's a dance Benjamin. It's a dance for two couples, very fashionable. You can be sure that you will, at some point, be called up to take part. You can't say no. So, to begin…,"

Desiree put her glass down, closed her eyes and began to dance around the stage.

"The quadrille is a tricky dance using four partners and it's divided into six parts. Part One is called 'The Pantalon' which runs thusly; theme A, theme B, theme A, theme C, theme A, then part two, 'Ete' which runs theme A, theme B, theme B, theme A, then the third part, 'Poule' - theme A, B, A, C, A, B, A, a brief two measure introduction brings in part four, the 'Trenis', theme A, theme B, theme B, theme A which is the same structure as the 'Ete', then 'Pastourelle', part five which is theme A, B, C, B, A and onto the sixth part, the 'Finale' which runs as theme A, theme A, theme B, theme B, theme A and ending on theme A again. Have you got that?"

She bowed to applause from Valerie and Claudia who were watching on from the wings. The dancer opened her eyes and hung her head in despondency. Benjamin had collapsed on the stage in confusion, the colour gone from him, sweat pouring. Desiree walked over and kicked him.

"Up you get, you silly man. I won't stand for it," she said in her teacher's voice.

Benjamin climbed back onto his feet. At the corner of the stage, Claudia and Valerie were giggling uncontrollably. Benjamin turned to them and attempted to shoo them off with a growl. They scurried to the safety of the curtained wings and looked on again. Desiree pulled a handkerchief from her dress and mopped his brow.

"You are a silly little man, aren't you?" she said with mild condescension in her tone.

"Yes Miss," he said with genuine schoolboy sheepishness.

"And we are going to begin again, aren't we?"

"Yes Miss."

"And you aren't going to have any more childish tantrums or panic attacks, are you?"

"No Miss."

"Good boy. If you do well, you can have a drink as a reward. So; to begin…"

———•———

"Is that too tight?" asked Tobias as he buckled the corset-brace around Antoine's back.

"No, it seems fine."

"Right, let's have a look at you."

The metallurgist stood back to look at the Frenchman. The leather corset had straps for suspenders and also straps to attach pauldrons and arm-greaves. Each panel had a series of tags and loops running in concentric hoops. Antoine attached the greaves and cuisses around his thighs. Antoine was now wearing a suit of leather armour. Tobias fingered a few loops to test their position and strength.

"I can adjust them, if you need. Here, try with these," said Tobias as he led the Frenchman to a side table. On it, there was an oily rag. Tobias whipped it away to reveal a twelve-piece cutlery set.

"Right," said the metallurgist, "let me get my watch and we can see how well you do." Tobias turned from the Frenchman, picked up his watch and turned back. The Frenchman stood with a huge, proud smile across his face. The cutlery was now stowed in the loops on his cuisse pieces. Tobias smiled in amazement.

"Well, they work. How about…"

He was cut short as the pieces were on the greaves.

"Wha…"

Around the breastplate.

"Perfect. But now the real test," said Tobias as he took all the pieces of cutlery off of Antoine and put them back onto the table.

"Lupe, if you will," said Tobias as Antoine turned to the door to see Lupe walking in holding a variety of shirts and trousers to try on.

"The real test," said Lupe with a devilish grin, "can you do what you do under concealment of a shirt?"

The Frenchman looked a little unsure.

———•◦•———

Anya tried to remain focused as she attempted the difficult tightrope walk. The downward trajectory of the wire was steep, and she knew that come the time when she would have to do it for real, the angle would be tighter and the pressure far, far greater.

She stood on the rafter and looked down along the wire. For a few seconds the world around the wire fell away. She thought about her destination, she thought about the distance, the elevation and angle and she thought about the sweet boy with the butterfly net. Her heart rate dropped significantly and her breathing was controlled. She stepped out onto the wire.

Before she began to walk, she stood still upon the wire, blotting out the image of Ananas and Desiree dancing below. She had observed briefly before committing to the walk and had laughed to herself at seeing the oafish dancer blunder around the stage as if his legs were stone. He had improved though. Desiree's firm instruction and sharp tongue had whipped him to shape. In a few more lessons he might be confident around a dance floor. These thoughts fell from her as she lifted her trailing foot out onto the wire. She froze for a few seconds, held her arms out for balance, took one final look at the path ahead, closed her eyes and began her descent.

———•·•———

Lupe and Tobias stood looking at Antoine. They had their arms crossed, heads lilting in the same direction.

"I think he looks good," said Lupe.

"Even passable," remarked Tobias, "how does it feel?"

Antoine stretched and flexed. He nodded a little. He felt good.

If anyone had walked into the workshop at that point and been asked to describe what they saw, they would have accounted for the props, the tools, the oil-stained metallurgist, the living cake and then commented on the out-of-place waiter. Antoine looked perfect in his costume.

"Right," said Lupe rubbing her hands, "let's see how you get the cutlery off the table and lashed to the braces without us noticing. Ready?"

Antoine hopped on the spot. A metallic jangle came from him. Tobias and Lupe looked in surprise at each other before looking at the table. There was no cutlery on it.

"When did you do that?" asked Lupe.

Antoine smiled. "While you looking at me!"

Tobias laughed loudly and clapped his hands, "magnificent!" he cried.

"Of course", said the Frenchman, "however, I cannot move without sounding like a symphony" and he jangled the hidden cutlery.

"That's no problem," said Tobias, "I can tighten everything. Let me go and get Benjamin. He needs to see this," and with that, the excited man went to leave.

"Tobias," called out Antoine. Tobias Strong looked back.

"You really are a genius" he said and bowed deeply, the knives and forks creating a pleasing tinkling sound. Tobias bowed back and rushed off to get their leader.

———•—•———

Anya had completed her tightrope walk and was sitting at the far end of the building with Danilov and Gertie. There were laughing at the sight on stage. Desiree had enlisted Srdjan to be Benjamin's dancing partner. The actor and stunt double made a perplexing partnership. From the dark end of the theatre, Danilov and Gertie could not tell where Srdjan ended and Benjamin Ananas began; their resemblance bordered on the unsettling. Still, Srdjan's assured steps and Benjamin's buffoonery marked them apart and brought a much needed comedy to the duality of it all. Gertie slapped his thighs.

"Right, I think I should get some drinks," he said as he stood up. He fished around in his pockets and found enough coins. He shook Danilov's hand, smiled at Anya and left. Tobias came onto the stage and threw double-take when he saw the dancers. Danilov laughed at the stage-dance and stood up to go join in the fun. He turned back to beckon Anya to join him. He saw that his sister was in a meditative state and so left her.

Anya was looking up at the wire, tracing its path back up into the darkness of the eaves. She was not happy with her technique. The descent had felt slightly off. Her muscles grumbled and her heart rate had been slightly erratic. It had not been a perfect performance.

She stood up and felt the bolt holding the wire into the ground. It felt strong. She had no idea what sort of strain the rafter was under. Danilov reached the stage and hopped up to join the gang, laughing and joking. Gertie had gone to get drinks. Anya was alone. She stepped up onto the tightrope, lowered her heart-rate and began her ascent.

Srdjan, Benjamin, Danilov and Desiree were dancing a fast jig around the stage when the sickening crack and groan echoed around the theatre. Tobias, Claudia and Valerie were sat in the wings laughing when their merriment fell away. The dancers stopped. Everybody looked around. Confusion and dread suddenly ruled the stage. There was another creak. Tobias stood up and hushed everybody. Valerie pulled Claudia in close to her.

The dancers broke apart, taking immense care not to make any heavy footsteps. A heavy, painful groan like a ship listing came. Desiree looked around and then up. She gasped. They all looked up. Anya was stationary on the wire. Eyes open: scared. She was in a dreadful no-man's land between the rafter and the floor.

Danilov shouted up at her and was met by an angry crack from the beam. Anya's wire flexed slightly and she almost fell to the side but managed to grab the wire at the last moment, swing herself fully round and back up again. Her arms waved as her balance wavered dramatically. She looked across at the distressed beam. She could see the split. It was catastrophic. She looked forward at the remaining thirty feet to safety. She could run which would definitely cause the beam to break. If she was fast enough, she could leap the last few feet and hope to grab onto the safe rafter. It was her best option. She bent her legs and prepared to sprint. Her heart was racing and so she thought of the sweet boy with the butterfly net. Her heart slowed. She opened her eyes to mark her route and looked down to him. He was not there and his trusty butterfly net was propped up against the stage thirty feet below her. She felt utterly alone. Anya realised that she could be in some very serious trouble.

Danilov looked up and saw the moment of panic flash across her face. He motioned to run. Benjamin shot an arm out to halt him. He shook his head.

"We are in a house of cards!" said Srdjan.

"She's going to fall!" whispered a desperate Danilov.

"We can get her!" called Tobias, from across the stage, "we need her net. I can reach it, and throw it to you!"

Tobias was the nearest to the net which lay leaning on the edge of the stage. There was twelve feet to traverse to get to it. Timing would be critical.

"I should get it!" responded Desiree who was the furthest from the net, "I'm lightest!" The wire above flexed and Anya shouted in fear. She lost her balance and fell onto the wire, wrapping her legs around it, clinging on for dear life.

"There's no time!" shouted Danilov, "get the net!"

Tobias turned his heels into the stage in preparation to bolt. He mouthed a silent prayer and took a step towards the edge of the stage.

"Halloo! I have drinks for us all!" yelled Gertie as he flung open the doors to the theatre. He did not have time to take in the sight before him. Everyone went to shush him. Tobias went for broke and ran for the net. Gertie saw Anya hanging on the wire. She looked over to him, her face tense with fear. Gertie dropped the bottles and ran down the aisle. Tobias grabbed the handle of the butterfly net. A crack, a groan, the wire lost all tension. Gertie screamed for Anya as she fell. Tobias swung the net up. Anya was nearly in the net when a portion of rafter broke free and smashed into Tobias, connecting with his hip and sweeping him ten feet into the air. The Players ran forward towards the incident as larger portions of the rafter smashed onto the stage. Valerie and Claudia fell backwards to safety. The flailing wire whipped down and cracked across Desiree's back as she fell to the side, slitting open her shoulder blade. Two javelin splinters missed Benjamin and Srdjan by inches. Anya saw the net fly pass her as she crashed into the front row of chairs, knocking herself cold instantly. Gertie threw the chairs aside as he reached her. Danilov arrived at the same time and they both went to work checking on Anya.

The noise of disaster brought Antoine and Lupe to the stage in moments. Lupe dashed over to Desiree and picked her up. The Umbrian dancer was delirious with the pain, blood flowing all over her. Antoine sprinted across the stage, leaping over Srdjan and Benjamin who lay twisted between the impaled javelins. He had his eyes on Tobias. The jangle of his cutlery, still attached to the leather corset he was wearing clattered furiously. The Frenchman leapt off the stage, clearing Danilov and Gertie who were almost in tears over Anya, and landed clean by Tobias.

The metallurgist had a distant, tired look in his eyes. Antoine lifted a chair off him and winced. He could see blood, ripped flesh and bone.

"You are alright, you are alright my boy, my genius, you're alright!" he said, cupping Tobias' face with his hands and trying his best to smile reassuringly.

Anya's eyes opened to see Danilov and Gertie leaning over her, the tears from her brother's eyes dappling her soft, white skin. The two men looked at each other hopefully. Anya took inventory of her senses. She was alive. Her limbs worked. But she was in pain. She smiled. The men sighed in relief.

"I need help!" Antoine's shouted. Srdjan and Benjamin helped each other up and rushed over to Antoine while Valerie and Claudia tried to mop up Desiree's blood, the hems of their skirts simply moving the pool around rather than absorbing it.

Benjamin and Srdjan arrived by Antoine's side and looked at him. Antoine shook his head gravely. Tobias, deliriously, told them that he was tired and that he really wanted to sleep. Benjamin, Srdjan and Antoine pleaded for the metallurgist to please, please, stay awake.

Tobias Strong promised them that he would only sleep for a while. He told them that he wanted to make a sword. He told them that God wanted him to live. He said that he really, really needed to sleep.

Chapter Nineteen

Thomas Moore

E very street corner was marked by extravagantly coloured piles of vomit and the stench from the stables mixed with the street markings and caked everything. One did not walk through Camden, one hop-scotched their way though. As soon as Herschel stepped out of the carriage at Mornington Crescent, he felt renewed. His youth returned to him. One always comes back to Camden.

Archie and Herschel had spent hours scouring the most notorious drinking holes of Camden Town and now, half past the witching hour, they sat at a small corner table in The Mother Red Cap, a gargantuan bar on Camden High Street. It was crammed with the sort of drinkers whose identity was known only by their odour. Collectively there were more stools to sit on than there were teeth left in their mouths to punch out. While Archie had folded his lapels up around his neck in an uncharacteristically defensive move, Herschel jovially reclined in his chair. He felt like a Lord.

"If I know him, he won't show. I'll wager two bottles on it...," slurred the playwright.

"He will show. I take your bet," said Archie, hoping he was right and so could get out of Camden. It was not how he remembered it.

"Good, as long as I can claim my prize here. I have come back, come back, come back to Camden!" cried Herschel with childish abandon.

"Just keep your head till your man shows up," advised Archie, nonplussed with the desperate madness of Camden Town.

"Old bastard, you mean!" giggled Herschel, loudly and brashly.

"Old bastard? The man is a genius."

"He's a snake, a windy snake in the grass. An arse-grape in my... oh! There he is!" Herschel's demeanour changed completely, his drunken snarkiness replaced by a wide-eyed rapture. Archie turned around to the door. Four large, hairy men were pressing hard against it - a force on the outside pushing in.

"Hold men! Hold!" they cried as the doors strained under the weight of the battering ram outside. Then, the force stopped.

Archie looked back at Herschel who had sat back, arms folded and with a big nostalgic smile over his face. The four men bracing the door eased off slightly. The rest of the drinkers went back to their glasses of amber sludge.

Archie opened his mouth to speak. His words were interrupted by a wooden crate smashing through the window. Everybody in the vicinity ducked for cover as the glass shards rained down. Then, in the space where the window had been climbed a giant man, clearing six foot four, broad shouldered, high forehead and long, thin nose. He stepped though the window, walking over tables and stepping on the backs of hunched, bemused drinkers. He reached the bar, dusted himself off and grabbed a bottle.

"Bravo!" shouted Herschel, "did you see that, Arch? Arch?" He looked around for his friend and found him hiding under the table. He helped him up.

"Bravo!" he shouted again. The giant man looked around to see who was cheering him. When he spied Herschel, he released a thunderclap of a laugh. The two men walked over to each other and hugged.

"Herschel, you prostitutes clap-rag! Come here!" boomed the giant as he hugged Herschel so tightly, that the playwright's back cracked in five places. He set him down.

"Are you alright, there?"

Herschel stretched to assess the pain. His back suddenly felt thirty years younger. He laughed and hugged the huge man again.

"Come on, I think we should go!" said the man as he noticed the four men dusting themselves down and approaching. Herschel and his pal hopped up onto the windowsill.

"Archie, let's go!" cried Herschel before hopping down into the night, giggling with his pal like too errant school boys. Archie swiped a few bottles from nearby tables, tipped his imaginary hat to the stunned patrons and leapt out after the two men.

Archie looked around the street. The Mother Red Cap stood on the corner of Parkway and Camden High Street. The dark streets were no help at all. The few lamps that flickered over pub signs barely made an impact in the fog. He was about to call out when he heard the thunderclap laugh of Herschel's friend. He darted off down Camden High Street towards them, assuming that they were heading for the lock. He hoped they would also be heading for a bar around Stables market as the canal dampened the air and caused him to shiver slightly.

He caught up with them outside the Candlelight Ballroom, a dance hall for the young and hopeful. The man had stopped to recite a poem to the queue of young dandies waiting to get inside. They all fawned after him, scribbling his words down on ragged bits of paper.

He finished and bowed to the line and they applauded hungrily. The man walked on as Archie caught up with Herschel.

"Ah, Archie, it's good of you to join us. May I present to you, the least reverend Mr Thomas Moore. Thomas Moore, this is my colleague and adventurer, actor and schemer, Mr Archibald Enfield."

Thomas Moore looked Archie up and down.

"Delighted to meet you, Mr Moore," said Archie, "I come with the regards of Mr Benjamin Ananas."

Archie bowed and Herschel gave a sly, vouch-safe nod to Thomas Moore.

"Up! Up! You fine fellow you! Bow not to the cobbles and my boots, for they are covered in pig shit!"

Archie stood up and the pair shook hands.

"Now!" said Thomas, "I would wager you chaps have coming seeking counsel or coin. Let us retire to a nearby hostelry and expose our agendas. Gentlemen, I know a den in the market. Follow me, good sirs, follow me!"

Thomas Moore strode off into the foggy night. Herschel threw his arm around Archie and the pair walked on after the mad poet.

———•◦•———

"How is she?" whispered Benjamin as he approached Herschel's bed where Desiree lay on her front. Lupe and Valerie had laid her down and were attending to her.

"I will be alright" said Desiree, "the laceration doesn't feel too serious. Not too deep."

Valerie was dabbing her back with a gin-soaked rag while Lupe stood in the corner of the room crushing some herbs in a pestle and mortar. The scent of lavender filled the room, but it carried with it another scent; that of dread, rather than serenity.

Benjamin leant over Desiree and looked at the slash across her back. It looked clean, but angry. He gently kissed the nape of her neck.

"You are a trooper my dear."

"How is Tobias? Is he alright?"

"He is fine," assured Benjamin. Lupe and Valerie looked over to him and understood that his grave expression told the truth.

"Let me see it, please," winced Desiree. Lupe held the bowl under her nose and she sniffed it. "A little more thyme."

Valerie handed up a pinch of thyme to Lupe who sprinkled it into the paste and pressed on.

"Has Herschel come home yet?" asked Desiree with an undeniably hopeful tone. Despite her bravery, she was in pain and needed her love.

"Not yet, my dear; he is on a mission!" said Benjamin softly, stroking her hair. Desiree smiled.

"I hope he is not with any maids, or in any trouble. I think it is ready now, Lupe."

Lupe gave the bowl to Valerie who scooped out a large dollop.

"Are you ready, my brave love?" said Lupe, clearly apprehensive of what was about to happen. Desiree nodded sternly. Lupe pulled a wooden peg from her wig and placed it in Desiree's mouth to bite on.

"I'm here my love." Said Lupe as she bent down to stare Desiree in the eye, "We are all here. Just look into my eyes and dream of Umbria. Of you and Herschel in your father's vineyard,"

Desiree nodded, her brow furrowed and fierce. She was ready.

"Benjamin?" said Lupe. Benjamin looked at her. Lupe nodded.

"After you," said the opera singer.

Benjamin took his cue and looked at Valerie. She looked back and nodded her readiness.

"One....two....three!" cried Benjamin and Valerie smeared the lavender paste into Desiree's wound. The ballerina screamed through the peg and they could see the muscles on her back contort in agonising revulsion to the medicine. Lupe held her head tight and looked deeply into her tear-filled eyes. That connection saved the Umbrian dancer from spitting the peg onto the floor and screaming the rest of the rafters down. The pain fell away.

"There, there, you are so brave, so brave, so brave!" said Lupe as she stroked the sweat and hair from Desiree's face.

Benjamin breathed out in relief that Desiree survived. He looked over to Lupe who raised her eyebrows in relief back, before turning her sympathetic eyes back to Desiree.

"My brave ballerina...just twelve more applications to go."

"One...two...three."

———•·•———

Tobias Strong had been laid out across his workbench. Antoine sat beside him, reading one of his notebooks, flicking through the pages and marvelling at the notations and sketches for all his ideas and dreams. He looked up to see Claudia peering around the doorframe. He beckoned her in. She looked at the sleeping metallurgist and was about to lift up the blanket draped over his legs when Antoine gently grabbed her arm and stopped her.

"Leave it, young one, it's not for your eyes."

"Will he die?"

"Oh goodness no, my dear. He will be fine. Although, but he may never dance again."

"That wouldn't be so bad," said Claudia, smiling in her irrepressible way. "He could muck around with Benjamin."
Antoine stifled his laugher and lifted Claudia onto his lap. He hugged her tightly and rocked her into a light doze.

Tobias winked open an eye and smiled at Claudia's joke. He closed his eye again and took his mind off the pain by building, breaking apart, and re-building Benjamin's sword design in his mind.

———•◦•———

Srdjan and Danilov had seen Anya to sleep. Her wounds were remarkably superficial. Her preternatural control over her body had enabled her to reflexively land, twist and roll to evade a much more serious collision. A less capable acrobat would have shattered their neck on impact. As Danilov laid her down and kissed her forehead, she looked around to see if Gertie was present. He was not. A twinge of pain ran threw her back which she attributed to his absence. She lowered her heart rate and closed her eyes and, as was one of her talents, fell asleep on command.

Danilov left her to recover. He walked out onto the stage to find Srdjan clearing away the debris. He went to help. Desiree's blood had been, for the most part, mopped up. The dryness in the air had evaporated the rest. The splinters had been moved into a neat pile and Srdjan was now trying to shift the large portion that had struck Tobias. Danilov grabbed one end and they managed to lift it up.

"Where's Gertie?" asked Danilov.

"He ran off, poor sod. I called after him, but he didn't stop."

"He must blame himself." said Danilov as they heaved the great log onto the heap of splinters.

"Should he?" asked Srdjan, trying to gauge how Danilov felt about the incident.

"He can't blame himself for the rafter."

"But?"

"But he can blame himself for not catching her. He should have had the net."

"Instead of Tobias?"

Danilov shrugged. "The net should have been in his hands in the first place. Gertie failed in his job." The acrobat dusted himself down and walked back to his sister, leaving Srdjan alone on the stage.

———•———

"Right then, my hearty tarts. Spit it out," said Moore as he dished out three pints of the rancid beer that Camden was infamous for. Archie leant in and flicked his glass. He counted four lumps of sediment, each one the size of a plum stone. He gritted his teeth and took a sip. As soon as the canal lager fell into his stomach his bowels almost voided. He gripped the table hard. Moore and Herschel laughed heartily and took huge glugs of their drinks.

"The poor sod can't handle his piss! What a little lavender. I should throw him to the canal-dogs and charge a penny for his arse. Drink your drink, you sissy boy!" demanded Moore.

"The Almack's Assembly Rooms," spluttered Archie, coughing and hitting his chest with his fist. Thomas Moore put his feet up on the table.

"Ah, I see, I take it Mr Ananas wants in. Wants a foot in the door?"

"In a manner of speaking."

"And you want me to have a wordsy with the Baronesses, I take it?

Archie and Herschel nodded.

"Are you serious? I am a man of standing within those rooms, it is true, but it is standing gotten through talent and verse. Which, though more noble than those who pay their way in, it also means that my favour can be rescinded in a flash of a Baroness's eye."

"All we need is a kinder, gentler panel. Just honey their ears about him and that's it. We can do the rest."

Herschel went to the bar and came back with three more canal-lagers. Moore took his pint and glugged away. Archie hadn't taken another sip of his first.

"I need a voucher of intent from you Mr Enfield," said Moore, seriously, "for if I do this and Ananas fails to impress them, then I will lose my voucher and find myself very much favourless."

"Once inside, he will be fine. He's a good sort is Ananas."

"That much is clear, but only to the likes of you and me. To the likes of those beau-bastards, he is the same as the shit on their shoes."

"£50" said Archie in a sudden, serious tone.

"Excuse me?" said Moore.

"And excuse me too," said Herschel, confused at Archie's declaration.

"We can pay you £50 for your services."

"If you could pay me £50 it means you could buy your way in anyways. It seems to me, Mr Enfield, that you are dancing me a maypole jig. I have a right mind to belt you, sir. Herschel, what do you mean to introduce me to this idiot?"

Thomas Moore necked his pint and stood up to leave. Archie stood up and grabbed his shoulder to stop him.

"I wouldn't do that boy, less you don't need your gonady's"

Archie felt a prod in his groin. He looked down to Thomas Moore holding a knife to his crotch.

"£50," reiterated Archie in a serious, fierce tone, "after we have done what we have to do. Our need to get Benjamin into the Almack's is the means to a greater end. I can assure you, three weeks after you have done your simple day's work, you will be sitting pretty on a nice little nest egg…and I hear that Miss Bessy has tastes as expensive as yours, sir"

Herschel was incredulous. He stood up to get inbetween the two men.

"Stand back, Herschel" said Archie, never once taking his eyes off Moore's. Herschel sat back down.

"Take my plums, if you will sir," continued Archie, "but take care for they are the most expensive you will ever take. £25 a pop."

Thomas Moore looked the young upstart over. He withdrew his knife

"All I do is line their ears, nothing more, just that for £50?" Thomas Moore sat back down. Archie followed suit.

"That's right, just put in a good word and that's it," said Archie trying to adapt his seductive voice to suit the poet. "Once he's inside, you don't even have to recognise him. Just a honey-word in the panel's ear is all we want. Get him the invitation, that's all."

Thomas Moore thought it over for a moment. Then he said, "I will do it," and held out his hand. Archie shook it and then took both pints of canal-lager and downed them in a single gulp apiece.

"Bravo!" yelled Thomas, clapping heartily.

———•◦•———

Dawn was approaching and their meeting with Thomas Moore had come to an end. The giant poet paid for their drinks, tipped his hat to them and left the two men alone on the street. As soon as Moore was out of sight, Archie turned to the gutter and bent over it. Herschel patted Archie on the back as the poor fop vomited his past lives into the gutter. There was no liquid left inside him, and yet still his body tried to squeeze out more. He could do nothing but lean over the canal and make a guttural growl that sounded like he was calling out for a girl named Ruth.

"You are a bold man, I'm proud of you," said Herschel stifling his laughter. Archie lifted his arm up and patted Herschel in thanks.

"You shouldn't be drinking in Camden unless your guts have had some experience in it. But well done, good sir, for giving it a good stab."

Archie finally stopping calling out for Ruth and stood up. He wiped his mouth and fixed his hair.

"How do you feel?"

Archie held up is finger for silence. He mentally checked his systems; all clear.

"I'll live. Regrettably," he said, hoarsely.

"Well, I must say, that was quiet the show. £50? You need a sanatorium. How are we going to cover that?"

"We will, we have to. We need to get into those rooms. If we can get in, we can rinse the Nelly's of everything over the next week or so. Once we start producing readies to Sheridan, we can negotiate a few extensions to cover Mr Moore, cover Sheridan and get some for ourselves."

"And if we can't get in?"

"I've never been kissed by a Cypriote, but that luxury will befall us all if we fail. £50 is nothing when added to our debt. To me, it sounded like a bargain."

"Jesus, we've got ourselves in a pickle by no means. What do we tell Benjamin?"

"We tell him Moore is onboard, but don't mention his payment. I will take care of that myself. He's got enough on his plate to contend with at the moment. Dance lessons for one!"

Herschel smiled at Archie and patted him on the shoulder. "Of all the scoundrels to fall in debt with," he said heartily, "you sir, always make it a little sunnier. Come, you mad drinker, we should get home. Time is drawing in and I miss my Desiree madly."

Herschel put his arm around Archie and they walked back into the foggy Camden night.

"We need to get you a girl, mate" said the playwright, hugging the actor closer to him.

"My Giselle is out there somewhere, my dear man. And if she is half the woman your Desiree is, then I will be a lucky man indeed."

"You're a good man, Archie, one of the better ones. We'll get you your Giselle…just don't take her drinking around Camden."

"You can be sure I won't do that. The people here are…"

Archie halted suddenly and began calling for Ruth once more. Herschel stopped and pulled his pipe out, stuffed and lit it. Archie vomited on.

Chapter Twenty

"He That Shall Live This Day..."

Sheridan strapped on his sword, threw on his overcoat and held up a candle to the mirror to inspect himself. He did not like his reflection. Not just for the sallow, tired skin and copper ringed eyelids, but for what lay beneath it - the void of his hollow soul. He called into himself. There was no echo. The man was a shell. There was a knock at the door and Ms Adberg entered. Sheridan was unsure if the candles were playing tricks on him, but in the flickering light, she looked quite reformed. There was colour to her cheeks that did not suggest an over-application of rouge. Her eyes sparkled with flecks of changing light and hue.

"Ms Adberg, you look quite beautiful" he said as he bowed earnestly. Ms Adberg curtsied back and they both smiled, instantly recalling a time and place when one did not do such a thing out of shocked surprise at receiving a compliment, but out of the pleasing warmth one receives when one sees a friend for the first time that day. They both shared a fleeting moment of happiness. Sheridan ushered her to quietly close the door. She obeyed.

"Quick," he whispered, "tell me about the play you saw again!"

Ms Adberg giggled and began to recount the tale of the sword fighting maniacs flying about on the listing ship.

Outside of Sheridan's office, Ms Siddons was carefully placing her needles into her hair. Kemble sat opposite her, sharpening his dagger across a stone. The two were staring at each other. Each, Peach, Pear and Plum were sitting in a circle playing cards together and all blatantly cheating.

Ms Adberg finished her story and the pair straightened their faces, put their serious masks on and left Sheridan's office. The troupe's leader strode purposefully across the stage, announcing his entrance with heavy steps. Kemble leapt to his feet and performed his sickening bow which turned Sheridan's stomach more than ever. Sheridan ignored him completely and turned to Ms Siddons. He kissed her on the forehead. She, Ms Adberg and Sheridan marched out of the theatre. Kemble boiled with rage at his master's snub. Each and Peach laughed at him. He snarled at them, ran his finger threateningly across his throat and hurried after the three.

Kemble climbed into the coach and pulled out his dagger to continue to buff it. He wanted to show Sheridan that he was ready for anything and that he was fierce and, when Sheridan saw that the Players were conniving blackhearts and he ordered their deaths, Kemble would be first in with the blade. Sheridan looked him over.

"Put the knife away, I doubt it will be needed tonight," he said.

"Well, you never know, my liege ain't none so devious as Benjamin and his villains. Best be prepared; might be a call for knife work." As he said this he looked over at Ms Siddons. "On the stage, or when they are sleeping," he continued, menacingly. "You give the word I will spill their gutties out for you, my master. Awake…or asleep"

Ms Siddons smiled at Kemble and fondled the wooden pommel of one of her eight-inch hair needles.

"Kemble, dear Kemble," said Sheridan, "you used to be such a sweet young thing! A great actor and fine fellow – you've had one too many kicks, you brute! Now you are a vicious demon! I'd wager we should all have to watch our necks around you!"

Sheridan and the two women laughed at him. Sheridan patted Kemble's knee and smiled. Kemble grinned back and put his dagger away.

"No dear boy," said Sheridan softly, "to save the bloodshed, you shall stay outside. Keep guard."

"But my Lord, what if you need me?"

Sheridan laughed again. "If I need a soliloquy, I will call!" The women laughed. Sheridan sat back against the carriage and wound his watch. Kemble mentally slaughtered the three bastards there and then. They underestimated him, as so many did. His bloodlust was threatening to consume him. He looked out at the window and diverted his rage to Benjamin, Archie and the black door of the Almack's.

Herschel entered Tobias's study still wiping his away his tears from seeing Desiree. Antoine sat with Claudia asleep against his shoulder.

"How is he?" whispered Herschel.

Antoine shook his head morbidly. "Srdjan has been sent to fetch..." he couldn't bring himself to finish the sentence.

"Oh Jesus...what about everyone else?"

"Gertie has vanished - run off into the night. He wasn't here to catch Anya and the boy is a mess. Danilov wants Sheridan's blood. Lupe and Valerie want to see the plan through. How is your Desiree?"

"She'll be alright. She is tough." Herschel pulled up a chair and sat next to the Frenchman. "What about you Antoine, do you believe in this, in what we are doing?"

Antoine covered Claudia's ears and leant across. "My family are balloonists," he said, "my three brothers anyway. My father, he was a carpenter. I had no interest in woodwork, or ballooning. I believed in myself and my skills though nobody else cared. From childhood to the circus, I was in a blackness... and then I met you. Do you remember?" Herschel smiled and nodded, "you saved me from that hell-hole. You did. And you brought me here and showed me The Roxy. And Lupe and Benjamin... and I started to believe in it, in this theatre and then more of us came along. We discovered Gertie under the stage, Claudia, like an angel from heaven, Srdjan the drunk; my friends. You believed in me and I believed in my family. I still do. But more importantly, I believe in life. What we are doing will save us all, unite us harder...but something more, Herschel, something much more!"

Herschel's eyes were no longer teary with sadness, but with pride. "What? What?" he whispered.

"We are going to rebuild this theatre. With the gems of those who don't care if we die in the gutter, those who are happy in their castles and towers. They are going to do something magnificent. With their donations, we all will rebuild the theatre and give back to our people some colour and hope; a free theatre, a free palace of light. We can make them all believe in life."

Herschel stood up and held out his hand. "I'd like to shake the hand of the finest man I know," he said proudly. Antoine stood up and shook Herschel's hand. He comforted Claudia who was lightly dozing and the left Tobias's room. Neither man saw that Tobias' eyes were open and that he was smiling. He was going to survive. God had spoken to him through the mouth of a Frenchman. Inside, Tobias laughed at the mysterious ways in which He worked and he started to sing a song.

Gertie had not fled The Roxy, contrary to the player's beliefs. Instead, he lay on his back, looking up at the underside of the stage, the light breaking through the cracks in the boards and crossing his face. Every once in a while a beam was broken by a footstep. The creak of the board sent dust onto the boy as he lay, unblinking, and sinking into a well of guilt, his love for Anya pulling him down further. He had gone back to the start - to the place where Herschel found him seven years prior.

He was a destitute, malnourished rat of a boy back then, orphaned and utterly forgotten by the rest of the world. From the age of six he had survived on stale bread crusts and ditchwater. He had no skill at thievery and a strange juvenile greenness to the world that did not sharpen fast enough to the harsh realities of London and so he had never found use for himself on the streets. He couldn't join a gang and he couldn't learn a wily street-trade, so he clung to the shadows and regressed into a Neanderthal state. He was a useless, pitiful creature. He had found The Roxyin the same way someone finds a door handle in the dark. He had been fumbling for years, looking for a sustainable place of shelter, and the seemingly disused theatre seemed perfect. Under cover of darkness, the snipe had crept in thinking it was abandoned, and looked around for a scrap and a blanket. Instead he found a pile of half-naked drunkards, snoring loudly. He looked them over. Their bodies seemed healthy and well fed. By the side of the stage he found a plate of soft bread which almost sent him into arrest when his lips tasted the sweetness of it. The boy was a stupid animal, but not so stupid as to not realise that the theatre offered warmth and food. While the pile of bodies slept, he crept around the stage, helping himself to food and drink until he came to a little hatch that led to the underside of the stage. He opened it and entered.

And there he stayed for five months unknown to the Players, living in the shadows under the stage, creeping out when the coast was clear and feeding himself. The Players had no idea the animal lived there. They shared everything, so when one of them found a roll they had been saving to have been eaten they naturally assumed one of the others had taken it.

This happy charade continued until the day Herschel was thrown out of bed by Desiree. Her temper was volcanic and she had chased the old man around the stage with a butterfly net. The boy had pressed his face up against the stage and peered through a crack to watch the action. Herschel, in a last ditch effort to evade her wrath, had found the hidden doorway and climbed under the stage. The playwright did not get far before spotting a large creature in the darkness. He scurried back out and received an almighty hit from the butterfly net over the back of the head.

Under the stage, the animal-boy was panicking. He tried to find a secure hiding spot but there were none to be had. He traced the footsteps above him, noting their unusual patterns and knew that he had been discovered. Above the stage, Herschel was explaining to the others that there was a bear-cub under the stage, probably escaped from the Russian Trappers who had come to Borough Market not three days before. The boy could not understand a single word that was being discussed, but he knew that the animals above him were colluding. He scrabbled around in the dirt, trying to dig downwards and throw some lose soil over himself for concealment. It did not work. After a few moments, the hatch door creaked open again and a tall man with a hairy face crept in. He tried to coerce the boy out, but it made him dig faster. Eventually, the hairy man grabbed the boy and yanked him out. He was confronted by a dazzling barrage of light, noise and faces looming in upon him. He bit the man's arm and tried to scamper away but only managed a few feet before another man dived in and grabbed his ankles. The animal-boy turned on his back and thrashed around. He struggled hard and had almost broken free when he noticed, high up on a rafter, a lithe figure glinting like a star. He was suddenly transfixed. The man released his ankle and the boy stood up. Still looking up at the figure on the rafter, he edged his way around the stage and picked up the butterfly net. Thoughts for his safety fell away, as did the figures from his vision and his proximity. The Players stood back and watched the curious animal-boy as he jumped and swung with the net, trying to catch the star. And that was how Gertie first came to be in The Roxy Playhouse.

But now, all those years later, he was back under the stage feeling the pain that only failed lovers feel. He could not breathe. He could barely move. In his mind he was standing in a black room under a pin spot, holding his net and catching a thousand falling Anya's. The image had been playing over and over in his mind from the moment he had first seen her. He closed his eyes and took a hammer to the image. He wanted to die for what he had failed to do. Then to him came the Devil who always appears brightest in the darkest of hours. A suggestion filled his mind and a tide of conviction came over him. *'Sheridan must die'* whispered the Devil into his mind's ear.

———•◦•———

Anya lay on her bed replaying her ascent over and over. She had lost her nerve and that in itself had rattled her. She had lost balance before, she had even lost momentum before, but she had never lost her nerve. The dark place halfway along the wire where one needed mental courage and fortitude the most was where she shone brightest. Her heart rate increased at the rising sense of doubt within her, which caused her bruises to inflame. She was on the verge of tears when a little melody floated through the wall and covered her like a blanket. It was the stirring, gentle voice of Tobias and her heart rate lowered again. She shifted her weight into a more comfortable position and began to sing along.

Gertie stood and looked through the slats. The stage was empty. He crept out of the hatch and, recalling the stealth of his youth, clung to the shadows as he made his way to Srdjan's quarters.

He knew what he was looking for and did not need to search for long. He grabbed the sharpest knife he could and stuck it in his belt. He crossed back over the stage and proceeded down the aisles until something caught his eye. His butterfly net was lying in the spot where Tobias had dropped it. He picked it up and looked it over. He knew every knot and grain of the thing. It was like another limb. He ran his hand along it and recalled every practice swing, and every successful catch. He thought about the one he wasn't there for. He took up the pole and smashed it across his knee and threw the pieces down in hatred before storming out of the theatre.

As he strode out into the night, he did not see Valerie returning with a bundle of rags for bandaging. She watched Gertie storm off into the night and, somehow, knew deep down inside just exactly what his mission was. The boy walked like one who had murder on his mind. Valerie ran into the theatre, dumped the rags on the empty stage and darted back out again to follow after him.

<hr />

Desiree was in Perugia once again. She was walking barefoot through the narrow, orange bricked streets carrying a basket of Tuscan bread. The scent from the sprigs of rosemary in her hair filled her nose and she was at peace. The sun was hot and dry and she stopped by a little water fountain on the edge of the deserted square. It was too hot for the older residents of town, but for Desiree it was perfect. She would go home, take her clothes off and walk through her house naked until she found Herschel.

As she drank from the fountain, letting the water droplets run down her neck and soak her cotton dress, she transformed them into the hands of the playwright. His was blessed with a writer's gentle touch and in their hot farmhouse, he would write his love over every inch of her. She finished drinking and let the last droplets run down her chin. She could hear singing. She looked around the deserted square. Not a soul, save her. The voices were soft and haunting. She recognized the voices and the song. Her shoulder blade began to itch. She realised then that she was dreaming.

Desiree woke up in the dark of her room, the slash across her back burning fiercely. She closed her eyes and tried to return to Perugia, but every time she arrived at the outskirts of the city the sky became more and more angry. She gave up trying to sleep. The song repeated itself. Tobias and Anya's words seemed to be the only thing around her, and so she too began to sing along.

⎯⎯•◦•⎯⎯

Benjamin, Archie, Lupe and Danilov were sitting in Benjamin's study when Herschel and Antoine entered. Antoine handed the sleeping Claudia to Lupe. Herschel handed a bundle of papers to Benjamin.

"What are these?" .

"That's your script. Learn it. Add it to your character. Become it."

Benjamin looked at the script heading and smiled. "Great title."

"Do you really think we can continue?" said Danilov before being halted by a strange sound wafting through the theatre. Claudia stirred awake and rubbed her eyes. The Players stood up.

"You hear that?" said Archie, leading the group out of the chamber and down into the theatre. The muffled noise soon became louder and more distinct: three voices. The Players hurried through the backstage area, following the voices until they reached the centre of the auditorium. The singing was loud and impassioned. The Players stood open mouthed and elated to hear the grand voices of Tobias, Desiree and Anya singing the old English tune based upon Henry V's St Crispin's Day speech filling The Roxy. The words filled them all with conviction, pride and belief.

"We continue," Danilov said, "we continue to the very end."

"And so say we all," said the Frenchman. The singing ended to rapturous applause from the Players. Tobias, Anya and Desiree knew that they had pulled everyone back together and pushed them, as one, into the right direction. They closed their eyes and fell into a warm, painless sleep.

The doors of The Roxy swung open and the Players turned to see Srdjan and another man. He was tall, plump and clearly sleepy. The bags under his eyes rested on his large cheeks like saddle bags over the hind legs of a horse and the few remaining silver hairs upon his head shot off in random directions. He was dressed in a shirt and waistcoat which was partially hidden by a blood splattered apron. In his hand, he carried a leather bag. The mood of the Players dropped slightly.

"Lupe," said Benjamin sternly, "take Claudia out for a midnight feast. Archie, go with them and, if you can find him so early, take this to the Irishman." He ripped a page out of Herschel's manuscript and handed to Archie. "It's my name," he said, "for the Almack's voucher". Archie took the paper and put his arms around Lupe and Claudia.

"What is going on?" asked the sleepy Spanish girl, "who's that man? He looks frightening."

Lupe took her hand and led her off with Archie. "Shush little one," said Lupe, "he is just a friend of Benjamin's. They have come to discuss part of his costume. Come on then, let's get you a muffin and some hot cocoa." Claudia did not entirely trust Lupe, or the stranger, but when Archie smiled at her she went along with it all because she always trusted Archie.

When Archie had led Lupe and Claudia out of the theatre, Srdjan ushered the strange interloper toward stage. When he got there, the stranger shook hands with Benjamin.

"Good evening Mr Coombes."

"Mr Ananas," said Mr Coombes authoritatively, "I will need assistance. Would you please take me to him?"

"Please, follow me," said Benjamin as he led Mr Coombes to Tobias's room. Antoine, Danilov and Srdjan stood in the stage looking gravely at each other.

"Where did you find a doctor at this hour?" asked Danilov. Srdjan did not reply.

"He's not a doctor" said Antoine, gravely, "he's a barber"

Chapter Twenty One

Blood

Gertie tried to storm across London Bridge, but even in the nowhere hours of the night the place was teeming. He was bashed and shoved from side to side, which soon turned his focused rage into frustration. He tried to push back and force his way through, but every time he shoved a person, three more seemed to shove back. He got his head down and drove on. Valerie tried to catch up with him. She was trailing twenty yards behind and was falling back even further due to the sheer amount of people on London Bridge.

It was approaching dawn and soon the world would come alive and thoughts of murder and retribution would fall away. Valerie knew that if she got to the boy she might have a chance to talk him down. If she could not, she trusted in the morning sun to assuage his dark intent. But how could she find him in this? She could easily walk right past him, or even bump into him and apologise and still not recognise him. She leant in and pressed on, craning her head every now and again to train her eyes on the back of him. Unfortunatly, Gertie was short and not wearing a hat so he blended into the murk but suddenly, Valerie saw him; the shape of the young boy being buffeted by some huge beast of a man. She was invigorated and so pushed and pulled at people in order to move further towards him. She called out his name, but her voice was lost instantly.

Gertie had started making real progress. He had dug deep and refocused his anger. The frustration of being lost amongst everybody subsided when he felt Srdjan's blade in his belt. He was almost halfway across when a carriage nearly struck him. He had been trudging with his head down, forcing onwards when a great shadow filled his peripheral vision. He looked up to see a two-horse drawn carriage push past him. The flank of the horse brushed his shoulder, spinning him outward and he would have been cleaved in two by the great wheel if it had not been for the short sharp yank that pulled him clear. The carriage pushed along across the bridge. Nobody looked twice for the young boy who almost died under its wheels. Had it been day time, and the carriage windows open, Sheridan, Ms Siddons, Ms Adberg and Kemble might have seen the young man they nearly trampled and three out of the four passengers therein might have wanted to offer assistance. Instead, they had no idea of whom they nearly killed and simply carried on towards Borough.

Gertie had been pulled into a cramped siding between two garrets. He struggled free of the person holding him and pulled out his knife. His rage and frustration fell into each other and he jabbed his dagger. He felt resistance, then give. He heard tearing of cloth and an ease into something soft. He gasped and pulled the knife back. It was coated in hot blood. Out of the darkness staggered Valerie. The colour had washed from her face. Gertie looked down at her side. Her white dress looked wet, heavy and black. Valerie looked down at her wound and pulled away the ripped clothing, looking at the sodden cloth with a curious child like stare. She poked her fingers into the gaping slice, prising it open as if she were peeking inside an envelope. She looked at Gertie. He was dumb-stuck. Valerie looked at her fingers, glistening in the moonlight and then held them up to her assailant.

"My hand is wet," she mumbled in a daze before slumping down. Gertie dropped the knife and grabbed her. He gently lay her down on the cobbles. Where had she come from? In all the madness of London Bridge, how had she run into him?

He searched through his mind for answers. All he found was dark, black rage. Gertie saw Anya falling and shattering on the floor. His mind was breaking too. He suddenly felt a polar shift in his senses. The young boy had lost something. He looked down at Valerie, lying on the floor holding her wound and murmuring. He forgot language. He forgot sense. In his delirium, the only words that seemed to emerge from the fog said; *'Sheridan must die' 'Sheridan must die' 'Sheridan must die'*.

All hope for the boy was lost; murder no longer a dancing thought, but the icon above his heart's altar. With his last flash of humanity he picked up Valerie and stepped back into the dawning hustle of London Bridge. He was now a creature of singular purpose: He would leave Valerie on the steps of The Roxy, go and kill Sheridan, thus releasing his old friends from bondage and then his debt will be paid. After that The Devil could come for him and He would find the boy smiling and ready. He looked down at her. She was murmuring, but still alive. He would have given her a prayer, or some comforting words, but they had erased themselves from his lexicon. He felt as if in a cold dream.

———•◦•———

Archie had left Claudia and Lupe in the relative safety of the George Inn, a keep-house directly opposite The Roxy and a pleasant enough den of lodging and sustenance. It was approaching dawn and he and Lupe knew that they could not stay in The Roxy. The Spanish girl was already back asleep in Lupe's arms. He bought Lupe and himself a pint and they sat at a secluded table in the rear.

"God, I'm glad I'm not inside there," said Lupe as she gently rocked Claudia.

"Me too."

"Do you think he will make it?"

Archie exhaled in doubt and drank.

"Where are you going now?"

Archie slid the folded bit of paper to Lupe. She picked it up and read it. She gave an approving flex of the eyebrow.

"That's a good name. Nice reference," she said in a desperate and transparent attempt at gallows conversation.

"It does fit, doesn't it?" said Archie, in the same tone of denial as his friend.

"Listen," he continued after another sup, "it's getting light and I should take a carriage. That lunatic Moore is probably floating around Muswell Hill by now, God help us, and I have to deliver the note. Take this."

He slid some coins across the table, "Old Howard will put you two up for the night. I would dearly like to stay with you both, and go back to look on our friends in the morning. But I cannot. Will you both be alright?"

"We will, dear boy, we will. You go…"

Archie put his coat on and kissed Lupe on the lips. It started as an innocent 'so long for now kiss' but quickly changed into a slow, deep and melancholy kiss that seemed to carry messages of longing and hope for their friends within it. Finally, their kiss came to an end and their lips parted, but Archie and Lupe could not bring themselves to pull their faces from each other. Archie cupped Lupe's hair with his hand and rested his forehead upon hers.

"Good night, dear Lupe," he whispered.

"Good night, sweet Prince, good luck."

Archie closed his eyes and kissed her on the forehead before sweeping out of the bar. Lupe fell into an introspective daze in which she danced through her memory in search of a warm place to take Claudia and free themselves from the knowledge of what was about to happen in their sacred home across the street.

———•••———

Mr Coombes looked over Tobias with a cold, steely gaze. Everyone else in the room shifted around nervously. The gentleman cleared his throat and opened his leather case. "alright Gentlemen," he began, "it is clear to me that this man's left shank must go. And go from above the knee at that."

"What are my chances?" whimpered Tobias, covered in a flop sweat.

"Good, good. As long as you survive the operation," said Mr Coombes as he pulled out a huge bonesaw from his bag. Antoine and Srdjan looked away in horror.

Danilov entered the room carrying a tray of bottles. He handed them around and each man took a swig for courage. Srdjan tilted up Tobias's head and Danilov poured a generous amount down his throat.

"Pass me one," said Mr Coombes. He took one from Herschel and smelt it. "That will do," he said, "put one aside please. I will try a method my friend recommends called 'sterilisation,'" and he poured a liberal dose onto both sides of the blade. "The alcohol should reduce the chance of infection." He put the blade down on the filthy work station.

"Herschel, could you please stay with Tobias? Throughout the procedure, I would like you to talk to him, mop his brow and keep his mind occupied. Can you do that?"

Herschel nodded. "Good man. Now, Danilov, once the leg is off and the artery clamped, I want you in there with the rags and the drink. What you are going to do will hurt Tobias a lot, but it's for his own good and, down the line, may actually save his life."

Danilov nodded.

"Alright," continued Mr Coombes, "what you have to do, once we're clear, is to tip an entire bottle of the strongest gin you have all over the stump. It'll hurt like Billy-Ho but it's going to stop the infection - hopefully. Can you do it?"

"I can."

"Good man. Now…is it Srdjan?"

"Yes Doctor," said Srdjan, nervously.

"Please," Mr Coombes said, putting up his hand to halt Srdjan, "Surgeon-Barbers are not Doctors, we are military men and you may call me Mr Coombes. Now, Srdjan, come round here next to me. I want you to hold Mr Strong's leg."

Srdjan obeyed.

"Lift it slightly,"

He did so and Tobias moaned a little. Danilov administered more drink to the metallurgist.

"Now," continued Mr Coombes, rubbing his eyes and sweeping his five hairs back across his head, "when that thing comes off, you will have the full weight of it. Have you ever seen combat before, Srdjan?"

"No, sir. Not off the stage…I mean not a war as such. Sorry, I'm blathering."

"That's alright. I would be concerned if you weren't a little nervous. Right then, when that leg does come off, the weight might surprise you. Not many people suddenly find themselves holding a severed limb, especially not one belonging to one of their friends. The natural tendency is to do one of two things," Mr Coombes held up a large, curved knife and inspected it, "one is to drop the leg on the floor and pass out in shock," he held up a hacksaw with his other hand, "the second impulse is to jam the leg back into the stump and try to 'glue it back on' out of sheer panic. I don't need to tell you which one is worse."

Danilov poured an even larger gulp down Tobias's mouth. Herschel was whispering in his ear to distract him. Benjamin was pushing down on Tobias's shoulders and Antoine was ripping up the pile of rags he had found dumped on the stage earlier.

"Ideally," continued Mr Coombes as he began to organise his tools on the bench, "the good assistant calmly, but quickly, takes the leg away - preferably in line with the stump. Just take the leg under your arm like it was a rope in tug-of-war and step backwards, as though you were taking his trousers off. If you whip it away and step to the side, you are likely to get in the way of Antoine here and he will not be able to attach the crow's beak around the artery, which will result in rapid blood loss and death. Clear?"

"Yes, sir."

"Show me"

Srdjan pretended to remove the leg by stepping backwards.

"Excellent. If you can do it just like that, it would be excellent. If, however, you resort to one of the two options I mentioned earlier, I would prefer you chose option one and just throw the leg somewhere," said Mr Coombes as he washed his hands in a bowl of water.

"Don't worry Srdjan," said Benjamin, "You are going to do it just fine."

"You can do it," agreed Danilov.

"Right," interrupted Mr Coombes, "Mr Ananas, your job is simple: Hold the patient down. He's going to struggle, naturally, and I need him steady."

Benjamin nodded and pressed down on Tobias's shoulders.

Mr Coombes turned to the magician who was handing the rags to Danilov.

"Now, Antoine, Mr Ananas tells me you have quick hands, is that so?"

Antoine thought of demonstrating his prowess, but instead simply nodded.

"Good because you are going to need them. Come around here please and stand inbetween the wicket keeper and the short mid on - the short leg if you were!" Mr Coombes smiled at his cricket analogy. Antoine looked baffled.

"Just stand in between Srdjan and Benjamin please." Antoine stood where he was told. Mr Coombes handed him a thin, three-inch jaw-pinned metal clamp.

"That's the crow's-beak. Now, as soon as I'm clear and Srdjan has stepped away with the offending limb, you have to clamp that little beauty around the main artery."

"How will I know which is the main artery?"

"The instant, three-foot jet of blood should point you in the right direction."

"Yes...yes, sorry."

"You have the fastest hands in the world," slurred Tobias. "The best I have ever seen. You'll be fine. I would not want any other man to stem the ebbing of my life-force than you."

Everyone in the room suddenly felt imbued with pride and confidence thanks to Tobias's courageous words.

"Alright, are we ready to begin?" asked Mr Coombes with a confident smile.

"Wait!" said Danilov, as he went to close the door. He opened the remaining bottles and handed one around. Everybody took a final swig. Herschel placed a leather strap in Tobias's mouth and held his head tightly, fixing his eyes upon the patient.

"Alright, wicket keeper, clamp, brace, bandages, moral focus...everybody ready?" said Mr Coombes, addressing each assistant with a concentrated stare. They all nodded. He picked up his thick curved knife and traced the cutting line just above Tobias Strong's knee.

"One...two..."

The surgeon-barber sliced in on 'three'. The blade of the razor-sharp knife almost disappeared into the flesh. Tobias bit on the strap and convulsed. Benjamin held him fast. Antoine blew the sweat off his fingers and Srdjan tightened his grip on the leg. The knife cut further in. Mr Coombes leant over the blade with all his might and angled the incision around the bone. They all heard a horrible pop and a crack as the tendons around the knee snapped like guy-ropes. Srdjan felt the leg loose tension. Tobias's screams faded as the pain overwhelmed him. Mr Coombes brought the blade back up to the top of Tobias's leg. He held it there for a single second then splayed the knife slightly to reveal the muscle and bone as yet uncompromised. The blood was pouring onto the floor. Benjamin gagged reflexively. Mr Coombes quickly discarded the knife back onto the bench and grabbed the bone-saw. The teeth of blade found a good bite into the bone. Mr Coombes bit his lip, pointed the saw downwards, leant upon it and pushed. The grating sound of blade on bone coarsed through the air. Tobias was yanked instantly from his comatose state and thrust into the excruciating reality of the moment. He screamed and bit down hard on his gag before convulsing slightly and falling unconscious once more.

The sudden awakening of Tobias shocked the Irregulars and they momentarily dropped their guards, but Mr Coombes was a good barber-surgeon and in four quick, but heavy, back and forths he was through.

"Now!" he cried as he pulled the saw up and stepped away. Srdjan breathed in, gripped the leg and yanked it free. He was slightly over-zealous in his duty and blood from the severed limb arched into the air, splattering into Antoine's eyes as he went in to the clamp the artery. The sting in his eyes threw the Frenchman for a split second.

"Now man, now!" called Mr Coombes as the artery in Tobias' leg began to spray everywhere. Antoine's instincts took over and he let his hands lead the way. They found the artery and clamped it. Antoine staggered backwards, trying to get the blood out of his eyes. Danilov was already there with the alcohol, pouring it all over the wound. He discarded the bottle and wrapped the bloody stump in a gin-soaked bandage.

Everybody stepped back, shocked and relieved that it was over. Mr Coombes inspected the wound and the bandage and finally Tobias who was still passed out.

"Gentleman," he said "I'd like to shake you all by the hand for an excellent job. I have rarely seen such professionalism in novices.

Hats off to you all" he shook their hands. Srdjan was still holding the leg.

"You can put that down, dear boy," Mr Coombes said, smiling at the wide-eyed Srdjan, "though I wouldn't leave it near the body. Dead flesh and all that. Come now, let us clean up and you can pour me a drink."

The men left Tobias's workshop and went to the auditorium. Srdjan was still a little shocked and could not seem to put the leg down. The rest of the Players too were in a dreamlike daze. The events of the day and the sight, sound, and smell of the inside of their friend's leg had possessed them. They were sleepwalkers.

Sheridan's carriage pulled up outside The Roxy just as the sun was coming up. They alighted.

"Pay the driver," said Sheridan to Kemble, who obliged through gritted teeth.

"Now, let's go see what the old fellow has been up to."

Kemble grabbed his dagger and grinned menacingly.

"You wait here," said Sheridan, "I told you!"

"I will not! I'm coming in, to do what you should have done long ago, master!"

"Do as your told, you ugly toad!" jeered Ms Siddons, "there's a good little wanker!"

Kemble turned on Ms Siddon's and slapped in her in the face. She whipped out two needles from her hair. Sheridan swung at Kemble with the back of his hand, connecting sharply and sending the greasy fop down the steps. Sheridan drew his sword and loomed over Kemble, pinning him to the ground with his blade.

"Damn you, Kemble! Cur! I take you in! I give you leave to come and go. And this is how you repay me? By striking a woman in my very presence?"

Kemble grovelled around on the floor, kissing and licking Sheridan's shoes.

"Forgive me! Forgive me! Spare your servant!"

"Pathetic worm, get up!" shouted Sheridan.

Kemble did and Sheridan sheathed his blade.

"Come, ladies" he said, offered an arm to each. Ms Siddons returned her needles into her wig and the three of them walked into the theatre.

Kemble crawled up the steps and sat against the wall. He took his knife out and began to sharpen it, adding three more names to his hitlist.

———•◦•———

The good surgeon and his assistants emerged onto the stage to be greeted by Sheridan, Ms Siddons and Ms Adberg who were walking down the centre aisle. Everybody froze. The Irregulars had not expected to have company and the Olympians had not expected to see a blood splattered group of men carrying a limb.

Srdjan dropped the leg to the floor. It squelched blood. It was clearly no prop. The Olympians took a cautious step backwards.

"Well," said Mr Coombes in a chipper fashion, "I can see you fine gentlemen and ladies have business to discuss. So I should bid you farewell. Good evening all."

"Good evening," said both acting troupes in an absent-minded unison. Mr Coombes walked down the aisle to leave.

"Mr Ananas," he called back, "I will be back to stitch up Mr Strong soon. In the meantime, change his dressings every half hour and clean the wound. Will you do that?"

Benjamin nodded.

Mr Coombes looked at his watch. "Would you look at that?" he said to nobody in particular, "it's nearly six in the morning. I will have a queue of beards to trim already. Good day to you, good fellows!" and with that, the surgeon-barber walked merrily into the breaking dawn.

The Irregulars and the Olympians stood for a few moments. Sheridan finally cleared his throat and stepped forward.

"Mr Ananas we came here to see how you are proceeding with payments. I can see that maybe I should have made an appointment. To my disgrace I did not. You are clearly...busy. We shall retire. I do apologise for this intrusion of ours, please, accept an extra week...an...an..." Sheridan was transfixed on the leg lying on the stage.

Benjamin and the rest of the Players wandered off of the stage like sleepwalkers.

"Hello Srdjan" called Ms Adberg.

Srdjan stopped and looked around at the baffled Olympians. He raised a blood-soaked hand.

"Hello Alexia," he said, as if he was talking to an apparition.

Sheridan looked around at the two ladies. Quietly the Olympians left. Tobias Strong's left leg remained lying on the stage.

Chapter Twenty Two

"We are Artists!"

Archie eventually caught up with Thomas Moore on Muswell Hill. He had scoured every drinking hole, brothel and opium den in the area looking for the poet but luckily, the elusive fellow had left a trail of breadcrumbs to follow: a bruised drunk here, a fawning idolater there. Eventually he found his man. Archie had been pointed into the park by a resting coachman whose boots looked too clean to be out at such an early hour of their own accord. The driver was lying across the riding bench with his feet up, hat over head and snoring gently. Archie tapped the carriage door. The horses acknowledged by taking their faces out of their nosebags, but the driver did not wake up. Archie wiggled the driver's boot and asked if he had seen Thomas Moore. The driver moaned and grumpily pointed into the park. Archie thanked him, patted the horses and entered through the gates.

There are not many sights that fill the Londoner with as much joy as Muswell Hill at dawn. It was almost deserted and so Archie felt as if he were walking through his own private garden, the warm sun giving life to him. He was a Lord of life. Archie knew that Mr Moore was in the park somewhere, but he was no longer in too much of a rush to find him and instead took some time to enjoy the walk. He passed through the trestles of ivy and into the Japanese Garden with its pretty rock features and gentle flower beds.

The chaos of the last week or so had not been given the chance to take root and as Archie walked peacefully through the garden, they chose their moment to strike. He was overcome with emotion. The beating at the hands and feet of Sheridan's cronies, the dark moment of his near suicide, the rescue of his soul via the glorious nature of Valerie Folk, the chaos of Regent Street and the vile drinks in Camden just a few hours before. He had been through a lifetimes worth of ups and downs in only a few hours. He was exhausted before he even factored in the trials and tribulations of his friends, especially those of poor Tobias.

He stopped for a moment and chastised himself as a tide of guilt swept through him. Here he was, the dreamer and architect of their troubles, enjoying a serene dawn walk through the park and only a few miles away one of his dearest friends was in the most excruciating pain imaginable. He cursed himself for his selfish nature and sank to his knees. For the first time in his life Archie Enfield prayed. He hoped God would not ignore him for calling only this once, but he knew that He would help if He knew it was for one of His children. Archie prayed for Him to watch over Tobias and to ease his pain. He penitently crossed himself and continued on his way through the gardens.

After half an hour, he neared the crest of the great hill. Upon its brow he saw someone sitting on a bench. He had found his man. Archie walked quietly up to join him. From the little hill he could see the whole of the park, and out, out, out across the whole of London. The sun was rising and the sky was cloudless. The warm morning beams kissed the tallest rooftops and spires and the orange hues fell down into the streets and bathed everything in a welcoming, maternal warmth. It was a stunning morning.

"Stop mincing around behind me, and sit down boy!" said Thomas Moore without even looking behind him. Archie obeyed.

"Good morning laddie, did not expect to see you so soon!"

"Don't you ever sleep?"

Thomas Moore, eyes red with heavy bags under them smiled as he inhaled the morning. The effects of his debauched lifestyle tried to take hold of his psyche, but the power and glory of London in the morning sun overcame everything.

"Beautiful isn't it?" said Archie, siding up to his man.

"Have you come for any reason other than to state the bleeding obvious and ruin my morning contemplations, young Enfield?"

Archie handed over the paper Benjamin had given him. Moore took it and read the single line.

"That's it? That's his name?" he handed the paper back to Archie.

"That's what we're going with, yes."

Thomas Moore thought for a few moments and then burst out laughing. He slapped Archie's leg so hard that he left a bruise that took a week to heal.

"It is a wonderful name! Utterly absurd and quite delicious! I'd wager if you had told me this last night, I would have done it for free! Just to hear the people whisper it... blast my eyes, I would have paid you for the privilege!"

"It's good isn't it?"

"It's wonderful. I just hope I can do my job and keep a straight face! May I?"

Archie handed back the paper. Moore looked at it again and burst out laughing once more. He wiped away a tear from his eye.

"Tell me, my dear sweet fool. Why are you doing this? What's so important to you?"

"Our necks."

"Besides that, everybody has a neck for Christ's sake. What else, come on, tell me something!"

Archie contemplated. Eventually he pointed out the view.

"Why are we the only people on this hill today? Is it because we are late to bed, or early to rise; maybe, but also for another reason. You, sir, are a poet, a master of verse, a grand creator. I, well I am nothing alone, but we together, you, me and my friends, we have something greater. It is a gift, a fire that we wield in our hands, something that everybody has, but very few ever hold."

"Tell me, dear boy, tell me!" said the enthralled Moore.

"We have the power to rise above the knock and bash of our lives and see the greater glory. We can come up to this hill and see that the world really is a wonderful place. We are artists, my friend. You ask me why we are doing this. I say we are doing this so that we can further our art, further ourselves. You ask me what is so important. I tell you that it is the world! The man, the woman, the child, we can give them performance, verse, song and portrait. We can illuminate them, as the world illuminates us. We can give back to the poor and the put upon, give them back hope and love on our stage. It might be for only a few moments, but it is there nonetheless. Sir, we do it for London!"

Thomas Moore thought over Archie's impassioned speech. Eventually he patted him in his bruised leg and stood up.

"If you had said that you were doing it for the money, I would have believed you!" he laughed. Archie smiled.

"Artists, indeed!" said the poet to himself with a quiet whimsy. Thomas Moore walked down the hill. When he was halfway down, he turned back and raised his arms.

"Look! The sun has risen, and the sun will set once more…and we will still be artists! Artists!" he bellowed.

"Artists!" Archie shouted back.

"Artists my boy! Artists! We are artists!" he laughed so loudly that the nearby birds flew out of the trees. Archie watched Thomas Moore skip into the sunshine and, for possibly the first time concerning their adventure, he thought that they might just be able pull it off and if they didn't, it would make a hell of a story nonetheless.

———•••———

Gertie laid Valerie down on the steps of The Roxy. The sun had brought colour to her cheeks and now that he could see her properly, he realised to his relief that the wound was not so deep and with a little treatment, she would be on her feet by lunchtime. He stroked the hair from her face. She smiled, still in her dream and wholly unaware of her wound and whereabouts. He took his overcoat and laid it over her before removing his jacket and folding it into a pillow for her head. Gertie had no thought to enter the theatre and confront the Players after what he had done. Although the morning sun had changed his attitude regarding his mission, it had not changed his mind as to its execution. Sheridan still had to die. However, Gertie felt that he would no longer commit the crime it out of rage, but out of cold necessity. The judge would see no difference and he would hang either way, but that was irrelevant. After he made the vow to himself to end their problems his life as he knew it had ended. Night time was for rage, morning for pragmatism.

Gertie kissed Valerie on the lips and whispered his apology. He asked her to forgive him for the wound, but not for the crime he was about to commit. She moaned slightly as some of his words filtered into her dreamscape. Gertie left her and walked into the city. He had to forge a plan. Getting past Kemble, Ms Siddons and Ms Adberg was one thing, besting Each, Peach, Pear and Plum was another matter altogether. He had a monumental amount to plan before he even got into Sheridan's study to slice his guts open. He needed not only a place to think, but also a place in which he could not be found should any Irregular come looking for him. He decided to lose himself amongst the wharves and docks. He could easily find a hull or pub to hide out in. He looked around and saw no suspicious eyes but still took off his scarf and wrapped it around the bloodied knife, said a final farewell to The Playhouse and made his way to hide out in Wapping.

Valerie lay on the steps of The Roxy for thirty minutes before she was discovered by Lupe and Claudia, returning home from their stay in the George Inn. Lupe picked her up and they ran into the theatre hollering and screaming for help.

———•••———

Desiree was awake and dressed when the screaming started. Her back felt strong and supple. She had performed some basic calisthenics and the stitches had fared well. She looked over to Herschel who had fallen asleep in his chair whilst watching over her. He had been too scared to lie next to her, which he so much wanted to do, in case he rolled over in the night and hit her wound. Instead he sat and watched, every once in a while, creeping over to her and giving her the smallest, softest trio of kisses on the nape of her neck. She had felt them too. Even in her deep sleep, the kisses had found their way to her. Desiree loved him even more that morning.

Lupe and Claudia's screams for help woke every player and they all rushed to the source.

Benjamin flew onto the stage to find Lupe and Claudia laying Valerie down.

"Get bandages!" cried Lupe as soon as she saw him. Benjamin rushed to the side of the stage, but could find none. They had used them all on Tobias.

"Benjamin, hurry!"

He gave up searching and instead ripped his shirt off and tore it into shreds in moments. He rushed back, half naked and holding the rags out. Valerie was awake.

"I'm alright, I'm alright." She whispered, bravely.

The other Players arrived at the same time.

"What's happened?" said Srdjan "is that Valerie?"

Danilov dashed over, nearly knocking Claudia over as he did so.

"Valerie, are you alive? Don't die, don't die; please don't die!"

Valerie smiled and reached up to stroke his face. "You do care! You'll make Archie jealous!"

Desiree arrived with a bowl of water and Herschel helped her bend down so that she could dress the wound. Everybody looked at the gash across Desiree's back. It had a green colouring due to the herbal paste. The Umbrian wiped a wet rag over Valerie's face.

"Desiree!" exclaimed Valerie, her eyes lighting up, "you're alright! You're better, I'm so happy!"

"Hush, my dear, I'm fine! I'm from Perugia. Women from Perugia live to one hundred and seventy five years without so much as a wrinkle!"

Benjamin leant in. Valerie eyed his masculine, assured frame and winked at him.

"Yes," said Lupe, "cover up!"

"Never mind that, what happened? Who did this? Sheridan? That bastard Kemble?"

"Yes," said Danilov, "tell us so I can avenge this!"

"It was nobody..."

"She was wrapped in these," said Claudia gravely as she held up Gertie's jacket and overcoat.

At that moment, the doors opened and a yawning Archie returned. There was no surprise in his expression when he saw the group huddled over a body. It was becoming an all too familiar occurrence.

"Archie! Valerie has been injured! Attacked!" cried Srdjan.

"By whom?"

Herschel looked around the stage. "Wait," he said, "Where *is* Gertie? Has he not returned?" everyone was suddenly hit with the same thought and expression. They had forgotten about the boy. They looked about the auditorium. Desiree put her ear to the boards and listened.

"He's not down there...where is he?"

Archie was about to join them on the stage when out of the corner of his eye he noticed an abnormality within the aisles. He scampered over a few chairs, throwing them aside like a burrowing animal.

"What?" called Benjamin, "what do you see?"

Archie stood up. He was holding the two pieces of Gertie's huge butterfly net. There was a stunned silence. Valerie closed her eyes. She knew they had figured it out.

"Forgive him. It was an accident." She whispered.

"What do you mean?" said Antoine, "where is the lad?"

"He has gone....gone...."

A rope fell to the side of the group and Anya, already back to the rafters, swung down. She looked terrified for the meaning of the broken net and Valerie's words.

"My God," whispered Benjamin. "He was armed, but not for you…."

"Then who?" said Antoine.

"Sheridan," said Benjamin, "he's going to kill Sheridan."

———•••———

Gertie had found himself inside a long, ancient bar on the Wapping Wall called The Town of Ramsgate. He had no idea how long the building had stood, but the creak of the beams and the list of the building suggested perhaps two hundred years. It backed right out onto the river and had a little hitching pier for small boats that was accessible via a few small stone steps. To the left of the pier he noticed an apt addition to the premises – a noose. He stared at it as it swung ominously in the breeze.

"For pirates!" said an old drunk slumped next to him, "catch 'em, hang 'em quick, no need for the beak. Best place for them!" He fell asleep before Gertie could engage him a proper conversation. Gertie took his drink and moved to another part of the bar.

He ran through every conceivable plan to exact his revenge, eventually narrowing it down to three options. The element of surprise – he could storm the theatre on his own. If he ignored the startled residents and made straight for Sheridan like an arrow, he might accomplish his goal before the others could react. If he stopped to engage them, it would be a short fight. The second option was to wait until the dead of night and burn the theatre down. It was an unknown quantity as people can survive fires. Besides, the theatre had done him no wrong. He could not burn a theatre to the ground as he was an assassin, not a madman. The third and most likely option was one of stealth. He recalled his ability to disappear. From his years as a starving shadow in the gutter, to his magical stage work where, thanks to the recognition and tutelage of Herschel, he was able to walk through a performance and change a prop or set without being seen or heard. Under cover of darkness, he could sneak into the theatre, locate Sheridan who would most likely sleep in his own quarters, creep up to him and slice his throat. It was the quietest way he could to do it.

———•—•———

Their carriage ride home had been a grating mix of bemused silence from Sheridan and the women, and the incessant chatter from Kemble. They mechanically nodded at his vows of hatred and his designs upon The Roxy Players. They smiled emptily at his declarations of love and passion for their unity. Sheridan did not pay any attention to Kemble who lurched forward and held his master's knees, kissing his thighs and repeating his vow of diligence. Instead, Sheridan looked vacantly out of the window and dwelled on the severed limb he saw on the stage, the amount of blood and the awful dead-eyed expression pasted upon the faces of The Roxy Players. What must they have been through? He recalled a long-buried time when he was friends with Benjamin. He recalled even a time when he did not mind his nickname of 'No Not' because the ribbing meant that he was loved. He was jolted from his dream by the carriage as it halted outside the Olympus. He looked over to Ms Siddons and Ms Adberg. They two had the same, distant gaze and all three seemed to share a unified connection. They each felt that they had gone too far in their current occupations and that, perhaps, it was time to about face and walk back into the light.

Kemble was still kissing Sheridan's thighs and mixing his sycophantism with his bile when Sheridan came fully to his senses. He looked down at the disgusting man and felt sick. He opened the door and almost fell out, desperate for air. Kemble fell forward and hit his face on the seat opposite. Ms Siddons and Ms Adberg stepped over him and alighted. Kemble felt his lip. He had bitten into it, splitting it open and spilling the blood into his mouth. He imagined that it was not his own blood, and as such it tasted all the more sweet.

From across the street, Gertie watched Sheridan stagger out of the carriage and walk into the theatre. The boy noted the strange lightness to the man's gait but did not pay heed to it. He had been waiting for a few hours, tucked in an alleyway behind a stack of barrels and had gone beyond the investigative nature of one on a stakeout. All he wanted to do was to see the man go inside so he could follow him in and then end him. His hand slid across his waist and gripped the handle of his dagger.

Sheridan wanted sleep. He could not remember a time when he needed it more. He walked into the theatre and was greeted by the rabble of Each, Peach, Pear and Plum. They ambled up to him, bantering and hitting each other. They had been kicking their heels all day. Without stopping, Sheridan flipped them a coin for drink and said that he was retiring. The buffoons ran out of the theatre like school kids running into a field of virgin snow.

Sheridan walked over the stage and into his quarters. As soon as he sat in his chair and put his feet on his desk, he fell asleep instantly. His dreams peopled with glorious marvels of art.

Ms Siddons and Ms Adberg held hands and drifted off to sleep together. In moments of disaster or enlightenment they had always gravitated towards each other. This moment was a combination of the two. They made love in a rhythm that suggested both instruments where playing the same melody, but only by chance.

Kemble watched the women leave. He looked to the doors: closed. He looked to the door to Sheridan's office: closed. He was alone on the stage and for some divine reason he was holding his knife.

Chapter Twenty Three

Death of a Dramatist

Kemble pushed open the door to Sheridan's office. It made no sound. He stepped inside, walking almost on point. Sheridan was dozing peacefully in his chair with his feet up on the desk and his head lolling backwards. Kemble's heart fluttered at the divine presentation of the body. Sheridan's neck was exposed and virtually begging to be slit. He left the door slightly ajar, lest the click of the lock awake the victim and spoil Kemble's grand moment. The sea change in his soul had been so sudden and complete that he did not stop to entertain doubt. His actions and motivations were as simple to him as a hungry man's motion to feed himself: you're thirsty, you drink, you're hungry; you eat, you're wronged; you kill. He could not conceive of the dark tunnel down which he was about to walk.

The simplicity of it all invited a strange curio to bubble up inside him. He felt a tangible sense of revelry sweep about his mind. His stance changed from creeping assassin to balletic performer as he glided around the room. He bowed to an imaginary audience before picking up Sheridan's hat and cane and prancing around in a mocking fashion. His performance became more angered and erratic as his madness grew. He began to bite his thumb and make rabid jabbing motions with his dagger. He leant in close and mouthed obscenities to his former Lord and Master. He pirouetted around the desk and stood like a barber behind Sheridan. It was then that he noticed that he had an audience after all. Gertie stood in the doorway, knife in hand and dumbstruck.

Kemble smiled an evil and twisted grin which showed all of his rotten teeth. His eyes glinted with the emptiness of a window pane at night.

"Murder, murder, betrayal!" he screamed. Sheridan's eyes shot open in fright. Kemble, fixing his stare on Gertie, dug his blade deep into Sheridan's neck, twisted it and dragged it jaggedly from ear to ear. Sheridan's eyes bulged as hot blood rocketed across the room, hitting the walls, ceiling and poor Gertie who was as a statue for fear.

"Murder! Siddons Come, come Ms Adberg!" yelled Kemble as he dug his fingers into the gap in Sheridan's neck and physically squeezed the life force from his windpipe. Sheridan's leg twitched and his eyes rolled to the side. The last thing he saw before the curtains fell down on his life's performance was the poster of his fine play, stuck to the wall by the door. Gertie came to his senses. He dropped his knife, turned and fled.

Gertie was halfway down the aisle when Each and his heavies ran in from the side of the theatre and blocked his exit. Ms Siddons and Ms Adberg came running out, swords drawn, to join them. A blood-soaked Kemble emerged onto the stage. He was carrying Sheridan and weeping.

"Foul murder! Most viciousness...our leader is slain!" He slumped to his knees and laid the former owner of the Olympus Playhouse onto the stage.

Srdjan, Archie, Danilov and Antoine stood in a semi-circle in 'the armoury'. Each one had on a fitted waistcoat and close cropped jacket. They looked lean and practical. Benjamin handed daggers to them. They stuck them in their belts.

"We don't want trouble, gentlemen, but if trouble comes looking, we'll make sure it comes only once." They all nodded. He handed them another dagger each.

"We need to find our boy and extract him before he does anything stupid. We have no idea where he is so we'll wait at the Olympus until he shows."

He handed each of them a rapier and scabbard. They attached them. Srdjan had to help Archie who was clearly not used to real-life danger.

"What if he has already done it? What then?" asked Antoine with fear writ large across his face. "You want he should…"

"Dear God, no, if we're too late, then it's a guilt we should all carry."

"What if they should discover us?" said Danilov. Benjamin handed each of them another sword.

"We go to get our boy. There is no other plan. If we are discovered, or if they have him…well…," he drew both his swords and pointed them to the middle of the circle.

"Let's get our boy," said Antoine and crossed his swords with Benjamin's. The rest of them followed suit and the heroes left the room.

The rest of the Players had lined the stage, awaiting the men to emerge from the wings. They did and they walked down the line.

"Go get the idiot," grumbled Herschel.

"And don't be angry!" said Lupe,

"He's only a boy. Boys do all sorts of mischief!" continued Desiree.

Valerie, awake and mobile despite the pain, kissed each man on the cheek. The men got to the edge of the stage and turned back to the line.

"Be careful, my dashing heroes," said Claudia.

The men, wanting to milk the situation, stood tall and proud, drew their swords and drew a large 'R' for Roxy in the air, before turning, jumping off the stage and running out of the theatre. The woman swooned and Herschel tutted.

"Idiots," he said and went to check on Tobias.

———•••———

The Olympians had encircled Gertie with club, blade, needle and broken bottle pointed at his jugular. Sheridan's body had been left on the stage and Kemble had joined the party. Gertie was panicked and sweating profusely. He scanned the eyes of his intimidators. They looked back with a steeled resolution underpinned with the burning fire of vengeance. He knew he could not talk his way out of this.

"He done him in! I saw it with my own eyes, curse me and pluck them from me so as I never see such a vicious sight again!" wailed Kemble, "he killed him in his sleep! He sliced open his throat!"

"He's a dead un!" growled Each.

"Death is too good for the assassin rat!" declared Kemble.

"Too good by half!" agreed Peach.

Kemble grinned. "Then you know what I say?"

The Olympians could barely contain their eagerness to hear Kemble's judgement.

"I say Cossack's Tea Party!" he declared. There were unanimous expressions of glee and anticipation for the forthcoming 'party'. Gertie swallowed in fear. It seemed that at the very mention of a

'Cossack's Tea Party', his sweat glands had erupted. He knew what was to come.

'The Cossack's Tea Party', in simple terms, meant a few choice slices across the face, notably under the eyelids and into which pure alcohol is poured in order to keep the victim awake and then, typically, much of the remaining ceremony consists largely of stamping and trampling on the body until it is more or less pulped. It is very time consuming and at great expense of the attackers energies. Such a tea party is not often orchestrated outdoors and so if one were to hear the threat shouted across the street, one could laugh it off. If, however, one were alone and outnumbered inside an abandoned building and the threat was issued, one would have to quickly reassess their short-term life goals.

Of course, Gertie could protest his innocence and accuse Kemble of Sheridan's murder but they Olympians would never buy it. Of all the fierce eyes staring back at him, Kemble's were the pair that carried an extra glint. They burned with a rapacious dementia and Gertie felt that behind these volcanic pupils, Kemble was twirling like a dervish around the fire of his madness. The man was lost to his crime, and so Gertie knew that he was lost to his fate. The circling Olympians began to drive Gertie back across the open auditorium, towards a dark and foreboding corner where chairs had been tossed like bodies in a mass grave. Each, Peach, Pear and Plum were all breathing hard, gripping and wringing their clubs as they pressed forward.

Kemble was barely able to contain his dementia and began to hopping from one foot to the other. Only Ms Siddons and Ms Adberg seemed to be calm. Their eyes carried the same anger and hatred as the other Players but, unlike them, the women's eyes offered a hint of falsity. The two women looked at each other, complicit in their intuitive understanding of the situation. They were great actresses.

Gertie sensed Death shrouding him as he stepped back into the pile of chairs. He watched a trickle of Sheridan's blood roll down the sharp contours of Kemble's face. It collected around the corner of his mouth and lay in a little pool. Kemble teased the pool with the corner of his tongue. The taste was sweeter than any wine and more enriching than any role he coveted. He looked over Gertie's heaving neck and focused on the boy's mountainous jugular. He lunged with his rapier.

It fell short my inches thanks to the parry from Ms Siddon's blade. She stepped forward and stood in front of Gertie.

"Just try it, you mugs!" she spat. Kemble mopped some blood from his brow and flicked it away, splattering it across the wooden boards.

"He done him in, you want we should let him go? He done in Sheridan!" protested Kemble.

Ms Siddons backed Gertie away from the chairs and towards the theatre doors, her blade darting between the necks of the others. "You're a blackhearted cunty one, Kemble! But I never thought you could murder no one!"

"Me? Me? Oh but Ms Siddons, up until a few moments ago, I could not have. But seeing this villain you protect do in our most beloved master, something must have... I don't know... snapped? Now I find myself quite taken with the old murdering. And, if I know that I will be doing in you as well as the boy, well, I will have two things to think about when I'm on my rod tonight!"

Ms Adberg winced at Kemble's disgusting patter.

Gertie backed into the theatre door and began feeling around for the handle.

"Boy," whispered Ms Siddons, "go outside and commandeer a carriage…go now!"

Gertie fumbled for the handle. He pulled the door open, the bright daylight flooding in and startling Each, Peach Pear and Plum who relaxed their clubs. Ms Siddons turned to follow Gertie out of the theatre when Kemble, quick as a thought, grabbed the dagger from his belt and hurled it at her back. It almost connected, but was denied by a deft swing of Ms Adberg's rapier. The dagger swung across the auditorium and stuck into a beam.

"Go now!" shouted Ms Adberg, grabbing Ms Siddon's and thrusting her out of the theatre and into the street. "I am right behind you," and with that she elbowed Ms Siddon's in the chest, sending her flying down the theatre steps. Alexia Adberg slammed the door shut.

Ms Siddons staggered backwards into the street, desperately trying to regain her breath. The sound of clashing blades and shouting from within the theatre filled her with fear that her friend was outnumbered and about to meet her end. She made to dash back in, but was grabbed by Gertie who flung her into a carriage displaying some surprising strength. Ms Siddons kicked and thrashed.

"No! We can't leave her!" she shouted.

"It's suicide! We must get back to The Roxy and then we'll come back for her!" Gertie hit the roof of the carriage and it sprung into motion, flinging Ms Siddons forward so that her head struck the door and she almost tumbled out.

Gertie sat back and reconciled his shame in leaving Ms Adberg and his offering of such a meek reason to do so, with the natural and overwhelming feeling of relief at surviving. He took a few moments to chart the different people he had been over the past twenty four hours from cold schemer to mutilator of women to avenging angel and now to coward. His shame overcame him and without thinking, he leapt over Ms Siddons, jumped from the carriage and ran back to the Olympus Theatre at full pelt. He charged up the steps and was about to throw open the doors when the job was done for him and he was almost crushed by a tumbling stampede of bodies, crashing down upon him. They all fell into the street and by sheer good fortune Gertie and Ms Adberg were thrown clear.

Each and Peach scrambled to their feet, their weight pitching them chaotically forward as they lunged for the woman. Gertie, lying next to her, swung his leg out and hit Peach square in the jaw, sending him barrelling into Each like a racehorse colliding into another. Both lugs hit the deck.

Gertie and Ms Adberg scrambled to their feet and ran off into the thick of Drury Lane. Kemble got to his feet and kicked the heavies to theirs, screaming at them to give chase. He raised his sword high in the air and screamed a demented wail which, given its twisted pitch, caused the nearby folk to clear out of his way. He belted off down the lane. Rejuvenated and feeding off Kemble's bloodlust, the four thugs scrambled up and followed him.

Gertie and Ms Adberg were pushing and pulling people out of the way, trying to move forward but it was like wading through thickening concrete. They could hear the bellows of Kemble and the others and, when they looked back, they could see the waving tips of their clubs and swords above the heads of the masses.

Gertie grabbed Ms Adberg's hand, bent low and dug his heels in. He charged forward like a young rhino, butting people to the side and dragging Ms Adberg behind him. They were making good progress when Ms Adberg felt a grip and a tug on her dress. Through the throngs engulfing her, she could see a blood splattered hand reaching out and pulling at her. She momentarily let go of Gertie, which sent him pitching forward and she reached into her hair and pulled out a needle and plunged it into the blood-soaked hand, spearing clean through the wrist. She heard a gurgling scream from close by and the hand let go and disappeared behind the sea of bodies. She spun round, helped Gertie back up and they pushed onwards.

Kemble tucked his hand into his jacket and pushed his way into a nearby doorway. Each and company followed him in.

"This is bullshit boss! We can't get to 'em!" despaired Plum. Kemble pulled Pear's neckerchief from him and wrapped it round his wrist.

"We can get the cunts! Follow me!" and with that, the actor leapt up onto some barrels and climbed onto a rickety wooden awning. Each, Peach, Pear and Plum caught his drift and smiled at each other. The whole street was lined with such awnings. They could hop from one to another and catch their quarry in no time. Kemble hopped onto the next awning and, once his balance was regained prepared to step to the next. Behind him, the heavies were living up to their name. A single awning could hold only one at a time and they staggered their ascent, hopping like frogs from one to another.

Ms Adberg looked back to see their pursuers rising above the masses. She gritted her teeth in preparation for more fighting. The bastards would be upon them long before they were free of Drury Lane. Gertie looked back also and a great fear rose in him, but he dug his heels in and readied his fists.

The enemy were almost upon them. Ms Adberg and Gertie were stuck in the crowd. Ms Adberg pulled the boy closer to him. "Stay close" she whispered.

"Why are you helping me?"

"You remind me of Srdjan when he was a young."

Gertie smiled and clenched his fists harder. He knew that he might not be a man in himself, but he could certainly pretend to be a man like Srdjan.

Kemble and the heavies were two crooked awnings from them. Kemble stood up and looked down at them. He raised his rapier and pointed to Ms Adberg and then to Gertie, smiling insanely. Ms Adberg spat on the floor and Gertie beckoned him with his fists.

Kemble screamed an awful warcry which shocked the crowd into making a confused gangway. The madman leapt down, sword extended. He landed hard well then charged at Ms Adberg and Gertie. Behind him, the heavies leapt off their gantries and too gave chase.

Ms Adberg graciously saluted with her sword and was about to engage when a great mass lurched in front her, partitioning Gertie and Ms Adberg from their assailants. Ms Adberg reeled backwards to avoid crashing into it. Ms Siddons' carriage! On the other side of it, Kemble's extended sword drove into its wooden door. Ms Siddons flung open the door on Gertie's side and stuck her arm out.

"Fancy a jaunt in a Hackney carriage?" she said with a wink and a flippancy that belied the present danger. They did not need telling twice. Gertie flung Ms Adberg into the carriage and jumped onto the running board. He hit the roof and the driver whipped the horses into motion. The carriage lurched forward, leaving the heavies for dust. Gertie breathed a sigh of relief.

Each, Peach, Pear and Plum shouted and cursed at their slowness.

"What a pile of donkey shit!" shouted Peach as he swung for Plum in frustration. He missed and instead hit Pear who, in turn swung and hit Each. They were about to fall into a bundle when Each looked around for Kemble.

"Wait, wait, where's that wanker?" They all looked around.

"There he is!" cried Pear, pointing into the distance. They all looked yonder.

As the carriage rattled out of Drury lane, they could see Gertie still standing on the kickplate and half slumped over the roof in exhaustion. Then, over the other side of the carriage, unseen to its occupants, they saw Kemble's sword impaled in the door and the mad actor still clinging onto it. He had wedged his foot on the mudrail for purchase and was negotiating standing fully upright.

Each and his friends rallied.

"Come on boys! Let's get the buggers!"

Peach turned round to see a parked carriage. The driver was enjoying a sandwich. He ran over and stopped the driver from enjoying being conscious with a sharp jab to the chin. Each, Pear and Plum ran over and hopped onto the carriage and gave chase.

Chapter Twenty Four

The Cypriote Kiss

A s the carriage thundered through Cheapside, Gertie clung onto the roof rail. To be out of the suffocating crowd was just as welcome as their escape from Kemble and Co. His heart rate slowed and the adrenaline faded. He became aware of his surroundings again. He prepared to climb inside the carriage and check on his rescuers. He steadied his grip on the rail and looked back down Cheapside. His heart sank, and the adrenaline spiked back up. A faster carriage was tearing after them like a gunshot rhino, and bouncing around on its back like giant ticks were Each, Peach, Pear and Plum all grinning madly and each swinging a sword or club above their heads.

Gertie flung open the carriage door and climbed inside. Ms Siddons had her back to the opposite door and was dabbing a wet rag against a cut on Ms Adberg's face. They both looked over and recognised from Gertie's pale and shocked look that they were far from out of the woods. Ms Adberg and Siddons nodded to each other and drew swords, ready for the melee that was about to unfold.

Ms Adberg put her blade out ready for Siddons to cross it and swear fidelity and honour and to fight to the death. Siddon's was just about to comply when her left eye twitched and half of her trussed up hair unravelled. She suddenly dropped her sword. A vacant expression crossed over her face. She made no motion to retrieve her sword from the cabin floor.

"Ms Siddons?" cried Gertie, leaning in and peering over Ms Adberg's shoulder.

"Sarah?" whispered Ms Adberg.

Ms Siddons motioned to speak. Her lips parted and a zephyr drifted out. The carriage rolled over a pothole and Ms Siddons jolted as if in the middle of a bout of hiccups. Her jaw fell open and Gertie and Ms Adberg saw, sticking out of her mouth, a smooth, eight-inch metal needle. Ms Adberg reached forward to touch Ms Siddons on the shoulder. Another pothole forced Siddons to slide forward and she fell into Alexia's lap. She and Gertie looked up in horror to see, in the carriage window, Kemble's blood-soaked face. He was grinning madly and holding one of Ms Siddons' eight inch needles. The blood ran down the needle and dripped over the door frame. Ms Adberg screamed in horror and Gertie backed away to the opposite side of the cabin. The body of Ms Siddons slumped off of Ms Adberg's lap and fell onto the floor. Kemble laughed and swung the door open.

Ms Adberg was frozen in horror, but Gertie was quick to act. He lunged forward and kicked the door, sending Kemble swinging outwards wildly. He clung on to the frame dearly as it swung and batted around as the carriage rumbled on. Gertie reached down and picked up Ms Siddons sword.

"Come on!" he yelled. "We have to go!"

Ms Adberg remained in a state of shock. Gertie, noticing Kemble regaining control of the buffeting door, leant in and impersonating Srdjan's voice whispered to her to rally and honour her friend's death by not joining her just yet. The timing was impeccable. Just as Kemble's door glided back towards the cabin, Ms

Adberg did indeed rally. She turned to Gertie and kissed him, before launching herself straight at Kemble. She crashed into him and grabbed hold of the inside of the door, the weight of both of them causing the cabin to pitch to the side. Gertie would have fallen forward, had it not been for the heavy and assured grip on the back of his collar. He turned to see the arm of Each grabbing him. He pulled up Ms Siddon's sword and jabbed it through the window. He did not feel the resistance of flesh, but he definitely cut through something as Each released his grip. Gertie turned and kicked open the door. The pursuing carriage was right alongside theirs. Gertie climbed out of the carriage and scrambled onto the roof. Ms Adberg and Kemble traded blows through the window and around the frame of the door as it swung back and forth. The carriage driver tried desperately to control the charging horses, all the while screaming blue murder at the roustabouts who had commandeered his vehicle. Despite the driver's efforts, the horses could not be trammelled as the sudden shifts in the cabins weight and Ms Adberg's scream had rattled them. As Ms Adberg and Kemble swung, pedestrians ducked and dived. Some managed to avoid the two; others were not so lucky and received a flailing boot or elbow as the carriage rocketed past.

Ms Adberg delivered a stunning headbutt to Kemble's nose, splitting it instantly. His bloodlust kept him from dropping his sword and falling under the wheels of the carriage, but it did not prevent him from dropping his guard. Ms Adberg spat in his face and bit down on his hand. He screamed in pain and she was about to bite down harder when she heard Gertie calling down to her. She looked up from her door to see him standing on the carriage roof, sword drawn and squaring off against Each and Peach who had climbed across from their carriage. She looked back into the cabin and saw Pear climb in to get to her. She gave up her assault on Kemble and used her inertia to swing the door towards its closed position. She stuck out both feet and swung into the cabin, kicking Pear in the chest and sending him sprawling onto the body of Ms Siddons. Ms Adberg grabbed hold of the roof rail and climbed up to stand next to Gertie.

Inside the cabin, Pear got to his feet and heard Kemble screaming at him for help. He climbed over the body and reached out to Kemble's leg and tried to grab him and pull him in.

Gertie and Ms Adberg stood on the small roof of the cabin. Each and Peach were showing remarkable balance to stand assuredly on the edge of the barrelling carriage.

"To the end?" said Gertie.

"To the damned end," said Ms Adberg and they engaged the two heavies. Gertie operated from a place of amateur rage, jabbing and swinging wildly. However, given the proximity and precarious nature of their makeshift piste, his approach was most effective and Peach found himself defending the blade with manic jumps as it swung low and sidesteps as he jabbed to the torso. Ms Adberg fought with a more measured and direct approach. Her intent was to either pierce Each or at least force him backwards, off the carriage to be dashed on the cobblestones. Each, easily the more skilled fighter of his friends was up to the challenge. He batted her sword away effortlessly and, using the driver's bench as an extra foothold was able to almost beat her back.

Gertie swung too wildly, throwing himself off balance and he fell backwards. Ms Adberg dived to grab him which in turn, caused her to miss the swinging club from Each. Gertie did not fall to his doom however, as his tumble was broken by Kemble and Pear who were climbing onto the roof. All three men fell down. Pear fell into the carriage and pulled Kemble in with him. Gertie was thrown out but managed to cling onto the swinging door at the last second.

Ms Adberg called out to him but could not reach. Each saw his moment and swung for her. Gertie shouted to her and she ducked without looking sending the club over her head and cracking into the back of the drivers, knocking him clean out. He dropped the reins and they fell off their holding and tangled themselves between the horse's bridles. This sent them into a mania and they bolted onwards. Everybody jolted and Each lost his balance slightly. Ms Adberg swung round and jabbed her sword straight into Each's thigh. He screamed and sunk to his knee.

Inside the cabin, Kemble regained his composure, leant out of the carriage and kicked at the door frame. His boot connected perfectly with Gertie's knuckles and the boy reflexively lost his grip. He fell off the door. Ms Adberg reached out and screamed, but the boy was gone.

Alexia Adberg stood up and backed away to the rear of the carriage roof. Each smiled and stood up to face off against her, using the pain in his thigh to fuel his rage. From either side of the cabin climbed Pear and Kemble. They scrambled up like two trapdoor spiders. From the other carriage, Plum let go of the reins and jumped over to the driver's bench of Gertie's. The other carriage careened off and smashed into a bakery window, sending glass shards out into the street and hungry street kids into the exposed shop.

Plum lay on the bench, trying to grab the reins and stop the carriage. Each, Peach, Pear and Kemble raised their weapons in unison. Ms Adberg, exhausted and bleeding, still had some fire inside her. She raised her sword to match.

"Come and get me, you pansies," she taunted and all four assailants lunged forward. Ms Adberg was not going to be defeated.

Not while her friend lay dead in the cabin and Gertie lay dashed on the cobbles some way back. She grabbed Each's club and pulled him towards her. He was not prepared for the move and leant forward, offering his face as a prime target. Ms Adberg elbowed him in the nose and he fell onto his back. She sidestepped Peach's club and backhand swiped her blade across his cheek. He screamed and dropped to the floor. She stepped over Each and drove her heel into his groin to make sure that he wasn't getting back up anytime soon. Pear swung his club downwards and she ducked to avoid while uppercutting him with her pommel. Pear spat two teeth into the air and fell down to join Peach and Each on the roof, leaving only Kemble to defeat.

Kemble bowed to her. Alexia bowed back. On any normal day, each opponent would have been easy to read. They had both fought each other many times on stage and seen each other fight in bars and opium houses. They knew each other's normal modus operandi with a rapier. Today, however, both carried an additional weapon which added a fierce and unpredictable edge to the duel: she was vengeance ridden and he was demented. They circled each other, stepping over the groaning heavies on the roof. They scanned each other's eyes. Ms Adberg's eye were focused and determined, Kemble's were dancing and his head twitching manically. They suddenly engaged in a whirlwind of steel as the carriage belted towards London Bridge.

Gertie's face was inches from the huge rear left wheel. He was clinging to the underside of the footrail like a monkey, his head hanging down. How he had grabbed the rail and not fallen to his death was more than the result of training or an example of great reflexive manoeuvring. It was a pure miracle. He could see the wheel, he could see the cobbles. All dashing passed him. The down force of the vehicle almost yanked him under, but he was stronger than he thought. He tightened his grip to the footrail and tried to reach around to gain purchase from within the cabin in order to pull himself up and around. It was no use. He looked to his right. The underbelly of the cabin offered a few exposed brace rails, some suspension mounts and the rumbling axles. It was traversable. He could climb across, under the cabin, come out the right way up on the other side, easily climb back up to the roof and, hopefully, surprise the bastards from behind. But first he would have to climb across the cabin belly. He was no acrobat. *'How would Danilov do it?'* he thought, trying to focus his mind.

Benjamin led his heroes through the melee of London Bridge. The speed of their exit from the playhouse had vanished as soon as they had hit the crowds. Now it was a case of hard marching like soldiers.

Benjamin remained focused and assured. His bear frame and powerful presence made him the natural choice to lead. Srdjan, being of a similar physique, flanked Benjamin but felt his thoughts betraying him somewhat as his mission mind kept Gertie front and centre, but his heart kept throwing up images of Alexia Adberg and what her remergence into his life might mean for both of them. He gritted his teeth and suppressed Alexia's face. Antoine, Danilov and Archie trudged like infantry behind Benjamin and Srdjan. Nobody spoke but they were all thinking the same thing; that Gertie had gotten himself killed and his blood would be on them all. Though they walked armed and with the pretence to rescue, each of them really knew that their duty was to claim their dead. They loved their friend and they wanted him back no matter what. The only one among them who carried the hope that he was alive was Benjamin. A curious power had arisen within him over the last few days. Before his birthday it was dark, foul and drunk. Now he felt alive, energised and imbued with that most mystical and empowering phenomena of all: belief. He knew what had to be done.

They had been trudging for almost half an hour when Danilov stopped. By the time the others noticed he wasn't with them, crowds had merged and taken his place.

"Wait!" called Antoine. "Where is the acrobat?" Archie stopped and looked around. He shrugged.

"Benji!" he called "Hold up, we have lost a man!" Benjamin and Srdjan did not hear, but instead pressed onward.

Antoine and Archie looked all around, suddenly feeling the separation from their unit and the suffocation of the crowd all too overwhelming. A slight panic began to entrench itself when Archie felt something strike the back of his head. He searched around to find the culprit who threw it. Then, over the din, they heard the familiar voice of the acrobat hollering for them. Antoine and Archie looked back to see Danilov standing on the roof of a rickety garret. He looked devilishly heroic, silhouetted in the sunlight. He was pointing to the north. Archie and Antoine craned to see what he was pointing at. They saw nothing. Danilov hopped from rooftop to rooftop to join them. Archie and Antoine pushed their way to the side of the road. Danilov leant down and hoisted both of them up in one smooth motion.

"What is it?" said Archie. Danilov pointed again to the north. Archie and Antoine squinted to see.

"Holy shit!"

"Mon dieu!

As they stood in the sunlight, above the crowds of London Bridge they watched the two duellists atop the runaway carriage bolting across the mouth of London Bridge and towards to the Upper

Pool docks. As one, the three men ran as best they could along the rooftops. They caught up to Benjamin and Srdjan and, after attracting their attention, hoisted them up and showed them the sight.

"That's Alexia!" cried Srdjan.

"No sign of Gertie!" said Archie.

"Kemble!" spat Benjamin and, with the squad reformed, they ran along the garret roofs on the side of London Bridge, never once losing footing, despite the ramshackle architecture of the buildings. The soldiers were dancers.

———•◦•———

Gertie was down in the belly of the beast; halfway from the safety of both footrail and clinging onto a suspension arm. His feet were wedged in the base guard by each wheel mount and his body was pressed tight against the underside of the cabin. He was at the point of no return. He had to keep moving forward. He closed his eyes and held his breath. His heart rate dropped. In his mind he was on a black stage. He was catching a hundred falling Anyas and without the aid of a butterfly net. He opened his eyes. He kicked his left foot free at the same time of releasing his grip on the rail and hopped his whole body across to the footrail on the other side of the cabin. He clung tight to it, his head millimetres from the ground. He sensed his hair brushing against the cobbles. The force and noise from the wheels were everything. He clung tighter and swung his outside leg up and hooked it around the topside of the footrail. He moved his outside arm to the same place. He was now half out from the underside of the carriage. He rocked his body in a thrice counting motion and on the third, swung it completely out. For a split second, his whole body was in mid-air, parallel to the carriage. His arm and foot holdings held true and he pulled himself up, onto the plate and then into the carriage. He laughed nervously as he caught his breath and took a moment to regain composure.

Above him, he could hear the clashing blades of Ms Adberg and Kemble. He looked down and Ms Siddons corpse. He could see the tiny entry wound in the nape of her neck from Kemble's Cypriote Kiss. It looked like a gnat's bite. She had died saving him. He spat on his hands, rubbed them together for grip, grabbed Ms Siddon's sword, clamped it between his jaws and prepared to climb up and join in the fight.

Benjamin and his men were almost at the mouth of the bridge. They could see the carriage heading towards them at great speed. They could see Ms Adberg and Kemble in the midst of an epic duel. Each, Peach and Pear were on the deck of the roof, but seemed to be getting to their feet. Plum was still clambering around on the driver's bench trying to grab the reins.

"Look!" shouted Archie and pointed to the door of the carriage. They were overcome with pride and joy to see Gertie alive and with sword in his mouth ready to fight. They thrust their swords in the air and huzzahed.

Their joy was cut short.

Gertie was half on the roof, eye to eye, with Each when they all heard Plum cry with joy as he grabbed the reins. They all looked wide-eyed. The idiot pulled them tight. Big mistake. The horses dug in and at that most unfortunate moment, the carriage front right wheel struck a huge divot in the road. There was a moment of silence. Then the horses buckled awfully and the entire carriage pitched forward with immense force.

Benjamin, Archie, Srdjan, Antoine and Danilov stood in horror as they saw their friends and enemies catapulted high into the air. They arched high and far, passing directly over the Players and clearing London Bridge easily, their arms flailed and legs kicked as they swam through the air.

Chapter Twenty Five

The Tall Ship 'Lady Colleen Anne'

As Gertie sailed through the air, passing high over London Bridge and faintly recognizing the shapes of his horror-stricken friends who stood, open-mouthed, on the roof of a garret, he thought of Anya and understood just why she chose to live her life high above everything else. For a few seconds he was as free as his love. He reached the zenith of his arc and the sensation of freedom was replaced with the mortal sensation of impending death. He could not see if Ms Adberg had survived the crash or if indeed she too was flying through the air. The same went for their pursuers. All he could see was the deck of the tall ship, moored next to the bank coming up fast upon him. He shielded his eyes and was, to his surprise, saved from death by the rigging. He flew into the mess of ropes and wires and almost passed straight through when his ankle snagged on a loose rope and the parabola of his descent became suddenly and violently acute. He swung upside down and back on himself. It was then, swinging back in the direction he had come from, that he saw the others coming towards him. In almost slow motion, he could see Ms Adberg, Kemble, and three heavies flying like a giant flock of birds towards him.

Unfortunate Plum did not find himself sailing through the air. Having been the one to pull the brakes on the carriage, he found himself to be in a very undesirable position. As the others were ejected from the carriage, the poor bastard was smashed face first into the cobblestones as the carriage up-ended on top of him. The last thing to pass through his mind was the hoof of a horse as it thrashed and kicked, entwined with the wreckage. The carriage frame impacted on his back and, with the forward momentum of the collision, smeared the thug along the cobblestones.

Ms Adberg, limbs flailing, was falling head first towards the mast but somehow managed to grab the halyard line and stop herself from smashing into the spar. Above her sailed Pear, heading straight towards Gertie. As the boy swung, time seemed to slow. He locked eyes with the bewildered Pear as he passed above him, crashing into the same rigging twenty feet above. The rope caught on his belly and he was slung, halfway through the mesh. The wind fell out of him as his momentum halted and it was pure instinct that managed to keep him from tumbling through the rigging and into the Thames.

Each and Peach flew past Ms Adberg, who was already scuttling down the halyard. The men reached the keel line. However, Peach's grasp was not as firm as Each's and he lost his grip. Each, hanging by one hand and with his leg wrapped over the line, reached out instantly and grabbed his falling friend. The poor man looked up at his saviour, almost hysterical at his new found vulnerability. Each tightened his grip and winked at Peach. With a monumental heave, he managed to hoist the flailing man up so that he could grab hold of the keel line. He did and they both hung there for a moment, swaying in the warm air.

Kemble's trajectory seemed to carry him higher and further than the rest. He flew almost to the top of the central mast, reached out and effortlessly grabbed a dangling cross-line which swung him around and upwards onto the yardarm. His balance was perfect and he landed on the beam, upright and confidently, seventy feet above the ground. He looked down at the spiders-web of netting and picked out Gertie and Pear, swinging upside down to the left of him and Each and Peach swinging half way down the keel line to his right. But there was only one person he was scanning for; Ms Adberg. He shielded his eyes from the bright sun and spotted her, scurrying down the halyard. She was only twenty five feet from the ground, directly in front of him. He took off his belt and wrapped it over the top of her line, which was attached around mast and yardarm that he was standing on.

Benjamin and his men stood in a line on a rickety garret roof with barely anytime to comprehend the madness in front of them. Benjamin Ananas took control and turned to his friends.

"Danilov?" he said, "would you be good enough as to get our boy down?

"Yes, I think I can do that. Antoine, come with me," and at that the two men leapt off the roof and fell fifteen feet down onto the deck of the boat.

"Well boys," said Benjamin to Srdjan and Archie, "will you help me drive these rats into the river?" Both men raised their swords unto the air, huzzahed and jumped down to the deck of the tall ship 'Lady Colleen Anne'.

———•••———

Kemble hooked his belt over the wire and pulled it tight. It held. He looked down at the rope, towards Ms Adberg then passed her and to the Irregulars who had boarded the ship. He snarled and jumped off the yardarm, zipping down the keyline towards Ms Adberg.

Gertie regained his composure and looked up to see Pear grinning madly at him and crawling face first down the rigging with a blade in his jaws demon spider. Gertie hunched up and desperately tried to free his snagged foot.

Each and Peach saw the Irregulars board the ship and nodded to each other in agreement of what had to be done. Each let go of the wire and the men plummeted to the deck. Their fall was broken by tarpaulin and they scrambled to their feet and charged at Danilov and Antoine who were rushing toward the fife rail around the mast which held Gertie's rigging. Danilov leapt onto a small deckhouse midway down the deck and grabbed a line. Antoine swung with his rapier and severed the tied end shooting Danilov into the air and swinging far and wide out over the Thames. The acrobat was immensely strong and held himself firmly in resistance to the inertia that pulled him outwards toward the river. The line pulled tight, then swung round, pulling him back towards the boat.

Antoine turned from the fife-rail and ducked just as Peach's club swung and whacked into the mast. Antoine dived to the side and rolled over the roof of a deckhouse, righted himself and prepared to engage Each and Peach.

Kemble slid towards Ms Adberg and screamed in delight as his feet connected with her ribcage. She flew off the keyline and into a stack of barrels, sending them rolling around the deck. Ms Adberg lay dazzled and dazed across the deck as Kemble loomed over her. He was about to drive the tip of his blade into her throat when Benjamin came diving from the side and tackled him to the ground. Both men skidded along the deck, trading blows with each other. Benjamin managed to get Kemble in a head-lock and attempted to choke the life from him. Kemble thrashed and kicked and was able to wrestle free enough to be able to sink his rotten teeth into Benjamin's arm. Benjamin released him and the evil actor scrabbled forward across the deck.

Srdjan ran over to Ms Adberg, knelt down to her and gently held her face. She smiled, as if half asleep, and kissed the palm of his hand. Archie came over.

"Is she alright, Old Love?"

Srdjan smiled, "Yes, she is going to be alright, go help Antoine!" Archie bowed and dashed over to the deckhouse to the Frenchman, who was struggling to fend off Each and Peach. Srdjan lifted Alexia Adberg into his arms and climbed onto the forecastle where he laid her down to rest. He brushed the hair from her face and revelled in the sight of her delirious blushing.

Pear was almost on top of Gertie. He had a firm grip on the boy's ankle and was presented with a choice. He could unravel the rope and send Gertie to his possible death, or he could stick his knife into him and finish the boy off for sure. It was an easy choice. He held the squirming boy firmly as he raised his dagger. He held it aloft for a few seconds while he selected his point of entry. Gertie was trying to struggle but he truly was between a rock and a hard place. He gritted his teeth in preparation for death when a shadow loomed into their peripheral vision. He and Pear looked to the side to see Danilov swinging in on his wire. He came out of the sun and almost blinded Pear. Gertie screamed out the acrobat's name as he watched him kick Pear square in the face as he landed on the rigging. The knife-wielding heavy spat his teeth into the air and fell from the mesh. Danilov, still swinging, grabbed hold of the unconscious man around his waist and brought him safely around and back onto the rigging and wedged him through it, making sure the thug was secure before going to tend to a relieved Gertie.

"Danilov! I'm so sorry! It's all my fault!" said Gertie panicking that he could die at any moment and desperate to spill out his final words. Danilov glared at him as he undid the boy's ankle and helped right himself onto the rope-net.

"I know why you did it and I know who you did it for. If it were me, I would have done the same...but fail in your job of catching my sister again and I'll kill you myself."

"It'll never happen again" said Gertie with a mature conviction that surpassed his young years. Danilov felt the sincerity in his voice and held out his hand. Gertie took it and they shook hands as men.

Below Danilov and Gertie, Archie and Antoine had their hands full with Each and Peach. Antoine was a skilled fencer. However, Each and Peach were not and attacked him like mad gorillas and with total disregard for the rules of engagement. Archie was, of course, a lover and not a fighter and while he had spirit and courage in his gut, he did not carry himself well in a scrap and as such, Antoine had to fight both Each and Peach and stop Archie from getting clobbered. The two heavies were pushing their opponents back across the deck of the boat, jabbing and swinging wildly.

Kemble and Benjamin had broken free of their brawling and were now fencing across the edge of the hull. Their 'piste' was just the one foot wide rail which separated them from the deck on one side and the murky Thames on the other. Kemble was a trained dancer and easily had the upper hand on Benjamin, however Benjamin was not as exhausted as Kemble and so his bear-strength was to great advantage. They cut and thrust back and forth, cutting lines and rigging with each errant swipe of a blade. The duel was measured but fierce.

Gertie and Danilov carried the unconscious Pear up the rigging and had tied him upside down to the mast. Once they were sure the thug wasn't going anywhere, they turned and looked down to see Archie and Antoine in a tight fix against Each and Peach.

"What do we do?" said Gertie.

Danilov looked down at the keyline in front of him. It ran all the way down to the deck, coming up from behind and in between Each and Peach as they pressed upon Antoine and Archie, forcing the Players towards the forecastle. Danilov kicked the line and assessed its durability.

"Climb on my back."

"What?"

"Climb on my back."

Gertie looked down the key line and the penny dropped.

"You have to be joking!"

Danilov turned to Gertie and smiled. "Only half," he said. Gertie sighed and climbed onto Danilov's back. The acrobat stuck his foot out and tested the tightness of the key line wire.

"Ready?" he said.

"No."

Danilov hopped off of the yardarm and began to walk down the wire towards his troubled friends with Gertie hugging his back.

Archie and Antoine were backing across the ship when Archie tripped backwards over one of the barrels that Kemble and Benjamin and sent scattering. His sudden shift in position threw Antoine's concentration and he turned to his friend. It was all Each needed and he jabbed the Frenchman in his stomach with his club and kicked him backwards. Antoine sprawled back over another barrel and fell on top of Archie. Each and Peach loomed over and were about to strike when Srdjan leapt down in between his fallen comrades and engaged Each and Peach.

The surprise of Srdjan's sudden appearance forced the heavies backwards. They turned around to seek higher ground. As they turned their back on Srdjan, they saw Danilov running down the keyline at full pelt with Gertie on his back. The Acrobat leapt off of the rope and landed in front of them. Gertie dismounted and he, Srdjan and Danilov surrounded Each and Peach.

Archie helped Antoine to his feet and they joined their friends. Each and Peach looked at their reinforced opponents. Then they looked at each other. They dropped their weapons and surrendered. The Irregulars uniformly stepped aside and presented Each and Peach with a tunnel that led to the little walkway onto the bank. Each and Peach didn't need a second invitation and they ran off of the boat and into the back streets of London, never to be seen again.

The Irregulars sheathed their swords, bowed and then hugged one another. Each one took it in turns to give the foolish Gertie a forgiving hug and a ruffle of the hair that proved to the boy how much he meant to the Players. When the congratulations were over, Archie looked around for Benjamin. He was not on the upper deck. Everyone looked around to see where their leader was. The sound of blades clashing enlivened the group once more and they unsheathed their swords and ran to the aft section.

Benjamin and Kemble had fought along the hull's edge and had ended upon the very edge of the poop deck. Kemble's exhaustion was almost overwhelming and he was operating from a place of pure raging hate. His swings were wilder than before and his balance was wavering but still he fought on. Benjamin, on the other hand, was a bear and his strength was seeing him through.

The Irregulars ran up to the stairs to the deck just in time to see Kemble make a foolish and ill-timed lunge. Benjamin parried it easily and riposted straight and true, the tip of his rapier spearing into Kemble's shoulder. The Roxy Players stopped dead in their track and watched as Kemble dropped his sword, wavered on the very edge of the deck rail before toppling overboard. Benjamin dived forward and just managed to grab the actor by the hand.

Kemble hung thirty feet above the water. The sun and the salt in his perspiration had congealed Sheridan's blood and Kemble looked like a barbarian in war paint. He breathed heavily as he swung. He looked up at Benjamin who was hanging half over the railing.

"Drop me, Ananas," snarled Kemble, "kill me! I will not be saved by you! Kill me! Kill me! Drop me! Do it!"

Benjamin's grip was loosening as he struggled to hold the actor.

"KILL ME!" yelled Kemble with a tone of utter conviction and desire. Benjamin gritted his teeth tried to hold on. He almost dropped the actor when another hand came to join his, and another, and another. He looked around him to see his Players surrounding and supporting him. His heart swelled with honour and pride. Together they heaved Kemble back onto the deck. He slumped against the railing, bleeding profusely from his shoulder wound and panting in rage, staring back at his 'saviours' who stood in a line in front of him

"Curse you! Curse you! Blackhearts! Curs!" he screamed, as he held his shoulder. The Irregulars stood over him, tipped their imaginary hats and turned to walk off the deck and towards home, arm in arm.

Kemble watched them all turn and felt a resurgent sense of strength and bloodlust rise inside his heart. He reached to his side and felt his second belt, groping for his dagger He felt its hilt and grinned. Kemble silently got to his feet and drew the blade, looking at the backs of the Irregular's as his mind's eye made an iris around the back of Benjamin's neck. He crept forward and raised the blade, ready to plunge it into the back of their leader's neck.

The Irregulars would forever argue about what had occurred first on that sunny day aboard the 'Lady Colleen Anne' as to whether they heard the shout before they felt the rush of the blade, or the other way round. The only thing they knew for certain was that, on that day, Gertie saved the life of Benjamin Ananas for the first time.

They walked towards the staircase arm in arm and happy when, suddenly, a cold rush befell upon young Gertie and, without even thinking, he thrust Benjamin to the side with the strength of four men. Benjamin tumbled to his right, knocking over Srdjan, Antoine and Archie like bowling pins. Kemble's knife, on the downswing, missed its intended target slashed through Gertie's forearm.

Gertie fell to the opposite side, clutching his arm. Suddenly there came a sharp gust of wind and an accompanying swoosh rocketed in front of Gertie's face as he fell backwards.

Kemble, inbetween Gertie and Benjamin suddenly halted his advance and dropped his knife. Time slowed. Benjamin, on top of Srdjan, Antoine and Archie looked over his shoulder to see Kemble standing beside him. Gertie lay on his back, clutching his arm and looking up at Kemble who was standing like a statue. The actor staggered back across the poop deck, clutching his throat and wheezing awfully. He backed against the railing and faltered for a few seconds. The Roxy Players looked over towards him in bemusement. Kemble groped at something protruding from his throat and pulled it out, sending a little arch of blood splattering across the decking. He looked at the object in his hands with bewildered eyes. He was holding an eight-inch needle.

Kemble gurgled slightly and dropped the needle to the floor. He tried to raise an accusative finger towards his attacker but could not muster the strength. Instead, Kemble toppled backward over the stern of the 'Lady Colleen Anne' and fell into the depths of the black Thames.

The Players looked at each other, and then looked into back towards the top of the staircase where stood Ms Adberg, half of her hair cascading over her shoulder. She casually reached up and pulled another needle out of her hair to send the other half tumbling down.

———•·•———

That evening saw a grand celebration inside The Roxy. The men returned heroes. Upon seeing them storm triumphantly through the theatre doors, Lupe shrieked and burst into a glorious rendition of that Prussian song about the Princess and her glass figurines. Claudia burst into happy tears and ran to Archie. Valerie, flushed with desire also ran toward Archie, however as she ran, she felt a more magnetic force upon her and she swerved from him and fell into the arms of a very surprised Danilov.

Desiree kissed Benjamin three times on each cheek and twice on the forehead as is one of the Umbrian ways. Gertie looked up to the rafters. Anya was up there, sitting on beam and swinging her legs. She waved at him and smiled.

They were all congratulating each other and revelling in their love and relief when they heard the unmistakable low and rumbling growl of Herschel clearing his throat. They stopped their hugging and looked to the back of the stage. There they saw Herschel standing behind a wheeled chair, smiling broadly. Everybody put their hands to their mouths and held back their tears of joy. Tobias sat in the chair, awake and grinning from ear to ear.

The Players rushed over to see him, bombarding him with endless questions and recounting and reenacting their daring rescue. Tobias was so giddy with happiness and drink that they all had to be ushered away to give him room. They dutifully obliged and stood back, basking in the marvellous way in which they had pulled each other through such dark times. It was in this moment that Lupe gave a knowing wink to Archie and the two of them snuck off backstage. Antoine went off to the other side of the stage to find his drinks trolley which he did, and to his wonderful surprise, he also found it fully replenished. He wheeled it back and readily dished out the booze to the thirsty and deserved Players. He opened his mouth to make toast when he found Archie's voice filling the stage instead.

"My loves, my Players, my brothers and sisters in arms," bellowed Archie, "I pray for your ears and eyes for but a few moments!"

They all turned to see the libertine dreamer standing next to Lupe in the centre of the stage. The Players backed up and flanked Tobias in his chair to listen to Archie.

"These few days have been amongst the brightest... and the bleakest of our history. When one of us felt alone in the dark, another would come with a candle to guide their way. We have flown and fallen and we have done it together and we have done it for a common purpose; mainly to get me out of the shit," the Players laughed and raised their glasses, "but also," he continued, "I believe for something greater and though it seems the debt is no more, I feel that we must carry on with our plans. For the love of our art, we have begun to stage a mighty production the likes of which London has never seen and, if all goes to plan, will never actually see, considering the necessary subterfuge we will employ. We few, we happy few, we band of Players who dream and love together and who are conspiring to steal from the rich to enrich the poor. However, now is the time where we stand together and we thrust a single man forward. One of us is about to both reclaim a past glory and forge a new one. One of us is about to take the lead in the performance of all our lives," Archie waved for Benjamin to step forward, to which

Benjamin humbly obliged. Archie turned him around so that he faced the Players.

"One man," he continued, "who has proven time and again to be the best of all of us, the light that guides us and the heart that pumps our blood. But, it is time that this man stood out on his own and became all he can be."

Archie stood behind Benjamin and kicked the back of his legs, buckling him and forcing him to his knees much to the delight of Claudia. Archie signalled to Srdjan who threw Archie a rapier. Archie caught it and walked around to face Benjamin.

"Say goodbye to Benjamin Ananas."

The Players all said their goodbyes as Archie tapped his sword on Benjamin's shoulders.

"And bow and bid welcome to the product of our art and the best of all of us."

Archie held his hand out and helped the humbled Benjamin to his feet. Lupe stepped up and draped the most beautiful coat over his shoulders. Everybody gasped at the garment, cut from the glorious curtains of The Roxy herself and embroidered with heartbreaking skill. Benjamin slipped carefully into the coat. It fit him perfectly and every member of the troupe felt pride, honour and love for the man before them.

"My loves," said Archie as he took a knee, bowing his head, but keeping his bright eyes fixed upon the Players

"Benjamin Ananas is dead; long live Count Abraham von Brandenburg."

Chapter Twenty Six

Love

Lupe led Count Brandenburg by the hand through to the costume department where she flung article after article at him. Shirts, cravats, breeches, waistcoats, hats; all manner were heaped upon him until, when she had finished and turned to look at him, she could not see the man but instead a mountain of velvet, fake silk and cotton. She unpicked the clothes and put them back on the railings, all the while chastising Brandenburg for not taking proper care of her clothes. When she reached the hand embroidered handkerchief, she asked him to show her how he would fold it and, when it was out of his pocket, how he would carry it. He folded it like a man who never considered handkerchiefs before and when he saw her face boil with rage, he asked her if he could try it again. He felt like a school boy who was being forced to eat cabbage. No matter how he tried, his folding could not satisfy Lupe, much to the delight of the Players who had been drawn to the costume department by the ever increasing volume of her protestations. She swore at the poor man in every language she knew.

Eventually, Lupe gave up and in a huff she snatched the hanky from Brandenburg, flung it at Srdjan in disgust and stormed out of the dressing room. Brandenburg looked utterly crestfallen. Desiree smiled and took the handkerchief from Srdjan's face, where it had landed, and told Benjamin that the details of his actions were where the real performance lay. With a softer voice than the one she employed while teaching dance, she kindly showed Brandenburg how to fold and carry the accessory so that, within an hour, the small little cloth had transcended its humble nature and was now an encyclopaedia of Brandenburg's history, mood and attitudes toward the future. When he was confident with the prop, Desiree marched him to Lupe's living quarters and, after she had promised the diva a foot rub and a rosewater manicure, Lupe let Brandenburg perform for her. He rose to the challenge and excelled in his task of folding the cloth. He finished and bowed. Desiree and Brandenburg held their breath while Lupe Darling ran a terrifying eye over his work. She regally stood up and walked over to him. He was hoping for a few kind words and, perhaps a congratulatory hug. Instead he got a ravenous and deep kiss which kidnapped all his senses for its duration. He reeled backwards when their lips parted. However mischievous a woman Lupe Darling was; the confusion in his groin and its refusal to reconcile with his brain was far more so. Desiree stifled her laugh and looked at her feet. Lupe stepped back from the kiss.

"Forgive me, dear Benjamin…I mean Count Brandenburg. For a moment you reminded me of someone. Long ago"

Her eyes fogged over with a glaze of sadness the depth of which he had never seen before. He reached out to touch her shoulder but she recoiled dramatically and sat back in her chair and buried her head in her boa. Desiree and Brandenburg looked at each other, unsure of what exactly what was going on.

"Please," whispered Lupe, "fetch Claudia, I need some peace. Oh, my heart! How you were him. Please, I need peace."

Desiree and Brandenburg bowed and crept out of the room.

"If you bring me one more cup of tea, I'm going to brain you, boy!" growled Herschel as Gertie brought him his eleventh of the hour. The boy was awash with guilt for all his actions over the last few hours. He placed the cup on Herschel's desk and took an eternity to walk back out. Herschel sensed that the boy needed a glimmer of hope of redemption and so, with much huffing and puffing, he put his quill down and told the boy to about face, sit down, spill the beans and chip off so that he could work.

Gertie started with begging for forgiveness which was met with a short sharp clip around the ear from his adoptive father.

"Cut the donkey mess, boy," snapped Herschel after Gertie's begging became too much, "you acted like a fool, that is true....but you acted for love and there has never been a man born who hasn't acted foolishly for love. When the heart is concerned, it's the only way to act."

"How do you cope with it, sir?"

"With what?"

"Well, you write beautiful plays and they're all full of love and your plays aren't foolish. They are intelligent, even if Archie says they are as clever as dung pie."

"Does he indeed? I will have to...thank him for his kind words later."

"So how do you get the fool inside to stop making decisions and get your head to take over? I mean."

"I know what you mean, boy. Come over...I will tell you a secret."

Gertie leant in close to Herschel who whispered to him a grand secret. Gertie's eyes widened as Herschel's words filled his soul. When he had finished, the playwright pushed him away.

"There you see. Now you know. Be gone and let me work," he said dismissively, his head already focused back on his papers.

Gertie was reborn. He stood taller, his heart beat more fervently. He had sought forgiveness and found so much more. Herschel saw a flash behind the boy's eyes and he was filled with paternal pride to see that behind those green pupils, there was a strong and noble gentleman approaching. He smile at the boy and waved him out of the door.

"Oh, one more thing," said Herschel, as Gertie was at the door.

"Yes?"

"Don't tell any old sod the secret I told you. It is Brigand's Law that you are only allowed to tell one person in your whole life."

"As you wish"

"And send in Mr Enfield please, I would like to talk to him about his critiques of my work."

———•◦•———

Srdjan lay Ms Adberg down on his bunk, kissed her on the forehead and went to leave. She stopped him by grabbing his hand. Her exhaustion from the day's exploits had relapsed and she needed rest.

"Please don't go," she whispered, already succumbing to her lethargy. "Stay until I fall asleep."

Srdjan obliged and carefully pulled a chair towards the bunk. He sat down and looked at her.

"Murder…it really takes it out of you," she said lethargically.

Srdjan smiled and held her hand. Ms Adberg's smile washed away and forlorn look rose in its place.

"I'm going to hell for what I did. I know that now." She turned her face from his.

Srdjan stood up and kissed her head once more. She fell asleep.

"Not without me, you're not," he whispered as he pulled a blanket over her and quietly left the room.

He walked through the theatre to the backstairs and up into Tobias's workshop. There he found the metallurgist playing cards with Antoine and sharing a drink. Tobias smiled when he saw Srdjan peering in through the doorway.

"Join us, dear friend! The Frenchman is not a frog...he is a fish!" Srdjan laughed and joined the two men.

"I cannot understand this!" declared Antoine as Tobias scooped another pot. "This man has one less place to conceal his aces, and yet still he wins. Damn the cripple! Damn him!"

Tobias and Srdjan clinked bottles and laughed at the stroppy Frenchman.

"The fish here tells me that Ms Adberg is back amongst us. How is she?"

Srdjan sighed. Tobias understood.

"We have all been through the ringer in these days. But from what Antoine tells me, none more so than Alexia. What a weight she must carry."

Srdjan nodded.

"Perhaps," offered Antoine, "When Tobias is ready to leave the theatre he could take Ms Adberg to confession, or to pray?"

"Damn you both!" smiled Srdjan "if you are not the most glorious of men. Tobias, when you are ready, I can think of nothing Alexia would like more than to go with you to pray."

The three men toasted and went back to their game.

"I didn't think she was a woman of God" said Tobias, casually as he dealt.

"She isn't" smiled Srdjan, "but they still do give free bread and wine, right?"

Desiree and Brandenburg were dancing on the stage when Claudia appeared and watched. Unfortunately, the performance was cut short when Brandenburg stepped on his 'wife's' foot and she kicked him in the shin.

"This is going to take forever!" she protested.

"I'm sorry, I could never do this. I remember now, a dance at the Whit Ball and I was prepared and focused. I had practised on my own for two weeks. Everybody danced except me, you see, and I wanted to impress. I needed to. I practiced so hard. I was ready. And then, when I arrived, a friend of mine told me that my name did not appear on anyone's dance card. Nobody wanted to dance with me. I gave up after that."

Desiree felt ashamed to have been so curt with Brandenburg and realised once again that old adage about there being no such thing as bad pupils, only bad teachers.

"I think you are doing very well!" called Claudia from the side of the stage.

Brandenburg bowed to her. "Thank you Little Mouse, now run to Lupe Darling. She was asking after you." The good girl picked herself up and skipped merrily past the dance couple and stopping only to kiss Desiree and smell her rose skin.

"What do you think is wrong with Lupe?" asked Desiree as they began to dance again.

"I don't know. A memory resurfacing no doubt, poor lamb. She has lived too long and done too much, perhaps. Her poor heart cannot cope."

"She is strong," said Desiree, "and you are too."

"I don't know about that."

"I do, Benjamin."

"It's Brandenburg now."

"Well, I was talking about Benjamin's heart. I have yet to see Brandenburg's."

Brandenburg bowed to her and the partners danced and this time he made no mistake. He danced like a man born to do so and the effect mesmerised Desiree so much that, by the end of their turn, if he had leant down and kissed her, she would not have refused. The Count Abraham von Brandenburg was truly coming together.

———•◦•———

Valerie had been sitting in the small attic space quietly for two hours before Danilov found her. She was looking out at the stars and trying to account for all her life's actions. She had no thoughts of leaping but instead offered up her sadness to the departed Sheridan. She rightly felt that, despite his monetary heart, the man was not deeply evil and perhaps deserved to be remembered as something more than a collector of debts. She thought about the quiet moments when she would see him play his harpsichord or murmur to himself. She would creep up behind and listen to the stream of words pouring from his mouth. There were great soliloquies, memorised and recounted in the private theatre of his mind. He acted tough and had sanctioned some terrible things, but he was not evil. Her nature demanded that she gave at least a few hours to his memory, to his smell, his funny ways and his sense of the dramatic.

"Goodbye, my misunderstood friend," she said quietly, "you will find your way back to the stage when you are in heaven. Good night." She blew a kiss to the night and turned to leave. She was startled to see Danilov half through the hatch, resting his head on his hand.

"What are you doing here?" she said, slightly flustered and desperate to wipe away her tears.

"I was looking for you. I was not spying."

"It's alright. I was leaving anyway."

"No," said Danilov, "stay. It's a beautiful night." He climbed through the hatch and stood in the attic, bathed in moonlight. "Come, sit down and tell me about him. I never had the chance to know him truly."

Danilov sat down on the floor and looked through the skylight. Valerie sat next to him and, over the course of the night, told him everything she knew about Sheridan and in doing so she felt that he would live forever and her heart was no longer heavy.

———•◦•———

Claudia found Lupe lying on the floor and staring up at the ceiling. The mad woman had a vacant look about her and for one awful moment, Claudia thought she had expired. Then she saw a tear wind its way through the wrinkles and cracks in her make-up.

"Lupe? What has happened?"

Lupe Darling lolled her head to the side and looked at the sweet Spanish girl. "Oh my dear Claudia, where have you been?"

"I ha.."

"Oh! How I need you! Help me up! Help me quick, my sweet!"

Claudia tried to heave Lupe up but the girl was not strong enough and Lupe was not helping. Eventually, and with great effort, she managed to roll the huge woman onto her side which enabled her to get to her feet. She did not waste a second and rushed over to the corner of her room.

"Come help me, my love, help me with this!" and she began to throw rags and clothes off of a huge pile.

"Help with what?"

"This! This!"

Claudia shrugged and went to help Lupe throw clothes around the room. After a few minutes, the treasure was revealed. Buried under the mound of clothing was a large and heavy elephant skinned trunk. Claudia's eyes lit up at the discovery.

"A secret treasure!" she beamed, "what is inside? Gold, pearls, rubies?"

"Better," said Lupe, "inside is a treasure more valuable than any other known to man, woman, or Scotsman!"

"If it's so precious, why don't you bury it? Someone could find it!"

Lupe wiped away her tear, her former glory marching back.

"Only I can open this chest!"

"You have a special key? I bet Antoine could pick the lock! He can pick anything!"

"Not this chest. See? No lock!"

Claudia gasped when she saw that Lupe was not lying. There was no lock. The trunk was sturdy, functional and without any exterior decoration of refinement.

"Go on, just try to open it! I will buy you a bun every day until your seventeenth birthday next month if you can open it!"

Claudia smiled. She was no fool. She inspected the case for a latch or release switch. She could find none and eventually slumped down in a huff.

"Show me then!"

"This, my dear, is a love chest! You have to say the magic word to open it!"

"What is the magic word?"

"Well I could tell you, but it wouldn't mean you could use it. Only those that bear the love can open it. It is just any old word to you. Say 'George' to it. I dare you."

Claudia leant into the chest and said, "George". Nothing happened. Lupe kissed the Spanish girl and then shoved her aside. She leant in and closed her eyes. Her lips trembled and she uttered "George" so quietly and with so much pain that the words almost refused to be heard. There was a click and a release of air that sounded like a sad groan. The lid of the trunk opened. Claudia cupped her mouth when she saw the contents; hundreds and thousands of memories - letters, scraps of paper and cloth, pressed flowers, buttons. It was the timeline of a love since past.

"Claudia, I have made love to three thousand, six hundred and twenty seven men. I have been in love eight times that many. But there has only ever been one man to have built a fortress in my heart and my soul. I loved him more than I can ever say. I would hope with all that is left of me that one day, you will love someone as fiercely. But I don't think you will. I don't think anyone will."

Her tears came back and the fell into the trunk and pattered on the envelopes like rain. Claudia reached out and held Lupe's hand. The Spanish Girl's touch brought Ms Darling back to life.

"Forgive me, my love, forgive me," whimpered Lupe, "I had buried the past for many years and earlier, when I saw Mr Ananas...sorry...Count Brandenburg with his handkerchief..." Lupe broke down totally and sunk to the floor, resting her back against the trunk.

"Nothing stays buried, not even the dead," she said, eventually.

Claudia sat next to Lupe and picked a letter from the trunk. She handed it to her.

"Bring him back to life, Lupe, bring him here. I'm not afraid of ghosts."

Lupe was overcome with regret for the past and with love for the gift from God that was Claudia Sanchez-Diaz. She took the letter and began to read it aloud.

Claudia crossed her legs and began to build bridges and answer questions to all her private, internal conflicts. She learnt about love.

———•◦•———

It was around four the morning when Archie heard the screams. He had been nursing the bruise on his jaw administered by Herschel after a stern chat about Archie's 'reviews' of the playwright's works and while he lay there, alone in his bunk, he had fallen into a melancholia. He was not very good at being alone at the best of times, but alone in bed was worst of all. He knew, vehemently, that if he was with his Holy Giselle, he would never feel alone again.

The temporary fulfilment he found in the arms of countless men and women had begun to become even more temporary. Of late, the after-love glow of satisfaction had begun to fade away faster than usual and the emptiness had begun to return faster and faster each time. He had built a fort around his solitude and his vivaciousness had always stood guard. He could never tell anyone, not even Benjamin, that most days Archie Enfield was dying of loneliness.

He was about to close his eyes and search his dreams for Giselle when the screams came. They chilled him instantly as he knew exactly where they came from and what they meant. He had not heard them for years and he had feared their return since he had pitched the scheme to the Players. He knew it might be unearthed and he had been proven right. The screams meant that Benjamin Ananas was having a nightmare - his old recurring nightmare about the harpy Abigail Hardwoode.

Chapter Twenty Seven

Regent Street Redux

His screams rattled the foundations of the Playhouse and the Irregulars, whether alone or sharing their bed, each clasped their hands over their ears and desperately tried to blot out the harrowing sound. They had not heard Benjamin's night terrors in a long time and it was a clear sign that the man was sober enough now to fell the force of his internal maelstrom.

He thrashed around on his bed, possessed by the memories of his youth. In his dream he was confronted by the nightmare of truth. If his dreamscape had been twisted and deformed, his rational mind may have been able to conclude that he was dreaming and therefore overcome the fear and pull himself out of the nightmare. Alas, it was not so; his dreamscape was a perfect reflection of what once was and the minutiae of his youth was recreated before him and duped his rational mind. He was totally within his dream.

Though the dreamscape was an exact representation of what went before, the actions within it were more representative of their emotional impact. His former friend Nathanial Whit bowed to him in an empty hall before running him through with his own sword. Benjamin felt the blade drive slowly into his gut, pulling his organs inwards as the suction of the blade attracted them. He felt the air leave his lungs and fall out of his mouth, his shirt becoming heavy with the thick, warm blood. It was real. Nathanial Whit bowed politely and before Benjamin's eyes, he fell into black smoke and drifted like a thick fog across the floor and down into the cracks in the floorboards. He tried to remove the blade but it was no use. The basket handle, shaped like a pineapple glistened and dazzled him before the light finally fell from his vision.

He awoke inside a hedged labyrinth. His feet were sunk into the earth up to his ankles. He tried to wade, but he could not. The sword remained only this time, the tempered steel blade had been replaced with twisted bark. His skin was brown and cracked. He was melting into the hedge. He could not move. He could not scream. As his veins became roots and tendrils, his eyes flicked up to the dark sky. There, swimming across the sky as if it were an endless pool was Abigail Hardwoode. Around and around she paddled, unobtainable and free. His eyes grew dark once more and became wooded gnarls.

He jolted out of bed, breathless and panicked. The sweat had soaked through his night shirt and even by the light of the guttering candles, he could make out the stain in his image upon his bedding. He desperately tried to reconcile his dream with reality and shut away the fear and pain but for a few awful moments, his mind and his dark chamber were one of the same and he still could not differentiate from nightmare and reality. He breathed heavily, trying to regulate his heart and mood and, after a few moments, he regained control of himself. He looked around his dark room. He could make out the sketches and notations pinned to the walls. He picked up a candle from his bedside table and passed it over the scribbles until the light fell onto a sketch of Brandenburg. He sighed at the image before him. The simple pencil line represented a distant island and he knew that in order reach it, he would have to travel through his nightmare wasteland. And travel alone. He placed the candle back on the bedside table and picked up a bottle of gin. He raised it to the sketch and took a long swig.

"You can do it, you have to or it's going to kill you," he said to himself. He finished the bottle and fell back onto the bed.

He slept undisturbed for the remainder of the night and, upon waking, felt a strange emptiness inside him. He was hollow and tired from the emotional purging the night before. He contemplated falling back asleep. He would have liked to, had Archie not bounded into the room and pretended as if nothing had happened during the night. He clapped his hands annoyingly and threw open the curtains.

"Five minutes, centre stage. Chop-chop Old Love," Archie placed a mug of coffee on the table and cleared away the empty bottle.

"What's going on?" replied Brandenburg.

Archie stopped at the door and smiled, "time to axe that Barnet! Not a moment to lose." He flounced out of the room leaving Brandenburg to heave himself out of bed.

———•·•———

Claudia stood back from the seated Brandenburg and considered his face, lilting her head and squinting at him. She hummed and scratched her chin as she took in the tired and hairy man in front of her. Claudia knew, like other Irregulars who had witnessed his mighty power when wearing his new coat that underneath the matted, long hair and the greying beard there shone a dashing man and it was her job to uncover him.

The rest of the Irregulars had assembled behind Claudia and were sharing coffee and buns. It was a rare sight to see the maestra wield her magic, and today the final touches of Brandenburg would emerge.

Claudia held out her hand and clicked her fingers to summon Gertie who dutifully stepped forward and placed an ornately decorated pair of scissors into her palm. He bowed his head and stepped back. Claudia tapped the scissors against her cheek as she began to walk around a visibly nervous Brandenburg. He tried to remain calm, but the eager faces of the Irregulars in front of him, and the inspecting eye of the Spanish girl unsettled him. He felt naked and on display. Claudia leant in and held out a lanky sliver of his hair. The audience held their breath, tense with anticipation of the first incision. Claudia sniffed the hair and tutted. She let go of it and carried on pacing around Brandenburg. She placed the scissors between her teeth and focused her attention on his face, mentally overlaying a thousand different hairstyles until the right one called out to her

Brandenburg motioned for a coffee and Archie stepped forward to offer a cup. He was halted by Claudia's arm.

"I'll just put this here," he whispered and placed the cup on the floor. Claudia ushered him back with a wave of her scissors. Archie tip-toed backwards and did his best to silently apologise. Claudia turned back to her sculpture in waiting.

"Now," she said, like a maestra about to perform, "we can begin." The Spanish girl walked up to Brandenburg and leant in closely, her eyes inches from his. She winked and he suddenly felt a lot less nervous. She didn't even take her gaze from his face she raised her scissors and made her first snip. A greasy lock fell to the floor, much to the joy of the Irregulars who clapped approvingly.

The floodgates were opened and Claudia's scissors became a blur. The Irregulars could not take their eyes off of the virtuoso display. They reflexively placed their hands over the brim of their cup as the air became thick with hair. Before their eyes, Brandenburg seemed to be growing younger. With each swipe and snip, years fell away. Claudia trimmed the hair to just above the ear, taking great care to finely trim and accentuate the hair line. She flecked out his grey streaks and gently feathered the back of his head until it fell neatly and fashionably into the nape of his neck. She straddled him and began to work on his fringe, running her fingers through his mop and pulling them along the full length in order to gauge how far she would need to go. She pulled a pin from her hair and pinned his fringe back to expose his large, furrowed forehead. She ran her fingers softly around his scalp, massaging and pulling out the knots, then she gently began to snip away the hair.

The Irregulars all craned around trying to see the haircut emerge, but they could not and so they murmured and hypothesised amongst themselves as to what style Claudia was employing. They did not have to wait long. Claudia made her final snip and threw her scissor down with a flourish. They embedded themselves into the floorboard with a twang. Lupe silenced the gossiping Players and they all looked on as Claudia climbed off of Brandenburg.

His hair was more than perfect. Short and feathered at the back and with an ultra-modern fringe that hung to the side of his face and had length enough to just be swept behind his ear. She had somehow magically concealed a lot of his grey hairs and those that she had left had been swept into the fringe. The Players were awestruck.

"It's perfect," said Valerie, "absolutely perfect."

"No, not quite," said Antoine as he stepped forward. "We have to do something about that beard. The hair is perfect but with that beard it just looks like we have put a crown upon a badger."

Claudia nodded and looked at Antoine, fixing him with a curious squint. She slowly bent down and pulled the scissors out of the stage floor.

"Antoine, would you be kind enough as to come here, please?" she asked.

Antoine stepped forward, suddenly filled with trepidation.

Archie leant into Valerie's ear and asked her to fetch water and a razor from Tobias' workshop and she scuttled off merrily. Archie then leant to the side of the stage and picked up a second chair and placed it next to Brandenburg who was clearly overcome with fear. He began pawing his beard.

"No...not the beard. Please! Not the beard!" he pleaded.

"Sorry Old Love," said Archie, "it's time for the soup catcher to go."

"You can't make me!" protested Brandenburg.

"PARA!" shouted Claudia, who only spoke in Spanish when she wanted to really assert her authority. Brandenburg shut up instantly.

"It will grow back, Old Love, it will grow back," said Archie, reassuringly, leaning over and patting Brandenburg on the shoulder.

Valerie returned with a bowl of water and razor and handed it to Archie, who placed it onto the floor next to the coffee cup, which he handed up to Brandenburg who refused it.

"I could use a real drink"

Archie looked over to Lupe who fished inside her huge wig until she found what she was looking for. She pulled out a bottle and tossed it over. Archie caught it, bit off the cork, took a swig and handed it to Brandenburg who glugged furiously all the while looking over at Claudia who was preparing the razor.

She looked over at Antoine and memorised his moustache. Archie stood behind Brandenburg and tilted his head back in preparation. The poor man had a genuine look of sadness and fear in his eyes.

"Buy you a pint after, Old Love," said Archie.

Brandenburg relaxed a little at the thought of a prize. Archie gave Claudia the nod to proceed and proceed she did. To the side of the stage, Srdjan cheered at the sight of Brandenburg's beard falling to the floor.

"I don't know what you are laughing at!" smiled Archie. "You're next!"

Srdjan's laugh fell away and he too felt his beard.

"What," he said, "why mine?"

"You're the understudy!"

"Yes, I am, in a way."

"And an understudy goes all the way," added Desiree, smiling to the side of the group.

"Well….you say that," weaselled Srdjan, "but do you really…."

"I hate that beard anyway" interjected Ms Adberg. Srdjan hung his head in defeat.

"Thank you, Ms Adberg," said Archie. Ms Adberg nodded back.

Claudia stepped away and flicked the water off of the razor. She wiped the stubble from Benjamin's forlorn face and gave him a kiss on each eyelid.

"Gaupo," she whispered.

Benjamin stood up and dusted himself off. The man was complete. After seeing the new and beautiful man before him, Srdjan raised his hand slowly.

"I'm in," he said and made to sit in the chair.

———————

Count Abraham Von Brandenburg stood in front of Lupe's twelve foot dress mirror. She had wheeled out Lord Mirror especially for him and for good measure had also positioned a few minor dignitaries so that he could see himself from every angle. His waistcoat fitted nicely and the sheen deflected light well, erasing a good three inches from his waist. His shirt was crisp and bright and his cravat was suitably ludicrous. He turned and tilted to take in the sight before him. Lupe stepped from beside Lord Mirror and helped him into his frock coat.

"You are amazing," she said, beaming with pride.

"It's all a costume," he replied, modestly.

"Nonsense, colour fades, cloth becomes threadbare," she said as she began to brush the velvet jacket and straighten his belt and braces, "but the man remains. Some things always remain." Lupe's voice wavered and Brandenburg saw an expression pass over her face. She inhaled heavily and rallied herself.

"Forgive me, dear Count," she said, "but you are the very ghost of someone. Forgive me, dashing spectre of love itself!"

Brandenburg bowed to her and Lupe Darling curtsied back. From the doorway, Archie cleared his throat. He was dressed as a gentleman. Not as fine as the Count, but adequate enough to be a well kept man-servant. He threw a polished cane to the Count.

"Show time, Brandy, you ready?"

Brandenburg looked at Lupe for some final reassurance and found it in her eyes. She truly believed in him.

"I'm ready," he said.

The two men left the dressing room and stepped out onto the stage. There, they found the rest of the Players, all eager to see their creation stride across their hallowed boards and out into the sunshine. Archie emerged first to wolf whistles and cat-calls which he batted back by blowing raspberries and sticking his fingers up at them. Brandenburg emerged to a stunned silence. The air in the theatre was sucked into the lungs of the Players as they gasped in unison. He stood in the wings and in one instant stole the hearts of every single one of them.

Herschel began to clap, overcome by seeing his words live. His character was alive, breathing before him. Soon the Irregulars were all clapping. Then cheers to accompany the claps. Brandenburg stepped fully onto the stage and bowed before them all. He smiled proudly before them and felt the touch of a something light fall onto his head. A single white petal fell to the floor. Then another, and then another. Soon, it was raining flowers inside The Roxy Playhouse. They looked up to see Anya on the rafters, sprinkling the petals onto her friends. Brandenburg saluted her, and together with Archie walked out of the theatre and into the warm afternoon sun.

"How do you feel?" asked Archie as he and Brandenburg stood at the mouth of Regent Street once more.

"I feel good, confident. I can do this."

"I was referring to last night and your nightmare."

"You heard that?"

Archie smirked.

"Just a dream. I'm fine."

"You sure?"

"Positive. Let's do this."

"Now remember," said Archie, "don't stand beside me, always in front. Don't look at me when you hand me hat or cane. If you engage in conversation with anyone, keep eye contact and remember the cardinal rule. Above all, you are the centre of the world. Savvy?"

Brandenburg nodded. "See you on the other side, my friend!" and he began to march off into the throng of Regent Street.

"Dear God help us" whispered Archie as he walked behind his man.

When one is clean, shaved and wearing a nice jacket, Regent Street becomes a totally different place. The Count had taken only a few steps before he saw a hat being tipped in his direction. He had already walked on before he had time to register the gesture. He turned to tip his hat in return but the man had already disappeared. Instead Brandenburg saw Archie looking at him and urging him to carry on. He turned back and continued further into the fray. A few more hats were tipped along the way and many, many fans were fluttered and eyelids batted in his direction. Indeed, the very same pair of women who scuttled past in disgust when they had originally walked down the street had this time gravitated towards him, pouting their lips and whispering into each other's ears. Brandenburg did not miss a beat and did his best impression of Archie with a smile and a wink which sent the women floating off into the afternoon. He was getting used to this persona. His stride grew in gait and confidence and he puffed his chest out and raised his chin slightly.

Archie was satisfied with the reactions of the passersby and he himself received a few nods and salutes from the various servants and dogsbodies. However, he was slightly concerned with the overt nature of Brandenburg. The man was revelling in his role, which was no bad thing, however the man was bordering on the ridiculous. His stride made him look like he was measuring a tennis court and his chin was so high in the air, his hat was in danger of falling off the back of his head. Archie whipped out his pocket book and began to make performance notes.

Brandenburg was in full swing when he took a side step to avoid a puddle and bumped into a man striding in the opposite direction. He turned to apologise and stopped dead in his tracks. His hat fell off of his head. The man whom he had collided with turned back to Brandenburg.

"I say sir, I do apologise. Forgive me," said the man as he bowed. Brandenburg remained frozen. Archie caught up with them and picked his man's hat up from the road.

The stranger, realising an apology wasn't coming from Brandenburg tipped his hat and walked off. A cold dread had overcome the Count. Archie handed him his hat.

"Your hat, sir"

Brandenburg didn't take it. He was like a stature. A cold sweat had broken out over his forehead.

"Your hat, sir!" repeated Archie waving the hat under Brandenburg's nose, "Benji..." he whispered forcefully, "take the hat!"

Archie looked around at the people walking by. A few had begun to notice the well dressed statue on the roadside.

"Archie," whispered the Count in a dry, cracked voice, "I really need a drink."

"Sure, sure, Old Love. We're almost out the other side. Come on now, let's be on our way."

Archie threw caution to the wind and sacrificed the rehearsal by putting his arm around his friend and leading him down the street.

The character of Count Abraham von Brandenburg had been all but dispelled by that chance meeting. The man whom he had just bumped into was none other than Nathanial Whit and with him he brought the curse of memory. Benjamin was shattered.

Chapter Twenty Eight

Brandenburg has an Idea

A rchie did not tell the other Players about Brandenburg's encounter on Regent Street. In all honesty, he was not sure entirely what had happened or what it meant. He took his friend for a few drinks around Tottenham Court Road in the hope that after a few scoops, the man's tongue would loosen. It did not. Instead, he had found himself drinking opposite an increasingly introverted man. By the time they stumbled back through the doors of The Roxy, Archie was nicely battered and Brandenburg seemed coldly sober. Srdjan and Antoine were sitting on the stage playing cards when the two men entered. They called for the others to come and join them in welcoming home the performers, only to be greeted by an entranced Brandenburg who walked straight passed them all and into the gloomy theatre to seek out his chambers. They tried to question the drunken Archie, but he waved them away with a casual flick of the wrist before tripping over nothing and falling onto the floor. He picked himself up and pushed his way through the crowd of performers and swayed through the stage. Only Claudia's voice seemed to penetrate his drunken fog and, upon hearing it, he reeled around and bowed to her.

"My loves. Forgive me...I appear to be....slightly discombobulated"

His loves folded their arms and rolled their eyes. Desiree cleared her throat in the way teachers do to get the attention of wayward students. Archie snapped to and smiled at her. She half-smiled back and raised her eyebrow.

"Yes, right, umm…" he said, finally, "it has come to my attention that a few…inconsistencies have arisen with our performer. And as such, we are closing production of Brandenburg until….until…." he lost his train of thought as he spied a little petal on the stage. He picked it up and ate it.

"Until when?" asked Desiree in a stern voice, "Archie, until when?"

Archie looked up from his meal and squinted at the congregation.

"Tomorrow…maybe the day after… maybe indefinitely. Take a break, have a drink! We are…" he wandered off into the backstage area and promptly fell over what sounded like a stockpile of cymbals. The Players turned to each other when Archie's voice drifted out once more.

"Hello my beauty, are ye married? You are? And where…" Archie's snores drifted from the under the pile of whatever it was he had collapsed into and the Players looked at each other despondently.

"Fantastic!" declared Herschel, "they've gone out on the piss! No doubt they sunk a few at our expense, wandered into some posh nob's eatery, made tits of themselves and blown the whole script! I knew we couldn't rely on those soaks!"

Desiree rubbed his back tenderly to calm him down. "I do not know," she said "Benjamin seemed…," she tried to find her words but could not.

"Pissed is the word you're looking for," growled Herschel. "He seemed utterly rollaxed!"

"Merde!" shouted Antoine as he threw his cards onto the stage. Lupe covered Claudia's ears instinctively. "What a pretty waste of time!" he shouted, "I was ready! I was going to be magnificent!" and he began to 'disappear' the remaining deck of cards up his sleeves.

Lupe whispered in Valerie's ear and she scuttled off to retrieve Antoine's drinks trolley. As soon as he heard the sound of the bottles he stopped playing with the cards.

"Yes! Yes!" he shouted in a happier voice, "a million times yes! We will drink and sing sad songs to the performance that never was! To the great Antoine, who never got his moment of glory!"

"Whatever gets your goolies in a Gondola, my foolish frog," said Herschel who took a bottle from the cart, "your trickery and sleight of hand was nothing compared to the grandeur of my character! Nothing! I'm drinking to the greatest script never bloody spoken!"

"Nonsense, you daft Billy-ho!" interjected Lupe, "did you not see his fine costume! And his hair cut? Your words would have been trapped within that great hedge around his face had it not been for my clothes that inspired Little Mouse here to do her work!"

The Players all began to argue about the validity of their input, each one declaring that their own contribution to be the jewel in the crown of Brandenburg.

Only Valerie drank quietly, knowing deep down that it was her wonderful passion that sparked the idea in Archie. If only they knew what a muse she was.

———•◦•———

As soon as he opened the door the smell from within slapped Brandenburg in the face and he awoke from his trance and fell into his chamber. The alcohol Archie had plied him with suddenly coursed through his veins and the room began to blur and swirl. He managed to close the door before tripping over a bottle and falling hard on the floor. He began to convulse and shiver slightly. He reached up and pulled the blanket from his bed and wrapped it over himself. He had not even kicked off his boots before he had fallen into a deep, gin-soaked sleep.

His dreamscape did not offer any solitude and, as with the night previous, he found himself traversing a land peopled with ghosts of the past. He was standing in the middle of a huge masquerade ball. All around him people danced, swooping in close to him, their pointed, evil masks scratching at his clothes and skin. He could not move. He looked down at his feet to see that they had melted into the floor. The wooden grain of the floorboards was weaving its way up his legs. He tried to scream, but no sound came out. Instead the swirling dancers began calling out his stage name.

"Welcome, Count Brandenburg," came one.

"How wonderful! You came," another said.

"Would you dance with us all?"

The voices grated at him and seemed to appear inside his soul before his ear. The panic began to rise up in his gut as he looked around the room. He recognised where he was. The ballroom was not a product of his sorrow's architect. The ballroom was a place he remembered; it was an actual - a physical construction. The panic subsided and he found that he could move. He lifted his feet out of the floorboards and, to his liberating joy he began to float above the dancers. The sensation of flying was palpable and seemed as real as the wooden panelling along the walls. He glided over the heads of the dancers and spun in time with the music. He looked over the portraits hanging on the walls and felt as if he was reacquainting himself with long lost friends. He knew exactly where he was and that he could control his dream. It was in that moment of divine realisation that he woke up.

He had not been sweating and he was certain that he had not screamed in his sleep. He sat bolt upright and his eyes flicked around the room as if they had seen a fairy dancing in the candlelight. He chased the dream and the idea it had sparked. He was battling that moment when one wakes from sleeping and watches one's dreams sail away. He held onto the moor line and pulled his dream back to the pier. He remembered the dream. The idea was saved. He laughed to himself. It was a free, relived laugh.

"Perfect...it's perfect" he said before scrambling to his feet and throwing his coat on.

———•••———

The Players were drunk and singing and had all but forgotten about poor Tobias Strong who was stuck in his workshop. Ordinarily, he was happy to spend his hours in there, but that was before he was denied the ability to stroll out the door. He could hear their revelry and focused harder on his work to blot out the noise. The pain in his stump was ever-throbbing and he had to bite his lip from not shouting in frustration. His faith saw him through the worse part and his work the other.

He was busy preparing a faux silver candelabrum, resplendent with roses in bloom to hold the candles. Claudia's recollection of the details of the flower had aided him greatly in creating the authentically moulded petals. He was happy with his work and truly felt the hand of God as he carved the intertwining stems into the trunk of the candelabrum.

"Tobias?" called Brandenburg from the doorway. No reply. "Mr Strong!" Tobias was jolted from his pious work.

"Benji…I mean, Count Brandenburg"

"What are you working on?"

"Ah, a candelabrum! A rose-bush candelabrum. Would you like to see?" asked Tobias, holding his work out for inspection.

"No time. Stop that project. Have you started the sword?"

"Not yet, I wanted to…"

"Start immediately. You have a fortnight."

The Count left the doorway. Tobias picked up the candelabra and wheeled it to the other side of the workshop. He opened a draw and pulled out Brandenburg's sketches for his spider-basket rapier. He inspected them and rubbed his chin.

The Count reappeared in the doorway.

"Thank you, Tobias, I did not mean to be so curt but I have had an idea."

And he left again. Tobias crossed himself and kissed his crucifix.

"And come with me!" came Brandenburg's voice from the wings of the stage. Tobias wheeled himself out of the room.

———•◦•———

Brandenburg entered to the stage area to find half of the troupe embroiled in an elaborate dance marshalled by Desiree and the other half huddled in the corner drinking and laughing. He cleared his throat and they stopped instantly.

"Sobered up, have we?" huffed Herschel.

Brandenburg ignored the playwright and clicked his fingers at Antoine and Srdjan.

"You two, come with me. You, Danilov, go help Tobias," and he turned and walked back into the storage area. Srdjan and Antoine shrugged and went after Brandenburg while the acrobat went to fetch the metallurgist. The rest of the group retreated to the edge of the stage where they gathered together into a tight pack.

"What's going on?" said Valerie, a note of concern in her voice. Lupe frowned and was about to respond when the cry of "Archie Enfield!" thundered through the theatre. The sound reverberated through the rafters and nearly sent Anya crashing to the floor. The Irregulars braced themselves, fearful that the ground was about to open up.

"ARCHIE!" the thunderclap came once more.

"I would say" whispered Herschel, "that our man Benjamin has had an idea."

There was a clatter and a tumble from stageleft and Archie Enfield sprung up from the gloom and bounced onto the stage.

"Husband? Has your husband come home? Has he found us? Cover up, my dear, we are being hunted by your hus..." he stopped when he realised where he was. He dusted himself off. He noticed the other Players staring at him. "I was... that was... I am... it was from a play... What's going on?"

"The bear has had an idea," said Herschel. Archie stopped dusting himself off.

"What? Has he said..."

"Not yet" said Lupe. "We can ex..."

"I HAVE HAD AN IDEA, WHY AM I WAITING FOR YOU PEOPLE?" yelled Brandenburg from offstage.

The Players hung their heads.

"What's going on?" said Valerie.

"It's Benjamin," said Danilov as he wheeled Tobias into the group and sidled himself up to Valerie, placing his arm around her shoulder.

"Every once in a while," interjected Herschel, "he has..."

"An idea" continued Desiree "and for a few moments…"

"The bear roars," finished Lupe.

"Don't worry", it won't last," Archie lied.

Srdjan and Antoine emerged from the storage area carrying two large, blank flats. They propped the twelve by six foot boards against the backdrop of the stage. Brandenburg stormed on stage and squared up to Archie.

"You're in my way. Go join the others."

Archie scuttled over to the Irregulars and scooped up a drink from the floor. Srdjan and Antoine righted the boards and joined the others also.

"It occurs to me, that of late," began Brandenburg with a stern and steady tone, "we have spent too much time focusing on the first act and not enough on the second."

Herschel went to protest but the look shot from Brandenburg made him think twice.

"We have our character, Count Abraham Von Brandenburg – a product of…"

All the Irregulars went to raise their hands to claim credit.

"…a PRODUCT, of all our efforts. However, we now need a purpose, a goal, a mark. We need to define our creation. Contrast him. Pit him a challenge. Something big, magnificent, not the petty thievery of trinkets and watches scooped up from second rate dance halls. We need a performance worthy of Count Abraham Von Brandenburg."

"Alright, what do you have in mind?" said Archie as he struggled to uncork his bottle of gin.

Brandenburg smiled, walked over to the boards and picked up a paint pot and brush. He dipped the brush into the thick, black paint and wrote 'NATHANIAL WHIT' in two foot letters across the flats.

The troupe murmured. Brandenburg put the paint pot down and turned to them. He rubbed his hands and smiled.

"Nathanial Whit?" said Archie, "that's our second act? Are you pulling our legs?"

"Who is he?" said Valerie.

"He's an old acquaintance of Mr Ananas," said Herschel gravely.

"You can say that again" said Archie in a serious and challenging tone. He stepped forward to stand in between the troupe and their leader.

"Wait a tick," he said, the penny dropping, "was that the fellow who gave you a Gorgon's stare earlier?"

"What do you mean?" said Herschel.

"Of course!" said Archie as the cork at last came out of his bottle both literally and metaphorically. "I see now!" and he turned to the others to address them. "You see, earlier today as you know we were on Regent Street. Our man here is swanning down about, making himself seen. He was doing alright too - if a little overt - tipping his hat here, bowing there. People are looking and I start to think that all this might work when he suddenly bumps into some posh tosser which sends his hat flying. I go over and hand him his topper only to find our man here stiff as a post, white as a sheet, marble. Proper scared rigid he was. I couldn't figure what had spooked him. It was the bloke, wasn't it? You bumped into Whit, didn't you?"

"I did" said Brandenburg firmly.

"Who is Mr Whit?" repeated Valerie.

"Mr Whit, dear Ms Folk," Archie said, "is only the fellow who kicked our man here hardest when he was down. Mocked him, threw him to the wolves. Cast him...well you get the idea. And now you have the fancy clothes and have seen him out and about, you want a bit of payback!"

"Performance!" cried Brandenburg.

"Performance or revenge?" asked Archie.

The Players froze. Nobody had ever challenged Benjamin on one of his ideas before, mostly because they were very good ideas, but also partly because it wasn't necessarily a good idea to stick ones head in a bear's mouth and then kick him in the privates.

"You are right, Mr Enfield, you are right," said Brandenburg, "he is right, Mr Whit was once a friend, and was indeed the man to whom I turned to in my darkest hour and who spat in my face. And I will not lie to you, I did once dream of my revenge upon him. But that was many years ago. I am an old man now, and revenge is a young man's game. Besides, I am not so arrogant as to put your necks on the line so that I can settle some pithy score. My dear Irregulars, I love you like children of my own. Each and every one of you and I would offer my life in an instant if it meant your safety and happiness. So, I beseech you, forget vendettas and whatever else you think I might be seeking for a second and contemplate what Mr Whit represents to us all. Not just me, but to all of us; to our future and the future of the Playhouse. I ask you to trust me now, trust in my love and my intentions here. He is our best opportunity at rebuilding this theatre and bringing some hope to Borough...and to London herself! Trust in me, I beg you"

Archie looked at his friend and saw conviction and truth in his eyes. He looked back at the Players who each seemed convinced that Benjamin's motive was more than revenge. He smiled.

"Well...when you put it like that," he said and patted Brandenburg on the cheek and handed him his bottle of gin.

"So then," said Herschel, "this acquaintance of yours. Why him, if it is not revenge?"

Brandenburg smiled broadly.

"Not just any old acquaintance, my good man but a very, very rich acquaintance. An acquaintance whose manor I have walked through, eaten in, slept in."

The group began to see the plan unfold. Herschel rubbed his chin and began to pace around the stage.

"I see," said the playwright, "the setting is known and the stage is already set. If you draw us a floor plan of that stage then maybe we go in one night, have a look-see at what trinkets they have. Take little Claudia."

"Halt thee there, Old Love," interjected Archie, "Claudia is front of house, where I can keep a watchful eye on her."

"No," said Claudia, "I can do this. Anya and Danilov will look after me. I can have a look around, see what sort of goodies they have, remember them all, come home then tell Tobias."

"Right!" agreed Antoine, "the master will make perfect replicas and then we go in a second time with the fakes, swap them over. Robert is the brother of the mother!"

The group looked at him.

"He means 'Bob's your uncle" said Archie."

"Why don't you just steal the stuff in the night?" asked innocent Valerie.

"We are not common thieves my dear!" scoffed Herschel, "we are artists. And besides, if we blagged everything it would make it a lot harder to fence."

"Indeed," continued Archie, "if they don't report nothing missing, nobody will come a lookin'. Easy as pie."

"And, if you think I'm performing the role of the Thief in the Night without an audience, you can think again!" declared Antoine. "No, no, no, right from under their noses, or not at all!"

"Herschel, what date is it?" asked Brandenburg.

"Fourteenth."

"That gives us three weeks to prepare. We will need stage-plans, Herschel, you can help me with that. Scouting; Anya, Danilov, Claudia and Srdjan. Transport; Gertie and Archie, we're going to need a carriage and horses. I trust you to acquire these items. Lupe, I'm going to need more costumes and Desiree too. I will need a wife. Mr Strong, Ms Folk, you two will be in charge of props. Once Tobias has his designs, I will entrust you to catalogue them all and make sure that whatever we take, we replace. Can you do that?"

Valerie nodded.

"Good girl. Ms Adberg, will you be so kind as to teach Desiree the finer points of swordplay. Herschel, it's just a precaution in case we run into any trouble. Trust me I have no desire to see danger at all. So, we have exactly three weeks tomorrow to get Brandenburg and his wife into the very thick of Society. Three weeks to entrench ourselves so deeply that people will not be able to utter a sentence without it having the name 'Brandenburg' hanging off of it. Any questions?"

"And what happens in three weeks?" said Archie.

"In three weeks time, our mark will hold his annual masquerade ball. It is the event of the calendar. Everyone will be there and it will be the perfect time to do what we have to do. Three weeks until curtains up."

There was a palpable sense of excitement in the air.

"Understand?" Everybody nodded and beamed. "Good...get to work" he turned and marched off the stage.

Before he left the stage, Brandenburg turned back to them and smiled at Desiree

"And one more thing, Ms Ricci, in three weeks time my dear, I want to be able to dance every reel, minuet, quadrille waltz and polka you know."

Count Abraham Von Brandenburg left the stage and The Roxy Players cracked open drinks to celebrate

"The game is afoot!" floated the Counts deep voice from backstage. And indeed, it really was.

Part Three

In Like Brandenburg

Chapter Twenty Nine

Training

The golden hour of light had come and gone London was bathed in the warm, magical hues of twilight. It was such an all pervasive tone that it and somehow seeped into the psyche of the Londoner and throughout the town, the general pace of life slowed somewhat and the attitude of the populous lifted. The harsh day was coming to a close and the night was drawing in and, as the ochre tones danced off of the Thames and dappled the eyes of the put upon, each and every single one took, in their own way and at their own speed, a little time to take stock and smell the roses. The collective, unspoken but understood consensus amongst the people was that, in fact, the world really was a wonderful place and London was the heart of it. You could hear it the in quiet clinks of the drinker's glasses as they brought them together and in the elevation of the cabbie's hats that tipped to all as their carriages rolled around the town. Even the doormen who kept guard at the more dangerous drinking holes managed to raise half a smile between them all.

The magical effect of twilight permeated The Roxy Playhouse easily and, as is the way with artists, they had become more susceptible to the power of shifting weather hues. A quiet industry had brewed in the theatre and everybody was happy with their work. However, there was no time to bask on the stage and drink wantonly from Antoine's drink trolley or gorge upon Desiree's rosewater sugar-glass props. There was work still to do, and preparations still to make. But, the mood of the world outside helped them greatly.

After three days intensive training in the art of stage fighting, Desiree was ready for inspection. Srdjan sat at the side of the stage, cutting chunks out of his apple as was his way and looking over her stance. Ms Adberg appeared from the dressing area, dressed in breeches and sporting a thickly padded torso-plate. She walked over to her student and saluted her. Desiree saluted back and stood on guard. Ms Adberg inspected Desiree's grip, running her eye down both sides of the Italian's blade, from foible to forte. Her position was sound. She walked around her pupil, inspecting her feet and legs which seemed loose yet coiled. She looked over her exposed, muscular back and ran her fingers over the long green scar left over from the rafter accident.

"Does this hurt you?" she whispered.

It did, but Desiree had spent too many years on point to let the pain show through her eyes.

"No," she said without any emotion.

Alexia straightened Desiree's neck slightly and raised her chin.

"Alright then," she said as she moved around to confront her student. She raised her sword. "Let's see what you can do."

Alexia Adberg did not treat her student with kid gloves and began to advance aggressively, driving Desiree backwards; step, step, step, faster and faster before delivering an explosive ballestra and lunge. Desiree, on the back foot, could not parry in time and caught the point in her breast.

"One point to me," said Alexia, turning her back on Desiree and without checking to see if she was harmed. Desiree rubbed her breastplate and rotated her shoulder. She looked over to Srdjan who offered no compassion but simply ate his apple.

"Watch your footwork," he called from the wings, "keep your head, keep cool. It is only a sword - it doesn't have a mind of its own"

Desiree shook off and nodded. She exhaled sharply and stood on guard once more.

"It's only a sword, it's only a sword." she whispered to herself as she focused on her opponent. *'I am the student, again'* she thought as she recalled the hardships she had endured at the dance academy. She remembered how unforgiving training was and, luckily, remembered how she had excelled in taking the knocks and realising that masters were being harsh for her own good. She knew it was time for business and so she did not protest or quit but instead took the pain of Alexia's strike and broke it apart so that she could learn and adapt from it. She clenched her teeth, focused her mind and the two fencers returned to their starting positions. They saluted and Alexia lunged in a flash. This time, Alexia did not land an easy point and Desiree managed to fend off her first attack. Her confidence rocketed and she was suddenly able to reconcile her inherent sense of balance with the new fencing skill set she had learnt. Srdjan stood up and clapped as the two women began to duel in a surprisingly well matched fight.

"Bravo!" he shouted, happy to be witnessing some good sport.

———•◦•———

"Which do you think?" said Lupe as she dangled two different coloured boas in front of Claudia's face. The Spanish girl was too engrossed in reading the letters from the secret George chest to pay much attention and she absent-mindedly pointed to the left boa. Lupe looked at it and suddenly felt as if she was looking upon the colour for the first time. She grimaced. "Oh no, not this, it is disgusting!" and she held it at arm's length, as if it was a rotting skunk. She sashayed across her dressing room and dropped it in the boa-graveyard by the dress mirror.

"No, no," she said to herself, "Desiree needs blue. Lightning blue! That is the colour of her heart, everybody knows that." The mad woman held out her arm towards a stack of poles resting against a dress rail and looked up to the clothes rack, high up in the rafters.

"Claudia, dearest," she said, still looking up to the eaves, "hand me the pole with the hook on it, please." She waited. No pole crossed her palm. She clicked her fingers impatiently. Nothing. She looked over to the girl by the chest.

"Honestly girl," she huffed, "I should never have…"

Lupe stopped talking the moment she saw Claudia's shoulders shaking and her head bobbing.

"My God, are you crying?" cried Lupe, clasping her hands over her mouth in horror.

Claudia sniffed and Lupe gasped again. She picked up her largest bear-fur shawl and rushed over to the girl, sank down next to her and threw the great, warm shawl around them both.

"What is the matter, dear Mouse? You poor girl, tell Lupe!"

Claudia gently folded the letter up and placed it back into the chest.

"Will I ever be in love?" she said through her sniffles. Lupe's heart nearly broke with melancholia. She pulled the Spanish girl in tight to her huge breasts.

"You have sailed all the seas and loved all the men and women of the world," whimpered Claudia. "Will I do that? What will become of me? Will I have a secret love chest like yours? Will I be happy? Will I grow up?"

Lupe gently rocked the young girl and kissed her head over and over again. "I don't know, young Claudia. I don't know...I am old, but I am not a fortune teller!"

Claudia tried to laugh through her tears.

"Can I tell you a secret?" said the Spanish girl in a quivering whisper.

"You can tell me anything, my angel"

"I love Archie...I really do! But he loves women, and I am just a girl."

Lupe smiled as the penny dropped.

"Oh my dear, you waste perfect tears on that fool; so sweet, so sweet!"

"But what am I to do?"

Lupe Darling broke off her hug and stood Claudia up so that she could wipe away the tears and clear the hair from her face. She sighed.

"My dear, with a face like yours and the years ahead of you, having a crush on Mr Enfield is the least of your troubles. You are going to break a million hearts just by breathing."

"But what am I to do now?"

"I remember my first love," sighed Lupe, "he was eleven and I was eight. He was a forest child."

"Forest child?"

"Yes, you see I grew up in a little town called Pushtia, surrounded on all sides by mountains and enchanted forests."

Claudia's eyes began to fire with interest and imagination.

"We called them the Woods of Bewilder. Anyway, he was a forest child all wild and clothed in ferns and moss, a huntsman and an archer. I used to stray into the woods to pick blossoms and seek out the imps and will o'wisps...and to seek out Karol, the boy. He would always find me first and together we would venture into the heart of the woods. We would talk to the trees. We would sit on giant lily pads and drift over the lakes. I loved him dearly, but his heart, well his heart was for the forest and not for me."

"How did you know? What did you do?"

"Well as I grew up a little and my feelings changed from a girl's love to a woman's love and I would try to keep him near. I tried to kiss him, tried to hold him, tried to grow up with him in an intimate way."

"And..."

"And nothing, my sweet. This is a story that had no tumbling and frolicking. After I realised that he did not feel things as I felt them, as I grew older I began to see less and less of Karol. I stopped wandering into the Woods of Bewilder and I started finding more intriguing and exotic boys in the village."

"That sounds sad."

"No, no, my angel, quite the opposite, you see. If I hadn't loved Karol and he hadn't rejected me, well, not rejected me; it isn't the right word. If he had considered me in the intimate way, then I would not have been able to understand heartbreak, and therefore I would not have been able to understand love and its value. By not loving me as I thought I wanted he gave me the gift of love that I really unknowingly needed. And because of that, I have this." Lupe hit the side of the secret George chest. "Everything I have ever loved or hated has sprung from the seed that I planted for Karol and which he watered. Everything. Do you understand, my love?"

Claudia shook her head.

"I do not, but I think that it is something I will not understand until I have learnt it."

Lupe Darling wrapped the bear-shawl around them both, and hugged Claudia close to her once more.

"Boys, my sweet Claudia, they are nothing but fools and thieves! But how fun are their games and how sweet their tongues."

————•◦•————

Herschel poured the rest of the bottle into two glasses and handed one to Brandenburg. He then placed the empty bottle on the corner of a large piece of paper. There were three more empty bottles pinning down the other corners. Brandenburg sipped his gin and looked over the paper. Upon it, there had been drawn a great floor plan of Eveltham House, the mansion of the family Whit. Herschel filled his pipe with orange tobacco and lit it.

"So we are here," said the playwright, pointing to the front entrance and exhaling the wonderful smoke into his study. "We have got ourselves to the front gate... and then?" He rolled an orange-papered cigarette in two seconds flat and handed it to Brandenburg. The Count lit his cigarette and looked over the plan.

"Well," replied Brandenburg, "once we're through the gate we have a fifty yard driveway with a steep bank on one side, and tiered garden on the other, which means we will not be able to park the carriage off the road here. Our best option is to follow the others all around the grounds and to the stables towards the rear. Then, once Desiree and I have alighted, the carriage can be moved here, at the back of the grounds by the copse. This is where we will load the takings, out of sight, out of the way. Now, the house itself..."

Brandenburg held out his empty glass and Herschel looked around for another bottle. He looked in his drawer and found his secret, after-love bottle of cheap wine. He went to pour it, stopping only to frown at the depleted amount within. Someone had been at his secret stock. He poured the wine all the same.

"So," continued Brandenburg, "from the main entrance, you will have a large reception room with a door leading to the direct right. That is a reading room, but will no doubt be used as a cloak room. The door at the back of that room leads into the huge library. The service door at the back, underneath the mezzanine, leads into a long corridor that almost circumnavigates the entire complex. The Whits like their servants to be neither seen nor heard, which is fine by us. We'll use this corridor to move from room to room. There is a door halfway down that also leads to the four bedroom servant quarters. They will, hopefully, be vacant, as all hands will be on the floor. This is a good, hidden spot to retreat to if things get awkward. There are windows that look out onto the copse and will provide us with cover should the need to escape arise. The corridor past the servant quarters, runs around the chapel into the main gallery. This stretches all the way down to the main entrance reception room. This gallery is wide with a high ceiling and dripping with finery. The Whits will line the walls with portraits, and under each will be vases, candelabras and all manner of trinket. This is where we mustn't get too crazy. The gallery will be packed with people so lifting will be harder. If we do it, I would suggest we do it when the gallery is cleared, perhaps for dinner, or when the dances are called. Before then, it should be used only by me and Desiree to make sure all eyes are on us and not on the silverware."

Herschel looked over the map while listening to Brandenburg's dizzying patter.

"To the right side of the gallery, if you are looking down it towards the main reception room, lies the dining hall where, when we are seated, Antoine will take centre stage and lift everything he can between courses. The room adjacent to the dining hall will no doubt be the drinks room. This will be a good spot to make contacts, pick up invites and lift some rings and pearls. Opposite the gallery entrance to the drinks room is a doorway onto the terrace. I'll come to that in a moment. Adjacent to the drinks room is the morning room where, one would imagine, the gentlemen will retire to after the dances to talk bollocks. I will have to be among them and so, from that point, the extraction will have to be initiated by Archie. As soon as I am in the morning room, we start to pack up and get the hell out of there. After good time, I will collect Desiree and we will leave. Savvy?"

Herschel nodded and poured more drink.

"Now," continued Brandenburg with barely a pause, "to the main hall. We have come back on ourselves and we are next to the main entrance. The main hall is directly to the left of it. In here we will dance for many, many tedious hours. This, I hope, is where Desiree will shine, gaining the trust and love of the men and women as we pirouette about the place. This is a good place to raise our profile a bit, while you lot are pilfering your guts out. And so, the conservatory, now this is the tricky part. As you can see, it looks directly out onto the lawn and to the very edge of the copse, where the carriage is parked. Now, hopefully, we will be under cover of darkness and nicely obscured, however, there will probably be a section of lawn that will be illuminated by the interior lights. What that effectively does, is give us a danger spot. There will be no other way of getting from the house to the carriage without being lit up like fireworks night. We will need to keep the loading runs to an absolute minimum. If some fop is out on the conservatory having a smoke and sees Gertie belting across the lawn with his arms stuffed full of silver, we'll be undone quick smart.

"Can't we go round?"

"We could, but it would take thrice as long for the same amount of loot. No, speed is what we need. Straight across the lawn, through the danger spot for maybe three runs. It's a risk, yes...but if we time it right, perhaps when everybody is dancing, then I think we should be safe."

Brandenburg and Herschel finished their drinks.

"Alright," said Herschel, "that is a plot structure that holds weight. I would write that."

"Good," said Brandenburg, "then let's redraft and start to think about the climax and the curtain calls. Exit strategy is going to be the key."

Herschel opened the bottom drawer to his desk and pulled out a tiny bottle. He uncorked it and let Brandenburg sniff the purple vapour. It almost burnt his face off. Herschel took a swig and coughed violently. He handed it to the count.

"Exit strategy, you say?" he wheezed. Brandenburg nodded in agreement before taking a swig of the mysterious tonic.

The backstage area was winding down after a hard day's toil and training. Desiree exhausted from fencing, swung in her hammock, rubbing rosewater into her aching joints and quietly singing that Florentine rhyme about the biscetta and the butcher's dog. Though she ached all over, she was happy and proud of her new found combat abilities. She had fought Alexia and lost every time, but with each new bout she had gained more ground against her opponent and taken great psychological advances in besting her fear of the blade. She had done well.

Next to her hammock stretched Danilov. He had spent the entire day locked in his training regime of press-ups and kettle bell rotations. He had worked past the point of fatigue and into that automaton state of muscle memory. Now, in the dimming hours of the evening, he was performing his stretching routine. From the shadows watched Valerie. She had studied him all day. His body was unlike anything she had seen before. His heart she had met a few times since walking through The Roxy's doors, but his body? The musculature was perfect, the poise sublime. Throughout the day, when she had become overwhelmed with his physicality, she had stolen herself away to the darkest recess of the theatre and privately investigated every contour of the acrobat within the ever expanding landscape of her fantasy. She looked at him stretching and noticed a small inch-square portion of skin, just below his left shoulder blade that she had not seen before and was about retreat to a private corner when the sound of theatre doors opening, followed by the sound of Archie's shouts rushed through the theatre.

"It's here! It's here! Get me to Brandenburg, it's here!" he bellowed as he ran down the aisles toward the stage, waving a piece of paper above his head.

"Clear the way, it is here, it is here; we are in business!" He leapt clean onto the stage and ran across it without breaking stride and belted through the back stage area shouting still. The Players had little time to react, let alone gather, before Archie rushed past them and burst into Herschel's room.

"Have you seen...oh, you're here!" he beamed upon seeing Brandenburg. Archie slammed the piece of paper down on the map and stopped to catch his breath.

"It's here," he gasped, "we have it!"

He began trying to drink out of the empty bottle paperweights. Herschel handed him the tiny bottle of purple tonic which Archie downed in one go. Brandenburg picked up the scrap of paper and inspected it.

"What is it?" asked Herschel.

"It's from our man, Thomas Moore. It's an invitation into the Almack's Assembly Room for one Count Abraham Von Brandenburg." said Brandenburg as he handed the paper to Herschel. Herschel looked amazed at Brandenburg and they both looked over to Archie who was trying to smile despite the volcano in his throat caused by Herschel's tonic. All three men laughed heartily.

There was a knock at the door which halted their festivities. The men turned to see Claudia standing there, eyes bloodshot and arms folded.

"Archibald Enfield" she said in a stern, teacher-like voice. Archie turned to her and smiled. She stamped her foot down hard and glowered at him.

"You can smile at me all you want," she ranted, "but you should know that there can never be anything between us. I am saving myself for a real man, not some forest boy like you! I love you, but only as a friend. Now that I have said that, I will leave you to you to your boys' games. I have places to go. Good evening gentlemen!"

The Spanish Girl lifted her chin and walked haughtily out of the doorway. Herschel and Brandenburg both looked at Archie who was dumbstruck.

"It seems to me," said Brandenburg with an undeniable sense of paternal love, "that our girl is no longer. Gentlemen, we have another woman in our midst."

Herschel dug out three further bottles of purple tonic and handed them to the two men. They each uncorked them and held them in the air.

"God help you Archie, and God help us all!" said Herschel and all three men drank and then heaved.

Chapter Thirty

The Way Their Love Is

L upe Darling scanned through her vast costume rack. Beside
her stood Brandenburg reviewing a scrap of paper. Archie
sat in Lupe's grand thinking-chair and was draping boas over
himself.

"I think the black shirt will work," she said to the room.

"Yes, I agree," said Archie, "black is the right choice,
mysterious yet assured and not wanting. That is the right attitude we
want to portray."

"Perfect, black it is, now what style?"

"What are the options?"

Lupe pushed a rail-rack aside and revealed a seemingly endless
line of black shirts. Archie's eyes widened. Brandenburg did not look
up from his paper.

"Let us see" said Lupe as she thumbed through the first three
hundred shirts at lightning speed, "we have fronted, backed, back
fronted, Wilcott style, autumn red wing, the Brekker folded seam,
three sleeved turn-around, deck hand's soup style....what else."

"That one" said Archie blindly pointing to a shirt halfway along
the line. Lupe took it out and looked it over.

"Mm, interesting choice" she said as she held the shirt against
Brandenburg. "The old Carolina stitched cross-around under-lined

Rickman cut. Simple, classic, understated. I see you are a man of taste after all Mr Enfield."

Archie fanned himself with a boa, soaking in the praise despite having no idea of what she had just said.

"Yes, this will be the shirt, now, to breeches!" she said as she pushed the shirt rack aside to reveal a rail of breeches twice as long and thrice as dense as the shirts.

"Do we go with round leg or square tapered; decisions, choices, options..."

———•◦•———

Gertie looked over the floorplan that Herschel and Brandenburg had drawn up the day before. He scratched his head as he studied it. "Antoine," he began, "do you think we can really do this?"

Antoine, who was currently drawing a huge pencil grid on the two Nathanial Whit inscribed flats, looked over to the boy.

"We can do this if we pull together and do as we are told."

"I hope I don't screw it up. I hope I don't make a mess of things as I always do."

"You will be fine" said Antoine. "Now pass me that paint brush."

Gertie did as he was told. "I'm not so sure," said the boy, "I think I will do something wrong. I always do."

Antoine took the paint brush and looked at him. Gertie had a forlorn and desperate look in his eyes. Antoine smiled at him.

"Well, it is clear that we will fail if we perform as boys and girls. Are you a girl?"

"No," said Gertie.

"Are you a boy?"

Gertie looked to the floor. Antoine used the brush handle to lift his friend's chin up.

"Gertie, I saw you, remember?"

"Saw me when?"

"I saw you on that carriage. You climbed onto the roof and stood beside Ms Adberg. I saw you fly in the air. I saw you fight side by side with Danilov and, when nobody else saw it, you saved Brandenburg from Kemble's knife. You saw it coming and you saved him when nobody else did. I saw you then and I see you now and, do you know what I see?"

Gertie shook his head. Antoine dropped the paint brush and bowed deeply and slowly to Gertie, all the time fixing his eyes on him.

"I see a man. I see a man whom I have the honour of knowing and the honour of aspiring to be like one day. You sir, are the best of all of us and the very hope for our future. I salute you sir, good man Gertie."

Antoine then performed a ridiculous salute which comprised of many complicated hops, bows, winks and hand gestures in the way that it's done in Gascony. Gertie bent down and picked up the paint brush and handed it back to Antoine.

"I will not fail you, or anyone else. I swear to you on the name of all I hold dear and true. I swear on The Roxy Playhouse that we will all perform as men and women!"

Antoine smiled at him. "Good man...now, help me scale up this map! We have much work to do!"

While Antoine and Gertie began to replicate Nathanial Whit's stage plan onto the huge flats, Anya sat above them in the rafters. She looked down at Gertie and smiled to herself. She cartwheeled back and forth along the beam, fifty feet in the air and with her eyes closed. Her heart rate was low and her nerves were steady. In her mind's eye the floor below looked like a huge butterfly net held by Gertie. *'Antoine is right,'* she thought, *'he really is a man.'*

———•◦•———

"What do you think?" said Lupe as she stood back from her work. Archie disentangled himself from the eighty-seven boas he had draped around his neck and sidled up to her.

"I think that if I didn't know him, I would fight tooth and nail to secure that man's plaything."

"Good!" said Lupe "If a little unsettling. How do you feel Count Brandenburg?"

Count Abraham Von Brandenburg, now resplendent in his perfect black shirt and cream breeches looked at himself in the giant dress mirror. He patted his gut.

"Where has my belly gone?

"That would be the secret of the Rickman Cut shirt…it is wondrous in stripping years and inches of a man. It is a mighty, mighty cut of a shirt. Good choice Mr Enfield!" said Lupe as she squeezed Archie's backside.

"I feel extraordinary!" exclaimed Brandenburg.

"And you look spectacular. Mr Enfield was right, if he wasn't here right now, I would lock the door and you would not escape the vice of my thighs for a fortnight. You are incredible."

Brandenburg put on his velvet jacket and turned to them both.

"The Count Abraham Von Brandenburg is complete. And it is all thanks to you both," he bowed to Lupe and Archie. They bowed back.

"Now then," said Miss Darling. "Who's on the panel these days? Who do you have to impress to get into the Almack's Assembly Rooms?"

Brandenburg handed her the piece of paper that he had been studying. Lupe Darling took it and raised an eyebrow.

"These seven witches, holy Lisboa, how did they ever get into that position? What is the world coming to? Right, sit down both of you and let's have a look at these harridans."

———•·•———

Ms Adberg reclined in Desiree's hammock while the Umbrian mixed some rose petals and oils into her signature lotion.

"I think it is time to say thank you to my teacher," said Desiree as she tasted the lotion, "I know, in the past, we have not seen so eye to eye. It is true that I said some awful things about you many, many years ago. But I hope that you can now forgive me."

Ms Adberg, swinging peacefully, smiled at her. "My dear," she said. "There is nothing to forgive. You were just looking after Srdjan and concerned for his heart. And you were right to do so. You were right to mistrust me. I was the snake. I poisoned him."

Desiree rubbed a small dollop of lotion on her wrist to test the temperature and consistency. "It was a difficult time for all of us," said the ballerina, "but I should not have said what I said."

"Time heals everything."

"Yes it does," agreed Desiree as she stood up with the bowl in her hands. "My dear for this," she continued, "you will need to be naked. Do not worry there are no prying eyes here."

Ms Adberg looked around and, after some thought, removed her dress. Desiree began to apply the lotion into her skin. Ms Adberg relaxed into the hammock.

"Srdjan" she whispered, "has he....since....you know?"

Desiree smiled, "the man has been with many, I will not lie to you."

Alexia's stomach turned at the thought. Desiree felt the knot as she gently rubbed the lotion over her belly.

She continued "But they all bore more than a passing resemblance to you. I am not making fun, it is true!"

"Really?"

"Really. I think when you stole his heart you replaced it with a portrait of yourself. Now, everything else has to be a copy."

The knot in her stomach untied itself. "Well, that is something I imagine, but tell me, Desiree...do you think that he wou...."

"Yes," replied Desiree before Alexia could finish her sentence. "In a heartbeat and you would not even have to ask him."

"Amelia Stewart, the Viscountess Casteleagh," said Lupe as she handed a bottle of wine to Brandenburg. The Count took it and poured himself and Archie a large glass.

"The last I heard of her, she was secretly entwined with that baker's son on Drury Lane," she said, "looks like his bread got stale rather quickly. She has a fast tongue and an evil eye. Watch out for her, she is tricky and untrustworthy.

"Could be good for a bribe then?" said Archie.

"Not likely. You're best hold over her is the baker's son. If you get a tricky question, or a raised eyebrow from her, drop a hint about her illicit past and watch her collapse like a flan in a cupboard. Who's next?"

"Sarah Villiers," said Brandenburg.

"That bitch!" shouted Lupe.

"I'm sure she's not th...."

"Her mother-in-law, Frances, used to bounce goolies with the King! That was when he was still himself, and a man. A dashing, handsome, beautiful...."

Lupe tailed off and her eyes fogged over with the unmistakable mist of nostalgia. Brandenburg elbowed Archie. Archie swallowed his wine and cleared his throat.

"Who is next, Miss Darling?"

Lupe snapped out of her reminiscence and looked back at the list. "Emily Lamb, she's the sister of Lord Melbourne."

"The Prime Minister?" said Brandenburg as he topped up their glasses.

"The very same," said Lupe as she took her drink.

"I've done her," said Archie. The other two looked at him with shocked surprise.

"Sorry, not meaning to be crass. That escaped me. How shall I say, I have held discussion with her."

"When?" asked Brandenburg.

"A few years back."

"Where?"

Archie blushed. "Well, if you must know, to start with it was up the lady-flute and then, as things heated up, she turned herself over and guided me towards the garden around the back!"

"Stop, stop, foul beast!" shouted Lupe, slapping Archie's chest, "I meant, where, geographically."

"Oh, in the speaker's chair."

"You're joking?" said Brandenburg, "in the Houses of Parliament?"

"It wasn't in the middle of Prime Minister's question time or anything," protested Archie.

"Well." said Lupe, "I would say that is leverage enough. Next up is Maria Molyneux. Now, I don't know her per se, but I do know the house of Molyneux is as crooked as Danilov's card playing. They are almost sunk in debt. If she is of that house, she will bat an eyelid and spread her pins for anyone who flashes a bit of wealth around."

"Nice," said Brandenburg.

"Well, a girl has to eat," said Archie. Lupe winked at him and clinked glasses.

"Indeed," she said, "a girl has to eat. The next one the panel is the Honourable Mrs Drummond Burrell; whom under no circumstances must be addressed as anything other than that which I have just said. She is fiercely proud of the 'honourable' epithet, despite the fact that she gained it though a deed so Machiavellian, that it would make the Devil stumble."

"How do we get to her?" said Archie.

"You don't," replied Lupe, "she is almost untouchable. She is the alpha bint. When you address the room, make sure you start by holding her gaze, before looking at the others. When you answer someone else's question, always make sure you look back at The Honourable Mrs Drummond Burrell after. She needs to love you instantly. She will decide it all."

"That's easy for you, Old Love," said Archie, ribbing his friend, "just give her a wink and smile and you're home and dry,"

"Hardly," countered Lupe, "the woman is as dry as a desert and wouldn't know what to do with a wink if it came with instructions. The bitch should have been a nun."

"I will be honest, sincere and noble," said Brandenburg.

"That's the ticket. Now, Dorothea Lieven is the wife of the Russian Ambassador. She has her eye on politics and I would not be surprised if she hadn't married into royalty by the time she's forty. She has a radical and outspoken way about her. I have heard that she has a great fondness of the common man and his plight."

"Perfect," said Archie, "you can side with her and create a powerful ally on the board. Be a little outspoken, be modern."

"Yes," said Lupe, "touch on your empathy for the common man; hint at a time spent in the fields, listening to peasants and serfs. Modernity is the key word here. Forward thinking and modern. If you can hit that, you will have Miss Lieven eating out of your hand and thusly have the whole of Russia behind you.

"I can do that," said Brandenburg as he uncorked another bottle of wine.

"And last and by no means least is, one Countess Esterhazy of Austria. You will never guess who deflowered her in the confessional box in Southwark Cathedral"

Brandenburg looked aghast at Archie.

"Don't look at me, Old Love!"

"Nope, not Archie" said Lupe.

"Not Srdjan?" said Brandenburg. Lupe shook her head.

"Not Herschel, Desiree would have sniffed that out, not Gertie, not Antoine because Austrian-Franco relations don't stretch that far. Danilov?"

Lupe shook her head. It dawned on Brandenburg.

"No!" he exclaimed.

"Yes!" said Lupe.

"Tobias? But he's quiet and sweet and silent: really?"

Lupe held up her hand "five times."

Archie laughed and poured more wines. "It's always the pious ones!" he exclaimed.

———•◦•———

"What do you think?" said Tobias as he handed the blade to Srdjan. The Dalmatian took the steel and ran his fingers down its length.

"It's astonishing! How do you fold the metal without furnace or fan?"

Tobias smiled and wheeled himself across his workshop to his bench. He picked up the unfinished Spider-Basket and looked over it. "It's a secret my father once told me."

Srdjan looked over the hilt-less blade and then to Tobias and the basket. "So, the basket will be a spider and the legs will be the quillons?"

"That's right"

Srdjan held the blade as if it were a completed sword. He swung and lunged.

"The weighting seems to be perfect already. I do not know how it is possible, but it is. With the handle, it is going to be incorrectly weighted, no?"

"That is correct. The basket, as it is designed in its full state will be grossly unbalanced. But I have been instructed to make it so, and so make it I shall."

"It will be a spectacular showpiece. I just hope he doesn't have to use it properly or else he will find himself wielding a blade attached to an anvil."

"Indeed. But we have taken that into consideration. Despite that, tell me Srdjan, have you noticed the inscribed notations?"

Srdjan tilted the blade so that the candle light reflected off it. He gasped as a beautiful twine of ivy and roses shone from the blade. He looked harder at the bewitching pattern and was aghast to see, upon the petals of the roses, the names of every Roxy Playhouse Irregular that was and had ever been. In an instant he recalled the faces of the fallen thirty-three friends and performers who had trod the boards and since departed. He fought hard to quell the tide of emotion that rose inside him. Forgotten friends remembered by the hands of Tobias Strong. Srdjan tilted the blade and the pattern vanished.

"I saw something, I really did, but it has gone now. It is invisible!"

"Until light catches it!" said Tobias. Srdjan bent the blade into the light and once more the names reappeared. It was magical.

"How do you do it?"

"I do not, God does it, and I am but his instrument, his chisel, his scribe."

"You make me believe in Him with your art."

"That is the way His love is," said Tobias as he rolled over to Srdjan. "But now, while I have shown you the secret to a great trick, you must also do the same."

"What do you mean?"

Tobias smiled and patted Srdjan on the hip.

"I see Ms Adberg is once again in our midst. Tell me about her."

Srdjan handed the blade back to Tobias who took it and placed it back upon the bench. He handed him back an iron goblet of gin.

"Yes, Alexia has come home," said Srdjan as he took his drink.

"How do you feel about that?"

Srdjan smiled. "I don't know. I feel undone and reborn at the same time. What am I supposed to feel?"

"I don't know. I am not so well versed in the ways of the heart. I have the Lord and not much else."

"True, you don't even have all your limbs either!"

"Touché, good man, touché, so, will you go to her and marry her?"

"It's a bit early for that. I think first I will just go to her."

"Don't let her get away again." said Tobias as he turned his chair back to his desk. "I let someone go once, and I didn't get another chance. You have, so don't waste it."

"I will try not to, my man, I will try not to."

Srdjan kissed Tobias's head and went to leave the room. "I must go and train and I can see you have much work to do."

The Dalmatian walked to the door and stopped. He pondered Tobias's request for a few seconds before turned back to him. "Tobias, you asked me to show you the secret of a great trick."

"I did, I did."

"Alexia Adberg is no secret and no trick. I cannot show you any more than what you already know and see. She is a woman, I am a man and through hell and high water we will fall for each other again. That's the way *my* love is."

He left the room and Tobias looked over at the doorframe. He kissed his crucifix pendant.

"Bravo, good man, bravo." He whispered before turning back to his alchemy, feling serene and light with the touch of God's love. His stump no longer ached.

Chapter Thirty One

Opening Night for Brandenburg

Count Abraham von Brandenburg and his right hand man, Mr Enfield left The Roxy Playhouse at half past six in the evening. They had allowed themselves ample time to get from Borough all the way to King Street in St James in order to make their appointment at the Almack's Assembly Rooms.

Archie left the theatre first and secured a carriage. Then, under the cover of a blanket, the Count dashed out of the theatre and into the waiting cabin. It was crucial that nobody witness the emergence of the dashing Count from the theatre lest it set the wrong sort of tongues wagging. Once inside the cabin, Brandenburg threw his blanket off and drew the curtains on the doors. Archie held up a mirror to him and he fixed his new hair style and checked his collar. As the carriage trundled over London Bridge, Archie and Brandenburg ran over the script and stage directions again and again. When he used to tread the boards, Benjamin Ananas was stickler for last minute checks. Archie, who preferred to trust in chance and fate, had always begrudgingly obliged his friend. On this occasion, however, even he understood the importance of Ananas' routine. There would be no room for errors. As soon as that carriage came to halt outside Almack's and Brandenburg alighted it would be show time. The audience behind that unassuming black door were vicious, critical and unwilling to overlook even the slightest of transgressions. It needed to be a perfect performance.

Once they had read over the script eight times, Brandenburg closed his eyes and began to calmly track each beat of the story. He conjured Brandenburg's history and took a stroll through every event in the character's life. It wasn't enough for Benjamin to simply remove his clothes, put on Brandenburg's and simply expect to become him. His art ran deeper than that. Herschel had provided a great script, filled with history and drama, and now it was up to Benjamin to imbue the creation with the humanity. Over the previous few weeks he had worked tirelessly to stay loyal and true to the spirit of the character and, in the moments leading up to the opening night, he felt a calm and satisfying glow around him. That knowing warmth that tells a man that he has done all he can do and he has done it well. The man was ready.

The carriage rolled to a stop at Piccadilly Circus under instruction of Archie as it was deemed more masculine and dignified to walk the remaining streets to the Almack. Brandenburg concurred and the two men alighted. The third time that they two friends attempted to walk down Regent Street was, indeed, the lucky time. As soon as the kick-plate had been raised and the carriage had rolled away, the Count winked at Archie and flashed a devilish smile that said 'showtime' and he strode off down the street. Archie kicked up his heels and followed after him, basking in the performance of his friend. Brandenburg's walk had changed totally since the last time they attempted the perilous catwalk of Regent Street. Brandenburg had focus and purpose. His strides where long and elegant and, as the sun began to set and the sky's hue changed to rich purples and reds, The Count Abraham von Brandenburg made an unmistakable impression upon the evening strollers of Regent Street. Archie counted at least thirty six hat-tips, fourteen nods of approval and at least sixty different sets of eyelids batted in Brandenburg's direction. It was a masterful sight to behold and his was truly proud of his friend, the great actor.

———•◦•———

"Hang on a tick, Old Love," said Archie as Brandenburg walked through St James square. The Count turned back to look at him. Archie looked around. The square was deserted. He walked up to his friend and handed him a rolled cigarette.

"Smoke this," he said. Brandenburg took it.

"Thanks."

"It's a good prop. It will give you a scent. The whiff of tobacco can be quite an alluring aphrodisiac, and it will lower your voice somewhat. Give it some gravel."

"May I have another one?"

Archie obliged his friend, and also took out his hipflask. He took a swig. Brandenburg's eyes lit up.

"Oh great, something to take the edge off," the Count reached for the hip flask only to have Archie snatch it away.

"No chance, there is no booze in the Almack!"

"What?"

"No booze in the Almack. It's a dry assembly room. Tea is all you're getting Old Love."

"You're joking!"

"Nope, remember that arse-grape Kemble?" said Archie, drinking away, "he was a member once, back when they served booze. One night, he had one too many...well, about twelve too many, tried to finger a baroness, got into a scrap and then pissed into a champagne fountain. Needless to say he lost his voucher, got booted out and they subsequently banned alcohol because it."

"Just for that? Sounds a bit harsh" said Brandenburg.

"I know, right?" agreed Archie, "still, that's the way it is now, Old Love."

"Jesus," said Brandenburg, "give me another cigarette then and let's get this over with."

Brandenburg lit his third and final cigarette of the evening and marched off through the square and onto Kings Street.

———•·•———

Antoine and Gertie stood back and admired their handiwork. Brandenburg's stage plan of Nathanial's mansion had been beautifully rendered onto the twelve foot flats and was now propped up against the stage. The two men clinked glasses and drank their well earned drinks. Valerie wandered onto the stage carrying a large bundle of cloth. She looked over the boards.

"Is it finished?" she enquired.

"Yes," said Gertie as he picked up the broken end to his butterfly net and used it as a pointer. "You see these areas here, here and here? It will be where the richies will be gathered."

"I see."

"And the backstage crew with be mainly consigned to this long ringed corridor here. It is a bit like a service tunnel. We should be unseen mostly."

"Mostly?"

"Well, when we are outside ferrying the loot to the carriage, we may have to cross this danger area here which will be lit up. But, it should not be a problem."

"Unless someone looks out of the conservatory window, or pops out to smoke," added Antoine, "anyway, I cannot stand around here all evening. I have a dress fitting with Lupe," he said before bidding the two good evening and walking off the stage. Gertie looked over at Valerie who was drifting back into a contemplative state.

"Are you alright?" he said as his lifted a hand to touched her shoulder. The contact awakened her senses and she smiled.

"Yes…yes, I'm fine. I just…I don't know. It isn't my place to say…"

"No, please, go on! We are the only ones here."

"Well I haven't been here all that long and I don't have no right to think as I do…I just…" she hung her head. Gertie lifted up her chin.

"You can say."

Valerie hugged the bundle of clothing tightly against her chest. "Oh!" she sighed, "I just know I am not a stage hand! I am grateful for the work, and I am in love with this theatre and all of you…but I want to be on stage! I want the action and adventure! I wouldn't even mind being a stage hand in the mansion. At least I will be there helping. Instead, I will be here waiting! Do you think if I asked Archie, he would find me a better job?"

Gertie grabbed her and hugged her tightly.

"I don't know, dear Valerie, I don't know, but when he comes home, you should ask him. And, if you want, I will go with you as moral support!"

Valerie beamed. "Will you really do that? What a friend you are!" She kissed him on the cheek and trotted off the stage, leaving Gertie to look over the map.

The seven women sat in a row behind an imposing oak table. Each one had a stern, unwavering business-like demeanour about them. The man on the other side of the table was holding his hat sheepishly in both hands and darting his gaze up and down from the floor to each of the seven panellists. The woman in the centre, the Honourable Mrs Drummond Burrell cleared her throat and shuffled a few bits of paper.

"Well Mr…" she looked at her cards. The woman to her right leant in and whispered in her ear, "Mr Bennet. Thank you for your time. After careful consideration, I am afraid we are going to have to pass on your application."

"But…"

"It seems that you are lacking certain…," the lady to her left leant in and whispered in her ear. "Quality of class."

"My father is the Duke of Argyll!"

"Yes well, it's is precisely because you presume to think that you're lineage alone is enough to grace our club that makes you undesirable here. I am talking about essence and dignity."

"And besides," chipped in Maria Molyneux, who was sitting on the very end of the line, "you're financially undesirable to this club." Maria Molyneux slowly and deliberately picked up the card with Mr Bennett's name on it and tore it in half. Then, each in turn and down the line, the panellists of the Almack followed suit until, on the centre of the table lay a small pile of scraps.

"Begads! You harridans! What an outrage! Mrs Drummond Burrell, you are a vomit. A large vomit!" and with that, Mr Bennett stamped his foot and stormed out. The women all cleared their throat in unison and each reached for the glass of water in front of them.

"Mr Warner," said Mrs Drummond Burrell to the serving man in the corner, "will you distribute these cards to the members so that they know Mr Bennett has come up wanting?" Mr Warner bowed and stepped forward. He scooped up the pile of scraps, bowed to the panel and left out of a side door.

"Who have we next?" said Amelia Stewart who was positioned next to Mrs Drummond Burrell on her left side. Mrs Drummond Burrell looked down the table to the designated Lady of Cards, Mrs Dorothea Lieven.

"Mrs Lieven, if you please," commanded Mrs Drummond Burrell. Mrs Lieven took next pile of cards in a line of four and looked at it. She raised her eyebrow and tilted her head before passing the pile down the line. Each lady took a card until it reached Miss Molyneux at the other end who received the last. Mrs Drummond Burrell nodded to the servant by the door to open it. The man opened the door and all seven ladies lost their composure for a split second. There was the tiniest of gasps as they saw Count Abraham von Brandenburg standing in the hallway. He stood motionless and heroic for a few seconds while the scent of liquorice tinged tobacco wafted into the room and over each lady. After what seemed like an eternity, Mrs Drummond Burrell nodded to the servant who took the Count's hat and led in into the room. Before the ladies could welcome him, he bowed a gracious and deep bow starting with Mrs Drummond Burrell and then, at random to each of them, so as they did not feel that there was any favouritism, aside for the leader. After his bow, he stood straight and posed with one hand on his belt, scooping his jacket behind his wrist, and the other hand resting on the hilt of Srdjan's best prop sword.

"And who stands before us?" said Mrs Drummond Burrell in an officious tone that belied the curious and hitherto alien sensation stirring in her belly.

"Abraham von Brandenburg."

Mrs Drummond Burrell looked down at her card, and back up to him, "it says you are Count Abraham von Brandenburg. Do you not care for titles?"

"Honourable Mrs Drummond Burrell, to my mother I was simply Abraham, her boy, her son." All seven women swooned and reflexively batted their eyelids at him.

"And a wife?" continued Mrs Drummond Burrell, determined not to succumb to the man, "what does she think of that?"

"Alas, I have not yet taken a wife," said Brandenburg improvising suddenly. The women sat up.

"So," chirped Amelia, "do you seek to find your mate within these rooms? Is that why you present yourself here?"

Brandenburg smiled at her and blushed. "Mrs Stewart" he began, "it is not the case. Though I would imagine within these walls are women of the greatest esteem and virtue. However, my heart is betrothed to another - a ballerina from Perugia who dances with the light of God in her heart."

"And yet you have not married her? Does her dowry not suit?" said Miss Molyneux.

"On the contrary, if it pleases one to know, my estate is plentiful and neither I nor my future wife and family will want for anything. If gold and silver are what my ballerina desired, I would have showered her with them. But she is not so keen a magpie. She is an artist and thoroughly modern and will not permit talk of marriage until she is certain that my intentions are pure and full of love and doubly so that the nature of her heart decrees it right to take my hand."

"And how will you prove your intentions?" said Miss Villiers, sitting next to Mrs Drummond Burrell on the right side.

"I will not prove anything for I have no need. I have told her that I am hers and hers alone and if she asks that I wait for her, then wait for her I will." The women smiled and made a few notes on their cards.

"And besides," he continued, "I would like my wife to be first a wonderful and trusted friend with whom to have great adventures and, at present, we are still working on our friendship." The women began to scribble more furiously on their notes.

"So in summation," said Mrs Drummond Burrell, "you care not for titles, you are unmarried, you are not man enough to take the one you want and she is to haughty to accept your obvious wealth and statue." The women squinted at the Count to test his reaction. He bowed to them again.

"My ladies, if that is your conclusion than I will not contest it. You are women of great reverence and I hear that what you say goes and so who am I to question your judgements? And so, if you have no further use for me, I will bid you goodnight. I have a pressing engagement with my haughty ballerina. It is a full moon tonight and the stars are unveiled. I have a mind to take her to the Serpentine so that she can teach me how to dance by starlight, as is the way in Perugia." He bowed once more and turned to leave.

Amelia and Miss Villiers both leant into Mrs Drummond Burrell's ears and whispered. The Count was at the door when their chairperson called for him to halt. They could not see his face and so didn't see the relief across it that his little gambit had paid off. He turned back to them.

"My ladies."

"Count Abraham von Brandenburg" said Mrs Drummond Burrell, "you do not walk out of the Almack without being told to do so." She held up her card and turned it over. He could see his name inked upon it.

"I must admit," she continued "that when Thomas Moore recited his new sonnet to us and we listened to the verse that extolled the virtues of the Count Abraham von Brandenburg and his velvet jacket we where bewitched. Such is the trickery of his art. When he told us the character was real, we were more than sceptical and when he told us that this character requested consideration of vouchering we were incredulous. Nobody has ever waltzed into the Almack. It takes years to build reputation. Some never gain an interview. And yet, against all reason, here you stand before us now."

"I will take that as a compliment, Honourable Mrs Drummond Burrell."

"It was not one."

"Nevertheless, I shall consider it one for you see, in the little town of Holstenwall, where I come from the glass is always half full and never half empty."

Mrs Drummond Burrell looked down the line to Miss Molyneux who held up her card. She let the moment wring out for an eternity before gently kissing the card and passing towards the centre of the table. Slowly each woman kissed their card and passed them along until there was only Mrs Drummond Burrell and her card.

She stepped out from around the table in a gesture that was clearly out of the ordinary as the remaining six women looked at each other in nervous uncertainty. Mrs Drummond Burrell stood in front of the Count and looked deep into his eyes. The smell of tobacco and the hypnotic slow rise and fall of his chest wooed her.

"Well," she whispered "some reputations are built on magic and mystery. And all the better for it, I say."

Brandenburg smiled and offered her the faintest of winks. She almost fell into his arms before snapping out of the spell.

"Well!" she said in a louder tone, "it seems my sisters have spoken," and with that she kissed her card and placed it in his breast pocket.

"Welcome to the Almack Assembly rooms, Count Abraham Von Brandenburg."

She nodded to Mr Warner to take Brandenburg through the doors at the back of the room. Mr Warner bowed and stood before the Count.

"Count Abraham von Brandenburg, by authority of the panel of Almack's, you are granted passage and voucher to enjoy the facilities within its walls in a manner that serves you and the Almack's reputation well. Be with grace and honour and you will find home. Be with debauchery and knavery and you will find home in the gutter. Accept you of these rules?"

"I do."

"Then please, sir, through these doors here you must now go."

Mr Warner opened the doors and led the Count into the assembly room. The sight before him was overwhelming but he remembered his training and his role and held himself together. He stood in the doorway to the inner sanctum as he had done before the ladies; one hand on hip, one on sword hilt.

Mr Warner stood in front of him.

"Ladies, Lords and Gentlemen, I present to you Count Abraham von Brandenburg," he boomed. There was a faint murmur of excitement and then the multitude of socialites went back to their tea and gossip.

The door closed behind Brandenburg and he spent a few seconds scanning the room. It was filled with red-cheeked faces. Some of whom he recognised some of whom he didn't. It wasn't until he had scanned the entire room and started back again that he noticed his mark. There, quietly in the corner and talking clandestinely to three serious men sat Nathanial Whit. He felt an acidic twinge of fear in his gut and for the briefest of moments he felt very, very alone. He rallied quickly by likening that fear to that of stepping on stage on opening night.

"Brandenburg!" a holler came from across the other side of the room. The Count looked over to see Thomas Moore ushering him over. The poet was surrounded by a small group of men and women. The Count nodded his head, breathed deeply and strode across the room to join them.

Chapter Thirty Two

Madhouse

B randenburg had spent three hours inside the Almack and had worked the room like a professional. After half an hour talking with Moore, Brandenburg felt confident enough to peel away from the group and to begin mingling on his own. He had noticed while sharing jokes and stories with Thomas Moore and his fine friends that other people had been casting looks his way. His stage training gave him acute awareness to the whereabouts and eyelines of his audience. He felt strong and powerful and his stage-laugh became louder, relaxed and more infectious. Eventually, when his moment arrived, Brandenburg politely excused himself from the group and began his working of the room.

By the time he had gone full circle and rejoined the poet, everyone in the room knew his name and felt that they had a new and pleasing friend in their lives. His patter was genuine and sincere, he listened attentively to each person and instinctively knew the right responses to questions and offered insightful and well received advice. Most importantly though was his focused and powerful stare that he fixed people with when shaking or kissing their hands. It was a vulgar technique and one, outside of a performance he was not so fond of. However, Antoine had always extolled the benefits of a vice like stare when shaking someone's hand. "It makes them look at your face, and not at your hands," he would say while demonstrating to

Brandenburg and relieving him of his rings. On this occasion, Brandenburg was not lifting jewellery, however, he knew that he would have limited opportunities to etch his face into their minds and each opportunity had to be seized aggressively. Luckily, his clean face, alluring moustache and devastating haircut made the confidence-stare much more enjoyable to those caught in its beam.

The only group of people he had not met were Nathanial's. They had built an invisible wall around themselves and Brandenburg knew that it would be counterproductive to go barrelling over and introduce himself. He thought it more prudent to orbit the room and let the gravity of his charm pull the target to him.

Brandenburg was halfway through an anecdote about his time hunting in India when a gong was struck. All conversation stopped and everyone turned to the door. The grandfather clock struck half past nine and the doors opened to reveal the seven panellists, redressed in different, but similarly themed crimson and cream dresses. Mr Warner did not introduce them, as it was not necessary and the women, led by the Honourable Mrs Drummond Burrell entered the room and splintered off to join various groups. As soon as the doors were closed, everybody returned to the conversations while, obviously accommodating one of the women into it, should they be fortunate enough to be blessed with their presence.

None of the ladies joined Moore and Brandenburg but as soon as the Count had turned his back to continue his anecdote he could feel all seven sets of eyes upon him. He finished his story to the delight of the others and the room was filled with their laughter. It had not even had the chance to die down before Thomas Moore threw in an unexpected counter to the story which whipped the laughter up again. By the time that resurgence had died down their little group had swelled as the two flanking parties had joined them. The young lady standing next to Brandenburg begged for another story while holding onto his arm and gazing adoringly at the man.

"Yes," came a voice from outside the group, "please, tell us all a story, Count".

The group hushed as Brandenburg turned around to see Honourable Mrs Drummond Burrell standing there. After a subtle glance from the Queen Bee, the woman holding Brandenburg's arm let go and slunk to the back of the group. Mrs Drummond Burrell took her place.

"Tell us all about how you met your ballerina."

"Ballerina?" Moore smirked.

"It seems our new member has some rather old fashioned views on his modern lady friend," said Mrs Drummond Burrell.

"This I have to hear," beamed Moore, folding his arms in delight.

"Yes, Count, please do tell us a story," said a random gent.

Brandenburg looked around at his audience. He had them in the palm of his hand, but had no story to tell. Then, as if Herschel himself had appeared on his shoulder and was whispering into his ear, inspiration came. The Count smiled a devilish smile at the group.

"Very well," he whispered to which the crowd clapped politely and leant in.

———•◦•———

Hidden in an alleyway, across the street from the Almack, sat Archie. He had his cigarettes and tobacco lifted from Herschel's study and also a couple hipflasks dotted about his person but he still felt a little sorry for himself. He would have loved to have been inside with his friend, working the room, laughing joking and securing some new beds for the night. Of course, manservants were not allowed in and so it was his charge to keep watch of the Almack and to make sure Brandenburg came off stage and back to the Playhouse as soon as he left the building. He pulled up his collar and wrapped his coat around himself to fend off the night breeze. He lit a cigarette and pulled out one of his hipflasks.

"At least" he said, "I can have a drink, while you're supping on tea. Here's one for you, Old Love," and he toasted Brandenburg and took a long swig.

The rest of the Players had decided, while they were waiting for Brandenburg to return, to take themselves to The Bishop. Antoine and Srdjan had covered the giant map and all props and costumes had been stowed. It was time for a well earned drink and Lupe wheeled Tobias out of theatre with the other Players in tow.

They had, as was their way, assembled around the small lounge area of the pub and instead of drinking games and cards, they sat in relative modesty. Quietly drinking their pints and taking it in turns to reminisce over past glories. When it came to Valerie, she told them that she had no story yet, but aimed to prove herself in the coming show. The group fell silent and looked to the floor. Each one crossed themselves and pinched the ear of the person sitting to the left of them. Valerie was about to continue when Danilov leant into her ear and whispered that it was incredibly bad luck to talk about future performances. Valerie whispered her apology and Danilov accepted it by kissing her ear softly and sweetly. He could not say what possessed him to do so, but Valerie's short and sudden gasp and the instantaneous rush of blood to her cheeks told him that it had been the right thing to do.

"And then she said, 'in Perugia the rabbit stays in the pot until spring."

Brandenburg finished his story and there was a moments silence before rapturous laughter and applause shook the building. All sense of propriety left the men and women as they roared with laughter, slapped their thighs and wiped tears from their eyes.

It was in the downturn of laughter that caused Brandenburg to drop his guard slightly and he let out one final burst. However, this laugh was not the Count's but the actors. The change in timbre and volume went unnoticed to all but three men in the room. Brandenburg realised his mistake instantly and cleared his throat and regained his composure and Thomas Moore shot him a look before turning his attention to a pretty young thing next to him.

The third man to notice was Nathanial Whit. Up until that point he had been deep in his business dealings and had paid no attention to the new member of the club, nor the riotous atmosphere his presence had created. But the sudden and unexpected sound of that laugh triggered his memory into action. Like catching the scent of a long forgotten smell that ignites the passion of nostalgia, Nathanial Whit suddenly found himself back in his early twenties, standing amongst his childhood friends and listening to them laugh at his jokes.

His sudden and sideswiping distraction caused him to lose the attention of his colleagues. They looked at each other in bewilderment.

"Mr Whit?" said one, "Mr Whit?" Nathanial's eyes had fogged over. He looked around the room.

"Mr Whit?" said another colleague and reached out and shook his shoulder. Nathanial Whit came back into the present with a jolt.

"Gentlemen, do excuse me. I must leave. I have a meeting with our Lord."

"Certainly sir, we will do as you have bid."

The five men stood up and shook hands. From across the room, Brandenburg bit his lip in self reproach at seeing his mark about to leave the room. He was about to walk over, when he noticed the curious handshake by which the five men said goodbye. It was inconspicuous to the layman, but this actor was schooled in looking for details. A simple shake, but the thumbs crossed over and their hands shook a purposeful yet strange seven times. Each man nodded to each other and watched as Nathanial Whit left the room before returning to their seats. Brandenburg wracked his memory to locate the origin of that peculiar handshake. In his research into his character, he had lifted an awful lot from the mannerisms of Nathanial Whit as a younger man. How had he not noticed that handshake? Or maybe he had? As he delved further into the memory, the sight of the shake became more and more prevalent, however Brandenburg knew that it wasn't a true memory but rather a contamination of what he had just seen imprinted over old memories. He dismissed it from his mind and returned to his conversation.

———•••———

Archie sat up and hugged the wall the moment he saw Nathanial Whit emerge from the club. He watched as the mark looked around the street before walking down a side alley. Archie thought about returning to his position of guard when an overwhelming sense of curiosity came over him. He had been sat on his own for hours, which wasn't any fun at the best of times and he had been itching for something to do. He looked around the street. It was deserted.

'Well,' he thought, as he finished his second hip-flask, *'it can't hurt to follow the little bugger, see where he goes to at night.'*

When the coast seemed clear enough, Archie dashed across the street and into the alleyway opposite. He clung to the walls like a stalking murderer, keeping his target in view but at safe distance. He had noticed the way Gertie moved across the stage and tried to incorporate it now. He attempted to place a footstep only when Nathanial did to mask the sound and to also somehow preternaturally guess his next movements and gestures. It was a good enough attempt and Archie managed to follow Whit for a good ten minutes before his quarry came to halt in the middle of a deserted cobblestone square. During the winding backstreet walk, Archie had lost his bearings and now had no idea where he was. He had to stay and continue his stalk and so he ducked down behind a barrel as Nathanial bent down to straighten the hem of his breeches. The full moon was bright and enabled Archie to view Whit in a good light. The man finished attending to his breeches, stood up and looked around. He did not see Enfield. The silence of the square seemed to be complicit with the foreboding sense of unease that this strange man created. Nathanial Whit pulled a silver cigarillo case from his jacket opened it. As the moonlight flashed across the lid, Archie caught a glimpse of a symbol that he could not place. It appeared to be a black cross.

Nathanial Whit took out a match, lit a cigarette and then held the match down by his side. He made no attempt to extinguish the flame. Archie ducked down a little tighter into the barrel as his unease grew. As soon as the match burnt itself out, a black carriage pulled silently into the square and stopped beside Whit. The door flung open. Nathanial Whit slowly tipped his hat and said, "My Lord."

Before Archie heard another word the air seemed to fall still and his blood ran cold.

"Good evening, Brother Whit," came a ghastly, demonic hiss from within the carriage. Nathanial dropped the match and stepped into the cabin.

Archie fought his dread and looked over edge of the barrel. Inside the cabin he could see a sickly and sallow hand rise up to Nathanial's face. Mr Whit kissed a glittering ring that hung loosely of a greying finger. Archie squinted to try and see whose hand it was. The other passenger was wearing a large black cowl that obscured his form completely.

"To Bedlam?" said Whit.

"To Bedlam," the awful hiss came. Nathanial tapped the roof of the carriage and it sprung into life. Archie had time for one decision to which is answer came almost as soon as he said it.

"Fuck it, why not!" he said to the night as he ran out of the alleyway, caught up with the carriage and managed to jump onto the luggage rail on the back. He held on tightly as the black carriage sped through moonlit streets.

The carriage came to a halt outside a great building just off Bishopsgate. The doors of the cab opened and Nathanial and the cloaked man alighted. Archie held fast until they had walked some distance before resuming his pursuit. The two men walked up the long driveway and up the steps to the building. Archie knew exactly where he was and it sent a shiver down his spine. He was standing on the steps to Bethlam Hospital, colloquially known as 'Bedlam' and even less affectionately known as the madhouse.

Why was he at a sanatorium? Why was he even contemplating following the two men inside? He had no idea why they called it a hospital as it was more an awful mixture of prison and circus where the rich would come to goad the wretched and insane and torment them still further. Is that what these two men were doing? Tormenting the tormented? He ran through the days of the week in his mind. They had been at the Almack which meant it was a Wednesday and the goading day was a Tuesday and so these men had other business. He looked around before pulling his collar tighter around his neck and walking into the madhouse.

The inside of Bedlam was a sickening mix of filthy brickwork, coated in an unnamed wet substance. Upon the walls, which twisted and contorted like a nightmare collapsing, hung wrought iron candelabra upon which mourned weeping red candles that offered little light, but instead issued their wasting bodies down to the floor where they amassed upon the heaped graves of former candles. The hospital looks like a mad amalgamation of building and some poor bastard's insides.

How does one act when walking uninvited through the corridors of hell? Does one walk like Dante and Virgil, bold and determined? Or does one try and be as a shadow lest they invoke the unwanted gaze of the demons and condemned? He walked with a mixture of both. He stuck to the shadows, but his armour did not buckle completely. The smell was unbearable. He almost vomited the instant he walked through the doors, but he knew he could not cover his face and show that he was not used to it. He had to be a regular. He remembered how Desiree could stand on point for hours on end and never let the pain show in her face. He channelled the ballerina's mental strength and beat back his bubbling insides and pushed forward into the labyrinthine prison. The two men remained in view, however Archie did not follow blindly as he had done outside the Almack. He wanted to be able to find his way out again and so remembered his marks as an actor would. Twelve steps, left turn, stop, down sixty three steps, right turn, fourteen steps, stop, and so on and so on.

The moans and wails of the inmates rattled his soul but his rational mind used the noises as aural checkpoints to coincide with his counted footsteps. He came down a great flight of steps onto a long, torch-lit corridor. He stopped at its mouth and hugged the wall. At the very end he could see Nathanial and the cloaked man stop by a huge wooden chamber door. The far end of corridor was flanked by twenty men in black cowls. Nathanial put on a black cloak and he and his accomplice opened the room. An almost supernatural light from within flooded out into the corridor. Inside, Archie could see a long table around which sat possibly forty men all dressed in sinister cowls. Nathanial and his friend entered the room, followed by the twenty other men. The door slammed ominously. Archie knew he had no chance of waltzing into that room and so decided that it was time to retreat. As soon as he made that decision, his heart began to take control over his rational side and the realisation of his whereabouts dawned. He began to panic slightly.

He ran back up the steps and desperately began to retrace his path however the twisting corridors and oppressive air crushed in on his mind and seemed to jumble up the map he had made. Bedlam asylum seemed to be alive, and eager to claim a new inmate. Archie became confused and scared as he ran through the maze of the asylum. The sensation of fear and desperation was nothing compared to the feeling of suffocation that came about, as he began to realise that he was a madman inside a temple of madmen. Where atriums before had three entrances, now they seemed to have thirty. Corridors suddenly grew steep and he had to scramble up them on all fours, the slime causing him to skid down and tumble into darker, uncharted tombs and corridors.

He was about to scream when his rational side stepped forward and slapped him in the face. He stopped running and gathered himself. He thought about Anya and her meditative tendencies. He thought about her tightrope walking and her total self-control. His heart rate slowed and he began to think of a way out of his fix. He thought about being on the stage and what he would do, if he ever lost his lines or his mark.

"Improvise, Old Love, improvise," he whispered and he opened his eyes again. Up ahead lay a fork in the corridor. He 'ippy dippied' his choices, shrugged and walked down the right corridor resigned to his fate, but determined to greet his imprisonment with the same devil may care attitude he greeted everything else.

His choice was fortuitous as, after forty-five minutes of wandering through the catacombs of the asylum, he passed a cell from within which he recognised the babblings of an unfortunate. He tipped his imaginary hat in thanks and walked with a more assured pace down the corridor and towards a welcoming spiral stairwell. He was about to walk up it when a new noise caught his attention. It was a painful, sad and slow wheeze. It sounded like a dying animal and, as he loved animals, he was overcome with the horrible feeling that perhaps humans weren't the only captives. The wheezing continued. Archie took a torch from its holding on the stairwell and shone it into the cells. The poor bastards inside all shied away from the light. Archie almost cried when he saw the state of them. They were filthy, crooked, ridden with boils and sores and half eaten by rats. The wheezing continued. He traced it with his light until he came to a bundle in the corner of a cell He could see that whatever creature it was, it was facing the wall in a foetal position. Its body rose and sank with each painful wheeze. Archie could not speak. He just held the light over the dying creature. After a few moments, the wheezing pattern changed slightly and the beast rolled around on its side to look at him.

Archie's eyes grew with horror and the colour ran from his face. He dropped the torch and fled the asylum and full pelt and without taking a single wrong-turn.

The figure wheezed and turned back to the corner of the cell.

Chapter Thirty Three

Knife Dancing

The minuet finished and the room filled with polite applause. Despite his restrained clapping Brandenburg was elated that he had managed to survive the entire dance without putting a foot wrong. He bowed graciously to his dance partner, a one Lady Bronwyn of Earley who curtsied back.

"You dance very well, Count Brandenburg," she said as she took his arm and led him over to a private table where she sat and he poured lemonade for her.

"Thank you, Lady Bronwyn,"

"Winnie, please call me Winnie"

"Very well, Winnie, how sweet a name."

Winnie blushed and made eyes at the Count over her drink. "So, tell me something," she said in a quiet, private tone, "how did you learn to dance like that? I can recognize the training of a professional."

"Can you?"

"Yes, the way your heel turns out, the angle of your thigh. It is a great technique." She blushed once more. "Excuse me, too many seasons at the ballet."

"Not at all, you have a good eye. It was my father who taught me the importance in dance. He was a strong, noble fellow with a stout heart and a fierce temper. But he loved life and had the most peculiar of obsessions."

"Like dance?"

"Exactly, he loved archery and fishing and sewing and dance. His obsessions bemused his peers. In the mountains of Holstenwall, where I grew up, such things were for children. But my father didn't care. He did what made him feel happy and without a care for what others might say. When his guests drank brandy and spoke of war and politics, my father would be seen dancing around the room with my mother in his arms."

Young Winnie was enthralled by the Count's story. Brandenburg was more than convincing. There was truth in his voice. He dug into the memory of his father and his idiosyncrasies that, up until recently, had seemed to be flaws to him. Now Brandenburg or Anasas that was, was slowly coming to reconcile the strengths his father possessed and which had been passed onto him. He was his father's son for perhaps the first time and that realisation anchored his story with a sincere gravitas. He did not look at Winnie when he told his anecdote, but to the middle distance as he drifted over his memories.

"When it came to dance, he used to say, 'Young Man, if you cannot take yourself for a turn on the floor, then you have no business owning legs. Now, dance with me or else its twenty lashes!' He would do this in private or in front of guests. It didn't matter to him. He wanted to dance with his son. Many times I almost died for embarrassment!"

Winnie put her hand on the Count's knee. "Well, I for one am sincerely glad you did not! You're father sounds like a great and unique man and there are so few these days."

Lady Bronwyn would never have normally been so honest with an acquaintance given that the slightest opinion to err on unfashionable was a dangerous practice in the Almack, but there was a refreshing quality to the Count that seemed to melt her sense of propriety. She leant in further to him. "It is hard to be one's true self I find. In any situation it seems to me that everybody is wearing a mask these days, don't you find?"

"My dear Winnie, you have no idea how right you are."

The music started and Brandenburg stood up and held out his hand. "Winnie, would care for a turn around the floor?"

Winnie smiled and put her lemonade down. "Do you know, I think I will!" She took his hand and the joined in with the other dancers.

"In Holstenwall we only wear masks at balls. We have the most sensational masquerades. You would be my guest of honour! Oh! How I miss masquerade balls," said Brandenburg leading the conversation.

"Well, if its masquerade balls you seek perhaps first you would try one in England? The Whit Ball is the place to go."

Brandenburg smiled. "I have heard that, I would so dearly like to attend." Winnie's eyes lit up.

"Well, it couldn't be simpler! I am having a little event on Friday and Mr Whit will be in attendance. I could introduce you."

"Oh, I couldn't presume to ask for an invitation."

"Don't be silly, Count Brandenburg, a charming gentleman like you would not need to ask. In fact, I am amazed that you have not been asked already. You must come to my event on Friday. You must."

The dance finished and the couple bowed.

"My Lady, if you could introduce me to the honourable and esteemed Nathanial Whit, I would be beholden to you." He leant down and kissed her hand, forcing her to momentarily forget that she was married. The blood ran to her cheeks.

———•◦•———

The Irregulars piled into the Playhouse as silently as they could. This was unsuccessful however as each person's 'hush' was met with a chorus of 'hushes' from everybody else. They barrelled down the aisle towards the stage.

Herschel, who was always extra sprightly when under the influence, led the way. When he reached the front row, he halted everybody behind him with an extra loud hush.

"Behold!" he cried with poor vocal projection, "the script!" and he raised his hands in glorious wonder towards the Nathanial Whit board that lay against the backdrop. The other Irregulars cheered a cheer that carried little enthusiasm.

"We've seen it all before," dismissed Lupe as she pushed passed the writer and walked up onto the stage. "Antoine Le Magnifique? I want to see something amazing!"

Everybody knew what she meant and cheered as they rushed passed Herschel to get onto the stage and secure prime seating.

"Very well!" cried Antoine, "I will because, by God, we are Kings and Queens of all we see! Come, Herschel, take Tobias's wheel here, I want everyone to witness this!" At that, Antoine rushed up to join the others, leaving Herschel and Tobias amongst the empty seats.

———•◦•———

Brandenburg left the Almack in secrecy. It had been hard to do so and had taken considerable cunning on his part to slip away. Inside

The Almack Assembly Rooms, his opening night had been a resounding success. He had danced well, something he had never dreamt he would do, he had talked and laughed appropriately and he had acted with dignity and poise at every turn. He patted his breast pocket and felt the thirteen invitations to coffee mornings, elevenses poker games, afternoon teas and all night 'ahems' that he had acquired over the evening. For one treacherous moment he thought that maybe things were better when one was off the wagon and in company of those who had heritage. A sudden flash of realisation blinded him. This was who he truly was. He had been slumming it for too long. It was time to cast off the wastrels whom he had clung to, and they to him, for the past twenty or so years and reclaim his rightful place amongst the elite.

He let the thought settle in his mind for a few seconds. He convulsed at the realisation of his thoughts and baulked. He held his stomach and threw a panicked look up and down the street. Fortune pitied him. King Street was deserted. Count Brandenburg dashed to the dark side of the street and let his extrusion gush forth from his belly. It was over in an instant and a welcome feeling of calm returned. He undid his collar and took a few deep breaths. By the time he had exhaled his fifth breath the reassuring desire for The Roxy returned. He looked around for Archie and hoped to tell him of his success inside the Almack and his sudden failing outside. Most of all, he wanted to have a few scoops with his mate. Archie was nowhere to be seen. Brandenburg didn't need to think about possibilities or alternatives. He knew his friend. Archie had probably grown bored of waiting and gone drinking or hunting Giselle, or got bored of waiting and gone Giselle hunting first and drinking after. He knew his pal was safe but he needed a drink to drown out that mutinous feeling he had had a few moments ago. How could he think that? The Almack was not that alluring. Not nearly as alluring as Herschel's vanilla tobacco, or Danilov's acrobatics, not to mention to the smell of Antoine's moustache wax or Lupe's almond breath. He really, really needed a drink.

He scuttled unseen through the back alleys until he could find the nearest drinking den possible. He soon came to 'The Savvy Goose', a tiny corner bar on the borders of the St Giles rookery. Brandenburg took his jacket off, turned it inside out and put it back on. The effect of wearing the tatty inner lining on the outside calmed him greatly and he felt he could walk into the bar and not get glassed within moments. It worked. Nobody cared for the idiot with the tatty jacket and unsettling haircut who skulked in, downed four pints and walked out again within the space of a few minutes.

The Irregulars milled around the stage as if they were an indifferent audience to a free play. Antoine set a single serving table in the centre of the stage and then stood behind it. He cleared his throat. No good. He cleared his throat again and Lupe looked at him.

"Oh really, Antoine, we are all passed that now, come and join us in talking about Herschel and his masterwork!"

"Yes do!" said Herschel, "get involved, mon amie, it's something new!"

Antoine put his hands on his belt and chewed his lips.

"Oh really,' he said with disdain, "something new, that's what you want? Well here is something new!"

Gertie, at the back of the crowd with Valerie, nudged her. "They've riled him up, watch this!" he whispered. Valerie stopped trying to fight her way into the Players chatter but instead turned her attention to Antoine.

"Right, that's it!" said the Frenchman and he slammed the table with his fists before running into the midst of the Players and grabbing the handles of Tobias' chair. He yanked him out of the centre of the crowd and pulled him around the little table and faced him toward the group. Everybody looked at everybody else and edged backwards, making a semi circle. Antoine moved around the table, positioning himself in between the audience and Tobias. He smiled at him. Antoine turned around to face the crowd.

"So then, something different, I see. I think I can oblige." He moved around the table and stood behind Tobias. "How about 'The Gascony Knife Dance' as you have never seen it?"

The ruse had worked. The Irregulars had performed a great sting operation and Antoine was the target. Their ambivalence to his preparation had ignited his passion and now they were in for a real show.

———•—••———

The huge door at the end of the corridor swung open and black-cloaked bodies filed out. Each man took a position along the corridor until a 'tunnel' was formed. When the last man had taken his place each one stamped their right foot once. Nathanial Whit and his hooded colleague left the secret room and walked down the corridor and up into the labyrinth of Bedlam.

"Tell me," hissed the cowl, "are the preparations set?"

"They are, my Lord; everyone will be at the ball."

The cloaked man stopped at a fork in the corridor. He turned and looked at Nathanial Whit.

"Peace be with you, brother," he hissed.

"Death be unto the other," snarled Nathanial. The man in the cowl turned and disappeared into the recesses of Bethlam Hospital

Antoine soaked up the applause with a proud smile and transferred it to Tobias via an unseen squeeze of the metallurgist's upper arm. His contact said 'trust me'. Antoine flicked his coat tails aside to reveal two eight-inch kitchen knives in his belt. He pulled them out, leant over Tobias and angled the points toward the metallurgist's hands which were spread on the tabletop.

The knife-dance began. The tips of the knives fell at a slow, introductory rate inbetween Tobias' fingers. The audience settled themselves into their positions, ready for the show ahead. Slowly, the knives came down harder and faster and faster and faster. Valerie was the first to gasp and she clamped her mouth in fear as the knives became a blur. Antoine was up to full speed and the tap-taps of the knives sounded like frenzied woodpeckers. The Irregulars held their own competition to see who could follow one blade and track its sequence. Antoine was too fast. The knives seemed to disappear, lost in motion.

———•◦•———

Nathanial Whit began the long ascent through the bowels of the asylum all the while contemplating the events that had occurred during the secret meeting between himself and his associates. His friend in the cowl was on the brink of magnificence and Nathanial had to pinch himself every few seconds to assure himself that he was, indeed, a witness to it all. He turned a corner and proceeded down a straight and filth-lined corridor. He was halfway toward the turning at the other end when a strange and unsettling wheezy vowel floated through the air. He stopped walking and listened.

"A…." came the wheeze again, louder and more pained than before, carrying an echo suggesting that it had travelled great distance. Nathanial turned and looked back down the corridor. There was another wheeze.

"N," it spluttered. Nathanial felt an odd sense of curiosity float up inside his mind.

"A," another wheeze came.

Nathanial picked up a torch from the wall and began to seek the source of the wheezing.

Antoine had his audience under his spell and so started to alternate the sequence changing rhythm and changing direction also. The left hand copied the right hand perfectly and then it mirrored it, replicating the sequence in a back-to-front order. The audience gasped. Desiree could hardly watch, but Claudia was wide eyed and trying her best not to jump up and down with giddy excitement and ready to break into rapturous applause, their communal desire for witnessing magic sated.

Then Antoine performed the impossible. He crossed over his arms and performed the entire sequence in reverse and back-to-front, and at double speed. He was sweating and concentrating hard but, ever the showman, he sometimes offered up a grimace or a sigh of relief at escaping a near miss. The audience lapped it up, everybody believing that Antoine was voyaging into the unknown and possibly just one jab away from impaling poor Tobias to the table.

Nathanial had ventured far into the catacombs of Bethlam hospital and was standing in a bricked atrium which presented three equally foreboding passages away from the one in which he had come.

He spun the torch around. The cobblestones reflected an impossible amount of etched tally marks and arrows. Nathanial stood in the centre of the room in horrified silence at the realisation that, perhaps, a thousand men had stumbled this way and had never been seen again.

"N," floated into the atrium. Nathanial swung his flaming torch toward the direction of the noise. Third entrance.

"...A..." drifted out.

Nathanial rallied, held his torch aloft and marched into the darkness.

———•••———

Antoine's performance ended with a shout of "Allez!" and he threw his knives into the air. They spun upward, reached their peak, turned over and descended point first, straight down towards Tobias. Everybody froze. Antoine blew gently on his fingers to dry the sweat, never once taking his eyes of the falling blades. A few worried looks were thrown to Antoine, the audience starting to lose their sense of confidence. Had the Frenchman gone too far? The blades fell and Desiree was about to call out, when Antoine shot his arms out. Desiree screamed. Everybody closed their eyes. They heard Tobias's panicked breaths turn to laughs of relief. They opened their eyes. Tobias was sitting there as before, hands flat on the table with a wild-eyed look of astonishment on his face. Antoine was standing over him, arms outstretched and holding the knives millimetres from Tobias's hands. He had caught them by the handles at the last possible moment. Everybody gasped and clapped. Antoine soaked up their adoration and bowed deeply.

The rapturous applause was halted by the sound of the theatre doors opening. The Irregulars turned in unison to see Archie, white as a ghost walk in. Immediately, Claudia rushed from the group, hitched up her dress and ran down the steps and along to the aisle to be with him. As she leapt at him, Archie grabbed her mechanically and held her close.

"This kiss is only for friend's love!" said Claudia as she kissed his neck.

"Friends love," parroted the sweat covered and ashen Archie.

From forty feet away and undercover of bad stage lighting, the Irregulars could still sense that something was not quite right.

"What is the matter, cockatoo?" chirped Lupe. Claudia climbed off of Archie and stood in front of him. His face was white.

"I'm tired," he said quietly, "I need to sleep."

And with that, Archie walked like a zombie through the stage and towards his quarters leaving the rest of the Players dumbstruck.

———•◦•———

Nathanial Whit crept into a Dutch-angled cell block. He had to tilt at an alarming degree to get through the opening. He folded himself into the room.

"Hello... who makes the alphabet at night?" There was silence. Nathanial Whit spat on the floor and went to leave.

"S....." suddenly invaded the gloom. Nathanial spun around and shone his torch towards the bars of the cells.

"Who said that?"

There was a giggle and a scratching. Nathanial moved his torch over the bars to illuminate the cell. He could not count the amount of people within the enclosure, only the mounds.

"Who is there?"

There was a shuffle in the corner. Nathanial moved his torch over. He saw a bundle jolt and wriggle. It rolled over and looked at him. Nathanial's eyes widened.

"Who are you?"

The wheezing stopped as the creature rolled onto its front and dragged its way towards Nathanial.

"A.N.A.N.A.S" said Mr Whit. "What does that mean?"
The creature rolled onto its back and pawed the air like an upturned beetle.

"Ananas, Ananas, Ananas," it cried.

Nathanial Whit was sideswiped at hearing the surname he had not heard in thirty years.

"Who? Speak you madman!"

The beast rolled onto its front and in a display of hitherto unseen strength pressed itself upright. It was a man. Nathanial Whit held the torch close to himself as the wheezing figure walked towards him.

"Ananas," it croaked.

"Ananas?" whispered Whit, suddenly reconciling the laugh he heard earlier to the name he heard now.

"What do you know of that name, madman?"

"I am no mad…man," wheezed the figure. "I am...an artist..."

"What do you know of that name? Tell me!"

The figure gently rubbed a hole in his throat. A trickle of puss sloped out.

"They call me river corpse. But in truth I am….more," he said as he wiped the sludge from his throat.

Nathanial cupped his mouth with his sleeve. The figure assumed an odd poise that hinted at past assurance.

"My name is Kemble," it said.

Chapter Thirty Four

Brandenburg's First Act

Nathanial Whit left the asylum as the sun was rising. He decided to walk for a while, so as to take some time to comprehend what he'd experienced. The strange inmate named Kemble talked in circles, as madmen do, but in his babbling had thrown up words that bothered Whit. Words like *'Ananas'*, *'Almack'* and *'deceit'*. How they were linked, he did not know. Nathanial's questioning had not garnered conclusive results. As well as the babbling, the inmate suffered from a most appalling condition where vile liquid seeped from his open throat wound whenever he spoke too much.

More curious than the few discernable words he had thrown up, was the look the creature had about him. There was a strange distant gleam in his eyes that was not so becoming of one who had lost their mind totally, but of one who was of sound reckoning and just so happened to be surrounded by insanity. He had the look of a killer about him. Nathanial concluded that the inmate may be of future use and so consigned the name 'Kemble' to his memory banks and hailed a carriage to take him the rest of the way home.

Brandenburg came back to The Roxy in the early hours of the morning. The Irregulars were already up and dressed and sitting on the stage, facing the Nathanial boards. Herschel was taking them through the floor plan room by room. The Players were all taking notes except for Claudia who was playing cat's cradle with some string. She had glanced at the map once and already had it firmly imprinted in her mind, such was her gift.

Herschel stopped mid sentence when he saw Brandenburg walking down the aisle. Everyone turned to him and stood up.

"My darling!" cried Lupe, "how did it go? And what did you do to Archie?"

"The performance was…bearable." Replied Brandenburg.

Herschel raised his eyebrow. "Don't be modest, it don't suit you like that jacket does."

Brandenburg beamed. "Smashed it."

The Players erupted and rushed over to him, all talking at once. Brandenburg hugged them all. "It was you, it was all you!" he gushed.

"Nonsense!" said Herschel, "my words are just ink on paper. You gave them life!"

"And my clothes are just rags and stitches, you give them grace!" shrieked Lupe as she showered him in kisses. Brandenburg raised his arms to calm the crowd down.

"Now, where is Archie? What were you saying about him?"

"He came home," said Desiree, "white as a sheet and went straight to bed!"

"I'll go see what the matter is," said the Count and squeezed his way through the crowd.

"Count Brandenburg?" called out Valerie. He turned to her. "Any news on the next performance?" she said timidly as she beckoned to the Nathanial board. The crowd murmured in agreement at her question. Brandenburg fished in his pocket and handed Valerie a card.

"On Friday I have an introduction to see the mark," he said, "Desiree, put on your best dress. This is your curtain call."

Desiree beamed with delight and flung her arms around Herschel.

"The rest of you," he began "will take Friday as a good opportunity to familiarise yourself with the stage plan." He tapped the Nathanial Board and bowed to the Players. They all bowed back and he left the stage. As soon as he was out of sight, they erupted into delirious chatter.

————•◦•————

Before attending to Archie, Brandenburg took a detour to Tobias's workshop. He peered around the door to see the metallurgist hunched over his workbench. He knocked politely on the doorframe.

"Come in!" cried Tobias upon seeing him, "I have something to show you!" Brandenburg entered as Tobias wheeled himself across the workshop and lifted the magical blade off its holding.

"See here!" he said as he handed it to the Count. The blade performed its magic trick for Brandenburg and he stood amazed at its beauty.

"How is this possible? Is it magic?"

"Only God's magic and my father's know-how."

Brandenburg smiled, "It is amazing what fathers know, isn't it?" He handed it back to Tobias who replaced the blade on the pedestal. "And the basket?"

"Over there."

Brandenburg walked to the other work bench and picked up the gold and bejewelled Spider's belly and held it close for inspection.

"This is a masterpiece! Will the mandibles form the quillons, as I designed?"

"They will. Everything is how you requested."

"Masterful," whispered the Count as he turned the gold spider over. "But there is one thing."

"What is it? Have I made a mistake?"

Brandenburg smiled and knelt down beside his friend. He held his hands and looked into his eyes.

"The blade, it is too fine. It cannot go with the basket."

"I don't understand"

"The basket is perfect, but the blade is too fine and I cannot wear it. I wish I could explain better, but you will have to trust me."

"You want me to destroy it?" Tobias said in a fearful tone.

"Oh dear God no, save it, please save it, but for this sword, I would like a modest, plain blade. Can you do that for me?"

Tobias looked to the floor, clearly devastated that his fine work would not see the light of day.

"My dear man, it will have its day, I promise you, but not yet." Tobias sighed and nodded. "As you wish," he said, "a plain blade it is."

"Thank you, my man, thank you" and he kissed his friend on the forehead and left the room. Tobias turned to the blade and, as if he were burying a loved one, gently laid an oil-stained rag over it.

Brandenburg made his way to Archie's quarters where he found him sat on his bed with his head bowed. The Count sat next to him.

"What's up, Mr Enfield?"

Archie relayed the events of the evening without any embellishment or artistic flourishes. He simply laid it down.

Nathanial and his mysterious friend, the strange symbol on the cigarillo case, the coach ride, the descent into Bedlam. Brandenburg took it all in without making a sound. His mind cogs were turning slowly as he processed the information.

"I wouldn't worry about it, dear boy" he said eventually, "who cares what nefarious dealings the wanker is dabbling in."

"That's not all" said Archie, "there is something else, something more about Bedlam."

"What?"

"Kemble."

"What?"

"He's alive. I saw him inside there. He's alive!"

Brandenburg saw the fear behind his friend's eyes and understood the implications of his discovery.

"What are we going to do?"

"The only thing we can do, Archie. We keep this between us. We can't tell the others. Imagine the fear it would spread. All we can do is keep it peeped and pray that the bastard rots inside that madhouse."

"What if he gets out?"

"Nobody gets out of Bedlam."

"But what if: he's defied death! He's in with the Devil now."

"We can't think like that! We can't let the fear take us, Archie. Now look, we are going to keep this between us, aren't we? We are going to be strong for the protection of the others, for Ms Adberg, for Claudia. Can you do that for me?"

Archie looked at him and nodded. "I can do that, Benji, I can do that."

"Good man," said the Count as he stood up. "Now, get some rest. We have a party to go to on Friday."

Archie perked up at the word *'party'*. Brandenburg smiled.

"That's right, dear boy. You're coming too. We're going to perform. Now get some rest."

The Count left Archie to his thoughts which were now on parties, wine and women in reverse order. Archie lay down on his bed and fell into a calmer sleep as all fears of Kemble sunk away.

———•••———

"Inspection!" yelled Srdjan at the top of his lungs. Five figures, decked head to toe in black, marched out onto the stage and stood to attention. Srdjan looked them over.

"Not bad, not bad, you are punctual, which is a start! Now, remove your hoods. Let's have a look at you!" the black figures obeyed. Srdjan stood back to see Gertie, Danilov, Antoine and Claudia standing before him.

"What is our mission?"

"Reconnaissance of the Whit Mansion" they shouted.

"What are our objectives?"

"Gain entry; scope for loot, walk the floor and exit."

"And what are we?"

"Shadows!"

"And who are we?"

"The Roxy Playhouse Irregulars."

The soldiers stamped their feet in unison.

"Alright Players, let's get to the playground!" and at that Srdjan pulled on his black mask and jumped off the stage. The Players donned their masks and rushed after him, full of military pep. From the wings, Herschel and Lupe chuckled to themselves.

"That idiot loves the Wellington routine!" said Herschel as he filled his pipe.

"Did you see Claudia?" said a fawning Lupe. "So sweet, I thought my heart would break! Do you think she will be alright?"

"I bloody well hope so," Archie's voice came from across the stage. He walked into the light to the laughter of Herschel. Mr Enfield was clean and well dressed with combed and parted hair. Lupe walked over to him, her pendulous hips swinging wildly.

"You look good enough to eat!" she purred, holding his cheeks in her hands.

"If only you would, my dear," said Archie with a wink. Lupe leant into his ear.

"If you don't get lucky tonight, come to my quarters. It's about time I gave you an opportunity to better yourself," and she slapped his backside. Herschel walked over and handed a pouch of tobacco to Archie.

"Take this, you will need a supply. It's a good ice breaker if you're caught milling around with the other man servants."

"Good thinking, cheers."

He pocketed the tobacco and straightened his coat. Herschel looked him over.

"For a second rate actor, you do make a first rate impression."

"Thanks, I think."

Brandenburg stepped onto the stage and stood beside Lupe. She tutted at him and flicked his cravat.

"What is this? Are you wearing boiled cabbage? No, no, no, this will never do," and she whipped the cravat off and, from her never-ending cleavage, she pulled out another and tied it on.

"Perfect," she said. The others nodded in agreement.

From the other side of the stage came a cough. They turned to see Ms Adberg standing in the wings.

"Ladies and gentlemen, may I present to you Lady Desiree Ricci of Perugia" she stood aside and, from the darkness behind her, floated Desiree. Heartbeats were skipped and time stopped. Desiree walked into the stage and stood before them. She was wearing a beautiful, dark blue off-the-shoulder dress that clung to her torso before falling off of her hips like a waterfall. Her perfect skin glistened in the light. The men slowly bowed to her, each one speechless and each one hopelessly in love with her in an instant.

"Giselle," whispered Archie. Desiree walked up to the group.

"Do I look alright?" she said without any hint of compliment fishing.

"You have never been more beautiful," said Brandenburg. "You are Grace incarnate."

Desiree blushed and looked at Lupe whose tears said more than any words could. Desiree nodded her thanks before turning to Herschel. "Do you think I look alright?"

"You are the reason for paint and canvas," he whispered. Desiree smiled broadly and turned to Archie. She rolled her eyes when she clocked his eager expression. He went to speak but she halted him.

"No," she said firmly.

"But…"

"Behave yourself tonight!"

Archie looked at his feet in disappointment. Desiree smiled.

"Unless we find ourselves in a cupboard…"

"You're also the reason God gave us castrating irons!" said Herschel, looking at Archie who caught his drift.

There was a sudden sound of rope being pulled tight and then the faintest of thuds. The Players turned around to see Anya making a rare appearance on the ground. She walked up to Desiree who turned to the acrobat and presented herself fully. Anya looked her over before winking at the Umbrian. Anya walked back to her rope and scurried back up to the rafters.

"Well then, on that note of approval," said Brandenburg, "to the dance we go. Lady Ricci if you please," and he held out his arm and she took it.

"Ladies and Gentlemen," said Brandenburg, "we shall return at a reasonable hour. Before we do, I suggest you go to Archie's quarters, move his bed and lift up the crooked floorboard. Under which you will find enough stored cash to have a party of your own."

"But…" protested Archie.

"Speak when you're spoken to, footman!" mocked the Count, "Have fun on his expense, my dears."

"We will, you can count on it" said Herschel.

Brandenburg led his fiancée and his bat-man out of the theatre and into the evening air.

Srdjan and 'The Backstage Players' had commandeered a mail coach and were currently rocketing out of town towards Nathanial Whit's mansion in Surrey.

"Are you ready, Little Mouse," said Antoine as he noticed Claudia looking a little tense.

"I am! I will not fail you!" she said.

"And we will not fail you," retorted the Frenchman. The other Players nodded in agreement. The safety of little Claudia was more important than anything else they could dream of.

"Wait!" said Gertie suddenly, "did you hear that?"

"No" said Antoine, "what?"

"That! Listen." The Players craned their ears to try and discern any out of place sound. All they heard was the sound of the carriage rumbling over an uneven surface.

"There!" said Gertie, "I can hear a rattle."

"Probably the axle," said Danilov. Gertie stuck his head out of the window.

"Look at the fellow!" said Antoine, "one little adventure on a carriage and suddenly he is a master!"

"Stop the carriage!" shouted Gertie. Srdjan heard him and pulled the reins. The horses pulled up and the carriage halted. Gertie held everyone in silence with his raised finger. They heard a thud.

"Right" said Antoine as he and Danilov threw the doors open, "let's see what that is!"

They cautiously climbed out of the cabin which had parked on a tree-lined country path. Antoine moved around the carriage until he came to the rear. "Hold it right there!" he said, "step off the carriage before you meet steel!"

The other Players climbed out to see who he was addressing. They backed around the carriage flanking the shadowed figure that was clinging to the back of the carriage. Srdjan drew his sword.

"Slowly!" he commanded. The figure alighted from the carriage and raised its hands.

"Unmask yourself!" said Antoine as he raised his fists and took a pugilist's stance.

The figure slowly removed its mask and the Players relaxed.

"Valerie!" exclaimed Gertie, "what the hell are you doing here?"

"I'm sorry, I didn't mean to, just I wanted to help is all, and be of use. I'm sorry, don't stab me!"

"We very nearly did!" said Srdjan has he sheathed his blade, "why didn't you just ask?" Valerie looked to the floor.

"Well, I for one am glad you are here," said Danilov. Valerie smiled at him.

"You are?"

"Of course, one more set of eyes to keep on the Frenchman here!" and with that he slapped Antoine's shoulder. The group laughed at his expense.

"Come on then," said Srdjan, "we can't stand around here all night. Everybody back on board."

The Backstage Players, now with the recruited Valerie, squeezed back into the carriage and it began to roll into the night.

"I need the toilet" said Valerie. The carriage jolted to a halt.

"Joke," she said.

———•◦•———

Archie stepped out of the carriage and kicked down the footplate. He held up his hand and Desiree took it and stepped down. He ran around the other side of the coach and helped Brandenburg alight. They were fifty yards from Lady Bronwyn's house. They could see the wonderful red brick mansion lit up with a thousand garden candles. To the left of it stood a huge conservatory where guests were already gathering.

The sight was magnificent and Archie fleetingly wished that he had been cast in Brandenburg's role. *'Maybe inside there is Giselle,'* he thought, *'no time for that now, there's a show to do!'*

He straightened his jacket, paid the coach driver to park and turned to look at Brandenburg and Desiree who were standing side by side as friends would. Archie crossed his arms and hung his head.

"Really!" he said dismayed.

"What?" Brandenburg said.

"Well, you don't exactly set my tongue wagging. You're a pair of librarians. Look at you two!"

Brandenburg and Desiree looked at each other and shrugged.

Archie threw his head back and muttered a few words to the heavens.

"Look" he said with great impatience, "I could sail a clipper between the pair of you. You're supposed to be in love." He gestured for them to stand closer. They edged closer to each other. He gestured again. They moved even closer. He gestured again.

"Look," said the Count, "If we were any closer, we would be inside each other!"

"Well that's precisely the point. You two are supposed to be in cataclysmic love. Right now it looks like you ain't never even seen each other. Get busy looking like you're fucking, or get busy fucking off! Now kiss!"

Brandenburg and Desiree looked at each other and nodded. For the sake of performance, Brandenburg kissed Desiree. Slowly and awkwardly at first but, after a few inquisitive movements, their tongues found each other and soon they were kissing like they had invented it.

"Alright, alright" said Archie has he separated them, "that was just unsettling. But at least you now look more the part."

Brandenburg and Desiree were flushed and breathing heavily.

"Are we ready, loves?" said Archie.

"I'm ready," said Brandenburg.

"I am ready," said Desiree.

"Alright then, let's get busy" and he led the actors up the driveway and towards the waiting Master of Ceremonies.

"If you tell Herschel about this, I will kill you," whispered Desiree.

"Me or him?" Archie said.

"Both of you."

Chapter Thirty Five

Reconnaisance

S rdjan pulled the carriage to a halt just outside the grounds of Eveltham House. He dismounted and walked the horses off the road and into the nearby copse. Once the carriage was completely hidden from view, he tied the horses off and opened the carriage door.

"Alright," he whispered, "we are a few yards from the house, but from here on in, as quiet as the dead. Ready?"

The Players looked at each other and nodded.

"Let's do this," said Valerie with an overt conviction. Antoine chuckled at her.

"As she said!" he declared, and they all piled out.

"Right," said Srdjan, "we'll flank the house and approach the service entrance from the east side. From there we will split up; Gertie, Danilov and Valerie?"

"Service corridor," said Gertie

"Perimeter," said Danilov

"What they said," concurred Valerie.

"Antoine and Claudia?"

"With you, watching her," answered Antoine.

"With him and you looking at the goodies," said Claudia.

"Perfect. One hour, maximum, in out and back here, ready?"

Everybody nodded.

"Let's go rehearse."

The Players huzzahed as quietly as they could and followed the Dalmatian as he ran into the copse.

———•·•———

Brandenburg and Desiree had been well received into the party. After they had been announced, Lady Bronwyn had swooped in to grab him. Brandenburg introduced his 'fiancée' and Desiree purred her hello in such a fashion as to strike and instant connection with Winnie. Brandenburg then, against all protocol, introduced his servant, Archie Enfield who bowed and said not a word as servants should. Winnie was stunned at first, but after Desiree touched her shoulder and said that it was one of Brandenburg's pleasant oddities that he liked to make his servants feel as friends she felt even warmer inside.

"Come," said Winnie as she took Desiree's hand, "let me show you around the room"

Desiree bowed her head in appreciation and the two women left Brandenburg and Archie alone. They had been standing around for nearly a whole second before a waiter appeared with a drinks tray.

"Champagne, sir?"

"Thank you," said Brandenburg as he took the glass. The waiter scuttled off and the Count turned to face Archie. He stood so close to him that their noses were touching.

"What are you doing, Old Love?"

"Here," said Brandenburg, "drink this! I can't get smashed!" and he thrust the champagne flute into his hand. "Quick, before anyone sees!"

Archie grabbed the glass and necked it. Brandenburg grabbed the empty flute from him and turned around as normal. He raised the empty glass to salute the nearby gentry and placed the glass in on a passing tray.

"I like this job," whispered Archie.

"Just remember it in the morning," Brandenburg whispered back, "right, the plan is to orbit the room a bit, press the flesh and move towards an introduction to our mark that is around here somewhere. Savvy?

"Savvy."

"Good man, come on, follow my lead."

"Before we go in, tell me something, Old Love," said Archie, grabbing his arm.

"What?" Brandenburg whispered.

"What was it like to kiss Desiree?"

"If I told you, you'd need a lie down."

"Herschel, that lucky bastard, I knew it."

"I know, anyway, let's go to work." Brandenburg spied a conversing group who seemed to be running out of steam and walked over to them. Archie, hands behind his back followed, making sure to not make eye contact with anyone who appeared to be of higher standing than his character.

Srdjan and the team had reached the edge of the copse and now faced the glass conservatory and the dreaded danger zone. As Nathanial and his wife were at Lady Bronwyn's event, the house was being run by the staff and so, barely any lights were on. The lawn was safe to cross.

"Alright, here we are. Good luck, Players," said Srdjan who was about to dart out into the night when Gertie grabbed his arm.

"What?"

Gertie grabbed him and pulled him close. "You make sure nothing happens to Claudia, understand?" Antoine stifled his laugh of pride as Srdjan looked at the boy with shocked surprise. Gertie's tone was firm and threatening. He relaxed his grip and Srdjan stood to full height.

"Gertie," he said, "I give you my word as your friend and peer, no harm will come to Claudia. Not under my watch."

"Good man," said Gertie.

"And not when we would have you to answer to," added Antoine with a wry smile as he ruffled Gertie's hair.

"Alright, alright," said Gertie. "Begone with you, Gentlemen!"

Srdjan nodded and he darted off across the lawn, diving and rolling like a fox. Antoine bowed ridiculously at the group and followed Srdjan, mimicking his moves with comic buffoonery. Claudia was about to leave when she turned to Gertie and kissed him on the lips.

"Thank you for your concern, Gertie. You are a fine man. If I wasn't betrothed to another, I would ask to you hold my hand," and at that Little Mouse skipped out across the lawn as if she was walking through a meadow in spring time.

"Shall we?" said Danilov, gesturing to Gertie to move off towards the other side of the house.

"After you, sir, after you."

Danilov smiled and saluted the young soldier before walking out into the moonlight. Valerie looked at his figure as he walked over the service entrance. Once again she was overcome with desire for the acrobat and gripped Gertie's arm.

"Sorry," she said, "I'm just nervous."

"Come on, let's go," he said and they both ran out across the lawn to join Danilov.

———•—•———

Archie had spent an hour standing beside Brandenburg as he talked and joked with a wide variety of guests whom, to Archie anyway, all seemed exactly the same. Same clothes, same topics of discussion and the same forced laughs. The rich were terrible actors he concluded and was suddenly, overwhelmingly, appreciative of Brandenburg's performance. How masterful his friend was at working the room in the face of such a depressing audience. He knew that his initial reaction in the carriage park had been wrong. He was thankful that he had not been cast in the dashing lead role.

Whether it was his boredom that triggered his guard to fall, or whether it was the power of her presence that broke though he could not tell and, even on his deathbed many years later he hadn't figured it out. But, as Archie Enfield stood beside Count Abraham von Brandenburg on that fateful night, he felt a presence in the room. He felt like he was suddenly in a dream, or in a fantasy of his own making. There was a person in the room who was unlike anyone else. There was an interloper, an imposter. He subtly looked around at the group laughing and snorting into their drinks. They hadn't noticed it. He diverted his concentration from Brandenburg's performance and onto the presence in the room. It was really there. He felt a seachange within him.

Archie looked beyond the group in front of him and around the room. The normal people turned to grey and faded from vision. His eyes tracked for colour. Then, in an instant he caught a flash of pink. A sudden shock of flesh passed between a crowd of people and then it was gone. He knew it meant one thing and one thing only: there was a woman in the room, a real woman. He gradually began to inch away from his mark beside Brandenburg and towards the back of the Gathering Hall in order to get a better view of the plain in which his prey walked.

———•◦•———

Antoine and Srdjan stood guard at the door of the reception hall. Claudia was already busy at work inside the room. The chamber was filled with trinkets and fine solid silver candelabras, gold plates, jewel encrusted goblets and fruit bowls. She walked over to each table and plinth and looked at the objects. Her eyes fogged over as she took a long, deliberate glare at each. Every dimension and detail was catalogued in her mind. She worked slowly around the room until, eventually, she was done. She trotted over to Srdjan in the doorway and tugged at his coat.

"Finished," she whispered.

"Good work, Mouse. Antoine, where next?"

"Dining hall," he whispered as he took Claudia's hand. Srdjan looked around before leading the two out of the room and down the corridor.

Danilov, Gertie and Valerie meanwhile where busy walking around the service corridor that circled the mansion. So far, they had neither seen nor heard anyone else.

"Servants must be asleep," said Gertie.

"Probably in their quarters having tea; it's only nine o'clock," said Valerie.

Danilov hushed them both as he approached a corner in the corridor. He peered around it and ducked back. "Someone's coming!" he whispered. Gertie and Valerie looked around the corridor for a place to hide.

"Quick, in here!" said Gertie as he opened a door to a dark room. The three of them piled in and closed the door just in time as two laundry maids walked past. They waited until for a full minute before breathing in relief. They looked around the room.

"Where are we?" said Gertie. The sudden panic having seemingly erased the map from their minds. They felt around the walls and floor.

"I can feel flagstones," whispered Valerie, "why are there flagstones inside?"

"We're in the chapel," said Gertie, "this must have been here first, and then the house annexed to it."

"We...," Danilov stopped. The door was opening. "Hide!" he whispered. Gertie dived under a pew and held his breath. Valerie stood in the aisle looking around.

"Val, hide!" whispered Danilov as the door handle turned fully. She was frozen.

Danilov reached out and grabbed the frightened girl and dragged her to the side. He fell backwards into the confessional booth and Valerie fell onto his lap. The door opened just as the she managed to pull the curtain closed. Four men entered and chose to sit on the pew under which Gertie was hiding.

———•———

"Count Brandenburg," said Winnie, interrupting his conversation. "Come, you need to meet some people. Gentlemen, do excuse me for dragging him away from you."

The group smiled in acceptance of her apologies. She dragged him away.

"You're fiancée is making quite the impression. Come to her." Winnie pulled Brandenburg through the crowd and thrust him into a group of which Desiree was holding court. The women were hating themselves for their jealousy and at the same time loving Desiree for her warmth, and the men were drowning in their envy that someone had won her heart before they had.

"Ladies and Gentlemen!" said Winnie, "please meet…"

"My dear!" interrupted Desiree, "how good of you to come and say hello!"

Brandenburg smiled at the crowd and stood next to Desiree. He kissed the nape of her neck in a gesture, he hoped, would convince the group that they were enamoured. It worked.

"My love!" said the Umbrian, "please meet Lord Rafe De Locke."

Lord De Locke, caked in make-up and wearing a lurid silk blouse bowed ridiculously to Brandenburg.

"My dear Count, what an honour! What a chime of angels! What a what! Your dear lady Desiree has spun us countless stories of your grand deeds!"

Brandenburg shot Desiree a little look of mistrust at the thought that she might have been building him up too much.

"Has she indeed!"

"Oh," said a voice to the side of De Locke. "It was nothing we had not heard before, and nay expected of you. We have also heard tell that you wooed all seven panellists at the Almack in twelve minutes flat!" Brandenburg turned to the voice.

"This," began Desiree, "is…"

"Nathanial Whit," said Brandenburg. A look of seriousness washed over Desiree but, luckily, it went unnoticed.

"You know me?"

"Only by reputation," said Brandenburg.

"Then you do me a great honour," said Whit locking eyes with the Count. There was a tense moment hanging in the air. The two men may have well drawn swords at that moment. Lord De Locke did not pick up on it at all.

"Well," he declared, "new friends meeting! Isn't this fun?"

Desiree smiled graciously at him.

Across the room Archie kept one eye on the Brandenburg and Desiree and another on the odd flashes of colour that permeated his vision.

———•◦•———

Srdjan signalled that the coast was clear before running back across the lawn and into the copse. Antoine looked down at Claudia. The concentration she had exerted in memorising every detail of every prized possession on the Whit Mansion had exhausted her. She leant against his leg and he saw her eyes become heavy.

"Come, Little Mouse," he whispered as he held out his arms. Claudia climbed into them and he lifted her up and held her close to his chest. The smell of his moustache wax and the security of his strong grip sent her into a happy sleep and, once he could hear her snore those sweet snores, he crept across the lawn to join Srdjan.

Gertie, Danilov and Valerie where not so lucky; they were still trapped in the chapel. Danilov and Valerie were stuck in the confessional box and Gertie was hiding under the occupied pew. The men sitting on it were annoyingly pious. Gertie closed his eyes and relaxed his heart in preparation for a long wait.

In the confessional booth Valerie, sitting on Danilov's lap, could not lower her heart. The possibility of being caught at any second filled her with volcanic adrenaline. Danilov held her tight and could feel her heavy breathing. The back of her head was resting against his shoulder and his nose was next to her ear. He could smell her skin and her hair. It was too potent a mix and, against his better judgment, his biology over came him.

Valerie fixed her gaze on the curtain that rested a few inches from her face and separated them from the men outside. Her heart was beating so loudly that she was sure they would hear it. Danilov tried to hold his breath to calm himself. He thought of waterfalls and frogs but it was no use. Valerie's eyes widened in panicked astonishment as she felt Danilov's arousal rise up and press against her thigh.

———•◦•———

"Count Brandenburg," said De Locke, "Lady Bronwyn tells me that Desiree is a ballerina by trade. Is it so?"

Brandenburg broke off his battling stare from Nathanial and turned to the foppish Lord. "Indeed she is. Perhaps the finest I have ever seen!"

"Well, that will remain to be seen. Tell me, Lady Ricci, will you dance for us?"

Desiree blushed and looked to the floor.

"I'm afraid," said Brandenburg, "that Lady Ricci is a stickler for preparation and could not possibly perform at the drop of a hat!"

"Ah! An artist! An artist!" declared De Locke in a shrill voice, "but I have just the solution. Mr Whit, you have a ball coming up don't you?"

"Maybe."

"Oh don't be so modest! You do! Now, be a good fellow and extend an invitation to the Count here and to his most wonderful Lady. I insist."

"But…"

"Ah! Who is the Lord? And besides, your masquerades are frightfully dull. An Umbrian dancer will be the highlight of the year, and it will give us a chance to get to know Count Brandenburg even better!"

De Locke reached for Desiree's hand, who offered it. The Lord took it and kissed each knuckle, leaving a plum smelling lipstick mark. "Come to Whit's ball, my dear," he pleaded, "I would love you to meet my dear wife Lady Jennifer-Joy who, alas, cannot be with us tonight."

Desiree bowed in acquiescence to De Locke's wish.

"Well, now that has concluded," said Nathanial, the only one among them to not share any enthusiasm for the agreement. "I must attend to some issues."

He held out his hand to Brandenburg. "I look forward to seeing you at the Whit Ball," he said. Brandenburg smiled wryly and shook his hands tightly. Nathanial then shook hands with the rest of the group. Brandenburg turned to Desiree and took her onto the dancefloor.

Archie watched Brandenburg and Desiree take to the floor and was about to watch them go for a turn when out of the corner of his eye, he noticed an oddity. He looked back at the group and noticed Nathanial Whit and Lord Rafe De Locke exchanging a particularly strange handshake. For a moment, he could swear that he recognised the hand of the Lord. He dismissed it quickly as he felt a warm hand brush against his neck.

"I would keep your eyes on your duties if I were you."

Archie turned around to see the owner of the honeyed voice and velvet touch. There was nobody there. He looked around the crowd of grey dullards and then, wonderfully, he saw a glimpse of a shoulder blade and a perfect neck. He craned his neck to see more. Then, magically, the woman turned back to Archie. Through the throng of guests, he could just catch a glimpse of her face. She looked like heaven. Her green eyes pierced straight into his heart and, before he could do anything, the woman winked at him and disappeared from view. Archie shuffled around the edge of the hall to try and catch a second glimpse but it was no use. She was gone.

He turned in resignation and, against propriety, snatched up a glass of champagne from a passing waiter and walked over to the window. Nobody noticed his indiscretion. Archie huffed as he drank his wine, looking out onto the dark lawn and trying to reconcile in his mind what he had just seen. As he drank the last drops from the flute, he saw something, a shape darting across the lawn rushing into the night; a black shape. It was almost imperceptible in the darkness. He squinted. Then he saw a flash of cream flesh. It was the mysterious woman. She was rushing off somewhere. Archie pressed against the window and looked harder, and just as soon as he had seen her, she was gone again. It seemed to him that she just turned into a plume of black smoke and dissipated into the night. Kemble looked down at the empty flute and sniffed it.

Chapter Thirty Six

After Show Love

Valerie's heart was beating so fast the she thought she would die. Her chest was heaving and she had to bite her lip and clamp her eyes shut from crying out. Danilov's arousal was pressing against her leg with force. She could feel its warmth and undeniable promise invade every thought. The curtain to the booth was waving slightly as her heavy breath fell against it. In the chapel, the penitent men did not notice. Gertie, under the pew craned his neck towards the booth. He could barely see the two pairs of legs behind that curtain and he certainly had no idea of the chaos that was overwhelming the universe therein.

Danilov cycled through every conceivable image to try and quell his excitement to no avail. It was there for her to feel and there seemed nothing that could be done about it. Valerie clenched her jaw and, like ghost floating over its newly vacated corpse, she felt a cold detachment wash over her. In her mind she was watching herself as her left hand, of its own volition, moved to the side and pressed on the bulge. She knew of the danger of their position, but she had as little control over her actions, as the ghost did over its body. She began to press her body against Danilov's and her hand began to rub against him. The situation was becoming frantic as she worked faster, desperately trying to find a way into his breeches without disturbing the curtain. Danilov bit his lip and nuzzled into her neck as her hand broke through the barriers and found its prize. They both let out a sigh as her movements began to slow a little, anxious to capture and keep every precious second and sensation.

Danilov's need to throw the curtain open and push Valerie onto the floor and ravage her was almost too much to bear. Her hand worked in a steady rhythm and each passing moment provided a more and more convincing argument to do so. He held her tightly, fighting the urge to kiss her neck, or to find a way to explore her sex. It would be catastrophic to do it, and so he nearly squeezed the very air out of her. He was on the edge of the cliff, seconds from falling into bliss when the curtain flung open.

"Coast is clear! Lets skidaddle!" said Gertie not noticing the advanced state of foreplay Valerie and Danilov were in. He darted from the booth to the chapel door and opened it slightly. The interruption had yanked Danilov from the edge and the sudden exposure of the world outside the booth had drawn Valerie's ghost back into her body. She was aware of her surroundings and what she was doing. She pulled her hand free of his breeches and he let her go. She stood up, shielding Danilov from any embarrassment while he calmed himself. He cleared his throat to signify the all clear and they both dashed over to the doorway where Gertie was waiting.

"Are you ready?" he whispered.

They both nodded.

"Alright, you two lovebirds, on the count of three, one...."

"What do you mean lovebirds?" whispered Valerie, firmly into his ear. Gertie turned and winked at her.

"Two...." he said.

"We're not... there was nothing..."

"I won't tell. Three!" and with that he dashed out into the service corridor and almost disappeared into the gloom.

Valerie and Danilov looked sheepishly at each other.

"That was," she began.

"It's alright. It was nothing" he lied, and left her alone in the chapel as he slunk out to meet Gertie. Valerie was left alone and embarrassed. She looked down at her hand and reconciled what had just happened. She smiled and shrugged. It was most certainly not 'nothing'. She crept out to join them.

Their escape through the dark recess of Eveltham House was completed without any further incident. When they came to the danger zone across the lawn, they found it to be pitch dark. Gertie still did not trust the cover and ran out, stooping low to the ground and at a good pace. Danilov peered out around the corner of the wall. The coast was indeed clear. He reached out and took Valerie's hand together they walked slowly out. They ignored the possible dangers of capture and instead took a few moments to slow their pace and look up at the bright night sky and search for constellations. It was a crisp and complete night and when Danilov squeezed her hand, they both knew that the stolen moment in the confessional box was theirs for keeps and, in their own time, they would relive it once more. They felt calm as they walked across the lawn and into the safety of the copse.

Srdjan, Antoine and Claudia had been waiting for thirty minutes and were wringing their hands with worry. Antoine and Srdjan had debated in hushed tones whether they should sit it out, or go back and investigate. All the while Claudia had been sleeping, which presented them with another problem. Do they leave her sleeping in the carriage, or do they take her with them. For certain, just one of them could not go and search the house on their own. They were on the brink of waking Claudia and together mounting a search and rescue operation when they spotted some movement in the copse. Srdjan shushed Antoine with his finger and gestured towards the movement. The two men flanked the parked carriage and prepared to draw swords. Srdjan's keen eyes trained on the moving shapes and when the unmistakable silhouette of Danilov hove into view. He breathed a sigh of relief and gestured to Antoine that there was no danger present.

Gertie, Danilov and Valerie skulked towards the carriage and were met with stern looks but warm, relieved embraces. Gertie shrugged and rolled his eyes, suggesting that it wasn't his fault despite his best efforts to lead and Srdjan and Antoine both noticed a new, strong sense of maturity to the boy. In the moonlight, he appeared taller and broader. Antoine ruffled his hair and everybody boarded the carriage. Antoine scooped up Claudia, who groggily climbed into his arms and carried on sleeping. Danilov sat opposite Valerie and each tried desperately to keep their eyes and hands to themselves and managed it with moderate success. Once all were aboard, Srdjan cajoled the horses into a quiet canter and the reconnaissance team drove back towards London and The Roxy Playhouse.

———•◦•———

Brandenburg, Desiree and Archie left Lady Bronwyn's party at the stroke of midnight as instructed by Lupe Darling as it was, clearly, the magical time to leave a party. "If you have played your part well," she had said, "then by leaving, the hosts will feel like they are releasing some bright birds free of their cages and into the wild, and though they are happy to be setting the bright and beautiful free, they will know that the rest of the party will be that more dull. That is the effect you must leave them." And so, as the clock began to strike, in true enigmatic style, Brandenburg suddenly cut his conversations short, bowed and said his au revoirs and, by the final chime of midnight, he was gone.

As soon as the carriage door was closed, Archie drew the curtains and fished in his trousers. Brandenburg and Desiree were a little shocked and disturbed to see the man rooting around in such a fervent manner. Desiree cleared her throat and Brandenburg began to whistle absent-mindedly. Archie held up his finger to request a moment while he continued to fish. He stopped suddenly and pulled. His arm seemed to be stuck. He pulled again. Desiree and Brandenburg looked at each other quizzically and were about to offer assistance when, with one almighty heave, Archie pulled free a bottle of wine. He tossed it to Brandenburg who caught it with wide eyes and a happy smile.

"You are incredible," he said, "when did you nick this?"

"Last thing, I figured there was a bit of extra room, you see."

"Extra room?" enquired Desiree. Archie winked back at her and put his arm back inside his trousers. After a little rummage, he pulled out a huge, circular bottle of brandy that had somehow managed to fit inside his tight trouser leg. He pulled the cork off with his teeth and handed it to her. She was about to take a swig when he stopped her.

"Let it breathe, you mad woman!" he declared.

"He's right" said Brandenburg, "it's been stuffed down his pants for three hours, and I would say it has earned a breather." And he handed to the wine to Desiree who drank it down in a manner directly opposed to the elegance of her being. Archie then took a long sip and together the three friends shared the quiet moment of reflective calm that comes after the curtain on the first night has come down. Brandenburg pulled his hands through his hair and sat back against the bench. Archie tapped his friend's knee affectionately.

"Bravo, Old Love, bravo."

"Yes," said Desiree, kissing his check, "You were wonderful. It was great performance."

"Please, it was all you, my dear. Herschel would have been in awe at your performance. I have never seen its equal."

"Thank you, that is very kind. But really, the roses should be thrown to you. You worked the room. You had dignity and grace. And you achieved the goal. You got the invitation to the Whit ball."

Archie cleared his throat. Desiree looked at him and smiled. She leant over and kissed his cheek.

"And who could forget you, dear Archie" she said with her brightest smile, "you were the perfect eyes and ears. You stood well, you did not get distracted, and you managed to steal the scene with your sleight of hand." She clinked bottles with him and sat back. Archie contemplated telling them both about the mysterious presence he felt in the room, or the pang of recognition he felt when he saw Nathanial shake hands with the foppish Lord De Locke. He looked over to Brandenburg and noted his friend's stern and distant look. He concluded it was best not to trouble the bear with his thoughts and let him ponder his performance and draw up his own reviews and conclusions.

Brandenburg was indeed in deep thought, however he was not thinking over his performance but instead thinking about Nathanial Whit. There was something that did not sit right with him. He was almost certain that he had not guessed Brandenburg's true identity, but still, there seemed to lurk a deep mistrust behind the old rival's eyes. Whether it was a mistrust of Brandenburg or a mistrust of the world in general, he could not be sure. But what he was sure of was that having gone face to face with his mark and enemy, he was certain that Nathanial Whit was not all that he seemed. This new underlying sense of wariness and dread tinged the success of the evening for him. He had secured the invitation to the Whit Ball thanks to the overbearing nature of Lord De Locke but he could not help but wonder at what price the ticket had been bought. He had a bad feeling about the upcoming performance. He decided that the brandy had breathed long enough and he took a large gulp of it. The warmth coursed through him and reflexively shuddered in that glorious and welcome way strong drink provokes.

———•••———

Lord Rafe De Locke stood alone on the balcony of Lady Bronwyn's house and watched Brandenburg's carriage roll down the long, winding driveway. He lit his cigarillo and inhaled deeply. The light from its tip revealed a new set of eyes. These were now deep-set and keen, unlike the wide and jovial set he had displayed inside. His stance had changed and his shoulders hunched slightly. He followed the coach and thought about the new and dashing Count he had just met. He pondered the man's curious dress, unlike any he had seen, he thought about his delightful and beguiling fiancée and how they had breezed into the party, seemingly on a whim. He mulled over their agenda and wondered whether he had been right to force Nathanial Whit to invite him to his ball. There was a curious nature about the Count; a strange and compelling duality. It was as if he belonged and yet, at the same time, not. He had certainly made an impression on De Locke. He prepared to return to the party. His shoulders relaxed and his stance began a little more dandyish. His keen eyes came forward and the fierce galaxy that swirled in them a few moments ago was replaced by a bright and naive glaze. He flicked the cigarette butt to the floor and as he exhaled the last of the smoke, a sickly and sinister wheeze escaped from him. He cleared his throat and swanned back through the balcony door and to the party.

———•·•———

Brandenburg did not return to The Roxy to find it buzzing with anticipation. The atmosphere upon his entrance was surprisingly muted for an after show party. Antoine had wheeled his drinks trolley out to centre stage but it was, at two in the morning, still healthily stocked. Herschel was sitting on the edge of the stage playing cards with Tobias, Srdjan, Ms Adberg and Antoine. Lupe was reclining in the corner, singing that gentle French lullaby about the vestry cat and dormouse to the sleeping Claudia and Gertie was drinking with Valerie who was staring at the back of Danilov's head. In fact, when Archie leapt onto the stage as was his way, it was barely noticed by the others. He took some more drinks from the trolley for the Count and Desiree and handed them out. Srdjan finished the hand of cards and Tobias begrudgingly picked up the trick. They slowly turned to acknowledge Brandenburg.

"So," said Herschel, finally, as he stuffed his pipe, "Seems little point to talk of their day, without first talk of yours."

Brandenburg looked his friends and smiled. "We got the ticket," he said. The Players audibly let out a sigh of relief.

"Good work," said Gertie with a stronger voice than usual. "We did our part marvellously. My boys, and girls for Claudia and Valerie came too, all did a sterling job!"

"Your boys?" Brandenburg smirked.

"Aye, my boys!" said Gertie raising his glass.

Brandenburg turned to Archie who shrugged in bafflement at this man in Gertie's skin who drank before them. The conversations began to flow with more verve and gusto as the night went on. Srdjan regaled them with tales of his stealth and cunning, Antoine made everybody laugh by pulling the rug from under Srdjan's yarns. Gertie grew to twelve feet tall while he spoke of his moment of dread, trapped in the chapel and to which Danilov and Valerie became suspiciously sheepish. Claudia, now awake, alive and drinking, told the enthralled Players about every article she had memorized and how Tobias had already replicated a trunk full. Archie heaped praise upon Brandenburg and Desiree and how they the other Players had regrettably missed out on the performance of a lifetime. He did not mention the secret handshake or the mysterious woman who had captured him. Similarly, Brandenburg spoke of how face to face he came with the mark, and how, come the following week The Roxy Playhouse Irregulars would have no problems rinsing the bastard Whit for all he was worth.

The evening came to a natural close as the sun began to rise. The Players had talked and talked and everyone seemed ready for the performance ahead. Brandenburg was the first to retire to bed, but not before he wheeled Tobias back up to his workshop where upon the metallurgist bestowed the *'Sword of Brandenburg'* upon the Count. The hilt was perfect and the blade was now dull. Brandenburg saw the disappointment in Tobias eyes at being forced to produce a substandard prop. But when the Count leant into his ear and whispered a great secret of the sword, the metallurgist's eyes widened with an explosion of understanding and he laughed heartily. Desiree and Herschel retired to her hammock where, swinging above a comatose Gertie, they made silent, devastating love.

That night in The Roxy Playhouse saw the making of much love. As well as Desiree and Herschel, Srdjan finally lay with Alexia and while they reacquainted themselves with each other's bodies, they made unshakable vows of love and fidelity. When they had finished, they lay naked and glistening with perspiration. They looked at the ceiling with the serene duality of post-coital emptiness and completeness.

"I think," said Alexia "that we should start writing our opera again." Srdjan showed his agreement by climbing back onto his soulmate for another physical conversation.

Of course, Danilov spent all of twelve seconds in his quarters before he could not resist any longer and he went searching for Valerie. He did not have to look far. As soon as he threw back the curtains of his room, he saw her standing in the bowels of the theatre half-naked, bathed in candle light and staring at him. She beckoned him to follow and he did, all the way to the store area until they found the rickety staircase that led up to the attic. Valerie opened the hatch and climbed into the tight space. Danilov was barely halfway through the opening before Valerie grabbed him with an unseen strength and pulled him clean through. In all the years of her life, until her final days in St Petersburg, Valerie Folk counted that first, violent and cataclysmic adventure with Danilov as the most groundbreaking. She matched his perfect nature and intimidating physical prowess with her boundless, sprung dam of passion. Again and again she came at him and never the same way twice. Throughout their private hours Valerie gave birth to myriad different variations of herself, doing things and behaving in ways in which she never thought she could. By the time they finished, they barely had the energy to stand and so, they collapsed in a naked heap on the floor and let the sun's energy flood though the hole in the roof and restore them.

Archie, upon request, had knocked on Lupe's door and hoped to find her in want of his services as she had been on her birthday all those years ago. And indeed she was. She had been sideswiped by his costume change and he decided to give him a second go on the carousel. However, twenty minutes into the games, and she felt her thighs run cold and her mind drift. She looked into the eyes of the great lover and suddenly realized something. She climbed off the surprised Archie and sat naked next to him.

"What is her name?" she said in a lamenting voice. She knew instantly, by looking into his eyes that Archie Enfield was forsaken in the labyrinth of unrequited and melancholic love. She saw herself in him and it pained her greatly. Archie, shocked to have been found out, and in such a manner, realised that it was foolish to deny anything. His eyes filled with tears as he began to comprehend just what had happened to him a few hours earlier.

"I don't know," he said. His eyes fell to the middle distance and Lupe leant in to hold him dearly.

Chapter Thirty Seven

Curtains Up for the Nathanial Whit Heist

The day of the greatest performance in the history of The Roxy Playhouse had finally come around. The week in between Lady Bronwyn's event and the Whit Ball had seen little necessary activity amongst themselves. Instead, they occupied their time performing checks and routines over and over like soldiers waiting to advance on an entrenched enemy. Srdjan and Ms Adberg continued to teach Desiree the art of the sword and by now she was more than competent. Indeed, on several occasions she had bested Alexia, much to the amusement of Srdjan whose experience and strength were still too much for the Umbrian ballerina. Danilov and Anya had walked along their high wires and tight ropes with a clockwork rhythm that was not once interrupted by thoughts of Valerie or boys with butterfly nets. As for the boy himself, Gertie had found a new net provided to him by Valerie who had shown a surprising ability in turning wood on Tobias' lathe. She presented Gertie with his new instrument and he was so overcome with joy that he immediately thrust it outwards in his favourite catching-stance and stuck poor Valerie in the gut, forcing her to tumble into the net. He offered his most profound apologies which she shrugged off with a gurgled, "at least the net works."

While Valerie turned the butterfly handle, she had spoken at great length to Tobias as he worked alongside her creating all manner of replica prop based on Claudia's detailed description. Indeed, while the rest of the Players had performed routine tasks, Tobias had been working like a man touched by the hand of God. The metallurgist was happy to have some company in the workshop and Valerie provided not only good conversation, but also tireless worker fetching him all manner of tool and material. While they worked they spoke of love, history and faith. Tobias told her of his past, and she told him of her future and while they disagreed on a few subjects, the two things that they did agree on where that love is good and God is great.

During that week of preparation, love truly was in the wine amongst the Players. The morning after going to war with Valerie's body in the attic Danilov had approached Archie and nobly told him that he and Valerie were as one. Archie graciously accepted that the better man had won her heart, bowed and walked away. His little performance was convincing enough. Danilov understood that Archie was not angry, but he had noted a distant whip of pain behind Archie's eyes that suggested that he was upset. This pleased Danilov slightly in that he would have felt incensed if he thought his friend Archie Enfield had shown dark colours by taking Valerie and casting her off without a second thought. That glimpse of pain reaffirmed that Archie was a good man, who treated everyone with love. In truth, he was right; however, the distant pain in Enfield's eyes was not related to losing Valerie. He did love Miss Folk and had loved her dearly that night she had become a muse. Since then, his love had morphed into an unshakable platonic love for her. He was happy she had found someone with whom she could find adventure and life, and he could think of none better than Danilov. When the acrobat had told him, a rattling gear deep inside Archie suddenly fell into place. Of course she should be with him. It was as obvious as sunrise. No, the pain in his eyes was for himself. He was in love with the flash of shoulder blade and the glimpse of cheekbone. It was a certainty that he had seen his one true Giselle and she had slipped away from him forever.

That week, he became closer to Lupe Darling than he ever became with Benjamin. They poured over the contents of the George chest and spoke endlessly on the calamitous nature of unrequited love. Over that week they made constant, soul enriching love upon her bed of boas. Sometimes Archie would be George, sometimes Lupe would be Giselle. It was a desperate partnership and a vital one too. When they finally emerged from her quarters on the day before the performance, they had quelled their aching love for long enough to get through the play. None of the other Players spoke to them about what had been going on behind her doors. They guessed that it was simple lovemaking. They would never understand, and Lupe and Archie knew this. They kissed each other as friends do and went about preparing for the day ahead. They never made love with each other again as they never needed to find each other in such a way for the rest of their days.

Brandenburg had spent much of the week in solitude. He had divided his time by revising his character and performance and remembering his past. A few weeks prior, the very act of remembering the death of his parents and the awful fire which had destroyed everything he loved was tantamount to suicide. But it was testimony to his deep reservoir of courage that over the weeks, he could now easily walk through the burning halls of his memory, visit every room and even look upon his parents lying on their martial bed, wreathed in flame. He could do all this without bursting into uncontrollable anguish or even dropping dead. He now had steeled focus. The last two days before the performance started, he had simply sat on the edge of his bed and turned his sword upon its point slowly, around and around, staring into the glinting spiders hilt. He was ready.

———•◦•———

And so the day came. They all stood on the stage and Archie handed a drink to each and every one. Claudia and Antoine were dressed in their servant outfits and ready for the first act. They were to be taken by carriage along with Anya, Danilov, Gertie and Herschel, who had taken the place of Tobias as the driver. Srdjan and Ms Adberg were still to remain behind as security to protect the metallurgist, Lupe and Valerie should any thieves or chancers attempt to break in.

The backstage crew were head to toe in black body stockings save for Herschel who refused to drive the carriage in anything other than his warmest coat which, incidentally had the largest storage capacity for pipe tobacco and hip flasks. The first act crew were ready to take off.

Count Brandenburg was not yet in costume so now Benjamin Ananas and Archie Enfield stood before them, drinks in hand.

"Ladies and gentlemen, fair Players," began Archie, The Roxy speechmaker, as he poured drinks for the first act crew. "You will soon going out there, on stage, in front of a blind audience. But do not be disheartened, my dear ones, by the ambivalence of the fools. I will be there. We will be there to watch you, and to love you. We will see you perform as you have never done before, on a stage of real and tangible danger. What an adventure! And what glorious adventurers you are!" He placed his hand on Antoine's shoulder and gave him a heartfelt squeeze which filled the Frenchman with pride.

"We are going into the lion's den, all of us!" continued Archie, "for our art, for our profession and for each other!" He held Claudia's cheek and tenderly kissed her forehead which completely eradicated the defiance of her feelings for him. Her crush returned and she sweetly blushed.

"We will be right behind you, and remember, behind us, behind all our prancing and dancing, is the strength and resolve of the unseen heroes!" And he poured an extra large glass for Anya, Danilov, Gertie and Herschel.

"These men, and this woman, will be our saviours, our true performers. Please, for they will not get the glory of performing to an audience, please give them some love now!"

The rest of the Players turned in unison and bowed solemnly at the backstage crew. The crew nodded in return. Archie was about to continue with his toast when Valerie suddenly stepped forward and kissed Danilov deeply on the mouth. The Players kicked their heels for a few seconds while the two lovebirds finished their activities. She broke of the kiss, whispered her love and desire for him to come home safely and stepped back to join the rest.

"Well," said Archie, trying to pick up from where he left off, "I suppose that leaves only one more thing to say. Ladies, gentlemen and Players, curtains up, drinks down and let's go show the bastards what art is! Huzzah!"

The Players downed the drinks in one go, placed the empty goblets on their heads and huzzahed their agreement. The backstage crew jumped off the stage and ran out of the theatre to begin the first act.

The rest of the Players watched them leave with the shared senses of joy and anxiety. Brandenburg turned from the stage and went to get into costume.

By the time Herschel's carriage rolled up, the sun was beginning to yawn. They had timed their arrival perfectly and had joined a long procession of service carriages shuttling all manner of party fare to Eveltham House. Some carried staff, others ingredients, some carried furniture and a large convoy carried the last few struts for the extended awning. Herschel manoeuvred the carriage inconspicuously to the side of the road halfway up the driveway. The cabin door opened and Claudia and Antoine jumped out and hid in the copse. As soon as they were clear, Herschel drove the carriage on through the ranks until he came around to the stable yard. When the coast was clear, Antoine led Claudia out onto the driveway and they slipped unseen amongst the throng of staff rushing about.

"Be careful now, Little Mouse," whispered Antoine as they approached the service entrance to the huge mansion house.

"You too, my magician."

Antoine looked round to check the coast was clear before giving the Spanish girl a hug and a kiss. "Let's go to work," he said, and they entered the house.

Once Herschel had parked amongst the carriages he hooked the nosebags over the horses and climbed inside the cabin. There he, Gertie, Danilov and Anya played cards using the large trunk of replica loot as a table until cover of darkness fell.

At around seven in the evening, Claudia had memorised every single room in the mansion. Under the guise of a chambermaid she had snuck in and out of each room and secured a good perimeter from which the back stage crew could operate. The service corridor was, of course, their main route of operation. However, there would be times when the loot would have to be ferried through the living areas of the house; up the main staircase, through the bedrooms and onto the balconied section that looked over the conservatory and out onto the lawn.

As she walked around in the well lit and decorated house, she could not help but be in awe of the splendour of Nathanial Whit's house. Everything was so clean and bright. Even the portraits seemed to be clean shaven and proud. The meeting gallery that joined the reception room to the dining hall, bar and drawing rooms was resplendent with heavy velvet and thick drapery. Claudia thought she was walking through the warehouse of all the riches of the world. She was not tempted to steal anything, despite the abundance of silver and gold on display but she did notice one young chambermaid pocket a tiny pewter otter but when Claudia gave her a stern look, the young girl replaced it.

After an hour's worth of working and snooping, Claudia found the room she was looking for; a hidden side study adjacent to a guest bedroom. She listened intently at the door before entering. The study was fairly bare in comparison to the rest of the house with just a modest bed, a roll top bureau, a black cowl hanging on the door and a few portraits of stern looking, sallow figures on the walls. The room was perfect for her needs. She quietly closed the door and made her way to the roll top desk. After a few minutes rooting around, she found the key to the door and locked it.

She looked over to the window and carefully opened it. There was a small, yet sturdy wrought iron balcony that was just large enough for matching table and chair. She moved them aside and looked down. Below her she could see the conservatory and inside that, she could see Antoine carefully setting the table. She took a moment to see if he was stealing the cutlery but she could not tell. She assured herself that he was not doing it just yet as the man would prefer to do under the noses of his audience like a true magician. She stowed away her admiration as there was work to be done and she looked out over the dark lawn towards the copse. The carriage was not yet there, but it would be soon. She had not a few moments to lose.

Claudia quickly removed her blouse to reveal a large leather belt. She took the clasp, unhooked it and pulled it taut. A coil of high-wire unravelled from the belt and she pulled it completely free of its leather holding and gathered it up in her arms before stepping out onto the balcony and tying one end of the line to the base of a iron bar. Once she was sure it was secure, she hoisted the wire over the balcony and let it drop down beside the conservatory. Once she was certain the wire was safe, she put her blouse back on and returned to her duties relieved that her first scene had gone well.

Inside the glass house, Antoine heard the wire clatter against a glass panel as it fell to the ground. Before the sound had carried all the way through his mind, his hands had acted and had knocked over a goblet onto a pewter serving plate. The resulting noise covered the clatter from outside. He looked around at the waiting staff nervously. They nodded disapprovingly at his clumsiness. Antoine apologised with a shrug and a grimace but on the inside, he smiled in relief and kissed the Spanish girl. He returned to laying out knives plated with silver petunia leaves.

———•◦•———

At a quarter to seven, Herschel lost a large hand of 'Joker's Bed Mates' and had to pick up a mean trick. He didn't want to and so declared that it was dark enough to go to work. Anya, Gertie and Danilov booed him for not conceding the game, but knew that it was probably time to get into character. Silent as the grave, Herschel unhooked the horse's nosebags and drove the carriage along the edge of the copse towards the back of the lawn slower than he would have liked, but the caution was a necessity. The ball had not begun and so the activity of the staff was an unknown quantity and he feared to drive past a groundsman attending to the copse and therefore get caught before the curtain had even gone up. He was right to do so as twice he had to halt the carriage as staff walked passed nearby carrying lawn candles. Eventually, he managed to drive the carriage safely to its position. From there, they could see the conservatory and the waiting staff busy in their preparation. The lawn candles were yet to be lit, but it was only a matter of time before they were.

Herschel and Gertie trained their eyes on the balconies above and saw Claudia fixing the wire. They looked to the floor through respect when they noticed that she was topless. After counting to a hundred, Herschel looked back up through the side of his eye to see the door to the study closing. The wire was there; time for action.

He turned to Gertie and shook his hand. "Make me proud."

"I will, you can count on me," and at that, the young man ran at full pelt across the lawn to the edge of the conservatory. He didn't even pause for breath when he got there but instead picked up the clasped end of the wire and ran back towards the carriage. As he did, a servant appeared at the far end of the lawn and began to light the lawn candles. Each one lit up a more and more grass and Gertie became more and more visible. The stage hand was in the middle of the lawn, and easily visible to anyone who cared to look out there. Herschel was hopping up and down on the carriage driving bench with worry. Danilov and Anya were holding each other in fear of their man being caught. As the sixth candle lit up, Gertie froze and closed his eyes. The servant casually walked right passed Gertie, whispering to the night and swinging a candle around by its wooden spike. The Players on the edge of the copse froze in horror. The servant passed across Gertie's path not two feet in front of him. Gertie was as still as the dead. Then, against all odds, the servant carried on walking to the other side of the lawn where he began to place a few more candles before lighting them up and throwing more light across the lawn.

Gertie looked to Herschel who beckoned him, in no uncertain terms, to move his arse. Move his arse he did and Gertie reached the safety of the copse before the candles were lit.

"Jesus H Christ" whispered Herschel, the relief beating back the fear, "you really are a stagehand! How come he didn't see you?"

"He wasn't looking" said Gertie, recalling how he managed to swap props and change sets mid performance without ever being seen by the audience. He handed the wire to Danilov

The acrobat took the wire and pulled it taut, tying it off against the axle of the carriage. Gertie and Herschel rotated the carriage and backed it far into the copse until the wire stretched, taut and unseen, all the way up to the balcony. Anya tested the tensile strength of the wire before nodding to Danilov. She looked over to Gertie, smiled at him and held out her hand. The young man took it and steadied Anya as she climbed up onto the wire. Once upon it, she calmly looked out at her path ahead. She lowered her heart rate and began to ascend taking careful, considered footsteps. They all held their breath until she reached the balcony and, like a shadow under a doorway, in an instant she was inside the room and invisible. Once she was safe, the three men went to the back of the carriage and heaved the trunk out. Herschel almost threw his back out trying to get the bugger out of the cabin. They placed it on the grass and looked up at Danilov with looks of doubt. The acrobat had his eyes closed and was performing his stretching routine. He was calm as a Hindu cow.

"Two drinks says 'no chance," said Herschel as he loaded his pipe.

"Four drinks says 'easy as a barmaid from the Barrow Boy and Banker," said Gertie.

"You're on," said Herschel, "Mr Kamilcova, you are up sir!"

Danilov's eyes opened slowly and he smiled. He was ready. He bent down and with one arm, heaved the huge trunk onto his back. He tested the weight, rolling back and forth before gauging the physics of his load. He nodded that he was ready and Herschel and Gertie stood back in amazement that the man could actually even lift the thing.

"See you on the other side, gentlemen," said Danilov as he stepped onto the wire. He took three laboured breaths before beginning his slow, arduous ascent. Herschel and Gertie stood amazed as Danilov carried the huge trunk on his back, up the wire towards the balcony. Once the acrobat joined his sister, Herschel held out his hand to Gertie.

"You called it," he said.

Gertie smiled and shook his hand.

Once he had scaled the wrought iron railings, Danilov threw the trunk down on the bed and caught his breath. Anya nodded her approval at his masterful feat before throwing open the trunk lid. Inside was a treasure trove of beautiful trinkets. To the eyes of the layman, the trunk was worth millions but to the Players, there were simply well made props. They began to unpack the replicas and line them up on the bed, ready for the next scene to unfold.

"What time is it?" said Gertie. Herschel looked at his pocket watch.

"A quarter past seven."

"Enter Brandenburg," said Gertie as Herschel handed him a hipflask.

Chapter Thirty Eight

Of Masks

Brandenburg and Desiree stood aghast in the grand entrance hall. In front of them milled two hundred and thirty three of the most dazzling Socialites in the Empire. The room was beautifully lit with maroon tinted gas lamps and bespoke ruby chandeliers. Above the crowd hung a web of golden garlands, stretching from each marble pillar and meeting at the base of the seven chandeliers. Towards the back of the room stood a raised platform upon which a few elderly manservants fussed about. Behind them, to the very left of the room, a huge velvet curtain hung sectioning off part of the hall. The Count felt confident in his character and his clothes. Neither he, nor Desiree looked out of place. Indeed, they appeared to be perfectly over-dressed for the occasion.

Brandenburg, elegant in black breeches, crisp white shirt and his velvet frock coat could not help but feel in awe at the theatricality of the decorations. Desiree, too, found it hard not to stare in disbelief at the grandeur of the hall. Before they were announced to the congregation, eleven suited men in masks swarmed around the Count and his fiancée each one holding large damask cushions upon which sat four differing Venetian masks. Brandenburg and Desiree bowed and curtsied respectively to the serving men before perusing the beautiful masks. Desiree opted for an exquisite Volto mask made of pure gold leaf and encrusted with pearls. The 'half mask' covered her forehead and eyes and came to a sharp curving end over the brim of her cheekbones leaving her perfect jaw and full Umbrian lips exposed. It was a ravishing choice. Brandenburg had no choice and went straight for the gothic Medico Delle Peste mask with its wonderful long, maroon beak and fierce, arched eyebrows. It was clearly the choice of mask for the dashing and mysterious Count.

Archie was about to bow his head to hide his disappointment at being excluded when to his right, a cotton cushion was pushed before him. Upon that sat a basic white Bauta mask which was to cover his whole face. He took the mask and put it on, happy to be included in the games. Once all three were suitably dressed for their entrance, the Master of Ceremonies announced them to the guests with an impressive baritone. The entire congregation stopped mid-conversation and turned to the new guests. The sight of two hundred or so masked people suddenly staring at the interlopers filled the three with dread and trepidation. However, the congregation all bowed politely and then turned back to the mingling. Brandenburg gripped Desiree's arm and stepped forward into the fray.

Archie, a few steps back, moved to the side of the hall to keep an overseeing eye on proceedings. He trained his eyes through the crowd until he made out the broad shoulders of Antoine who was masked as he was. The Frenchman was working through the crowd offering drinks to the guests. Archie squinted and thought he saw the magician's sleight of hand, but he could not. He had no idea if the magician was performing his turn or his prestige. Archie stepped to the side and stood amongst the ranks of manservants. He was offered a complimentary glass of wine which he gratefully took. He looked up and down the line of men and felt sorry for the poor buggers, forced to stand out on the edge and watch the fun. But he had a job to do, and right now, the job was to disappear amongst the White Masks and keep a watchful eye out for his friends. So far, he had not felt the invading sense of the mysterious 'Giselle'.

———•◦•———

Upstairs, in the private study, Anya was loading some silverware into the trunk. There came a coded knock at the door. She opened it and let Danilov in. He was holding three silver plates and a candelabrum that he had swapped from a nearby guest bedroom. He piled them onto the bed and together they wrapped them up in some rags and stowed them away in the trunk. He tested it for weight and deemed it not nearly full enough. Danilov looked at the replicas on the bed and selected the silver handled hair brush, and ivory comb and a golden letter opener as he had passed the room where the real versions lay. He stuffed them into his belt and handed a pewter mirror to Anya. He went to the door and peeked out into the corridor: deserted. Danilov and Anya both snuck out and hugged the wall of the upstairs corridor as they made their way towards the next guest bedroom. They reached it in minutes and pressed their heads against the door. It was empty. They crept inside.

The room was of generous proportions with a huge solid oak four posted bed and an ornate chandelier in the centre of the room. To one side of the room sat the dresser and wardrobe and opposite that were two floor-to-ceiling windows leading out onto a balcony big enough for two people to stand on and admire the gardens. Upon the dresser they saw the items they were looking for. They began to replace the real items with the forgeries and were almost done when they heard a creak and a tap coming from the balcony. They looked over to the window. Outside was nothing but darkness. They approached the window cautiously but were suddenly halted when they saw the railing wobble slightly before a dark figure climbed over the edge. Danilov and Anya looked at each other and turned to rush out of the room. They had no time and the French windows flung open. Danilov immediately grabbed his sister and threw her up into the air, where she managed to grab hold of the cut-glass and ormolu chandelier. Anya weighed less than a feather and the chandelier was not troubled to hold her. Danilov leapt and pulled himself up onto the roof of the four-poster bed and lay there looking out at the figure picking the lock of the French windows. The doors opened and the slender figure slunk into the room. The person was dressed like Anya and Danilov; head to toe in black and had a small black pouch slung over their shoulder. Danilov looked over to Anya who was clutching onto the chandelier swaying directly above the mysterious intruder.

The black figure stood in the centre of the room for a few moments before whipping off the black hood. Danilov gasped as a bountiful tumble of raven hair fell luxuriously about the figure's shoulders. The figure looked in the mirror, and from his angle, the acrobat could see her face. It was a perfect collection of features - large green almond-shaped eyes, sharp, angular cheekbones, full bee-stung lips and a nose of sculpted perfection. She took off her pouch and placed it on the dresser before sitting down and opening it. Anya and Danilov were mesmerized as this mysterious woman took out some make-up articles from her bag and begin to accentuate her sultry features. She worked fast and after two minutes she was done. She stood up and pulled at a little cord that clasped her black body stocking at the nape of her neck. After a little shimmy, the entire body stocking unravelled into a pile of thread as if it were attached to a loom working in reverse. Danilov and Anya were wide-eyed at the miraculous transformation before them. Somehow, underneath the skin-tight body stocking, the raven-haired beauty was wearing a full ball gown of stunning quality. She held out her toned, cream coloured arms and pirouetted on the spot. The motion caused the dress to puff out to its full circumference. The corseted dress exposed her sleek shoulders, collarbone and shapely chest. She fixed her hair and checked herself in the mirror before reaching into her pouch and pulling out a thin stick no bigger that a cigarillo. With a sharp flick of the wrist, the stick magically unfolded into a delicate Columbina mask. She tied the mask off and swept out of the room.

Danilov and Anya waited for a few moments before descending from their hiding spots. Anya bent down and picked up the bundle of black thread. As soon as he touched it, the whole lot evaporated into a plume of odourless black smoke. They looked incredulously at each other before gathering the rest of their loot and leaving the room.

———•◦•———

Brandenburg and Desiree moved into the depths of the congregation, bowing and tipping their glasses every which way. The room was packed and they could barely move. When they had seemingly reached the centre of the room, a monumental gong sounded. Everybody turned at once to the end of the hall where the Master of Ceremonies stood on a raised platform and was flanked by two couples dressed in finer clothes than anyone else. Despite the masks, Brandenburg recognised the two men to be Nathanial Whit and Lord Rafe De Locke. Nathanial was dressed in a cream jacket and breeches and his wife matching in a large dress that, to Brandenburg and Desiree both, resembled a wedding cake. Their masks matched in design and pattern: black and white harlequin chequers on a Volto style mask. Lord Rafe De Locke was draped in a long myrtle-green cloak that was pinned with golden clasps down the front to his waist whereupon it fanned out dramatically revealing well fitted black breeches and highly polished court slippers. The woman standing next to him, who Brandenburg and Desiree agreed to be his wife Lady Jennifer-Joy, was wearing a matching green dress that sparkled at the seams. Around her neck she sported silver latticed necklace upon which dangled twelve emeralds. De Locke's mask was a severe black Medico Delle Peste which carried a far more sinister look about it than Brandenburg's. The beak sneered at the left nostril and the eyebrow above was raised to match. Desiree gripped Brandenburg's arm a little tighter when she noticed that awful detail.

"My Lords, Ladies and Gentlemen," boomed the Master of Ceremonies, "Please will you receive the Lord Rafe De Locke and Lady Jennifer-Joy," the congregation bowed deeply as De Locke and Jennifer-Joy gracefully alighted off of the platform and glided into the crowd.

"And now, with great pleasure, may I introduce you to your glorious hosts for this evening, the very honourable and esteemed Mr and Mrs Nathanial Whit,"

Nathanial and his wife bowed to the audience, who bowed back. They stepped down off the platform and moved into the crowd, nodding and bowing wherever necessary until they were just a few people away from Brandenburg and Desiree. The gong sounded again and, instinctively, the guests spread a little apart, finding room wherever they could.

Archie, still in regimented line amongst the other White Masks looked over to Antoine who tapped his pocket to signify that he was full of loot already. Behind his mask, Archie smiled. It was working. He looked around the room until he found the line of serving girls who were the only ones not to be wearing masks. He saw little

Claudia standing in the middle with her hands held by her waist in a true servants pose. He desperately wanted to call out and wave to her. He resisted of course. Little Claudia, at the back of the audience, saw out of the corner of her eye, Archie looking over to her. She couldn't see his face, of course, but she could feel his eyes on her and could imagine his smile and wave. She allowed herself to break protocol and she quickly waggled her index finger at him and winked. Her message got through because she could see his shoulders jiggling from stifled laughter. She bit her lip and looked to the floor.

There was another sound of the gong to which the audience turned back to the platform. The Master of Ceremonies pulled on a golden cord and a heavy velvet curtain that cordoned off the rear left section of the hall fell to the ground to reveal the orchestra. The audience applauded heartily while an octogenarian conductor took to his podium. He tapped his baton three times, raised his arms dramatically and the music and dancing began.

Danilov and Anya were sitting in the study room contemplating the strange woman who had broken into the mansion when they heard the secret knock on the door and Antoine entered. They did not have time to explain what had happened before the Frenchman had offloaded all manner of bejewelled trinkets and left again to rejoin his post. Anya and Danilov packed the jewels into the trunk which took up the remaining space. Danilov closed the lid and tried to lift it. It was an immense weight, but he managed to hoist it onto his back. Anya opened window and guided her brother out onto the rope. He balanced on the balcony, seventy feet above the conservatory before taking his regulatory deeps breaths and preparing his descent. When

Herschel and Gertie felt the wire wobble, they put down their cards and looked up into the darkness. For a few moments they could not see anything and then, through the gloom they saw the shape of Danilov calmly walking towards them with the trunk on his back like a wire-walking atlas. His descent was easily made and he hopped off at the end and rested the trunk onto the floor with a loud thud. He flung the lid open and to the gasps of Herschel and Gertie. Danilov caught his breath before starting to unload the goods.

"What are you doing?" said Gertie, sure that they had blagged enough.

"We're going back again. This is only half of what he had prepared. Unload boys, stuff more props in and back we go!"

Herschel and Gertie shrugged and quickly began to help the acrobat unload the trunk, load up the carriage and reload the trunk with more fakes. They had barely closed the cabin doors before Danilov was racing back up the wire with the new consignment on his back. Herschel handed Gertie a fresh hip-flask and they toasted the performance that, from the wings, seemed to be flowing effortlessly.

———•◦•———

Brandenburg and Desiree had been forced to split up and take new dance partners, as the music had dictated. Brandenburg had been trying desperately to get close to Nathanial so that, once the dance finally came to an end he could look into his eyes once more. He wanted to test himself and his ability to slap his enemy in the face, without the bastard even knowing it. As he danced around, keeping an eye on his mark, he felt his calmness fade away and a wealth of anger rise up. He was spinning in the dance and desperately needed to catch sight of Archie to help quell this rage, but he could not see him. All he could see was the harlequin mask of Nathanial Whit moving in and out of his vision. He took a final turn and stopped dead in front of a new partner.

The music rested for a few seconds, to allow the dancers to bow to their new partners. Brandenburg was now facing Lady Jennifer-Joy and, when she bowed, he could see that Whit was directly behind her and about to dance with Desiree. It was perfect. This would be the last rotation. All they needed to do was keep in time, see it through and then he and his 'fiancée' would be face to face with the enemy. The music started and the dancing began once more, this time at a slower more regal pace to which Brandenburg was most thankful as it allowed him time to gradually calm down and get his head back into the play.

Archie was keeping a close eye on the dancers and he could see Brandenburg tense up during the middle stages of the dance. He tried to make himself visible to his friend, but to no avail. However, the final part of the dance had started and, apparently, that meant it was time for the regiments of servants to break ranks and begin preparing chairs and drinks for the dancers. Antoine had managed to return to the ranks of White Masks unseen, and when they all began to mingle, he, Archie and Claudia managed to meet up.

"How are we doing?" whispered Archie.

"A piece of pie, easy as cake!" boasted Antoine. "We have already made one delivery and the acrobats are piling up for another!"

"Yes, it is going well," said Claudia, "we are…." she tailed off when she noticed a distraction descend upon Archie's face. His head was craned, his eyes sharp and his eyebrows arched. She reached out to him.

"Are you alright?"

Archie ignored the Spanish Girl and followed his nose into the crowd. Antoine and Claudia looked at each other and shrugged. They drifted back to their positions and continued in their performances.

Archie was lost to his senses. She was here. He could feel the presence of the woman who had captivated his soul with all but the merest hint of a shoulder blade. She was in the room, somewhere, and he was a slave to the magnetic attraction. He forgot all sense of place and moment as he broke protocol and began to walk like a ghost amongst the dancing socialites. After a few seconds ducking and weaving, he saw her; a vision in lightning blue, jet black hair and cream skin. She danced in elegant and enticing swirls, the light gliding over her collarbone and shimmering in her hair. He was a few feet from her when she noticed him. His heart stopped and his feet became as stone. As he stood, rooted to the spot, the other dancers sashayed around him. The mysterious woman grabbed her partner and began to pirouette on the spot, faster and faster and all the while whipping her head around to fix her masked stare on Archie. She was dancing for him and he was bewitched.

An accidental elbow from a passing gentleman woke Archie from his dream and a cold panic overwhelmed him when he realised that he was standing in the middle of the dance floor. He turned to dart to the side of the room and back to his stage mark when he felt a warm breath on his neck.

"We meet again," a voice came in a honeyed accent that he could not place. "You always seem to be in places you shouldn't be." The voice was so close to his right ear that he could have sworn he felt her full lips brush against his lobe. He turned around to see the mysterious woman but she was not there. He looked around whilst backing out of the crowd and back to his mark. Was she a ghost?

Was he imagining things? He was locking away his moment of madness when, out of the corner of his eyes, he saw the raven haired woman standing at the back of the room, shielding her masked face with a black fan.

Brandenburg had not noticed the Archie Enfield statue in the middle of the dancefloor as he was concentrating on keeping a steady head in the presence of his enemy. Nathanial Whit was being held well by Desiree and every time the two couples spun, he would swing passed Whit and come within perfect striking distance should the Count wish to plunge a dagger silently into his side. He controlled his breathing and diverted the murderous portion of his mind towards his dance partner and, to his surprise, felt a strange and pleasing calmness granted to him by Lady Jennifer-Joy. She danced well and had a pleasing form. The smell of her skin hinted at a vanilla lotion and he could not help but imagine her applying it. She seemed graceful and poised and her smile was calming and delicate. The Count was about to initiate a conversation to see whether her voice was as serene as her temperament when the huge gong sounded once more and the dance came to a halt.

"Lords, Ladies and Gentlemen," boomed the Master Of Ceremonies, "the dance is over and dinner is to be served after drinks. And so, it has come that time! On behalf of Mr Whit, now is the time....unmask!"

There was a sigh of relief and the guests all whipped off their masks. Count Abraham von Brandenburg, on seeing the true face of his dance partner stumbled backwards and almost fell to the floor. Desiree looked over to see all the colour wash from his face and the character of Brandenburg dissolve. Benjamin Ananas was standing in front of Abigail Hardwoode.

Chapter Thirty Nine

Brandenburg Goes Off-Script

L ady Jennifer-Joy reached for the stumbling Brandenburg and managed to grab his arm. A jolt of electricity passed through them, making her shudder. The man was pale as the dead and his eyes seemed to be changing colour in front of her. As she held his arm, she saw them change from her dashing and competent dancer partner to those of someone she once knew but could not place.

"Are you quite right, Count Brandenburg?" she said. Brandenburg stood up, inhaled and dug into his improvisation experience.

"I'm fine Abi...."

Jennifer-Joy's eyes widened slightly and her lips parted.

"I'll be quite right, Lady Jennifer-Joy. I just came over a little grey; quite fine indeed." Brandenburg reached for Desiree's arm and yanked her close. The Count's cold and clammy grasp almost turned the Umbrian to ice. She looked up into his wide eyes and across to the Lady. She was about to ask to be introduced when the gong sounded and an announcement came ringing through.

"Ladies and Gentlemen, upon request of Lord De Locke, and to the delight of us all, we have a special performance for you all."

Desiree's eyes widened as she recalled an off-the-hand comment Lord De Locke made at Lady Bronwyn's event.

"Amongst us we have a creature of purity and grace and, we are told, a dancer of heavenly talent."

Desiree tried to disappear as she stepped closer to the frozen Brandenburg, but he offered no protection for he was lost to the sight of Abigail before him.

"And so," the announcer continued as the crowd began to part around Desiree, "please ask with your hearts if the Lady Ricci would be gracious enough to gift us with a performance!"

Desiree's heart sank as the crowd parted. Archie, Antoine and Claudia looked at each other in shock, each unsure of what was happening or how they would improvise their way out of it. As the crowd made way for Desiree, the Players could see her standing in fear and alone. Brandenburg was ashen white and completely out of focus.

Desiree looked around the room and caught sight of Archie, Antoine and Claudia individually. Their look of bemusement somehow galvanised a conviction inside her. It was her time to perform. She grew an extra few inches in confidence, smiled at her friends, turned and walked to the stage to the rapturous applause of the guests. As the crowd closed the gap and turned to face the stage, Brandenburg was locked in amongst them and the panic of being mere inches from Abigail Hardwoode threatened to detonate his very fibre. He looked around for his friends but could not see them. He was drowning in panic.

Herschel was stuffing his pipe for the twelfth time that evening when an unmistakable Gallic whistle stung through the quiet night. He pricked his ears up and looked to the source. There, illuminated by a lawn candle stood Antoine. Herschel stood up on the driver's bench and waved at him unsure quite why the Frenchman was so out of position. He strained his old eyes to see his friend waving back and pointing to the large windows over to the east. Herschel looked to where the Frenchman was pointing and dropped his pipe. He slowly climbed down from the carriage and walked into the middle of the lawn. Gertie whispered out to him, but it was no use and so he walked out and joined Herschel.

The two men stood next to each other, illuminated and free in the centre of the lawn and looked through the large windows to see Desiree dancing on the stage. Herschel shed tears as he recognised the dance. Desiree, as if she had somehow known he would be watching, had chosen to dance her secret dance which was reserved only for Herschel. It was a melancholic and pained dance that demonstrated no great technical ability, but instead oceans of artistic interpretation, with every gesture, step and motion conjuring experiences specific to the two lovers. He saw in her performance, their first meeting, their arguments, his prayers for his departed wife and his new love watching over him. He saw a past and present love and he saw flashes of a blissful and content future. He saw everything.

From the edge of the lawn, Antoine smiled and tipped his imaginary hat for Herschel and snuck back into the hall to watch the performance first hand. Inside the hall, it seemed that everybody was transfixed by the dancer, each other traversing their own memories, conjoined in a blissful dream like solitude where the room had become entirely populated by somnambulist lovers. It was a serene moment and Antoine would remember it always. Desiree held the world in her hands for seven whole minutes, and when she finally finished her routine by sinking to the floor and receding into her dress like a butterfly falling back into the chrysalis, the crowd remained in stunned silence for several minutes longer.

Slowly, as if unwilling to destroy the illusion, a ripple of applause began to seep through the hall. It gathered momentum and soon the portraits were rattling on their mountings. Desiree bowed graciously to her audience and flashed honest and heartfelt smiles to Archie, Claudia and Antoine who all bowed subtly back to her. She stepped off the stage and as she did she caught sight of a rotund figure standing in the gloom of the night. She knew then that Herschel had watched her perform and she felt complete.

Brandenburg had missed the entire performance, a fact that would forever haunt him, as he was lost in the labyrinth of painful nostalgia. Abigail Hardwoode was alive and standing just two feet from him. She had a new identity and did not recognise him, but he knew who she really was and what she was like. He had two enemies in the room and knew instantly that he had not the strength to fight them both. He was undone. He stood stricken with fear as the crowd parted once more to form a corridor down which Desiree glided. She walked up to the Count and, wanting to remain in character, stood on tip-toes and stage-kissed him on the lips. It was the kiss of life and Brandenburg was brought back into the room. She saw the colour of his eyes in a state of flux as the green of Ananas was slowly beaten back by the grey of Brandenburg. She squeezed his arm reassuringly and led him, along with the rest of the crowd, into the reception room where they would take drinks before dinner. Along the way, Lady Jennifer-Joy slipped away from the Count and rejoined De Locke. She felt safer near him then she did with her strange dance partner. Something about his eyes had sparked an unwanted and hitherto buried curiosity inside her. She kept a keen eye on Brandenburg as they made their way to drinks.

The reception room was wide with high ceilings. There were white clothed trestle tables lining the walls and every few feet were stacked crystal wine glasses next to wine bottles arranged in attractive triangle formations. The bar, at the far end of the room was the height of fashion. Bartenders stood in lines and flamboyantly prepared very strange and very vibrant drinks which were presented in very strangely shaped and annoyingly small glasses. The majority of the crowd congregated around the bartenders, whereas a few older folk hung around the old fashioned wine tables. Archie had positioned himself in the far corner and, when he was sure nobody was looking, had taken a few glasses for himself. Brandenburg came barrelling into the room with Desiree barely touching the floor behind him. He went straight for the first pyramid of glasses and before Desiree had finished one glass, he had finished the rest. He breathed heavily and colour returned to his cheeks. He looked over at Archie in the corner who fixed him with a wide eyed stare that told him to sort himself out. Brandenburg nodded, picked up a glass and turned to the crowd. He took Desiree by the arm and pulled her into the midst of them all.

Archie had lost sight of the Players as they mingled and had focused his attentions on the mysterious, raven beauty who was working the room as if she owned it. Kissing hands, curtseying and bowing with such grace that men became agitated and women became flustered. He could not draw his eyes away from that magnetic green stare of hers and he thought that, every once in a while, she had been casting curious glances towards him. He was sure she was. She must have been. He looked around him to see if anything more interesting might be drawing her gaze. There was not. She was looking at him. His heart was racing.

Antoine stepped over and cleared his throat. Archie did not move. Antoine flicked his ear. That got his attention.

"Keep your eyes on that one," whispered Antoine, gesturing to the mysterious woman.

"I am."

"No, I mean, keep your eyes on her, especially her hands."

"They are nice aren't they? Like perfect...silk."

"Yes, nice...and fast. She is a thief and a good one; though not as good as us."

"What do you mean?"

"The man in the corner, the idiot with the red waistcoat; see him?"

Archie nodded.

"Well, he came here with three signet rings on his left hand, he now has none. The woman with the silk gloves talking to the man with the big nose was wearing a pearl necklace and matching bracelets. Not anymore. The Major at the bar is no longer as highly decorated and his wife's slippers no longer have the ruby buckles. Actually, I don't know how she got those."

"Are you sure?"

Antoine raised his eyebrow.

"Masterful!" whispered an enamoured Archie.

"Dangerous," countered Antoine before stepping back to his post. Archie watched the raven haired woman meet and greet and as he focused, he picked up on her techniques. He agreed that she was not as magical as Antoine, but she was still highly skilled and far, far more alluring than the Frenchman.

The gong sounded for dinner and the guests finished their drinks and filed through the huge doors and into the banquet hall. Archie kept his eyes on the mystery woman who made towards the doors, but at the last second ducked through a service door to the side. Archie seemed to be the only one to notice. He wanted to follow after her, pin her against a wall, introduce himself and then ravish her and be damned to the consequences. He motioned to do so but halted when he noticed Brandenburg staggering towards the banquet hall.

As the crowd funnelled through the doors, Brandenburg pushed his way towards De Locke and Lady Jennifer-Joy until he was standing behind her. As the group got caught in the traffic, he leant into her ear and whispered quietly, "I know who you really are".

Lady Jennifer-Joy's heart skipped a beat at the sound of his words. A fear swept through her but her secret training kicked in and she remained calm. Lady Jennifer-Joy ignored the drunkard behind her and waited patiently to file into the dining hall with her husband.

———•◦•———

The raven-haired woman floated down the service corridor like a ghost until she came to a small wrought iron candle holder bolted to the wall. She pulled out a scrap of paper from a concealed pocket and held it up to the light. She squinted at the crudely drawn map, turning it over and over until she was orientated. She looked around. The coast was clear. The raven haired woman ate the piece of paper, leant on the wall and pulled on the candle holder. There was a grating of stone on stone and a portion of the wall opened up to reveal a secret passage. She stepped through the opening and the door closed. It was if nothing had happened.

There was a spark. Then another, before a third which grew into a flame, which then ignited a small torch. The dark passage was illuminated. It was narrow, with a low ceiling and dank. It offered no hint of a beginning or end. The raven haired woman looked down into the gloom before hitching up her dress and making her way down it.

She had walked for twenty yards before she came across a wooden panel. She inspected it with the light from the torch until she came across a handle. She turned it and the wood panel slid directly upwards. She thrust her torch into the opening and peered in. She was looking into one of the confessional booths in the chapel. She withdrew and closed the hatch and moved on. After a further twenty yards, the passageway opened up into a large chamber. She walked into the middle and spun the torch around to gauge her surroundings. Upon the walls hung an arsenal of weapons; blades, muskets, pistols and daggers. She inspected them all, taking in all the details of the weapons. The blades edges were fierce and chipped and none of the swords carried any embellishment or decoration. This was an arsenal built for business. The raven-haired woman walked around the room until she came to a thick black cloak hanging on the wall. She smiled, doused the torch and pulled on the cloak hook. A silent door opened and she looked out into the empty master bedroom of Nathanial Whit. She stepped through and closed the secret door behind her.

The dinner was well underway and Brandenburg was drunk. He was sitting diagonally down by two from Lady Jennifer and Lord De Locke and down a further two from Nathanial Whit and his moribund wife who said not a word and looked into her food as she ate. Desiree was looking to Archie to suggest he think about giving the signal to call it a day, and Archie was beginning to agree with her. Brandenburg was falling apart. He was drinking heavily and hitting the table hard to emphasise his increasingly slurred points. The only reason why Archie did not drop the curtain was because he wanted to watch the magician at work. It was worth a few more moments to see

Antoine perform. A little bell rang and the guests, whether finished with their course or not sat back. Except for Brandenburg who, much to the disgust of his nearby guests and to the dismay of Desiree carried on eating his soup. The Umbrian stamped on his foot and the Count dropped his spoon and sat back grinning like a child, all the while casting overt glances at Lady Jennifer-Joy who did not give him the satisfaction of looking back. Archie gritted his teeth and looked over to the waiting staff, of which Antoine was first in line. Archie looked around and beckoned to Claudia who walked solemnly over and stood beside him like a good serving girl.

"Thank you" she whispered without moving her lips, "this is a much better view." Archie stroked her hair and she rested the full weight her head into the palm of his hand.

Desiree squeezed her foot into Brandenburg's and placed her hand on his leg to help keep his focus. Antoine started without any gusto which was as beguiling to the Players as any of his tricks. He simply walked up to the foot of the table and began replacing cutlery. Behind him, a team of waiters began replacing plates, bowls and glasses. The guests all began conducting polite conversations to the people next to them. Except for the Count and Desiree who were transfixed by the nondescript waiter who was making has way down the table. They watched his face and recognised the look of concentration. They watched his hands and saw no evidence of trickery. He moved with purpose and without stopping. They were in awe of his concentration. He moved down the table and, when he passed them and took their knives, Desiree whispered, "You are a genius" under her breath which was not met by any response. He simply moved on. They tried to watch the switch, they tried to see where the cutlery went and they tried to hear the clatter of metal as he worked. They could not.

Antoine finished his performance and turned to the foot of the table and, while the guests all nattered, he gave them a triumphant grin and a little bow. Desiree and Brandenburg looked at him and acknowledged his performance. The Frenchman was filled with pride and elation before turning to join the procession of waiters filing around the room and back to their regiment position. As he walked passed Archie and Claudia he looked to them for their reviews. Archie gave a so-so gesture and Claudia yawned and looked at her nails. Antoine flicked his teeth and walked on, out of the room.

———•◦•———

The guests had just started to eat their next course when Brandenburg hit the table with his hand.

"So, Lord De Locke!" he said loudly and across the table. "Tell me how you came to meet your wonderful wife."

Desiree angled her heel into Brandenburg's foot but it made little difference to him. He was armoured with booze. Lord De Locke looked down the table at the Count and at the startled guests who had not all but forgotten their food and were waiting for a response. De Locke let out a little sickly wheeze before regaining his voice.

"We met, six years ago, didn't we my dear?"

Lady Jennifer-Joy nodded into her drink.

"Out of the blue we met, at a ball in Oxford. I was wearing red and you...what were you wearing?

"Red" she uttered quietly.

"That's right! Red! What a coincidence!"

"Yes!" said Brandenburg, "What a coinky-dink indeed!" and he raised his glass to disapproving looks before downing the contents and picking up another.

"And tell us more, what about the wedding?"

Lord De Locke poured a drink to make it seem like Brandenburg was not alone and obliged the drunkard with an answer. "Well, as much charm as I have, it was not enough secure the woman's hand in marriage upon the instant of meeting her. As I'm sure you would have, dear Count."

Brandenburg fixed Lady Jennifer-Joy with a piercing stare and for a moment she knew his true identity.

"Oh yes," he said, "it seems that not even a man of the House of Brandenburg would have the charm to trammel such a free bird!" He winked at Jennifer-Joy; a gesture that did not go unnoticed amongst the other guests.

"Perhaps..." interjected Nathanial Whit, "that such...."

"That such conversations are best reserved for other times?" countered Brandenburg. Desiree shot a look to Archie to call curtains on this. He was not looking at her instead; he was looking at the other guests and trying to find the mysterious raven-haired woman. Desiree had no choice but to drive her heel harder.

"Where I come from, Mr Whit," continued the drunk Count "we say what we mean, and we say it wherever, at table, at study, at dance and at rest!" and at that he downed another drink.

"Well, perhaps thankfully, we are not where you are from. But in fair England where propriety is King" said Nathanial with a stern tone.

"Really, I thought a madman was your King!" and at that he roared with laughter.

Archie darted his gaze towards Brandenburg and instantly gave the signal to call curtains on the shambles. Antoine and Claudia registered the nod and began to sidle towards the door. Brandenburg roared with laughter again and it was his laugh that was the signal to end things. It was not the laugh of Brandenburg, but the loud, brash and unmistakable laugh of Benjamin Ananas that broke through.

Chapter Forty

Extraction

L ady Jennifer-Joy ran cold at the sound of the laugh, looked over at the Count and she saw before her the grown man who used to be the boy she loved. She lost all sense of training and she fumbled a glass, spilling it across the table. The waiters darted over to attend to the minor disaster. Lady Jennifer-Joy apologised to Lord De Locke and the other guests profusely and her apologies were brushed away with polite disregard. Only Nathanial Whit remained undisturbed by the laugh. He looked over at the phoney Count and knew that he had in his own house, a rat that needed disposing off. Desiree gave one final stamp on Brandenburg's foot and, finally, she got a response.

"Well," said the Count as he stood up from the table, drank two drinks in quick succession and dropped his napkin over his untouched food. "It appears that I have said too much, perhaps on account of the drink, perhaps on account of my history. As it stands, and as I sway, I will bid that you grant me leave for a few moments while I take in some air. Lords, Ladies, Gentlemen…" he stepped backwards and almost tripped over his chair. Desiree stood to leave with him. The Count stopped her and sat her back down. "No, my darling," he slurred, "You stay and eat. I will be back in a few moments. You eat. Besides, you could use a good meal!"

The guests gasped as Brandenburg weaved off towards the doorway. Archie was stricken with stage fright. The play was tumbling out of control and he did not know what to do.

"Lord De Locke!" called Brandenburg before he left. The Lord graciously looked over to him and smiled a hate-smile.

"Look out for that one," he said, pointing to Lady Jennifer-Joy. "She has secrets. I can tell! She is a woman, and as we know in Holstenwall, women are like snakes…but with less of a spine!" he laughed again and left the banquet hall.

The doors to the banquet hall closed behind Brandenburg, leaving him alone in the reception hall. As soon as he heard the click of the latch his demeanour changed. He no longer swayed and his eyes regained focused. He looked around, keen and alert. He stretched his neck and tried to work out the kinks that the last two hours of drinking. He closed his eyes and flicked out the tension in his hands, transforming himself back into the Brandenburg he was before. In his mind he was racing through the stage plan of the house, trying to locate the room he needed. He found it and his bloodshot eyes snapped open and he dashed off through the empty house.

———•◦•———

Archie nodded to Desiree and she understood that the gesture meant that she was to stay at the table. She complied and turned her attention to her food and to the pitiful looks given to her by the guests who felt her embarrassment at the way her man had behaved. She acted accordingly and looked humbly into her glass.

Archie made his way to the service door and slyly beckoned to Antoine and Claudia to join him. He had initiated the final scene and now, it was time to pack up and leave the Whit Ball and hope that they had secured enough loot to rebuild The Roxy and execute their endgame.

As Archie led the Antoine and Claudia out of the banquet hall, he could not help but entertain his anger at Brandenburg for his behaviour. He marched onwards with a long and purposeful stride. Antoine kept pace, but Claudia had to run every few faces to catch up with the striding actor. The trio walked through the empty gallery and around to the grand central staircase and ascended it without paying any attention to who may have been watching them. They rounded the top of the stairs and carried along the mezzanine and through the long corridor where the private rooms and guest bedrooms were. Archie reached the door to the study and opened it, foregoing the secret knock which startled Anya and Danilov greatly. He held it open for Antoine and Claudia and they hurried in. He threw a cursory glance down the corridor before closing the door.

"What's going on?" said Danilov, surprised at their sudden entrance and sensing Archie's agitation.

"Pack up. We're done." said Archie sharply.

"But we've at least two more trips to make!" protested Danilov.

"Were done," said Archie firmly and turned to the door.

"Where are you going?"

"To find that arse-wipe, Ananas" and with that he left the room, slamming the door behind him.

"What's happened? Antoine, what's going on? Where's Desiree?" Danilov asked with an exasperated tone. Antoine lifted his arms up and Anya began to carefully unbutton him.

"Brandenburg has destroyed the play!"

"Did he forget a line?" asked Danilov as took a leather harness from the inside lid of the trunk.

"No chance! The fool got drunk and made an idiot out of himself for no reason!"

"There must be a reason!" protested Claudia as Danilov attached the harness around her waist.

Anya finished unbuttoning Antoine and pulled his shirt out of his waist band and to reveal his leather corset stocked with silver cutlery.

"I don't know," he said, "we will find out later."

"And Desiree?"

"I will get her out. We'll meet them around the front."

Antoine and Anya began to unhook the cutlery from his brace and pack it away in the trunk. Danilov tightened the harness around the Claudia and strapped it to himself like a backpack.

"Are you ready, Little Mouse?" he said looking over his shoulder to her. She nodded.

"Alright, let's go!" and the Acrobat hopped up onto the wire and walked off down into the darkness towards the waiting carriage. As she disappeared into the night, Claudia waved back to Antoine who blew her a kiss.

———•◦•———

As Desiree sat in silence she recoiled at the way in which the Socialites had already forsaken her. The initial looks of pity had all but washed away and now she sat in the middle of the banquet table while all around her, the gossips gossiped. She put down her knife and fork and picked up her wine glass and, over the rim, she judged each person and felt great comfort in the love she felt in her hammock, safe in The Roxy and far, far away from these beasts. The wine fell down her throat and, to her, each cascade felt like Herschel's kisses.

As her eyes moved from face to face, they finally fell upon Lady Jennifer-Joy and there they stopped. Desiree looked at her beautiful face and was stunned to realise that the woman was an actress too; the tension in her jaw when she chewed, the tiny film of sweat along her hairline, the calculations behind her eyes that gave away the mania of an improvising actress struggling to keep the plates spinning upon their poles. Most importantly of all, Desiree realised that Lady Jennifer-Joy was trying desperately not to look at her. What was her secret? What was she hiding? Desiree diverted her attentions from the love of Herschel and the Playhouse and her disdain for the rest of the tiresome guests at the ball and focused them all on Lady Jennifer-Joy and an attempt to mentally storm the woman's battlements and uncover all her secrets.

———•·•———

Danilov hopped off the wire and Gertie rushed over to unclip Claudia. Herschel, now happily drunk on cheap booze and the spectacle of witnessing Desiree's performance, sat on the driver's bench.

"Didn't expect to see you two so soon!" he said as he patted himself down, searching for another hipflask. "Did you see her? Did you see Desiree, oh the wonders! The…"
Gertie hushed the playwright with his hand as he noticed the stern look on Danilov's face.

"What is it?"

"It's over. Brandenburg's gone off-script and Archie is dropping the curtain!"

"What the hell happened?" said Gertie, unclasping Claudia from Danilov's back.

"Don't know. Something spun him and he started hitting the bottle."

"I could have predicted that! Dumb soak!" scoffed Herschel, "well, we've done our jobs. Got loot a' plenty. Is there an emergency scene we need to act out?"

"Archie is looking for the errant lead actor, Antoine is going to get Desiree out and we'll meet them around the front."

"What, all of us in one carriage, with the booty; are you out of your walnut, mate?" slurred Herschel. Gertie lifted Claudia off the harness and put her on the grass.

"Dani, go back for the last load," he said. "We'll drive around the front, nick another carriage. Antoine, Desiree, Archie and Brandenburg can take that. Savvy?" Everybody looked at everybody else and nodded.

"Agreed." said Danilov and he ran back up the wire to retrieve the last trunk from the study.

———•◦•———

Brandenburg stood in the middle of the armoury which was hidden away at the far end of the mansion, behind the library. It was a private and magnificent room. The ceiling was twenty feet high and the walls were adorned with shields, insignias and colours of every regiment in the Empire. Lining the armoury stood forty suits of armour and through the middle of the room stood huge glass display cabinets housing every conceivable weapon from all four corners of the globe. Brandenburg only had one weapon on his mind. His adrenalin had calmed the effects of the booze and he scoured the cabinets quickly, until he found what he was looking for.

Hidden in a nondescript cabinet and displayed without any pomp or circumstances was a rapier with a gilded basket fashioned in the shape of a pineapple. His eyes welled upon seeing it and he was suddenly a child again, seeing the sword upon the wall in his father's study. He clenched his jaw and bit his lip as he then recalled the moment that he sold his soul and offered the heirloom to the young Nathanial Whit who paid for it with a few coins and a barrowful of scorn. Brandenburg rested his forehead against the glass pane and ran his hands down it, hoping somehow that he could melt through the glass, grab the sword, step back in time and hand it back to his young self.

"Forgive me, father, for my youth and my desperation. I was not a man as I should have been. Forgive me," he whispered.

The Count then reverted to a silent prayer whereby he asked God for forgiveness for all his sins and thanked the Almighty for bestowing upon him the chance to redeem himself. Once the prayer was finished his melancholia lifted and a calming sense of righteousness came over him. He stepped back from the cabinet and ran his fingers over the seams until he found the latch. He clicked it open and the glass door swung out. He was in touching distance of his father's sword. The Count ran his fingers down the blade and felt alive and free. The blade was his. He looked down at the Spider Basket sword Tobias had made him, drew it and held it up in comparison to the Pineapple basket. He smiled, gripped his sword by the forte with one hand, and with the other, snapped off one of the mandible shaped quillons. He rested the piece in the cabinet and began snapping off first the other mandible and then all the legs until only the spider's body remained. He smiled at Tobias's work and thanked him for following the designs perfectly. He held the broken sword up to the sword of Ananas that was still hanging in the cabinet. Without the mandibles and legs, the true design of the sword was revealed. It was an exact replica of his father's sword. Brandenburg unclipped the hanging sword and sheathed it before hanging up the replica.

The end of dinner had barely been called when Nathanial Whit stood up and left the room while the rest of the guests filed into the conservatory to take drinks and compliment each other. Brandenburg's performance had eradicated all goodwill towards Desiree and she found herself alone in the room. She looked out onto the lawn and saw, in the gloom, the carriage being loaded with loot. She felt confident that nobody would see them as one would really have to know what they were looking for, and strain as well, to make them out. Around her the guests mingled. However, Lady Jennifer-Joy also stood alone. Desiree continued to study the strange Lady as she looked out into the gloom of the copse. Desiree could see the Lady's lips moving and strained to read them. She could pick out a few words, but they made no sense. Clearly, Lady Jennifer-Joy was rattled by something and was desperately trying to reconcile her thoughts. Desiree decided to keep a keen eye on her while she waiting for Antoine to come and extract her from the play.

Nathanial Whit stalked through the rooms of the lower section of his house, trying to find the drunken Count. With every step he became more convinced of Brandenburg's true identity as that booming laugh reverberated through his mind, but he needed true confirmation, and he needed it through confrontation. He started his sweep in a logical fashion, systematically checking room after room until in a moment of divine inspiration he realized just where he would find his man. He left the lower study and hurried towards the armoury.

———•••———

The raven haired woman was sat at Nathanial Whit's desk in his private room. The secret passage had opened out into the room via the giant portrait of his grandfather. The man was tall, lean and stern. He was decked in black armour and bore a large scar across his cheek that the artist had made no attempt to conceal. If anything, it was more likely accentuated at the command of the man sitting before him. The woman did not pay any attention to the work of the artist, nor did she pay any reverence or respect to the powerful figure. She had simply wedged the portrait door open with a chair and gone straight to the desk whereupon she had picked the lock in seconds and begun riffling through his papers until she had found what she was looking for; a small black leather pocket book emblazoned with a silver sword crossing an arm. She scanned over the various diary entries, notations, maps and diagrams working at great speed that was not executed through fear of getting caught, but through ingrained training. She finished the diary and cursed to herself. She had not found what she was looking for. The woman replaced the diary and tried to re-fit the drawer. It did not slide all the way in. She tried a few times, but something was jamming it. She took the drawer out, reached in and pulled out the blockage. It was another book, smaller than the diary but carrying the same emblem. She flicked through the pages and her eyes widened in astonishment. The pages were full of near unintelligible scribbles, symbols and diagrams. She kept on flicking until she came to the centre pages. A large, folded page fell out. She held it up and smiled at her discovery. The gatefold page displayed a giant floorplan of a huge building. The map was annotated with strange symbols and codes that she could only assume was some sort of battle plan. Written across the top of the map, in capital letters were the words 'Brighton Pavilion'. She looked out of the window at the night sky. The position of the moon told her that she was running out of time. The woman smiled, pocketed the secret book and slid the drawer back into its place before disappearing into the dark passage, forgetting to replace the chair properly and let the portrait door close behind her.

Archie cursed under his breath as he crept around the house, looking and listening for any sign of the drunken actor. He could have sworn he had checked every room at least twice and was on the verge of quitting and leaving his idiot friend behind when his better nature won out and he decided to give the house one more sweep. It was an unknown miracle that Archie had not run into Nathanial during his search of the house and, indeed, on several occasions, one had left a room via one door just as the other had entered through another. Archie, of course, had no idea that Whit was on the prowl for the Count and so he dashed back to the staircase and took the door underneath it that lead to the service passage as it was the quickest way to get around to the front of the house and begin the sweep.

The corridor was dark and empty when he entered it at the far end of the house. He made his way quickly and quietly, stopping every once in a while to listen for any stumbling, clattering, drunken noises. The corridor was deadly still. He moved forward again. Suddenly, he heard the unexpected sound of stone grating on stone.

At first it was a tiny, almost imperceptible noise. He froze like a predator catching scent of his prey. He held his breath. The scrape came again, this time, long and steady. It was coming from behind him. He spun around, expecting to find Brandenburg staggering about and was sideswiped to see a feminine shape emerge. The darkness of the corridor blighted Archie's presence and the woman rushed out into the corridor and, before she could react, collided with the man. They both tumbled to the floor. The woman's instincts took over and she rolled the man onto his back, pinned him down cupped his mouth with her hand. The only light available in the corridor found its ways to her eyes and Archie caught a glimpse of the green emeralds. They were fierce and focused. He raised his hand to give her a little wave when an unwelcome 'snick' sound and the cold touch of steel against his throat forced him to reconsider. Her eyes told him that, if he made a sound, it would be his last. The woman slowly removed her hand from his mouth. They were both breathing heavily, faces inches from each other. Archie smiled at her and she rammed her lips against his and thrust her tongue into his mouth. He closed his eyes for a few seconds and allowed himself to succumb to the bewitching woman. He felt the knife relax a little from his throat and his hands found themselves drifting up to her waist. The woman's passion intensified for a few moments before suddenly ceasing altogether. Archie opened his eyes. She was not there. He sat up to see a shape darting off down the corridor.

"Wait!" he called out, rather pathetically, "at least tell me your name!"

"Another time, another place, perhaps by the sea!" she called back in that beguiling accent of hers. Archie scratched his head.

"Odd thing to say" he said to himself as he looked down and smiled. He had stolen from her all the jewels and rings that she had pick-pocketed earlier.

Chapter Forty One

A Shot in the Dark

L ady Jennifer-Joy was holding the seams of her dress so tightly that her knuckles had turned white. She could feel the line of cold sweat running down her shoulder blades and soaking her dress. She was looking out at the blackness outside and felt the void swelling inside her to be greater than the darkness behind the window. She had spend her entire life in training and the previous six years entrenched in an assumed identity that it was now shattering to conceive of the return of Benjamin. Could it really be him? The Count Brandenburg was dashing and well informed regarding dance patterns which almost convinced her that it was not him. However, that wild laugh, and those eyes which married with his sudden sallow skin tone and electric touch fought a desperate vanguard action in her soul. It could be him! A thousand others erupted in her heart at every question. Why him? Why now? Did he really know who she was? Was he working for them? Would he ruin it all? She tried to the think of the bigger picture, of her mission and her charge and she prayed that the Count Brandenburg was nothing more than a passing resemblance to the man she once loved. She had a mission and it was paramount that she saw it through. She must bide her time. Though she wanted to grab her husband by the arm and march him home, she knew she could not. She had to weather this storm.

"Benjamin," she whispered, "if it's really you, wait one more week, and then come for your revenge. I beg you."

Desiree, studying Lady Jennifer-Joy from across the conservatory picked out every word of her admission fearful of what it meant and knowing with dread that she was right to fear. She looked around to see Archie but he wasn't there. All she could do was to wait and so she returned to her study of the actress in front of her.

Lady Jennifer-Joy was so lost in her thoughts that she felt not the warm hand glide down her right arm and rest against her hip. The hand squeezed playfully and pulled her close. Lady Jennifer-Joy smiled and maintained her position, looking out onto the lawn. The raven haired woman was standing next her, looking out into the darkness also.

"A good evening?" whispered Lady Jennifer-Joy.

"Pleasant," said the woman, running her tongue over her lips and recalling the taste of Archie Enfield, "very pleasant."

Desiree watched as the raven-haired woman slipped a small article to Lady Jennifer-Joy who took it and concealed it in a secret pocket.

"Meet me under the moon, when the starlight is westerly," Lady Jennifer-Joy said, cryptically. The raven haired woman laughed and ran a hand through her hair.

"You spies and your secret passwords and phrases," she said, quietly, "don't worry, I'll find you...before Brighton."

"Brighton?" said Lady Jennifer with a hushed seriousness. The raven-haired woman walked over to the window, unclasped it and stepped out onto the lawn. Before disappearing she turned back to Lady Jennifer-Joy and blew her a kiss.

"Brighton," she whispered, and she was gone.

Desiree tried to follow the figure walking out into the darkness. Contrary to her rational mind but completely in tune with her romantic streak, Desiree would swear until the day she died that the dark haired woman who walked across the lawn, disappeared into a plume of black smoke and was gone into the night.

————•••————

With the sword of Ananas back in the scabbard of its rightful owner, Brandenburg felt renewed. The effects of the alcohol had subsided and he had even managed to quell the panic and nausea that had been swirling inside him since he saw Abigail Hardwoode. Indeed, he felt as if the interim years between his youth and now had been washed away. As if he had fallen asleep and awoken the next morning. He had fulfilled his destiny and his father's legacy was restored to him. He exhaled in relief and moved his mind onto his next mission; getting the Players out of the house, into the night safely and on with their bright futures.

His hand rested on the hilt and he rounded the corner of the hallway and onto the main gallery when he stopped dead in his track. Nathanial Whit was standing in the centre of the room just left of the central staircase, and he had his sword unsheathed.

"Count Brandenburg" he whispered as he looked, head bowed and eyes fierce. He lifted the point of his sword.

"I have no quarrel with you, good sir," said Brandenburg in a faux tone of innocent surprise. Brandenburg needed to retain his cover, get his Players out of the house and escape as soon as possible. He believed the best way to do that was to feign cowardice and, perhaps, talk his way out of it. Nathanial Whit smiled and stepped up to the Count, lifting his sword to neck height.

"That is a nice weapon….Ananas."

The cover was blown, Brandenburg was had. Whit swung with his sword. Brandenburg jumped backwards, craning his head up to avoid the blade which swung so close that it cut the top button off of his collar. The Count jumped to the side to avoid the follow through and swung his fist out, connecting sharply with Nathanial Whit's jaw which sent the man crashing down to the floor. The Count wasted no time and motioned to flee down the corridor. He made two steps before he felt Whit's hand on his ankle, yanking his leg backwards. Face first, the Count fell onto the carpet, his arm shielding his face from the impact. He rolled onto his back as Whit got to his knees. Brandenburg kicked him square in the gut and Whit was driven onto his back also.

Brandenburg looked down to the hallway to see Archie running towards him to help out. Brandenburg silently motioned him away, pointing towards the reception room. Archie halted his charge and understood. He had to go and get Desiree out without breaking cover of the performance. He nodded and darted into a side room, just as Whit managed to get to his feet and, thankfully raise his head too late to notice Archie.

The Count ran at Whit and tackled him to the floor again and they began trading blows to the midriff as they rolled around on the carpet. Brandenburg knew he had to end the scuffle quickly and decisively, and that meant playing dirty. He rolled Nathanial onto his back and administered an almighty knee to the groin in a wonderfully cathartic move. The impact knocked years off of Whit and he gasped, releasing his grip on the Count. Brandenburg got to his feet and fled down the gallery.

He reached the door to the conservatory just as Archie was leading Desiree out of the room. He grabbed both their hands and led them towards the main entrance hall.

Nathanial Whit expelled the air from his lungs and regained himself in time to see 'Brandenburg', his fiancée and man-servant leaving the gallery and entering the entrance hall. He spat on the floor and staggered towards the main staircase and ascended it, three steps at a time.

———•·•———

Anya kissed her brother on the forehead for luck and watched as he climbed onto the wire for his final descent. All the loot had been loaded and it was time to for the last two to go. In the darkness, beyond Danilov, she could see the carriage with Herschel, Gertie and Antoine waiting for her. Once Danilov had reached the carriage and stepped off the wire, she prepared herself to leave. She had not taken a walk in a good few hours and so quickly ran through a stretching routine. When she was ready, she stepped onto the railing and lowered her heart rate. The walk was simple. She began.

Anya had taken only five steps when she heard the door to the study fly open. The unexpected noise caused her to wobble slightly and she looked back to see Nathanial Whit standing in the room staring, dumbfounded at her. They locked eyes for a second.

On the ground, Gertie squinted to see the figure on the wire motionless.

"Something's wrong," he uttered. Herschel and Danilov were busy stowing the loot.

"Something's wrong," he said, louder. They did not hear him.

Nathanial Whit looked at the odd little woman suspended in the darkness. He looked at the railing and saw the knot. His mind turned in an instant. He was being robbed. He leapt for the wire and frantically began to untie it, causing the wire to shake violently.

Gertie threw his cigarette to the floor and grabbed his butterfly net from the roof of the carriage. His sudden burst of movement stirred the others into noticing what was happening. Before anyone could react, Gertie was already pelting across the lawn towards the acrobat. As he ran he yelled over his shoulder back to the other.

"Go! Get out now! I will get her and get another carriage! Go! Go!"

Herschel slapped Antoine on the back and they threw the rest of the loot into the cabin.

"Go get her Gertie!" shouted Danilov, "you can do it!"

Danilov's words lit a fire under Gertie's feet and he moved at a gazelle's speed. Anya was battling her fear and trying to remain calm and balanced as she watched Nathanial Whit attempting to untie the wire. She could not run down, as it was shaking too vigorously. All she could do was sway with it, keep balance and pray for Gertie. In frustration Nathanial Whit gave up with the knot and drew his sword. As she saw the blade glint in the moonlight Anya's eyes widened in fear. Nathanial brought it swinging down to the wire. Anya closed her eyes and leapt up into the air, performing a blind back flip and plunging down towards the floor.

Gertie tracked her arc of descent and felt a tuning fork ring in his heart. He dove forward, his net stretched out far in front.

Nathanial Whit craned his neck over the railing to see the robber fall into a net and roll out onto the floor and into the arms of an unknown. He shouted in rage and wracked his mind. He was being robbed at one end of his mansion, and at the other, Benjamin Ananas was escaping. He looked to the copse to see the outline of a carriage begin to roll towards the front of the house. It seemed the two parties were converging. He gritted his teeth and ran out of the study.

Nathanial belted along the upper corridor of his mansion until he came to the door to his private quarters. He near barged through it and ran over to the large portrait and entered his secret arsenal. He wasted no time in grabbing his trusted flintlock Baker Rifle from its mount. He continued through the arsenal and back along the secret passage with the intention of emerging at the back of the mansion and, if he was fast enough, into the path of the oncoming carriage. He was fast on his feet and faster with the rifle. A good rifleman could discharge three rounds a minute with the Baker rifle. Nathanial, formerly of the 95th once shot four dragoons in forty-five seconds in high winds. He would get Ananas in his sights and cut the head off of the snake. His heart raced with vengeful fire as he ran down the cold stone corridor.

Brandenburg, Archie and Desiree were already in the carriage compound while Gertie was on the other side of the house catching Anya. They had left the ball as discreetly as possible and had picked up their pace the farther from the mansion they had got. Archie explained that they had been made and needed to escape fast. Both Desiree and Archie had questions in their minds regarding Brandenburg and his motivations to go off script in such a disastrous manner. Archie's mind was spinning and thoughts of the danger that Claudia could have been in thanks to Brandenburg's behaviour began to rise up inside him.

As they entered the compound and ran towards the nearest suitable carriage, Brandenburg removed the nosebags from two beasts and flung the reins up to the driver's carriage. He was about to mount when anger overcame Archie and he grabbed hold of Brandenburg and pulled him down. He pinned the Count against the carriage and against his nature he stuck him hard across the face. Brandenburg fell to the floor and Desiree gasped in shock. The Count did not retaliate, instead lying in the muddied straw-bedded ground.

"What the hell happened? It could have been perfect! I knew it was about revenge!" shouted Archie as he went to grab Brandenburg, pull him up and administer another punch. He was interrupted by Gertie and Anya falling into the compound. They stopped on their heels when they saw Archie, fist raised to strike and Brandenburg breathing hard and bleeding out of the corner of his mouth.

"What the hell is going on?" demanded Gertie with an authoritative tone that took the two men down a peg or two. "We've got to get out of here. Punch the idiot later, I'll help, but for now, we have Claudia to get to safety. Stop fucking about and let's go!"

Gertie lifted Anya onto the driver's plate and looked down at the shocked actors. He rolled his eyes and kicked open the carriage doors.

"Fancy a jaunt in a Hackney carriage?" he shouted, remembering what Miss Siddons had said to him that day on Drury Lane, moments before she died at the hands of Kemble. The actors did not need asking a second time and Archie and Desiree climbed inside. Brandenburg jumped onto the footrail and Gertie kicked the horses into life.

The two black steeds reared up and kicked open the compound doors. The carriage lurched forward and out into the courtyard. They rode out and halted just on the driveway.

"What are you waiting for?" shouted Archie, leaning out of the window.

"Convoy!" replied Gertie and pointed towards the dark copse towards the rear of the mansion. Anya sat close to Gertie as the carriage sat on the driveway waiting for the welcome sign of the loot-filled carriage to come rumbling around the corner.

Herschel and Danilov sat on the driver's bench and beat the horses mercilessly. Alas, the weight of the carriage combined with the weight of Antoine and Claudia pressed down onto the axles something fierce. Their turning circle was huge and it had taken a few attempts to swing the carriage around the corners of the mansion until they could see, ahead, the waiting carriage of Brandenburg. Danilov hit the roof of the carriage.

"I can see them, we're on our way Antoine; we're on our way"

"Formidable," whispered the Frenchman as he held Claudia tightly and rested his feet on the trunk of loot in the cabin.

"I can see them!" said Gertie, pointing to the edge of the mansion. Brandenburg swung around to see Herschel driving the heavy coach towards them. The relief was palpable. Brandenburg stuck his head into the cabin and smiled at Archie and Desiree.

"We're all here, we're on our way."

Desiree smiled and fell into the arms of Archie who held her tight and laughed. Brandenburg stood back up on the foot plate. Gertie looked around to him, his face easing into a relaxed smile. Brandenburg smiled at him.

"Alright, Gertie, let's...." The Count was cut short by Gertie's hand thrusting into his face, pushing him clean from the carriage.

Brandenburg had not even hit the ground before the shot whistled past him and into the woods. He rolled onto the floor and looked up at the balcony to see Nathanial Whit, kneeling down and reloading a long rifle. Brandenburg got to his feet and grabbed Gertie's extended arm and jumped back onto the carriage. Gertie whipped the horses into motion and the carriage rolled forward just as Herschel's pulled up alongside.

"Get moving Herschel!" shouted Brandenburg. Herschel and Danilov whipped the horses harder and managed to motivate them more. Both carriages pulled into the long driveway and into the night.

"We're clear, we're clear," said Brandenburg as the carriages drove into the night. He chanced a glance back and, through the woods, he could barely make out the house, let alone the balcony from which Nathanial had positioned himself.

———•◦•———

On the balcony, Nathanial Whit was reloading his rifle with a sleek automaton motion. While his hands worked, his eyes remained closed as they factored in the weather conditions, elevation and visibility of his position. His second shot would not miss. He finished reloading and opened his eyes. By now the carriages were racing away from him, into the night. He could make out the general shape of the two carriages, but, as they passed under the cover of trees and darkness, he could not make out any discernable mark. He exhaled and focused his mind on the most likely positions of his targets. He opened his eyes slowly and lifted his rifle up to his shoulder. He ran his hand down the wooden stock and rested his cheek along its body. It was an extension of himself; a living, breathing organism in symbiosis with himself. His finger caressed the nickel coated trigger.

The tree-lined canopy flicked moonlight over everything. Brandenburg looked over to Gertie and Anya who looked back at him with nervous relief, the stroboscopic light ticker-taping their expressions. Brandenburg turned to his side and looked over to the carriage rushing alongside his. Through the dull window of the cabin, he could see Antoine holding Claudia. The both looked at him and seemed scared but safe. The Count looked up at Danilov and Herschel, sitting upon the driver's bench. Danilov was laughing and drinking out of Herschel's hipflask. He took a swig and handed it over Brandenburg. The Count reached across the divide and took the flask and drank heartily. Nobody heard the crack of Nathanial Whit's impossible shot.

Danilov leant out to grab the hipflask from Brandenburg when he suddenly felt the left side of his face become doused in liquid. For a few moments, he thought Herschel had played a trick and spat drink over him. He looked around and saw that the playwright was not there. Time slowed. The acrobat looked around. No Herschel. He looked back around to Brandenburg's carriage. Gertie, seemingly in slow motion, was still driving the coach onwards. He looked at the Count who seemed to be routed to the spot, arm extended holding the hipflask at arm's length, a look of shock on his face. The moonlight flicked over his face and showed it to be glistening red. Danilov touched his left cheek. His hand too, was glistening red. He stomach turned as he looked back around to Herschel. His body was there, slumped in the driver's seat, but his head had been detonated over Danilov and Brandenburg.

The last image Benjamin Ananas ever saw of Herschel Barnabus was of him roaring with laughter as he drove that carriage through the wooded lane. The moonlight took a snapshot of the happy playwright. And then he was gone.

Part Four

Brandenburg and the Big Bad

Chapter Forty Two

A Chill Wind

Nathanial Whit opened his eyes and raised his rifle. He breathed steadily. He could not see his target, but he knew his shot was true. His senses chimed in unison and he knew he had hit something. He stood on the balcony and looked out at the peaks of the trees ahead and the moonlight that dappled their top leaves. Somewhere underneath them lay either Benjamin Ananas or one of his accomplices. He shouldered his weapon and left the room to return the trusted Baker rifle back to the arsenal.

———•◦•———

Danilov and Brandenburg locked eyes in shocked despair as the two carriages began to veer away from each other. Brandenburg reached out and tried to grab Danilov's arm but it was no use. The carriage's kerb side wheels hit a rut, throwing the coach off balance and rattling the charging horses. Danilov was flung clear in an instant as the horses crumpled onto each other. As he tumbled and skidded along the muddy track he caught flashes of the carriage bumping and jolting before snagging on a rut. The next thing he saw was a tree trunk. He smashed into it and tumbled into a ditch, passing out in the three inches of freezing, stagnant water.

The crack of the axle was loud enough to get the attention of Gertie who had, up until that moment, been unaware of Herschel's demise. He turned from his driver's bench and looked in horror as the second carriage pulled up on two wheels and rolled along upon a knife edge. He saw Danilov fly clear and tumble onto the path but he could not see Herschel. All that he could see was some strange, limp rag doll lolling about on the bench. He pulled hard on the reins and his horses dug into the muddy road.

The driverless coach swerved violently and Claudia and Antoine were flung over the trunk in the cab and onto the bench opposite. Claudia screamed as the coach bumped and rattled. Antoine desperately tried to shield her, but the inertia was too great and they were both pinned against the wall of the cabin. They felt an almighty crack and strange, otherworldly sense of weightlessness as the flickering moonlight darted through the windows. Everything seemed to spin. Claudia and Antoine were suddenly gifted with a slowed vision of the trunk shooting upwards to the roof of the cabin and breaking open. They tilted their heads at the strange gravitational phenomena and looked in wonder as the silverware and jewels began to fall out. Time then seemed to resume its normal speed and they crashed to the cab floor, inbetween the benches as the loot fell upon them. Antoine, with paternal instinct, rolled onto Claudia and saved her from the falling trunk as he took the burden on his back. There was no pain. As the carriage upturned and rolled along on its side, Antoine's vision faded to black.

The overturned cabin slid along the ground, piling up mud and earth in front of it and the horses tumbled and collapsed into each other. Brandenburg's carriage came to a turning halt just a few yards from it and the cab door flung open. Desiree flew out and began to run blindly towards the carriage calling for Herschel. Her mad hysteria blinded her to the present danger and she did not hear the shouts of Brandenburg to stop. Archie came darting out of the carriage and grabbed Desiree and dived to the side of the road, rolling clear as the flailing legs of the horses kicked, bucked and thrashed madly. Archie rolled Desiree to safety as Gertie, Anya and Brandenburg rushed over to the overturned carriage. Gertie leapt up onto the 'roof', flung the door open and looked into the darkness. Anya ran on back down the road to her brother.

She reached Danilov and slid down the ditch to her brother. She grabbed his shoulders and fell back against the muddy slope, pulling his face out of the water. Then she scrambled backwards up the verge and onto the road before laying him down and slapping his face. After a few seconds, her brother coughed up a mixture of blood and ditch water. Anya laughed in relief and hugged him tightly, which caused him to recoil from the pain his ribs. She rested him back down and sat beside him while he looked up at the night sky and regulated his breathing and systematically checked his bones and musculature for fractures and strains. Once his breath had returned and the dizziness subsided, he reached over to his sister. She took his hand and heaved him to his feet. The stinging pain in his side almost made his knees buckle, but the support from Anya with her arm around his shoulder helped him to remain upright. They slowly made their way to the crashed carriage.

Brandenburg had run around to the back of the carriage and tried to heave the buckled doors open, but they would not budge. Archie ran to help him and together they braced and pulled. It was no use. Gertie climbed into the cabin, taking great care not to tread on the unseen bodies inside. He held onto the door frame and managed to wedge himself across the ceiling, a few inches from the mountain of loot on top of the Players. He called out to them and managed to discern the muffled cry of Claudia. Gertie reported back to Brandenburg and Archie that she was alive and they yanked on the back doors with more urgent vigour. Gertie shuffled his way over the precarious heap and towards the back door. He wedged his hands against each wall and gave the inside of the doors three huge kicks with both legs. On the third, they flew off their hinges, almost knocking the Count and Archie to the ground.

As the doors flung open, the mountain was disturbed and an avalanche of gold and silverware poured out of carriage. The treasure held no currency as Archie and Brandenburg kicked it aside, trying to get to the trunk. The moonlight flooding into the carriage afforded Gertie a better view of the situation and he could see a safe spot of bench to stand on. He climbed over and began to the throw the debris out of the cabin to reveal the upturned case. Brandenburg climbed into the cab as best he could and grabbed the handle of the trunk. Gertie straddled the benches and the trunk, reached down and awkwardly managed to grab the other handle. After a nod to three, Gertie delicately lifted the trunk from his end while Brandenburg did the same. Archie bent down and peered under it. He could only see the small bald patch on Antoine's head and the locks of Claudia's hair. He looked up to Brandenburg and nodded. Slowly, the Count and Gertie began to move the heavy trunk over and out of the carriage. When it was clear, Gertie managed to get down inbetween the benches and inspect the body of Antoine. Archie and Brandenburg looked on nervously.

Behind them, Anya was helping Danilov back to the carriage. He was clutching his side and limping, but he was alive.

Gertie rested his head on Antoine's back and listened carefully. He smiled in relief. The man was alive. He gently slapped the Frenchman on the cheek and he soon came around. Gertie helped the man up and Brandenburg and Archie helped him out of the cabin and into the fresh air. He wobbled for a few seconds as his grogginess subsided but soon recovered his faculties. When he regained his memory of where he was, he pushed his way back to the cab to see to Claudia. Archie held him back and cleared the path as Gertie carried her out. She was fine. Antoine had saved her. Anya and Danilov reached the upturned cabin and everybody hugged.

It was only when Claudia looked confusingly at Danilov and Brandenburg's blood spattered faces that the hearts of the Players sank. They looked at each other realised two people were missing. They walked round to the other side of the carriage to see Desiree standing in shock over the body of her beloved Herschel. Archie grabbed Claudia and covered her eyes, picking her up and holding her tightly into his chest.

At three minutes past midnight Alexia Adberg swung her rapier at Srdjan who matched her move. The action was the culmination of an epic battle that had raged across the auditorium, over the stage, through the backstage area and back onto the boards. The ebb and flow of the battle had been a wonderful ballet showing two dancers at the very top of their game. Their blades clashed in the decisive move but they did not meet the expected resistance. Both blades shattered like glass. Ms Adberg and Srdjan dropped the remnants of their swords in shocked confusion. Alexia was about to speak when a bitter wind swept through the theatre extinguishing all the lamps and candles. The chill infected the two lovers to the core and in the silence they stepped into each other's arms.

Valerie was sat in her private little spot in the attic, looking out at the moonlight when the chill crept under the hatch and ran up her spine. The temperature fell dramatically and she felt an unease sweep over her. She looked around the dark attic and could have sworn someone was there. The attic was full of dread. Valerie looked back up to the moon. She could feel the hairs on her neck stand up and her breath became visible. She closed her eyes and thought about Danilov and the energy and warmth they had generated in that very attic a week before.

Lupe Darling was alone in her quarters, reading some love letters from the George Chest. She held little desire to socialise with the other Players and, as the performance started, stowed herself away to her chambers and to more welcoming times. The other Players realised that she was not to be disturbed as they recognised the jet-black boa tied over her chamber door which meant that beyond that border there was only endless solitary love. And so there Lupe was when the unwelcome and uninvited chill wind seeped under the door and enveloped her. Her heart became like ice and her blood ran cold. When she felt her thighs freeze she knew instantly that death was in the room with her. She wrapped her shawl around her and curled up against the George Chest, pulling it close to her hoping the cold touch of Death would not rifle through her belongings.

Tobias Strong had an acute awareness that something terrible had happened. He was attuned with the spiritual and he felt no fear when the wind blew out the candles. At the moment his neck ran cold and the candles blew out, he calmly removed his multi-lensed goggles and placed them carefully on an oily rag. He turned his chair towards the dark doorway and calmly cleared his throat. The metallurgist gripped the edge of his bench and slowly heaved himself up, using the desk to lean against. He was balanced and steeled and felt that power of the Lord with in him.

"Behold the Cross of the Lord!" he began in a bold and unwavering voice "Be gone you evil powers! The Lion of the tribe of Judah, the Root of David, has conquered. Alleluia!" and he crossed himself three times. The chill recoiled at his words and fell away. The temperature rose and all the candles and lamps reignited. Tobias sighed in relief and sank back down in his chair. He sat there for a few moments before Valerie cautiously walked into the room, clearly rattled at the supernatural encounter. Tobias beckoned her over to him and she held his hands, surprised at how warm and welcoming they were.

"What happened?" she whispered.

Tobias looked up at her with a heavy heart and held her hands tight.

"Take me onto the stage, dear Valerie"

She obliged.

Srdjan and Ms Adberg were still in their embrace, but it had changed its meaning since the chill had left the theatre and the light had returned. Where they held each other in dread before, they now stood embraced in melancholia. Ms Adberg buried her head deep into Srdjan's chest and he rested his cheek on her crown, swaying her gently.

Lupe arrived on the stage, arms folded and shawl wrapped uncharacteristically tightly. She walked over and stood by Srdjan and Ms Adberg who made room for her in their hug. After a few moments, Valerie pushed Tobias onto the stage to the sight of her three friends hugging in the centre.

"What happened?" she whispered to them. Lupe broke away from the other two and held her hands out for them to join. It was when all five were together that Lupe confirmed what the others knew. Something dreadful had happened. Ms Adberg, Tobias and

Srdjan had guessed it, having succumbed to the perceptive superstitions of the theatre, but poor Valerie was green to the signs and omens that plague all thespians and performers. It was only when she looked at their grave and sad expressions that she understood. Someone was not coming back.

———•◦•———

Brandenburg stood amongst the Players and looked over at Desiree. He knew that her soul had irrevocably shifted and that, in the final analysis, it was his fault. He had shot Herschel. He did not pull the trigger physically, but he was just as culpable. He looked to either side of him, taking in each broken expression of his friends' faces as they looked on at Desiree. He had betrayed their trust and loyalty and had fallen far beyond their love. He knew it. He felt numb. He motioned to step forward, but his legs felt like stone, anchoring him to the ground. Eventually, Archie handed Claudia slowly over to Antoine and stepped forward towards the Umbrian ballerina. Nobody knew what reaction he would be met with. She was unpredictable; a lion lady. He inched towards her.

Desiree was in the Void. As she stood above the body of Herschel she felt numb and apathetic. The body was not him. It had no laugh or growl. No groan or wheeze. It was useless. She lilted her head and inspected the body in the moonlight, testing its state by tapping and pushing it with her foot. The body lolled. She didn't see the other Players edging towards her and she didn't hear Archie's soft voice whispering to her. It was only when he gently touched her on shoulder that she looked over to him, her eyes as distant as the moon. She mouthed a phrase in Italian and, like a marionette whose threads have been severed, she fell to the floor.

Life returned to Brandenburg and he managed to step forward from the back of the group. He took off his jacket and handed it to Archie before bending down and picking up Desiree. The other Players looked on in tears as Mr Enfield laid the jacket over the body of their friend.

"Will I say any words?" Archie said in a voice barely audible from the shock. Brandenburg shook his head and carried Desiree over to the coach. The other Players watched as he gently rested her down, walked back to the upturned carriage and began to load the loot back into the trunk.

"What are you doing? Have you no respect?" said Archie, his words bursting with incredulity. Brandenburg ignored him and carried on loading the trunk. Archie stepped forward and motioned to grab Brandenburg. Quick as a whip the Count rose to his feet, drew his sword and held the point out to Archie's throat. The other Players gasped and stepped back. Brandenburg looked deeply into Archie's eyes, burning his way into his soul. He then looked over to the rest of the Players, staring each one down with a look of pure resolve. Slowly, Archie raised his hands and stepped backwards and around to the remaining plates and candelabras scattered around the ground. He began to pick them up and place them back in the trunk. Brandenburg stepped back and one by one The Roxy Players joined their man in packing up their taking.

They knew what was coming next and none motioned to prevent it. Once the carriage was loaded with the trunk, Danilov and Antoine picked up Herschel's body and laid it on the bench opposite the sleeping Desiree. Gertie and Anya climbed onto the driver's bench while Danilov, Archie and Antoine, holding Claudia, flanked it. Count Brandenburg walked to the rear of the cabin and peeled back his jacket and looked down at the body of his old friend. Desiree was still unconscious. Brandenburg drew his sword and laid it over the body before closing the door. He stood back from the Players and watched as Gertie looked over, threw Brandenburg a 'good luck for the future' nod before nudging the horses into a funereal pace. Antoine, Danilov and Archie looked at Brandenburg and each one would have gladly given their own lives to have prevented the course of the evening. But they could not. They bowed politely and turned to walk beside the carriage as it trundled off towards London.

Claudia looked over Antoine's shoulder as he carried her along and could not pull her eyes away from the sight of Count Brandenburg standing on the muddy road, bathed in moonlight and utterly alone. She did not know if she would ever see him again, but she knew that he had caused the death of Herschel and that he could not come home.

Benjamin Ananas watched as the only people whom he had ever, truly loved, left him alone in the woods. It was for the best and his fate, just as Herschel's death was entirely of his own making. He held little hope that he would ever see them again. He had fallen too far from grace to climb back up to heaven. He was done for. As the carriage rolled into the darkness, he looked to the side and into the dark forest. A sudden, cold wind rose up inside him. It seemed to start within his soul and spread outwards. Around him, leaves flicked up into the air and the gust rose and fell. He looked once more to the funeral carriage. It had disappeared entirely and he sighed heavily. And thus, Benjamin Ananas stepped off of the path and into the wilderness.

Chapter Forty Three

Into the Void

Benjamin, shivering without his jacket, trudged through the woodland. He had no destination he simply wanted to trudge. He had no strength in him for revenge. Though he fantasised about kicking down Nathanial's door and caving in his skull with a rock, he knew that it would be futile. He was exhausted and had no advantage. The further into the wood land he walked, the denser it became, the canopy folding in over him, blotting out the moonlight and beating him down further into his abyss. Progress began to slow, and yet still he trudged, holding his arms tight around his muddied and bloodied shirt. The evil twigs and snide branches scratched and jostled him as if the trees themselves were a baying mob of accusers. He swung out and tried to defend himself but time after time lost his balance and fell to the mud. Still he ventured further until his path was totally blocked by a huge fallen oak trunk that lay across from him as dead as Herschel. The chill wind rose up again and the dead leaves whipped all around him. He pulled his collar up around his neck, though it did little to deflect the cold. He looked all around. All he could see was darkness and the occasional accusative branch, lurching out of the gloom towards him. He sneered at the branches and spat on the floor before turning to back to the trunk and swinging his leg over it.

As he sat, straddling the dead tree, he looked up at the canopy, desperately trying to find the moon. He held a primal belief that if he could locate the moon, then he could locate himself and therefore give order to everything. He needed to re-establish the divine connection between himself as man, and the moon in the universe. He could not see it, for the darkness was all pervasive. He was in the void. The Count leant back and lost his balance, falling off the trunk and, instead of hitting the ground where he expected, he found himself tumbling down a seemingly endless slope. He thundered over and over, crashing over vine and root, limbs flailing and head spinning. He eventually came to a stop at the bottom of the ditch, landing hard on his back, the wind gusting out of him. He could barely move from the pain. Above him, he heard a thunderous crack and then the heavens opened. He lay on his back and the freezing rain fell on him, hammering at his skin and causing him to convulse and shiver. Still he could not move. The ground around him began to turn to sludge and the sound of the rain drops on the leaves began to sound like a million marching drums. If he was to drown in the mire, then so be it. He was about to resign himself to being swallowed up by the evil woodland marsh when he felt an object grow unnaturally warm in his pocket. He moved his arm, with all his might, to his trouser pocket and felt inside. As soon as his hand touched the object, it pulsed with heat - a warm, inviting, almost magical glow. Brandenburg pulled it out and held it up to the darkness. A beam of moonlight penetrated the black and fell upon the object in his hands; Herschel's trusted hipflask. The raindrops danced off its silver case, glistening and sparkling in the moonlight. He unscrewed the cap and drank to the friend whom he'd got killed.

As The Roxy Playhouse Irregulars walked alongside the carriage, its pitch and yawl lulled them each into a dreamlike sense of detachment. Claudia, in Antoine's arms with her head over his shoulder, could not smell his moustache wax, nor feel the pulse in his neck. He could have been anyone. The crunch of dried leaves and snap of twigs under his boots were distant and echoed and the moonlight blurred everything. Her eyes were heavy and she felt drained and devoid of emotion. She craned her head to the side and looked at the black doors of the cabin and tried to cry. No tears came, even though her cheeks felt wet. It had begun to rain and yet nobody had noticed. She continued to stare at the side of the cab and, through the murky window, she could make out the heap that was Herschel and the sleeping Desiree next to him. She longed to see both one roll over and drape an arm over the other as sleeping lovers often do but something inside her had shifted and though she looked frantically inside herself for that magical sense of childish whimsy, but she could not locate it. Instead, as the rain beat down upon all of them, she just looked at the two bodies and felt old for the very first time.

———•◦•———

It was well into the night when the Players first set weary eyes on Borough. They had walked funereally slowly from Eveltham house, through the copse that merged into Dulwich Woods and down the cold and heartless marshlands set among the villages of Walworth and Newington until they had at last come home. Nobody had spoken and the rain had failed to slap any awareness into them. They trudged like the newly dead who have missed the boat man and now have to walk to the afterlife. Desiree had not stirred from her sleep and when they halted the carriage outside Borough Market Stables, the horses brayed quietly and the Players awoke. They looked at each other and then to the doors of the theatre a few yards down the road, and with heavy hearts they alighted from the carriage. Gertie helped Anya from the driver's bench and she immediately walked over to Danilov and put her arms around him. Archie and Gertie walked around to the back of the carriage and after a solemn nod to each other, they opened the door. It had been an unspoken agreement that they would all walk into The Roxy together. And so, Archie carefully lifted the comatose Desiree and held her as gently as possible and Gertie, bravely fighting his tears, picked up the limp body of his mentor. He shuddered at the lack of anima and warmth.

The Players in the theatre were sitting in a tight circle in the middle of the stage. Lupe had fetched one of her larger shawls and Valerie and Ms Adberg were tucked inside it, trying to relax into the almond scent of her skin. Tobias was next to her with Srdjan resting against his wheel. They had been there for countless hours, just as before when Benjamin had rushed to Sheridan's Olympus Theatre to rescue Archie. It all seemed like lifetimes upon lifetimes ago. The candles fluttered and the doors to The Roxy creaked open with a lamenting sigh. The Players on the stage stood up. Even Tobias managed to push himself up onto one leg and balance on his chair.

"My God!" whispered Lupe as the returning Players walked into the light. Valerie put her hands to her mouth and bit her lip to stop crying as she craned her neck hoping that Danilov was there. She saw him limping into the light and bit down so hard on her lip to suppress her joy that she drew blood. The procession of Players filled up the stairs onto the stage and they all stood in a circle. Srdjan looked over at Tobias and received a nod of encouragement. The Dalmatian stepped forward and lifted the jacket that was draped over Herschel's head. He baulked slightly and replaced it. His look told his friends all they needed to know. Herschel Barnabus, playwright, dreamer, widower and lover had not returned to them. They stood around the body and each of them drifted into a private abyss of sorrow.

———•◦•———

Whit replaced his Baker rifle and stepped through the portrait-door and into his bedroom. He intended to give a cursory sweep of the residence and take stock of what had been stolen, return to his guests as if nothing had happened and then, while his wife slept by his side, he would plot his revenge on the cur formally known as Brandenburg. He intended to do all this and was already planning it all when he stopped by the doorway. Something in the room was not right. He turned around and saw the upturned chair that the mysterious woman had used to prop open the portrait door. He looked at it, and then across to the space where it should have sat. And then back to it. Someone had been in his private room, and they had come through the passage. Only someone with intelligence would have known about the passageway and, therefore, knew what they were looking for. A panic rose inside him as he instantly dared to think of what it meant. He dashed to his desk and threw open the drawers, emptying their sacred contents brazenly onto the floor. He rifled through them, noting that each one seemed to be present. That could mean only one thing. He clenched his jaw and reached into the drawer-hole. His heart sank and he cursed aloud when he felt that the space was empty. His pocket book had been stolen.

Chapter Forty Four

Sight by Firework

The chill in the theatre made poor Valerie Folk feel as though she herself were dead. The Roxy Players did not seem to notice the cold air it but she did. *'Must be because I'm an outsider,'* she concluded forlornly. Despite her efforts over the previous weeks and no matter how welcomed she had felt, in that moment, staring at her friends and at the body of Herschel she felt utterly alone, almost dead, but still alive. She likened the feeling to Archie's notion of being naturally naked. Now she felt unnaturally dead. She wanted to speak. To ask questions, to wail and mourn but nothing seemed appropriate. As she looked around at them all, her eyes fell upon Claudia and she was filled with sadness. The young girl who had at first been hostile and then warmed to her, the very heart of the theatre was as stone. She looked ancient. More ancient than Lupe in the morning, more ancient than the Egyptian pyramids she had painted on the stage flats. It seemed to Valerie that all the wonder of the future had been taken from the little girl. As the tears began to well in her eyes, Claudia turned her cold face towards Valerie. She looked not only ancient, but tired. Valerie's mouth opened in an attempt to say something, anything, but no sound came out.

After perhaps fifteen minutes of silence and stillness, the Players began to look at each other. No signal had been given to release them from their stillness. No clock had chimed. They just broke free of their state at the same time.

Firstly, Antoine took the handles of Tobias's chair and wheeled him back to the end of the stage. He didn't make a sound, or motion to the others. Then Srdjan and Ms Adberg turned and walked to their quarters, together but apart. Lupe next, she took Claudia's icy hand and walked her to her quarters. They did not wail and they did not hug. They walked like the dead walk to the Other Side: calmly, slowly and without expectation. Gertie then turned to Archie and took Desiree from his arms. She was still in her deathly sleep. He looked at her face and tried desperately to find a glimmer of hope; a vague signifier that, in her dream, she was safe and happy. She gave no such indication. He took her to her living quarters and laid her in her hammock and then climbed in and lay next to her in the way a caring son lies next to an ailing mother. He gently rocked the hammock and counted her eyelashes until he fell asleep.

Danilov was the only one of the Players to recognise Valerie. As Anya strapped a harness to him and began to winch him up to the rafters where she could take better care of him, he looked at her and tried his best to smile. As he disappeared up into the dark eaves, Valerie caught the light glinting off his eyes and she knew that he loved her and that he would come back soon and in that glint, she too held a glint in her heart that, perhaps, they would all come back from this.

And so, there Valerie stood on the stage with just Archie and the body of Herschel upon the boards. Valerie didn't know where to look or what to do. Archie gave no indication as to whether he wanted peace and solitude, or company and distraction. She watched as he looked over the body, rubbing his stubble. After a few seconds, he bent down low to the corpse and lifted the jacket from his face. He held it up, shielding the wound from Valerie's view, bent in close and whispered his last goodbye into the ear of the dead playwright. Valerie could not hear what was said and never asked. She stood and watched as Archie rose from the body with traces of blood on his beard. He looked at her. She could not help but gesture toward his face. He ran his hands over his mouth and felt Herschel's cold blood on his lips. Archie looked at his fingers vacantly as he rubbed the blood into them and then, trance-like, he turned to leave.

"Please," called Valerie through a clenched jaw, the sounds of her voice almost deafening in the dark theatre, "where is Mr Ananas?" She instantly put her hands to her mouth. Archie stopped at the edge of the backstage area, half into the darkness.

"When is he coming back?" she asked.

"He isn't." replied Archie in a bleak tone that seemed to be offered to the theatre, for its information, rather than directed solely to Valerie.

"Why not?"

Archie turned to her, tears falling. "He can't come back. Not after this. Brigand's Law."

"I don't understand!" Valerie's tone became more desperate and less concerned with the oppressive sanctity of the environment.

"It's the way it must be. Our man is dead because... because... he cannot come home."

And with that Archie turned and disappeared into the gloom leaving Valerie alone with Herschel.

The unexpected ruthlessness of the Players and their apparent apathy at throwing one of their own, their leader no less, to the wolves destroyed everything that she had built inside her. She didn't understand and felt even worse than she did while they were standing as statues. Before she was an outsider who wanted to get in, now she wasn't sure if she wanted even that. '*Who are these people?*' she thought as she looked to the entrance to The Roxy and it's powerful invitation to her to flee the place. Instead of running, she lay down next to the corpse of the playwright and fell asleep presently.

———•◦•———

The Whit Ball was still going strong when Lord De Locke was summoned away by a rattled Nathanial Whit. To everyone else, he seemed fine, but to Abigail Hardwoode, he seemed on edge. She had a trained eye and a keen sense of her surroundings and the moment she saw him walk into the room, his stride urgent and his hand on the hilt of his sword she knew that something was amiss. She carried on laughing politely to the gentlemen prattling on to the group she had joined but kept a sharp eye and a tuned ear to the two men talking in the corner. She was almost certain that Nathanial Whit had discovered that his secret journal had been taken. Had her accomplice been so careless as to leave evidence to lead him to find it missing so soon? Had she betrayed her? She could feel the journal in her secret pouch and knew it was safe, but for how long? She tried to lip read, a skill she had not had to rely on for years and as such, was rusty. She made out the words 'stolen' 'shot' and 'gone' which told her that it was time to leave. She made her excuses to the group and began to walk calmly through the crowd and over to the conspiring men. As she got closer she could make out snippets over their speech.

"It was him...but not 'him'...it wasn't Brandenburg. It was some fool called Ananas!"

Abigail stopped in shock at the sound of the name and quickly took a drink from a passing waiter so that she could stand and listen to more.

"He's taken it. He and a crew of others! I don't know...I don't know how, or why. Nobody has seen that cur for years. And now this! He is an agent. I know it. I fought him, and I chased him and I saw that he had a team. I shot one in the dark, an impossible shot! But a felled one! I can only pray it was Ananas!"

Abigail steadied herself at the barrage of information she was overhearing and the possibility that the return of her young love into her life had been all too brief.

"Who is this Ananas, who will ruin our masterpiece?" said Lord Rafe De Locke in a cold and wheezing voice, instead of the usual fey tones. A chill ran over Abigail. She loathed and feared that secret voice in equal measure.

"He is with a team...nobody has heard of him in years. I have no intelligence."

"Find him. Find them all. Destroy them."

Nathanial's eyes widened as he recalled a buried detail.

"Wait...wait, I know a name. I met a man, a madman who spoke of Ananas."

"Take me to him."

At that, Abigail finished her drink and walked up to the two men. Lord De Locke's demeanour changed instantly as he saw her. "My dear," he beamed, "are you having fun? Isn't this wonderful?"

"Yes, yes! Wonderful!" she said as she hugged him.

"But," he said as she broke away from the embrace, "I'm afraid that our good friend and host Mr Whit has a rather enticing business proposition for me that cannot wait until morning!"

Abigail pouted. She was a good actress.

"Oh my dear, why don't you stay? Mr Whit, is that a good idea?"

"A wonderful suggestion; there are planned fireworks later."

"She would love to see those, would you not, my love?"

Abigail smiled and nodded.

"It is settled then. My love, I will leave my carriage for you and I will adjourn in Nathanial's." He bent and kissed Abigail's hand. She suppressed her instinct to vomit expertly. After six years undercover and in the bed of that devil, it was almost instinctual.

"Good night, Sweet Lady Jennifer-Joy."

"Good night my Lord."

Nathanial Whit bowed to her, "A goodnight to you Lady Jennifer-Joy. Enjoy the fireworks."

Abigail nodded her thanks and they two men exited the room. Abigail turned to the rest of the party. Though she wanted to leave instantly, she knew she could not. She had the journal secure and there were no other threats in the room. For the sake of appearances, she decided to wait until the fireworks had started and all eyes were on them before she would slip away unnoticed.

———•◆•———

The rain had halted and Brandenburg had finished the hipflask. He had not planned his life past that moment and, as he lay, caked in mud and looking up at the canopy above, he realised that he was indeed lost in every sense of the word. This realisation sparked an odd motivation inside of him and he pocketed the hipflask. There was no desperation to his situation anymore. He was lost, but he had nowhere to go and nowhere to get back to and so all that was left to do was simply get on with things, whatever they where. He struggled to his feet. The deep mud and the injuries sustained in the tumble down the deep slope made it an ungraceful process. He did, however, finally manage and looked around at the environment. The booze and the rainfall had cleansed him and the anguish and been flooded with a sense of acceptance. He breathed out and looked up at the slope. It was at least twenty feet high, but climbable thanks to the roots and rocks that had battered him on his descent. He planned simply to climb up, get back to the road, get back to London, find a home, and plan his revenge. He looked up at the moon and tipped his imaginary hat. The acceptance, in a flash, had turned into conviction.

"Thank you moon and rain," he said aloud, "I am dead anyway but before I consign myself to the reaper, know this. Nathanial Whit will die."

After he said the words, he was struck with a momentary understanding of how Gertie must have felt after the incident in The Roxy and the injuring of Valerie when he vowed to kill Sheridan. He dusted himself off and scrambled up the slope.

After the protracted scramble which had sent him crashing back down to the bottom on seven occasions, Ananas eventually made it to the top and over the fallen trunk. From up there and now under cover of moonlight, the woodland seemed slightly less oppressive. He could see a way through and despite being turned around in the darkness he figured the general direction of the road. He set off and trudged for a further thirty minutes without any clue of his true whereabouts when the sound of a horsedrawn carriage filled up his ears. It was close. He scooted down and looked through the bracken for the light on the driver's bench. He spotted it to the left and about fifty yards ahead. He tracked the carriage and was surprised at its speed. However the light did not intensify nor dissipate but moved in a steady glow along through the woodlands. He was parallel to the road. He stood up and tried to run as fast as he could towards the road. He needed to reach it before the light disappeared from view. If he did not, then who knows when the next carriage would come along to illuminate his way? He ran like a feral beast, ducking and jumping branches and logs until the light was almost upon him. He ran onto the road as the carriage rocketed past. It did not stop. Ananas never knew how close he had come to Nathanial Whit just hours after he had murdered his friend. If he had known who was in that cabin, he would have leapt onto the footrail and torn through the carriage like a hurricane.

Ananas watched it go and then looked around to gauge his position. He did not need to look for clues. He could see the wheel of the upturned carriage poking out of the ditch on the other side of the road. The two horses had died from the injuries. *'Poor beasts'*, he thought. He was about to step forward when an almighty bang made him leap out of his skin and dart back into the undergrowth. Was that another gunshot? He looked around for a muzzle flash or signs of a shooter. Another bang, this time an eerie, supernatural green glow descended over the woodland. Another bang followed by a cackle of pops and fizzes. He looked up. The sky was ablaze with phosphor. A great shower of purples, greens and reds falling over the dark sky like a detonating Borealis. Ananas stepped onto the roadside and approached the crash site as the glorious firework display lit up the sky.

———•◦•———

As the crowds of guests made their way from the conservatory and onto the lawn to watch the fireworks, Abigail Hardwoode drifted to the back and while everyone was "ooohing" and "aaahing", she slipped back into the mansion, through the main hallway and out towards the waiting carriages. She climbed aboard and was onto the road in two minutes. As soon as she felt safe from any possible intrusion, she extracted the journal from her secret pocket. The lights of the fireworks spilled into the carriage and provided usable reading light. She began. After three pages of scribbles, symbols and notes, she began to skip pages, skimming for relevance and revelations. She got to the middle and the centrefold fell open. As did her jaw. As the greens and purples of the fireworks outside filled her cabin, she sat aghast at the magnitude of the information in front of her. She looked intently at the floorplan of Brighton Pavilion and of the markings and stratagems scrawled across it.

"My God," she said to herself, "we'll need an army!" she flicked through the rest of the book frantically looking for any sign of a weakness or way to undo the plan. There was none. She sat back, eyes wide with shock and was about to pocket the book when the carriage came to a jolting stop. She lurched forward and leant out of the window.

"Driver," she whispered, "What's the matter?"

"Ahead Milady" he whispered back. Abigail Hardwoode looked into the gloom and saw nothing.

"Wait!" said the driver, pointing to the sky. Abigail caught his drift and looked to the sky, waiting for a rocket to burst and give a glimpse of what was a head. After a few seconds, a grand golden starburst poured over everything. Abigail gasped. Up ahead lay an upturned carriage.

"Stay here, driver" she said as she stepped out of the carriage.

"Bu..."

"Trust me...just stay put. I will be fine." Abigail walked cautiously towards the wreckage. As she approached she began to discern shapes in the ever changing light; a wheel here, an axle there. She kicked a few silver plates and trinkets that lay strewn over the road. She stopped dead in her tracks when a red burst illuminated the unmistakable silhouette of a man standing by two dead horses. She could not tell if he was facing her or not and so approached with extreme caution.

Abigail was twenty feet away from him and concentrating on deciphering his form so intently that she did not see the small silver carriage clock resting against the silver tray. Her left slipper struck it and the clatter alerted the man to her presence. She froze as the figure stood up, alert and turned to her.

A silver shower burst over head and she gasped as a muddied, bedraggled and broken Count Brandenburg stood before her.

"Benjamin?" she whispered as the figure stepped into the light, "is it really you?"

"Yes, it's really me," he said in his true voice.

Chapter Forty Five

Greiving

A bigail Hardwoode coaxed Benjamin into her carriage like a gamekeeper wrangles beasts. She was cautious, she was stern and she was calm as she walked backwards, fixing the unknown and unpredictable animal in her stare. Benjamin in turn made no attempt to fight or flee but instead followed her like a sleepwalker. The sound of the fireworks and their supernatural light seemed to fall away from them as they focused on each other. Abigail opened the carriage door and gently beckoned him inside. Benjamin did not tip his hat, or insist that she go first. He drifted inside and sat in the corner quietly, like a tired child disappearing into the dark shadows of the cabin. Abigail stepped up onto the running plate and signalled to the driver to continue. He kicked the horses into life and they continued on their passage through the wooded road.

Ten minutes passed with Abigail staring at the blank Benjamin Ananas as he stared into the gloomy woodland. She was battling with a million questions and theories colliding and repelling in her mind. Where had he been? Who was he now? Who was the Count Brandenburg and why? Was he with them? Was he with another agency? Was he to be trusted? Did he remember her? Did he hate her? Did he love her? She ran over a multitude of scenarios in her mind as to how to initiate a conversation and where it might take them before she fell upon the most pressing issue and decided to go straight for the jugular.

"Who are you and why are you here?" she said without any hint of their shared history. This was her interrogation mode. Her trained, emotionless machine for gathering intelligence overwhelmed any natural emotional desire to ask her personal questions. Benjamin did not break from his gazing out of the carriage.

"Who do you work for?" she pressed, "an agency?"

There was nothing. She studied his eyes. Though they appeared blank, they were not blocked. She could see into him. He was in turmoil and rage; a volcano under a calm sheet.

"Nathanial Whit..." she began inquisitively. Benjamin's reflexive twitch in the corner of his eye betrayed him.

"He shot at you," she said, "he missed you."

Benjamin twitched once more.

"But he did hit something...didn't he?" Abigail continued, softly.

Benjamin sprung. He leapt onto Abigail, drew a dagger from his belt, thrust her head backward, using his weight to pin her to the bench and held the blade close to her throat. He was breathing heavily and his eyes were wild like the fires of hell and damnation.

"Not something," he hissed, "Someone; someone good, someone grand, someone."

Abigail did not shrink in the face of Benjamin and did not try and wriggle her neck away from his blade. She held his manic stare and calmly raised her hands to his face and gently brushed his sodden hair from his eyes.

"I can help you. I can help you. Let's talk, Benjamin. Just talk."

Benjamin pressed the knife harder, his eyes searching for answers. Hers were calm and true. He could not see a lie behind them. She brushed his cheeks.

"I can help you," she whispered in a honeyed tone. He relaxed the blade and fell back onto the bench. She looked at the fierce man as he regressed from avenging demon to broken mortal as quickly as he had snapped. He felt pity and pain. Genuine sympathy overcame her and she was stung with the realisation that for perhaps the first time in twenty five years someone else's welfare was her utmost concern. She became instantly fearful of the weakening feeling.

"Tell me about this grand person," she said with a genuine interest. Benjamin looked at her with bloodshot eyes. His lip wobbled and his faced creased.

"His name was Herschel Barnabus and the best man I have ever met. He was my friend."

He began to cry. Abigail Hardwoode found herself moving to sit next to him and holding him tightly. She had faced down uncounted foes in her life, but holding Benjamin Ananas in that state, after twenty five years of being apart undid her. She was defenceless.

"Can I take you home?" she said as she stroked his hair. He pressed his face into her lap and sobbed harder. She instinctively knew that he could not go home, though she knew not why.

"I know a place I can take you, somewhere safe." Benjamin's tears were spent.

He wiped them from his face and composed himself. He sat up and looked at her.

"Tell me about him," she said.

Then, unexpectedly, Benjamin broke into the widest and brightest smile.

"He was...he was...no, I have to tell you everything," and he giggled as he recalled in his mind the myriad stories and adventures that he and Herschel had encountered.

And so it came to pass, that Benjamin Ananas eulogised his friend Herschel Barnabus on the day of his death to the most unlikely of people and as the carriage rolled into London his stories expanded to incorporate more than just the playwright, but the other Roxy Irregulars too. Abigail was giddy with delight at the onslaught of vivid storytelling and bold adventure that the raconteur spun about his friends. He laughed and giggled and talked at a thousand miles an hour staging tiny productions and impersonations for her. He did not once mention himself and he did not once mention her and she did not even think to ask. By the time the carriage pulled to a halt, Abigail Hardwoode felt as if she knew each player by name and held them all close to her heart. They waited in the stalled carriage and looked at each other. So much history and they hadn't even begun to talk about themselves. Abigail looked out at the breaking dawn.

"It's getting light; a poor time for storytelling."

"Where are we?"

"Whitechapel, I have a room here. You can rest there. You will be safe. Go to the red door, knock three times and when the man with the limp asks you for the directions to the Prussian Embassy, you will tell him 'I don't know, I just work here, but I hear that the door handles there are made of wheat.' Understand?"

"No, not at all."

Abigail smiled and opened the door for him. He climbed out.

"Do it, you will be safe. Don't leave. There are provisions there. I will be back in a few hours. I will come and meet you there."

Benjamin stood on the muddy street and looked up at Abigail as she leant out of the window. He was completely confused as to what exactly was happening. Abigail smiled at him.

"Trust me," she said. Benjamin smirked.

"Who are you?" he said.

Abigail Hardwoode leant out of the window and pressed her full lips against his ear.

"All in good time" she whispered, before sitting back into the carriage, closing the curtain and hitting the roof. The driver tipped his hat to Benjamin and kicked the carriage into life. Benjamin watched it drive off into London before looking around to see if there were any witnesses about who could confirm to him just what exactly had happened. The street was deserted. He looked to his left and saw a tatty red door. He shrugged and approached it. When he knocked, a strange and ancient man sporting a ragged eye patch opened it an inch and then asked him the way to the Prussian Embassy. Benjamin replied as per instructed and made sure he imbued the words with a sense of hushed seriousness that he thought befitting such a situation. The door opened and he stepped into the dark corridor. The old man looked him up and down.

"You look like shit," the old man said.

Benjamin looked back at ancient fellow.

"And you look like a badly shaved ball bag, you mean old bastard."

"Drink, sir?" said the old man and he thrust a glass of water under Benjamin's the nose. He took it and drank it in one go. He handed it back to the man, who took a step backwards. Benjamin felt the room spin and contort. He looked at his hands as they seemed to grow to ten times their normal size.

"Giant...hands," he said before collapsing unconscious onto the floor. The old man put the glass onto a little side table and with unbelievable strength and vitality, hoisted Benjamin over his shoulder with one hand and carried him into the dark abode.

Gertie lay on his side studying Desiree. He had barely slept a wink, lest she awoke up to find herself alone. He brushed her hair to the side and she smiled and kissed his hand. He felt a rush of blood to his head and suddenly knew just how lucky Herschel was to have those lips on his. She opened her eyes and they seemed to be bright and full of joy and spirit. And then the dream fell from her mind and the reality of her situation returned. Her eyes dulled from brown to ashen grey. She looked at Gertie. He continued to bush her hair with his hand.

"Did I sleep long?" she whispered.

"You did."

"Is he still gone?"

Gertie clenched his jaw and Desiree's eyes misted over.

"Then I did not sleep long enough," and she rolled onto her back. The hammock swung gently as the morning light began to find ways into the theatre.

"I have woken up a widow," she said in a surprisingly matter-of-fact way, "I need coffee."

And just like that, the Widow Ricci rolled off of the hammock and unclasped her dress. It fell to the ground and she stood naked before a blushing Gertie.

"I must go to Lupe," she said and walked off into the backstage area.

Upon the rafter, Danilov lay on his front looking down at the stage below and to Valerie who had remained next to Herschel's corpse all night. Anya straddled him and was administering a very deep massage. Her magic touch pushed and pulled his muscles and the extensive bruising caused by the crash seemed to be wiped clean. He did not feel any pain and instead watched Valerie sleep.

"She is wonderful, isn't she?" he said. Anya nodded.

"I love her. I will love her forever," he said. Anya rolled her eyes at his melodramatic statement as she kneaded the last of the bruises out of his back. She slapped his shoulder and climbed off, throwing the harness to him. Danilov sat up and attached the harness and descended down to the stage.

Valerie was awoken by the acrobat's gentle touch on her shoulder. She rolled over and smiled at him. He unclipped the harness and scooped her up. She pulled in close to his chest and he carried her into the backstage area, up the stairs and into their secret room in the attic where they made quiet and solemn love for several hours.

———•••———

Benjamin awoke from his drug induced slumber with a head that felt like a tumbling boulder. His vision was blurry and his back ached.

"Never drink water, again," he said as he stood up. His vision returned. He did not remember entering the room he was in, and indeed had no recollection of the building it was situated in. The last thing he remembered was the conversation in the carriage and the kiss on his ear. He took comfort in the remembrance of that particular event. It had not been a dream.

He rubbed his eyes and looked around the room. It was extraordinarily plush. The oak panelled walls were lined with the usual stern portraits of long dead dignitaries, the carpet was a deep, blood red and there was a globe and a chaise-lounge in the corner. There were no windows and no door. He looked around for an exit but could not find one. He banged on the walls and called for help but none came.

"This is ridiculous," he said in frustration, "every way in has a way out." He tore the portraits off the walls and attempted to find a secret passage from every conceivable spot. After half an hour he gave up and sat on the chaise lounge and spun the globe in frustration. His despondency did not last long. A firm spin of the globe gave back the delightful sound of clinking glass. His eyes lit up and he felt around the edge of the globe's oak frame housing for a latch. He found it. He flicked it. It opened. He was reborn. Inside was a glorious collection of spirits from all four corners of the Earth and representing every colour he could conceive off.

"Thank Christ for that," he said, "Herschel, I'm drinking to you," and with that he picked up a bottle of lurid and gloopy purple liquor, ripped the cork off and took a swig.

———•·•———

Lupe had managed to make Desiree laugh against all odds. The two women had spent the morning and afternoon selecting and preparing an extensive wardrobe of suitable mourning clothes for all and had now amassed enough outfits to last the death of eight hundred lovers and husbands.

"You can stop now! Please!" said Desiree as yet another black veil fell over her like a giant tissue. Lupe was high above on top of her ladder amongst the upper rails.

"Just a few more, a few more, a few, a few, few more!" she trilled back.

Desiree smiled and thanked God that the theatre was there and her friends were inside it. She was destroyed in grief, it was true, but she was not destroyed in spirit and it seemed as though it had manifested itself in the form of The Roxy Playhouse Irregulars. As fourteen more veils drifted down from the eaves, the Widow Ricci believed that she was mother to them all, mother to the theatre, mother to the world. She would weather the storm.

The last veil fell onto her and she felt the touch of its thread to be a baptism of life. She breathed in the almond air of Lupe's quarters.

"Come down!" she called "Come down and help me choose!"

Up high, Lupe smiled to herself and thanked God for bestowing Desiree Ricci with the power, depth and grace of a thousand women. Lupe had, in her life, known two thousand widows, and herself been one fifteen times over and each one was a precarious balance. Many times she had seen widows fall into death and despair while others had revelled in the freedom and the devil-may-care liberties bestowed on them. Desiree was the first to tell her, spiritually, that she was going to be alright. Whether good times or bad, she was going to be alright. Lupe blew a kiss for the Almighty and a little one for the baby Jesus before wrapping her insteps around the outer edge of the ladder and gliding down to the floor.

Lupe was about to teach Desiree about the veils and how and when to wear each one when the sound of laughter filtered through the air. They looked at each other and then around the room trying to source it. Lupe took Desiree's hand and they left the quarters in haste.

———•·•———

Antoine was sat on Herschel's deck, Tobias was next to him and Archie was in the playwright's chair with his feet up on a huge stack of manuscripts. Gertie was pouring out the wine. They were all leafing through papers and reciting lines and notations to each other and laughing heartily to each other.

"Lo! It came to pass that on the eleventh day, Bill did indeed lay with Monica and in glorious spasms their love did end!" proclaimed Antoine to which Archie howled with laughter.

"I tell ye something," countered Tobias, reading from a page, "that I wager any man a groat and a go on my wife if ye can best me at hang-ball. Enter Caesar wearing a gorilla suit."

Everybody laughed. Gertie handed out the glasses and noticed Lupe and Desiree standing in the doorway. He cleared his throat. They all looked over and saw the women. They snapped out of the revelry and looked sheepishly to the floor.

"Forgive me. Forgive us lady Ricci," began Archie, "we mean no..."

Desiree stepped forward and slapped him in the face. Archie looked to his feet and stood from the chair. Desiree looked around at everyone. She sat down in her beloved's chair and ran her fingers over the edge of his desk until she found what she was looking for; a switch. She flicked it and a hidden drawer opened revealing a dusty bottle of whiskey. She took it out and slammed it down onto the table. Everybody jumped.

"Gertie" she said sternly

"Yes ma'am?"

"Get some glasses," she beamed. Gertie smiled and scurried off, "Mr Enfield, continue please," she commanded. He bowed to her and began to read Herschel's verses aloud to much cheering and laughter.

Gertie returned in minutes and as they poured, a heavenly sound descended upon them. Claudia, from somewhere in the theatre, was playing her violin for Herschel. The Players looked at each other and took in the sounds of her playing. When Claudia finished, the Players poured, drank, performed and laughed. Grief is what you make of it.

Nathanial Whit led Lord De Locke through the tight, stone clad corridor. The passage was narrow and twisted at a nauseating angle. They turned left and right and descended and rose until, finally, Nathanial led the Lord out into a circular room where a beam of light fell onto a small corner. There were iron bars segregating sections of the chamber, and in those bars were slumped bodies. It was a prison. Nathanial Whit waved his torch around the room, throwing light on the disgusting inhabitants. He stopped when it lit up a body in the corner. It was breathing a sickly wet breath.

De Locke stepped forward to the bars.

"You there, inmate," commanded Nathanial. "Come hither." The shape did not move.

"I want parlay. Now!" The shape remained breathing and facing the wall. De Locke cleared his throat in frustration.

"A" began Whit. "N...A..."

"NASSSSS" replied the body. "Ananas." It rolled over and stood up.

"We need information on somebody," said Nathanial. The body ticked and jerked.

"A name you said. A name you know."

The figure reached up and fingered its throat. A leaking substance glistened on the beam of light.

"I know your man," it said, "I know your man."

"Who is he?"

"Why should I tell you?" wheezed the creature.

"What would you want?

"Everything."

"Granted," hissed De Locke in his true voice.

Into the light stepped Kemble, smiling his awful, twisted smile.

Chapter Forty Six

Black Arm

S rdjan poured the wine and Alexia Adberg watched the candlelight flicker over his deep set eyes. The bar was dark and dank and they had secured a precious table in the corner. 'Grambo's Wine Bar' on Villiers Street in Charing Cross was a dirty place where drinkers, writers, poets and dreamers gathered to forget the sunlight and make art by candlelight. It had once been a store cellar and was been saved from obscurity by a forward thinking drinker who dreamt of a haven that was not affected by time or fate but simply was. And he succeeded too. The drinker won ownership of it through a lucky streak at cards and had turned the unused space into the paradise he'd always wanted. The cellar bar was always stocked with drink, always busy and always thought upon of times of need.

Srdjan and Alexia needed that wine bar. At midday they had been lying in bed, silently holding each other and thinking over the events that had brought them together all those years before and the circumstances that forced had them apart and ultimately brought them back together again. As they laid there contemplating the tapestry of life, they heard Claudia's violin sing its song for their dearly departed friend. The music was haunting and just. Over and over she played. After two hours of continued playing, Srdjan finally rolled over to Alexia and said: "We should leave."

Alexia understood that to mean they should leave the theatre and go for a walk. Srdjan meant something else. And so they sat in the dark corner of 'Grambo's Wine Bar' and poured wine.

"I remember the first time I met Herschel. He was thinner," said Alexia as she accepted Srdjan's glass.

"What was the production, again?" he asked.

"'Merchant of Venice', Archie was Shylock"

Srdjan face palmed. "Not his finest hour," he sighed. They laughed and clinked glasses.

"Herschel was so furious at Archie's interpretation. Furious; I remember him throwing his hipflask onto the stage and jumping up and down until it was flat like a plate!"

"I remember it!" laughed Srdjan. "You were wearing a black dress with a purple trim. I remember thinking, 'who is this woman and why is she wearing purple on stage, does she want to curse us all?"

"I didn't know about purple! I really didn't!"

"Brigand's Law," he retorted and they clinked glasses. As they drank, his smile dropped away and a look of severity dawned over his face. Alexia put her glass down.

"What's the matter?"

Srdjan held out his hands across the table and found hers. He squeezed them tightly. "Let's leave," he said softly.

"What, the bar? We still have a bottle to get through."

"I meant The Roxy. I mean leave The Roxy. Leave London, you and me. We'll elope and live a life of adventure. You and me. Me and you."

Alexia withdrew her hands and sat back. Srdjan tried to gauge her response. She took her drink and drank it all in one go before putting it down, topping it up and repeating. Srdjan bit his nails. After the third, she slid empty glass across the table and smiled at him.

"I thought you'd never ask," she said and they kissed.

———•·•———

Benjamin was neither drunk nor sober but residing in that drinker's purgatory betwixt the land of the sober and the land of the free. He was slumped on the floor resting against the back of the chaise lounge. He had finished off the purple gloopy substance and turned his attention to the absinthe. There were no windows in the room and he had no idea of what time it was. He gave the benefit of the doubt in favour of Absinthe o'clock. He poured a glass and was about to dedicate the drink to Herschel's aborted adaptation of 'Don Quixote' entitled simply 'Windmill!' when there a curious tap came and a scrape. He looked around groggily to locate the source. Suddenly, the chaise lounge shifted to the left by four feet, forcing Benjamin to fall backwards. He rolled over and tried to focus his disbelief as the chaise-lounge moved a further two feet of its own volition and rotated itself ninety degrees counter clockwise and then upturned. There was another scrape. Benjamin, the fear now taking him, scrabbled to his feet and backed against the wall as the chaise-lounge upended on its side and a hatch in the floor opened. He looked at the bottle and then wiped his eyes before looking back at the open hatch. He took a step towards it and was about to peer in when Abigail Hardwoode suddenly emerged. Benjamin shrieked like a girl and leapt back, clutching his bottle close to his chest. Abigail stopped halfway through the hatch and looked at him.

"Are you alright?"

"Yes, yes, right as rain. What?" he said in a tone that sweated with machismo. Abigail shook her head and climbed into the room.

"Sorry about the situation. Protocol and everything," she dusted herself off and walked to the globe.

"No problem, no problem at all," said Benjamin in a confused tone as he hugged his bottle a little tighter. Abigail Hardwoode poured herself a drink. The hours between their reunion and his breakdown had recharged her. She had regained her composure and was not at all rattled by the man before her whom she used to love what seemed like a million lifetimes before. She took a sip of vodka and turned to him.

"I would imagine, Mr Ananas, that you have many questions and that you perhaps feel you deserve some sort of explanation."

Benjamin took a large swig of absinthe.

"I will take that as a 'yes'. Please take a seat" He obliged her. She continued, "I will be brief. I am a spy."

"That was brief."

"I work for - well, you don't need to know that. I have been doing so for many years now, twenty five to be exact."

"You mean..." Benjamin could not bring himself to finish the sentence.

"Yes, since you and I..."

"Were in love."

"Since you and I knew each other. I was recruited into the service by a man named Hilary. He was a friend of the family. A great man, noble, just. Like your father. Certain circumstances came to light when you and I were together. I had to leave and go into the service. Hilary recruited me and told me to give you that awful 'Dear John' letter. It was hard for me."

"I bet it was."

"It *was* hard for me, I was seventeen years old and thought my future was going to be full of happiness and light...then, something happened and, well, here we are"

"What was it that happened?"

"I can never tell you"

"Protocol?" sneered Benjamin. Abigail hung hear head as ghosts of the past filled her heart.

"No, it is too painful" she said quietly and Benjamin was struck by her sudden melanchoclia, noting her had absently reach up to stroke the nape of her neck, as if to fondle a pendant or necklace that no longer hung there.

Abigail snapped out of her pensive state, smiled and shrugged. She drank her drink and poured another.

"Anyway," she continued, "I was recruited and my disappearance was orchestrated by Hilary. I wrote you the letter and delivered it to you."

"I remember."

"It was hard for me too, truly. You must accept this, if we are to work together."

"Excuse me?"

"I have been undercover for six years. Deep undercover, trying to bring out an organisation called The Black Arm."

"Never heard of 'em."

"Dissidents, united, armed and determined. They have lived in the shadows for generations, recruiting only the darkest and emptiest men and women around the world to carry out their master schemes.

They are entrenched deeply into every society on the globe and they are about to strike."

"Sound's like a ball."

"They are going to destroy the country."

"Country's already knackered. What's it got to do with me?"

"I need you."

Benjamin double took. Abigail cleared her throat.

"I need you," she continued, "and your players. I have acquired the enemy's plans and I know what we are facing. Unfortunately, they also know our every move, our every tactic. They know how we Other Agents operate."

"Other Agents?"

"It's what we are called in the service. I am an Other Agent of Command, an Active Four Season, designation Summer."

Benjamin furrowed his brow and lolled his head back against the chair, "you know I much preferred you when you were an eight armed harpy plaguing my existence."

"They will expect everything...except you and your players."

Benjamin sat up and looked sternly at her. "They aren't my players, and you have not the right to even utter their names."

"We can pay you. Whatever you want, whatever you desire."

"You haven't even got the carriage fare to cover what anyone of us desires. You people. You have no art! No honour! No fire! A plague on all of you!"

Benjamin spat on the floor, tossed the empty bottle onto chaise-lounge and made for the hatch. He was halfway down when Abigail played her trump card.

"They killed your family," she said in a tone that suggested her words were a last ditch gambit.

Benjamin stopped and looked at her. His eyes burned with fury and they battered her defences. She gulped and her blood ran cold, still she held her nerve.

"Be careful, Other Agent."

"The Black Arm' killed your family. Your father and mother were invited, they declined, so pure their hearts were. The Black Arm burnt your mansion to the ground. Nobody denies 'The Black Arm."

Benjamin gripped the ladder hard and clenched his jaw. "You knew this, all these years?"

Abigail bowed her head. "I did. To my eternal shame, I did."

Benjamin smirked and muttered under his breath.

"After it happened," she reasoned, "you went to ground. People assumed you were dead. I tried so hard to find you. Every year, from wherever I was, I would come back to London on your birthday to see if you had surfaced, to see if you alive and to tell you. As soon as I learned that the Black Arm had tried to turn your family, I vowed to hunt them down and bring them to justice. For you, for your family," She slowly began to approach Benjamin.

"To carry that weight, that pain," she said softly, "such pain you had. I could not bear to think of you out there alone and broken. And then I saw you at the party. I didn't know if it was you at first. You could dance so well."

Benjamin looked down into the dark hatch, "I had lessons," he said absently.

"Well, they worked. Your mask was impeccable, I could not penetrate it. But there was something about Count Brandenburg, something about his manner, his demeanour. He offered me a glimpse of the man Benjamin Ananas could have grown up to be."

"A character," he said, "nothing but a charade".

Abigail had reached the hatch and she bent down to him and offered him her hand.

"I searched the world for you. And now you are here. Alive, strong and now you are armed with the truth."

He looked at her hand and then to her face.

"What happened to this Hilary fellow?"

Abigail's eyes grew sad and she hung her head. "Captured. Tortured. Murdered."

"The Black Arm?" he said.

"The Black Arm."

"And Whit and De Locke are among them."

"They are."

"Then they just dallied with the wrong drinker," he said sternly. He took Abigail's hand and she pulled him back into the room. Abigail smiled at Benjamin. He leant in to kiss her. She stood back.

"Careful Mr Ananas," she said. "This is business, not some romance novel."

"Sorry. It just felt right."

"It's alright," she said, "it happens to me all the time."

"Yes, err... me too."

Abigail chuckled to herself and stamped on the floor. As soon as she did, the walls shifted away like wheeled stage flats to reveal a large, empty warehouse stocked with weapons, armour and odd machines of war. Huge maps of obscure countries were tacked on the walls. Benjamin mouthed an obscenity as he looked around at it all.

"Right then," said Abigail as she took his hand, "let's get to work...we can talk about the kiss later."

Danilov was still sleeping when Valerie left him. They had made love for hours and he was utterly spent. She, on the other hand, had the sort of energy reserves that only the early risers possess. It was late afternoon and Claudia had just finished playing her violin. Valerie kissed Danilov on the cheek and left him to sleep. The sunshine beamed in through the hole in the roof and bathed him like a lion in the plains. She blew him a final kiss and climbed down the ladder.

She walked through the theatre and around to the far end and ascended the back staircase. She didn't know why, but in that moment she was inexplicably drawn towards Benjamin's sleeping quarters. She climbed up, passed the landing and peered into Tobias's workshop. He was not there. She carried on up to the top of the stairs, opened the door and entered.

Claudia was sitting on Benjamin's bed, wrapped in his old bear coat. It swamped her entirely and only her large brown eyes were visible from within. Valerie almost didn't notice her when she entered. It wasn't until she nearly sat on Claudia's violin that the bear-coat moved and Valerie nearly leapt out of her skin.

"I'm sorry. I'm sorry!" she whispered as she fell backwards into Benjamin's quick-sand chair.

"Why are you here?" Claudia whispered back.

"I don't know. I was drawn here."

Claudia heaved off the large bear skin coat and shook her hair, "Me too," she whispered.

"I've never been in his room before," said Valerie looking around at the scribbles and notations pasted onto the wall. "It's a wonderful room. Full of life!"

Claudia looked at the floor, "it's a shrine now, a tomb for Benjamin Ananas."

"What happened? Why isn't he coming home?"

"It's Brigand's Law" said Claudia.

"What is that?"

"It's the way of things," said Archie Enfield from the doorway. The two girls jumped a little at the surprise sound of his voice. Claudia picked up her violin and left the room, ducking under Archie's arm and running her hand over his leg. He stroked her hair as she passed.

Valerie struggled to get out of the chair, managed it and stood up. Archie stepped forward and opened his arms to her. She stepped away from his embrace.

"What has happened to you?" she said with obvious disdain, "how can you throw him out? After he saved you from Sheridan? I don't understand! It was my fault that time, and I'm here, but why isn't Benjamin here?"

"Brigand's Law."

"Yes, yes, I've heard this a thousand times but it still doesn't mean anything to me!"

Archie sat down on the bed. He patted the blanket, gesturing for her to sit next to him. She folded her arms and stood defiantly instead.

"Brigand is Our Father Who Art in Theatre."

"What?"

"Reggie Roxy, Captain Brigand, the Man with Caftan. He founded The Roxy Playhouse many moons ago. Benjamin met him once, Herschel too. They were the original Players. He set the rules we live by – rules for drinking games, cards, performance etiquette...and also rules of a more serious nature I guess you could say. Allow by your actions the death of a friend to occur and you must go west to seek your forgiveness."

Valerie slunk back into the chair in despondency, "that makes no sense! Mr Ananas has to go away because Herschel died but he didn't shoot him, that Mr Whit did, right? I don't understand."

"It was Benjamin's production, his sword to fall upon."

"It's a stupid rule it makes no sense at all!"

"I wouldn't worry about it. I'm sure he will find his way."

"Find his way back here you mean?"

Archie winked at her and stood up.

"The world is a hard place. But it is a forgiving one." He kissed her on the forehead and left her alone in Benjamin's room. Valerie moved over to the bed and wrapped herself in the bear-coat.

"The world is a forgiving one," she said to herself and lay on the bed to sleep for just a few moments.

———•◦•———

"I want riches. And power. And honour and respect," wheezed Kemble. "I want to stand at the head of the table and be looked upon with fear. People will know the name of Kemble and understand its might. I want that!"

"You shall have it all," said De Locke through the iron bars, "now, tell us what we need to know!"

Kemble laughed and a globule of pus fell out of the hole in his throat.

"I am in a sanatorium, but I ain't barmy," he said, "I know who you want, but I won't tell you about him simply on promise of reward...get me out of here and I will lead you to him. Show you him. I will even kill him should you desire my Lords. Just get me out of here."

De Locke nodded at Nathanial before flinging his cowl over his head and exiting the chamber. Kemble looked back at Nathanial.

"You must be his secretary," Kemble sneered, "where do I sign?"

"You want to get out, so you can get in?"

Kemble began to hop on one foot to the other at the prospect, licking his lips vilely. "Yes! A million times over, yes! Get me out, I will kill for you, kill for you, my Lord. Oh! How I am a killer, an artist in it!"

"I will need some sort of token of trust."

"Anything, my Lord. Anything for you!"

"If you can escape, you can sit at the table of 'The Black Arm'."

"And be mighty?"

"And be mighty"

Kemble's eyes burned with fire. "How do I escape? I have no key! No chance. I would have done so earlier if I had but a needle."

"You could escape with a needle?"

"Oh, I'd wager, my Lord. There ain't much I can't do with a needle. I can do your dirties for you with a needle, my Lord."

"Very well," smirked Nathanial Whit as he unclipped a small broach from his lapel and placed it on the crossbar to the cell. Kemble picked it up.

"Find your way out of here and present yourself to me at the Serpentine in Hyde Park by midnight tonight and you will have your glory."

Kemble picked up the tiny brooch. The pin was barely an inch long. He ran it over is fingers and held it up to the light.

"And you shall be delivered unto the House of Ananas by twelve thirty my Lord." Kemble looked back from the brooch-pin to Nathanial Whit. The Black Arm dissident had already left.

Chapter Forty Seven

Bone Hill

B enjamin Ananas stared in wonderment at the maps and diagrams pasted over the walls of the warehouse.

"How did you come by all this information?" he asked.

"Years of careful research and intelligence gathering. It's isn't all glamour, the spy game," said Abigail who was pouring over a map of some obscure European province.

"Yes. I can imagine. When we build characters, we do so through meticulous research also, mining our memory, adding and subtracting elements. Honing everything we have learned and channelling it through our hearts."

"It sounds exhausting."

"It is. But it's what needs to be done. You can understand that?"

"I can," said Abigail as she plotted a red line from the centre of the province across other strange and bewildering countries until she came through a place whose shape Benjamin recognised. He looked over her shoulder.

"Ah, France! Paris, how I adore Paris!" he said, trying to appear worldly and wistful at the same time. Abigail looked at him.

"You have never been, have you?"

"What makes you say that?"

"If you had, you wouldn't adore it. It's a wretched pit of devilry. A hellmouth if ever I saw one."

Benjamin saw Abigail's hand move up to touch the pendant that wasn't there. He looked at her strange, angry and pensive stair before taking a moment to study every detail of her face. Abigail smiled and shook her anger off and brushed her hair befind her right ear and Benjamin noted that a large portion of her helix was missing."

"What happened to your ear?"

"Dog," she lied, brushing her hair back over her damaged ear.

Benjamin knew that she was lieing, but did not pursue a pursue a line of questioning.

A soldier carrying an armful of rolled up parchments stepped up to the table.

"For you, Captain Hachette" he said, dumping the papers onto the desk. Abigail nodded her thanks and the soldier dismissed himself.

"Captain Hachette?" asked Benjamin.

"When i joined the service after what had happened to me, it was deemed necessary to create a new identity for me. To all intents and purposes, Abigail Hardwoode died when she was seventeen and Andrea Elise Hachette was born"

"Andrea? After your..."

"Yes" snapped Abigail, cutting Benjamin short and rolling out a map. Benjamin understood that talk of the past was no longer welcome in the war room and he looked down at the map.

"What are you doing anyway?"

"I'm working."

"Sorry to bother you." he said, sensing her frustration at his small talk.

Abigail put her red marker down and looked at him. She pointed to Paris. "This is where we believe the heart of The Black Arm resides. Paris. From here they can infiltrate London, Northern Spain and, of course into the Germanic lands and soon, if they are successful, they will have nothing stopping them securing trade routes into India, and China and eventually the New Worlds."

"So that's what they are after, dominion of the world?"

"Something like that, although we cannot be sure. It's our best guess."

"What about Bonaparte?"

"Nosey's done us a favour on that one. The Black Arm though is much more dangerous than that runt of a Frenchman."

"How so?"

"You've heard of Bonaparte, right?"

"Of course, who hasn't?"

"And before I told you of their existence, had you knowledge of The Black Arm?"

"No. You know I didn't."

"Exactly, what you don't know can hurt you a lot more. The Devil is dancing in your parlour and you're all off watching a stumpy Frenchman jolly around Europe."

Ananas tutted, "dissidents" he said, jovially, "I hate these lads."

"You could try and take things a bit more seriously."

"How can I take this seriously? Yesterday I see you for the first time in twenty odd years, then my friend gets murdered, then you take me here and tell me you're a spy and that these Black Arse fellows murdered my family and my friend, and are intent on bringing the world to its knees and that you want my help and the help of The Roxy Playhouse Irregulars because, for some reason, the army can't handle it so you need some band of half-witted performers and thespians to sneak in and do the job for you."

"That's about the size of it, yes."

"Well forgive me, Lady Hachette, Other Agent, She of Twenty Names, if I am not overly enthused with a sense of understanding and willingness to act in a manner befitting the gravity of the situation."

"Well you should because you and your players are all that stands in the way of them and total victory."

Benjamin burst out laughing. The volume was such that Abigail clenched her jaws.

"They killed your friend, they killed your family. You want revenge. I can give it to you. To all of you," she said.

"The Roxy Irregulars are artists. They are above revenge. I am not. I am base and low so I will help you but The Players, they are far nobler! I will not be able to convince them."

"You should try," Abigail folded the map closed and leant over the table. "You can be sure that in any normal circumstances I wouldn't consider this, but the skills you have shown in infiltrating the Social Scene in three weeks and getting up close to De Locke and Whit shows you all to be remarkable assets."

"Thank you."

"Remember, your revenge is your motivation, but not mine. You are assets."

"Thank you. That's...comforting."

"Needs must as the Devil dances, Mr Ananas."

———•◦•———

Lupe adjusted the black veil around Desiree's face and stood back to survey her work. The Widow Ricci looked elegant and respectful in her black dress and gloves. The design of the dress was neither austere nor blasé. Her shoulders were exposed, but the cut was not too suggestive or alluring. The dress did not fan out or cling too closely to her hips, but fell in a sad and calm fashion down to the ground. Lupe stepped forward and turned Desiree around so that she could see herself in the dress-mirror.

"Thank you," said the ballerina, "I look how he would have wanted me to."

Lupe stood behind her and wrapped her arms around her waist and kissed the neck softly. There came a knock at the door and the two women turned around to see Gertie standing in the doorway, resplendent in a black frock coat and tie holding his hat in his hands. He had greased his hair to the side and made a best attempt to polish his ragged shoes. Lupe and Desiree sighed in delight at the sweet young man.

"Time to go," he said quietly. Desiree held out her arms to him and he stepped forward into her embrace. She held him tight and whispered into his ear her thanks for his courage and her pride at his strength and resolve. She kissed his neck three times as is the Umbrian way and broke off the embrace to hold him at arm's length for inspection.

"What a man," she said proudly, "Lupe, what do you see before you?"

"I see a Heracles, I see Hector. I see Diomedes himself."

Gertie looked sheepishly to the floor, "we should go, my ladies."

"Yes," agreed Desiree with a tone of conviction mixed with dreaded trepidation, "Gertie?"

"Yes, my lady?"

"Will you do Herschel and I the honour of holding my hand and standing by my side today?"

Desiree held out her hand and Lupe welled up with pride.

"My lady, it is I who should be so honoured," Gertie took Desiree's hand, bowed and kissed it. Lupe reached for her black-dyed peacock fan and hid her face from view as she wailed dramatically and fanned herself furiously. Desiree and Gertie laughed and put their arms around the gargantuan woman and led her out of her quarters and onto the stage.

The rest of the players were standing in a semi-circle around Herschel's coffin which Tobias had constructed. It was traditionally shaped, however the joins were not dovetailed but instead held together by a hexagonal design which Tobias had invented and which was strong and unique to his skill. It was in this tiny detail that Tobias said his goodbye to his friend. The coffin sat atop a table in the centre of the stage. On top of the coffin lay articles given to the departed by the other players. Srdjan and Ms Adberg had each laid a practice epee, Danilov and Anya had laid a gilded buckle from on their harnesses. Antoine had laid a deck of cards and Tobias a chisel. Archie had folded one of his waistcoats and Valerie, who had no possessions of her own, had written a poem about the departed and rolled it up and tied off with a long lock of her own hair. Claudia had donated one of her silver earrings and as Lupe approached, she pulled one of the peacock feathers from her fan and laid it across the lid. Gertie was handed one of his practice butterfly nets by Srdjan and he placed it next to the other articles. The Widow Ricci was the last player to arrive at the coffin and, of course, she did not place any article on top because they all knew that her heart and soul were lying inside. Once the players had assembled, they all bowed their heads and gave a silent prayer to Herschel.

After three minutes of prayer, Archie, Srdjan, Antoine and Danilov stepped forward and picked up the coffin and rested it on their shoulders. Valerie walked around to Tobias's chair and the procession left the theatre with Desiree the last to go, walking five paces behind the pall bearers.

Nobody in Borough had known exactly how Herschel Barnabus had died, but news of his demise had spread like a midnight whisper and as soon as the doors to The Roxy opened and the procession stepped out into the sun-drenched street, it seemed as if all London had come to a standstill. Old Man Peacock, who took care of the stables next to Borough market had donated a dual horse-drawn hearse and was sitting on the driver's bench bedecked in black. The street traders, hustlers and whores that normally spent their days rushing about had stopped in their tracks and had bowed in respect. The silence in the street was overwhelming.

Desiree stood on the top step of The Roxy's entrance and looked out at the mourning masses. She was overcome with emotion and almost collapsed, had it not been for the strengthened grip of Gertie, holding her tight and bursting with pride for his adoptive father and the sight of all the lives he had touched along his way.

The pall bearers loaded the coffin and stood around the carriage. Gertie leant into Desiree's ear and whispered a few words of encouragement. Desiree took a deep breath and made her first step outside. The silence was shattered with a thousand cheers and hollers. The bakers and butchers on the high street banged their pots and pans, the street sweepers hit their broom handles against anything nearby that would make a noise. The children shouted and cheered and through the windows of every bar, the Players could see that every barmaid had stood up on the bar and were applauding enthusiastically. Herschel's name rang out in Borough and the noise was deafening.

As soon as Desiree reached the carriage, she was helped up onto the driver's bench by Gertie who then joined her. Old Man Peacock checked that everyone was ready and then drove Herschel's body to its final resting place. The residents of Borough did not stop cheering and shouting until the carriage had rolled clean out of sight. When it had, they looked around at each other and uniformly decided that it was far too much of an occasion to go back to work. The pubs flung their doors and curtains wide and the market traders threw away their signs. From out of every doorway and window came flooding barrels and bottles of wine and baskets of bread and wheels of cheese. An impromptu street party commenced on Borough High Street and there people gathered to talk about Herschel and the Playhouse and to embrace their fellow Londoners and break bread. It was the first time it had ever happened.

———•·•———

Benjamin Ananas and Abigail Hardwoode stood unseen from the other players as they observed the funeral. For the nonconformist Londoner, there was only really one place in which to be buried: the non-consecrated ground at Bunhill cemetery in Islington, or 'Bone Hill' as it was 'affectionately' known.

The players stood around the shallow grave as the coffin was lowered. There were no tears, but instead embraces. Gertie and Desiree together, Lupe, Antoine, Tobias in a strange bundle over his chair, Danilov, Anya, Srdjan and Ms Adberg, Valerie and Claudia.

Only Archie stood apart and Benjamin Ananas was overcome with sadness that he was so. He wanted to run over and stand by his pal, but he knew he could not. Eventually, when everyone had finished hugging their partners, they then exchanged and this time, Archie found the arms of Claudia into which he held the Spanish girl so tightly that she almost suffocated.

Abigail looked up at Benjamin and saw his sadness. Despite her desire to maintain a professional relationship with the asset, she couldn't help but succumb to the feelings of love and concern for him that she had felt against her better judgement in the carriage the night before. She reached over and took his hand. The touch of his skin in that private moment was electric and she felt invigorated with a barrage of returning memories. She remembered their meeting in the labyrinth and their walks in the garden, their secret meetings and their innocent love. She felt sad that the girl she was then, in love and full of verve, was not within the woman she was now. She could feel that, fundamentally, Benjamin had not really changed at all and still carried that creative fire of youth but she did not. She was a machine, not a woman. However, as he squeezed her hand and reflexively ran his thumb over her knuckles, she felt an insurgence of excitement flutter through her and her heart skipped a beat. She looked up at his misty eyes and across to his mourning friends and then back down to their joined hands. She smiled to herself and felt a tiny pang of hope for the future. Maybe there was a way to find that youthful little girl inside her once more.

"That one there is Archie," whispered Benjamin and pointed with his eyes to his man. Abigail looked over to him.

"And that little woman is Claudia. Look, there is Lupe Darling and Antoine Le Magnifique! Oh, has it been only a few hours since I saw them last them, how beautiful they are. Look! Srdjan!"

Abigail looked over at the Dalmatian and was struck by how closely he resembled Benjamin and then she remembered his stories he had told her in the carriage. Suddenly, she was elated to discover that the faces he had drawn in her mind were exactly as they were in reality.

"And that must be young Alexia, and I suppose young Valerie. And the acrobatic siblings," she said in a hushed and excited tone, as if she was witnessing for the first time a rare secret meeting of magical beings.

"Yes! That's right. I hope one day you can meet them."

"Yes, I would like that," she said, her tone changing to a more serious one, "perhaps in another life and not under these circumstance."

Benjamin remembered what was to come and let go of her hand. The bond between the players, him and her severed and the cold light of day returned to her. She would not be meeting the magical creatures under any circumstances other than those of wartime. She sighed. Benjamin watched as the players finished the service and as a family, linked arms and walked away. Only Desiree stood for a few moments. The group turned back to her. Desiree lifted her veil and looked up the heavens. She had never shined as brightly nor appeared as graceful. Slowly, she began to dance around the grave; the sombre and melancholic dance that she had performed at the Whit Ball. Abigail held her mouth and fought back the tears as she recalled seeing it for the first time and now seeing it for the second and understanding its importance. Desiree danced for seven minutes and the world seemed to stop and watch. Benjamin did not hold Abigail's hand this time, instead his hand found its way up to the back her head and he ran his fingers through her hair. As Abigail watched the mourners dance, she rested the weight of her head into the hand of her long lost lover.

----•·•·•----

The sun was setting and light began to dim inside his cell. Kemble had retreated from the shaft of light and had sat in the dark corner all day fondling the brooch pin. The time was almost upon him. As he fondled the brooch in one hand, he fingered the disgusting hole in his throat with the other. He ran his finger over the wound and felt the warm discharge run down his hand and began to fantasise about his revenge. He had to deliver Ananas that much he could not jeopardise, but Ms Adberg, Archie Enfield and all the other players? His heart beat fast and he grew erect at the prospect of the orgy of violence that was his justified destiny. Through the light he could make out a half-drunk guard approaching his cell holding a small bowl of river water and a lump of soggy green bread. Kemble smiled and stood up. The guard stood by the bars and rattled the bowl against them.

"Grub's up inmate," he growled. Kemble stepped up to the door and smiled his vicious smile.

"Thank you Ogle, thank you kindly, what is it today?"

"Foie gras, ostrich goolies and the cup of Aphrodite's tit milk."

Kemble licked his lips, "my favourite."

"Take it then, bell-end," Ogle said and thrust the bowl between the bars. Kemble grabbed Ogle's hands and snapped his thumbs clean to the side with two sharp and sickening cracks. Poor Ogle went to scream but the lightning-fast Kemble let go of Ogle's hands, took the broach from his lapel and jammed the pin into Ogle's Adam's apple. Ogle could not scream to raise the alarm, but gurgled and tried to stagger backwards. Kemble showed no signs of emotion as he reached through the bars and pulled Ogle close. The gurgling man lurched forward and clanged against the bars. Kemble clamped his hands around the side of his head and looked deep into his eyes. Ogle's were wide and filled with fear and pain. Kemble's were calm but bright. The vicious actor smiled as his thumbs slowly brushed across the guard's cheeks. Ogle strained his eyes to see where the thumbs were going and he began desperately to try and push Kemble away, but his broken thumbs took care of that possibility. Ogle squirmed and tried to scream but it was no use. Kemble's thumbs moved up to Ogle's eyes and forced their way into his sockets. They pressed into his eyes and further still into his skull cavity. Ogle gurgled awfully and kicked feebly before falling limp. Kemble pulled his thumbs from Ogle's face and let the body slump down in the floor.

Kemble licked his thumbs clean of the jelly and bent down to the dead guard. He turned him over and found his keys. He unclasped them, unlocked the cage and dragged the body into the cell and stuffed it into a dark corner. He reattached his brooch and fixed his filthy cravat, cricked his neck and walked out of the cell, making sure to lock it before he left.

Chapter Forty Eight

Midnight

Nathanial Whit stood by the Serpentine lake in Hyde Park and checked his pocket watch; almost midnight. It was a clear night and the moon was full, casting its silver beams over the light and draping Hyde Park with an almost mystical hue. Nathanial was alone. The park was closed to the public and the ageing watchmen had gathered the destitute and the lost that had sought a soft flowerbed to sleep on and thrown them onto the hard cobbles. The thieves and chancers that had evaded the watchmen, lurked mainly around the peripheries, hiding in the bushes and hedges lining the park, looking to grab a purse or wallet belonging to some unsuspecting fool who happened to walk on the pavement, a little too close to the bushes.

Whit bent down and fanned his fingers through the crystal water. It was cool and crisp. He splashed his face and let the gentle breeze dry it off. He bent back to the water and rippled his hand through it once more. He watched as his reflection broke apart in the water. When it reformed he saw a ghoulish figure stare back at him. He turned to the side and jumped backwards, drawing his rapier instinctively. In front of him stood some awful, mad blood-soaked creature that was breathing heavily. Nathanial was about to run it through when a moonbeam glinted off of a brooch on its lapel. He recognised it and lowered his sword.

"Mr Kemble. Right on time."

The creature smiled and stood up to its full height and Nathanial looked him over. His features were obscured by the mixture of dried and fresh blood, grime and mud.

"I escaped as you commanded, sire" wheezed Kemble as he unpicked the brooch and handed back to Nathanial.

"Keep it."

"Oh! Thank you, my Lord!" gushed the madman as he fell to his knees and began kissing the ground around Nathanial's feet.

"Get up, you wretched man."

Kemble climbed to his feet.

"How did you escape?"

"With the brooch. First the guard, then the inmates nearby, then I stalked the corridors snuffin' out all the wretched life I came across, all the guards in the whole of Bedlam."

"You are a beast!"

"I am an actor! An artist! And I have come to claim my prize, my glory!"

"You have passed the first test, it is true. But now you need to fulfil the rest of your duty. Take me to Ananas and you will receive your initiation into The Black Arm."

"And I will sit by your side at the table?"

"You will sit by my side at the table."

"Then it is this way," said the mad creature, backing into the darkness. Nathanial Whit did not sheath his sword, lest the blood-crazed creature lure him into a dark corner and spring a trap. He followed cautiously.

The street party in Borough was still going strong when the bells of Southwark Cathedral rang out. The Roxy Players had danced and drank and sang with the revellers and had, come ten o'clock, fallen into The Bishop and were currently sitting in the reserved section at the back. There had been an endless procession of well wishers and condolers who paid their respects with drinks and the players' table was stacked high with glasses.

Desiree was sat in the main chair, facing the procession with Gertie by her side. The other players flanked her and the mood of the evening was jovial and relaxed. Claudia was braiding Valerie's hair who was casting overt looks to Danilov who was playing cards, and losing because of her distraction. He didn't mind though. She was beautiful. Antoine and Tobias also minded not as they took it in turns to lay trick after trick down on Danilov. Srdjan sat with Alexia on his lap and they were involved in a deep and private conversation, whispering in each other's ears and nodding enthusiastically as they began exchanging dreams for plans. Anya, as always, was sat between the lamp and the busted piano in a meditative state. Lupe and Archie had stolen themselves away from the rest of the troupe and were propping up the bar and sharing a large punchbowl.

"Tell me more, tell me more, dear love!" proclaimed Lupe in the quietest voice she could which still loud enough to be heard by the tables nearby.

"She had skin like milk and honey and eyes of emerald green! Our eyes locked and instantly I knew that she was the one. That my years of searching were over! It was love, true everlasting love!"

Lupe blushed and fanned herself. "And how did you feel down there?" she said, gesturing to his groin.

Archie smiled, leant in close and whispered the more erotic thoughts that had came to him during his encounter with the mysterious raven-haired woman. Lupe's eye-lids fluttered as he whispered all the details and she gripped the bar to steady herself as his words almost brought her to the brink.

"Oh my love," she whispered as she bit her lip. "Oh my love, ooh la la, that is amour! That is true love and desire. That is how I felt about my George!"

Archie broke away from his dirty story and poured more punch for them both. Lupe was fanning herself heavily, her enormous chest flushed red.

"My Archie, what a way you have with words, what a divine control you have over your body and soul. An instrument of love! And what was her name?"

"She told me not!" he said, sadly "she disappeared into the night and wished that we'd meet again, someday soon."

"Oh how devilish and perfect a creature!"

"She said we'd meet by the seaside!"

"Ah the seaside, a place built for lovers united! What times I have had by the sea...and you will too. Let us drink and talk more of our love, my dear soulmate, Archibald Enfield!"

Archie clinked glassed with Lupe and they linked arms, pouring their cups down each other's throats.

Back at the main table, Alexia climbed off of Srdjan's lap and helped him to his feet. He turned to the group and announced that there were turning in for the night, and wished the players luck for the rest of the evening, though in his heart he was really wishing them luck for the future as it had been decided that the pair of them would elope. The players raised their glasses and bid the two goodnight, unaware that they were about to run away forever. Srdjan bent in close and embraced Desiree tightly and kissed her cheek. He told her that he loved her dearly and was honoured to have met

Herschel. She thanked him for his kind words and turned to Alexia who did the same as Srdjan.

"Goodbye, Players," said Srdjan finally.

"Goodnight!" they cried back.

Srdjan took his darling Alexia's hand and they walked out of The Bishop. As they walked away, Valeria watched them stop and hug Archie and Lupe. A sudden sad realisation washed over her.

"They are going away forever," she whispered. Only Claudia heard and when she asked her how she knew, Valerie simply said: "Some things are plain to me."

Claudia looked over and noticed a slight contradiction in the eyes of her departing friends. Their eyes bore a glint of excitement, which could be attributed to the uncertainty of their future, but also a well of sadness that could only be caused by the melancholia of leaving something behind. Claudia agreed with Valerie, but she did not say so. The possibility was too much to bear and she put it from her mind and returned to braiding Miss Folk's hair.

<hr />

Abigail Hardwoode and Benjamin Ananas fought through the throng of the crowds on Borough High Street. They could barely believe the sights and sounds of the usually beat upon area. Benjamin laughed loudly and squeezed Abigail's hand.

"This is for him!" he said proudly. "This is for Herschel Barnabus, my man!" He laughed again and pulled Abigail in close to him. "Does your husband know where you are, Lady Jennifer-Joy? Does he?"

She smiled at the devious glint in his eye and the infectious mood of the unusual wake.

"No, Count Brandenburg! He does not! He is at the Almack Assembly Rooms making plans for the world!"

"The fool!" boomed Benjamin, "does he not know that the world is right here?"

"He must not! We should show him! We should round up a group of artists and show him how the world really is!"

"We must!" said Benjamin, overcome with the charade. He pulled Abigail in tightly and kissed her. The years in between their separation and reunification melded into each other and the individual pains and joys morphed together to create a kiss so powerful that for its duration, both parties realised that two plus two equalled five. It was a sea-changing kiss. When they broke it off, they realised that world hadn't ended, nor changed and the party continued around them. They looked at each other for a few seconds before bursting out laughing. As they laughed, but three feet from them, Srdjan and Alexia pushed through the crowd trying to make their way back to The Roxy. They had no idea how close they had come to each other and never would have the chance to realise it.

———•◦•———

The silence in The Roxy was oddly contrasted to the chaos outside and as Alexia and Srdjan fell through the door and slammed it shut, the world outside fell away. They took a few moments to look around the empty theatre and recall all the glorious times she had provided. They held hands and walked down to the stage and climbed upon it.

"Before we go," said Alexia, unclasping her dress, "let us make love on the stage to say goodbye to her."

Benjamin took a moment outside of The Bishop to compose himself.

"You will be fine. You will walk in, say what you have to say and that will be it," said Abigail as she looked over his shoulder and peered through the murky window of The Bishop.

"You make it sound so official."

"It is how I have learned to deal with the hardest things, my dear."

"You know, we still haven't spoken about us. Our time together and..." said Benjamin.

Abigail kissed him again, "you think too much. You distract yourself too much. Instead, be the arrow. Now, go!"

She patted his cheeks and his smiled.

"Here we go" and with that Benjamin entered The Bishop with Abigail behind him.

Inside he began to advance towards the back room where he knew the players to be. Each footstep was heavy with fear and trepidation. He got as far as the bar when an arm reached out and blocked his path.

"Come begging for forgiveness?" said Archie as he turned around to face Benjamin.

"Begging ain't my business."

Archie nodded and looked at Abigail.

"I recognise her."

Abigail held out her hand. "Lady Jennifer-Joy De Locke". Archie took her hand and kissed it.

"So, what brings you two here? If it is not on Brigand's business, then perhaps you can be granted parlay."

"Revenge," said Benjamin. Archie looked him over.

"Miss Darling" he said over his shoulder. Lupe turned around and momentarily smiled at the sight of Benjamin but remained stony faced when she realised that it was not appropriate.

"Revenge, says he," said Archie.

"Revenge you say? Sound's positively..."

"Useless" came Desiree's voice from across the way. She had seen Benjamin enter and stood up from her chair. The bar fell silent as she walked forward.

"We will honour his memory not through more death, if that is what you seek," she said in a graceful tone. Benjamin looked at the floor.

"We shall honour his memory with performance and love as he would have wanted."

Benjamin took to his knee and bowed his head.

"Forgive me Miss Ricci. Roxy Players, forgive me for everything, I have gone west as under Brigand's law and I have learned much, but not enough to deserve your love. I beseech you, drink hard, perform hard and fill The Roxy from this day to the next with all the light of the world. I bid you all goodbye." He stood up and turned to leave.

Archie rolled his eyes, "well, at least stay for a drink, you melodramatic tool."

"Alas, I cannot. There is work to do."

"Oh really?"

"Yes, I wish to involve you no more. They only know the name Brandenburg, not of The Roxy . I wish to leave you in safety."
He motioned to leave when Abigail stepped forward. "Not just by name!" she said.

"What do you mean?" said Archie.

"Lord De Locke."

"Who?"

"Lord De Locke and Whit, there were talking. Whit said he knew someone who knew you. Someone who knew the real you."

Benjamin looked at her and back to Archie, already realising what she meant. That one detail they had forgotten about. The colour washed from Archie's face.

"Who?"

"He said only that he was a madman."

Benjamin looked at Archie. The recognition of the gravity was picked up by Desiree and Lupe.

"What does that mean?" said Desiree, stepping forward into the bar proper. The rest of the players followed her.

"Kemble," whispered Archie. Lupe gasped and Antoine instinctively pulled Claudia close to him. Archie turned around to the players.

"Kemble. He is alive. I saw him, in Bedlam. I followed Whit there. They must have met."

The players naturally moved in close to each other like a herd of animals after one has spotted a tiger in the glade.

Benjamin looked around the group. "Where are Srdjan and Ms Adberg?"

"They left," said Lupe. Archie and Benjamin looked at each other and turned to the bar.

"Barkeeper Neil!" shouted Archie. The tall, wiry bar manager peered around the corner.

"Arms!" declared Benjamin. Neil nodded, reached under the bar a pulled up a filthy rag bundle. He slammed it down upon the bar and unravelled it to reveal its contents: a dozen dirty rapiers. Benjamin and Archie grabbed them and threw them to the Players.

Alexia and Srdjan lay naked on the stage, breathing hard and giggling.

"That was quite a goodbye," said Srdjan as he traced his finger over her belly.

"We should leave more often."

They did not see the entrance to theatre creak open and a figure dart inside. Srdjan got up and pulled his breeches on. The darkness in the theatre was all pervading. He lit a candelabrum and placed it near his love. She looked perfect in the candlelight, naturally naked and glowing with love.

"I'm going to pack some things" he said.

"Ok, my love. Don't be long. We can take the night boat to Cairo if we hurry."

"As you wish, my love," he blew her a kiss and walked off the stage.

From the edge of the auditorium the figure watched the man walk into the moonlight and the naked woman stand up, fetch a chair from the side of the stage and place it next to the candelabrum. She sat in it and tilted her head back, looking up at the eaves. The figure made his way towards the stage.

Alexia Adberg was reclining in her excitement for the future when she felt a pair of cold hands around her neck. Her eyes opened wide as the smell of a dead man filled her nose.

"Hello, Ms Adberg," hissed Kemble as he appeared from the darkness behind her. His face was resting against hers, his breath foul. Alexia was overcome with fear.

She tried to call out but his grip on her throat was too tight.

"Have you thought about me at all?"

Ms Adberg began to cry.

"I have thought about you, Alexia. Thought about you a lot," He peered over her shoulder and down at her naked body. He licked his lips.

"Thought and thought and thought." He relinquished one hand from her neck and made an attempt to fondle her breasts. She thrashed around in the chair as his slimy hand made its way over her body. Quick as a whip, Kemble pun himself around and swung his leg over her so that he was straddling her, his face inches from hers, the wound from his neck dribbling onto her cheeks and lips. He sniffed her and looked down at his groin. She tried to shake her head.

"Mm" he said "it seems you have no effect on me in that way. Perhaps my thoughts about you were not directed towards your coos. That can mean only one thing."

With his free hand, he pulled a long, thin needle from his greasy hair. Alexia knew what was about to happen. He ran the point of the needle across her face and around the back of her head until its point was resting against the nape of the neck.

"Tell me something," he hissed, "any last words?"

Kemble loosened his grip on her throat. Alexia knew she was staring the Devil in the face. She smiled.

"You were a shit actor." And she spat in his face.

Kemble's smile turned to rage and he drove the needle into Alexia's neck until it pierced through the other side, extinguishing her life instantly.

The mad actor dismounted her, drew the needle out of her body and licked it clean. He positioned her body so that she looked like she was sleeping and ran off of the stage.

———•◦•———

Nathanial Whit was hiding in the shadows of the theatre. He had entered as Srdjan had walked off the stage and witnessed Kemble's assassination of Ms Adberg. Kemble slunk up to him and bowed.

"I believe," he said, "that Mr Ananas is somewhere inside."

"Yes, I saw him leave the stage."

"What orders now, my Lord, my one and only?"

"Wait outside. Find me a carriage."

"Will you destroy him utterly?"

"I will, and the theatre too."

Kemble's eagerness waned, "but my Lord...burning a theatre?"

Nathanial looked at him. "You are with The Black Arm now Mr Kemble. We are born of fire. Find me a carriage."

Kemble reluctantly bowed and left the theatre. Nathanial Whit drew his sword and walked through the dark theatre to hide in the shadows and wait to introduce Ananas to the Reaper.

Chapter Forty Nine

The Understudy in the Inferno

Srdjan had packed some things and as a memento of the great performance that never was, he picked up the replica Brandenburg coat that Lupe had made him. He put it on and buttoned it up. He put on some black breeches and fixed his hair. He sighed at the magnificence of his replication of the lead character and they chance he never got. The Dalmatian picked up the bags and left the backstage area to rejoin his love and escape to destiny.

He walked onto the stage and saw Alexia sat in the chair, head slumped to the side. He smiled.

"My love, this is no time for sleep! There is a night boat to catch, and love to make. We must sleep later!" He put the bags down and walked over to her.

He stroked her head and reeled in horror as it lolled backwards and a thin trickle of blood ran out of her mouth and from the tiny exit wound in her neck.

"Alexia?" he whispered. He shook her. "We have to go. Come on. Stand up." He held her, the tears falling already. She was not as warm as she should be.

"Stand up," he whimpered, "please." Her head lolled back. He pulled her tight and pressed her naked, lifeless body next to his and screamed his horror into her thick hair.

His muffled screams did not mask the sound of steel being unsheathed. His keen senses snapped into action and his eyes widened. The murderer was in the theatre. He let go of Alexia and stood to his full height and his hand found its way to the sword by his side.

"Show yourself!" he declared, standing tall and firmly in the centre of the dark theatre, resplendent in his fine costume. He heard the sound of footsteps circling him in the darkness. He drew his sword and pointed it to the sound of the moving steps.

"Show yourself, cur!"

"Ananas" came a voice that he had never heard before, "I have found you!"

Srdjan squinted in the darkness, trying to locate the source of the voice.

"That is not my name, my name is the Devil. My name is vengeance. My name is your fury. Step into the light, your destroyer has come!"

"So be it," the voice came.

Srdjan adjusted his grip and controlled his heartrate. There was a yell and a swoosh of steel as Nathanial Whit leapt from the darkness and swung at Srdjan, who only just managed to deflect the blade as he fell to the side. Whit flew passed in a flash and the follow through of the swing struck the candelabra. Srdjan rolled to the side and watched in horror as the candelabra teetered awfully. He scrambled to his feet and grabbed the iron stand and prevented it from toppling.

There was another dash and swing of steel as Whit dove from the darkness once more. Srdjan, still holding the candelabra ducked as the blade swung over his head and cleaved the five candles in half, sending the ends flying through the air.

The candle ends landed and rolled slowly towards the back of the stage. Srdjan ran for them but was cut short by another attack. This time, Srdjan managed to engage properly and both blades met, forte to forte. In the pitch dark, he could not see his attacker's true identity. Whit, also in the dark, believed that he was fighting Benjamin, so similar were Srdjan's mannerisms. The men, locked together, pushed themselves apart.

The theatre was silent. Srdjan, knowing his geography perfectly, backed across the stage, sword raised until he was standing over Alexia's body, protecting it.

He trained his eyes to the gloom. There was a whoosh and a glow of orange from the far corner of the stage. The glow of orange spread and intensified. Srdjan began to panic. He lost concentration for a second and Whit rushed out again and slashed at the Dalmatian's arm. The wound was deep and Srdjan fell to one knee, clutching his shoulder. The blood ran freely down his arm and collected over the grip of the sword. His eyes stinging and the smell of burning wood filled his nostrils. There was a sickening crack and a sinister hiss. Srdjan looked in despair as the back stage erupted into a flame. The Roxy was doomed.

Srdjan looked around the stage. The flames were already creeping along the boards and up the proscenium arch. He thought fast. He wanted to fight, but Alexia's body was sacrosanct. He clenched his jaw and rallied himself, screaming in conviction as he got to his feet. His attacker was nowhere to be seen and so he lost not a moment. He dashed over to her body and scooped her up. The heat was building and the smoke was now creeping across the floor and falling off the stage and blanketing the auditorium.

"Come on, my love let me get you out here. We have a boat to catch."

He held her close and ran across the stage, leaping seven feet into the air and landing hard and well. He belted down the centre aisle and kicked open the doors to the theatre.

The party outside was still heaving and nobody had noticed the ominous glow breaking into the night sky. Srdjan stood on the steps holding her naked body and looking down at the revellers. Something clinked deep in his heart. The pain in his arm fell away in a second. He nodded solemnly to the London skyline and laid Alexia Adberg's body on the steps and covered her with his coat.

"I will see you in a few moments, my love" he said and kissed her forehead. Srdjan stood, turned around, opened the door to the theatre and stepped back inside the inferno. The heat haze warped his vision and the smoke stung his eyes. Still, he stood firm, drew his sword and screamed an animalistic call to arms.

Onto the stage, up ahead stepped his unknown attacker. Nathanial Whit stood in the centre, wreathed in flame and smoke, as if the very Devil himself had drawn a sword and ascended to do battle.

Srdjan raised his sword and pointed it at the Devil, screamed once more and charged down the centre aisle. Nathanial Whit dug his heels into the burning stage, unaffected by the heat and chaos after years in combat and raised his sword up and held it close to his face. To him, Benjamin Ananas was charging towards his doom.

Srdjan was eight feet from the stage when he leapt up and, using the back of a chair as a springboard propelled himself up into the air, somersaulting up and over an aghast Whit and down behind him onto the stage. He wasted no courtesy of allowing his opponent to turn and face him. Srdjan swung his rapier. Whit, who had tracked his flight, was not as unready as Srdjan suspected and managed to turn on his ankle and parry the swing and buy himself a few vital seconds to regroup.

Srdjan gave him nothing and unloaded a barrage of attacks, mixing together every discipline and style he could muster in a dazzling display of swordplay. Nathanial was on the back foot. It seemed to him that Ananas had been touched with the sword hand of Ares himself and was desperately fending off his the flurry of steel.

There was a tremendous crack and fortune smiled upon Whit as a huge flaming rafter broke free and thundered down, skewering the stage in between the fighters, sending a cascade of splintered boards into the air. Srdjan dived to the side as Nathanial dived backwards, sliding along on his back. Both men got to their feet and surveyed the situation. The entire theatre was coming down. Both men wanted the other dead. It was just a question of who was willing to die for it. Srdjan and Nathanial ran and dived over the chasm in the stage and clashed midair. They fell down into the hole and rolled around onto the floor, kicking and punching each other.

———•◦•———

The rest of The Roxy Players were making slow progress through the throngs of the street party. For every step Desiree made, she was hounded by another well-wisher offering her another anecdote involved Herschel. She was grateful and courteous, of course, but there was a more pressing issue on her mind. The Players rounded onto the High Street and dropped their swords. Archie sunk to his knees and Claudia screamed. Ahead of them all and behind a sea of people they saw their home ablaze.

Srdjan elbowed Nathanial in the face and climbed off of him. He leapt up and grabbed hold of a broken board and lifted himself out of the hole and back onto the stage. The inferno was all around him and the smoke almost overwhelming. He coughed and wheezed and looked around to get his bearings. The blaze had destroyed all markings and his sense of geography was shot. Below him, Nathanial spat blood on the floor and climbed back up.

The two men were exhausted. The heat haze masked Srdjan's true features and Nathanial was still convinced that he was fighting his nemesis.

"Ready for hell?" asked Whit through a grin.

Srdjan spat on the floor.

"I'm already here," he replied and the two men engaged once more. This time, their duel was not fuelled by rage, but by discipline. They were physically exhausted and knew that if they were to finish this, they would have to rely on their training, and that meant precise and practiced movements. The two men fenced back and forth across the stage. The fight was measured and yet still fierce, each man inflicting wounds upon the other. Another rafter broke free and swung down, smashing into the stage and wedging itself firm. The moon in the night sky was beginning to cloud over as the smoke billowed out of the hole in the roof.

Nathanial Whit moved forward with a perfect crossover movement which wrong footed Srdjan slightly and gave Whit the advantage. He pressed forward and bore down on the Dalmatian whose strength was depleting. Srdjan looked around and saw the wedged rafter to the side. It led straight up and out into the night air. He parried Whit's lunge and angled the fight so that he was retreating towards the beam. Still Nathanial pressed Srdjan backwards and the two men moved across the stage and up onto the diagonal beam.

Benjamin raised his sword a roared like a bear. The entire street stopped dancing and collectively realised that the theatre was on fire. There was a sudden outburst of shouts and screams and then the real chaos ensued. Benjamin, sword still raised, roared again and charged into the melee towards the theatre. His ferocity inspired the Players. Claudia screamed next and ran after him. Archie got to his feet and joined. And the rest of the Players charged forth as well, picking up Londoners along the way that had heard the call to rescue and sought to help save the theatre.

———•••———

Srdjan had backed up the beam and both men were now duelling across the burning skeleton of The Roxy. Below them, some vestiges of the other levels remained in a strange, cross section of the Playhouse. Srdjan and Nathanial fought back and forth above the burning costume department, the living quarters and the workshops. Srdjan was backing up along the beam, under pressure from Nathanial's relentless advance when a large portion of the roof alongside him fell away. Both men wobbled on the beam but held balance. The fallen roof offered a view across the theatre and out towards Borough High Street. Srdjan and Nathanial were now duelling atop a beam seventy five feet in the air and supported by little else but two burning struts.

———•••———

Benjamin, his Players and a large crowd shielded their faces from the crashing roof as it thundered into the shell of the theatre and burst through the doors. The splinters and beams rained down upon the crowd. Antoine dived over Claudia, and Danilov was pushed to safety by Valerie. Gertie, Desiree and Anya ducked and covered themselves from the burning embers and Tobias tipped his chair over pulling Archie out of the way of a falling beam that shattered onto the cobbles. Abigail pushed Benjamin to the floor as the last of the heavy debris fell to the ground and gentle shower of embers followed.

Benjamin got to his feet and pulled his hair over his head in despair. He looked at the twisted doors and noticed something buried under some wood. He picked himself up and dashed forward, shielding himself from the heat. Abigail called to him to stop. Archie saw what he was running towards and followed him.

Benjamin ran up the steps, skidded across the stone threshold and grabbed the burning beams that had fallen down on top of a something that resembled a body. He gripped the wood, burning his hands instantly. He screamed in pain and clenched his jaw and grabbed the wood once more. He heaved with all his might but it would not budge. He lay on his back and slid under in an attempt to press the wood upwards. It moved slightly and he expelled the air from his lungs and pushed again. It was suddenly easier and he looked to the side to see Archie, Danilov and Antoine by his side. They counted to three, gripped the scorching wood and heaved it clear to reveal the body of Alexia Adberg. There was no time to grieve. Archie scooped her up and the four men dashed down the steps and handed the body along a line of desperate Londoners who made sure it was ferried to safety.

The Players stood as close to the blaze as they could bear and held each other and watched in horror as their world burned. Another beam fell away and Claudia screamed and pointed. The Players looked to where she was pointing and the whole of Borough looked up see Srdjan and Nathanial duelling on the roof.

Claudia's screams pierced through the smoke and distracted Srdjan who lost his balance and fell off the rafter. He grabbed the beam, wrapping his arms around it, hugging it tightly. He was now was at the mercy of Nathanial Whit. The Black Arm dissident looked down at his opponent who looked back up with eyes that forbade him to extend any favours. Whit looked to his left and saw, behind The Roxy, hidden from the throngs to his right, his man Kemble standing on the roof of a carriage. The mad bastard had come through with an escape vehicle.

Nathanial Whit looked back at Srdjan and asked him if he had any last words. Srdjan, knowing that his opponent still thought him to be Ananas smiled and spat. "You think I am one? I am two! Death is just the first act and I will be return" Srdjan winked at Nathanial who raised his sword in a slow, controlled upswing.

The gathered crowd saw one of the fighters fall and grab onto the rafters. Benjamin knew what was about to happen and once again drew his sword and charged toward the theatre.

As he ran under the shadow of the theatre, his view of the fighters became obscured. It didn't matter to him. He ran up the steps and launched himself against the barricaded doors and busted through in an explosion of wood. He landed on his side and rolled expertly onto his feet and stood up just in time to see Nathanial Whit swing his sword down towards the dangling Srdjan. Nathanial's swipe removed Srdjan's head from his body as if he was gaily picking a daisy.

The Black Arm dissident watched as the body fell down below and turned to his left and looked at the waiting carriage. Kemble performed a ridiculous bow atop the carriage and stepped to the side. Nathanial Whit leapt off the beam and fell seventy feet, landing as if he was made of feathers. Kemble booted the back of the driver and the carriage quietly rolled away into the night.

Benjamin stood in the burning shell of The Roxy Playhouse and saw the head and the body of his friend fall into the bowels of hell. Above him Nathanial Whit casually wiped his blade and jumped down out of view and was gone.

The fires carried on burning and The Roxy silently fell to pieces. Benjamin dropped his sword and fell to his knees. He stayed there until he felt a hand on each shoulder. He looked to his left and saw Archie standing next to him. He looked to his right and saw Desiree. They helped him to his feet and together, the three marched into the dying embers of The Roxy Playhouse to retrieve their friend.

The residents of Borough had started their day with a funeral proceeded through a wake to remember and were now right back where they had started. They stood in silence and watched the doors of the theatre waiting for a sign of life. The Roxy Players held each other and wept at the tragedy.

After a few minutes the barricaded doors fell apart and Desiree climbed out, covered in soot and grease. She walked down into the crowd and joined her lovers. Then, Archie emerged holding the body of Srdjan. The crowd looked to the floor partly in respect and partly in revulsion at seeing a headless corpse. Archie, with a broken and ashen expression, descended the steps and the crowd parted. He stepped onto the pavement and looked around, waiting for Benjamin to emerge. He did so and Abigail put her hands over her mouth. The

Players held each other tighter and cried. He was cradling the head of their friend, the great swordsman and actor. The lover and defender of The Roxy Playhouse Irregulars: Srdjan Krupkal.

Benjamin walked down to join Archie and the two of them carried their friend's remains through the parted crowd and to the resting body of Alexia Adberg. They laid him down next to her, and positioned his arm under her, turning her into his chest. Then, Archie and Benjamin removed their coats and draped them over the two lovers and granted them both a final, everlasting privacy.

———•◦•———

Archie and Benjamin stood up and looked at each other. Archie held out his hand. Benjamin slapped his hand aside and pulled him into an embrace. The two men reformed their bond over that one hug and when they broke it off, they felt renewed. The crowd parted further and presented the two men with the rest of The Roxy Playhouse Irregulars who were no longer holding each other and weeping. They were stood in a line an each baring arms.

Archie walked over and joined them. He looked them over and each one gave him the look he wanted. He turned back to Benjamin and nodded.

"Finish this, Old Love?" he said, with tired tears.

"Till the end," cried Desiree.

The rest of the Players declared their agreement with a stamp their feet.

Benjamin Ananas thumped his heart in pride and he gestured to Abigail who had never witnessed such a scene of courage and tragedy. She had worked alone all her life and never knew what it was to work amongst one's lovers. She knew then that her entire life had been empty. She stepped forward and stood beside Benjamin.

"Till the end!" reiterated Benjamin and he turned to face Abigail, "and this woman is our way. Roxy Players, Abigail Hardwoode, Abigail Hardwoode, Roxy Players."

The Roxy Players stamped their feet once more. Abigail bowed to them and saw them all no longer as expendable assets to her endgame. She was honoured to stand beside them all.

Chapter Fifty

To Hell with Brigand's Law

The Roxy Players linked arms and stood on the bottom step of the theatre. The sun was beginning to rise, but her rays were blotted by the ashen cloud rising up from the ruins. Sad wisps of black smoke arched and weaved into the air and fine specks of ash fell solemnly all around. Benjamin was in the middle of the line. He looked to the left and to the right and took in the devastation writ large upon the faces of his friends. Nobody was crying. The exhaustion had taken care of the need to do so.

Abigail's final words were still ringing in Benjamin's ears as he looked at each player. Before leaving, she had formally introduced herself to the Players in as much detail as the situation permitted, which was in fact, very little detail outside her true name and the fact that she was more than 'on their side', she now *was* their side. Desiree, upon hearing her true name, felt a large piece of a puzzle fall into place. She remembered lip reading Abigail's conversation at the Whit ball and being confused by the exchange. Now she understood a little more and she realised that they had perhaps stumbled into something far greater than they could have ever known. She felt a great shame at silently inciting Brigand's Law and sending Benjamin west for his involvement in Herschel's death. He was no more to blame than any of them. She bowed her head and listened to

Abigail's words, vowing to herself that forever more she would never be sorry again, instead she would be accurate.

The Spy Hardwoode instructed the Players to salvage what they could and to relocate everything to an address in Whitechapel. She had told him that they would be safe there, taken care of and would be able to recuperate. The need for food, drink and a bed was great. Their limbs ached and their mouths had a coating of ash. They could each taste the lacquer from the stage flats, the oils from Tobias's workshop and the faintest taste of Lupe's almond candles.

Benjamin released his grip on Archie and Lupe who were standing either side of him and stepped forward and ascended the stone steps and climbed in through the wrecked doors. One by one the Players followed, silent, destroyed but still together. They each had many questions and doubts. Not least about their immediate future and what exactly they would do next. They had pledged fealty to the cause of revenge, but that was a few hours past. Now it was cold hard work and with no light of salvation to push them forward except the sight of Benjamin forging ahead, and the sight of each other following. They began to sift through the rubble and attempt to salvage what they could. There was no inventory, or need to salvage anything in particular. Their mandate was to simply take what wasn't ash.

They formed a production line with Benjamin, Archie and Gertie venturing into the still smoking bowels and passing forth what they could find. At first it was simple props that had been ignored for years. Play swords and daggers from a long since forgotten performance; a fake crocodile, a sarcophagus, a futuristic miniature flying machine. As the objects passed down the line and were fondled by each player, the memories of their past glories rose like phoenices in their hearts. In the death of the theatre, the trinkets that had survived meant more to the Players than they could possibly describe. As such, the work was slow. Claudia would hold props for minutes on end, running them over in her mind and recalling their use and the world around it. Indeed, simply by holding a mundane hairclip salvaged from Lupe's dressing room, she was able to conjure in her mind the exact moment Lupe had worn it, for what purpose and what had occurred that day. The theatre rebuilt itself in her mind. So as not to offend, and to speed things up, Valerie took her position and Claudia was sent out of the theatre and given the task of organising the piles on the street.

The street party obviously had come to an abrupt end and the revellers too ashamed to continue or to abandon the Players in their state, had silently taken it upon themselves to help. It started with Old Man Peacock who meekly walked up the steps and joined in the line. Soon, more men, women and children joined and before long, there were over one hundred people in several lines, each one headed up by a Roxy Irregular, passing trunks and flats, costumes and props out into the street where Claudia, now finding herself surrounded by people, had conscripted a small army of street children and was overseeing their filing of the objects into their appropriate pile.

Lupe Darling had been deathly silent the whole time. Though she worked tirelessly with the others, she did not utter a single word. She had a distant, dreamlike gaze about her and passed the objects along the line in an automaton fashion. Even before they had begun, Archie had sensed her despair and when he looked into her eyes a few hours prior when the theatre was ablaze, he knew exactly what was on her mind.

In the back of the theatre Archie worked frantically. He heaved great beams and rafters aside as if they were matchsticks. He was responsible for sniffing out all manner of article that brought relief to all the Players. He found seven of Herschel's hipflasks and, remarkably, three pouches of tobacco untarnished by the flames. The Irregulars had organised themselves into several lines, and depending on which player fronted the line dictated what type of recovered possession would be passed along it. For example, tools, weapons and artefacts of a metallurgical nature passed straight to Tobias' line. Harnesses, ropes and buckles to Anya's, Herschel's belongings to Desiree and so on. Though Archie's work was for the benefit of all, there was only one item he was desperate to locate and, as he progressed farther and farther into the theatre, the hope of its retrieval grew fainter and fainter. But he was Archie Enfield and he was not one to give up, and so continue he did, for Lupe and for himself.

Abigail Hardwoode arrived back at the De Locke residence in the small hours of the morning. She unlocked the door and crept into the house. As soon as she had stepped inside, she breathed a sigh of relief. Her heightened senses had told her that her 'husband' was still out. She sniffed the air and smiled. The scent in the house told her that someone else was there.

"The starlight isn't westerly yet" whispered Abigail.

"Depends where you stand," an exotic voice came from the corner of the room. The raven-haired woman stepped out and approached. Abigail relaxed instantly and took her shawl off and kicked off her slippers.

"Have you had a chance to review the take?" said the mystery woman. Abigail raised her eyebrows.

"It's going to take..."

"You're not wrong..."

"Have you got any..."

"I'm working on it."

"Will you need me, at all?"

Abigail rested against a bureau next to the door and folded her arms. She raised a single eyebrow in suspicion.

"Perhaps" Abigail said, "it isn't like you to ask for work."

"I can see that you have your hands full with Brighton."

"You read the book?"

"I glanced at it. You will need all the help you can get. If you do not use...what is that phrase? Big Ben timing? Then the place will turn into a bath of blood!"

"It's under control."

"I'm sure it is."

The raven-haired woman looked at her nails and shrugged coyly. "So you won't need my services at all? Disregarding my skills, my aptitude and my knowledge of the Pavilion? You don't need me? Fair enough." She went to leave.

"I need you."

"And my fee?"

"It will be the usual. Whatever you take, you take. The King's Specials and I have many eyes and we can turn a blind one every now and again."

"Actually, you can keep your fee."

Abigail raised both eyebrows in suspicion. "Come again?"

"You can keep your fee. I have set my sights on a particular jewel."

Abigail rolled her eyes, "what is his name?"

The raven-haired woman smiled a devilish smile, "his name is 'mine.'"

"Whatever you say"

Abigail stood up from the bureau. "Now, I'm going to take a bath. I'm filthy and tired. I must bid you good day, my dear."

The woman blew her kiss and turned to leave. She stopped and turned back.

"You know that when De Locke has his ducks in a row he will kill everyone in the room?"

"I do," replied Abigail.

"And you too."

"That's my job," sighed Abigail

"And the King?"

"It's a risk. But I'm working on an exit strategy."

The mystery woman laughed and shook her head. "That has to be one hell of an exit strategy."

"Well, I too am getting my ducks in a row."

The mysterious woman nodded. "I hope your exit strategy understands. Good day to you, dear spy." And with that, the woman stepped into the shadows and was gone, leaving only the tiniest whisper of black smoke trailing across the floor.

"Good day, Giselle," said Abigail to herself as she contemplated her ducks and what exactly she was lining them up in front of. She exhaled and went to take a bath.

———•◦•———

Kemble had stood in some relatively plush rooms and halls in his life. More often than not, in his later years, it was mainly because he was stealing from them or seeking to find a chambermaid in which to press himself upon under the grandeur of the room. He stood now, in the centre of a hall mightier than he ever had conceived. He felt as if he was in the halls of Olympus. The walls were painted a deep red and lined with numerous portraits of faces he did not know. Their pose and expression were all the same, facing directly outwards and with eyes of thunder. They looked down upon Kemble and he felt judged by them all. He would have run around the room with his needle and dagger and slashed and scraped every face so that they could judge him no more, if he did not focus on what was about to be bestowed upon him.

He stood and waited for an hour. He did not move, judging rightly, that it could be some sort of test. His face was still caked in blood from Bedlam and grime and oil from the fire. To occupy his mind while he waited (and to remove it from the glares of the portraits) he ran over the details of Sheridan's, Ms Siddon's and Ms Adberg's murders and the glorious performances they had been. The various inmates and the entire guarding staff in Bethlam had felt like ants to him and didn't feature in his recollection. But his three 'Big Ones' were searing and powerful in his mind. He felt almost euphoric when he played over the sensation of digging daggers and needles into flesh. He had sacrificed his ultimate prize of Benjamin to Nathanial Whit but the end outweighed the means. He would soon be at the head of the table and then, in a fantasy he dared not dream because its power was too great, he would visit himself upon every single Roxy Player starting with the little Spanish Girl whose name he did not recall, but who was loved so dearly by the rest of them. Archie would be last as he was the one he hated most, after Benjamin. He wanted Archie to suffer the greatest and so he planned to strip away everything from the dandy fool. It was going to be a glorious ascension for Kemble. He was about to step into the light.

The full hour's wait rushed passed as he visited vengeance upon the Irregulars. There was a sudden crack and creak which awoke him from his fantasy. He looked around the room and saw, underneath each portrait, a crack of eerie green light appear. He turned around on the spot, unsure of what to expect next. Slowly the cracks opened wider. Secret doorways! In unison they opened until he was left standing in the middle of a columned room with almost countless bright green passages leading into the unknown. He felt a tinge of trepidation and his left hand instinctively fall down to his rapier's hilt.

After a few seconds, figures appeared in the passageways. Blurred at first and then growing in form and depth. He squinted at them and tightened his grip until, eventually, the figures emerged and stood in the passageways blocking any means of escape, should he need one. Dozens of men wearing sinister black cowls surrounded him. He dug his heels into the ground and readied himself for the unexpected.

And, as is the way with the unexpected, he felt a surprising cold hand gently find its way over his own hand and calmly prise his fingers off of the rapier hilt. Kemble swallowed and spun round to see two men in black cloaks standing behind him. They removed their cowls. Lord Rafe De Locke, in his sickly pale and sunken form stood next to Nathanial Whit who was dressed, underneath the cowl in a fine medal adorned jet black suit with white piping. Kemble fell to his knees.

"Up," hissed De Locke. "You are Black Arm. You never fall to your knees. Not in servitude. Not in death. Not in afterlife."

"Afterlife," a unified reiteration came from the surrounding figures. Kemble slowly stood up.

"Are you ready, Master Kemble, to join our brotherhood? Through the fire, walk, and out again into the light?"

"I am, my Lords."

De Locke looked at Nathanial Whit and nodded before stepping back and putting up his cowl. Nathanial Whit stepped forward.

"You have proved yourself, Master Kemble. You have done well. And you shall be rewarded. Tell us what you desire."

"I want respect, glory, honour, justice."

"And what of blood?"

"Oh, I want that, too!"

"Very well, you can have that, but first, you have to have ours."

With that Nathanial Whit, quick as a whip, drew his sword and before Kemble could react it was back in its scabbard. Kemble furrowed his brow and his hand went back to his hilt. He could not grip. He felt cold and giddy. A flop sweat hit him and the room began to spin. He looked down at his hands to see two delicate slits open up along his wrists and hot blood flowing out. He felt woozy and the last thing he saw before falling over backwards was De Locke's shadowed face looming over him. The Lord's mouth opened wide and a torrent of blood vomited out over Kemble's face and down his throat.

———•—•———

Kemble awoke on a straw mattress in a stone walled room, groggy but alive. When his senses returned, he leapt to his feet and reached for his sword. Of course, it had been taken. He looked around the room and saw, hanging on the wall, a black uniform and a cloak. He went to grab it and noticed the scars on his wrists. The slits from Nathanial's blade were cleanly stitched up. He held each one in turn and tested his grip. He felt his strength returning and his mind felt keen and alert. He smiled to himself and put on the uniform which fit perfectly.

As soon as the last silver clasp was fastened on his tight, high collar, a stone passage way opened up and a green light fell into the room. This time, there was no cloaked figure blocking the way. Kemble looked at the light. He felt an undeniable attraction towards it. He resisted as best he could, but it was to no avail. Kemble stepped into the passageway and as soon as he was fully inside, the stone door closed and instantly sealed all evidence of its existence.

The salvage operation was drawing to a close. On Borough High Street there stood remarkable piles of objects and articles. A surprising number of possessions had been saved. One by one, the supply lines had dried up and now everybody, save for Lupe's line, were out in the street.

Old Man Peacock had kindly donated five carriages to the Players in order to transport their articles to the address Abigail had given. Gertie made sure he was driving the carriage with all the loot from the Whit Heist, not through mistrust of the Londoners, but through a sense of commitment in seeing his job done to the end. Desiree had climbed up and sat next to him and, when Anya climbed up and sat close to Gertie, the Umbrian felt a tiny glimmer of happiness.

Antoine and Danilov helped Tobias up into another carriage and secured his chair. Of all the Players, Tobias had done the best with regards to possessions regained. Yet he wasn't even slightly aware of the fact. Antoine patted his knee and told him not to worry and that God had saved the best for last. Tobias looked at the magician quizzically and then, with his trademark beguiling smile and wink combination Antoine clapped his hands loudly. Tobias was started slightly and, following Antoine's suggestive eyes, looked down to his lap. Across it lay the glorious and magical blade he had forged for

Brandenburg's sword; his masterpiece. He welled up and thanked God and thanked His vessel, Antoine Le Magnifique.

The other carriages were loaded up and the Players boarded. Eventually, Benjamin led a deathly quiet Lupe out of the theatre and helped her up onto the carriage. She sat next to Claudia, who fell into arms. Lupe held her tightly and kissed her routinely. For the first time ever, when she was holding and kissing Claudia she felt as if she was somewhere else. They both felt it. Benjamin then climbed up onto the lead carriage and led the procession out of Borough for perhaps the last time.

It took twenty yards for Valerie to suddenly realise that Archie was not amongst them. She stood up from her driver's bench next to Danilov and shouted to wait. As soon as they halted, everybody realised that Archie was still inside the theatre, digging around for remains. Benjamin turned around to climb off of the bench when he stopped. He smiled and laughed to himself. Lupe, who was sitting next to him with Claudia in her arms, received a gentle tap on her shoulder. She looked around to see Benjamin gesturing to her that she should look yonder. She turned around and a flash of life returned to her eyes. She climbed up and stood atop the carriage with Claudia standing by her side.

Up ahead, finally leaving the playhouse strode Archie Enfield. He was swigging from a charred bottle of brandy with one hand, and with the other he was holding the George Chest. It was complete and unharmed. Lupe and Claudia began to cry and then, much to his quiet delight, the whole of Borough began to applaud him. He reached the lead carriage and handed the chest up to Lupe who rested it on the carriage roof, whispered 'George' to open it and began to inspect its contents. Archie climbed onto the driver's plate and looked up to Benjamin.

"That whole Brigand's Law thing," he said to Ananas.

"Yeah?"

"Balls to it," he said and handed the bottle to his friend. Benjamin led the Players out of Borough to the ongoing applause of their neighbours. As they left, Lupe and Claudia remained on the carriage roof, poring over the contents of the George Chest.

Chapter Fifty One

The King's Specials

A dense fog had fallen by the time the procession of carriages had made their way into deepest Whitechapel. The area was a dangerous warren, dimly lit with any number of villains lurking in the multitude of doorways, culverts and alleys. It was the perfect place to lose one's self. It was an area which The Roxy Players had avoided for that simple reason. If the criminals and opportunists didn't get the better of you, the labyrinthine streets would certainly spin you around until you were lost beyond all hope. Lupe Darling had always likened the tight streets of Whitechapel to those of Venice. However, these were darker and more deadly; the Demon version of the angelic Venice. But now that the Players had nowhere to go, Whitechapel presented an attractive alternative. Collectively, the Players had abandoned most hope for the future and had resigned themselves to the act of revenge. They had nothing else to live for, other than to fulfil their immediate destinies. To a soul, they were fine with it. And so, when one has cast off all love and hope and seeks only to perform a few last dark actions, where better to reside, then amongst the deadly and devious? Whitechapel was their haven.

The procession moved slowly and cautiously through the thick fog. Before crossing into it, Anya, Claudia, Lupe and Desiree had been helped off of the driver's benches and placed, against their wishes, into the cabins. The men had climbed out onto the railings to protect them. Though they protested, the women of the former Playhouse were secretly thankful that the men had puffed up their chests and sought to protect them. It was eerie and silent and the slow moving convoy gave them all the impression that it was wholly too quiet and that they were walking into some sort of ambush.

The men, covered in soot and still exhausted from the events of the past few days, managed to combine their strength and resolve and share it equally back to each other through a series of terse nods of encouragement and resolve. Gertie, Danilov and Tobias drove the three carriages while Benjamin took the lead on foot through the fog like a daring adventurer walking into the arctic. Archie and Antoine stood on the footrails and kept a weather eye out.

Visibility for Benjamin was only around three feet in front of him and he walked on slowly. After twenty minutes trudge through the silent streets, Benjamin suddenly halted the convoy. Up ahead, through the fog, he could make out the tiny glow of a lamp bobbing and swinging towards them. He gripped the edge of his sword in preparation. Inside the carriages, the women held each other close while looking through the windows and scanning the fog for any signs of danger.

The light grew and grew until Benjamin could recognise it as a lantern being held by an unknown. The light halted five feet in front of him. Benjamin squinted at the glow and tried to define the person holding it. He could not. For all intents and purposes, the lantern could have been some sort of fairy or sprite coming to inspect them.

"Halloa, who goes there? Friend or foe?" whispered Benjamin. The sprite did not move. Benjamin then recalled the words Abigail had whispered to him, before she had left him to begin the salvage following the lantern until they came to halt in front of large disused warehouse. The monolithic wooden doors were heaved open and, from the depths of the fog, rolled the three carriages carrying The Roxy Players. They were led by the lantern-bearing old man and Benjamin, two steps behind. The warehouse was cavernous and cold. The old man led the three carriages into the centre of the space and halted them. He walked to each of them and banged hard on their doors, signalling for the inhabitants to alight, which they did timidly like children being called out to an assembly hall on the first day of school. The old man walked back to the huge doors and, with a show of unnatural strength, heaved them closed and walked back towards Benjamin without even once looking over the rest of the Players.

The old man didn't stop as expected by Benjamin, but proceeded to walk off towards the far end of the cold warehouse. Benjamin looked back at the rest of the Players, clearly unsure of the situation. He turned and followed the old man. After a few paces, Archie led the rest of the Players up to join him. They finally reached the far end and were led up to a tiny wooden door. The Old Man bent down to the keyhole and exhaled onto it, his breath condensing in the air. He stepped back and waited. There was a clunk and a scrape and the wooden door creaked open. He stepped back and gestured to the Players to enter. Nobody wanted to. The old man rolled his eyes and was about to contemplate kicking them in the behind to spur them on, when he noticed Claudia peering out from behind Antoine and Lupe, sandwiched between the two. He was old and mean, but not above the compassion. He saw the genuine trepidation mixed with sadness in her eyes and winked at her (the best he could muster). It seemed to work and Claudia regained a tiny iota of wonder. She stepped out from behind Antoine and Lupe and approached the doorway, out of which there was now pulsing a curious multi-coloured glow. She stepped towards it but was halted from entering by the strong hand of Benjamin. He pulled her back from the brink and bent down to her. He smiled and brushed her filthy hair from her face before turning and stooping through the door.

As ever, Archibald Enfield followed wherever his friend went. Then, with a firm conviction and a bold stride went Desiree. Next Antoine came holding Claudia's hand, followed by Danilov and Gertie who helped Tobias through the gap. Anya followed, leaving only Lupe and Valerie behind. Lupe Darling offered the way to Valerie who bowed a true Roxy bow and darted through the opening. Lupe realised her error. She was at least three times the size of the doorway without factoring in the volume of her dress or that she was carrying her beloved George chest. She looked over to the Old Man who pretended to look the other way. Lupe huffed and rolled her eyes before ripping off the dress and throwing it through the doorway. The Old Man, upon seeing the huge woman in only her underwear, had no qualms about getting behind her and giving her a push through the doorway.

Lupe popped through eventually and was handed her dress by Valerie. Lupe turned to thank the old man, but was greeted instead by the door slamming shut behind her. She turned back to put on her dress but when she saw the room she was in, she dropped it and the George Chest onto the floor as if they were meaningless.

The Roxy Players were standing in a room twice the size of the previous one, but the difference now was the sheer loudness and hustle of activity. They stood in a line against the wall and witnessed the military equivalent of a Roxy Playhouse pre-production phase. The place was alive with people scurrying around. Tobias followed a group carrying blades as they rushed to one end which seemed to be a station for a huge armoury. Lupe clasped her hands over her mouth upon seeing a wardrobe twice the size of hers against one portion of the far wall. Above Anya and Danilov swung highly trained soldiers, zipping around the upper ceiling on precarious wires and being barked orders at by a huge commander standing atop a giant pair of stilts. Antoine's gaze was drawn to yet another section of the room where a series of stern looking cloaked men were throwing projectiles at a wall, each one exploding into bright, colourful phosphorous light. In the middle of the room battled at least forty troops utilising swords, daggers and practice weapons that fired balls of paint which, upon impact, amused Valerie and Claudia no end.

"Where the Devil are we?" said Archie transfixed at the commotion in front of him.

"The Devil cannot tell you!" a male voice came from somewhere. The Players looked around to locate the source.

"That's right," another, more familiar voice came from above. The Players looked up to see a cable thrown down a few feet in front of them and a figure dressed in a black bodystocking zipped down the line, cutting itself free forty feet from the ground, somersaulting three times then landing perfectly in front of the stunned group. The figure pulled a seam of the suit and it unravelled itself and fell to the floor. Abigail Hardwoode stood before them. She bowed.

"The Devil could not tell you where we are, and that's the way it stays. Ladies, Gentlemen, Roxy Irregulars, welcome to Command HQ. What you see around you is the hive. The brain centre of it all, the..."

"The beginning, planning and execution of events that don't exist" the strange male voice came. The group looked around again, but still could not see its source. Anya nudged Danilov who stepped forward and picked up the unravelled black stocking suit. As soon as he touched it, it disappeared into black smoke.

"Wait, wait, wait," said Archie stepping forward. "Who exactly are you again? Why are we here? What is this place?"

Invisible Noel looked over at Benjamin and pointed to him. The others turned to him, looking for answers.

"We want revenge; these are the people that will help us. They are the King's Specials and we are helping them," said Benjamin.

"Helping them to do what?" said Gertie.

"Have you ever heard of The Black Arm, master Gertie?" said Invisible Noel. Gertie shook his head.

"They are the Devil. They are why we are here. We are the tip of the sword and also the shield. Do you sleep safely at night, young Senora Sanchez-Diaz?"

"I used to," said Claudia.

"The Black Arm took your home, killed your friends, killed this poor bastard's entire family [pointing at Benjamin] and destroyed his life. Some of us fight in the shadows [pointing to Abigail] to keep you in the light. All of you."

"Why do you need us?" said Danilov, "If you are tip of the sword, why us?"

"You have done things. I have been informed by Agent Hardwoode. This Brandenburg creation, it's quite something, quite a piece of strategy. Yes. And from minimal tools and a fraction of the time, you managed to infiltrate into the upper echelons of The Black Arm. Of course, you didn't know that then. I believe you were, robbing? Is that right? Robbing the rich?"

"To entertain the poor!" cried out Valerie, "for a good cause, sir!"

"Exactly!" said Invisible Noel pleased that she had caught on. "For a good cause, and now you have another one, a cause for the poor, and for yourselves and your theatre...and your fallen friends!"

"But we ain't soldiers!" said Archie. "We're actors, performers, artists!"

"And we are not?" countered Invisible Noel. "Come with us, help us and go where we go. I can guarantee you a performance grander than any other you will undertake!"

The Players' ears pricked up.

"What do you mean?" asked Archie.

"The chance to perform for your lives, in a play of life and death, on the very edge of all you hold dear, in the face of all adversity with only your talent, love and passions as weapons! A chance to defy it all and live free and well; doing all you love. And who knows, if you can do that, you might even survive."

The Players looked around each other and a surge of nihilistic conviction ran through them all.

"Death," said Benjamin wistfully, "the only great performance left."

"Aye, aye!" said Gertie.

Archie looked around at the other Players who were now fired up and on board.

"Well my loves," said Archie, "if we can avenge Herschel, Srdjan and Ms Adberg, save the realm and possibly see our friends once more in the afterlife, I say it's no question at all."

The Players turned back to Invisible Noel and performed The Roxy Bow to which, alongside Abigail, he saluted the King's Special Salute.

"So then, together, we will unite," said Noel proudly, "defeat The Black Arm, defy Death and The Devil himself...and save good Mad King George; for he is where we are going! Yes soldiers, we are going to meet the King!"

There was a gargantuan crash at the back of the group of Players. They all turned round in shock to see Lupe Darling lying in the floor out cold and clutching the George Chest.

Chapter Fifty Two

Exit Strategy

Claudia had brought Lupe around with a string of soft kisses and gentle whispers. When she had come too, white as a sheet and talking in whispered tongues, Abigail had shown the Players the way to some sleeping quarters where they could rest up. Claudia and Valerie stayed with Lupe and, when she was well enough to laugh and drink, she sat the two young women on her lap and began to tell them a thousand stories from her epic past. The women had heard most of the adventures, but were happy to hear them once more. Neither woman mentioned that it could possibly be the final time of anecdotage from Lupe Darling given what they now faced.

———•—•———

Upon request of Tobias, Desiree had taken him around the room towards the armoury where he met the metallurgists and watched them ply their skills. Desiree had previously held little interest in the intricacies of Tobias' skills and instead had found beauty in the finished article. However, on this occasion, when she saw his eyes ignite in excitement at the way in which they scored the baskets of rapiers, she understood that his piety and divine connection to God was present clearest of all in his work, and all afternoon she let him whisper in her ear everything he witnessed. The working metallurgists did not mind the audience and were happy to show him and Desiree new techniques and they listened avidly to the humble suggestions Tobias bestowed upon them and, when they tried a few of his techniques and saw the vast improvement in their work, they each declared him to be a master of the trade above all others. Desiree was warmed to find the absolute lack of vanity inherent in the small metallurgical community and sent a heartbeat up to her departed Herschel and a thought that told him she had learned what it was to be a true creator like Herschel was in his writing.

Danilov and Anya, of course, had made themselves very welcome amongst the high-wired commandos and, upon instruction of the stern Commander, had demonstrated their skills. The soldiers were astonished at the confidence of Anya and Danilov who perform so well on untested wires and without harnesses. But they moved too slowly for the soldiers' taste and so they decided to demonstrate their talents. They whistled down to the caped men with the ballistics and between them organised an impromptu wirewalking manoeuvre under heavy fire. Back and forth they ran and oftentimes leaping from one wire to the next all the while loud and bright explosions erupted all around them. Danilov and Anya were terrified to try it at first, but when Anya saw Gertie below with his net, she felt confident enough to commence her run-under-fire. And she succeeded nervously, but successfully none the less. Danilov, not wanting to be outdone by his sister, ran across the wires also and made it across to which they received great applause. But the Commander was hard to please and demanded that they perform it again and again until they were exhausted. Finally he called a day on the proceedings and offered them a rope to climb down. Danilov obliged but Anya remained. When he asked her why, she simply nodded down towards Gertie.

"That boy with the net?" scoffed the Commander, "don't be daf..." He did not finish his sentence as his jaw remained open. Anya smiled and back-flipped off of the wire and fell eighty five feet and landed perfectly into Gertie's net. She rolled out and waved back up at the soldiers who were too stunned to react.

"Right then, you 'orrible lot!" shouted the Commander back to his men. "By the end of today, I want forty jumps a piece. Any man who doesn't do it right..." he looked down to the floor. "...is gonna be brown bread!"

Then men all stood in silence and looked at each other.

"Mooooove it!" he shouted. And that was how Gertie spent the rest of the day and a portion of the night teaching the men his techniques until inspection came and every soldier, in a rapid succession completed all forty of his jumps without any injury. The Commander was more than impressed, but showed it only by saluting Gertie and then slapping him on the shoulder which left a week-long bruise.

———•◦•———

In the late evening, Lupe had finished her tales and the women all felt like they had lived and loved a thousand more times over.

"Right then," said Valerie, standing up and with the help of Claudia, heaving Lupe Darling to her feet. "Work to be done."

"Yes," said Claudia, "work to be done indeed!" And the three women left the quarters and rejoined the training camp. As they walked in, the two young girls made a beeline for the soldiers with the paint guns, giggling in excitement as they went. Lupe, like a reluctant parent, followed with trepidation. The training soldiers saw the three women approaching and halted proceedings. They jeered and smiled at them in the way soldiers do when met with giggling girls.

"Oi oi, little ladies, coppin' a look at our weapons are we?" one men jeered. Valerie tried to hide her blush but their uniforms got the better of her.

"Gosh, what lovely pistols!" said Claudia, batting her eyelids in her impossible-to-ignore way. "May I see?"

The soldier winked at his mates and handed her the pistol. "Careful now little lady, that one is easy to release!"

Claudia looked over the weapon with a faux innocence.

"Now, if you want a weapon that takes a little longer to release but is much more fun, come wiv Ol Simmons back to me barracks."

The men all laughed and jeered. Valerie giggled and Lupe smiled politely as she knew what was coming next. Claudia fingered the trigger.

"What does this little thing do?"

"Careful darlin' that there is the trigger! Don't want to be messin' with that! Dangerous, honey! Give it to ole' Simmons, 'ere."

"Alright," said Claudia and she shot Simmons in the groin at point blank range. He fell to the floor in agony, clutching a bright green paint splatter. The other men roared with laughter.

Above them all the unmistakable roar of Ananas came. The soldiers and the girls looked up to see Benjamin, Archie, Antoine, Noel and Abigail observing the whole camp from a high gantry. The three Roxy Players were cheering and clapping. Except for Archie who was only cheering, unable to clap having grabbed his own groin in a sympathetic act of solidarity.

"Bravo! Bravo! Little Mouse" cried Antoine.

"That's gonna leave a mark," winced Archie.

The three ladies bowed to the gentlemen, as Desiree left Tobias to join them. Claudia turned back to the men who were helping Simmons to his feet.

"Now then," she said in her haughty Spanish voice. "Which of you boys is going to let this women train with them?"

The men uniformly made way and offered plenty of room and advice to the women, now including Desiree, in the art of ballistics. In turn, Desiree schooled them all in the art of fencing to which, surprisingly, she felt herself recall all of Srdjan and Ms Adberg's schooling and impart through her, their mastery onto the novice soldiers. The sadness of their passing seemed to not arrive when she expected it, but instead there came an exaltation in recalling their knowledge and skill. For the few hours that Desiree taught the soldiers, Srdjan and Alexia lived and burned brightly

———◆———

"They are a good group of potentials," said Abigail from the gantry with a surprised tone. The men looked down to see all of the Players now schooling the King's Specials.

"Roxy Players or Kings Novices?" said Archie as he slapped Antoine's back, making the Frenchman puff out his chest in pride. Abigail smirked.

"Talented, yes, in danger..."

"They have seen their fair share," said Benjamin, clearly confident in their abilities.

"Not like this," said Invisible Noel. "Come, Master Ananas, come Mr Enfield and Mr..."

"Le Magnifique," said Antoine, still with his chest puffed out.

"Come, Mr Enfield and Antoine," said Invisible Noel which deflated the Frenchman somewhat, "I have details to go over."

The men went to leave. Archie stayed with Abigail. Benjamin turned back. "Archie?"

"You go, Old Love; I'll be at your heels momentarily. Just want a little word in Agent Abi's shell-like"

Benjamin looked over to Abigail who nodded that it was fine. The men left the other two on the gantry. Abigail looked Archie over and then turned to look over the railings and down to the training below. Archie studied her profile for a few seconds, taking in the calculating eyes and the tense jaw. He too, turned to look out over the rail.

"It isn't what you think, Archie."

"Call me Mr Enfield," he said smoothly, as he began rolling a cigarette from a pouch. He finished and gave it to her. Abigail took it.

"So she smokes," he said in a slimy tone he instantly regretted employing.

"Yes, and she dresses herself and cuts up her own food," she retorted in deserved disdain.

Archie struck a match off of the hand rail and lit her cigarette and then his. The liquorice and orange tinged tobacco worked wonders and she instantly felt a little more relaxed. She glanced at the corner of her eye. Archie was looking out elsewhere. She studied his keen eyes and the faltering border between his kohl ringed eyelids and the smudged soot from the fire. He glanced at her and she darted her eyes back to the melee below. He curled a side smile.

"So tell me something," he said quietly, leaning in close to her. She felt her heart rate increase slightly and for no apparent reason.

"Where is your husband in all this?"

"He's not my husband."

"How do you keep it from him?"

"We all must have secrets," she whispered, "I am good at keeping them."

"I know that, indeed, you are quiet the mysterious one, an enigma."

"You can't seduce me, Mr Enfield," she said, leaning in perilously close to his lips.

He handed her another cigarette. He lit a match and the flame's glow caught his sharp cheekbones and his devilish eyes wonderfully. Abigail leant in and lit her cigarette.

"And why ever not?" he said, edging even closer.

"Because," she whispered into his ear, "I'm not that stupid" and with that she broke off the exchange and took a few steps back to the railing.

"You thought you could test me, didn't you? You thought no woman could resist you! And if there was ever a creature alive that could, well heavens! She must be on the level!"

Archie laughed, pulled out a hipflask and tossed it to her. She caught it and took a swing.

"Something like that, something like that. I am an arrogant so and so, it is true."

Abigail handed back the hipflask. "No," she said smiling, "you're a good sort and you were protecting your friend. Beside's, I don't blame you. I am a catch."

"Indeed my lady, if one can only catch you and keep you!"

Abigail's expression changed to one of pure melancholia.

"Yes...indeed. I made my choice. I choose the greater good, at an even greater cost."

"Your own happiness?"

"No, his, I would have made him so happy. I would have been good and kind and he would have been caring and noble. But it wasn't to be. I have done many terrible things for the cause, but leaving him? That was the greatest sacrifice I made."

Archie wanted to chastise her and take her to task over her decision to choose action and death over love, but he could not. The obvious regret, coupled with the deep set resolve that she still held told him that she had done the right thing and, perhaps, had suffered more than Benjamin. He finished his cigarette and stubbed it out. He reached across and stroked her hair. She leant the weight of head into his hand and felt comforted by the gesture.

"The world is a wonderful place," said Archie as he stroked her hair.

"Is it?"

"Yes it is," and he went to leave, before turning back to her. "Of course, if we live through this and you mess it up with him again, I'll kill you myself. You have my word," and he winked and left.

Abigail knew he was serious and swooned at his parting shot. She instantly thought of a woman she knew who could possibly be perfect for that rogue's charm. She smiled and looked back down at The Roxy Players training her Specials.

———•◦•———

"One more thing," said Benjamin, as he stooped over the large plan of Brighton Pavilion.

"Yes?" said Invisible Noel

"Are you, in anyway, joking?"

Invisible Noel shook his head. "I'm afraid not, my friends. It is how it is."

Archie, who had joined them an hour previous, hung his head in despondency and put his hands on his hips, "bollocks!"

Antoine was stood in the corner, looking over the map.

"Indeed, gentlemen," said Noel, "if you're here and the bridge is not up, then it's curtains for sure!"

"And our window is to get from here," said Benjamin pointing to one end of the map, "to here," pointing to the other end, "in half a tick?"

"Give or take," said Noel, gravely.

"Give or take what?" said Benjamin.

"Give or take how many there are of you left; less people making the run, less people to worry about."

"Perfect," said Archie.

"It is what it is, gentlemen."

"Suicide is what it is."

"It's the only exit strategy there is. Believe me, gentlemen, we are all making sacrifices. None of the men outside that door expect to come out alive. Make no bones about it; the King and the Devil are our only concerns. Our lives are entirely expendable. I cannot lie to you. This is your decision entirely."

Benjamin hit the table in conviction, "As long as we have accomplished our goal, I am happy with that." He said firmly.

Archie stepped forward, "Wait a minute Benji, all very well putting oneself on the line, but Lupe? Valerie? Claudia? Do you want to put them through this?"

Benjamin weighed the possibility in his mind for a good two minutes. Finally he stood up from the table and took a sip of wine.

"We all make our own choices on this one. We've stood in front of them for long enough. There comes a time when you must let the ones you love and protect go out into the world and face the fire. We are all making our own minds up on this. I will put it to each of them individually. I cannot ask you to go with me on this one, brothers, but have too much invested."

Archie understood his friend and knew he was right, despite how dreadful a thought it was to put Claudia in direct danger.

"But let me talk to Claudia," Archie said, "I want to be the one to do it."

There was the sound of a throat clearing. The men looked around. Abigail had gathered the rest of the Players and quietly filed them in. Claudia stepped forward.

"Mr Ananas, Mr Enfield," said the Spanish girl, "I will lay down my life, for what it is, to see the performance through to the last orders, to the very end, the final curtain. For The Roxy Playhouse and our friends who's part in our great performance has come to a close. I haven't lived long enough to offer anything, but what I do have to offer, it is yours. To the very end" And she bowed. The rest of the Players bowed down in solidarity.

"To the very end, the final curtain," they said in unison.

Archie and Benjamin bowed back. The Players stood up and parted to give a path to Tobias. Abigail wheeled the metallurgist up to the table. Tobias grabbed the armrests of his chair and pulled himself up onto his leg and held the edge of the table.

"Mr Ananas, I knocked something up for you, something for all of us. I speak for each Irregular when I ask you, when you accept this, to do us all one thing."

"Sure, Tobias, sure," said Benjamin, confused at the proceedings. Tobias smiled and reached down into the back of his chair and pulled out along object wrapped in an oily rag, which Benjamin took and unwrapped. The room was filled with light.

Benjamin held in his hands the Sword of Ananas. The pineapple basket glowed and sparkled in the dark room. But it was not the sword as he remembered it. His delight at seeing the familiar basket once more turned to astonishment and overwhelming emotion when he saw the blade. It was new. It was the glorious and magical blade that Tobias had forged in the Playhouse. Benjamin welled up as he held the blade over a candle flame. As before, the names of every Roxy Player past and present revealed themselves.

Abigail cupped her mouth and Invisible Noel sat down in shock at the sight of it. Benjamin balanced the blade on his finger twixt basket and forte. It was perfectly weighted.

"Mr Ananas, as you have accepted our sword, you must now do one thing for us all. Will you, sir?"

Benjamin wiped a tear from his eye and held the sword up to his face in a gesture of fealty to them all.

"Anything you command, I am your servant" he said quietly.

Tobias looked around to see Desiree give him an encouraging nod. Tobias smiled at her and turned back to Benjamin. "When we go to war, brother, you must go as the Count Abraham von Brandenburg for his is the best of all of us. A symbol of our talent, verve, passion and loves combined into one, pure-hearted spirit. Will you do this?"

Benjamin's tears rolled out of his eyes, which triggered gentle tears to fall across the faces of all the Players. Abigail herself swore she saw Benjamin grow inches in height and a great presence swelled up inside her heart. He had moved in for good.

Benjamin let the names on the blade dance across his eyes and took a few seconds to recall all their faces and, to him, their ghosts appeared around the rest of the Players, pulled forth from Heaven to charge him with the great honour of leading the Last Roxy Players through their final performance and to bring them home, across to the

Other Side. He smiled at all the faces he saw, before sheathing the blade in a blinding flash.

"It will be the greatest honour of my life," said Count Abraham von Brandenburg

Part Five

Roxy Avengers

Chapter Fifty Three

Betrayal

The war room, as Invisible Noel called it, was empty and the air hung still. The table in the centre had a schematic plan of Brighton Pavilion pasted upon it. The heavy annotations and declarations of duty and task now meant nothing. A war room without people to fight is just a shell.

The door creaked open and Antoine stepped inside, taking great pains not to make a sound as the latch closed. He turned to the table and leant over it. He looked around the room, to make sure he was truly alone, before he reached into his breast pocket and retrieved a small pair of spectacles. He curled his lip as he put on the wretched things. He rarely used them and none of The Roxy Players had ever seen him in glasses, and he wanted it to remain like that. His eyesight was failing and, he had noticed, his hands had begun to lose their dexterity. At that moment, they were shaking almost uncontrollably through fear and through shame of what he was about to do.

He looked over the map with sad eyes and he bit his lip when he realised the futility of the plan. They were all doomed to die in the Pavilion and he wasn't ready just yet to do so. He wanted to flee. He wanted to abandon everything and run home to his father and mother and play with his brothers. He rarely thought of them, but now, just hours before he was to march to his death, their faces and the welcome scent of the home and hearth filled all his senses. His eyes filled with tears as he took his glasses off and pocketed them. To the Frenchman, there was no choice to be made. He would sneak away in the dead of night, without saying a goodbye, and stow himself back to his home in Gascony.

As soon as the decision became resolute in his heart, the sense of abandonment and shame lifted. It had to be done and be done it should be. He breathed out in relief and dried his eyes. After giving the map a final cursory glance he bade it adieu and left the room. He was walking across the gantry above the training ground when he saw Archie Enfield approaching.

"What you up to, Old Love?" halloed his friend. Antoine stowed his secret resolution and beamed a convincing smile back to his pal while grabbing his extended hand and shaking it heartily.

"Nothing, dear man, nothing at all."

"Going over the plan?"

"Yes, yes, going over the plan."

"It's a right old rum kipper and no doubt!" said Archie with a jovial whimsy.

"It is not half!" agreed Antoine. "What are you doing here, anyway?"

"Oh, right yes! Looking for you actually, come, we are having a drink to celebrate something, plenty to go around. Come!"

"Oh no, not for me, I'm tired," replied Antoine which rattled Archie somewhat.

Antoine instantly registered that his unusual response elicited suspicion that something was up in Archie's raised eyebrow and quickly made up for his gaff with a hearty laugh and a shoulder-slap.

"Making a fun!" he declared, "a drink sounds good!"

"Good man! Come with me." Archie grabbed the Frenchman by the hand and led off the gantry.

"What are we celebrating, our impending doom?"

"Not that, something much more agreeable!"

"Then what?"

"You will see, no more questions!"

Archie led Antoine down the staircase and across the training camp and to the little crooked doorway that led to the huge abandoned warehouse. They climbed through the door. The warehouse on the other side was no longer empty. Antoine stood amazed as Archie walked ahead of him, arms raised in adoration. The warehouse had been decked out with huge red drapes and strings of lights and candles. The carriages had been parked in a horseshoe configuration and across them had been spun golden garlands. The Players were sat underneath, drinking and laughing. The whole scene looked like a tiny mockup of The Roxy Theatre. Antoine put his hands over his mouth.

"Mon Dieu!" he cried, "The Roxy lives!"

"Indeed!" cried Archie, "The Roxy lives!" to which was met a huge cheer for the Players. "At least for tonight, anyway," he said to the Frenchman as they walked over.

"Who did this?"

"It was Valerie's idea."

"Ah! A true player!" cried Antoine as he beamed at Valerie.

The two men arrived at the makeshift theatre and sat down amongst them.

"Where is the Count?" said Antoine as Danilov and Gertie shifted aside to give him room. It was then that one of the carriage doors opened and the Count stepped out, dressed in his old costume. The group cheered. Lupe followed the Count out of the makeshift dressing room.

"It is not perfect," she said in a tone that practically begged for the Players to disagree.

"No, it isn't" said Archie, to which he received a clip around the ear from Claudia.

"It is perfect!" she said to Lupe, "don't listen to that booby. It is wonderful and perfect and you have done an amazing job as you always do!"

Lupe blushed and fanned herself with her peacock fan. "You tease me!"

"No, it is! Perfect! Perfect!" said the Spanish Girl as she got up to kiss Lupe.

"How do you feel, Old Love?" said Archie to the Count. Brandenburg cricked his neck and straightened his collar.

"I feel ready. I feel good. I feel..."

"Thirsty?" a voice came from the back of the warehouse. The Players looked at each other and shrugged. There then came a thud, as if someone had hit the ground with a wooden pole, then another, then another. The group stood up and looked around the edge of their 'theatre'. They saw Tobias, and he was walking unaided. Everybody roared with laughter and cheered relentlessly when they saw his new wooden leg.

"Those boys can knock up a peg leg!" shouted Tobias, "after I showed them how to do it, of course!"

Everybody cheered and, to show off, Tobias danced a little jig, hoping from one foot the other and spinning around, which was met with thunderous applause. Desiree instantly ran up to him and almost tackled him to the ground such was the ferocity of her embrace. No sooner had she grabbed him then he was leading her around the huge warehouse in a lovely, if a little awkward, dance routine. The Players needed no further invitation and they grabbed each other and began to dance feverishly around the warehouse.

Unseen to them all, in a dark corner of the space, stood Abigail and Invisible Noel looking on at the revelry.

"They know how to spend their last night, don't they?" said Invisible Noel, half melting into the shadows.

"Yes they do, yes they do" said Abigail with unrestrained melancholia.

"You love them, don't you?"

"Yes, I do. They are good people. Good people."

"And the Count?"

Abigail looked on at the reborn Count Abraham von Brandenburg as he danced wonderfully with little Claudia.

"Do you love him also?"

Abigail's eyes filled with tears. Invisible Noel looked to the floor.

"You will have to let him go, Agent Hardwoode. This is war. What can I say?"

"War or not, one thing will always remain the same."

"And that is?"

"You will always hurt the ones you love."

Invisible Noel placed a hand on her shoulder and the pair of them stepped back into the shadows, disappearing from view.

———•·•———

"We are all done for, you know that?" said Archie to Brandenburg as they sat atop one of the stagecoaches, dangling their legs over the side. In front of them the Players danced, drank and laughed. Brandenburg took a long glug from a hipflask.

"Yes we are," he agreed, "When we get to the roof, the curtain will come down on us."

"If we ain't snuffed in the ballroom first."

"Well quite," said Brandenburg, drinking again. "As long as Whit, De Locke and that 'dead rat scurrying' Kemble are twisting in Hell before that, we can call the performance a success."

"It's going to be one hell of a show, eh, Old Love?"

The pair clinked hipflasks and drank heartily.

"Yes, yes it will, before the day is done, they will know of The Roxy Players alright."

"And while they are reeling from that, we'll on our way to the greatest performance of all, death!"

"To dying," toasted Brandenburg, "the greatest of all adventures!"

The pair drank and hugged each other, resting their foreheads against each other.

"I love you, you big bear fool!" said Archie quietly.

"I love you to, Mr Enfield, thank you for saving me, saving us all. Thank you."

Archie was about to continue the long goodbye when they felt a tug at their boots. Their stifled their tears and looked down to see Gertie and Desiree standing below them.

"You two poor bastards been crying?" said Gertie.

"No, no we haven't. Don't know what you mean," said Archie. Desiree extended her arms up and opened her hands to them.

"Come, my dears, we shouldn't be separated tonight. Let's dance and drink and talk of the good times."

Archie and Brandenburg looked at each other. "Yeah, alright," said Archie and both men hopped down. Brandenburg stood up tall to Gertie and loomed over him.

"Bastard, eh, Gertie?" he said in a mock stern voice intended to put the young man in his place. Gertie curled a smile and grew a few inches.

"Poor bastard, actually," he said before smiling and turning back to the group. Desiree and Archie were stifling their laughter.

"You know," said Brandenburg, with his hands on his hips. "I liked him better when he lived under the stage."

"Come on!" called Lupe from the crowd, "what are you waiting for?"

Archie gave precedence to Brandenburg to lead on, and lead on he did, into the hearty embraces of all his beloved friends.

———•••———

The nighttime hung low over Whitechapel, beating the fog down to ground level where it clung, like a thick carpet over the cobblestones. Abigail Hardwoode walked out of a little side entrance to the secret training facility and stepped out onto the street. It was unusually quiet and tranquil. A few people chanced by her as she stepped out onto the street proper. She paid them no heed as they walked off through the fogged street. She looked around. She was totally alone. Her demeanour changed, her shoulders sank her back hunched a little, her lips became tighter and more hag like, and her eyes changed to a sickly grey shade. The sudden and almost imperceptible shift in demeanour resembled that of someone shaking of the rigours of a false persona and, knowing that they are alone, dropping their guard and removing their mask. In fact, it was the opposite. It was time to get into character. She pulled her collar around her neck and walked off into the warrens of Whitechapel.

She had not been walking far before she came to 'The Ten Bells', a disgusting dive bar populated with unsavoury Londoners.

Outside of the bar there slumped a dozen drunks and two dozen more whores and honey trappers, ransacking their clothes for coins and keepsakes. Abigail stepped over one unfortunate and walked up the couple of steps then made an attempt to enter. The doorway was blocked by two unshaven and foul smelling men. Abigail was about to try and squeeze passed when one blocked her way with his arm.

"Goi..." he didn't finish his sentence as Abigail stuck him in the throat and elbowed his friend in the nose. Both men fell onto the cobblestones, one choking and spluttering, the other wailing and gushing blood. Abigail looked around with fierce, keen eyes. Nobody on the street cared about what she had done. Abigail pushed open the doors and stepped into the pub while behind her, a pack of whores finished off the doormen with their heels before going through their pockets.

It was a rowdy joint with three pianists playing a single, battered, upright piano. All around her, chancers and townies were either starting fights or finishing them. The acrid air stung her eyes and her ears throbbed with the continuous sounds of shouting, jeering and smashing glass. She walked around the tables, passed the rum-addled sailors, around the whores displaying their wares to the prospective clients and passed the pimps who took their days takings. She walked unchallenged around the bar and through to the back where she came across a door painted with thick black gloss paint. She looked behind her. Nobody in the bar cared about her. Nobody had noticed her. She reached into her pocket and pulled out a long, twisted key and placed it into the lock. She turned it and opened the door. A strange and awful green light spilled out. Abigail Hardwoode pulled a thick, black cowl from a hidden seam in her dress and she put it on, pulling the brim down over face. She stepped into the green corridor and closed the door behind her.

The Players had passed out in heap. Some were naked, some were fully clothed and some in a state somewhere in between. The party had ended and the drink had overcome them all. The last of the orange and vanilla scented candles salvaged from the ruins of the theatre was now guttering on the floor. Bodies rose and fell as one.

Antoine Le Magnifique was not amongst the heap, and he was not in any of their states of dress. He was leaning against the carriage, looking them over. He was fully dressed with an overcoat, tall hat, cane and small bag of personal belongings that he wanted to take with him.

He looked over the pile and recognised every body part; Lupe's breast which was Valerie's pillow, Archie's foot that was resting over Gertie's belly, Tobias's back bent over Anya's thighs. He didn't need to see their faces, and was thankful that he could not as he knew he could not bear to see the look upon them.

He quietly stepped forward and uttered a few words to them all. He told them that he loved them, and that he was sorry to abandon them, but that he had to do what he had to do. He did not ask for forgiveness and he renounced Brigand's Law. He said his final goodbye before bending down and planting the softest kiss he could upon a body part belonging to every Roxy Player. When he came to Claudia, whose face he could see, his eyes well up and his heart broke. He did not kiss her, instead, he let his tears fall and get lost in her thick brown Spanish hair. Whether she could feel them, and whether in whatever dream world she was in, she could understand them, he could not tell. He reached down to stroke her hair but his hand was shaking uncontrollably. He let two more tears fall onto her, before stepping away from the group. In Claudia's dream, the forest she was playing in turned black and fell to ash, leaving her alone in barren, nightmarish landscape.

Antoine Le Magnifique exited the secret warehouse in the darkest part of night. He did not look around to take stock instead he headed straight for the wharves where he stowed away upon the first ship he could find that was bound for France. He hid himself under a tarpaulin, relieved that his abandonment of The Roxy Players had gone without a hitch. He closed his eyes and fell asleep presently.

———•·•———

Abigail Hardwoode walked down a steep and narrow stone staircase and along a passageway. The green light that filled it did not fall from any recognisable source, and yet that did not faze her. She knew where she was going. She walked with a purposeful and committed stride and with each step she took into the labyrinth she took a greater step in her mind away from the training camp, away from her duties and away from Brandenburg and his Players. She pondered his face for a few seconds and how he looked when he stepped out of the makeshift costume carriage. She pondered what Invisible Noel had said to her. She dismissed Brandenburg and his Players as she knew full well that there were now consigned to death.

She rounded a corner without paying any attention to the other passageways and stepped through an arch and into a large atrium. The walls went up thirty feet and in the centre there was a grated hole, over which the oblivious Londoners trudged. The moonlight darted in through the gratings, creating angular shafts that cut through the eerie green hue.

Abigail Hardwoode stood in the centre of the atrium for a few seconds, before a sickly wheezing crept across the room and chilled her. The breathing became louder as Lord De Locke stepped through the archway opposite her and removed his cowl. He smiled at her, his green eyes burning and almost becoming the source of the ambient light.

"Welcome home, my love."

"Everything is in place," she said with a strange, hissing tone that seemed frighteningly natural. She looked up and locked eyes with her husband. She smiled and the very colour from her cheeks seemed to vanish.

"All of the King's Men will be there, my love. All of the King's Men and all of his jesters," she hissed.

Lord De Locke stepped up to her and rested a bony finger under her chin. He raised her head up and looked deeply through her eyes and into the depths of her soul.

"What a servant to The Black Arm you are, my love!" he whispered.

Abigail Hardwoode's skin grew even more sallow as she smiled a twisted and broken smile.

"The Black Arm is my very soul," she said as she leant in and kissed Lord De Locke deeply.

Chapter Fifty Four

To Brighton

Nobody spoke of it. The pain was too great. Over the last few days they had lost Herschel, Srdjan, Ms Adberg and The Roxy Playhouse itself but the desertion of Antoine Le Magnifique was too much to bear and so the Irregulars buried the despair deep down and turned it over in their hearts and rebuilt the anguish into conviction. His desertion proved to them one thing: that what they were doing had to be done, no matter the cost. They all had choices to make, and they had made theirs just as Antoine had made his. While his path took him home, theirs took them into the jaws of death.

There was little preparation to be executed and even less rehearsal. Everybody knew what had to be done, and what their individual parts were. They dressed themselves in their favourite garments and armed themselves to the teeth. It was time.

They lined up for inspection in front of their carriages. Dressed in his tailcoat and favourite frilled shirt and breeches Archie Enfield walked down the line. He had nothing to say to them and so, as he felt compelled to, stooped at each one and kissed them fully on the lips. Each kiss was different. Each one held years of shared history, happiness, joy and sadness for the fate ahead. It was all he could do to show them that they were all in his heart and he in theirs. He got to the end of the line and stopped at Claudia. She had discarded her usual dress for a sleek trouser suit and customised jacket used for foil practice. It was black and brass buttoned in an asymmetrical line from waist to shoulder. Her hair was up and her large, brown eyes were full of the avenging spirit of a woman twice her age. Archie, for the first time, was stung with a pang of love and lust at the vision of womanly assertion that Claudia now presented and his heart broke at the thought that she may never grow into that woman. He kissed her on the forehead and, despite Lupe's wise words about finding a man suitable for her, Claudia threw caution to the wind, grabbed his face with her gloved hands, pulled him down to her mouth and kissed him so passionately that she obliterated years from him. He was sixteen again.

She broke off the kiss and Archie was dazed to discover that the woman remained and that he was the giddy one. She cleared her throat and adjusted her collar, her eyes still, focused and stern. Archie, lost for words, stood beside her and cast his eyes back along the line. The Players were all desperately trying to remain serious and prepared despite witnessing what they would like to have named The Roxy Kiss, should they have survived the assault on The Black Arm. Archie regained composure in just enough time before the Count entered the hall.

Count Abraham von Brandenburg was dressed in his one surviving maroon velvet jacket, black shirt, cream breeches and gold belt. He was armed with two pistols and three daggers in his belt. By his side hung the Sword of Brandenburg, reforged and glowing ready for action. He walked up to the line and stood before them. It was time. He bowed his head slightly, and the Players bowed back in expectance of a rousing speech that would call them to arms, and warn the Other Side that there were to be more souls at the table that night.

Count Abraham von Brandenburg simply drew his sword and pointed it at the necks of each player, one by one moving down the line and fixing each one with his fierce eyes. To each he quietly said "till death?" and every Roxy Player answered back, "till death".

When he came to the end of the line, he sheathed his sword. "Till death," he said aloud, before mounting the lead carriage. The Players followed. Ahead of them, the old man opened the doors to the secret Command HQ and The Roxy Avengers rolled out into a sunset bathed London.

Abigail Hardwoode was standing in front of her dress mirror. She was wearing a black bodystocking. It fitted her well and she looked prepared. However, her eyes seemed lost in a sea of confusion. There was a knock at the door.

"I am nearly ready, my love," she said, the colour washing from her face. She listened for a response. None came. Instead she heard the sounds of footsteps walking away on the other side of the door. The colour returned to her face. She looked down at the bed. Upon it lay a grand dress, resplendent with encrusted jewels and pure gold damask embroidery. She looked back at the mirror, her eyes becoming bright and her cheeks becoming flushed and plump. She smiled a golden smile.

"Showtime, Old Love. One last show," she whispered as she began to put the ball gown on over her tactical suit.

———•◦•———

Of all the sights in the realm, Brighton Pavilion ranked amongst the most overwhelming. Not just for its scale and architectural precision, but the unabashed opulence that sighed off every fixture and fitting as it were a jewel in Aphrodite's belly chain. The bulbous spires glinted in the moonlight and the various pathways criss-crossing over the vast topiary-hedge lined entrance lawn were illuminated by starlight capturing gems, harvested from all four corners of the globe. It was a palace of lust and decadence and there was not a brick or beam that did not know it.

The line of carriages leading up to Brighton Pavilion seemed to never end. It twisted and weaved like a giant snake as the esteemed guests politely waited to enter the grounds. Up and down the line patrolled stern and alert guards, checking each carriage for invitations and credentials. First the driver, then the batmen, then upon granted request, the inhabitants of each cab. Of course, they were only too happy to hand over their names and lineage to the guards as the added security gave the event an even greater sense of exclusivity.

Once through the gates, each carriage was led privately by a suited stable lad to its designated parking marquee. No expense was spared and once the carriage was parked, the horses were unbridled and led to hand-painted enamel drinking troughs and a team of stable hands began rubbing them down and preparing their food. The guests were then taken by a waiting valet from the marquee and across the lawn towards the event itself. While walking over the lawn, the valets politely informed the guests of the order of events, important codes of etiquette, the feast menu and even recounted the wine list with particular attention to personal choices based upon the individual tastes of the guests. By the time each dignitary had made their way across the lawn, through the Japanese gardens and towards the back lawn, they felt so pampered and loved, that they almost believed that they owned the Pavilion.

The back lawn was the evening's beginning venue. It was intended that guests would mill around, drinking and socialising while the garden orchestra serenaded them all with fanciful, but not intrusive music. Should the guests wish; there was also a large lake area on which they could take a row boat, carved in the shape of a giant swan and row around taking drinks from the private barman assigned to each waiting swan. In the middle of the lake there was a pretty island. The lawn itself was flanked by huge palm trees imported specifically for the event. There was a maze, a life size chess board and a white washed gazebo for every tenth guest, discreetly positioned around the edges of the lawn and in amongst the shrubbery. There were even beds hidden within the maze should any amorous and adventurous lovers wish to utilise them.

As the first guests emerged onto the rear lawn, they were greeted by an army of white shirted and slick haired waiters holding trays of magically sparkling wine presented in crystal flutes. And, of course, there was food. The 'dining' area of the lawn held ultra fashionable trestle tables stocked with delicious foods from all known corners of the world. There was to be no sit-down feast and guests were encouraged to help themselves to as much, or as little as they wanted, whenever they wanted. There was everything for everyone. The guests soon adjusted to the unusual method of socialising and an hour after the last guests were on the lawn, people were standing, talking, drinking and eating at the same time. The whole scene was so unheard of and so modern that, at first, many felt ridiculous and too self conscious to even try it. However, after a few crystal flutes, a forward thinking and very hungry woman from Dorset broke precedent and went to the buffet tables. After she had taken the plunge, the rest followed. The armies of waiters worked tirelessly as did the catering staff who ferried silver tray after silver tray from the kitchens and out onto the lawn.

Of course, the conversation was hushed and instilled with an air of undeniable expectancy. The King was yet to emerge and nobody, despite how hungry, thirsty or amorous wanted to be absent when he arrived. They talked and moved fluidly as if they all knew each other, which they did not, however none had known such opulence and decadent living, and so they all felt a conjoined sense of wonder. New friendships were made, businesses formed and broken, engagements announced and addresses exchanged and all of it as an afterthought or distraction to the main event.

Without warning, suddenly the band stopped playing. The guests noted instantly despite their conversations, as they all had one ear alert for any indication of his arrival. As soon as the conductor sat down, a deathly hush descended upon the crowd. They waited in eager silence for thirty three agonising seconds. And then there was an almighty clang of a gong.

The crowd gasped and looked up at the centre dome of Brighton Pavilion, in front of it, upon the huge balcony, stood a hitherto unnoticed gong, twenty feet in diameter. A man built like a galleon and wearing nothing by a leopard skin leotard hoisted a ridiculous sledgehammer and struck the gong a further three times. The sound was deafening.

Upon the last strike, he threw the hammer to the balcony floor and stepped back into the shadows. The sound of the gong was still ringing in the ears of the guests when, directly below the centre dome, on ground level, opened a set of inconspicuous French windows. Compared to the size of the gong and pomp and circumstance of its reveal, the doors seemed insignificant in comparison. Nevertheless, they opened and through them strode the King unaided and walking as if he was a man without a care in the world taking an early-morning stroll. The guests uniformly gasped at the audacity and misdirection of his entrance. He casually walked across the lawn and through the gobsmacked crowd, who parted like the Red Sea. He strolled, hands in pockets and whistling, through them all and up to the bank of the lake, where upon he stepped onto a swan boat and was handed a huge flute of champagne. The oarsman pushed off and rowed the King out forty feet into the lake. The King looked around at the water, at the oarsman, at the night sky and at the guests. He drank his flute down in one go and tossed the glass high, high, high into the air.

The guests watched its ascent as it flew ever higher and seemingly in slow motion. When it reached the zenith of its flight and teetered for a split second on that impossible brink between flight and gravity there then came a crack, a sudden whistle and the glass shattered. The crowd gasped and turned back to the balcony to see a marksman with a smoking rifle. They turned back to the King who was standing proudly on the swan boat as the shards of crystal peppered the water around him like a light shower. He raised his arms slowly and dramatically. He held them up and looked over his guests who were overcome with emotion and anticipation. He smiled.

"Welcome," he said, calmly. And at that, an Armageddon of fireworks erupted around the garden, from the Pavilion and from out of the lake itself. The guests gasped in shock at the sudden burst of sound and colour, and as the spectacle rained down around them, they cheered and laughed and hugged in delight and euphoria, each one acutely aware that they were the right people, at the right time, and the right place. They were the chosen ones.

The King, enraptured with his entrance and his guests' reaction, gave the signal to the oarsman to row him back to the shore. When he alighted, and the waiters stepped in to offer a sparkling green drink with diamonds floating in the glasses to each guest, the King took his time to meet and greet every single guest. And it wasn't a cheap stunt. He genuinely wanted to meet them all, and he remembered their names, and paid attention to their stories of how they came by an invitation and was respectful and dignified when they all gushed with adoration for him. He truly was mad as a box of frogs, but in the most perfect way possible. He was giddy as a child at Christmas to be surrounded by such decadence and light.

The Roxy Avengers rolled towards Brighton in silence. Through the window they could see the horizon explode in multicoloured light. They pressed themselves as best they could against the windows, and those on the driver's bench stood up to see. They each looked at each other in worry. Had they arrived too late? Had all been lost? The sky burned green and purple in a ferocity that, to them, could mean only apocalypse. The orange illuminations stabbed the hearts of each of them as the image of the burning Roxy superimposed itself over their eyes.

"Is that hell?" said Gertie who was stood next to Brandenburg on the driver's bench of the lead carriage. Brandenburg surveyed the skyline.

"If it is," he said finally, "it's quite a welcome!" and he slapped Gertie on the shoulder. Gertie smiled and nodded before sitting back down. He geed up the horses into a light canter.

In the second carriage Lupe sat opposite Claudia, who was turning a sword over upon its point and staring into the hilt. Lupe looked over the Spaniard and though she felt pride that the girl was now sitting there as a woman, she also felt sad that the new look in her eyes told Lupe that the young Claudia, the sweet young girl was now long gone. Lupe leant across and held Claudia's chin. Claudia looked up at Lupe's face, caked in a ton of make-up but still as expressive as ever.

"Claudia" she said, with tears in her eyes. "I never had a daughter..."

Claudia didn't let her finish her sentence. She craned her face to the side and kissed Lupe's thumb with a trio of little kisses. "Yes, you did" she said before returning back to her sword meditation.

In the last carriage, Archie was trying desperately to appear calm. In truth, he was no fighter but a lover and though he was quite prepared to die for his lovers, he was riddled with fear. Desiree, next to him, could sense it. To the Umbrian it was louder than cannons. She shuffled up to him and put her hand on his jigging knee.

"Sorry...I'm sorry," said Archie.

Desiree turned his head to hers. "You will be fine" she said.

"I don't want to..."

"Die? Nobody does...but we will."

"Let you down," he said as he looked to the floor. "Let you down. Let all of you down. I don't want to do that. I want to fight. Even though I am rubbish with a sword...I don't want to let you all down."

Desiree looked across at Danilov, Anya and Valerie who were stung by Mr Enfield's heartfelt honesty and open vulnerability. Danilov turned to Anya and nodded to her. The acrobat leant across the carriage and leant into Archie's ear and whispered something. Archie's leg stopped jigging, his eyes became furnaces and his shoulders rose from their slumped stature. Anya sat back, winked at him and closed her eyes, returning to her normal meditative state.

"I shall be brave," said Archie Enfield, stamping his foot. Nobody in the carriage doubted him for a second.

The lead carriage rolled over the brow of a hill and stopped. Below them and a few miles ahead, they could see Brighton Pavilion.

The fireworks were still painting the sky a thousand colours. Gertie and Brandenburg looked at each other.

"Are you ready?" said the Count. Gertie looked at the Pavilion ahead and contemplated for a few moments. He hopped off of the driver's bench. Brandenburg looked down to see where he was.

"Gertie?"

There was no answer. Brandenburg was about to alight himself when he heard a ruffle, a latch, a creak and chink. Before he could look back over the edge of the bench, Gertie hopped back up and plonked a crate of bottles on the seat. The young man pulled one out, uncorked it and took a monumental swig.

"Well," said Gertie, recoiling from the strength of the booze, "if we're headed to Hell, better we don't arrive thirsty and in need of libation. Cheers!" Gertie threw more booze down his neck. Brandenburg laughed and slapped his thigh.

"Gertie, you fine man, you are the best of all of us!" and he took a bottle from the crate. They clinked and they drank. When they had finished their bottles, Brandenburg dismounted. Gertie walked to the other two parked carriages and banged on the doors. The Players alighted assuming it was time to get into character. Instead, they were greeted by the Count holding a crate of bottles. He rattled them.

"We're about to go to war, Roxy Avengers, my advice to you now is to drink heartily and toast to life."

"'Cos you ain't going to get another chance!" finished Gertie.

The Roxy Playhouse Irregulars did not need asking a second time. They dived into the crate and sat under the multi-coloured night sky and drank their last drinks, finding a few last remaining jokes and anecdotes to share. It was a good half hour.

Chapter Fifty Five

Uninvited Guests

The King had made the rounds and the celebrations had upped a gear. The guests were drunk on the euphoria of the event and from the exceptional sparkling wine. Collars became unbuttoned and chests became flushed. The King was in his element, pinballing from guest to guest, roaring and gorging and wild-eyed with joy. Around the edges of the lawn, his personal guard stood stoically, keeping track of the mad King. Many women, and a few drunken men, had approached the guards and tried to distract them with kisses to the cheeks, or gropes to the groins. The guards remained as statues. Only one of them moved when a former Colonel attempted to grab the soldier's sword and inspect its cleanliness. The guard simply stepped to the side and the Colonel fell face-first into a hedge. The soldier stood back to his position as a few guards hidden in the bushes dragged the Colonel into the foliage and carried him around to the front of the building and ejected him from the party. They watched as he staggered into the Brighton night, swaying and swearing at nothing in particular.

It was approaching ten o'clock when the King, slightly bored of the crisp seaside wind, decided to walk inside. He did so without pomp or circumstance. He looked up at the sky, breathed in, tossed his flute to the grass and walked towards the Pavilion mid-conversation. The guests looked at each other, slightly bemused at his erratic behaviour. The guards flanking the guests moved in subtly and quietly behind the party and tightened their circle, politely forcing the guests to gather together and proceed to follow the king into the great venue.

The guards then checked the perimeter and then followed the guests in, locking the doors to the lawn behind them and bolting them shut. The King kicked open the grand ballroom door and marched into the ballroom which his chest puffed out and his hands on his hips. The room was enormous. The door way led directly under the mezzanine level which held a giant staircase that snaked around the walls and down onto the floor in a giant horseshoe shape. Directly opposite the entrance in which the King had strode, faced another set of doors. These led into the reception hall and out onto the front lawn. In effect, the King had led his guests into the main ballroom via the back entrance. He walked across the giant dance floor towards the main entrance doors, stopped and turned around. The guests all filed in, aghast at the splendour of the room. Like the lawn, there were trestle tables of food lining the walls. However, the main attractions were the wine fountains. Great spouting solid silver pools and fountains shaped like Lilly pads with mermaids reclining on them, spitting red and white wine high into the air and down into the Lilly-pond shaped fountain baths. In total there were six positioned around the edges of the central dance area. Above the fountains hung grand crystal chandeliers which reflected the dazzling light of the silver fountains and mixed it with the moonbeams shining in from the oval skylights. The room was bathed in silver light. The guests felt as though they had walked into Olympus itself and quietly dispersed around the fountains.

Once inside, the guards, silent and discreet, filed in and stood around the edges of the room. The King picked up a silver bucket from a waiter and scooped it into a white wine pond. He roared with laughter and heaved the bucket into the air, letting the entire contents cascade all over him. The guests cheered and they began drinking wildly from the fountains all around them.

The King laughed once more and clapped his hands, sending an echo louder than the giant gong above the pavilion around the room. The guests jumped in shock. Suddenly, the left wall fell to the ground. But it did not fall as if it was made up brick and mortar. It fell as it was made of cloth. An intricate and masterfully painted matte curtain that duped the guests into thinking the room was solid on all sides. As the curtain fell to the ground, it revealed another ballroom of equal size and with another six wine fountains. The Pavilion, it seemed was some sort of magical venue that held unimaginable possibilities. At the far end of the double-sized ballroom sat a full orchestra who struck up an unusually fast paced and chaotically arranged piece of music that none of the guests had ever heard, but the beat was so infections and overbearing that they held no control over their feet and they all ran into the space and began to dance furiously, drunk now on more than just sparkling wine and the King's presence but also on the evidential proof that magic existed in the world and they were a part of it.

———•———

The waves lapped against the shingle shore on the Brighton waterfront. Most of the culverts were closed and the port slept. Those culverts that had been converted into bars and live music venues were still serving a few young and happy people, dressed in radical clothes and enjoying coloured drinks that smelt of pineapple and vanilla. They hung close to the bars and let the sound of the lapping shore remind them of where they were.

The darkness of the night masked the carriages rolling across the shoreline. Occasionally, a moonbeam might catch a horse's bridle, or glint off a silver running board, but generally, the convoy of black carriages rolled unseen through the breakers.

They were swift and silent. The wheels had been replaced with skids and the horses pulled them along with ease. The drivers, hidden in the darkness, were all wearing black cowls. The Black Arm moved as shadows towards their goal.

Lord De Locke, Abigail and Nathanial Whit sat in silence in the lead carriage. They were in their uniforms and ready for their ascension. Even De Locke's wheezing breath had fallen away. They were ghosts. Above them, Kemble sat next to the driver. He was sharpening the blades of his throwing knives against a pumice stone. The blades were painted black and did not reflect anything other than the murderous desire of their master. He wanted death, and they were eager to find it for him. His finished sharpening the throwing knifes and attached them to a customised strap on his bicep, making them available for use at the blink of an eye.

As the convoy of Black Arm dissidents rolled through the breakers the drivers could see, to their left, the glow of the culvert bars, the distant din of drunken revelry, and beyond that, the light of Brighton Pavilion. There was only one other object that remained unseen even to them. High above the convoy there sailed a strange futuristic flying contraption. It was a large, triangular shaped winged sail under which hung its pilot. The gliding wing swooped and circled around the convoy. The pilot was wearing a tight black suit and mask.

The wing swooped low, bringing up the rear of the convoy. The pilot navigated the approach to the rear carriage and, as it was about to fly over it, the pilot pitched the nose up, bringing it to sharp, silent halt. The pilot landed at the back of the carriage, the driver remaining oblivious of the hijacker behind him. The pilot pulled a metal clasp on their chest and, just as a gust of wind came, the wings detached, caught the breeze and flew out to sea, lost and unseen. The pilot scooted down on the carriage and crept up behind the driver. There was little time to lose. The pilot listened to the sound of the waves breaking against the shore and, on the third wave, in time with the breaker, a dagger was drawn and run across the driver's throat killing him instantly. The pilot grabbed the reigns and the carriage carried along its path, horse and passengers oblivious to what had occurred. The pilot lifted the dead driver off of the bench and laid him down on the roof and tied his ankles to the handrail so that he didn't fall off and draw attention. The pilot turned back to the horses and removed their mask. The cascade of raven-hair fell down and her fierce green eyes glinted in the moonlight. The convoy was almost at its destination.

A hundred soldiers hidden in the dense woodland at the very edge of the grounds to Brighton Pavilion waited. They were young, dedicated, trained and ready. They were dressed in the garments of the King's Specials: blood red tunics with black piping and the special insignia upon their shoulders - that of a prancing horse and a spear wielding knight. Though their tunics were red, they were not bright enough to penetrate the gloom of the dense forest.

"How long now?" one whispered to his squad leader. The squad leader looked up at the moon and then across to the platoon commander. The platoon commander did not turn around, instead held up his hand and gave a series of bizarre hand signals. The squad leader turned back to his man.

"Soon," he whispered. He looked around to the rest of his squad and nodded. Along the line of men there came an almost imperceptible 'schnickt' of steel as bayonets were fixed. Like Kemble's throwing knives, these were painted black to avoid catching the moonlight. A shadow moved among them. The men could not quite see it, but they knew it was there. As the shadow passed them, they stood to attention. The shadow passed by and drifted up to the platoon commander and rested next to him.

The platoon commander, face smeared in boot-polish and chewing on a bullet looked out at the edge of the Pavilion grounds.

"In position, sir" he whispered to the shadow next to him.

"Perfect" said the shadow, in the voice of Invisible Noel.

"Will our ringers do their jobs?"

"They will," said Invisible Noel.

"What is the signal to advance?"

"Red flare, fired from the centre dome."

"Understood, sir"

The shadow drifted away from the platoon commander and back into the forest.

———•·•———

Brandenburg, Archie and Desiree had penetrated the perimeter of the grounds, crossed the lawn and were now outside a service entrance to the Pavilion. They had left the rest of the Players on the hill. They each had their roles, and Brandenburg and the other two had to get into the building. The mission was too important to run with only a single man on point, and so Brandenburg, his fiancée and their batman were the perfect three to get inside. Brandenburg and Desiree were known and expected and so would not be challenged.

"Ok, my loves," said Brandenburg, "This is it, curtains up."

Archie breathed out nervously.

"Just keep your eyes on each other, and on your surroundings. Desiree, Archie, when it's time: I expect nothing from you except acts of extreme violence. This is real. We are no longer artists, we are lions. There are a lot of innocents in there and there is a little window of opportunity to get them out. We have to act fast and hard. Save as many as you can."

The two accomplices nodded.

"Alright," said the Count, "see you in the Other Side." He bent down and picked the lock to the door. It creaked open and they slipped inside.

———•—•———

The Black Arm convoy halted beside a dark culvert hidden underneath a wooden pier. As the carriages stopped, the raven-haired woman quickly grabbed the black cowl from the dead driver lashed to the roof and put it on. She alighted as the rest of the dissidents stepped out of the carriages.

Nathanial Whit walked up to the iron grate at the culvert's entrance and opened it. De Locke and Abigail stepped inside, followed by Whit and Kemble and then the rest of The Black Arm.

The culvert was wide enough to walk two abreast. Nathanial lit a torch and used it to light six others that had been prepared and were hanging on the sides of the stone passage. He handed them down the line and they began to progress along the stone tunnel. At the rear, the raven-haired woman began to make her way up the line until she was walking behind Nathanial and Kemble. There she stayed as they walked.

The dancing and revelry was at its height. People had abandoned most of their manners and were simply enjoying being alive. Men and women splashed and paddled in the fountains and openly kissed and fondled each other by the trestle tables. The King, drunk and half naked was dancing with fourteen topless women who were spinning each other around and laughing like possessed nymphs. The guards looked on with stern and unremitting eyes.

The Black Arm marched down the stone passage until it opened out into large, arched vaults. As they walked through the vaults, Abigail looked around her to see barrels and barrels of gunpowder and dynamite. Her heart leapt as she realised that they must be below the Pavilion and that The Black Arm had rigged it with enough explosives to blow the whole place from memory. This was not in any of the notes and plans in the diary. This was new.

Lord De Locke halted in the centre of a great atrium and looked up. They were directly below the Pavilion. The Black Arm filed into the atrium and stood around the edges. Lord. De Locke removed his cowl and let the cold water drip from the ceiling onto his grey, shrivelled face. He stuck out his vile tongue and tasted the acrid water.

"We are here, down in the bowels of the beast. We are soon to be reborn." He hissed as he put his cowl back on and turned to Abigail. He stroked her face.

"My dear, look how far we have come."

"It is upon us, our greatest moment!" she whispered.

"No, my dear, not your greatest moment," said De Locke as Nathanial Whit stepped to the side of her and removed her cowl. De Locke stepped in close and rested his face against hers.

"You have been a busy, busy, busy little bee, haven't you?"

"My love?"

De Locke smiled his sickly smile. "Fighting to the last, you spies, so brave but so, so badly trained."

"What are you saying, Rafe?"

"The King's Specials are waiting outside, aren't they? Do you think you could stay next to me for six years and think I wouldn't know who you really are?"

Abigail froze. She had been made. She motioned to protest. De Locke shushed her with a cold finger.

"You have done everything I wanted. Now, we will take the King, kill the rest and destroy the Specials too. All thanks to you, my love!"

A Black Arm dissident took their cue and stepped up. De Locke nodded to Nathanial who held Abigail tightly from behind. Abigail did not scream, but instead spat in the face of her fake husband.

"See you in hell," she hissed. De Locke nodded to the dissident who wasted no time in drawing a dagger and plunging it into Abigail's stomach. Abigail lurched and gurgled. The knife went in a further three times. Nathanial felt her body grow limp and he released her. She slumped to the floor and lay in a freezing puddle. The Black Arm killer casually tossed the murder weapon onto the body.

Lord De Locke looked over her body. He watched as her eyes greyed over and her skin became sallow. He kicked her. She slumped onto her face. He looked around to the rest of The Black Arm.

"Now," his hissed, "let us step out of the shadows."

He turned and rushed down a small tunnel to the left of the atrium with Nathanial Whit close by his side. The rest of The Black Arm followed them, stepping over the body of Abigail Hardwoode as they ran.

—•—•—

The remaining Roxy Players stood on the brow of the hill and looked out over the Pavilion. They had finished their drinks and were feeling happily confident. And they needed to be. Gertie helped Danilov onto the driver's bench and handed him a looking glass. Danilov looked over the upper windows of the compound until he found something suitable. He handed the glass back.

"There's our entry point," he said, "three to the left, top level, iron balcony. You see it?"

Gertie looked through the eye-piece, "I see it. Christ Danilov, that's one helluva way. Can you get us there?"

"Trust me."

Danilov and Gertie jumped off of the carriage and faced the other Players.

"Alright," said Gertie, "we have our way in. High window, long walk. But you know..."

"Nothing is ever easy," said Lupe.

"Exactly," agreed Gertie.

"My man can do it!" said Valerie enthusiastically, "he can do anything!"

"Well alright then!" said Gertie, laughing. "Let's get into position!"

The time had come. The guests were now behaving in an orgiastic manner. The guard atop the mezzanine level nodded to the guard by the main entrance. That guard turned around and pulled down a giant crossbeam. The guard by the windows received a nod from the lead guard on the stairwell and turned to the windows and pulled the shutters closed and barred them. The lead guard walked down the steps and passed the guests who were too busy taking off clothes to notice what was happening, and walked towards the door underneath the mezzanine level. He opened it to see Lord De Locke, Nathanial Whit, Kemble and one hundred and twenty three hooded and cloaked Black Arm dissidents waiting. The Lead Guard smiled as De Locke walked passed him.

As soon as he entered the main hall, the rest of the Kings Guard's took off the tunics and unbuttoned their collars to unpack a hidden black cowl. They turned their jackets inside out to reveal the jet-black lining and draped them back over their shoulders, clasping them at the neck. The Black Arm now numbered over two hundred.

Of course, the King and his guests had noticed none of this. Lord De Locke led his personal Black Arm troupe into the main hall and turned them all to face the orgy. He signalled to the guards flanking the hall who all drew their pistols and fired them into the air. The sound was deafening and was instantly met with screams from the guests.

Lord De Locke raised his arms.

"Lords and ladies!" he said calmly. The screams continued.

"Lords and ladies!" he repeated a little louder.

The shocked crowd calmed down a little bit. Lord De Locke removed his cowl to the disgusted gasps from the guests. His green eyes glinted and his smiled curled up the side of his haggard face.

"Now then," he whispered, "where is your King?" A hush descended upon the room.

None of The Black Arm noticed one of their number slip back, unseen out of the entrance from whence they had come.

Chapter Fifty Six

Heads Roll

A thin man stood up from the centre of a red wine fountain.

"I am the King!" he said in a stern and brave voice. De Locke squinted at him and smiled.

"I am the King!" came another from the back of the room as a fatter, older man stood up.

"No, I am the King!" four more shouts came.

"Six kings?" De Locke smirked. "How blessed we are." He signalled to The Black Arm guards lining the room to marshal the six men forward. They did so and brought them towards De Locke and Whit.

De Locke looked them over.

"Lords Smithe, Wellingbourgh, Field Marshal Stebson-Peet, Commander Brakespeare, Sir Remington, and that means you must be General Stewart."

Lord De Locke smiled as the men looked at the floor.

"The King's own protectors, his favourites, and his loves, how noble and sweet of you to protect him." Lord De Locke stood up and walked passed them and into the main hall proper. Behind him Kemble stepped up to the six kneeling men.

De Locke walked amongst the drunk and scared men until he found what he was looking for. King George cowered underneath a pile of naked women.

"There you are," he said as he fished the King out and stood him up. De Locke turned him to face the six men. He nodded to Kemble who drew his sword.

Brandenburg, Desiree and Archie crept through the Pavilion, surprised at its desertion.

"Where is everyone? Are we too late?" said Desiree as they rounded a corridor. Brandenburg looked in a side room. It was impeccable. Not a soul had been in that room since it had been decorated. He stepped back into the corridor.

"This is a little eerie, Old Love," said Archie as they walked on. As they rounded a second corner, Archie, bringing up the rear, turned back to see if they were being followed. Suddenly a flash of black caught his eye as a figure darted across the adjacent corridor. He turned back to Brandenburg and Desiree. There were not in front. He was standing at a crossroads.

"Benji" he whispered, "Desi?" He was alone. "Bollocks!" he looked back down the corridor to where he had seen the flash of black. He swore under his breath and dashed off to follow it.

Brandenburg entered a private chamber, decked in canary yellow paint and with a solitary harpsichord in the corner. At the other end of the room there was yet another door.

"That leads out into the ballroom. Onto the mezzanine," he whispered. Desiree swallowed.

"After you," she said.

Brandenburg looked back "Where's Archie?"

Desiree looked into the corridor. "Archie!" she whispered.

"Balls!" said Brandenburg, He looked at his watch, and then back to the door, then back to Desiree.

"Do it," she said. Brandenburg nodded and walked slowly over to the door.

———•◦•———

The Roxy Players had driven their carriages to the edge of the copse and were parallel to the front east face of the Pavilion. Gertie secured the lead carriage, bolting it into the ground and leading the horses into a secluded paddock to graze. Lupe and Valerie heaved a large trunk out of the back and opened it. Claudia lifted the contents out and handed them to Anya who laid them out on the floor. Once the trunk was empty the Players crowded around it.

"Right," said Gertie, "how do you build the bugger?"

Tobias tutted and then bent down. He studied the parts, looking over the rivets and bolts pulling everything apart and placing it together again. He went to work and before the Players could sigh in understanding of it all, he had constructed the huge surface-to-air-crossbow. He held out his hand and clicked her fingers. Valerie placed a large bolt in his hands. Tobias loaded it.

"Wait!" said Lupe, "you have to tie it off," and she bent down and tied a wire to the end of the bolt and handed the other end to Anya who tied it to the top rail of the carriage.

"Alright!" said Valerie, "Let's go!"

Tobias nodded and turned to the sights. He wound the gauging wheels which controlled the elevation and direction until he was satisfied. He stood up and turned to face the Players. They held up their crossed fingers and closed their eyes. Tobias tutted at their mistrust and, without looking, kicked the release with his wooden leg. The crossbow fired, sending the bolt and wire into the night sky.

From the far area of the woods, the platoon commander watched through his looking glass, tracking the bolt as it flew. He smiled in amazement as the bolt hit the railings of the balcony and wrapped around it eight times, pulling the wire tight.

The Roxy Players applauded as quietly as they could after Gertie had verified the hit, and Anya and Danilov had verified the capabilities of the wire. Tobias bowed.

"No time to hang around, friends," said Gertie as he jumped off the driver's plate and began strapping on weapons.

"Anya," he said, "you go first, secure the balcony and count us in."

Anya smiled coyly at the confident and take-charge stage hand. She jumped up onto the rope and scuttled up into the night.

———•·•———

Archie stalked through the corridors trying desperately to track the black shape that had caught his eye. He drew his sword and held it out. The point was shaking as his fear was getting the better of him. The sweat began to break out across his forehead. Every sound he thought he heard every movement he thought he saw made him leap and jab into the emptiness. He stopped for a second to compose himself. He jabbed the sword into the floor so that it stood upon its point. He jumped up and down on the spot and shook off, alternating his facial expressions from grimace to gurn.

"Big man face, small man face, big man face, small man face," he repeated over and over again. He soon calmed down. He drew the sword out of the carpet and was about to advance when he heard the slide of wood on wood and a gush of wind. He spun around to see, twenty feet down the corridor an open window and a wisp of black material shoot out into the night air. He dashed down the corridor to the window and stuck his head out. There was no balcony or foot rail, but instead a sheer sixty feet drop. He turned over and looked up to see, directly above him, the same wisp of black material disappear over the wall and onto the roof.

"You have to be joking," he said as he put his sword between his teeth and swung his leg out over the window ledge. He looked around for some way of scaling it. There was a series of concrete gargoyles running up the side of the wall eight feet away. They were small perhaps protruding only ten inches from the wall.

"Alright Archie boy, time to meet Old Nick!"

Archie leapt from the window and cleared the eight feet, just, and managed to grab one of the gargoyles with his left hand. He laughed hysterically for a few moments as he dangled from the gargoyle. He composed himself and managed to gain a better purchase upon it. He placed his feet upon the wall and managed to 'walk' himself up the wall until the gargoyle above was in reach. He grabbed it and carried on his ascent until he reached the finale gargoyle. He managed to scramble up onto it, so that he was standing, precariously, upon it and pressed flat against the wall. He looked up. The edge of the wall was two feet out of reach. He would have to spring, and hope to grab it.

"Jesus," he said to himself, through the sword blade still between his teeth.

"Nothing is ever easy, is it?"

He sprung as best he could and threw his arms up to the edge. He was short by six inches. He reached the peak of his flight and his eyes widened as he realised he did not have it in him to clear the distance. He was about to begin his descent when an arm appeared over the edge and grabbed his wrist. He hung there, suspended in midair for two seconds. He looked up. He could not see who was holding him.

———•—•———

The water from the vault ceiling dripped onto Abigail's body. She convulsed suddenly and sat up, spluttering the cold puddlewater from her lungs and struggling to catch her breath. She ripped the cloak from her as it was pressing against her throat and hindering her recovery. She looked around. To the side lay the murder weapon. She picked it up and touched her finger against the daggers tip. She pressed it. The blade disappeared into the hilt; a stage knife. She coughed and spluttered again as she got to her feet and ripped off her dress to reveal a vest with four empty pigs bladders attached, the bloody contents of which smeared down the rest.

"Thank you, Giselle," she said as she unclipped it. It slopped to the floor. She wriggled out of her dress to reveal her black suit underneath. She tied her hair up and looked around at the barrels of gunpowder and dynamite. She approached the largest pile.

"Right then, you son of bitch" she said, blowing on her fingers to dry them out, "you want to play rough with me?"

Brandenburg opened the door to the mezzanine level and he and Desiree crept out onto the landing. They moved with the grace and delicacy of highly trained backstage personnel. The guards on the landing did not notice as they crept along to the far side, away from them. For that vantage point, they could peer through the banister. Below them, they could see the back of Kemble as he stood over the six kneeled men. Ahead of Kemble, they could see a gargantuan room containing a hundred or so guests in varying states of undress. Then they saw the two hundred or so men and women in black cowls. Finally, they located The King, standing next to Lord De Locke.

"My God," whispered Desiree, "what do we do?"

Brandenburg sat back against the banisters and tried to think. He was lost.

"Say goodnight to your favourites," floated De Locke's wretched voice through the hallway.

Brandenburg and Desiree looked back through the banisters to see Kemble swing his sword down hard and true. A man's head left its body and spiralled into the air. There was an instantaneous outburst of screaming. Desiree went to join in, but Brandenburg grabbed her mouth and pulled her into his chest and turned his back on the awful scene below.

——•◦•——

Abigail had worked feverishly in disarming the barrels and now a large majority of them had been safely decommissioned. It was delicate work, but despite her cold hands and fearful heart, her training and experience saw her through.

Only a few remained and she had stacked them according to how she wanted them. Though she was not the munitions expert that Invisible Noel was, she was more than competent in the intricacies of structural engineering. She knew what she needed to do to achieve what she wanted. She had carefully rolled four barrels into position on the blind side of a column, far away from the rest. Her plan was to detonate them, blow the tunnel to block any escape that way, direct the blast upwards into the Pavilion and, as she had estimated it, away from the hostages and towards an area that would cause the most panic and disruption. The King was there and he needed to be extracted. The only way she could do that was through chaos. Like the arrow that finds its target through the melee of war, she was focused on him. Create confusion and get to the King. Everything else would take care of everything else. She believed in Invisible Noel and his ultimate endgame.

Abigail carefully prised off the lid of the fourth barrel and scooped out some gunpowder. She then carefully made a trail along the dark corridor, away from the vault and towards the entrance into the Pavilion. From there she would light the fuse, enter the Pavilion and wait for the chaos to really start. She made five more trips with the scoop of gunpowder to make sure the trail would ignite and continue over the damp cobblestones.

"What do you want with us?" whined the King as De Locke held him tight.

"With us? Nothing," said De Locke, "with you, everything. Mr Whit, if you will!"

Nathanial Whit bowed and forty dissidents stepped forward, weapons raised on the guests.

"Ladies and Gentlemen!" cried Nathanial.

The desperate crowd fell silent.

"Now that we have your attention..." he kicked the head of the executed guest into a fountain, "if you would come with Mr Kemble here."

Kemble bowed to them all. The dissidents rounded up the guests and proceeded to march them out of the hallway leaving De Locke with the King and The Black Arm Guards.

Above them, Brandenburg and Desiree turned back in dismay at the sound of Kemble's name mentioned and there they saw their nemesis leading the guests out.

"They are going to execute them all," whispered Brandenburg.

"No they're not," said Desiree and she leant across and kissed Brandenburg on the forehead. "For the Playhouse," she kissed him again, "for me," and then she placed her third kiss on his lips "for

Herschel. See you on the other side, indeed" and she disappeared to track Kemble and the guests. Brandenburg turned back to watch the events below.

———•••———

Archie grabbed the arm that was holding him with his other hand for extra security. The arm heaved and he managed to get his feet against the wall. The arm heaved again and, with its help, he managed to walk himself up until he could reach the edge. He grabbed it and pulled himself up and over. He fell down the other side, collapsing on his back upon the roof, panting wildly. He looked to his side to see a 'Black Arm' dissident standing over him. He scrambled to his feet and went to grab his sword. It wasn't there. He looked down before realising it was still in his teeth. He spat the sword out and caught the handle, and raised the blade to his rescuer's throat.

"Thank you for saving me...but now we must duel! En Garde!" he declared as menacingly as he could. The Black Arm dissident laughed an exotic laugh which carried an accent he could not place. His sword lowered. The dissident lowered their cowl and Archie's eyes widened in shock.

"You!" he said to the raven-haired woman. "I didn't expect to see you here," he said incredulously. She stepped into a moonbeam and revealed to him her perfect features.

"Did I not say we would meet again by the sea?"

"Oh yes...you did."

"And here we are."

"Yes...here we are," said Archie, completely forgetting the real reason why he was in Brighton and on the roof of the Pavilion.

"So, you are with them!" he said, trying to not fall under her spell. She shook her head.

"Then you are with *them*?" he said, slightly confused. She smiled and shook her head.

"Who are you with?"

"It's complicated," she said, "I'm freelance."

"Oh, I see. So, tonight?"

"Tonight, I'm on your side," she said, winking at him.

He smiled. "Oh, alright," he said jovially as he sheathed his sword. He held out his hand.

"My name is Archie" he said with his best grin. The woman stepped up to him and took his hand.

"My name is Giselle" she said and before he had time to react, she pulled him into a long, deep kiss. As they did so, Giselle drew a pistol into the air and fired. There was no gunshot, only a slight whistle followed by a plume of grey smoke which shot up one hundred feet into the clear night sky before exploding into a bright red starburst.

From the edge of grounds, the red flare signalled to the waiting troops. Suddenly, the shadow that lingered amongst them became front and centre. Invisible Noel raised a sword and, without a rallying cry, ran forward towards the Pavilion. The troops silently followed.

———•◦•———

Kemble and a troupe of cloaked men led the guests through the Pavilion and into a stately library. Along the way, a few of the more courageous guests had attempted to seize a weapon only to be beaten down and held there long enough for Kemble to come back from the front of the group to the troublemaker and slit his throat and spray blood over the terrified guests less they think about trying something similar. After the third occasion he found the guests to be completely compliant. They were his and he had never felt as respected and

awed. He had never felt so alive. He opened the door to the library
and the guests were marched in. Kemble then positioned eighteen
Black Arm guards by the doorway to prevent any escape attempts.
The guards knew it was a suicide post and they accepted their charge
with no protestations. Once all the hostages were inside the library,
Kemble told them, quietly and calmly but with undeniable relish, that
they were standing directly above a very large and angry stockpile of
dynamite and that since they served no real purpose to the plan, there
were about to become tinder to the forthcoming apocalypse. He
smiled as he closed the door on them and disappeared down the
corridor.

From a side room, Desiree watched as Kemble marched on. She
looked back at the corridor. She needed the Players to assist her.
From the room she was hidden in, she had only one way out; the
small window on the far side. She walked over to the curtains and
opened them. She smiled. On the balcony on the other side stood
Anya.

Desiree opened the window pulled her in, hugging her tight.

"What a stroke of luck! I was just in need of you!" she said.
Anya pointed out to the gloom. Desiree squinted and nearly burst out
laughing to see, from within the darkness, Danilov trudging up the
wire carrying Lupe Darling on his back. It was such an effort that he
did not have the strength to place her daintily into the balcony, but
instead heaved her over his shoulders and dumped her into the room.
The gargantuan woman rolled into the chamber, burying Desiree and
Anya inside the folds of her dress. She rolled over and up onto her
feet in a single fluid motion and stood up in front of a mirror and
started checking her make-up. She paid no attention to the reflection
of Desiree and Anya helping each other up or Danilov turning on his
heel and running back to collect the next player. Instead she kept

fixing her hair and make-up and repeating "Dear George, I am here, I am here, I am here."

———•·•———

Abigail backed herself against the wall and looked down at the trail of gunpowder. She took a match from her pocket and struck it against the wall. It lit first time. She dropped it onto the trail, igniting it instantly. It rocketed along. She blew a kiss to the barrels up ahead and opened the door, disappearing into the Pavilion.

———•·•———

De Locke frogmarched The King over to the remaining five men, still held and bowed at the feet of Nathanial Whit who had taken over execution duties from Kemble.

"What do you want from me?" whimpered the King, trying to keep pace despite his trousers being held around his ankles.

"We want this," said De Locke, running his bony finger over his throat. "We want these" running his finger over the Kings arms. "Do you know who we are?"

The King whimpered.

"We are The Black Arm and we have lived in the shadows since time began. And now, we will reveal ourselves."

He brought the King to the five men and kicked him in the back of his knees so that he fell down to face them. De Locke stood above The King, revelling in his moment.

"These lovers, your guests, they mean nothing. We will dispose of them, tonight. We will use them to fuel our fire. To baptise us! We are 'Black Arm'. We are born of fire. And we will use your vain and sick socialites to birth us. We will rise up. But do not worry, you will survive this. We have no reason to kill you."

De Locke nodded to Nathanial who promptly decapitated the hostage facing the King, spraying him with blood. The remaining hostages struggled to get free, but there were held fast. De Locke kicked the trembling King in the ribs, forcing him to move along to the next hostage while the body of the last slumped to the floor in a wet heap.

"You will be spared and tomorrow, when the nation is reeling from the deaths of their elite, you will be presented to the public."

Nathanial Whit cut another head off and the King, breathing heavily and eyes panicked, was moved along to the next hostage.

"The beaten, the poor, the dirty and the dying, those are the ones that matter. And to them we will present you upon London Bridge."

Another head flew through the air.

"You will be hung, drawn and quartered"
Another head. The King began to cry as he came face to face with the last, General Stewart.

"Why? Tell me why?" wailed the King. De Locke and Whit laughed maniacally

"My King!" said General Stewart through gritted teeth, "My King, look at me. Stop crying. Look at me!"

While the dissidents laughed, the King looked at the General. "Be strong" he said. The King clenched his jaw.

"Why?" said De Locke? "The why is for us!"

"BE STRONG! Shouted General Stewart before his head flew from his body. It slumped down to the side.

Lord De Locke helped the King to his feet.

"Time to go, my King" he said.

Above them all, Brandenburg rallied himself. He had sat and watched six men executed and done nothing about it. He was overcome with despair. He grabbed his sword and leapt up onto the banister rail, high above and behind the bastards and screamed the first words that came to his mind. De Locke and Nathanial turned around and looked up to see Count Abraham von Brandenburg stood high on the banister rail with his sword in the air. Whit dropped his sword in disbelief at seeing the Count alive and ready for action.

"BEHOLD! BRANDENBURG!" he bellowed again, sending his words booming around the hall and sending fear straight into the hearts of all.

"My God" whispered Whit. "He's alive"

Brandenburg pointed his sword at Whit and prepared to leap off the banister and take them all on.

The trail of flaming gunpowder reached the kegs and Brighton Pavilion exploded.

Chapter Fifty Seven

Behold! Brandenburg

Invisible Noel was leading the charge across the lawn when the explosion decimated the left wing of the Pavilion, sending masonry and mortar two hundred feet into the air, scattering out over land and sea. As the debris rained down around them, the army charged on, undeterred. Inside the Pavilion, however, it was a different matter.

Kemble, who was on his way back to join his master was the nearest to the blast. As he ran down the corridor, he felt the floorboards ripple unnaturally. There was a sudden suction of air. He stopped running and turned around. The end of the corridor seemed to contort and buckle. He tilted his head like a confused dog, before the blast tore through the building and blowing the vile wretch through a window and out into the bushes by the lake.

Inside the main hall, Brandenburg, standing high on the banister and brandishing his new sword was blown forward, falling twenty feet, and crashing into a red wine fountain. The Black Arm guards, De Locke, the King and Nathanial were blown back across the cavernous dance hall as the wall supporting the great staircase upon which Brandenburg had stood, exploded into the room. The banisters whizzed and spun like deadly spears through the air, pinning some unfortunate guards and skewering them to the walls and floor. The force rushing into the room swept the first great chandelier clear of its mount.

Nathanial Whit, with his trained reflexes, dived across the room and rolled over the King and De Locke, protecting them from the shower of crystal shards that fell all around. The chandelier's skeleton smashed into the ground and peppered four unfortunate guards, shearing their exposed skin from their bodies. After the detonation came the fireball. Brandenburg was getting to his feet, as were the others, when an awful hiss and backwind suddenly swept through the hall and back into the gaping hall where the staircase used to be.

Nathanial picked up De Locke and the King and, with all his might, shoved them into a fountain and dived in on top of them. Brandenburg turned back to the hole in the wall and gasped as he saw an inferno storming forth. He dived back into the wine-pool as the fire belched into the hall in one monstrous blast of flame.

———◆·◆———

Danilov had just managed to carefully place Tobias in the room when the whole building rocked and the iron balcony gave way under the strain. The wire went slack instantly and Danilov lost his balance and toppled to the side. Before anyone else could react, Tobias, finding himself half in the room and half hanging out where the balcony used to be, reached out and grabbed Danilov's hand. The weight of Danilov carried Tobias out of the window and he, in turn, was grabbed by Gertie and Valerie. Desiree, Anya and Lupe rushed over and grabbed hold of Gertie's belt and as one, they heaved the rest of the Players into the room and they fell into a relieved heap on the floor.

"What in the blazes was that?" said Gertie.

"Twelve barrels of dynamite on a shape-charge," said Tobias matter-of-factly, "most likely placed against a supporting vault structure, designed to direct the blast upwards. There will be a flash fire, and then it will burn itself out,"

The rest of the Players looked at him, quizzically.

"I would imagine," he continued, "that it was controlled to block something, a stone passageway, perhaps an escape route. Keep people here. Doubtful it was designed to do more than that"

"That's sure one way of ensuring people don't leave!" spluttered Valerie

"I think," countered Tobias, "That they did somewhat overbake the cake. Amateur"

Desiree and Gertie helped the others to their feet and they checked them for wounds. Finally, they all turned to Lupe, who was beached on her back and all heaved her onto her feet.

Desiree went to the door and peeked into the corridor. The eighteen guards were still standing firm. She went back into the room and drew her sword.

"How many?" Gertie said.

"More than ten, less than twenty, I think" she said.

The Players drew their swords and were about to charge out when there was an almighty smash and a large bundle tumbled through the skylight and landed on the four-poster bed with such force that the canopy collapsed down upon the object. The Players fell back in shock, the glass from the almond shaped window falling all around. Desiree was closest to the bed and first on her feet. She drew her sword, on the other side of the bed stood Gertie. They nodded to three and, with the tips of their rapiers, lifted the canopy and threw it aside. Their swords dropped and their eyes rolled: the bundle that had fallen through the ceiling was none other than Archie

Enfield underneath some mystery woman, entangled in an amorous embrace.

Gertie cleared his throat. Archie's hand stopped moving over the woman's back, and moved up to her hair. His left hand moved some of the thick, glossy hair to the side to reveal his bright eyes looking out. They widened when he saw Gertie and then Claudia next to him with her raised stern eyebrow.

Archie tapped the woman on the shoulder. She looked around and, seeing that they were no longer standing on the roof, climbed off of the man.

"My loves!" said Archie, struggling to do up his belt and appear focused, "it's not what it looks like, honest!"

Giselle gracefully climbed off of the bed and paid no attention to the dumbstruck Players and went straight to the mirror to fix her hair. Archie, still trying to recover his composure, went to roll off the bed however he got caught in his scabbard and fell off onto the floor. He instantly sprang to his feet seemingly back to his old self. He brushed his hair to the side and marched to the door.

"Right then, Old Loves, to war!" he said.

Desiree cleared her throat. Archie turned back to the room and shrugged. The raised eyebrows directed him towards Giselle, who was now applying some make-up.

"Oh yes, ladies and gentlemen, this is...this is...she is...er" he didn't quite know how to introduce the woman, as he didn't quite know who she was. Giselle turned to the room, adjusting her weapons belt. She walked over to the door and peeked out. She looked back into the room, and from her belt pulled two coin sized discs. She kissed them both, opened the door and threw the discs down the corridor. Giselle side-stepped beside the door and slowly sunk to her knees, placing her hands over her ears. She looked up at the incredulous and confused room full of Players.

There was an explosion in the corridor, and the door to the room blew off its hinges. The smoke billowed into the room, and by the time it had cleared, Giselle had gone. The Players coughed and wheezed and staggered into the corridor.

The corridor stank of powder and the smoke was thick. Up ahead they could make out the shape of a figure bent over some bodies. The smoke died down and Giselle was standing amongst the dead guards. She had harvested their cloaks and cowls.

She walked up to the Players and dumped the cowls in Gertie's arms before running off down the corridor. Archie ran after her.

"Where are you going?" shouted Lupe.

"To the King, to save the King!" he shouted back. "Save as many as you can, Old Loves!" and he disappeared into the smoky corridor.

"The King!" said Lupe to herself, "the King! My Georgie!" and she hitched up her dressed and ran off into the smoke.

"Lupe!" shouted Gertie who then followed after, hotly pursued by Anya and Danilov.

Valerie and Claudia went to give chase when Desiree stopped them.

"What are you doing?" they said in unison.

"We have to get the people out!" said Desiree, "we have to rescue them! Toby and I can't do it on our own!" She turned to the door and began barging it open.

Claudia and Valerie looked off into the smoke, desperate to go to the aid of their foolhardy friends, but they knew in their hearts what was to be done. Claudia turned to the door, pushed Desiree and Tobias to the side and pulled a pin from her hair. She bent down and jammed the pin inside the lock. Within two seconds, the latch clicked and the door opened. The four Players rushed into the room to see the terrified, tired and cowering guests.

"We're The Roxy Players!" shouted Valerie, full of conviction and pride, "and we're here to save you! Follow us!" and she turned into the corridor. The guests all looked at each other in utter confusion.

———— • • ————

Archie managed to catch up with the super-fast Giselle as she darted through the corridors, turning left and right like a fox giving chase. Archie was hot on her heels when Giselle came to a sudden halt by a door. He almost crashed into her, but managed to stop in time, just as the door flung open and a charred and exhausted Abigail Hardwoode burst into the corridor, trailed by a plume of black smoke.

"Perfect timing," spluttered Abigail upon seeing her accomplice.

"Hello!" waved Archie from behind Giselle.

"Hello, Mr Enfield" she gasped as she fell against the wall, he eyes darting around clearly overcome from the shock and smoke of the blast. She grabbed Giselle's arm for support.

"Yeah, that whole explosion thing?" wheezed Abigail, "that probably wasn't my best idea."

Giselle smiled and pulled a little pill from her waist, cracked it and shoved the two halves under Abigail's nose. A green vapour floated out and Abigail inhaled it sharply. It made her gasp and convulse, her eyes burning red, then green and finally resting back on their natural colour. Abigail was back to her old self.

"Jesus on the cross, that stuff is strong! Thank you," she said drawing her sword.

"Now let's go to the King!" she said before rushing off down the corridor. Giselle winked at Archie and patted his cheek before the two of them rushed ahead.

The ringing in his ears cleared and the fire had burnt itself out. Brandenburg staggered out of the wine fountain. He pinched this nose and shook the stinging from his senses. He looked over to see the entire Black Arm opposite him. He looked to the upper level of the room. The fireball had not burnt itself out entirely and he could already see the flames that had remained begin to lick up the walls, creeping like death and clinging to anything for sustenance.

Behind him lay only the decimated ruins of half of the dance hall and the fires that had now moved downwards, catching the remnants of the banisters and spreading across the skirting boards and across the fittings. He was soon to be in the very belly of hell. Count Brandenburg smirked to himself and held his hand up to ask for a few more seconds, before reaching back into the wine to retrieve his sword. He held it out, the blade catching the light and revealing the hidden names engraved thereon. As the fire spread and the heat began to dry his sodden clothes, he concluded that, perhaps, it wasn't such a bad way to go. The fire behind his eyes then burnt brighter than the fire in the room. He smiled and looked over at the mass of cloaked enemy, shimmering in the heat haze.

"Alright, you bastards," he glowered, "this is how we do things down in Borough," and he charged down the hallway, sword raised ready to engage De Locke, Whit and the hundred or so Black Arm awaiting him.

The enemy screamed and charged forward all except De Locke who grabbed the King by his throat and dragged him to the side of the hallway and up the side of the great stair case that was still intact.

Brandenburg wailed and swung his sword as approached the army. He was sixty feet from them and closing fast when, Abigail, Giselle and Archie burst in through the destroyed wall beside him, swords raised and screaming. They leapt through the fire and ran alongside their man. His army was now four. They ran behind him and The Black Arm did not slow down. Nathanial Whit lead and was almost upon their meagre opponents when the great entrance doors flew off their hinges and the platoon of King's Specials, lead by Invisible Noel poured into the hall. Nathanial and The Black Arm dug their heels in, shocked at the sudden entrance of the Specials. They did not have time to divert their charge, or prepare for a large onslaught as the two amassed armies crashed into each other.

Nathanial Whit and Brandenburg flew at each other, clashing blades instantly. Brandenburg was stronger and his charged forced Whit backwards, into the thick of his own Black Arm ranks.

Giselle and Archie peeled off from Brandenburg and Abigail and remained close to each other engaged while they engaged the enemy. Archie was flailing his sword wildly, parrying blades with more luck than skill. Giselle, near him was fighting as if it was as simple as breathing but she could sense that Archie was in trouble. She began to back up to him until they were back to back.

"Having a trouble, little one?" she said with a wry smile as she defeated three enemies with one swing.

"I'm an artist not a fighter," he said as he held off an attack by grabbing a dissident's wrist, "if we make it through this, I'll show you!"

"If you can survive this," countered Giselle, "I'm all yours"

That was all he needed to hear. Archie was suddenly engorged with adrenaline and desire to live. He headbutted his attacker and ran him through before engaging five more dissidents. It was as if his arms were not his and he was Diomedes himself. Giselle, with her back still pressed against Archie's, likewise defended herself against a constant stream of multiple enemies. They worked as a partnership and, despite their three encounters, somehow appeared to share a deep set language. When Giselle wanted to round kick an enemy, Archie somehow knew and would bend over, so that she could lean on his back and swing her leg high to her target. Likewise when an enemy, unseen to Giselle lunged at her, Archie, without looking would hook his arm in hers and swing himself in front, parrying the blade and diverting it into the side of the enemy next to him, while thrusting his own blade into the attacker's throat. They were untouchable.

Abigail Hardwoode had no time to watch Brandenburg's back. She could see, ahead, passed the masses of cloaked enemy, Lord De Locke with a small personal guard, heave the King away from the battle up the stairs. She shouted and railed harder against the enemy, cutting a vicious sway through them. Her blade was an instrument of economic death as it pierced and slashed its way through their ranks. Dissidents fell around her, but their numbers were many and soon she was engulfed, defending herself on all sides from The Black Arm.

The King's Specials followed closely behind Brandenburg, regimentally advancing upon the ranks of The Black Arm who, in turn held fast with gritted hate-filled determination. The fire was spreading over the walls and across the ceilings, reducing the battleground slowly and compressing the combatants. Walls began to creak and groan under the strain and the ceiling began to crack and buckle. Chunks of plaster began to fall all around and still they raged on and the cacophonous sound of battle shook the foundations more so than Abigail's explosion.

Lord De Locke and his bodyguards dragged the King up the stairs and across the landing. Below them the battle raged. De Locke could see the King's Specials advance through his army. He looked around him, the fire on the staircase was intensifying and his chances of escape were reducing. He shouted to his men to block the staircase in front. The bodyguards battled through the blaze to the edges of the landing and, despite the flames, tore down the burning portraits that lined the landing and toppled over the grandfather clocks and pulled down the statues until the stair case was completely blocked by the flaming barricade.

Now De Locke and the King were cut off from the melee below, on both sides. On one side by the stair case destroyed by the explosion, and on the other by the second stair case now blockaded with burning furniture. He had now only one escape route; the double doors on the centre of the landing, directly to his left that led into the upper corridors. He gave a final look down, from the flames, to the battle below. Through the haze, he saw Abigail fighting. She looked up at him. He laughed and kicked open the door, disappearing from the battle.

Abigail screamed in anger, only to receive a slash blade across her back. She wailed in pain and sunk to her knee. Brandenburg, out of the corner of his eye, saw Abigail fall to her knee. He screamed out to her, but she could not hear him. Nathanial Whit pressed upon Brandenburg and fought him backwards, taking advantage of Brandenburg's distraction.

Abigail, now on one knee, was overwhelmed by 'Black Arm' dissidents, intent on finishing her off. They swarmed in upon her, but she was not the sort to die on her knees and she swung her sword up and parried the blades on one, full three-sixty swing. She managed to get to her feet before a second slash raked down her left arm.

Nathanial Whit was pushing Brandenburg backward and soon the Count had lost sight of Abigail. To his side and further away, Giselle and Archie were still fighting as one. Archie felled a dissident with a slash across the face. The body fell backwards to reveal Brandenburg on the back foot, shouting for Abigail. Archie looked to his left and saw a swarm of black cloaks swinging and hacking at an unseen enemy.

"Giselle!" shouted Archie.

"Yes, my dear," she said, as she ran her blade through an enemies gullet.

"Follow me!" and Archie began to advance forward through the ranks towards Abigail. Brandenburg saw Archie and Giselle advancing through his peripheral vision and it gave him the resolve to hold fast against Nathanial Whit's onslaught.

Abigail Hardwoode was almost undone. She was down on her back, looking up at the faceless cowls as they swung and jabbed down at her. She parried as best she could, but they moved fast. She blocked three jabs to her waist just as she saw a blade glint over her face begin its descent down towards her neck. She had no time to pull her sword up to deflect it. The blade was almost on her neck when it was halted by another. She looked up to see Giselle and Archie standing over her, fighting off the dissidents with passion and ferocity. They swung and hacked and beat a perimeter around her. Once a path had been cleared, Archie turned to Abigail, picked her up and threw her over his shoulder.

Giselle backed him up as he ran through the flaming battle field to the relative safety under the staircase. He laid her on the floor. Giselle handed him a first aid package and a couple of the reviving pills she had used on Abigail before.

Giselle held the perimeter, while Archie Enfield bandaged her up.

"You 'ave been in the wars, ain't you, Old Love?"

"Patch me up, Archie...I have to save him."

Archie ripped a bandage from the kit and stuck into the gash on her back. She buckled in pain. He turned her over.

"Give me a pill, I have to save him, I have to save him."

Archie wiped the sweat from his brow and cracked the vapour pill under her nose which, as before, recharged her fully. She leapt to her feet.

"Giselle, Mr Enfield," she shouted, as she picked up her sword. "Secure the King" and she turned back to the melee.

"I have to save Brandenburg!" and she charged back into the fray towards her man.

Giselle and Archie stood under the stairwell and watched as Abigail disappeared back into the fight.

"To the King?" he asked.

"To the King" she agreed.

"Can I have one of them pills?"

"No." answered Giselle sternly.

Chapter Fifty Eight

From Bad...

Abigail, energised by the vapour pill and with Brandenburg in her sights, fought back through the battle. The King's Specials were by now, almost on top of The Black Arm, their training winning out. They had forced the dissidents to retreat further into the centre of the inferno. Abigail fought forward and joined Brandenburg's side as he continued to fight with Nathanial. The battle was almost won when, to the side of the hall there came another catastrophic explosion as a portion of the ceiling collapsed down, ripping a great hole in the wall behind the enemy. Nathanial seized upon the moment and kicked Brandenburg in the gut and backhanded Abigail across the face, sending them both staggering back. He raised his sword in the air and bellowed for The Black Arm to disperse. And, like spiders running to safety, the black-cloaks disappeared through the new hole in the wall and into the depths of the Pavilion. The battle was over. Invisible Noel walked up to Abigail and Brandenburg who were breathing hard.

"We're in serious trouble now," he said. Abigail spat blood on the floor and looked to Brandenburg who was exhausted. He nodded to her and she turned to the remaining King's Specials.

"Men of the Realm," bellowed Abigail, "our enemies have gone to ground. We must hunt them down. The rally point is the island on the lake. Break into squads, stay sharp and remember there are civilians here!"

A huge beam fell down on the far side of the hall, belching yet more flame into the hallway. The men shielded their eyes from the furnace. Abigail and Invisible Noel looked at them. There were tired and each wounded. Brandenburg stepped in front of them all.

"You are among the bravest men I have ever known," he said with galvanising sincerity, standing tall amongst them and with a Lordly, piercing gleam in his rejuvenated and fierce eyes, "Braver than mere soldiers, you are artists of courage. My friends are in there," he said pointing to the hell mouth. "There are innocent people in there. Your King is in there. Those of that are done, make your way to the rally point knowing that you fought like lions today, those of you still with fight inside of you, follow me now, follow your friends... into hell and to death and glory!"

Every last one of the surviving Specials roared with conviction and Brandenburg led Abigail, Invisible Noel and the rest of the King's Specials into what was left of the Pavilion.

———•◦•———

Archie and Giselle ran through a service corridor at the far side of the Pavilion. Through the windows they could see the lawn and the lake with the swan-boats bobbing calmly in the water. Giselle stopped Archie. "Look," she said.

Archie looked out. "What?" he said.

"Look at the water?"

Archie squinted and his eyes widened. While the boats bobbed gently, he could see that the water was not dark and reflective of the moonlight. It was orange and angry, reflecting only the flames from the building.

"The whole Pavilion is ablaze," said Giselle.

"Then we have even less time," said Archie, grabbing her hand, "come on!" and he pulled her along the corridor. They rounded a corner and almost bumped into a squad of King's Specials. The soldiers raised their swords to attack. Giselle readied herself.

"Wait!" said Archie, "we're on your side!"

"Mr Enfield!" said one of the soldiers, stepping forward. "It's me, Private Simmons, sir."

Archie offered his hand cautiously.

"Your little Spanish girl shot me in the unmentionables."

Archie's eyes lit up in recognition.

"Simmons, good man, good man!"

"Squad, at ease!"

The squad lowered their arms.

"What's going on?" asked Archie.

"The bastards scattered, they are everywhere."

"And the King?" said Giselle.

"Don't know, ma'am."

"And the guests?" asked Archie.

"Don't know, sir. But the rally point is the island on the lake. I think that's where the civilians are."

"The island is empty!" said Archie.

"Then they are still inside. Squad!" shouted Simmons. He was about to command them when Archie leant into his ear and whispered. The others looked at each other while the two men spoke. They could see Simmons shaking his head, and Archie trying to subtly nod his head towards Giselle without her noticing. Simmons eventually hung his head in resignation and nodded. Archie stepped back.

"Squad!" shouted Simmons, "search and rescue operation and Mr Enfield has point, because is a brave and noble fellow!" Simmons could not help but imbue the last remark with a strong hint of sarcasm.

The squad proudly stood to attention and Archie led them down the dark corridor. Simmons shrugged and rolled his eyes at Giselle as he passed her. Giselle couldn't help but smile at Archie and his ways.

———•◦•———

Desiree, Valerie and Claudia rushed through the conjoining chambers until they came to a large dormitory; the servants' sleeping quarters. They led the guests in, the rear being brought up by Tobias, rushing as fast as he could on his wooden leg.

Desiree stood by the door as the guests hurried in. Tobias came in and Desiree slammed the door. Up ahead, Valerie rushed to the next door. She was about to open it when Tobias shouted for her to stop. She touched the handle and opened the door. A blast of flame belched into the room, sending Valerie and the door back twenty feet into the room. The guests screamed as the young girl bounced over two beds and into the corner. Claudia rushed over, while some of the guests ran to the fire and attempted to put it out with the bedding.

Desiree, Tobias and Claudia heaved the charred door of Valerie to find her alive but stunned. Tobias exhaled in relief.

"Lucky for you that's a sturdy door," he said as he helped her to her feet.

"What now, what now?" shouted a frantic guest. The Players looked at each other. They had no time to answer as the door they had come in through began to shudder on its hinges. Something on the opposite side was trying to get in. The battering intensified. They were cut off.

"Back up, back up!" shouted Desiree as the guests moved away from the door and towards the fire. There was a scream from behind them and they turned to see twenty 'Black Arm' dissidents leap through the fire and impale the brave guests who were attempting to douse the flames. The guests panicked and scattered like chickens as the foxes in the coop ran amok. The barricaded door continued to suffer a battering from the enemy outside eager to get in on the action.

The Black Arm were drunk of battle frenzy and seemed to not care about escape, only for bloodshed and they hacked and slashed dementedly. Tobias instinctively stood in front of Desiree, Claudia and Valerie as he backed them into a corner. A dissident felled an unarmed guest in front of Claudia, spraying their blood on her face and mouth, she screamed reflexively. The dissident looked up, its black faceless cowl fixing on Claudia's horror stuck face. It charged forward.

Tobias screamed and jumped at the dissident, swinging wildly. His paternal rage for Claudia overcame his enemy and he ran him through. The dissident fell down dead and Tobias turned back to his friends. He was about to rejoin them when he halted. His eyes bulged.

Valerie screamed in horror as a blade emerged from his stomach and arched high in the air, lifting Tobias clean off the ground. The blade retreated and Tobias fell to the floor.

Desiree, Valerie and Claudia were overcome with rage and they dashed forward to engage the enemy.

———•—•———

De Locke dragged the King into a banquet hall that seemed to be as yet unaffected by the fire. It was large, empty and remarkably silent.

The guards flanked their master and their quarry and they advanced across the open space. They were halfway through when the opposite doors opened and in walked Gertie, Lupe, Anya and Danilov. They halted in surprise.

"Georgie?" said Lupe. "Georgie, Georgie!"

"Lupe? Lupe Darling?" shouted back the King.

Lupe barged passed Anya, Danilov and Gertie and ran up to the King, forgetting the situation. De Locke and the guards were dumbfounded at the surreal moment. The King was clapping excitedly.

Lupe got halfway across the hallway and there was a strange twist and creak.

"Lupe, stop!" shouted Gertie. But it was too late. The seemingly safe room was wholly unsafe. Nobody had noticed the bubbling wallpaper, the drooping portraits or the way the main dining table was listing. The entire floor gave way and crashed down to a lower level. The floor below did not survive the impact and they crashed through that too. Danilov's vision became a disorientating collage as debris flew passed him and walls and ceilings seemed to merge as he tumbled through the air. He caught sight of his friends and enemies all too briefly as he turned to see the ground rush up on him. They all landed in cold water, inside a dark stone cellar, the splash breaking their fall.

Gertie was the first to come around. He stood up in the water and looked up at the hole in the ceiling. He could see up three floors, through the roof and out into the night sky. He looked around to find Danilov. He roused him slowly. The acrobat got to his feet. Everybody else was out cold. Gertie pointed to the ceiling, and then tapped his waist.

Danilov looked up and surveyed the unspoken idea. He nodded to Gertie. Gertie put his finger to his lip as he slowly unclasped his belt, unthreaded it and handed it to Danilov, who unhitched his own belt and tied it to Gertie's, producing a long, leather strap. They walked slowly through the water towards the King, checking on their friends as they went. The King, like the Players was alive but unconscious.

Gertie bent down and scooped up the King so that he was sitting upright. He was a gargantuan weight.

In the dark, Danilov surveyed the route one last time and stretched off. Gertie attached the leather strap under the King's arms and Danilov took the ends, and tied them around his chest. He looked like a snail with a man-shaped shell. He counted to three and stood up.

Gertie held his breath as Danilov stepped over the unconscious De Locke and his bodyguards and walked over to the cold wall. He ran his fingers over the edges of the stones until he found a purchase. He lowered his heart rate and began to climb. Gertie watched as Danilov scaled the vault like a spider and climbed out of the hole and began to scale up the wreckage towards the open roof.

Danilov's muscles were burning but still he climbed. He eventually came to the highest point he could. The beam he was holding onto jutted into the highest room of the Pavilion. The hole in the roof was ten feet away and around four feet above him. He was exhausted, but he had to do it. Below him, Gertie crossed his fingers and prayed.

Danilov thought of seeing Valerie one last time before compressing his muscles, and springing in the air. He dived, with the king on his back, clearing the crumbing building below, and grabbing the edge of the roof. He hung there for a few seconds, took a few deep breaths before pulling himself up, using his biceps alone.

The exhausted acrobat fell onto his front breathing heavily and felt his muscles burning hotter than the room he had just climbed through. He unclipped his harness and the King rolled onto his side and woke up. He looked over and saw his presumed rescuer lying on the roof and kindly dragged him away from the hole and propped him up against the small wall. The King sat next to him and they both took a few seconds to evaluate what had just happened

"King George" said the King offering a hand to shake. Danilov took it without looking and shook it almost in a delirium.

"Danilov" he said.

"Thank you"

"Don't mention it...can you do me a favour Your Majesty?"

"Name it"

"Would you be so kind as to help me find a length of rope?"

Gertie breathed a sigh of relief to see Danilov and the King disappear over the edge of the roof, high above. He crept around to Anya and stroked her face. Her eyes opened and she smiled. Gertie helped her to her feet and they walked quietly over to Lupe. Gertie clamped his hand tightly over her mouth, sure that when she came to she would scream. Her eyes opened to see Gertie and Anya with their fingers over their lips. She understood. She got to her feet and looked around. Gertie tapped her on the shoulder and pointed upwards. They looked up to see The King and Danilov peering down. Danilov threw down some rope that they had found. It fell all the way down through the holes and splashed into the water. Gertie grabbed it and tied it around Lupe Darling. In ten seconds, she was being hoisted up into the hair towards Danilov and her darling Georgie.

Nathanial Whit led his men away from the rest of the dissidents and they doubled backed on themselves. He was coming to realise that the night was lost, but before he would be taken in, he sure as hell that he would take Benjamin Ananas down first. He led them back to the main hall as he knew, eventually, his enemy would come back there and walk into his trap. He dispersed his men into the room, of which the fires were burning with less intensity having eaten up most of the fuel and moved to seek more. The smoke from the charred wood covered the room and it was nearly impenetrable. It was perfect for an ambush. They dispersed and waited.

Abigail and Brandenburg led a troop of Specials into the very bowels of the Pavilion. They had encountered a few dissidents along the way and dispatched them easily as the progressed in their pursuit of the enemy. As they had descended further and further, the heat had intensified and by now, it was so hot that the grips of their swords burnt their hands but they did not complain. They stalked from room to room until finally they came to a single doorway at the end of a corridor. Abigail approached it and ran her hand over it. It was burning hot.

A soldier tossed her his neckerchief and she wrapped it around her hand before opening the door. The other side was a burning room far, far too intense to attempt to cross.

Brandenburg kicked the wall. "We can't go on!" he spat. "We have to double back! Dammit!"

"Beggin' pardon, sir" said a quiet soldier, "but if we can't go on, how can they?"

Abigail looked at Brandenburg who looked at the soldier, who in turn looked sheepishly at the floor. "I mean, they ain't demons or anyfink..."

Brandenburg kicked the wall again and pushed through the soldiers and began to run back down the corridor. "Come on!" he cried.

"Where are we going?" Abigail called back

"Back to the hall, it's a trick, they've doublebacked! We have no time!"

Abigail threw the neckerchief back to the soldier, and patted the cheek of the chap who provided the 'eureka' moment for Brandenburg. She led the soldiers back the way they came, through the bowels and out to the main hall.

Desiree had killed two dissidents and saved the lives of four guests and still the black cloaks kept coming. Valerie and Claudia had tried to wade in, but their meagre skills were no match for the size and ferocity of the enemy and they had found themselves pinned back against the wall. The situation was becoming hopeless. They were vastly outnumbered and the only door out of there was being battered from the outside by yet even more black-cloaks. It was Desiree's last stand and she knew it. The thought that she would probably be meeting Herschel in a matter of moments calmed her fears, but she absolutely needed to save Valerie and Claudia from a terrible fate and that kept her sword arm feeling strong. She fought on. However, after dispatching two more dissidents, she found herself surrounded by five more. She was undone and about to receive a blade to her chest when the doorway shattered and in poured The King's Specials led by Archie and Giselle.

Claudia and Valerie were backed against a wall, fending off a vicious dissident. Archie ran over and removed the assailant's head from his body. He looked down at the girls and asked if they were alright. They were wide eyed with shock. He stood in front of them and looked around. The King's Specials were taking care of The Black Arm. He saw Desiree dispatch a foe.

"Desi!" he shouted. She turned to him.

Archie elbowed one of the windows, shattering it instantly. He pointed towards a mattress. Desiree caught his drift and rushed over to him. Together they heaved the mattress out of the window and threw it down, fifteen feet to the floor.

Desire ran over to Valerie and Claudia who were hugging each other. She shouted at them and slapped them both. They came to their senses. Desiree picked them up and threw them out of the window. They landed on the mattress and rolled to safety.

Archie ran forward and joined the squad. Giselle was fighting the front line. He grabbed her collar and pulled her backwards, yanking her from the fray.

"I think it's time we skidaddled my darling!" he said. She did not argue and, as he took her place, she retreated back and began marshalling the remaining guests. She stood by the window with Desiree and helped each guest jump out. They were halfway through rescuing them, when the ceiling cracked and the plaster began to fall.

"We ain't got much time, Desi!" shouted Archie, holding a dissident's arm as his blade threatened his neck.

A second crack came and a large chunk of masonry fell down, crushing the foe that was pinning Archie to the wall.

Desiree and Giselle began to throw the guests out of the room at double time. Below them, Valerie and Claudia helped them to their feet and directed them over to the swan-boats on the lake. The last of the guests got clear.

"We're done!" said Giselle

"Not yet," said Desiree as she rushed over and heaved Tobias's body onto the ledge. The two women heaved him out and he landed onto the mattress. The last two guests helped pick up the body of their rescuer and carry him to the lake. Desiree leant out of the window and yelled for Claudia and Valerie to go and get to the island. As she leant out, Giselle took her moment and pushed Desiree out. Desiree fell onto the mattress and rolled onto the grass.

Giselle turned back to Archie.

"Come on, Mr Enfield, time to go!"

"Don't wait for us!" he called back as the squad began to move back towards the window, still struggling with their enemies. Giselle waited. Archie turned and looked at her.

"Go!" he shouted.

"Don't be long!" she said as she jumped out of the window.

"Time's a wasting, boys!" shouted Archie as the ceiling began to dip and twist.

"As one, lads!" shouted Simmons, as the line of Specials made one last offensive move on their enemies. Their unity and strength won out and the last of them fell. Archie and Simmons marshalled the troops to the window and they jumped. On the ground, they ran alongside the guests and made sure everyone made it to the island. Desiree and Giselle waited for Simmons and Archie.

Inside the room, Archie and Simmons remained. Archie offered the window to the soldier. "After you, Mr...".

The roof finally gave way caved in on Archie Enfield and Private Simmons.

On the island, The Roxy Players and guests watched in horror as a ball of fire burst out of the window. Desiree and Giselle, still on the lawn under the window, were blown to the ground by the impact. Desiree's ears were still ringing as she got to her feet and saw Giselle trying desperately to climb the sheer wall back up the window. She grabbed her waist and pulled her down onto the ground. Giselle rolled Desiree onto her back and was about to throttle her through madness when the Umbrian's eyes told her that there was still a job to do. Giselle let her go and they helped each other up and ran across the lawn as more explosions rocked the Pavilion.

Simmons and Archie were gone.

Chapter Fifty Nine

...to worse...

Danilov and the King heaved Lupe onto the crumbling roof and she fell into his arms. They rolled around showering each other in kisses and gropes. Danilov broke up their reunion to drag them over the far edge of the roof, towards the back of the Pavilion which was the only place still stable. They stood against the wall and looked out. Over the lawn, through the smoke, they could see Desiree and another woman rushing towards the lake. Upon the island they saw the saved hostages. The King pointed with glee.

"Look, look my long lost love, look, there are my guests!"

Danilov and Lupe looked over to island, far away, and then down the wall to the ground. It was far, far too high to jump. Danilov looked at Lupe and shook his head. She understood what that meant and she turned to the King and embraced him, filling his heart with all the love she had stored for him over all the years of their separation.

Danilov looked back over the rooftop to see Anya, climbing through the hole. He dashed over to help her climb up. When she was over the edge, they turned back and peered into the furnace swirling below, and down further still into the vault below where Gertie was.

Below, Gertie was relieved to see Anya climb to safety. He spat on his hands and grabbed the rope, ready to ascend. He worked as fast as he could hand over hand, out of the vault and into the flaming room above. It felt like a kiln, but he bore the burning and climbed on. He was halfway through the room when he felt something tugging on his boot. He looked down to see Lord De Locke holding the rope and clawing at his ankle. Above him Anya screamed and Danilov threw his leg over the edge and prepared to descend for help.

Gertie looked down at the Lord and saw deep into his fierce and burning green eyes. The hem of his cloak had caught fire and was licking all around them both. Gertie felt as if he was being pulled into Hell by the Devil himself. And below them further, he could see the squad of 'Black Arm' guards climbing up the rope. Gertie had only one option. He looked up at Danilov and then to Anya who shook her head vigorously, understanding what he was about to do.

Gertie winked at her and mouthed 'I love you' before pulling a dagger from his belt and holding it to the rope just above his head.

Danilov screamed for him to wait, but Gertie fixed him with a resigned smile and cut the rope. The stagehand, Lord De Locke and The Black Arm squad fell back down through the flames and into the vault.

Danilov, suspended above the fire looked around, there was no way down. The flames ignited the end of the rope and began to lick upwards. He had to cut his loss and so scrambled back up onto the roof, dragging a sobbing Anya towards the end of the roof where they sank into the arms of the King and Lupe Darling to await their imminent death.

Desiree reached the shore and stepped onto a swan boat, untying it from its moorings. She turned back to Giselle and held out her hand for her. Giselle took it, but suddenly her grip loosened and she halted. Desiree looked at her, the green falling from her eyes. Suddenly, she fell down, face first into the boat, a dagger sticking out of her back. Desiree screamed as she saw standing ten feet behind her, Kemble, awake, alive and breathing hard. The monster was covered in soot and filth and the discharge running from the wound in his neck was as black as tar.

Desiree swallowed her fear, untied the boat and pushed off just as Kemble ran towards her. She rowed fast, the dying Giselle across her lap. Kemble reached the shore and leapt. Desiree tracked his arc and stood up, bringing her oar back and swinging it. She connected with the actor and smashed him across the chest, sending him crashing into the lake. She sat back down and rowed fast to reach the shore. The actor scrambled in the water and finally made it back to shore were he snarled and swung at the water's edge with his sword.

Desiree managed to get to the island and instantly Claudia and Valerie ran to her aid. Together they lifted Giselle out of the boat and onto land. The mysterious woman was breathing erratically and her eyes were panicked. For the first time in many, many years she felt cold mortal fear run through her. She didn't want to die and so she gripped the hands of the girls beside her tightly. A soldier knelt beside her and together they turned onto her front and he went about making safe her wound.

Desiree clenched her jaw in rage, stood up and turned to look at Kemble who was scanning the shore line. He spotted another boat and ran to it. She looked over to the soldiers.

"Right then, lads!" shouted the captain. "Make ready arms and drop that son of a bitch!" The soldiers took a knee and raised their guns. "Fire!"

The five rifles unloaded, the bullets whizzing passed Kemble who was too fast for them. One passed his ear and shot off towards the other end of the lawn. It struck a tiny funnel sticking out of the lawn and suddenly ignited four rows of giant Roman Candles, left over from the fireworks display. They lit up in sequence from the shore, down to the Pavilion. Kemble jumped onto the boat and cut the rope free.

"Right, you lot! To swords!" said the captain.

The Soldiers threw down their rifles and drew swords, jumping onto the boats to meet Kemble on the water.

———————•—•—•———————

Abigail and Brandenburg halted their squad by the entrance to the hallway. They had indeed doublebacked and where now by the exploded hole in the wall. The main hall beyond was thick with smoke. Abigail looked in, and then back at the men.

"We're not coming out of this one," she said with a smile as she loaded two pistols and repositioned her knives so that they were more accessible.

The soldiers looked at each other and shrugged. "It's been a lovely war," said one.

"Aye," said another, "let's give 'em one final kicking."

"Christ, I need a drink," said Brandenburg.

"Shame we make it through this, sir," said the squad leader, "my old man would've bought you a few. He owns the 'Bandy Bull' on Old Compton Street."

"Really?" asked Brandenburg in a sudden, happy tone.

"Yeah," agreed the soldiers, jovially. "He does this fing where you get two pints for the price of one, between five pm and six pm on fersdays," said one soldier. The others all agreed with him.

"That's a good deal!" said Brandenburg, "I've always..."

Abigail cleared her throat, snapping the men back into the reality of the situation.

"Sorry, ma'am" said the squad leader.

Abigail rolled her eyes before nodding to the count of three. She slipped out first, silently into the smoke filled room. Brandenburg went next, and then followed the soldiers.

The squad walked in formation through the centre of the room. It was silent save for the odd crack and twinkle of dying embers. The soldiers held out their weapons, training their eyes on the deep smoke. From the edges of the room, the waiting 'Black Arm' guards watched, with keener eyes, as their targets walked passed them, their black cloaks providing great cover.

Abigail and Brandenburg were in front of the squad heading through the room and towards the grand staircase. Through the mist they passed the fountains which loomed out eerily as they passed by, the waters running red with blood and wine. They took care to step over the bodies of the fallen soldiers and dissidents, alike now in death. Abigail suddenly stopped Brandenburg with a raise of her fist when she recognised a body. She bent down and turned the corpse over. Her long time friend Invisible Noel had met his end. She knew that there was no time to grieve and instead reached into his breast pocket to find his note of will and buriel requests.

"See you on the Other Side old friend" she whispered before pocketing his will and standing up. She was about to give the signal to advance when there came a quick sudden, quick swish of steel followed by four ominous thuds. Abigail and Brandenburg turned around to see four heads of their squad come rolling through the smoke. Then, as if it were conspiratorial in the trap, the smoke parted slightly to reveal the fifteen strong troupe of Whit's guards, but no Nathanial amongst them. Abigail sidestepped next to Brandenburg and, as the enemy slowly made their way through the mist, her hand fell to the side and found his. Their fingers intertwined and squeezed tightly.

The soldiers on the lake, standing on a swan-boat each, had encircled Kemble and were jabbing and swinging wildly, unable to mount a solid attack due to the unstable footing. Kemble, however, had an actor's balance and was sure of foot as he moved with the pitch and yawl of the boats. As they encircled him, he had no trouble dispatching the first two with a single slash that crossed both their throats. They fell backwards, tipping their boats and capsizing them, the resulting wake unsettled two more soldiers who Kemble dispatched with two single lunges. He spun around to face the captain. The soldier raised his sword and swung downwards, attempting to slice across Kemble. It was a foolish move and Kemble dodged it easily by sidestep. He jumped forward onto the captain's boat, and landed nimbly onto the edge, holding onto the swan's neck for balance and hacking his sword down, decapitating him.

The guests screamed in resignation as the body of their last saviour fell into the red water. Kemble stood up on the boat and picked up and oar, he looked over to Desiree and raised his sword to her, challenging her to best him. Claudia dived forward and grabbed Desiree's ankle, sobbing that she should not go. Desiree bent down to her.

"It's alright, little Mouse, it's alright, you have to look after the others now. You have to take care of them all," and she kissed her on the forehead. She turned to Valerie who was crying and hugging her knees. She blew her a kiss. "Roxy Playhouse Irregular," she said, tapping her heart three times, which was her solemn blessing to Valerie. Valerie Folk tapped her heart three times in return. Desiree stepped onto a swan-boat and pushed it out onto the lake to engage Kemble.

———•◦•———

Abigail and Brandenburg were back to back, fending off the onslaught of The Black Arm. The attack was relentless, but Abigail and Brandenburg fought well, choosing their moments to strike and not giving an inch to the bastards. Wounds were inflicted on all sides, but slowly, Abigail and Brandenburg dispatched a few of the more foolhardy dissidents. Abigail looked up to the rickety stair case. Atop she saw a figure move: Nathanial Whit.

"Higher ground!" she shouted.

"Right ho!" agreed Brandenburg.

"Three...two...one!" she shouted and they turned around so that they were side by side. The change in stance sent two of their assailants' off-balance and Brandenburg grabbed one by the neck and slashed his throat before shoving the body into the oncoming Black Arm. It was now two versus three.

"You have these clowns?" said Brandenburg.

Abigail kicked one in the groin and drew a second sword. "Oh yes!" she cried, "Now go kill that son of a bitch!"

"Gladly!" said Brandenburg and he turned and dashed up the staircase, leaping over the smouldering barricade until he came onto the landing to face Nathanial for the final time. There were no words, or gestures. Brandenburg did not even break stride and charged straight at his man who charged in return. Brandenburg swung his blade, but Nathanial saw it coming, almost in slow motion and hopped up onto the banister and kicked the passing Count in the jaw sending him sprawling to the side and his sword flying into the air. Brandenburg watch in horror as his sword spun over and over, before falling perfectly into the hand of Nathanial Whit.

———•◦•———

Two of the four guards had died on impact. After Gertie had cut the rope, they had plummeted face first into the stone floor, dashing their brains out. The other two landed on the first and so managed to have their fall broken by the bodies. De Locke landed on his feet and Gertie plummeted into the two feet deep water behind him, landing on his back and knocking the wind out of him. His vision swirled as he adjusted to the darkness around him, and the swirling fire in the rooms above. He came to his senses.

The two guards rushed to De Locke to see if he was alright, he was. He drew his sword and turned around to where Gertie had fallen. He jabbed into the murky water. But there was nothing there.

"Where are you, boy?" he hissed. "Where are you hiding?"

Gertie, using his stagehand stealth had stowed himself away into a recessed culvert in a dark adjacent atrium. He picked up a stone and threw it into a nearby puddle. The foolish guards were drawn to it and dashed over. As soon as they were in range Gertie leapt out and stabbed them both with his dagger. He was so fast that there were looking down at their guts, before they even realised they had been spilt. They slumped down on top of each other. Like a ghost, Gertie moved to another shadowed corner.

Upon seeing his men fall, De Locke bit his tongue and threw off his smouldering cape. He drew dual swords as he stepped into the darkness to meet the boy.

Gertie controlled his breathing and looked out from his hiding spot and around at his surroundings. Down in the depths of the vaults he could see a tiny shaft of light signifying a possible exit. He wanted to run. He wanted to run and keep on running. He gripped his little dagger and stepped out into the atrium ready to not run, but to stay and fight. He stepped forward. There was a swish of steel from somewhere and his shirt became instantly heavy and wet. He looked down. It was dark and glistening. There were two more swishes across his back and he fell down onto his knees. De Locke stepped out of the darkness, his eyes burning, his swords dripping with Gertie's blood.

———•◦•———

Desiree was fighting with all her might, but Kemble was just too good. For every attack, he countered twice as fast and in a differing style to hers which threw her off balance. He dealt no killing blows but instead intricate little cuts and scrapes to maximise the pain. She was tired, but still fought on, her rage taking over as, with every little wound inflicted by Kemble was being matched by his buffoonery and mocking. He was leaping about and cooing wildly, dancing like a lunatic while he made long work of his brave adversary. She summoned her last remaining strength and got to her feet. Her arm was heavy and she could barely lift it. The blood was running freely from every part of her. Still, she managed to raise it purposefully enough for Kemble to stop his dance and tut at her, before leaping across, point outstretched and directed at her heart. Desiree closed her eyes as she felt the air around her change slightly as Kemble's blade pierced through it. She deflected the killing blow and managed to score a slash across his cheek. She staggered backwards and opened her eyes. Kemble scrabbled to his feet, clutching his cheek. Desiree opened her eyes groggily and looked at his wound. She smiled. Kemble felt his face and screamed at her. Desiree swayed and smiled back at him, before the tiredness overcame her. She staggered backwards and fell to her knees.

Valerie stood up and looked around for a weapon. All she could find were some small pebbles. She picked up a handful and desperately threw them at Kemble. They bounced off him. He turned to her and waggled his finger at her remonstratively. Claudia picked up some stones and threw them too, joining Valerie and beginning to wade through the lake, which was deeper than they expected. Still they tried. Kemble smiled and stood behind Desiree, resting his hand under her chin and craning her neck back into his groin, presenting her throat to the oncoming girls. With his other hand he threw down his sword and picked up his dagger. He held it up to the moonlight, ready to bring it down into her neck.

———•◦•———

Abigail ran her sword through the final dissident and pulled him in close to her so that he could see who was sending him into the inferno. The dissident spluttered and fell to the ground. She wiped the blade clean and turned round to face the balcony. The smoke was beginning to clear and she could see Nathanial Whit facing off against an unarmed Brandenburg. She shouted his name and began to run up the stairs to try and save him.

Nathanial Whit turned and smiled at her before impaling Brandenburg through the gut. The wind fell from the Count and he instinctively grabbed the blade as it slide into him. Abigail screamed in horror as Nathanial Whit booted the Count off of his sword. Brandenburg stumbled backwards before falling down, clutching his stomach. Abigail was climbing over the barricade, desperately as Nathanial Whit stood over Brandenburg. She climbed onto the landing in time to see Whit smile crookedly at her again, before jamming Brandenburg's own sword into him and skewering him into the landing.

The Count gasped a deathly gasp as the sword fell through him and suddenly all the bravado and heroic intention that had gone before were suddenly replaced with the fearful cold realisation that, in the final analysis of it all, he was mortal and rapidly about to expire. His mind whirred and fought on, but his body was growing cold and he felt a terrible lethargy overcome him.

Abigail stopped in horror as Nathanial Whit twisted the blade into Brandenburg squeezing the life out of him. He let go of the Pineapple basket. It swayed slightly but remained upright, skewering Brandenburg to the landing. Nathanial spat on him then stepped aside to face-off against Abigail.

———•◦•———

The roof was creaking and falling away and a great schism ran along its length and moved like a snake towards Lupe, the King, Anya and Danilov. They had pressed themselves as far against the wall as they could and were a matter of moments from death. Danilov held his sister tight. Lupe held the King. They stood up, and climbed onto the walls ledge, barely one foot wide. Behind them, a sheer drop, in front of them, and gaping chasm to hell opening up. Danilov looked at Anya and then to Lupe with a glance that suggested they fall backwards over the edge. Lupe closed her eyes and nodded. They all held hands and prepared to jump when suddenly, the King let go and pointed up high into the night.

"What is that coming towards us?"

The other three opened their eyes and looked towards the distance. Up ahead, swaying through the night sky appeared three strange orbs.

"I don't believe it," whispered Danilov.

Chapter Sixty

...to the Magnificent.

From the air, Brighton Pavilion resembled a war zone. Most of the roof had collapsed, save for a thin stretch along to a leading wall. Most of the upper floor was exposed, and in certain areas one could see deep down through the levels and make out the stony vaults blow. The updraft was immense, with swirling black plumes drifting up and merging with the black sky.

The three balloons floated silently over the wreckage, moving slowly and gracefully. The pilot of the first balloon, a tall, thin man with a ridiculous moustache peered over the edge, as they flew over the first section of the Pavilion he scratched his chin and looked all the way over to the far end of the building. He pointed with one hand and slapped his passenger on the chest with the other. Up ahead they could see some people, standing on the ledge of the roof.

Lupe and Anya peered through the smoke at the approaching balloon. Danilov waved his arms to attract it.

"Halloa! Halloa there! Over here, over here!"

Lupe and The King began to wave and shriek too and then, through the night sky there bellowed a most welcome voice.

"Roxy Players!" it roared in a wonderful French accent, "Roxy Players!"

On the island by the lake, Kemble relaxed his sword and looked around. Desiree's eyes lit up. Valerie and Claudia stopped wading and looked yonder to the distance.

"Roxy Players!"

Brandenburg, skewered to the floor opened his eyes, a resurgence of life beaming through them.

"Roxy Players!"

Gertie, on his knees in the belly of the Pavilion sat up and smiled. De Locke looked up to the burning roof to the source of the odd voice that seemed to become louder than everything around.

Inside the servant's quarters, Archie woke up. The beam across his chest did not burn so much and did not feel so heavy at all. He looked around. Next to him, Simmons lay crushed.

"Roxy Players!" once more.

Archie screamed out in delight and heaved the beam off of his chest as if it weighed nothing. He climbed to the window and looked down at the mattress below. He turned back to the fallen soldiers and saluted them before jumping out onto the lawn. He landed hard and he landed well.

Upon the roof, Danilov and Lupe yelled in joy, as through the plumes of smoke sailed the balloon, and there, standing on the edge of the basket, holding the guy-rope with one arm and waving his hat with the other stood Antoine Le Magnifique.

"Antoine! Antoine!" yelled Danilov. "Go Antoine!"

The balloon drifted over the roof and Antoine threw a rope down to them. He leant over and looked down at his friends, waving his hat frantically.

"Didn't I always tell you?" he beamed, "my family are balloonists!"

Danilov held his sword in the air and screamed in appreciation. The rope fell down to them and Anya grabbed it, tying it around the King quickly. Lupe pointed to the island and Antoine gestured to the other two balloons to fly over. They obeyed.

Desiree took her opportunity and slammed her head back into Kemble's groin, forcing him to fall backwards onto the boat. She scrambled on top of him and both rolled into the water. Claudia and Valerie looked at each other and dived into the lake to search.

Underwater, Kemble and Desiree scrambled with each other, the coldness of the water and disorientating loss of sound making it near impossible to gain a good purchase on each other. Still they thrashed and struggled, sinking deeper down until Desiree managed to find an arm near her mouth. She opened her jaws, flooding her mouth with freezing water and clamped her teeth down on Kemble's limb. The numbness of the water did little to abate his pain as the ferocity of the Umbrian's vice-like bite caused him to release his grip of her. Desiree let go of his arm and kicked hard, making for the surface. She scrambled up and pulled herself out of the lake and onto the island. A few guests heaved her clear and opened her dress slightly so that she could breathe more easily.

Neither Valerie nor Claudia could see anything underwater but still they felt around, trying to locate Desiree. Soon however, the need for air overcame Valerie and she swam up to the surface and was pulled back onto the island.

Desiree and Valerie sat huddled together and shivering on the edge of the lake watching in fear for signs of Kemble and Claudia. The wash drifted away and the waters became clear. Up ahead they could see a hot air balloon coming in low ready to rescue them. The pilot dropped a line that hit the ground and trailed along.

Still there were no signs of life. Suddenly, on the opposite bank scrambled up Claudia, alive and unhurt. She coughed and spluttered and got to her feet.

"Claudia!" shouted Desiree as she looked around for a boat; the only usable ones where on her side.

"Climb on a boat, little one!" she shouted. Claudia nodded and ran to one. She put one foot aboard when, like a beast from the depths, Kemble lurched out of the water and grabbed her ankle. Claudia screamed and fell back. Desiree looked around for a rifle. Giselle reached over to one lying by her side and threw it to her. Desiree caught it and knelt down to reload.

Claudia backed across the lawn while Kemble scrambled towards her, drooling and scrabbling like a maniacal beast. She looked up to see the balloon drift over and the wire it trailed moving beside them. Kemble was on top of her. He held her neck and pressed her head into the ground. She arched backwards, craning her head back. She could see the Pavilion, upside down now, and the roman candles still firing into the air.

Desiree reloaded the rifle, took aim and fired. The bullet was true and thundered into Kemble's shoulder blade. He flew forward, screaming in pain and releasing Claudia who scrambled to her feet. Kemble stood up and faced her, his back to the pavilion with Claudia now facing him on the banks of the lake. He drew a sword. Desiree began to reload fast.

"Kemble!" came a cry from far behind him. The actor turned around. Claudia's heart almost exploded, as did Valerie's, Desiree's and Giselle's as they saw Archibald Enfield, back from the dead and running at full pelt with his sword raised. Either side of him, the rows of Roman candles showered him with golden light. Kemble hissed and grabbed his throwing knives. He hurled them at Archie who deflected all three with his rapier without breaking stride.

Kemble screamed and drew his sword ready to engage. Archie was running now at full pelt and his desire to save his friends made him feel invincible. It was almost in slow motion for him. He could see Kemble, he could see Claudia on the bank, and he could see the balloon gliding just overhead with the wire trailing. He could see the saved prisoners on the river bank with Valerie, Desiree and Giselle watching him with eyes that told him he was a true hero.

'Okay, Old Love,' his heart said to him, *'this is your moment, don't balls it up now!'*

At the peak of his stride he leapt into the air just as Kemble swung his blade. Archie grabbed hold of the trailing wire and hoisted himself above Kemble and out of range of the bastard's attack. The dumbfounded actor looked up to see Archie sail overhead and swing down with his sword at a sharp and true angle.

The last thing Kemble ever saw were the smiling eyes of Archie Enfield looking down upon him as he sailed overhead wreathed in sparks of golden light. And then all went to black as Kemble's head flew off of his body and arched high and landed in the water. Archie, on the back end of his swing sheathed his sword and bent down to scoop up Claudia. She grabbed onto his arm and he carried her over the lake and placed her down on the ground.

Valerie and Desiree ran over to him and hugged him. The prisoners all cheered and clapped and Archie ate it all up. After the hugs and kisses had finished, he went to see Giselle. She had gone.

"Where did she go?" he said, deflated.

Everybody looked at each other and shrugged.

"Ah what!" he said, sitting down on the lawn, "I really fancied her too."

The Players laughed and Claudia threw her arms around him. "You still have me, old Archie, my love," Archie held her tight and kissed her forehead.

The balloon landed and additional rope ladders were cast over board. Group by group, they were ferried off the island and to safety until only the Players remained.

"Wait here, good man," said Archie to the pilot, "We'll all go together."

"Oui, oui" said the pilot who then proceeded to pull a deck of cards out of his pocket and shuffle them extravagantly.

Down in the vault of the Pavilion, Lord De Locke swung his two swords in an attempt to decapitate the boy. Gertie, imbued with the collective spirit of The Roxy Playhouse Irregulars, lifted his hands quicker than lightning and clapped loudly.

De Locke stopped his swing in sudden shock. He smirked.

"A foolish distraction" he hissed as he went to swing. Nothing happened. He wasn't holding anything. He looked in bemusement at his empty hands. The touch of a steel blade rested against his chin. He looked up to see Gertie standing beside him, holding both swords.

"How did you? I..." De Locke was lost in confusion at the impossible display, "Devilry" he spat.

"Roxy magic" whispered Gertie with a sly smile.

He backed away from De Locke, keeping him at arm's length until he reached the darkness of the tunnel that led to the small beam of light. De Locke stood aghast in the light as Gertie disappeared into it.

De Locke smiled to himself and drew an unseen sword from his belt and dashed into darkness to chase. Gertie had anticipated this act of cowardice and had hidden behind a pillar in the darkness. As De Locke dashed passed, Gertie stepped out with his swords raised from the hip. Lord De Locke impaled himself upon them. He gasped as he slid down the blades. Gertie looked deeply into his faltering green eyes.

"You can't...kill...me," he spluttered as he tried to raise his sword and swing for Gertie's head.

Gertie twisted the swords and De Locke screamed his final scream. Gertie kicked him off of his blades and the vile Lord slumped into the murky water.

"On behalf of The Roxy Playhouse, get bent you tool" said Gertie proud of his final put down but a little disappointed that nobody was around to hear it.

He bent down to the body to make sure he was dead. De Locke was no more. Gertie was about to leave when he saw the curious signet ring on the Lord's hand. He slipped it off and pocketed it before dashing off to the beam of light at the end of the corridor.

When he reached it, he saw a crawl space just wide enough for him. He threw away his blades and squeezed into the hole and scrambled through. When he reached the other side, he found himself crawling out into the shell of the chamber. There was no roof to speak of, only four walls.

Nathanial Whit ignored the odd voice booming through the pavilion and stepped towards Abigail who, against all her training, was overcome with grief at seeing her man on the floor and his more powerful killer advancing on her. She drew a second sword and spat at him. Nathanial prepared to engage.

"Mr, Whit!" came a voice from behind him. Whit's brow furrowed in confusion and he turned around. Count Abraham von Brandenburg was standing up. He grabbed the basket of his sword and yanked it clean out of him. Nathanial snarled and raised his sword to strike. Brandenburg reached up and grabbed Nathanial's wrist, preventing his strike. He pulled him close, looked him deep in the eyes and drove his sword through the bastard's guts.

"That's for my family, you son of a bitch," he said through a gritted smile. He drove it even further in. Nathanial inhaled involuntarily as his insides felt the suction of the blade. He gurgled and slumped forward. Brandenburg pulled the sword out of his enemy and watched him slump to the ground, rolling onto his back, gurgling and spitting blood.

"I ...I am...Black Arm," he winced.

"I'm a Roxy Avenger," said Brandenburg as his enemy's eyes closed. The Count smiled and turned to Abigail and fell into her arms. She grabbed him and kissed him relentlessly.

"You're alive, you're alive, you're alive."

"Just a scratch," he said, and got to his feet before slumping back down, "a really...painful scratch."

Abigail kissed him deeply on the mouth and heaved him up. "On your feet, you big Nancy, on your feet and let's get you out of here."

They stood up and looked over Whit's body. Abigail wriggled her arm free from Brandenburg's and pulled out a pistol from her belt. She did not hesitate in discharging it into Nathanial's forehead.

"Such an arsehole," she said, tossing the weapon onto the body. Then, as if it had been planned all along, a rope fell through the roof and landed neatly next to them. Brandenburg looked up and saw the balloon hovering overhead.

"After you, Agent Hardwoode," he said, pulling the rope in. She looked up at the waiting balloon.

"No," she said, "I've left you behind enough already," and she grabbed the rope, tugged it and pulled Brandenburg in close. The balloon ascended and, as they kissed passionately, they were pulled clear of the Pavilion.

They floated over the wreckage and passed Antoine's balloon which was still loading the King, Lupe, Anya and Danilov. Antoine waved as Brandenburg and Abigail passed by.

"Bravo, Antoine, bravo!" shouted Brandenburg.

"No, monsieur, bravo you! Hats off to Brandenburg!" he said, watching as they sailed towards the island.

Archie sat on the lawn and tried to be nonchalant as he watched Brandenburg and Abigail drift over. He lay back on the grass and put his hands behind his head, whistling to himself.

Brandenburg alighted with Abigail to hugs all round.

"Where is he? Where's Enfield? Did he make it?

"Did he make it?" scoffed Valerie, "You should have seen him! He was a god, he was Diomedes, and he was a myrmidon! No, he was Achilles himself!" she gushed. Brandenburg ruffled her hair as he walked passed, clutching his wounds with one hand, and hanging onto Abigail with the other. They walked over to Archie and looked down at him.

"I hear you did good, young man!" he said.

Archie remained on his back and inspected his dirty nails.

"It weren't nothing," he said casually. Brandenburg smirked and turned from him. Archie leapt to his feet.

"Oh my lord!" he gabbled, "there was this fight and swords and then Kemble, foul beast, and a balloon and fireworks..."

Brandenburg hugged him tightly, happy to see him alive, and also to stem his ramblings. Brandenburg looked around at everyone. His smiled dropped. Desiree nodded to a little grass mound where lay Tobias's body. The Roxy Players and Abigail linked arms and walked over.

"He died saving us" said Claudia.

"He died saving many" said Desiree. Brandenburg drew his sword and laid it on his body.

"Be with your Lord, sweet artist. Be at peace," said the Count.

"Just a flesh wound actually" said Tobias, before breaking out into a huge smile and opening his eyes. Everyone leapt back, startled out of their wits. Tobias began to laugh loudly, though the pain in his gut prevented him from truly letting go.

"And you thought I was just a metallurgist and not an actor also. Shame on you!"

Brandenburg roared his true laugh and Desiree and Valerie bent down to help him sit up, letting their tears of joy fall freely. They then all turned to the edge of the lake to face the burning Pavilion and await their friends who remained unaccounted for.

Lupe and the King were safe with Antoine and the pilot in the basket of the last balloon while Danilov and Anya were still on the roof. Time was running out.

"Come on, sister" said Danilov through his tears. "We have to go." He went to grab her, but she pushed him away, her watery eyes still trained on the gaping remnants of Brighton Pavilion, scanning beyond hope for the boy with the net.

"Come on, my friends!" called Antoine, "there is no time!"

Danilov stroked his sister's hair. "He died so we should live, come on, we must leave," he whispered. Anya bowed her head and slowly grabbed the rope. They both climbed up into the basket.

Gertie was not dead, but by no means safe having found himself at the far end of the complex inside a crumbling and burning room. The first of the four walls fell down next to him and he dived to the side to avoid the masonry, rolling back onto his feet. He looked around. There was only one way out of the deathtrap: upwards. He was no climber so he tried to think like Danilov and look around for a route out of there. He saw a beam resting against the remnants of a wall at the far side of the 'room'. He wasted no time and ran towards it. He dived over the collapsing floor and grabbed onto the beam as everything below him fell away. The beam slid back down and he almost fell back into the vault. However his drive for survival won out and he scrambled up the beam like a rat. He was now seventy feet in the air, precariously on the end of beam that rested on an unstable wall. On the other side of the room lay his best way out – there was a platform just six feet below the last remaining exterior wall. From there, along the edge, he could run all the way to the far side of the building to where the ballon had flown. But he had to get there first. He balanced on the beam's tip and looked around. There was only one cross-beam lying six feet from him, flaming and crippled, but reaching all the way back across to the platform. He spat on his hands and leapt for the beam, grabbing onto it and swinging wildly. The burning wood seared his hands, but he held on, swinging his legs and pulling himself up until he was standing on top of the beam. He looked down.

It was now or never. He stuck his arms out, as he had seen Anya and Danilov do a million times, lowered his heart rate and walked out onto the flaming beam.

"We cannot wait any longer!" said the pilot to Antoine, who had ordered his brother to hold for a minute more.

"We have a King here...an English king...but a King all the same! We must go!" and with that, he loosened the guy ropes and the balloon ascended.

"Here they come!" shouted Claudia, pointing to the balloon. The Players all breathed a sigh of relief and hugged each other. Abigail drew a looking glass from her belt and put it to her eye.

"The King, he is there! They've got him!" Everybody cheered.

"Who else?" Valerie said. "Is Danilov, my love there? Danilov, the strong one! The beautiful one?"

Abigail looked back and smiled.

"Yes! He is there. And Lupe, and Anya...and Antoine! There are all safe." The group cheered.

"Gertie" said Brandenburg, "what about Gertie?"

Abigail looked back through her glass. She knew he wasn't there, but looked anyway. She replaced her eye glass and looked at Brandenburg.

"I'm so sorry," she said. The Irregular's mouths fell open in dismay as they turned back to the balloon.

Gertie was eleven feet from the platform when the beam gave way. He was walking with his eyes closed, sensing every movement and moan from the beam. He was, as Danilov had once described to him, at one with the walk. As soon as he felt it buckle, he knew it was gone for good. He dived forward just as it fell and landed on the platform which, of course, buckled under the weight, he sprung up and grabbed the wall ledge, hoisting himself up onto it. He had not spared a moment. As soon as he was upright, the entire left side of the room crumbled in on itself. The impact of the masonry and rubble broke through the remaining layers throughout the pavilion and new air was breathed onto the fire, turning it back into an inferno. The flames belched up all around him. Up ahead he had only the wall and nothing else. Through the fire balls, he could see the balloon drifting away without him. He ran.

Danilov couldn't bear to look at his sister, who was still looking out of the exploding wreckage as they flew away. Anya held the basket tight and wept. Antoine looked out towards the island, like Danilov, too heartbroken to look back. The balloon began to ascend.

Gertie ran along the wall as everything exploded all around him, fire spewed ahead of him and behind and masonry erupted from the cavern below as it was some angry volcano. He leapt over an eight foot gap in the wall and did not break stride. He could see the balloon now. He could see it.

Behind him, the Pavilion wall gave way, crashing down at his heels.

The balloon rose a little higher to escape the updraft. Suddenly, Anya grabbed Danilov's arm, he turned around to see her jumping up onto the basket's edge.

"Anya, what are...," he stopped when he saw what she was pointing to. Antoine turned also.

"Mon Dieu" he cried.

From the balloon, they could see young Gertie running like a man possessed inches ahead of the collapsing wall. Antoine threw a length of rope to Danilov who quickly tied it around Anya's ankle and then around the base of the basket.

On the island Abigail looked back, when the others had turned away.

"Look," she said, "wait!"

The Irregulars looked back and they could see Gertie belting along the wall.

"Oh my God!" cried Lupe, grabbing Claudia and pulling her close.

"Come on boy! Come on!" shouted Brandenburg.

Gertie was out of time. He felt the wall give way behind and in front of him. He looked up at the balloon and saw Anya, standing high upon the basket and glinting like a star. He reached the edge of the wall and leapt over the edge, and into nothingness.

Upon seeing Gertie dive into the air, Anya too leapt clear of the basket. Her form and technique were perfect. She flew into the night sky, her back arched, her arms out-stretched and her chin pointing to the heavens. At the peak of her flight she bent herself into dart and rocketed back down towards the ground.

Gertie had flown as far as his flailing body could take him, his legs and arms stopped trying to grab extra air and he looked up at the balloon as he began to fall. He reached his arms up above him and clenched his jaw as the wind began to rush up on him.

Anya cut through the night air like an arrow and just as Gertie was about to close his eyes, he saw through her beautiful face come rocketing down towards him like an avenging angel from heaven. He reached up with all of his might and grabbed a hold of her arm. Antoine and Danilov cheered and hugged each other. The Roxy Players jumped up and down and hugged and kissed each other when they saw the catch that would prove to be the greatest feat a Roxy Irregular had ever pulled off.

Gertie swung, forty feet in the air, hanging onto Anya. He looked up, eyes panicked and gasping for air.

"You caught me!" he gasped. "You caught me!"

Anya shrugged serenely at the boy. "Of course," she said, in a voice he had never heard before, "I love you."

Her delivery was so matter-of-fact that Gertie did a double take.

Anya pulled Gertie up so that he could grab hold of the rope. He wrapped his feet around the rope and hung upside down and face to face with Anya.

As the balloon floated towards the island, Anya held Gertie's face and kissed him softly. They didn't hear the cheers from the rest of the Players, but were told at a later date that they were the loudest that they had ever produced.

Antoine and his brother piloted the balloon to safety and Brandenburg and Archie helped Gertie and Anya onto their feet.

Brandenburg looked at Gertie and ruffled his hair.

"Good man," he said proudly, "good man."

Antoine landed the balloon and climbed out to adulation from the Players. He soaked it up. Claudia stormed up to him and kicked him in the shins.

"Why didn't you tell me you were planning this?" she said, haughtily.

Antoine picked her up and held her tight. "Well, what kind of an entrance would that have made?" he said to the crowd. They applauded in rapturous agreement.

Abigail stepped up to him to offer her hand. Antoine was about to shake it, when behind him there was a commotion. Everybody turned to see Antoine's brother being thrown out of the basket and landing on the lawn in a heap.

Lupe and the King stood up inside the basket and the gargantuan singer grabbed a line and pulled, sending the balloon up into the air. She winked at the Players and turned back to the King, pulling him down into the basket.

The Players laughed and cheered as the reunited lovers floated off to find a quite spot for some noisy privacy.

Abigail turned and walked back to the shore, a look of seriousness falling over her. Brandenburg and the Players stepped up beside her.

"What's wrong?" asked the Count, running his hands through her hair.

"De Locke" she said gravely, "he's still out there."

Gertie stepped up next to her and held out his hand. "I wouldn't worry about that, Miss Abigail," he said, opening his hand to reveal Lord De Locke's signet ring. Abigail burst out laughing and hugged the boy.

"One last thing!" shouted Antoine, before the hugs went on too long. The Players looked around. Antoine nodded to the three brothers who went over to the remaining balloons. "We cannot celebrate just yet!"

"Why not?" said Archie.

Antoine nodded once more to his brothers and the pulled a guy rope on each balloon and stepped aside. The baskets suddenly rose two feet in the air, of their own volition and hovered. The men pulled another rope, and the sides out the baskets folded out and the bottoms slid back down the ground. The Players gasped.

"Magnificent," said Brandenburg in astonishment.

"Heavenly," whispered Archie.

The Players moved in together to witness it. The balloon baskets had transformed themselves into gloriously well-stocked bars. Antoine smiled and nonchalantly pulled out a bottle of champagne and handed it to Brandenburg. The Players waited for a great speech. Instead, the Count just smiled, ripped the cork off and sprayed them all with the glorious drink.

And there they stayed for the rest of the night, on the island next to the burning Pavilion, recounting the heroic deeds and dark moments they had all endured until they had passed out in a huge pile amongst countless empty bottles.

Chapter Sixty One

To Roxy Playhouse by Royal Appointment

The curtain came down on the opening night of Valerie's first play entitled *'Hats off to Brandenburg'* and the audience in the newly restored Roxy Playhouse sat in stunned silence for two whole minutes. Then they erupted into monumental applause that shook the foundations of the theatre and burst out into the street, floating over the whole of London Town. The curtain came up and Desiree, Lupe, Claudia, Anya, Antoine, Tobias, Gertie, Danilov and Valerie took to the stage and were pelted with roses. As they stood there, in a line, holding hands they felt never more alive and in love with the world. As the applause continued, they one by one took to the centre stage for their own moment in the sun.

First stepped Gertie, the hero of Brighton to which he received a standing ovation. In the audience, the King himself roared and stamped his feet. Gertie bowed respectfully to the auditorium, and also to the three new tiers that had been constructed by order of his Highness in grateful thanks to The Roxy Avengers. He stepped back into line and grabbed Anya for a kiss which sent the audience berserk.

Next up stepped Tobias who received a similarly enthusiastic cheer not just for his loyalty and courage but also for his searing debut performance in the play which saw him play the part of both Nathanial Whit and Sheridan with an uncanny ability.

Then Desiree glided up to take her moment. She was hit with a thousand roses and in thanks to the crowd she performed a small solo dance just for the audience who thanked her with more cheers.

Next up sashayed Lupe Darling who treated the audience to a race up and down the scales in an operatic fashion so fierce that the chandeliers rattled on their mounts. Of all the adventures she had been on, of all the curtain calls that one was the most overwhelming. She turned to the line and beckoned over Claudia, who gracefully stepped up to join her. In the short six months since Brighton, she had matured greatly and had somehow managed to evolve her girlish wonder into a beguiling new energy that made the audience gasp. She stood beside Lupe, looked at her and winked. The two women bowed to the audience and then rejoined the line.

Anya and Danilov stepped up next to the rapture. Danilov, standing behind his sister, picked her up and she climbed up onto his head and balanced there for a few seconds. Then she leapt high into the air as Danilov bowed to the audience. In the air she performed three somersaults before landing back onto Danilov's head as he stood up from his bow. She climbed off her brother and stood to the side as Antoine stepped up and, as is the Gascony way, performed an ornate and intricate bow for the audience. When he stood up, there was a sudden eruption of laughter and clapping as the crowd realised that, during his bow, he had somehow changed his costume inside out and was now dressed in a white suit.

Then came Valerie's turn and she shyly stepped up to the applause. In the six months leading up to opening night, Valerie had found that she had a secret talent for writing. It had come to her one day in a dream and she had awoken and produced the first draft of the play in a single morning. She handed it around the Players who had taken temporary residence in The Bishop and, by evening, they had already cast the play and learnt their lines such was the magnificence of her writing. When asked how she had managed such a feat, she had simply turned to Desiree, smiled and said; "Herschel's voice came to me in a dream," to which Desiree responded that she knew and had, the night before, told him to do so. Valerie stood on the stage and though the applause filled her with joy, it was nothing in comparison to the elation she felt in seeing her play come into fruition under the skilled guidance of all the Players.

She stood in front of the stage and turned back to the Players and beckoned them all forward, to which they responded and stood as a line once more. They looked at each other and smiled, linked arms and took one long, deep bow as one.

They stood up and Gertie unlinked his arms, and held them up in an attempt to hush the audience slightly. His new-found confidence worked a treat and the applause died down a little.

"Your Majesty," he said in a strong, deep voice that seemed to carry a hint of Srdjan's about it, "my Lords, Ladies, gentlemen and lovers, if you would please now show your appreciation to The Roxy Playhouse herself, rebuilt and gleaming."

There was a loud cheer.

"And, as is The Roxy way, would you please now take a moment to show your love to the brave and beautiful Players who could not make it here tonight: To the honourable Miss Sarah Siddons and Miss Alexia Adberg!"

There was a respectful round of applause.

"To the dashing and courageous Srdjan Krupkal and," he hung his head for a moment and looked back up with tears in his eyes, "to the greatest man we knew, and to whom inspired us all, my adoptive father and the love of Miss Ricci's life, to Mr Herschel Barnabus."

The audience leapt to their feet and applauded arduously. Gertie looked around the audience and smiled.

"And, before we retire to our after-party, if you would please turn your attention to the back of the auditorium," Gertie pointed to the doors and a large, modern spotlight swung down to illuminate it. The crowd turned and gasped.

"I give you," said Gertie, proudly, "Lord Benjamin Ananas and Lady Hardwoode…and, of course, the irrepressible Sir Archibald Enfield."

Benjamin, Abigail and Archie stood at the entrance of their theatre, resplendent in fine clothes and looked down the aisle to see their friends, bathed in light and beckoning them forward like angels into heaven.

Lord Ananas looked over at Sir Archie.

"After you, my man?" he said, smiling.

"No, no, Old Love, after you," said Archie stepping aside to let Lord Ananas and Lady Hardwoode walk down the centre aisle to rapturous applause. They took to the stage and turned back to the audience. Archie looked around the crowd, soaking it all in, before striding up to meet his friends. Once they were all together, they bowed once more and the curtain came down.

———•◦•———

The after-party was in full swing and the Players were dancing and performing as was their way. It was a magical feeling for them all and nobody noticed the door to the theatre open and a slight figure walk in. The Players continued to laugh and sing as the figure approached the stage.

Antoine was about to start a knife-dance when they suddenly heard the sound of someone clearing their throat. They all turned around in surprise to see a young man, dirty and bedraggled standing by the stage holding his cap in his hands.

"Yes, my good man," said Antoine bending down on the stage to meet the intruder and offering his hand to shake. The young man took it. "What can we do for you?"

"Beggin' your pardon sir," said the man in a soft, timid voice, "but I thought you might need a musician. I'm a travelling one, see, and I've come to seek roots."

"A musician you say," said Gertie from the wings, "what do you play?"

"Anything I 'spose, but I only have this here one violin" he said, holding up a tattered and worn instrument.

"What's your name, son?" asked Antoine, looking over the young man and noting his bright blue eyes and blonde hair.

"Lanford, sir," replied the stranger, "Freddie Lanford."

"Well then, Freddie Lanford," said Antoine, "what are you waiting for? Play on!"

The Players sat down and the young man began to play. From the backstage area, Claudia was restocking the drinks trolley when the violin's tone floated into her ears. She put the bottles down and followed the melody until she walked onto the stage and locked eyes with the newcomer. She put her hands on her hips and tilted her head as she looked at him. She never expected it to happen so casually and she shrugged in happy resignation at the blindingly lassaiz-faire way in which life treats the heart. She had fallen in love in an instant. *'Oh good'* she simply thought and pushed her trolley to deliver her drinks and meet the filthy violinist. He stopped playing when he saw her.

"When's the date, Old Love?" said Archie as he walked with Benjamin and Abigail up the stairs towards his quarters. Benjamin looked at Abigail.

"Eight months from now, in the spring," said Benjamin.

"Yes, on the day that I left him in May," added Abigail, the light from the candles dancing off of her wonderful engagement ring.

"Any hot bridesmaids going?" said Archie, hopefully.

"Twenty seven" replied Abigail, smiling.

"Ah, you are good to me!" he said as he opened the door or Benjamin's chamber. All three stopped dead in their tracks. The window was open and the cold night air was blowing papers around. They looked to the ledge to see a black-cloaked figure leap out of the window, into the darkness. The three friends dashed into the room and over to the window. Benjamin and Archie craned their necks out to see who the intruder was. There, standing on a carriage-roof, rushing off into the night stood the figure, looking back up at them, its black-cowl covering its face.

Inside the room, Abigail looked around to see if anything had been taken. Upon the desk, under a paperweight, she found a tatty piece of cloth that she did not recognise. She picked it up and looked at it. She smiled to herself and handed it to Benjamin who, in turned, smiled and handed it to Archie.

Archie opened it up to reveal a crudely drawn map of Italy with two large 'X's in the centre of it. He furrowed his brow and looked back out the window.

The figure on the carriage roof removed their cowl and two bright-green almond shaped eyes shone back at him.

"Giselle," he whispered.

It was indeed Giselle, and she waved, blew him a kiss and the climbed into the carriage and disappeared around a corner leaving behind a trail of black smoke. Archie leant back into the room. He looked over at Benjamin and Abigail.

"Eight months, you say?"

They nodded. Archie mulled it over, before swinging his leg over the ledge.

"Plenty of time," he said. "So my loves, look after yourselves and look after The Roxy!"

Benjamin smiled and nodded and Abigail blew him a kiss for luck.

Archie caught the kiss and winked before leaping out of the window. Benjamin and Abigail looked out to see Archie Enfield land hard and well. He turned to them and tipped his hat before taking off into the night to give chase to his love.

Lord Ananas and Lady Hardwoode looked at each other, laughed, and then left the room to rejoin the Players and have a drink.

The End

Count Abraham von Brandenburg and The Roxy Playhouse Irregulars will return.

Also by the same author

TheNeverPages

Master G_'s dearly departed Lucy is lost within TheNeverRealm: The transitory wasteland between here and the ever-after where memory does not exist. He knows because he has dreamt it. He must track her down and save her, but TheNeverRealm is already infiltrating his psyche and turning his memories into sand.

If Master G_ is to rescue Lucy, he must not only overcome his mental entropy, but also survive the chaos that awaits him in Pripyat: The city that anchors every reality in the Multiverse

TheNeverPages is a journal that explores our internal and external landscapes. It is about our position in space and time and our perception of the universe.

Above all, *TheNeverPages* is about the lengths we go to for love.

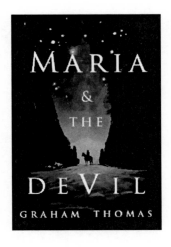

Maria & The Devil

The Devil, Montana's most feared outlaw has left his secret lover, Maria, alone in their secluded house deep in the wilds. If she had known that she was pregnant, the Devil might have stayed. That was almost nine months ago and Maria is still awaiting her lover's return and the arrival of her child.

But while Maria waits for the Devil, a vengeful band of gunslingers are hunting him. Led by the relentless Rickman Chill, the gang have ventured deep into the dark wilds of Montana and they will stop at nothing to bring the Devil to Justice.

It is not long before the Chill gang happen upon a house in the woods where a pregnant woman seems to be the only inhabitant. Vengeance is a dangerous game, but as the Devil said to Maria before he left her: "there is nothing more dangerous than lovers"

Maria & The Devil is a supernatural thriller about motherhood, vengeance, solitude and self-preservation.

OUT NOW IN PAPERBACK AND FOR KINDLE

www.mariaandthedevil.com

Lightning Source UK Ltd.
Milton Keynes UK
UKOW052250140412

190771UK00001B/1/P